KENILWORTH

SIR WALTER SCOTT

1771-1832

KENILWORTH

SIR WALTER SCOTT

With an Introduction by

SIR H. J. C. GRIERSON

LONDON AND GLASGOW

First published, 1821
This edition, 1952
Latest reprint, 1969

PRINTED IN GREAT BRITAIN
COLLINS CLEAR-TYPE PRESS

SIR WALTER SCOTT

WALTER SCOTT was born in Edinburgh on the 15th of August 1771.
He was the ninth of twelve children (of whom the first six died
in childhood) of Walter Scott, a successful lawyer who, in 1758,
had married the eldest daughter of John Rutherford a professor
of medicine in Edinburgh University. Both on his paternal and
maternal side Scott was descended from some of the oldest
families of the Scottish Border Country.

As an infant he contracted the infantile paralysis which left him
permanently lame in one leg. However, he recovered health and
vigour thanks mainly to the open-air life which he led at his
grandfather's farm at Sandyknowe near Smailholme. As a boy he
was remarkable for his precocious intelligence, vivid imagination
and a powerful retentive memory. At a very early age he became
an omnivorous reader, especially of ballads and historical romances,
and together with his interest in the historical past, he developed
a strong desire for a life of action and adventure. He spent four
years at the High School in Edinburgh (1779–83) and attended for a
time the Grammar School in Kelso. Proceeding to the University of
Edinburgh, he took classes in Humanity, Greek and Logic (1783–86.)

In 1786 he was apprenticed to his father, who was a Writer to
the Signet, for five years. He returned to the University in 1789
for classes in Scots law and Moral Philosophy and remained there
until 1792, when he was called to the Bar. Apart from his
professional studies, Scottish history, antiquity, and walking
expeditions into the Highlands and the Border Country constituted his most serious pursuits. Thus he acquired the immense
knowledge of history, local legends, people and conditions which
went into the writing of his ballads and novels.

Around 1790 he fell passionately in love with Williamina
Belsches, daughter of Sir John Belsches. Though the young lady
at first reciprocated his feelings, she ultimately married Sir William
Forbes, a rich young banker (1797). The same year Scott, after a
brief courtship, married Charlotte Charpentier, a French girl then
living under the guardianship of Lord Downshire.

Soon after his marriage he took a house in Castle Street

Edinburgh (which remained his residence until 1826) and also acquired a cottage at Lasswade near Edinburgh, which he occupied until 1804. During those years, which were among the happiest of his life, Scott made his literary *début*. Having translated Bürger's poem *Lenore* and Goethe's play *Goetz von Berlichingen* and contributed some ballads to Lewis' collection *Tales of Wonder*, he published his first work of importance, *The Minstrelsy of the Scottish Border* in 1802. Two years later he edited the old romance *Sir Tristram* and in 1805 came his first original work, the poem *The Lay of the Last Minstrel*. Its success was decisive in making Scott adopt literature as the main work of his life. Yet his real ambition was not literature, nor the Law, nor the commercial activities in which he became involved about that time. All these were to him the means to an end. His real ambition—which to a large extent he realised—was to live the feudal life of a Scottish Border laird.

In 1799 he was appointed Sheriff of Selkirkshire with a salary of £300 a year; some years later he became Clerk of the Sessions which eventually increased his income by another £1300. He counted on earning at least another £1000 a year by his pen; the balance—the very large balance—was to come from his business activities. Thus in 1805 began his secret financial association with James Ballantyne the printer (and later publisher) which was decisively to influence his whole literary (and consequently also his social) career in that it enabled him at the cost of ever greater literary exertions, to create and to maintain a deceptive fabric of wealth which finally however crumbled into dust, leaving him at the age of fifty-five to face crushing liabilities. To the reduction of these liabilities he applied himself with superhuman effort during the last years of his life—literally writing himself to death.

In 1804 Scott moved his summer abode from Lasswade to Ashestiek on the Tweed where he remained until 1812. Among the works written during that period were *Marmion* (1808), the *Life of Dryden* (1808), and *The Lady of the Lake* (1810), the most popular of his narrative poems.

In 1812 he bought land on the Tweed near Melrose where he built his famous house Abbotsford—the home of his triumphs, of his far-reaching ambitions, and of his final heroic fight with misfortune. In 1813 he published *Rokeby*; in 1814 *The Life and Works of Swift* and *Waverley*, the first of his 'Scotch Novels' all of which were to appear anonymously. In the years to follow appeared among others, *The Lord of the Isles* and *Guy Mannering* (1815); *The Antiquary*, *The Black Dwarf* and *Old Mortality* (1816); *The Heart of Midlothian* (1818); *The Bride of Lammermoor*, *The Legend of Montrose* and *Ivanhoe* (1819). The four last named were written while Scott was ill, suffering from cramps in the stomach which at times were so severe as to make it impossible for him to hold his pen.

With the publication of *Ivanhoe* Scott had reached the peak of his popularity and fame. He had become 'The Great Unknown.' In 1820 he was created a baronet by George IV and in 1822 he took a leading part in arranging the monarch's official visit to Edinburgh. In 1820 Scott published *The Monastery*, his first recognised failure which was partly redeemed by the success of *The Abbot*, its immediate sequel. The next few years saw the publication of, among other works, *Kenilworth*, *The Pirate* (1821); *The Fortunes of Nigel* (1822); *Redgauntlet* (1824). In 1825 he began his *Journal* which he continued until shortly before his death.

The year 1826 brought the combined failure of Scott's secret business associates, the firms of Ballantyne and Constable, and with it Scott's own financial ruin. Henceforth he worked for his creditors, retaining for himself only his official salary and such earnings from his writings as the trustees would from time to time concede to him. In 1826 also Lady Scott died. At the time when the financial catastrophe overtook him, Scott had been working at the completion of *Woodstock*. It proved an immediate and outstanding success and its very large earnings went wholly towards the reduction of the debt.

Other works followed in unbroken succession. To name only the most important ones: *The Life of Napoleon* (in nine volumes); the first series of *Chronicles of Canongate;* the *Tales of a Grandfather* in four successive series (1827–1830). Scott's last two works were *Count Robert of Paris* and *Castle Dangerous*, both published in 1831.

In 1830 Scott had suffered his first paralytic stroke, and from then on his health and mental powers rapidly declined. A second, more severe seizure followed in 1831, and a third, which finally incapacitated him, in May 1832 while he was in Germany on his return from a trip through the Mediterranean and Italy.

Back in Scotland he lingered on in a semi-conscious condition for several months and died at Abbotsford on September 21st 1832.

Three children, Sophia, Walter and Charles survived him.

H. d. R.

INTRODUCTION

THE shining success of Ivanhoe with the public, if not with some more critical readers such as Coleridge, was succeeded by the first admitted failure, *The Monastery*, followed in the same year, 1820, by the better received *The Abbot* and in that year also Constable collected and issued a volume of *Miscellaneous Poems*. Each novel in succession was composed and published to meet accumulating bills: 'Moreover,' he writes to James Ballantyne 'if I turn rich or even easy I should get lazy withal and that would suit none of us.' (August 1820). Before *The Abbot* was out he had drawn £2,500 in advance on the anticipated profits; and was hard at work on *Kenilworth* for a like purpose. 'This matter' (the proofs of *The Abbot*) 'is very nigh done, you will receive a dozen pages on your return, so you may crush on boldly. As to *Kenilworth*, I mean to go on with it but as one must have some breathing, it is possible there may be intervals'. (August 1820) In letters to Constable of 20th August and 10th September we see him hard at work: 'The Progresses (i.e. of *Queen Elizabeth*) are doing me yeoman service, for I am in *progress* myself . . . What was the name of Dudley Earl of Leicester's first wife, whom he was supposed to have murdered at Cumnor Hall in Berkshire? . . . In Lyson's *Magna Britannia* there is something about this same Cumnor Hall. I wish you would have it copied out for me, and should like to know anything that occurs to you about the village of Cumnor, its situation etc.' *Kenilworth* was out early in 1821.

In *Kenilworth*, as in *Ivanhoe*, Scott is in England and no Scot plays any part in the story. But the period was one with which he was much more familiar. With history he takes the same freedoms as in others of the novels. When the historical Amy Robsart died at Cumnor Hall in 1560, by accident or design, Robert Dudley was neither Earl of Leicester nor proprietor of Kenilworth. It was in 1534 that he was created Baron of Denbigh and immediately after that Earl of Leicester. It was in 1575 that Queen Elizabeth visited the Earl at Kenilworth, and was so gorgeously entertained. His marriage next year with the Widow of the Earl of Essex, by whom he was already believed to have

9

had two children while her husband was in Ireland, brought on the anger of the Queen who disapproved of the marriage of any of her favourites. But dates are of little importance to Scott. He had hold of the main facts of the situation, that Leicester was married and that the Queen's favour led him to dream of further possible advancement between which and fulfilment the existence of his former wife would prove an impediment. The general belief was that attempts were made to poison her, so the Spanish embassy reported, and Scott has not overlooked the suspicion; and her death by falling downstairs and breaking her neck was believed to have been arranged just as Scott represents, though he makes the Earl repent of his intention too late to prevent its accomplishment by followers who hoped to benefit by his advancement. The central interest of the story is this conflict in Leicester's mind between love, for he does love Amy Robsart, and ambition.

For the background of his story Scott has drawn on his familiarity with the Elizabethan age, but with much the same freedom as regards dates. Even in 1575, and Scott writes as of an earlier period, Shakespeare was a boy of eleven 'creeping like snail unwillingly to School,' which is exactly the picture Scott gives of himself in a letter: 'My little boy,' he wrote in 1809, 'is just entering the High School, and my imagination, like that of Leontes in *The Winter's Tale*, is running back thirty years and recollecting when I first crept through George Square with Robert Dundas to learn tasks to which I could annex neither idea nor utility.' But Shakespeare is in *Kenilworth* already the author of the beautiful *Midsummer Night's Dream*.

If Leicester is the most interesting figure, the only one involved in the inner conflict which gives its central interest to the actual hero of a story (for Tressilian is like other of Scott's conventional heroes, a somewhat colourless person), Queen Elizabeth is, after all, the most arresting figure. Scott had Shakespeare always more in his mind than any of his predecessors as novelists. It was from Shakespeare's plays that Scott learned how to bring together real historical characters and the creations of his own imagination, to mingle scenes of court life and battles with more intimate pictures of tavern and street. Where Scott differs from Shakespeare is that he is concerned with the setting, both of place and time, as Shakespeare is not. But it is in drawing Kings and Queens and

Princes that he most recalls his great model. Allowing always for the vast difference in beauty of diction, between the poet and the prose writer, Scott's regal figures are not unworthy to stand beside Shakespeare's—Mary, Queen of Scots; Elizabeth; James the First; Louis XI of France; the Duke of Burgundy; Richard in *The Talisman*. And of them all Elizabeth is the most impressive; so human and yet so royal, so much the man and yet also the woman. No Queen of history, Thomas Hardy has said, is quite so impressive and real as the Elizabeth of *Kenilworth*. But Shakespeare is also in Scott's mind in the character of Varney, the Iago of the story. Scott was also one of the few persons who had read Goethe. He had been a member, if impatient of grammar, of the German class which the Man of Feeling had made popular for a time in Edinburgh. He had translated, if with some notable blunders, *Goetz von Berlichingen;* and in the seventh chapter here, where Amy is indulged with a view of her husband's orders, Scott is borrowing from *Egmont*, Act. III. 'Walter Scott,' Goethe said to Eckermann, 'used a scene *from my Egmont*, and he had the right to do so; and because he did it well, he deserves praise. He has also copied the character of my Mignon in one of his romances' (*Peveril of the Peak*) 'but whether with equal judgment is a question.' Goethe had a great respect for Scott, if it yielded later to the general Continental passion for Byron: 'He passed on to Byron, praised his *Cain*, especially the scene of the slaying: "Byron alone will I let stand by myself. Walter Scott is nothing beside him"' (October 23). Of Scott he said again a little later: 'I have read two romances of Scott. I now understand what he can do with you. He would always amuse me, but I can learn nothing from him. I have time only for the first-rate.' The two were probably, judging by the date, *Kenilworth* and *The Fortunes of Nigel*.

H. J. C. GRIERSON

KENILWORTH

AUTHOR'S INTRODUCTION

A CERTAIN degree of success, real or supposed, in the delineation of Queen Mary, naturally induced the Author to attempt something similar respecting 'her sister and her foe,' the celebrated Elizabeth. He will not, however, pretend to have approached the task with the same feelings; for the candid Robertson himself confesses having felt the prejudices with which a Scotsman is tempted to regard the subject; and what so liberal an historian avows, a poor romance-writer dares not disown. But he hopes the influence of a prejudice, almost as natural to him as his native air, will not be found to have greatly affected the sketch he has attempted of England's Elizabeth. I have endeavoured to describe her as at once a high-minded sovereign, and a female of passionate feelings, hesitating betwixt the sense of her rank and the duty she owed her subjects on the one hand, and, on the other, her attachment to a nobleman who, in external qualifications at least, amply merited her favour. The interest of the story is thrown upon that period when the sudden death of the first Countess of Leicester seemed to open to the ambition of her husband the opportunity of sharing the crown of his sovereign.

It is possible that slander, which very seldom favours the memories of persons in exalted stations, may have blackened the character of Leicester with darker shades than really belonged to it. But the almost general voice of the times attached the most foul suspicions to the death of the unfortunate Countess, more especially as it took place so very opportunely for the indulgence of her lover's ambition. If we can trust Ashmole's *Antiquities of Berkshire*, there was but too much ground for the traditions which charge Leicester with the murder of his wife. In the following extract of the passage the reader will find the authority I had for the story of the romance:—

'At the west end of the church are the ruins of a manor, anciently belonging (as a cell or place of removal, as some report) to the monks of Abington. At the Dissolution, the said manor, or lordship, was conveyed to one —— Owen (I believe), the possessor of Godstow then.

'In the hall, over the chimney, I find Abington arms cut in stone, viz., a patonee between four martlets; and also another escutcheon, viz., a lion rampant, and several mitres cut in stone about the house. There is also in the said house a chamber called Dudley's chamber, where the Earl of Leicester's wife was murdered; of which this is the story following:—

'Robert Dudley, Earl of Leicester, a very goodly personage, and singularly well featured, being a great favourite to Queen Elizabeth, it was thought, and commonly reported, that had he been a batchelor or widower, the Queen would have made him her husband; to this end, to free himself of all obstacles, he commands, or perhaps, with fair flattering intreaties, desires his wife to repose herself here at his servant Anthony Forster's house, who then lived in the aforesaid manor-house; and also prescribed to Sir Richard Varney (a prompter to this design), at his coming hither, that he should first attempt to poison her, and if that did not take effect, then by any other way whatsoever to dispatch her. This, it seems, was proved by the report of Dr Walter Bayly, sometime fellow of New College, then living in Oxford, and professor of physic in that university; whom, because he would not consent to take away her life by poison, the Earl endeavoured to displace him the court. This man, it seems, reported for most certain, that there was a practice in Cumnor among the conspirators, to have poisoned this poor innocent lady, a little before she was killed, which was attempted after this manner:—They seeing the good lady sad and heavy (as one that well knew by other handling, that her death was not far off), began to persuade her that her present disease was abundance of melancholy and other humours, etc., and therefore would needs counsel her to take some potion, which she absolutely refusing to do, as still suspecting the worst; whereupon they sent a messenger on a day (unawares to her) for Dr Bayly, and entreated him to persuade her to take some little potion by his direction, and they would fetch the same at Oxford; meaning to have added something of their own for her comfort, as the doctor upon just cause and consideration did suspect, seeing their great importunity, and the small need the lady had of physic, and therefore he peremptorily denied their request; misdoubting (as he afterwards reported), lest, if they had poisoned her under the name of his potion, he might after have been hanged for a colour of their sin, and the doctor remained still well assured, that this way taking no effect, she would not long escape their violence, which afterwards happened thus. For Sir Richard Varney above-said (the chief projector in this design), who, by the Earl's order, remained that day of her death alone with her, with one man only and Forster, who had that day forcibly sent away all her servants from her to Abington market, about three miles distant from this place; they (I say, whether first stifling her, or else strangling her) afterwards flung her down a pair of stairs and broke her neck, using much violence upon her; but, however, though it was vulgarly reported that she had by chance fell downstairs (but still without hurting her hood that was upon her head), yet the inhabitants will tell there, that she was conveyed from her usual chamber where she lay, to another where the bed's head of the chamber stood close to a privy postern door, where they in the night came and stifled her in her bed, bruised her head very much, broke her neck, and at length flung her down stairs, thereby believing the world would have thought it a mischance, and so have blinded their villainy. But behold the mercy and justice of God in revenging and discovering this lady's murder, for one of the persons that was a coadjutor in this murder was afterwards taken for a felony in the marches of Wales and, offering to publish the manner of the aforesaid murder, was privately made away in the prison by the Earl's appointment; and Sir Richard Varney the other, dying about the same time in London, cried miserably, and blasphemed God, and said to a person of note (who hath related the same to others since), not long before his death, that all the devils in hell did tear him to pieces. Forster, likewise, after this fact, being a man formerly addicted to hospitality, company, mirth, and music, was afterwards observed to forsake all this, and with much melancholy and pensiveness (some say with madness), pined and drooped away. The wife also of Bald Butter, kinsman to the Earl, gave out the whole fact a little before her death. Neither are these following passages to be forgotten, that as soon as ever she was murdered, they made great haste to bury her before the coroner had given in his inquest (which the Earl himself condemned as not done advisedly), which her father, or Sir John Robertsett (as I suppose), hearing of, came with all speed hither, caused her corpse to be taken up, the coroner to sit upon her, and farther enquiry to be made concerning this business to the full; but it was generally thought that the earl stopped his mouth, and made up the business betwixt them; and the good Earl, to make plain to the world the great love he bare to her while alive, and what a grief the loss of so virtuous a lady was to his tender heart, caused (though the thing, by these and other means, was beaten into the heads of the principal men of the University of Oxford) her body to be re-buried in St Mary's church in Oxford, with great pomp and solemnity. It is remarkable, when Dr Babington, the Earl's chaplain, did preach the funeral sermon, he tript once or twice in his speech, by recommending to their memories that virtuous lady so pitifully *murdered*, instead of saying pitifully slain. This Earl, after all his murders and poisonings, was himself poisoned by that which was prepared for others (some say by his wife at Cornbury Lodge before mentioned), though Baker in his Chronicle would have it at Killingworth, anno 1588. *

The same accusation has been adopted and circulated by the author of *Leicester's Commonwealth*, a satire written directly against the Earl of Leicester, which loaded him with the most horrid crimes, and, among the rest, with the murder of his first wife. It was alluded to in the *Yorkshire Tragedy*, a play erroneously ascribed to Shakespeare, where a rake, who determined to destroy all his family, throws his wife downstairs, with this allusion to the supposed murder of Leicester's Lady—

> The only way to charm a woman's tongue
> Is, break her neck—a politician did it.

The reader will find I have borrowed several incidents as well as names from Ashmole, and the more early authorities; but my first acquaintance with the history was through the more pleasing medium of verse. There is a period in youth when the mere power of numbers has a more strong effect on ear and imagination than in more advanced life. At this season of immature taste the Author was greatly delighted with the poems of Mickle and Langhorne, poets who, though by no means deficient in the higher branches of their art, were eminent for their powers of verbal melody above most who have practised this department of poetry. One of those pieces of Mickle, which the Author was particularly pleased with,

---

* Ashmole's *Antiquities of Berkshire*, vol. i. p. 149. The tradition as to Leicester's death was thus communicated by Ben Jonson to Drummond of Hawthornden:—'The Earl of Leicester gave a bottle of liquor to his Lady, which he willed her to use in any faintness; which she, after his returne from court, not knowing it was poison, gave him, and so he died.'—*Ben Jonson's Information to Drummond of Hawthornden MS.—Sir Robert Sibbald's copy.*

is a ballad, or rather a species of elegy, on the subject of Cumnor
Hall, which, with others by the same author, were to be found
in Evan's *Ancient Ballads* (volume iv. page 130), to which work
Mickle made liberal contributions. The first stanza especially had
a peculiar species of enchantment for the youthful ear of the
Author, the force of which is not even now entirely spent; some
others are sufficiently prosaic.

CUMNOR HALL

The dews of summer night did fall:
    The moon, sweet regent of the sky,
Silvered the walls of Cumnor Hall,
    And many an oak that grew thereby.

Now nought was heard beneath the skies,
    The sounds of busy life were still,
Save an unhappy lady's sighs,
    That issued from that lonely pile.

'Leicester,' she cried, 'is this thy love
    That thou so oft hast sworn to me,
To leave me in this lonely grove,
    Immured in shameful privity?

'No more thou comest with lover's speed
    Thy once beloved bride to see;
But be she alive, or be she dead,
    I fear, stern Earl, 's the same to thee.

'Not so the usage I received
    When happy in my father's hall;
No faithless husband then me grieved,
    No chilling fears did me appal.

'I rose up with the cheerful morn,
    No lark more blithe, no flower more gay;
And, like the bird that haunts the thorn
    So merrily sung the live-long day.

'If that my beauty is but small,
    Among court ladies all despised,
Why didst thou rend it from that hall,
    Where, scornful Earl, it well was prized?

'And when you first to me made suit,
    How fair I was you oft would say!
And, proud of conquest, pluck'd the fruit,
    Then left the blossom to decay.

'Yes! now neglected and despised,
    The rose is pale, the lily's dead;
But he that once their charms so prized,
    Is sure the cause those charms are fled.

'For know, when sick'ning grief doth prey
    And tender love's repaid with scorn,
The sweetest beauty will decay—
    What floweret can endure the storm?

'At court, I'm told, is beauty's throne,
    Where every lady's passing rare;
That Eastern flowers, that shame the sun,
    Are not so glowing, not so fair.

'Then, Earl, why didst thou leave the beds
    Where roses and where lilies vie,
To seek a primrose, whose pale shades
    Must sicken when those gauds are by?

''Mong rural beauties I was one,
    Among the fields wild flowers are fair;
Some country swain might me have won,
    And thought my beauty passing rare.

'But, Leicester (or I much am wrong),
    Or 'tis not beauty lures thy vows;
Rather ambition's gilded crown
    Makes thee forget thy humble spouse.

'Then, Leicester, why, again I plead
    (The injured surely may repine),—
Why didst thou wed a country maid,
    When some fair princess might be thine?

'Why didst thou praise my humble charms,
    And, oh! then leave them to decay?
Why didst thou win me to thy arms,
    Then leave to mourn the live-long day?

'The village maidens of the plain
    Salute me lowly as they go;
Envious they mark my silken train,
    Nor think a Countess can have woe?

'The simple nymphs! they little know
    How far more happy's their estate;
To smile for joy, than sigh for woe—
    To be content, than to be great.

'How far less blest am I than them?
    Daily to pine and waste with care!
Like the poor plant that, from its stem
    Divided, feels the chilling air.

'Nor, cruel Earl! can I enjoy
    The humble charms of solitude;
Your minions proud my peace destroy,
    By sullen frowns or pratings rude.

'Last night, as sad I chanced to stray,
    The village death-bell smote my ear;
They wink'd aside, and seem'd to say,
    "Countess, prepare—thy end is near!"

'And now, while happy peasants sleep,
    Here I sit lonely and forlorn;
No one to soothe me as I weep,
    Save Philomel on yonder thorn.

'My spirits flag—my hopes decay—
    Still that dread death-knell smites my ear;
And many a boding seems to say,
    "Countess, prepare—thy end is near!"'

Thus sore and sad that lady grieved
    In Cumnor Hall, so lone and drear,
And many a heartfelt sigh she heaved,
    And let fall many a bitter tear.

And ere the dawn of day appeared,
    In Cumnor Hall, so lone and drear,
Full many a piercing scream was heard,
    And many a cry of mortal fear.

The death-bell thrice was heard to ring,
    An aerial voice was heard to call,
And thrice the raven flapp'd its wing
    Around the towers of Cumnor Hall.

The mastiff howl'd at village door,
    The oaks were shatter'd on the green;
Woe was the hour—for never more
    That hapless Countess e'er was seen!

And in that Manor now no more
    Is cheerful feast and sprightly ball;
For ever since that dreary hour
    Have spirits haunted Cumnor Hall.

The village maids, with fearful glance,
    Avoid the ancient moss-grown wall;
Nor ever lead the merry dance
    Among the groves of Cumnor Hall.

Full many a traveller oft hath sigh'd,
    And pensive wept the Countess' fall,
As wand'ring onwards they've espied
    The haunted towers of Cumnor Hall.

Abbotsford, 1st March, 1831.

I am an innkeeper, and know my grounds,
And study them; Brain o' man, I study them.
I must have jovial guests to drive my ploughs,
And whistling boys to bring my harvests home,
Or I shall hear no flails thwack.—'*The New Inn.*'

IT is the privilege of tale-tellers to open their story in an inn, the free rendezvous of all travellers, and where the humour of each displays itself, without ceremony or restraint. This is specially suitable when the scene is laid during the old days of merry England, when the guests were in some sort not merely the inmates, but the messmates and temporary companions of mine host, who was usually a personage of privileged freedom, comely presence, and good humour. Patronised by him, the characters of the company were placed in ready contrast; and they seldom failed, during the emptying of a six-hooped pot, to throw off reserve, and present themselves to each other, and to their landlord, with the freedom of old acquaintance.

The village of Cumnor, within three or four miles of Oxford, boasted, during the eighteenth year of Queen Elizabeth, an excellent inn of the old stamp, conducted, or rather ruled, by Giles Gosling, a man of a goodly person, and of somewhat round belly; fifty years of age and upwards, moderate in his reckonings, prompt in his payments, having a cellar of sound liquor, a ready wit, and a pretty daughter. Since the days of old Harry Baillie of the Tabbard in Southwark, no one had excelled Giles Gosling in the power of pleasing his guests of every description; and so great was his fame, that to have been in Cumnor, without wetting a cup at the bonny Black Bear, would have been to avouch oneself utterly indifferent to reputation as a traveller. A country fellow might as well return from London without looking in the face of majesty. The men of Cumnor were proud of their host, and their host was proud of his house, his liquor, his daughter, and himself.

It was in the courtyard of the inn which called this honest fellow landlord, that a traveller alighted in the close of the evening, gave his horse, which seemed to have made a long journey, to the hostler, and made some inquiry, which produced the following dialogue betwixt the myrmidons of the bonny Black Bear.

'What, ho! John Tapster.'

'At hand, Will Hostler,' replied the man of the spigot, showing himself in his costume of loose jacket, linen breeches, and green apron, half within and half without a door, which appeared to descend to an outer cellar.

'Here is a gentleman asks if you draw good ale,' continued the hostler.

'Beshrew my heart else,' answered the tapster, 'since there are but four miles betwixt us and Oxford. Marry, if my ale did not convince the heads of the scholars, they would soon convince my pate with the pewter flagon.'

'Call you that Oxford logic,' said the stranger, who had now quitted the rein of his horse, and was advancing towards the inn door, when he was encountered by the goodly form of Giles Gosling himself.

'Is it logic you talk of, Sir Guest?' said the host; 'why then, have at you with a downright consequence,—

'The horse to the rack,
And to fire with the sack.'

'Amen! with all my heart, my good host,' said the stranger; 'let it be a quart of your best Canaries, and give me your good help to drink it.'

'Nay, you are but in your accidents yet, Sir Traveller, if you call on your host for help for such a sipping matter as a quart of sack—were it a gallon, you might lack some neighbourly aid at my hand, and yet call yourself a toper.'

'Fear me not,' said the guest, 'I will do my devoir as becomes a man who finds himself within five miles of Oxford; for I am not come from the fields of Mars to discredit myself amongst the followers of Minerva.

As he spoke thus, the landlord, with much semblance of hearty welcome, ushered his guest into a large, low chamber, where several persons were seated together in different parties: some drinking, some playing at cards, some conversing, and some, whose business called them to be early risers on the morrow, concluding their evening meal, and conferring with the chamberlain about their night's quarters.

The entrance of a stranger procured him that general and careless sort of attention which is usually paid on such occasions, from which the following results were deduced:—The guest was one of those who, with a well-made person, and features not in themselves unpleasing, are nevertheless so far from handsome, that, whether from the expression of their features, or the tone of their voice, or from their gait and manner, there arises, on the whole, a disinclination to their society. The stranger's address was bold, without being frank, and seemed eagerly and hastily to claim for him a degree of attention and deference, which he feared would be refused, if not instantly vindicated as his right. His attire was a riding-cloak, which, when open, displayed a handsome jerkin, overlaid with lace, and belted with a buff girdle, which sustained a broadsword and a pair of pistols.

'You ride well provided, sir,' said the host, looking at the weapons, as he placed on the table the mulled sack which the traveller had ordered.

'Yes, mine host: I have found the use on't in dangerous times, and I do not, like your modern grandees, turn off my followers the instant they are useless.'

'Ay, sir?' said Giles Gosling; 'then you are from the Low Countries, the land of pike and caliver?'

'I have been high and low, my friend, broad and wide, far and near; but here is to thee in a cup of thy sack—fill thyself another to pledge me; and, if it is less than superlative, e'en drink as you have brewed.'

'Less than superlative?' said Giles Gosling, drinking off the cup, and smacking his lips with an air of ineffable relish—'I know nothing of superlative, nor is there such a wine at the Three Cranes, in the Vintry, to my knowledge; but if you find better sack than that in the Sheres, or in the Canaries either, I would I may never touch either pot or penny more. Why, hold it up, betwixt you and the light, you shall see the little motes dance in the golden liquor like dust in the sunbeam. But I would rather draw wine for ten clowns than one traveller. I trust your honour likes the wine?'

'It is neat and comfortable, mine host; but to know good liquor, you should drink where the vine grows. Trust me, your Spaniard is too wise a man to send you the very soul of the grape. Why, this now, which you account so choice, were counted but as a cup of bastard at the Groyne, or at Port St Mary's. You should travel, mine host, if you would be deep in the mysteries of the butt and pottle-pot.'

'In troth, Signior Guest,' said Giles Gosling, 'if I were to travel only that I might be discontented with that which I can get at home, methinks I should go but on a fool's errand. Besides, I warrant you, there is many a fool can turn his nose up at good drink without ever having been out of the smoke of Old England: and so ever gramercy mine own fireside.'

'This is but a mean mind of yours, mine host,' said the stranger; 'I warrant me, all your town's folks do not think so basely. You have gallants among you, I dare undertake, that have made the Virginia voyage, or taken a turn in the Low Countries at least. Come, cudgel your memory. Have you no friends in foreign parts that you would gladly have tidings of?'

'Troth, sir, not I,' answered the host, 'since ranting Robin of Drysandford was shot at the siege of the Brill. The devil take the caliver that fired the ball, for a blither lad never filled a cup at midnight. But he is dead and gone, and I know not a soldier, or a traveller who is a soldier's mate, that I would give a peeled codling for.'

'By the mass, that is strange. What, so many of our brave English hearts are abroad, and you, who seem to be a man of mark, have no friend, no kinsman, among them?'

'Nay, if you speak of kinsmen,' answered Gosling, 'I have one wild slip of a kinsman, who left us in the last year of Queen Mary; but he is better lost than found.'

'Do not say so, friend, unless you have heard ill of him lately. Many a wild colt has turned out a noble steed. His name, I pray you?'

'Michael Lambourne,' answered the landlord of the Black Bear; 'a son of my sister's—there is little pleasure in recollecting either the name or the connection.'

'Michael Lambourne!' said the stranger, as if endeavouring to recollect himself—'what, no relation to Michael Lambourne, the gallant cavalier who behaved so bravely at the siege of Venlo, that Grave Maurice thanked him at the head of the army? Men said he was an English cavalier, and of no high extraction.'

'It could scarcely be my nephew,' said Giles Gosling, 'for he had not the courage of a hen-partridge for aught but mischief.'

'Oh, many a man finds courage in the wars,' replied the stranger.

'It may be,' said the landlord; 'but I would have thought our Mike more likely to lose the little he had.'

'The Michael Lambourne whom I knew,' continued the traveller, 'was a likely fellow—went always gay and well attired, and had a hawk's eye after a pretty wench.'

'Our Michael,' replied the host, 'had the look of a dog with a bottle at its tail, and wore a coat every rag of which was bidding good-day to the rest.'

'Oh, men pick up good apparel in the wars,' replied the guest.

'Our Mike,' answered the landlord, 'was more like to pick it up in a frippery warehouse, while the broker was looking another way; and, for the hawk's eye you talk of, his was always after my stray spoons. He was tapster's boy here in this blessed house for a quarter of a year; and between misreckonings, miscarriages, mistakes, and misdemeanours, had he dwelt with me for three months longer, I might have pulled down sign, shut up house, and given the devil the key to keep.'

'You would be sorry, after all,' continued the traveller, were I to tell you poor Mike Lambourne was shot at the head of his regiment at the taking of a sconce near Maestricht?'

'Sorry!—it would be the blithest news I ever heard of him, since it would ensure me he was not hanged. But let him pass—I doubt his end will never do such credit to his friends; were it so, I should say—(taking another cup of sack)—Here's God rest him with all my heart.'

'Tush, man,' replied the traveller, 'never fear but you will have credit by your nephew yet, especially if he be the Michael Lambourne whom I knew, and loved very nearly, or altogether, as well as myself. Can you tell me no mark by which I could judge whether they be the same?'

'Faith, none that I can think of,' answered Giles Gosling, 'unless that our Mike had the gallows branded on his left shoulder for stealing a silver caudle-cup from Dame Snort of Hogsditch.'

'Nay, there you lie like a knave, uncle,' said the stranger, slipping aside his ruff, and turning down the sleeve of his doublet from his neck and shoulder; 'by this good day, my shoulder is as unscarred as thine own.'

'What, Mike, boy—Mike!' exclaimed the host;—'and is it thou, in good earnest? Nay, I have judged so for this half-hour: for I knew no other person would have ta'en half the interest in thee. But, Mike, an thy shoulder be unscathed as thou sayest, thou must own that Goodman Thong, the hangman, was merciful in his office, and stamped thee with a cold iron.'

'Tush, uncle—truce with your jests. Keep them to season your sour ale, and let us see what hearty welcome thou wilt give a kinsman who has rolled the world around for eighteen years; who has seen the sun set where it rises, and has travelled till the west has become the east.'

'Thou hast brought back one traveller's gift with thee, Mike, as I well see, and that was what thou least didst need to travel for. I remember well, among thine other qualities, there was no crediting a word which came from thy mouth.'

'Here's an unbelieving Pagan for you, gentlemen!' said Michael Lambourne, turning to those who witnessed this strange interview betwixt uncle and nephew, some of whom, being natives of the village, were no strangers to his juvenile wildness. 'This may be called slaying a Cumnor fatted calf for me with a vengeance. But, uncle, I come not from the husks and the swine-trough, and I care not for thy welcome or no welcome; I carry that with me will make me welcome, wend where I will.'

So saying, he pulled out a purse of gold, indifferently well filled, the sight of which produced a visible effect upon the company. Some shook their heads, and whispered to each other, while one or two of the less scrupulous speedily began to recollect him as a school-companion, a townsman, or so forth. On the other hand, two or three grave sedate-looking persons shook their heads, and left the inn, hinting, that if Giles Gosling wished to continue to thrive, he should turn his thriftless godless nephew adrift again, as soon as he could. Gosling demeaned himself, as if he were much of the same opinion; for even the sight of the gold made less impression on the honest gentleman, than it usually doth upon one of his calling.

'Kinsman Michael,' he said, 'put up thy purse. My sister's son shall be called to no reckoning in my house for supper or lodging; and I reckon thou wilt hardly wish to stay longer, where thou art e'en but too well known.'

'For that matter, uncle,' replied the traveller, 'I shall consult my own needs and conveniences. Meantime, I wish to give the supper and sleeping cup to those good townsmen, who are not too proud to remember Mike Lambourne, the tapster's boy. If you will let me have entertainment for my money, so—if not, it is but a short two minutes' walk to the Hare and Tabor, and I trust our neighbours will not grudge going thus far with me.'

'Nay, Mike,' replied his uncle, 'as eighteen years have gone over thy head, and I trust thou art somewhat amended in thy conditions, thou shalt not leave my house at this hour, and shalt e'en have whatever in reason you list to call for. But I would I knew that that purse of thine, which thou vapourest of, were as well come by as it seems well filled.'

'Here is an infidel for you, my good neighbours,' said Lambourne, again appealing to the audience. 'Here's a fellow will rip up his kinsman's follies of a good score of years standing. And for the gold, why, sirs, I have been where it grew, and was to be had for the gathering. In the New World have I been, man—in the Eldorado, where urchins play at cherry-pit with diamonds, and country wenches thread rubies for necklaces, instead of rowan-tree berries; where the pantiles are made of pure gold, and the paving-stones of virgin silver.'

'By my credit, friend Mike,' said young Lawrence Goldthred, the cutting mercer of Abingdon, 'that were a likely coast to trade to. And what may lawns, cypruses, and ribbons fetch, where gold is so plenty?'

'Oh, the profit were unutterable,' replied Lambourne, 'especially when a handsome young merchant bears the pack himself; for the ladies of that clime are bona-robas, and being themselves somewhat sunburnt, they catch fire like tinder at a fresh complexion like thine, with a head of hair inclining to be red.'

'I would I might trade thither,' said the mercer, chuckling.

'Why, and so thou mayst,' said Michael; 'that is, if thou art the same brisk boy who was partner with me at robbing the Abbot's orchard—'tis but a little touch of alchemy to decoct thy house and land into ready money, and that ready money into a tall ship, with sails, anchors, cordage, and all things conforming; then clap thy warehouse of goods under hatches, put fifty good fellows on deck, with myself to command them, and so hoist topsails, and hey for the New World.'

'Thou hast taught him a secret, kinsman,' said Giles Gosling, 'to decoct, an' that be the word, his pound into a penny, and his webs into a thread. Take a fool's advice, neighbour Goldthred.

Tempt not the sea, for she is a devourer. Let cards and cockatrices do their worst; thy father's bales may bide a banging for a year or two, ere thou comest to the Spital; but the sea hath a bottomless appetite, she would swallow the wealth of Lombard Street in a morning, as easily as I would a poached egg and a cup of clary—and for my kinsman's Eldorado, never trust me if I do not believe he has found it in the pouches of some such gulls as thyself. But take no snuff in the nose about it; fall to and welcome, for here comes the supper, and I heartily bestow it on all that will take share, in honour of my hopeful nephew's return, always trusting that he has come home another man. In faith, kinsman, thou art as like my poor sister as ever was son to mother.'

'Not quite so like old Benedict Lambourne her husband, though,' said the mercer, nodding and winking. 'Dost thou remember, Mike, what thou saidst when the schoolmaster's ferule was over thee for striking up thy father's crutches?—it is a wise child, saidst thou, that knows its own father. Dr Bircham laughed till he cried again, and his crying saved yours.'

'Well, he made it up to me many a day after,' said Lambourne; 'and how is the worthy pedagogue?'

'Dead,' said Giles Gosling, 'this many a day since.'

'That he is,' said the clerk of the parish; 'I sat by his bed the whilst—He passed away in a blessed frame, "Morior—mortuus sum vel fui—mori"—These were his latest words, and he just added, "my last verb is conjugated."'

'Well, peace be with him,' said Mike, 'he owes me nothing.'

'No, truly,' replied Goldthred; 'and every lash which he laid on thee, he always was wont to say, he spared the hangman a labour.'

'One would have thought he left him little to do then,' said the clerk; 'and yet Goodman Thong had no sinecure of it with our friend, after all.'

'*Voto a dios!*' exclaimed Lambourne, his patience appearing to fail him, as he snatched his broad, slouched hat from the table and placed it on his head, so that the shadow gave the sinister expression of a Spanish bravo, to eyes and features which naturally boded nothing pleasant,—'Harkee, my masters—all is fair among friends, and under the rose; and I have already permitted my worthy uncle here, and all of you, to use your pleasure with the frolics of my nonage. But I carry sword and dagger, my good friends, and can use them lightly too upon occasion—I have learned to be dangerous upon points of honour ever since I served the Spaniard, and I would not have you provoke me to the degree of falling foul.'

'Why, what would you do?' said the clerk.

'Ay, sir, what would you do?' said the mercer, bustling up on the other side of the table.

'Split your throat, and spoil your Sunday's quavering, Sir Clerk,' said Lambourne, fiercely; 'cudgel you, my worshipful dealer in flimsy sarsenets, into one of your own bales.'

'Come, come,' said the host, interposing, 'I will have no swaggering here. Nephew, it will become you best to show no haste to take offence; and you, gentlemen, will do well to remember, that if you are in an inn, still you are the innkeeper's guests, and should spare the honour of his family. I protest your silly broils make me as oblivious as yourself; for yonder sits my silent guest, as I call him, who hath been my two days' inmate, and hath never spoken a word, save to ask for his food and his reckoning—gives no more trouble than a very peasant—pays his shot like a prince royal—looks but at the sum total of the reckoning, and does not know what day he shall go away. Oh, 'tis a jewel of a guest! and yet, hand-dog that I am, I have suffered him to sit by himself like a castaway in yonder obscure nook, without so much as asking him to take bite or sup alongst with us. It were but the right guerdon of my incivility, were he to set off to the Hare and Tabor before the night grows older.'

With his white napkin gracefully arranged over his left arm, his velvet cap laid aside for the moment, and his best silver flagon in his right hand, mine host walked up to the solitary guest whom he mentioned, and thereby turned upon him the eyes of the assembled company.

He was a man aged betwixt twenty-five and thirty, rather above the middle size, dressed with plainness and decency, yet bearing an air of ease, which almost amounted to dignity, and which seemed to infer that his habit was rather beneath his rank. His countenance was reserved and thoughtful, with dark hair and dark eyes—the last, upon any momentary excitement, sparkled with uncommon lustre, but on other occasions had the same meditative and tranquil cast which was exhibited by his features. The busy curiosity of the little village had been employed to discover his name and quality, as well as his business at Cumnor; but nothing had transpired on either subject which could lead to its gratification. Giles Gosling, headborough of the place, and a steady friend to Queen Elizabeth and the Protestant religion, was at one time inclined to suspect his guest of being a Jesuit, or seminary priest, of whom Rome and Spain sent at this time so many to grace the gallows in England. But it was scarce possible to retain such a prepossession against a guest who gave so little trouble, paid his reckoning so regularly, and who proposed, as it seemed, to make a considerable stay at the bonny Black Bear.

'Papists,' argued Giles Gosling, 'are a pinching, close-fisted race, and this man would have found a lodging with the wealthy squire at Bessellsley, or with the old Knight at Wooton, or in some other of the Roman dens, instead of living in a house of public entertainment, as every honest man and good Christian should. Besides, on Friday, he stuck by the powdered beef and carrot, though there were as good spitchcock'd eels on the board as ever were ta'en out of the Isis.'

Honest Giles, therefore, satisfied himself that his guest was no Roman, and with all comely courtesy besought the stranger to pledge him in a draught of the cool tankard, and honour with his attention a small collation which he was giving to his nephew, in honour of his return, and, as he verily hoped, of his reformation. The stranger at first shook his head, as if declining the courtesy: but mine host proceeded to urge him with arguments founded on the credit of his house, and the construction which the good people of Cumnor might put upon such an unsocial humour.

'By my faith, sir,' he said, 'it touches my reputation that men should be merry in my house, and we have ill tongues amongst us at Cumnor (as where be there not?), who put an evil mark on men who pull their hat over their brows as if they were looking back to the days that are gone, instead of enjoying the blithe sunshiny weather which God has sent us in the sweet looks of our sovereign mistress, Queen Elizabeth, whom Heaven long bless and preserve.'

'Why, mine host,' answered the stranger, 'there is no treason, sure, in a man enjoying his own thoughts, under the shadow of his own bonnet? You have lived in the world twice as long as I have, and you must know there are thoughts that will haunt us in spite of ourselves, and to which it is in vain to say, begone, and let me be merry.'

'By my sooth,' answered Giles Gosling, 'if such troublesome thoughts haunt your mind, and will not get them gone for plain English, we will have one of Father Bacon's pupils from Oxford, to conjure them away with logic and with Hebrew. Or, what say you to laying them in a glorious red sea of claret, my noble guest? Come, sir, excuse my freedom. I am an old host, and must have my talk. This peevish humour of melancholy sits ill upon you— it suits not with a sleek boot, a hat of a trim block, a fresh cloak, and a full purse—A pize on it, send it off to those who have their legs swathed with a hay-wisp, their heads thatched with a felt bonnet, their jerkin as thin as a cobweb, and their pouch without ever a cross to keep the fiend Melancholy from dancing in it. Cheer up, sir! or by this good liquor we will banish thee from the joys of blithsome company, into the mists of melancholy and the land of little-ease. Here be a set of good fellows willing to be merry; do not scowl on them like the devil looking over Lincoln.'

'You say well, my worthy host,' said the guest, with a melancholy smile, which, melancholy as it was, gave a very pleasant expression to his countenance—'You say well, my jovial friend; and they that are moody like myself, should not disturb the mirth of those who are happy. I will drink a round with your guests with all my heart, rather than be termed a mar-feast.'

So saying, he rose and joined the company, which, encouraged by the precept and example of Michael Lambourne, and consisting chiefly of persons much disposed to profit by the opportunity of a merry meal at the expense of their landlord, had already made some inroads upon the limits of temperance; as was evident from the tone in which Michael inquired after his old acquaintances in the town, and the bursts of laughter with which each answer was received. Giles Gosling himself was somewhat scandalised at the obstreperous nature of their mirth, especially as he involuntarily felt some respect for his unknown guest. He paused, therefore, at some distance from the table occupied by these noisy revellers, and began to make a sort of apology for their licence.

'You would think,' he said, 'to hear these fellows talk, that there was not one of them who had not been bred to live by Stand and Deliver; and yet to-morrow you will find them a set of as painstaking mechanics, and so forth, as ever cut an inch short of measure, or paid a letter of change in light crowns over a counter. The mercer there, that wears his hat awry, over a shagged head of hair that looks like a curly water-dog's back, goes unbraced, wears his cloak on one side, and affects a ruffianly vapouring humour,—when in his shop at Abingdon, he is, from his flat cap to his glistening shoes, as precise in his apparel as if he was named for mayor. He talks of breaking parks, and taking the highway, in such fashion that you would think he haunted every night betwixt Hounslow and London; when, in fact, he may be found sound asleep in his feather-bed, with a candle placed beside him on one side, and a Bible on the other, to fright away the goblins.'

'And your nephew, mine host, this same Michael Lambourne, who is lord of the feast, is he, too, such a would-be ruffler as the rest of them?'

'Why, there you push me hard,' said the host; 'my nephew is my nephew, and though he was a desperate Dick of yore, yet Mike may have mended like other folks, you wot—And I would not have you think all I said of him, even now, was strict gospel— I knew the wag all the while, and wished to pluck his plumes from him. And now, sir, by what name shall I present my worshipful guest to these gallants?'

'Marry, mine host,' replied the stranger,—'you may call me Tressilian.'

'Tressilian?' answered my host of the Bear, 'a worthy name; and, as I think, of Cornish lineage; for what says the south proverb—

'By Pol, Tre, and Pen,
You may know the Cornish men.

Shall I say the worthy Mr Tressilian of Cornwall?'

'Say no more than I have given you warrant for, mine host, and so shall you be sure you speak no more than is true. A man may have one of those honourable prefixes to his name, yet be born far from Saint Michael's Mount.'

Mine host pushed his curiosity no further, but presented Mr Tressilian to his nephew's company, who, after exchange of salutations, and drinking to the health of their new companion, pursued the conversation in which he found them engaged, seasoning it with many an intervening pledge.

Talk you of young Master Lancelot?—*Merchant of Venice.*

AFTER some brief interval, Master Goldthred, at the earnest instigation of mine host, and the joyous concurrence of his guests, indulged the company with the following morsel of melody:—

'Of all the birds on bush or tree,
    Commend me to the owl,
Since he may best ensample be
    To those the cup that trowel.
For when the sun hath left the west,
He chooses the tree that he loves the best,
And he whoops out his song, and he laughs at his jest;
Then though hours be late, and weather foul,
We'll drink to the health of the bonny, bonny owl.

'The lark is but a bumpkin fowl,
    He sleeps in his nest till morn;
But my blessing upon the jolly owl,
    That all night blows his horn.
Then up with your cup till you stagger in speech,
And match me this catch though you swagger and screech,
And drink till you wink, my merry men each;
For though hours be late, and weather be foul,
We'll drink to the health of the bonny, bonny owl.'

'There is savour in this, my hearts,' said Michael, when the mercer had finished his song, 'and some goodness seems left among you yet—but what a bead-roll you have read me of old comrades, and to every man's name tacked some ill-omened motto! And so Swashing Will of Wallingford hath bid us good-night?'

'He died the death of a fat buck,' said one of the party, 'being shot with a crossbow bolt, by old Thatcham, the Duke's stout park-keeper at Donnington Castle.'

'Ay, ay, he always loved venison well,' replied Michael, 'and a cup of claret to boot—and so here's one to his memory. Do me right, my masters.'

When the memory of this departed worthy had been duly honoured, Lambourne proceeded to inquire after Prance of Padworth.

'Pranced off—made immortal ten years since,' said the mercer; 'marry, sir, Oxford Castle and Goodman Thong, and a twopenny-worth of cord, best know how.'

'What, so they hung poor Prance high and dry? So much for loving to walk by moonlight—a cup to his memory, my masters—all merry fellows like moonlight. What has become of Hal with the plume?—he who lived near Yattenden, and wore the long feather—I forget his name.'

'What, Hal Hempseed?' replied the mercer, 'why, you may remember he was a sort of a gentleman, and would meddle in state matters, and so he got into the mire about the Duke of Norfolk's affair these two or three years since, fled the country with a pursuivant's warrant at his heels, and has never since been heard of.'

'Nay, after these baulks,' said Michael Lambourne, 'I need hardly inquire after Tony Foster; for when ropes and crossbow shafts, and pursuivant's warrants, and such like gear were so rife, Tony could hardly 'scape them.'

'Which Tony Foster mean you?' said the innkeeper.

'Why, he they called Tony Fire-the-Fagot, because he brought a light to kindle the pile round Latimer and Ridley, when the wind blew out Jack Thong's torch, and no man else would give him light for love or money.'

'Tony Foster lives and thrives,' said the host. 'But, kinsman, I would not have you call him Tony Fire-the-Fagot, if you would not brook the stab.'

'How! is he grown ashamed on't?' said Lambourne; 'why, he was wont to boast of it, and say he liked as well to see a roasted heretic as a roasted ox.'

'Ay, but, kinsman, that was in Mary's time,' replied the landlord, 'when Tony's father was Reeve here to the Abbot of Abingdon. But since that, Tony married a pure precisian, and is as good a Protestant, I warrant you, as the best.'

'And looks grave, and holds his head high, and scorns his old companions,' said the mercer.

'Then he hath prospered, I warrant him,' said Lambourne; 'for ever when a man hath got nobles of his own, he keeps out of the way of those whose exchequers lie in other men's purchase.

'Prospered, quotha!' said the mercer, 'why, you remember Cumnor Place, the old mansion-house beside the churchyard?'

'By the same token, I robbed the orchard three times—what of that?—It was the old Abbot's residence when there was plague or sickness at Abingdon.'

'Ay,' said the host, 'but that has been long over; and Anthony Foster hath a right in it, and lives there by some grant from a great courtier, who had the church-lands from the Crown; and there he dwells, and has as little to do with any poor wight in Cumnor, as if he were himself a belted knight.'

'Nay,' said the mercer, 'it is not altogether pride in Tony neither—there is a fair lady in the case, and Tony will scarce let the light of day look on her.'

'How,' said Tressilian, who now for the first time interfered in their conversation; 'did ye not say this Foster was married, and to a precisian?'

'Married he was, and to as bitter a precisian as ever eat flesh in Lent; and a cat-and-dog life she led with Tony, as men said. But she is dead, rest be with her, and Tony hath but a slip of a daughter; so it is thought he means to wed this stranger, that men keep such a coil about.'

'And why so?—I mean, why do they keep a coil about her?' said Tressilian.

'Why, I wot not,' answered the host, 'except that men say she is as beautiful as an angel, and no one knows whence she comes, and every one wishes to know why she is kept so closely mewed up. For my part, I never saw her—you have, I think, Master Goldthred?'

'That I have, old boy,' said the mercer. 'Look you, I was riding hither from Abingdon—I passed under the east oriel window of the old mansion, where all the old saints and histories and such like are painted—It was not the common path I took, but one through the Park; for the postern-door was upon the latch, and I thought I might take the privilege of an old comrade to ride across through the trees, both for shading, as the day was somewhat hot, and for avoiding of dust, because I had on my peach-coloured doublet, pinked out with cloth of gold.'

'Which garment,' said Michael Lambourne, 'thou wouldst willingly make twinkle in the eyes of a fair dame. Ah! villain, thou wilt never leave thy old tricks.'

'Not so—not so,' said the mercer, with a smirking laugh; 'not altogether so—but curiosity, thou knowest, and a strain of

37

compassion withal,—for the poor young lady sees nothing from morn to even but Tony Foster, with his scowling black brows, his bull's head, and his bandy legs.'

'And thou wouldst willingly show her a dapper body, in a silken jerkin—a limb like a short-legged hen's, in a cordovan boot, and a round, simpering, what d'ye lack, sort of a countenance, set off with a velvet bonnet, a Turkey feather, and a gilded brooch. Ah! jolly mercer, they who have good wares are fond to show them. Come, gentles, let not the cup stand, here's to long spurs, short boots, full bonnets, and empty skulls!'

'Nay, now, you are jealous of me, Mike,' said Goldthred; 'and yet my luck was but what might have happened to thee, or any man.'

'Marry confound thine impudence,' retorted Lambourne; 'thou wouldst not compare thy pudding face, and sarsenet manners, to a gentleman and a soldier!'

'Nay, my good sir,' said Tressilian, 'let me beseech you will not interrupt the gallant citizen; methinks he tells his tale so well, I could hearken to him till midnight.'

'It's more of your favour than of my desert,' answered Master Goldthred; 'but since I give you pleasure, worthy Master Tressilian, I shall proceed, maugre all the gibes and quips of this valiant soldier, who, peradventure, hath had more cuffs than crowns in the Low Countries. And so, sir, as I passed under the great painted window, leaving my rein loose on my ambling palfrey's neck, partly for mine ease and partly that I might have the more leisure to peer about, I hears me the lattice open; and never credit me, sir, if there did not stand there the person of as fair a woman as ever crossed mine eyes, and I think I have looked on as many pretty wenches, and with as much judgment, as other folks.'

'May I ask her appearance, sir?' said Tressilian.

'Oh, sir,' replied Master Goldthred, 'I promise you, she was in gentlewoman's attire—a very quaint and pleasing dress, that might have served the Queen herself; for she had a forepart with body and sleeves, of ginger-coloured satin, which, in my judgment, must have cost by the yard some thirty shillings, lined with murrey taffeta, and laid down and guarded with two broad laces of gold and silver. And her hat, sir, was truly the best-fashioned thing that I have seen in these parts, being of tawney taffeta, embroidered with scorpions of Venice Gold, and having a border garnished with gold fringe;—I promise you, sir, an absolute and all-surpassing device. Touching her skirts, they were in the old pass-devant fashion.'

'I did not ask you of her attire, sir,' said Tressilian, who had shown some impatience during this minute description, 'but of her complexion—the colour of her hair, her features.'

'Touching her complexion,' answered the mercer, 'I am not so special certain; but I marked that her fan had an ivory handle, curiously inlaid;—and then again, as to the colour of her hair, why, I can warrant, be its hue what it might, that she wore above it a net of green silk, parcel twisted with gold.'

'A most mercer-like memory!' said Lambourne; 'the gentleman asks him of the lady's beauty, and he talks of her fine clothes!'

'I tell thee,' said the mercer, somewhat disconcerted, 'I had little time to look at her; for just as I was about to give her the good time of day, and for that purpose had puckered my features with a smile——'

'Like those of a jackanape, simpering at a chestnut,' said Michael Lambourne.

'—Up started of a sudden,' continued Goldthred, without heeding the interruption, 'Tony Foster himself, with a cudgel in his hand——'

'And broke thy head across, I hope, for thine impertinence,' said his entertainer.

'That were more easily said than done,' answered Goldthred indignantly; 'no, no—there was no breaking of heads—it's true, he advanced his cudgel, and spoke of laying on, and asked why I did not keep the public road, and such like; and I would have knocked him over the pate handsomely for his pains, only for the lady's presence, who might have swooned, for what I know.'

'Now, out upon thee for a faint-spirited slave!' said Lambourne; 'what adventurous knight ever thought of the lady's terror, when he went to thwack giant, dragon, or magician, in her presence, and for her deliverance? But why talk to thee of dragons, who would be driven back by a dragon-fly. There thou hast missed the rarest opportunity!'

'Take it thyself, then, bully Mike,' answered Goldthred. 'Yonder is the enchanted manor, and the dragon and the lady all at thy service, if thou darest venture on them.'

'Why, so I would for a quartern of sack,' said the soldier—

'Or stay—I am foully out of linen—wilt thou bet a piece of hollands against these five angels, that I go not up to the Hall to-morrow, and force Tony Foster to introduce me to his fair guest?'

'I accept your wager,' said the mercer; 'and I think, though thou hadst even the impudence of the devil, I shall gain on thee this bout. Our landlord here shall hold stakes, and I will stake down gold till I send thee linen.'

'I will hold stakes on no such matter,' said Gosling. 'Good now, my kinsman, drink your wine in quiet, and let such ventures alone. I promise you, Master Foster hath interest enough to lay you up in lavender in the Castle at Oxford, or to get your legs made acquainted with the town-stocks.'

'That would be but renewing an old intimacy; for Mike's shins and the town's wooden pinfold have been well known to each other ere now,' said the mercer; 'but he shall not budge from his wager, unless he means to pay forfeit.'

'Forfeit?' said Lambourne; 'I scorn it. I value Tony Foster's wrath no more than a shelled pea-cod, and I will visit his Linda-brides, by Saint George, be he willing or no.'

'I would gladly pay your halves of the risk, sir,' said Tressilian, 'to be permitted to accompany you on the adventure.'

'In what would that advantage you, sir?' answered Lambourne.

'In nothing, sir,' said Tressilian, 'unless to mark the skill and valour with which you conduct yourself. I am a traveller, who seeks for strange rencounters and uncommon passages, as the knights of yore did after adventures and feats of arms.'

'Nay, if it pleasures you to see a trout tickled,' answered Lambourne, 'I care not how many witness my skill. And so here I drink success to my enterprise; and he that will not pledge me on his knees is a rascal, and I will cut his legs off by the garter.'

The draught which Michael Lambourne took upon this occasion had been preceded by so many others, that reason tottered on her throne. He swore one or two incoherent oaths at the mercer, who refused, reasonably enough, to pledge him to a sentiment which inferred the loss of his own wager.

'Wilt thou chop logic with me,' said Lambourne, 'thou knave, with no more brains than are in a skein of revelled silk? By Heaven, I will cut thee into fifty yards of galloon lace!'

But as he attempted to draw his sword for this doughty purpose,

Michael Lambourne was seized upon by the tapster and the chamberlain, and conveyed to his own apartment, there to sleep himself sober at his leisure.

The party then broke up, and the guests took their leave; much more to the contentment of mine host than of some of the company, who were unwilling to quit good liquor, when it was to be had for free cost, so long as they were able to sit by it. They were, however, compelled to remove; and go at length they did, leaving Gosling and Tressilian in the empty apartment.

'By my faith,' said the former, 'I wonder where our great folks find pleasure, when they spend their means in entertainment, and in playing mine host without sending in a reckoning. It is but what I rarely practise; and whenever I do, by Saint Julian, it grieves me beyond measure. Each of these empty stoups now, which my nephew and his drunken comrades have swilled off, should have been a matter of profit to one in my line, and I must set them down a dead loss . . . I cannot, for my heart, conceive the pleasure of noise, and nonsense, and drunken freaks and drunken quarrels, and smut, and blasphemy, and so forth, when a man loses money instead of gaining by it. And yet many a fair estate is lost in upholding such a useless course, and that greatly contributes to the decay of publicans; for who the devil do you think would pay for drink at the Black Bear, when he can have it for nothing at my Lord's or the Squire's?'

Tressilian perceived that the wine had made some impression even on the seasoned brain of mine host, which was chiefly to be inferred from his declaiming against drunkenness. As he himself had carefully avoided the bowl, he would have availed himself of the frankness of the moment, to extract from Gosling some further information upon the subject of Anthony Foster, and the lady whom the mercer had seen in his mansion-house; but his inquiries only set the host upon a new theme of declamation against the wiles of the fair sex, in which he brought, at full length, the whole wisdom of Solomon to reinforce his own. Finally, he turned his admonitions, mixed with much objurgation, upon his tapsters and drawers, who were employed in removing the relics of the entertainment, and restoring order to the apartment; and at length, joining example to precept, though with no good success, he demolished a salver with half a score of glasses, in attempting to show how much service was done at the Three

Cranes in the Vintry, then the most topping cavern in London. This last accident so far recalled him to his better self, that he retired to his bed, slept sound, and awoke a new man in the morning.

3

Nay, I'll hold touch—the game shall be play'd out,
It ne'er shall sup for me, this merry wager;
That which I say when gamesome, I'll avouch
In my most sober mood, ne'er trust me else.
                                        The Hazard-Table.

'AND how doth your kinsman, good mine host?' said Tressilian, when Giles Gosling first appeared in the public room on the morning following the revel, which we described in the last chapter. 'Is he well, and will he abide by his wager?'

'For well, sir, he started two hours since, and has visited I know not what purlieus of his old companions; hath but now returned, and is at this instant breakfasting on new-laid eggs and muscadine; and for his wager, I caution you as a friend to have little to do with that, or indeed with aught that Mike proposes. Wherefore, I counsel you to a warm breakfast upon a culiss, which shall restore the tone of the stomach; and let my nephew and Master Goldthred swagger about their wager as they list.'

'It seems to me, mine host,' said Tressilian, 'that you know not well what to say about this kinsman of yours; and that you can neither blame nor commend him without some twinge of conscience.'

'You have spoken truly, Master Tressilian,' replied Giles Gosling. 'There is natural affection whimpering into one ear, "Giles, Giles, why wilt thou take away the good name of thy own nephew? Wilt thou defame thy sister's son, Giles Gosling? wilt thou defoul thine own nest, dishonour thine own blood?" And then, again, comes Justice, and says, "Here is a worthy guest as ever came to the bonny Black Bear; one who never challenged a reckoning (as I say to your face you never did, Master Tressilian—not that you have had cause), one who knows not why he came, so far as I can see, or when he is going away; and wilt thou, being a publican, having paid scot and lot these thirty years in the town of Cumnor, and being at this instant headborough, wilt thou suffer this guest of guests, this man of men, this six-hooped pot (as I may say) of a traveller, to fall into the meshes of thy nephew, who is known for a swasher and a desperate Dick, a carder and a dicer, a professor of the seven damnable sciences, if ever man took degrees in them?"—No, by Heaven! I might wink, and let him catch such a small butterfly as Goldthred; but thou my guest, shalt be forewarned, forearmed, so thou wilt but listen to thy trusty host.'

'Why, mine host, thy counsel shall not be cast away,' replied Tressilian; 'however, I must uphold my share in this wager, having once passed my word to that effect. But lend me, I pray, some of thy counsel. This Foster, who, or what is he, and why makes he such mystery of his female inmate?'

'Troth,' replied Gosling, 'I can add but little to what you heard last night. He was one of Queen Mary's Papists, and now he is one of Queen Elizabeth's Protestants; he was an on-hanger of the Abbot of Abingdon, and now he lives as master of the manor-house. Above all, he was poor and is rich. Folks talk of private apartments in his old waste mansion-house, bedizened fine enough to serve the Queen, God bless her. Some men think he found a treasure in the orchard, some that he sold himself to the devil for treasure, and some say that he cheated the Abbot out of the church plate, which was hidden in the old Manor-house at the Reformation. Rich, however, he is, and God and his conscience, with the devil perhaps besides, only know how he came by it. He has sulky ways too, breaking off intercourse with all that are of the place, as if he had either some strange secret to keep, or held himself to be made of another clay than we are. I think it likely my kinsman and he will quarrel, if Mike thrusts his acquaintance on him; and I am sorry that you, my worthy Master Tressilian, will still think of going in my nephew's company.'

Tressilian again answered him, that he would proceed with great caution, and that he should have no fears on his account; in short, he bestowed on him all the customary assurances with which those who are determined on a rash action are wont to parry the advice of their friends.

Meantime, the traveller accepted the landlord's invitation, and had just finished the excellent breakfast which was served to him and Gosling by pretty Cicely, the beauty of the bar, when the hero of the preceding night, Michael Lambourne, entered the apartment. His toilet had apparently cost him some labour, for his clothes, which differed from those he wore on his journey, were of the newest fashion, and put on with great attention to the display of his person.

'By my faith, uncle,' said the gallant, 'you made a wet night of it, and I feel it followed by a dry morning. I will pledge you willingly in a cup of bastard. How, my pretty coz, Cicely! why, I left you but a child in the cradle, and there thou stand'st in thy velvet waistcoat, as tight a girl as England's sun shines on. Know thy friends and kindred, Cicely, and come hither, child, that I may kiss thee, and give thee my blessing.'

'Concern not yourself about Cicely, kinsman,' said Giles Gosling, 'but e'en let her go her way, a' God's name; for although your mother were her father's sister, yet that shall not make you and her cater-cousins.'

'Why, uncle,' replied Lambourne, 'think'st thou I am an infidel, and would harm those of mine own house?'

'It is for no harm that I speak, Mike,' answered his uncle, 'but a simple humour of precaution which I have. True, thou art as well gilded as a snake when he casts his old slough in the spring-time; but for all that, thou creepest not into my Eden. I will look after mine Eve, Mike, and so content thee. But how brave thou be'st, lad! To look on thee now, and compare thee with Master Tressilian here, in his sad-coloured riding-suit, who would not say that thou wert the real gentleman, and he the tapster's boy?'

'Troth, uncle,' replied Lambourne, 'no one would say so but one of your country-breeding, that knows no better. I will say, and I care not who hears me, there is something about the real gentry that few men come up to that are not born and bred to the mystery. I wot not where the trick lies; but although I can enter an ordinary with as much audacity, rebuke the waiters and drawer as loudly, drink as deep a health, swear as round an oath, and fling my gold as freely about as any of the jingling spurs and white feathers that are around me,—yet, hang me if I can ever catch the true grace of it, though I have practised for an hundred times. The man of the house sets me lowest at the board, and carves to me the last; and the drawer says,—"Coming, friend," without any more reverence or regardful addition. But, hang it, let it pass, care killed a cat. I have gentry enough to pass the trick on Tony Fire-the-Fagot, and that will do for the matter in hand.'

'You hold your purpose, then, of visiting your old acquaintance?' said Tressilian, to the adventurer.

'Ay, sir,' replied Lambourne; 'when stakes are made, the game must be played; that is gamester's law, all over the world. You, sir, unless my memory fails me (for I did steep it somewhat too deeply in the sack-butt), took some share in my hazard.'

'I propose to accompany you in your adventure,' said Tressilian, 'if you will do me so much grace as to permit me; and I have staked my share of the forfeit in the hands of our worthy host.'

'That he hath,' answered Giles Gosling, 'in as fair Harry-nobles as ever were melted into sack by a good fellow. So, luck to your enterprise, since you will needs venture on Tony Foster; but, by my credit, you were better take another draught before you depart, for your welcome at the Hall, yonder, will be somewhat of the driest. And if you do get into peril, beware of taking to cold steel; but send for me, Giles Gosling the headborough, and I may be able to make something out of Tony yet, for as proud as he is.'

The nephew dutifully obeyed his uncle's hint, by taking a second and deeper pull at the tankard, observing, that his wit never served him so well as when he had washed his temples with a deep morning's draught; and they set forth together for the habitation of Anthony Foster.

The village of Cumnor is pleasantly situated on a hill; and in a wooded park closely adjacent, stood the ancient mansion occupied at this time by Anthony Foster, of which the ruins may be still extant. The park was then full of large trees, and, in particular, of ancient and mighty oaks, which stretched their giant arms over the high wall surrounding the demesne, thus giving it a melancholy, secluded, and monastic appearance. The entrance to the park lay through an old-fashioned gateway in the outer wall, the door of which was formed by two huge oaken leaves, thickly studded with nails, like the gate of an old town.

'We shall be finely holped up here,' said Michael Lambourne, looking at the gateway and gate, 'if this fellow's suspicious humour should refuse us admission altogether, as it is like he may, in case this linsey-wolsey fellow of a mercer's visit to his premises has disquieted him. But, no,' he added, pushing the huge gate, which gave way, 'the door stands invitingly open; and here we are within the forbidden ground, without other impediment than the passive resistance of a heavy oak door, moving on rusty hinges.'

They stood now in an avenue overshadowed by such old trees

as we have described, and which had been bordered at one time by high hedges of yew and holly. But these having been untrimmed for many years, had run up into great bushes, or rather dwarf-trees, and now encroached, with their dark and melancholy boughs, upon the road which they once had screened. The avenue itself was grown up with grass, and, in one or two places, interrupted by piles of withered brushwood, which had been lopped from the trees cut down in the neighbouring park, and was here stacked for drying. Formal walks and avenues, which, at different points, crossed this principal approach, were, in like manner, choked up and interrupted by piles of brushwood and billets, and in other places, by underwood and brambles. Besides the general effect of desolation which is so strongly impressed, whenever we behold the contrivances of man wasted and obliterated by neglect, and witness the marks of social life effaced gradually by the influence of vegetation, the size of the trees, and the outspreading extent of their boughs, diffused a gloom over the scene, even when the sun was at the highest, and made a proportional impression on the mind of those who visited it. This was felt even by Michael Lambourne, however alien his habits were to receiving any impressions, excepting from things which addressed themselves immediately to his passions.

'This wood is as dark as a wolf's mouth,' said he to Tressilian, as they walked together slowly along the solitary and broken approach, and were just come in sight of the monastic front of the old mansion, with its shafted windows, brick walls, overgrown with ivy and creeping shrubs, and twisted stalks of chimneys, of heavy stonework. 'And yet,' continued Lambourne, 'it is fairly done on the part of Foster too; for since he chooses not visitors, it is right to keep his place in a fashion that will invite few to trespass upon his privacy. But had he been the Anthony I once knew him, these sturdy oaks had long since become the property of some honest wood-monger, and the manor-close here had looked lighter at midnight than it now does at noon, while Foster played fast and loose with the price, in some cunning corner in the purlieus of White-friars.'

'Was he then such an unthrift,' asked Tressilian.

'He was,' answered Lambourne, 'like the rest of us, no saint, and no saver. But what I liked worst of Tony was, that he loved to take his pleasure by himself, and grudged, as men say, every drop of water that went past his own mill. I have known him deal with such measures of wine when he was alone, as I would not have ventured on with aid of the best toper in Berkshire—that, and some sway towards superstition, which he had by temperament, rendered him unworthy the company of a good fellow. And now he has earthed himself here, in a den just befitting such a sly fox as himself.'

'May I ask you, Master Lambourne,' said Tressilian, 'since your old companion's humour jumps so little with your own, wherefore you are so desirous to renew acquaintance with him?'

'And may I ask you, in return, Master Tressilian,' answered Lambourne, 'wherefore you have shown yourself so desirous to accompany me on this party?'

'I told you my motive,' said Tressilian, 'when I took share in your wager,—it was simple curiosity.'

'La you there now!' answered Lambourne: 'See how you civil and discreet gentlemen think to use us who live by the free exercise of our wits! Had I answered your question, by saying that it was simple curiosity which led me to visit my old comrade Anthony Foster, I warrant you had set it down for an evasion, and a turn of my trade. But any answer, I suppose, must serve my turn.'

'And wherefore should not bare curiosity,' said Tressilian, 'be a sufficient reason for my taking this walk with you?'

'Oh, content yourself, sir,' replied Lambourne; 'you cannot put the change on me so easy as you think, for I have lived among the quick-stirring spirits of the age too long to swallow chaff for grain. You are a gentleman of birth and breeding—your bearing makes it good;—of civil habits and fair reputation—your manners declare it, and my uncle avouches it; and yet you associate yourself with a sort of scant-of-grace, as men call me; and, knowing me to be such, you make yourself my companion in a visit to a man whom you are a stranger to, and all out of mere curiosity forsooth? The excuse, if curiously balanced, would be found to want some scruples of just weight, or so.'

'If your suspicions were just,' said Tressilian, 'you have shown no confidence in me to invite or deserve mine.'

'Oh, if that be all,' said Lambourne, 'my motives lie above water. While this gold of mine lasts,'—taking out his purse, chucking it into the air, and catching it as it fell,—'I will make it

48

buy pleasure, and when it is out, I must have more. Now, if this mysterious Lady of the Manor—this fair Lindabrides of Tony Fire-the-Fagot, be so admirable a piece as men say, why there is chance that she may aid me to melt my nobles into groats; and, again, if Anthony be so wealthy a chuff as report speaks him, he may prove the philosopher's stone to me, and convert my groats into fair rose-nobles again.'

'A comfortable proposal truly,' said Tressilian; 'but I see not what chance there is of accomplishing it.'

'Not to-day, or perchance to-morrow,' answered Lambourne; 'I expect not to catch the old Jack till I have disposed my ground baits handsomely. But I know something more of his affairs this morning than I did last night, and I will so use my knowledge that he shall think it more perfect than it is. Nay, without expecting either pleasure or profit, or both, I had not stepped a stride within this manor, I can tell you; for I promise you I hold our visit not altogether without risk. But here we are, and we must make the best on't.'

While he thus spoke, they had entered a large orchard which surrounded the house on two sides, though the trees, abandoned by the care of man, were overgrown and mossy, and seemed to bear little fruit. Those which had been formerly trained as espaliers, had now resumed their natural mode of growing, and exhibited grotesque forms, partaking of the original training which they had received. The greater part of the ground, which had once been parterres and flower-gardens, was suffered in like manner to run to waste, excepting a few patches which had been dug up, and planted with ordinary pot-herbs. Some statues, which had ornamented the garden in its days of splendour, were now thrown down from their pedestals and broken in pieces, and a large summer-house having a heavy stone front, decorated with carving representing the life and actions of Samson, was in the same dilapidated condition.

They had just traversed this garden of the sluggard, and were within a few steps of the door of the mansion, when Lambourne had ceased speaking; a circumstance very agreeable to Tressilian, as it saved him the embarrassment of either commenting upon or replying to the frank avowal which his companion had just made of the sentiments and view that had induced him to come hither. Lambourne knocked roundly and boldly at the huge door of the mansion, observing at the same time, he had seen a less strong one upon a county jail. It was not until they had knocked more than once, that an aged, sour-visaged domestic reconnoitred them through a small square hole in the door, well-secured with bars of iron, and demanded what they wanted.

'To speak with Master Foster instantly, on pressing business of the state,' was the ready reply of Michael Lambourne.

'Methinks you will find difficulty to make that good,' said Tressilian in a whisper to his companion, while the servant went to carry the message to his master.

'Tush,' replied the adventurer; 'no soldier would go on were he always to consider when and how he should come off. Let us once obtain entrance, and all will go well enough.'

In a short time the servant returned, and drawing with a careful hand both bolt and bar, opened the gate, which admitted them through an archway into a square court, surrounded by buildings. Opposite to the arch was another door, which the servant-man in like manner unlocked, and thus introduced them into a stone-paved parlour, where there was but little furniture, and that of the rudest and most ancient fashion. The windows were tall and ample, reaching almost to the roof of the room, which was composed of black oak; those opening to the quadrangle were obscured by the height of the surrounding buildings, and, as they were traversed with massive shafts of solid stone-work, and thickly painted with religious devices, and scenes taken from scripture history, by no means admitted light in proportion to their size: and what did penetrate through them partook of the dark and gloomy tinge of the stained glass.

Tressilian and his guide had time enough to observe all these particulars, for they waited some space in the apartment ere the present master of the mansion at length made his appearance. Prepared as he was to see an inauspicious and ill-looking person, the ugliness of Anthony Foster considerably exceeded what Tressilian had anticipated. He was of middle stature, built strongly, but so clumsily as to border on deformity, and to give all his motions the ungainly awkwardness of a left-legged and left-handed man. His hair, in arranging which men at that time, as at present, were very nice and curious, instead of being carefully cleaned and disposed into short curls, or else set up on end, as is represented in old paintings, in a manner resembling that used by fine gentlemen of our own day, escaped in sable negligence from under a furred bonnet, and hung in elf-locks, which seemed strangers to the comb, over his rugged brows, and around his very singular and unprepossessing countenance. His keen dark eyes were deep set beneath broad and shaggy eyebrows, and, as they were usually bent on the ground, seemed as if they were themselves ashamed of the expression natural to them, and, were desirous to conceal it from the observation of men. At times, however, when, more intent on observing others, he suddenly raised them, and fixed them keenly on those with whom he conversed, they seemed to express both the fiercer passions, and the power of mind which could at will suppress or disguise the intensity of inward feeling. The features which corresponded with these eyes and this form were irregular, and marked so as to be indelibly fixed on the mind of him who had once seen them. Upon the whole, as Tressilian could not help acknowledging to himself, the Anthony Foster who now stood before him was the last person, judging from personal appearance, upon whom one would have chosen to intrude an unexpected and undesired visit. His attire was a doublet of russet leather, like those worn by the better sort of country folks, girt with a buff belt, in which was stuck on the right side a long knife or dudgeon-dagger, and on the other a cutlass. He raised his eyes as he entered the room, and fixed a keenly penetrating glance upon his two visitors, then cast them down as if counting his steps, while he advanced slowly into the middle of the room, and said, in a low and smothered tone of voice, 'Let me pray you, gentlemen, to tell me the cause of this visit.'

He looked as if he expected the answer from Tressilian; so true was Lambourne's observation, that the superior air of breeding and dignity shone through the disguise of an inferior dress. But it was Michael who replied to him, with the easy familiarity of an old friend, and a tone which seemed unembarrassed by any doubt of the most cordial reception.

'Ha! my dear friend and ingle, Tony Foster!' he exclaimed, seizing upon the unwilling hand, and shaking it with such emphasis as almost to stagger the sturdy frame of the person whom he addressed; 'how fares it with you for many a long year? What! have you altogether forgotten your friend, gossip, and playfellow, Michael Lambourne?'

'Michael Lambourne!' said Foster, looking at him a moment,

then dropping his eyes, and with little ceremony extricating his hand from the friendly grasp of the person by whom he was addressed, 'are you Michael Lambourne?'

'Ay; sure as you are Anthony Foster,' replied Lambourne.

"Tis well!' answered his sullen host; 'and what may Michael Lambourne expect from his visit hither?'

'*Voto a Dios*,' answered Lambourne, 'I expected a better welcome than I am like to meet, I think.'

'Why, thou gallows-bird—thou jail-rat—thou friend of the hangman and his customers,' replied Foster, 'hast thou the assurance to expect countenance from any one whose neck is beyond the compass of a Tyburn tippet?'

'It may be with me as you say,' replied Lambourne; 'and suppose I grant it to be so for argument's sake, I were still good enough society for mine ancient friend Anthony Fire-the-Fagot, though he be, for the present, by some indescribable title, the master of Cumnor Place.'

'Hark you, Michael Lambourne,' said Foster; 'you are a gambler now, and live by the counting of chances—Compute me the odds that I do not, on this instant, throw you out of that window into the ditch there.'

'Twenty to one that you do not,' answered the sturdy visitor.

'And wherefore, I pray you?' demanded Anthony Foster, setting his teeth and compressing his lips, like one who endeavours to suppress some violent internal emotion.

'Because,' said Lambourne, coolly, 'you dare not for your life lay a finger on me. I am younger and stronger than you, and have in me a double portion of the fighting devil, though not, it may be, quite so much of the undermining fiend, that finds an underground way to his purpose—who hides halters under folk's pillows, and who puts ratsbane into their porridge, as the stage-play says.'

Foster looked at him earnestly, then turned away and paced the room twice, with the same steady and considerate pace with which he had entered it: then suddenly came back and extended his hand to Michael Lambourne, saying, 'Be not wroth with me, good Mike; I did but try whether thou hadst parted with aught of thine old and honourable frankness, which your enviers and backbiters called saucy impudence.'

'Let them call it what they will,' said Michael Lambourne, 'it is the commodity we must carry through the world with us. Uds daggers! I tell thee, man, mine own stock of assurance was too small to trade upon, I was fain to take in a ton or two more of brass at every port where I touched in the voyage of life; and I started overboard what modesty and scruples I had remaining, in order to make room for the stowage.'

'Nay, nay,' replied Foster, 'touching scruples and modesty, you sailed hence in ballast. But who is this gallant, honest Mike?—is he a Corinthian—a cutter like thyself?'

'I prithee, know Master Tressilian, bully Foster,' replied Lambourne, presenting his friend in answer to his friend's question, 'know him and honour him, for he is a gentleman of many admirable qualities; and though he traffics not in my line of business, at least so far as I know, he has, nevertheless, a just respect and admiration for artists of our class. He will come to in time, as seldom fails; but as yet he is only a neophyte, only a proselyte, and frequents the company of cocks of the game, as a puny fencer does the schools of the masters, to see how a foil is handled by the teachers of defence.'

'If such be his quality, I will pray your company in another chamber, honest Mike, for what I have to say to thee is for thy private ear. Meanwhile, I pray you, sir, to abide us in this apartment, and without leaving it—there be those in this house who would be alarmed by the sight of a stranger.'

Tressilian acquiesced; and the two worthies left the apartment together, in which he remained alone to wait their return. *

---

* *Note A.* Foster, Lambourne, and the Black Bear.

4

Not serve two masters?—Here's a youth will try it—
Would fain serve God, yet give the devil his due;
Says grace before he doth a deed of villainy,
And returns thanks devoutly when 'tis acted.—*Old Play*.

THE room into which the master of Cumnor Place conducted his worthy visitant, was of a greater extent than that in which they had at first conversed, and had yet more the appearance of dilapidation. Large oaken presses, filled with shelves of the same wood, surrounded the room, and had, at one time, served for the arrangement of a numerous collection of books, many of which yet remained, but torn and defaced, covered with dust, deprived of their costly clasps and bindings, and tossed together in heaps upon the shelves, as things altogether disregarded, and abandoned to the pleasure of every spoiler. The very presses themselves seemed to have incurred the displeasure of those enemies of learning, who had destroyed the volumes with which they had been heretofore filled. They were, in several places, dismantled of their shelves, and otherwise broken and damaged, and were, moreover, mantled with cobwebs, and covered with dust.

'The men who wrote these books,' said Lambourne, looking round him, 'little thought whose keeping they were to fall into.'

'Nor what yeoman's service they were to do me,' quoth Anthony Foster—'the cook hath used them for scouring his pewter, and the groom hath had not else to clean my boots with this many a month past.'

'And yet,' said Lambourne, 'I have been in cities where such learned commodities would have been deemed too good for such offices.'

'Pshaw, pshaw,' answered Foster, 'they are Popish trash, every one of them,—private studies of the mumping old Abbot of Abingdon. The nineteenthly of a pure gospel sermon were worth a cart-load of such rakings of the kennel of Rome.'

'Gad-a-mercy, Master Tony Fire-the-Fagot!' said Lambourne, by way of reply.

Foster scowled darkly at him, as he replied, 'Hark ye, friend

Mike, forget that name, and the passage which it relates to, if you would not have our newly-revived comradeship die a sudden and a violent death.'

'Why, said Michael Lambourne, 'you were wont to glory in the share you had in the death of the two old heretical bishops.'

'That,' said his comrade, 'was while I was in the gall of bitterness and bond of iniquity, and applies not to my walk or my ways, now that I am called forth into the lists. Mr Melchisedek Maultext compared my misfortune in that matter to that of the Apostle Paul, who kept the clothes of the witnesses who stoned Saint Stephen. He held forth on the matter three Sabbaths past, and illustrated the same by the conduct of an honourable person present, meaning me.'

'I prithee peace, Foster,' said Lambourne, 'for I know not how it is, I have a sort of creeping comes over my skin when I hear the devil quote Scripture; and besides, man, how couldst thou have the heart to quit that convenient old religion, which you could slip off or on as easily as your glove? Do I not remember how you were wont to carry your conscience to confession, as duly as the month came round? and when thou hadst it scoured, and burnished, and whitewashed by the priest, thou were ever ready for the worst villainy which could be devised, like a child who is always readiest to rush into the mire when he has got his Sunday's clean jerkin on.'

'Trouble not thyself about my conscience,' said Foster, 'it is a thing thou canst not understand, having never had one of thine own; but let us rather to the point, and say to me, in one word, what is thy business with me, and what hopes have drawn thee hither?'

'The hope of bettering myself, to be sure,' answered Lambourne, 'as the old woman said, when she leapt over the bridge at Kingston. Look you, this purse has all that is left of as round a sum as a man would wish to carry in his slop-pouch. You are here well established, it would seem, and, as I think, well befriended, for men talk of thy being under some special protection—nay, stare not like a pig that is stuck, man; thou canst not dance in a net and they not see thee. Now I know such protection is not purchased for naught; you must have services to render for it, and in these I propose to help thee.'

'But how if I lack no assistance from thee, Mike? I think thy modesty might suppose that were a case possible.'

'That is to say,' retorted Lambourne, 'that you would engross the whole work, rather than divide the reward—but be not over-greedy, Anthony. Covetousness bursts the sack and spills the grain. Look you, when the huntsman goes to kill a stag, he takes with him more dogs than one—He has the staunch lyme-hound to track the wounded buck over hill and dale, but he hath also the fleet gazehound to kill him at view. Thou art the lyme-hound, I am the gaze-hound, and thy patron will need the aid of both, and can well afford to requite it. Thou hast deep sagacity—an unrelenting purpose—a steady long-breathed malignity of nature, that surpasses mine. But then, I am the bolder, the quicker, the more ready, both at action and expedient. Separate, our properties are not so perfect; but unite them, and we drive the world before us. How say'st thou—shall we hunt in couples?'

'It is a currish proposal—thus to thrust thyself upon my private matters,' replied Foster; 'but thou wert ever an ill-nurtured whelp.'

'You shall have no cause to say so, unless you spurn my courtesy,' said Michael Lambourne; 'but if so, keep thee well from me, Sir Knight, as the romance has it. I will either share your counsels or traverse them; for I have come here to be busy, either with thee or against thee.'

'Well,' said Anthony Foster, 'since thou dost leave me so fair a choice, I will rather be thy friend than thine enemy. Thou art right, I can prefer thee to the service of a patron, who has enough of means to make us both, and an hundred more. And, to say truth, thou art well qualified for his service. Boldness and dexterity he demands—the justice-books bear witness in thy favour—no starting at scruples in his service—why, who ever suspected thee of a conscience?—an assurance he must have, who would follow a courtier—and thy brow is as impenetrable as a Milan visor. There is but one thing I would fain see amended in thee.'

'And what is that, my most precious friend Anthony?' replied Lambourne; 'for I swear by the pillow of the Seven Sleepers, I will not be slothful in amending it.'

'Why, you gave a sample of it even now,' said Foster. 'Your speech twangs too much of the old stamp, and you garnish it ever and anon with singular oaths, that savour of Papistrie. Besides, your exterior man is altogether too deboshed and irregular to become one of his lordship's followers, since he has a reputation to keep up in the eye of the world. You must somewhat reform

56

your dress, upon a more grave and composed fashion; wear your cloak on both shoulders, and your falling band unrumpled and well starched—you must enlarge the brim of your beaver, and diminish the superfluity of your trunk-hose—go to church, or, which will be better, to meeting, at least once a month—protest only upon your faith and conscience—lay aside your swashing look, and never touch the hilt of your sword but when you would draw the carnal weapon in good earnest.'

'By this light, Anthony, thou art mad,' answered Lambourne, 'and hast described rather the gentleman-usher to a puritan's wife, than the follower of an ambitious courtier! Yes, such a thing as thou wouldst make of me should wear a book at his girdle instead of a poniard, and might just be suspected of manhood enough to squire a proud dame-citizen to the lecture at Saint Antonlin's, and quarrel in her cause with any flat-capped threadmaker that would take the wall of her. He must ruffle it in another sort that would walk to court in a nobleman's train.'

'Oh, content you, sir,' replied Foster, 'there is a change since you knew the English world; and there are those who can hold their way through the boldest courses, and the most secret, and yet never a swaggering word, or an oath, or a profane word in their conversation.'

'That is to say,' replied Lambourne, 'they are in a trading co-partnery, to do the devil's business without mentioning his name in the firm? Well, I will do my best to counterfeit, rather than lose ground in this new world, since thou sayest it is grown so precise. But, Anthony, what is the name of this nobleman, in whose service I am to turn hypocrite?'

'Aha! Master Michael, are you there with your bears?' said Foster, with a grim smile; 'and is this the knowledge you pretend of my concernments? How know you now there is such a person in *rerum natura*, and that I have not been putting a jape upon you all this time?'

'Thou put a jape on me, thou sodden-brained gull!' answered Lambourne, nothing daunted; 'why, dark and muddy as thou think'st thyself, I would engage in a day's space to see as clear through thee and thy concernments, as thou call'st them, as through the filthy horn of an old stable lantern.'

At this moment their conversation was interrupted by a scream from the next apartment.

'By the holy Cross of Abingdon!' said Anthony Foster, forgetting his Protestantism in his alarm, 'I am a ruined man!'

So saying, he rushed into the apartment whence the scream issued, followed by Michael Lambourne. But to account for the sounds which interrupted their conversation, it is necessary to recede a little way in our narrative.

It has been already observed, that when Lambourne accompanied Foster into the library, they left Tressilian alone in the ancient parlour. His dark eye followed them forth of the apartment with a glance of contempt, a part of which his mind instantly transferred to himself, for having stooped to be even for a moment their familiar companion. 'These are the associates, Amy,'—it was thus he communed with himself,—'to which thy cruel levity—thine unthinking and most unmerited falsehood, has condemned him, of whom his friends once hoped for other things, and who now scorns himself, as he will be scorned by others, for the baseness he stoops to for the love of thee! But I will not leave the pursuit of thee, once the object of my purest and most devoted affection, though to me thou canst henceforth be nothing but a thing to weep over—I will save thee from thy betrayer, and from thyself—I will restore thee to thy parents—to thy God. I cannot bid the bright star again sparkle in the sphere it has shot from, but——'

A slight noise in the apartment interrupted his reverie; he looked round, and in the beautiful and richly-attired female who entered at that instant by a side-door, he recognised the object of his search. The first impulse arising from this discovery, urged him to conceal his face with the collar of his cloak, until he should find a favourable moment of making himself known. But his purpose was disconcerted by the young lady (she was not above eighteen years old,) who ran joyfully towards him, and, pulling him by the cloak, said playfully, 'Nay, my sweet friend, after I have waited for you so long, you come not to my bower to play the masquer— You are arraigned of treason to true love and fond affection; and you must stand up at the bar, and answer it with face uncovered— how say you, guilty or not?'

'Alas, Amy!' said Tressilian, in a low and melancholy tone, as he suffered her to draw the mantle from his face. The sound of his voice, and still more the unexpected sight of his face, changed in an instant the lady's playful mood. She staggered back, turned as pale as death, and put her hands before her face. Tressilian was himself for a moment much overcome, but seeming suddenly to remember the necessity of using an opportunity which might not again occur, he said in a low tone, 'Amy, fear me not.'

'Why should I fear you?' said the lady, withdrawing her hands from her beautiful face, which was now covered with crimson,— 'why should I fear you, Master Tressilian?—or wherefore have you intruded yourself into my dwelling, uninvited, sir, and unwished for?'

'Your dwelling, Amy!' said Tressilian. 'Alas! is a prison your dwelling?—a prison, guarded by one of the most sordid of men, but not a greater wretch than his employer.'

'This house is mine,' said Amy, 'mine while I choose to inhabit it—If it is my pleasure to live in seclusion, who shall gainsay me?'

'Your father, maiden,' answered Tressilian, 'your broken-hearted father; who despatched me in quest of you, with that authority which he cannot exert in person. Here is his letter, written while he blessed his pain of body which somewhat stunned the agony of his mind.'

'The pain!—is my father then ill?' said the lady.

'So ill,' answered Tressilian, 'that even your utmost haste may not restore him to health; but all shall be instantly prepared for your departure, the instant you yourself will give consent.'

'Tressilian,' answered the lady, 'I cannot, I must not, I dare not leave this place. Go back to my father—tell him I will obtain leave to see him within twelve hours from hence. Go back, Tressilian—tell him I am well, I am happy—happy could I think he was so—tell him not to fear that I will come, and in such manner that all the grief Amy has given him shall be forgotten—the poor Amy is now greater than she dare name. Go, good Tressilian—I have injured thee too, but believe me, I have power to heal the wounds I have caused—I robbed you of a childish heart, which was not worthy of you, and I can repay the loss with honours and advancement.'

'Do you say this to me, Amy? Do you offer me pageants of idle ambition, for the quiet peace you have robbed me of? But be it so—I came not to upbraid, but to serve and to free you. You cannot disguise it from me; you are a prisoner. Otherwise your kind heart—for it was once a kind heart—would have been already at your father's bedside. Come—poor, deceived, unhappy maiden —all shall be forgot—all shall be forgiven. Fear not my importunity for what regarded our contract—it was a dream, and I have awaked—But come—your father yet lives—Come, and one word of affection,—one tear of penitence, will efface the memory of all that has passed.'

'Have I not already said, Tressilian,' replied she, 'that I will surely come to my father, and that without further delay than is necessary to discharge other and equally binding duties? Go, carry him the news—I come as sure as there is light in Heaven—that is, when I obtain permission.'

'Permission?—permission to visit your father on his sick-bed, perhaps on his death-bed!' repeated Tressilian, impatiently; 'and permission from whom? From the villain, who, under disguise of friendship, abused every duty of hospitality, and stole thee from thy father's roof!'

'Do him no slander, Tressilian! He whom thou speakest of wears a sword as sharp as thine—sharper, vain man—for the best deeds thou hast ever done in peace or war, were as unworthy to be named with his, as thy obscure rank to match itself with the sphere he moves in. Leave me! Go, do mine errand to my father, and when he next sends to me, let him choose a more welcome messenger.'

'Amy,' replied Tressilian calmly, 'thou canst not move me by thy reproaches. Tell me one thing, that I may bear at least one ray of comfort to my aged friend— This rank of his which thou dost boast—dost thou share it with him, Amy? Does he claim a husband's right to control thy motions?'

'Stop thy base unmannered tongue!' said the lady; 'to no question that derogates from my honour do I deign an answer.'

'You have said enough in refusing to reply,' answered Tressilian; 'and mark me, unhappy as thou art, I am armed with thy father's full authority to command thy obedience, and I will save thee from the slavery of sin and of sorrow, even despite of thyself, Amy.'

'Menace no violence here!' exclaimed the lady, drawing back from him, and alarmed at the determination expressed in his look and manner; 'threaten me not, Tressilian, for I have means to repel force.'

'But not, I trust, the wish to use them in so evil a cause,' said Tressilian. 'With thy will—thine uninfluenced, free, and natural will, Amy, thou canst not choose this state of slavery and dishonour —thou hast been bound by some spell—entrapped by some deceit —art now detained by some compelled vow. But thus I break the charm—Amy, in the name of thine excellent, thy broken-hearted father, I command thee to follow me!'

As he spoke, he advanced and extended his arm, as with the purpose of laying hold upon her. But she shrunk back from his grasp, and uttered the scream, which, as we before noticed, brought into the apartment Lambourne and Foster.

The latter exclaimed, as soon as he entered, 'Fire and fagot! what have were here!' Then addressing the lady in a tone betwixt entreaty and command, he added, 'Uds precious! madam, what make you here out of bounds? Retire—retire—there is life and death in this matter. And you, friend, whoever you may be, leave this house—out with you, before my dagger's hilt and your costard become acquainted. Draw, Mike, and rid us of the knave.'

'Not I, on my soul,' replied Lambourne; 'he came hither in my company, and he is safe from me by cutter's law, at least till we meet again. But hark ye, my Cornish comrade, you have brought a Cornish flaw of wind with you hither, a hurricanoe, as they call it in the Indies. Make yourself scarce—depart—vanish—or we'll have you summoned before the Mayor of Halgaver, and that before Dudman and Ramhead meet.' *

'Away, base groom!' said Tressilian—'And you, madam, fare you well—what life lingers in your father's bosom will leave him at the news I have to tell.'

He departed, the lady saying faintly as he left the room, 'Tressilian, be not rash—say no scandal of me.'

'Here is proper gear,' said Foster. 'I pray you go to your chamber, my lady, and let us consider how this is to be answered—nay, tarry not.'

'I move not at your command, sir,' answered the lady.

'Nay, but you must, fair lady,' replied Foster; 'excuse my freedom, but, by blood and nails, this is no time to strain courtesies—you must go to your chamber. Mike, follow that meddling coxcomb, and as you desire to thrive, see him safely clear of the premises, while I bring this headstrong lady to reason. Draw thy tool, man, and after him.'

'I'll follow him,' said Michael Lambourne, 'and see him fairly out of Flanders—but for hurting a man I have drunk my morning's draught withal, 'tis clean against my conscience.' So saying, he left the apartment.

* Two headlands on the Cornish coast. The expressions are proverbial.

Tressilian, meanwhile, with hasty steps, pursued the first path which promised to conduct him through the wild and overgrown park in which the mansion of Foster was situated. Haste and distress of mind led his steps astray, and instead of taking the avenue which led towards the village, he chose another, which, after he had pursued it for some time with a hasty and reckless step, conducted him to the other side of the demesne, where a postern-door opened through the wall, and led into the open country.

Tressilian paused an instant. It was indifferent to him by what road he left a spot now so odious to his recollections; but it was probable that the postern-door was locked, and his retreat by that pass rendered impossible.

'I must make the attempt, however,' he said to himself; 'the only means of reclaiming this lost—this miserable—this still most lovely and most unhappy girl—must rest in her father's appeal to the broken laws of his country—I must haste to apprise him of this heart-rending intelligence.'

As Tressilian, thus conversing with himself, approached to try some means of opening the door, or climbing over it, he perceived there was a key put into the lock from the outside. It turned round, the bolt revolved, and a cavalier, who entered, muffled in his riding cloak, and wearing a slouched hat with a drooping feather, stood at once within four yards of him who was desirous of going out. They exclaimed at once, in tones of resentment and surprise, the one 'Varney!' the other 'Tressilian!'

'What make you here?' was the stern question put by the stranger to Tressilian, when the moment of surprise was past. 'What make you here, where your presence is neither expected nor desired?'

'Nay, Varney,' replied Tressilian, 'what make *you* here? Are you come to triumph over the innocence you have destroyed, as the vulture or carrion-crow comes to batten on the lamb, whose eyes it has first plucked out? Or are you come to encounter the merited vengeance of an honest man? Draw, dog, and defend thyself!'

Tressilian drew his sword as he spoke, but Varney only laid his hand on the hilt of his own, as he replied. 'Thou art mad, Tressilian—I own appearances are against me, but by every oath a priest can make, or a man can swear, Mistress Amy Robsart hath had no injury from me, and in truth I were somewhat loath to hurt you in this cause—Thou know'st I can fight.'

'I have heard thee say so, Varney,' replied Tressilian; 'but now, methinks, I would fain have some better evidence than thine own word.'

'That shall not be lacking, if blade and hilt be but true to me,' answered Varney; and, drawing his sword with the right hand, he threw his cloak around his left, and attacked Tressilian with a vigour which, for a moment, seemed to give him the advantage of the combat. But this advantage lasted not long. Tressilian added to a spirit determined on revenge, a hand and eye admirably well adapted to the use of the rapier; so that Varney, finding himself hard pressed in his turn, endeavoured to avail himself of his superior strength, by closing with his adversary. For this purpose, he hazarded the receiving one of Tressilian's passes in his cloak, wrapt as it was around his arm, and ere his adversary could extricate his rapier thus entangled, he closed with him, shortening his own sword at the same time, with the purpose of despatching him. But Tressilian was on his guard, and unsheathing his poniard, parried with the blade of that weapon the home-thrust, which would otherwise have finished the combat, and in the struggle which followed, displayed so much address, as might have confirmed the opinion that he drew his origin from Cornwall, whose natives are such masters in the art of wrestling, as, were the games of antiquity revived, might enable them to challenge all Europe to the ring. Varney, in his ill-advised attempt, received a fall so sudden and so violent, that his sword flew several paces from his hand, and ere he could recover his feet, that of his antagonist was pointed to his throat.

'Give me the instant means of relieving the victim of thy treachery,' said Tressilian, 'or take the last look of your Creator's blessed sun.'

And while Varney, too confused or too sullen to reply, made a sudden effort to arise, his adversary drew back his arm, and would have executed his threat, but that the blow was arrested by the grasp of Michael Lambourne, who, directed by the clashing of swords, had come up just in time to save the life of Varney.

'Come, come, comrade,' said Lambourne, 'here is enough done, and more than enough—put up your fox, and let us be jogging. The Black Bear growls for us.'

'Off, abject!' said Tressilian, striking himself free of Lambourne's grasp; 'darest thou come betwixt me and mine enemy?'

'Abject——by——' repeated Lambourne; 'that shall be answered with cold steel whenever a bowl of sack has washed out memory of the morning's draught that we had together. In the meanwhile, do you see, shog—tramp—begone—we are two to one.'

He spoke truth, for Varney had taken the opportunity to regain his weapon, and Tressilian perceived it was madness to press the quarrel further against such odds. He took his purse from his side, and taking out two gold nobles, flung them to Lambourne; 'There caitiff, is thy morning wage—thou shalt not say thou hast been my guide unhired. Varney, farewell—we shall meet where there are none to come betwixt us.' So saying, he turned round and departed through the postern-door.

Varney seemed to want the inclination, or perhaps the power (for his fall had been a severe one), to follow his retreating enemy. But he glared darkly as he disappeared, and then addressed Lambourne: 'Art thou a comrade of Foster's, good fellow?'

'Sworn friends, as the haft is to the knife,' replied Michael Lambourne.

'Here is a broad piece for thee—follow yonder fellow, and see where he takes earth, and bring word up to the mansion-house here. Cautious and silent, thou knave, as thou valuest thy throat.'

'Enough said,' replied Lambourne; 'I can draw on a scent as well as a sleuth-hound.'

'Begone then,' said Varney, sheathing his rapier; and, turning his back on Michael Lambourne, he walked slowly towards the house. Lambourne stopped but an instant to gather the nobles which his late companion had flung towards him so unceremoniously, and muttered to himself, while he put them up in his purse, along with the gratuity of Varney, 'I spoke to yonder gulls of Eldorado— By Saint Anthony, there is no Eldorado for men of our stamp equal to bonny old England. It rains nobles, by Heaven—they lie on the grass as thick as dew-drops—you may have them for gathering. And if I have not my share of such glittering dew-drops, may my sword melt like an icicle!'

5

————He was a man
Versed in the world as pilot in his compass.
The needle pointed ever to that interest
Which was his loadstar, and he spread his sails
With vantage to the gale of others' passion.
                    The Deceiver—a Tragedy.

ANTHONY FOSTER was still engaged in debate with his fair guest, who treated with scorn every entreaty and request that she would retire to her own apartment, when a whistle was heard at the entrance-door of the mansion.

'We are fairly sped now,' said Foster; 'yonder is thy lord's signal, and what to say about the disorder which has happened in this household, by my conscience, I know not. Some evil fortune dogs the heels of that unhanged rogue Lambourne, and he has escaped the gallows against every chance, to come back and be the ruin of me!'

'Peace, sir,' said the lady, 'and undo the gate to your master.— My lord! my dear lord!' she then exclaimed, hastening to the entrance of the apartment, then added, with a voice expressive of disappointment, 'Pooh! it is but Richard Varney.'

'Ay, madam,' said Varney, entering and saluting the lady with a respectful obeisance, which she returned with a careless mixture of negligence and of displeasure, 'it is but Richard Varney; but even the first gray cloud should be acceptable, when it lightens in the east, because it announces the approach of the blessed sun.'

'How! comes my lord hither to-night?' said the lady, in joyful, yet startled agitation, and Anthony Foster caught up the word and echoed the question. Varney replied to the lady, that his lord purposed to attend her, and would have proceeded with some compliment, when, running to the door of the parlour, she called aloud, 'Janet—Janet—come to my tiring-room instantly.' Then returning to Varney, she asked if her lord sent any further commendations to her.

'This letter, honoured madam,' said he, taking from his bosom a small parcel wrapt in scarlet silk, 'and with it a token to the Queen of his Affections.' With eager speed the lady hastened to undo the silken string which surrounded the little packet, and failing to unloose readily the knot with which it was secured, she again called loudly on Janet, 'Bring me a knife—scissors—aught that may undo this envious knot.'

'May not my poor poniard serve, honoured madam,' said Varney, presenting a small dagger of exquisite workmanship, which hung in his Turkey-leather sword-belt.

'No, sir,' replied the lady, rejecting the instrument which he offered—'steel poniard shall cut no true-love knot of mine.'

'It has cut many, however,' said Anthony Foster, half aside, and looking at Varney. By this time the knot was disentangled without any other help than the neat and nimble fingers of Janet, a simply attired maiden, the daughter of Anthony Foster, who came running at the repeated call of her mistress. A necklace of orient pearl, the companion of a perfumed billet, was now hastily produced from the packet. The lady gave the one after a slight glance to the charge of her attendant, while she read, or rather devoured, the contents of the other.

'Surely, lady,' said Janet, gazing with admiration at the neck-string of pearls, 'the daughters of Tyre wore no fairer neck-jewels than those—And then the posy, "For a neck that is fairer,"—each pearl is worth a freehold.'

'Each word in this dear paper is worth the whole string, my girl—But come to my tiring-room, girl; we must be brave, my lord comes hither to-night. He bids me grace you, Master Varney, and to me his wish is a law—I bid you to a collation in my bower this afternoon, and you too, Master Foster. Give orders that all is fitting, and that suitable preparations be made for my lord's reception to-night.'—With these words she left the apartment.

'She takes state on her already,' said Varney, 'and distributes the favour of her presence, as if she were already the partner of his dignity. Well—it is wise to practise beforehand the part which fortune prepares us to play—the young eagle must gaze at the sun, ere he soars on strong wing to meet it.'

'If holding her head aloft,' said Foster, 'will keep her eyes from dazzling, I warrant the dame will not stoop her crest. She will presently soar beyond reach of my whistle, Master Varney. I promise you, she holds me already in slight regard.'

'It is thine own fault, thou sullen uninventive companion,'

answered Varney, 'who know'st no mode of control save down-right brute force. Canst thou not make home pleasant to her, with music and toys? Canst thou not make the out-of-doors frightful to her, with tales of goblins? Thou livest here by the churchyard, and hast not even wit enough to raise a ghost, to scare thy females into good discipline.'

'Speak not thus, Master Varney,' said Foster; 'the living I fear not, but I trifle not nor toy with my dead neighbours of the churchyard. I promise you, it requires a good heart to live so near it; worthy Master Holdforth, the afternoon's lecturer of Saint Antonlin's had a sore fright there the last time he came to visit me.'

'Hold thy superstitious tongue!' answered Varney; 'and while thou talk'st of visiting, answer me, thou paltering knave, how came Tressilian to be at the postern-door?'

'Tressilian!' answered Foster, 'what know I of Tressilian? I never heard his name.'

'Why, villain, it was the very Cornish chough, to whom old Sir Hugh Robsart destined his pretty Amy, and hither the hot-brained fool has come to look after his fair runaway; there must be some order taken with him, for he thinks he hath wrong, and is not the mean hind that will sit down with it. Luckily he knows naught of my lord, but thinks he has only me to deal with. But how, in the fiend's name, came he hither?'

'Why, with Mike Lambourne, an you must know,' answered Foster.

'And who is Mike Lambourne?' demanded Varney. 'By Heaven! thou wert best set up a bush over thy door, and invite every stroller who passes by to see what thou shouldst keep secret even from the sun and air.'

'Ay! ay! this is a court-like requital of my service to you, Master Richard Varney,' replied Foster. 'Didst thou not charge me to seek out for thee a fellow who had a good sword, and an unscrupulous conscience? and was not I busying myself to find a fit man—for, thank Heaven, my acquaintance lies not amongst such companions—when, as Heaven would have it, this tall fellow, who is in all his qualities the very flashing knave thou didst wish, came hither to fix acquaintance upon me in the plenitude of his impudence, and I admitted his claim, thinking so to do you a pleasure—and now see what thanks I get for disgracing myself by converse with him!'

'And did he,' said Varney, 'being such a fellow as thyself, only lacking, I suppose, thy present humour of hypocrisy, which lies as thin over thy hard ruffianly heart as gold lacquer upon rusty iron—did he, I say, bring the saintly, sighing Tressilian in his train?'

'They came together, by Heaven!' said Foster; 'and Tressilian—to speak Heaven's truth—obtained a moment's interview with our pretty moppet, while I was talking apart with Lambourne.'

'Improvident villain! we are both undone,' said Varney. 'She has of late been casting many a backward look to her father's halls, whenever her lordly lover leaves her alone. Should this preaching fool whistle her back to her old perch, we were but lost men.'

'No fear of that, my master,' replied Anthony Foster; 'she is in no mood to stoop to his lure, for she yelled out on seeing him as if an adder had stung her.'

'That is good. Canst thou not get from thy daughter an inkling of what passed between them, good Foster?'

'I tell you plain, Master Varney,' said Foster, 'my daughter shall not enter our purposes, or walk in our paths. They may suit me well enough, who know how to repent of my misdoings; but I will not have my child's soul committed to peril either for your pleasure or my lord's. I may walk among snares and pitfalls myself, because I have discretion, but I will not trust the poor lamb among them.'

'Why, thou suspicious fool, I were as averse as thou art that thy baby-faced girl should enter into my plans, or walk to hell at her father's elbow. But indirectly thou mightst gain some intelligence of her?'

'And so I did, Master Varney,' answered Foster; 'and she said her lady called out upon the sickness of her father.'

'Good!' replied Varney; 'that is a hint worth catching, and I will work upon it. But the country must be rid of this Tressilian—I would have cumbered no man about the matter, for I hate him like strong poison—his presence is hemlock to me—and this day I had been rid of him, but that my foot slipped, when, to speak truth, had not thy comrade yonder come to my aid, and held his hand, I should have known by this time whether you and I have been treading the path to heaven or hell.'

'And you can speak thus of such a risk!' said Foster; 'you keep a stout heart, Master Varney—for me, if I did not hope to live many years, and to have time for the great work of repentance, I would not go forward with you.'

'Oh! thou shalt live as long as Methuselah,' said Varney, 'and amass as much wealth as Solomon; and thou shalt repent so devoutly, that thy repentance shall be more famous than thy villainy,—and that is a bold word. But for all this, Tressilian must be looked after. Thy ruffian yonder is gone to dog him. It concerns our fortunes, Anthony.'

'Ay, ay,' said Foster, sullenly, 'this it is to be leagued with one who knows not even so much of Scripture, as that the labourer is worthy of his hire. I must, as usual, take all the trouble and risk.'

'Risk! and what is the mighty risk, I pray you?' answered Varney. 'This fellow will come prowling again about your demesne or into your house, and if you take him for a house-breaker or a park-breaker, is it not most natural you should welcome him with cold steel or hot lead? Even a mastiff will pull down those who come near his kennel; and who shall blame him?'

'Ay, I have a mastiff's work, and a mastiff's wage among you,' said Foster. 'Here have you, Master Varney, secured a good free-hold estate out of this old superstitious foundation; and I have but a poor lease of this mansion under you, voidable at your honour's pleasure.'

'Ay, and thou wouldst fain convert thy leasehold into a copyhold —the thing may chance to happen, Anthony Foster, if thou dost good service for it. But softly, good Anthony—it is not the lending a room or two of this old house for keeping my lord's pretty paroquet—nay, it is not the shutting thy doors and windows to keep her from flying off, that may deserve it. Remember the manor and tithes are rated at the clear annual value of seventy-nine pounds five shillings and fivepence halfpenny, besides the value of the wood. Come, come, thou must be conscionable; great and secret service may deserve both this and a better thing. And now let thy knave come and pluck off my boots. Get us some dinner, and a cup of thy best wine. I must visit this mavis, brave in apparel, unruffled in aspect, and gay in temper.'

They parted, and at the hour of noon, which was then that of dinner, they again met at their meal, Varney gaily dressed like a courtier of the time, and even Anthony Foster improved in appearance, as far as dress could amend an exterior so unfavourable.

This alteration did not escape Varney. When the meal was finished, the cloth removed, and they were left to their private discourse—'Thou art gay as a goldfinch, Anthony,' said Varney, looking at his host; 'methinks, thou wilt whistle a jig anon—but I crave your pardon, that would secure your ejection from the congregation of the zealous botchers, the pure-hearted weavers, and the sanctified bakers of Abingdon, who let their ovens cool while their brains get heated.'

'To answer you in the spirit, Master Varney,' said Foster, 'were—excuse the parable—to fling sacred and precious things before swine. So I will speak to thee in the language of the world, which he, who is King of the World, hath taught thee to understand, and to profit by in no common measure.'

'Say what thou wilt, honest Tony,' replied Varney; 'for be it according to thine absurd faith, or according to thy most villainous practice, it cannot choose but be rare matter to qualify this cup of Alicant. Thy conversation is relishing and poignant, and beats caviare, dried neat's-tongue, and all other provocatives that give savour to good liquor.'

'Well, then, tell me,' said Anthony Foster, 'is not our good lord and master's turn better served, and his ante-chamber more suitably filled, with decent, God-fearing men, who will work his will and their own profit quietly, and without worldly scandal, than that he should be manned, and attended, and followed by such open debauchers and ruffianly swordsmen as Tidesly, Killigrew, this fellow Lambourne, whom you have put me to seek out for you, and other such, who bear the gallows in their face and murder in their right hand—who are a terror to peaceable men, and a scandal to my lord's service?'

'Oh, content you, good Master Anthony Foster,' answered Varney; 'he that flies at all manner of game must keep all kinds of hawks, both short and long-winged. The course my lord holds is no easy one, and he must stand provided at all points with trusty retainers to meet each sort of service. He must have his gay courtier, like myself, to ruffle it in the presence-chamber, and to lay hand on hilt when any speaks in disparagement of my lord's honour——'

'Ay,' said Foster, 'and to whisper a word for him into a fair lady's ear, when he may not approach her himself.'

'Then,' said Varney, going on without appearing to notice the interruption, 'he must have his lawyers—deep subtle pioneers—to draw his contracts—his pre-contracts, and his post-contracts, and to find the way to make the most of grants of church-lands, and commons, and licences for monopoly—And he must have physicians who can spice a cup or a caudle—And he must have his cabalists, like Dee and Allan, for conjuring up the devil—And he must have ruffling swordsmen, who would fight the devil when he is raised and at the wildest—And above all, without prejudice to others, he must have such godly, innocent, puritanic souls as thou, honest Anthony, who defy Satan, and do his work at the same time.'

'You would not say, Master Varney,' said Foster, 'that our good lord and master, whom I hold to be fulfilled in all nobleness, would use such base and sinful means to rise, as thy speech points at?'

'Tush, man,' said Varney, 'never look at me with so sad a brow—you trap me not—nor am I in your power, as your weak brain may imagine, because I name to you freely the engines, the springs, the screws, the tackle, and braces, by which great men rise in stirring times. Sayest thou our good lord is fulfilled of all nobleness? Amen, and so be it—he has the more need to have those about him who are unscrupulous in his service, and who, because they know that his fall will overwhelm and crush them, must wager both blood and brain, soul and body, in order to keep him aloft; and this I tell thee, because I care not who knows it.'

'You speak truth, Master Varney,' said Anthony Foster; 'he that is head of a party, is but a boat on a wave, that raises not itself, but is moved upward by the billow which it floats upon.'

'Thou art metaphorical, honest Anthony,' replied Varney; 'that velvet doublet hath made an oracle of thee—we will have thee to Oxford to take thy degree in the arts. And, in the meantime, hast thou arranged all the matters which were sent from London, and put the western chambers into such fashion as may answer my lord's humour?'

'They may serve a king on his bridal day,' said Anthony; 'and I promise you that Dame Amy sits in them yonder, as proud and gay as if she were the Queen of Sheba.'

''Tis the better, good Anthony,' answered Varney; 'we must found our future fortunes on her good liking.'

'We build on sand, then,' said Anthony Foster; 'for supposing that she sails away to court in all her lord's dignity and authority, how is she like to look back upon me, who am her jailer as it were, to detain her here against her will, keeping her a caterpillar on an old wall, when she would fain be a painted butterfly in a court garden?'

'Fear not her displeasure, man,' said Varney. 'I will show her that all thou hast done in this matter was good service, both to my lord and her; and when she chips the egg-shell and walks alone, she shall own we have hatched her greatness.'

'Look to yourself, Master Varney,' said Foster, 'you may misreckon foully in this matter—She gave you but a frosty reception this morning, and, I think, looks on you, as well as me, with an evil eye.'

'You mistake her, Foster—you mistake her utterly. To me she is bound by all the ties which can secure her to one who has been the means of gratifyng both her love and ambition. Who was it that took the obscure Amy Robsart, the daughter of an impoverished and dotard knight—the destined bride of a moonstruck, moping enthusiast, like Edmund Tressilian, from her lowly fates, and held out to her in prospect, the brightest fortune in England, or perchance in Europe? Why, man, it was I—as I have often told thee—that found opportunity for their secret meetings. It was I who watched the wood while he beat for the deer. It was I who, to this day, am blamed by her family as the companion of her flight, and were I in their neighbourhood, would be fain to wear a shirt of better stuff than Holland linen, lest my ribs should be acquainted with Spanish steel. Who carried their letters?—I. Who amused the old knight and Tressilian?—I. Who planned her escape?—it was I. It was I, in short, Dick Varney, who pulled this pretty little daisy from its lowly nook, and placed it in the proudest bonnet in Britain.'

'Ay, Master Varney,' said Foster, 'but it may be she thinks that had the matter remained with you, the flower had been stuck so slightly into the cap, that the first breath of a changeable breeze of passion had blown the poor daisy to the common.'

'She should consider,' said Varney, smiling, 'the true faith I owed my lord and master prevented me at first from counselling marriage—and yet I did counsel marriage when I saw she would not be satisfied without the—the sacrament or the ceremony—which callest thou it, Anthony?'

'Still she has you at feud on another score,' said Foster; 'and I tell it you that you may look to yourself in time. She would not hide her splendour in this dark lantern of an old monastic house, but would fain shine a countess amongst countesses.'

'Very natural, very right,' answered Varney; 'but what have I to do with that?—she may shine through horn or through crystal, at my lord's pleasure, I have naught to say against it.'

'She deems that you have an oar upon that side of the boat, Master Varney,' replied Foster, 'and that you can pull it or no, at your good pleasure. In a word, she ascribes the secrecy and obscurity in which she is kept to your secret counsel to my lord, and to my strict agency; and so she loves us both as a sentenced man loves his judge and his jailer.'

'She must love us better ere she leave this place, Anthony,' answered Varney. 'If I have counselled for weighty reasons that she remain here for a season, I can also advise her being brought forth in the full blow of her dignity. But I were mad to do so, holding so near a place to my lord's person, were she mine enemy. Bear this truth in upon her as occasion offers, Anthony, and let me alone for extolling you in her ear, and exalting you in her opinion. —*Ka me, ka thee*—it is a proverb all over the world. The lady must know her friends, and be made to judge of the power they have of being her enemies—meanwhile, watch her strictly, but with all the outward observance that thy rough nature will permit. 'Tis an excellent thing that sullen look and bull-dog humour of thine; thou shouldst thank God for it, and so should my lord; for when there is aught harsh or hard-natured to be done, thou dost it as if it flowed from thine own natural doggedness, and not from orders, and so my lord escapes the scandal. But hark—some one knocks at the gate. Look out at the window. Let no one enter—this were an ill night to be interrupted.'

'It is he whom we spoke of before dinner,' said Foster, as he looked through the casement; 'it is Michael Lambourne.'

'Oh, admit him, by all means,' said the courtier, 'he comes to give some account of his guest—it imports us much to know the movements of Edmund Tressilian. Admit him, I say, but bring him not hither—I will come to you presently in the Abbot's library.'

Foster left the room, and the courtier, who remained behind, paced the parlour more than once in deep thought, his arms folded on his bosom, until at length he gave vent to his meditations in broken words, which we have somewhat enlarged and connected, that his soliloquy may be intelligible to the reader.

"'Tis true,' he said, suddenly stopping, and resting his right hand on the table at which they had been sitting, 'this base churl hath fathomed the very depth of my fear, and I have been unable to disguise it from him—She loves me not—I would it were as true that I loved not her—Idiot that I was, to move her in my own behalf, when wisdom bade me be a true broker to my lord! And this fatal error has placed me more at her discretion than a wise man would willingly be at that of the best piece of painted Eve's flesh of them all. Since the hour that my policy made so perilous a slip, I cannot look at her without fear, and hate, and fondness, so strangely mingled, that I know not whether, were it at my choice, I would rather possess or ruin her. But she must not leave this retreat till I am assured on what terms we are to stand. My lord's interest—and so far it is mine own—for, if he sinks, I fall in his train—demands concealment of this obscure marriage—and besides I will not lend her my arm to climb to her chair of state, that she may set her foot on my neck when she is fairly seated. I must work an interest in her, either through love or through fear—and who knows but I may yet reap the sweetest and best revenge for her former scorn?—that were indeed a masterpiece of court-like art! Let me but once be her counsel-keeper—let her confide to me a secret, did it but concern the robbery of a linnet's nest, and, fair Countess, thou art mine own.' He again paced the room in silence, stopped, filled, and drank a cup of wine, as if to compose the agitation of his mind, and muttering, 'Now for a close heart, and an open and unruffled brow,' he left the apartment.

6

> The dews of summer night did fall,
> The moon, sweet regent of the sky,
> Silver'd the walls of Cumnor Hall,
> And many an oak that grew thereby.—*Mickle.*

FOUR apartments, which occupied the western side of the old quadrangle at Cumnor Place, had been fitted up with extraordinary splendour. This had been the work of several days prior to that on which our story opened. Workmen sent from London, and not permitted to leave the premises until the work was finished, had converted the apartments on that side of the building, from the dilapidated appearance of a dissolved monastic house, into the semblance of a royal palace. A mystery was observed in all these arrangements; the workmen came thither and returned by night, and all measures were taken to prevent the prying curiosity of the villagers from observing or speculating upon the changes which were taking place in the mansion of their once indigent, but now wealthy neighbour, Anthony Foster. Accordingly, the secrecy desired was so far preserved, that nothing got abroad but vague and uncertain reports, which were received and repeated, but without much credit being attached to them.

On the evening of which we treat, the new and highly-decorated suite of rooms were, for the first time, illuminated, and that with a brilliancy which might have been visible half a dozen miles off, had not oaken shutters, carefully secured with bolt and padlock, and mantled with long curtains of silk and of velvet, deeply fringed with gold, prevented the slightest gleam of radiance from being seen without.

The principal apartments, as we have seen, were four in number, each opening into the other. Access was given to them by a large scale staircase, as they were then called, of unusual length and height, which had its landing-place at the door of an antechamber, shaped somewhat like a gallery. This apartment the Abbot had used as an occasional council-room, but it was now beautifully wainscoted with dark foreign wood of a brown colour, and bearing a high polish, said to have been brought from the Western

Indies, and to have been wrought in London with infinite difficulty, and much damage to the tools of the workmen. The dark colour of this finishing was relieved by the number of lights in silver sconces, which hung against the walls, and by six large and richly-framed pictures, by the first masters of the age. A massy oaken table, placed at the lower end of the apartment, served to accommodate such as chose to play at the then fashionable game of shovel-board; and there was at the other end an elevated gallery for the musicians or minstrels, who might be summoned to increase the festivity of the evening.

From this antechamber opened a banqueting room of moderate size, but brilliant enough to dazzle the eyes of the spectator with the richness of its furniture. The walls, lately so bare and ghastly, were now clothed with hangings of sky-blue velvet and silver; the chairs were of ebony, richly carved, with cushions corresponding to the hangings, and the place of the silver sconces which enlightened the antechamber, was supplied by a huge chandelier of the same precious metal. The floor was covered with a Spanish foot-cloth or carpet, on which flowers and fruits were represented in such glowing and natural colours, that you hesitated to place the foot on such exquisite workmanship. The table, of old English oak, stood ready covered with the finest linen, and a large portable court-cupboard was placed with the leaves of its embossed folding-doors displayed, showing the shelves within, decorated with a full display of plate and porcelain. In the midst of the table stood a salt-cellar of Italian workmanship, a beautiful and splendid piece of plate about two feet high, moulded into a representation of the giant Briareus, whose hundred hands of silver presented to the guests various sorts of spices or condiments, to season their food withal.

The third apartment was called the withdrawing-room. It was hung with the finest tapestry, representing the fall of Phaeton; for the looms of Flanders were now much occupied on classical subjects. The principal seat of this apartment was a chair of state, raised a step or two from the floor, and large enough to contain two persons. It was surmounted by a canopy, which, as well as the cushions, side-curtains, and the very foot-cloth, was composed of crimson velvet, embroidered with seed-pearl. On the top of the canopy were two coronets, resembling those of an earl and countess. Stools covered with velvet, and some cushions disposed in the Moorish fashion, and ornamented with Arabesque needle-work, supplied the place of chairs in this apartment, which contained musical instruments, embroidery frames, and other articles for ladies' pastime. Besides lesser lights, the withdrawing-room was illuminated by four tall torches of virgin wax, each of which was placed in the grasp of a statue, representing an armed Moor, who held in his left arm a round buckler of silver, highly polished, interposed betwixt his breast and the light which was thus brilliantly reflected as from a crystal mirror.

The sleeping chamber belonging to this splendid suite of apartments, was decorated in a taste less showy, but not less rich, than had been displayed in the others. Two silver lamps, fed with perfumed oil, diffused at once a delicious odour and a trembling twilight-seeming shimmer through the quiet apartment. It was carpeted so thick, that the heaviest step could not have been heard, and the bed, richly heaped with down, was spread with an ample coverlet of silver and gold; from under which peeped forth cambric sheets, and blankets white as the lambs which yielded the fleece that made them. The curtains were of blue velvet, lined with crimson silk, deeply festooned with gold, and em-broidered with the loves of Cupid and Psyche. On the toilet was a beautiful Venetian mirror, in a frame of silver filagree, and beside it stood a gold posset-dish to contain the night draught. A pair of pistols and a dagger, mounted with gold, were displayed near the head of the bed, being the arms for the night, which were presented to honoured guests, rather, it may be supposed, in the way of ceremony, than from any apprehensions of danger. We must not omit to mention, what was more to the credit of the manners of the time, that in a small recess, illuminated by a taper, were disposed two hassocks of velvet and gold corresponding with the bed furniture, before a desk of carved ebony. This recess had formerly been the private oratory of the Abbot; but the crucifix was removed, and instead, there were placed on the desk two Books of Common Prayer, richly bound, and embossed with silver. With this enviable sleeping apartment, which was so far removed from every sound, save that of the wind sighing among the oaks of the park, that Morpheus might have coveted it for his own proper repose, corresponded two wardrobes, or dressing-rooms as they are now termed, suitably furnished, and in a style of the same magnificence which we have already described. It ought to be added, that a part of the building in the adjoining wing was occupied by the kitchen and its offices, and served to accommodate the personal attendants of the great and wealthy nobleman, for whose use these magnificent preparations had been made.

The divinity for whose sake this temple had been decorated, was well worthy the cost and pains which had been bestowed. She was seated in the withdrawing-room which we have described, surveying with the pleased eye of natural and innocent vanity, the splendour which had been so suddenly created, as it were, in her honour. For, as her own residence at Cumnor Place formed the cause of the mystery observed in all the preparations for opening these apartments, it was sedulously arranged, that until she took possession of them, she should have no means of knowing what was going forward in that part of the ancient building, or of exposing herself to be seen by the workmen engaged in the decorations. She had been, therefore, introduced on that evening to a part of the mansion which she had never yet seen, so different from all the rest, that it appeared, in comparison, like an enchanted palace. And when she first examined and occupied these splendid rooms, it was with the wild and unrestrained joy of a rustic beauty, who finds herself suddenly invested with a splendour which her most extravagant wishes had never imagined, and at the same time with the keen feeling of an affectionate heart, which knows that all the enchantment which surrounds her is the work of the great magician Love.

The Countess Amy, therefore—for to that rank she was exalted by her private but solemn union with England's proudest Earl,—had for a time flitted hastily from room to room, admiring each new proof of her lover and her bridegroom's taste, and feeling that admiration enhanced, as she recollected that all she gazed upon was one continued proof of his ardent and devoted affection. 'How beautiful are these hangings! How natural these paintings, which seem to contend with life! How richly wrought is that plate, which looks as if all the galleons of Spain had been intercepted on the broad seas to furnish it forth! And oh, Janet!' she exclaimed repeatedly to the daughter of Anthony Foster, the close attendant, who with equal curiosity, but somewhat less ecstatic joy, followed on her mistress's footstep—'Oh, Janet! how much more delightful to think, that all these fair things have been assembled by his love, for the love of me! and that this evening—this very evening, which grows darker and darker every instant, I shall thank him more for the love that has created such an unimaginable paradise, than for all the wonders it contains!'

'The Lord is to be thanked first,' said the pretty puritan, 'who gave thee, lady, the kind and courteous husband, whose love has done so much for thee. I, too, have done my poor share. But if you thus run wildly from room to room, the toil of my crisping and my curling pins will vanish like the frost-work on the window when the sun is high.'

'Thou sayest true, Janet,' said the young and beautiful Countess, stopping suddenly from her tripping race of enraptured delight, and looking at herself from head to foot in a large mirror, such as she had never before seen, and which, indeed, had few to match it even in the Queen's palace—'Thou sayest true, Janet,' she answered, as she saw, with pardonable self-applause, the noble mirror reflect such charms as were seldom presented to its fair and polished surface; 'I have more of the milk-maid than the countess, with these cheeks flushed with haste, and all these brown curls, which you laboured to bring to order, straying as wild as the tendrils of an unpruned vine—My falling ruff is chafed too, and shows the neck and bosom more than is modest and seemly—Come, Janet—we will practise state—we will go to the withdrawing-room, my good girl, and thou shalt put these rebel locks in order, and imprison within lace and cambric the bosom that beats too high.'

They went to the withdrawing apartment accordingly, where the Countess playfully stretched her upon the pile of Moorish cushions, half sitting, half reclining, half wrapt in her own thoughts, half listening to the prattle of her attendant.

While she was in this attitude, and with a corresponding expression betwixt listlessness and expectation on her fine and intelligent features, you might have searched sea and land without finding anything half so expressive or half so lovely. The wreath of brilliants which mixed with her dark brown hair, did not match in lustre the hazel eye which a light brown eyebrow, pencilled with exquisite delicacy, and long eyelashes of the same colour, relieved and shaded. The exercise she had just taken, her excited expectation and gratified vanity, spread a glow over her fine features, which had been sometimes censured (as beauty as well as art has her minute critics) for being rather too pale. The milk-white pearls of the necklace which she wore, the same which she had just received as a true-love token from her husband, were excelled in purity by her teeth, and by the colour of her skin, saving where the blush of pleasure and self-satisfaction had somewhat stained the neck with a shade of light crimson.—'Now have done with these busy fingers, Janet,' she said to her hand-maiden, who was still officiously employed in bringing her hair and her dress into order—'Have done, I say—I must see your father ere my lord arrives, and also Master Richard Varney, whom my lord has highly in his esteem—but I could tell that of him would lose him favour.'

'Oh do not do so, good my lady!' replied Janet; 'leave him to God, who punishes the wicked in his own time; but do not you cross Varney's path, for so thoroughly hath he my lord's ear, that few have thriven who have thwarted his courses.'

'And from whom had you this, my most righteous Janet,' said the Countess; 'or why should I keep terms with so mean a gentleman as Varney, being, as I am, wife to his master and patron?'

'Nay, madam,' replied Janet Foster, 'your ladyship knows better than I—But I have heard my father say, he would rather cross a hungry wolf than thwart Richard Varney in his projects—And he has often charged me to have a care of holding commerce with him.'

'Thy father said well, girl, for thee,' replied the lady, 'and I dare swear meant well. It is a pity, though, his face and manner do little match his true purpose—for I think his purpose may be true.'

'Doubt it not, my lady,' answered Janet—'Doubt not that my father purposes well, though he is a plain man, and his blunt looks may belie his heart.'

'I will not doubt it, girl, were it only for thy sake; and yet he has one of those faces which men tremble when they look on—I think even thy mother, Janet—nay, have done with that poking-iron—could hardly look upon him without quaking.'

'If it were so, madam,' answered Janet Foster, 'my mother had those who could keep her in honourable countenance. Why, even you, my lady, both trembled and blushed when Varney brought the letter from my lord.'

'You are bold, damsel,' said the Countess, rising from the cushions on which she sat half-reclining in the arms of her attendant—'Know, that there are causes of trembling which have nothing to do with fear. But, Janet,' she added, immediately relapsing into the good-natured and familiar tone which was natural to her, 'believe me, I will do what credit I can to your father, and the rather that you, sweetheart, are his child. Alas; alas!' she added, a sudden sadness passing over her fine features, and her eyes filling with tears, 'I ought the rather to hold sympathy with thy kind heart, that my own poor father is uncertain of my fate, and they say lies sick and sorrowful for my worthless sake! But I will soon cheer him—the news of my happiness and advancement will make him young again. And that I may cheer him the sooner'—she wiped her eyes as she spoke—'I must be cheerful myself. My lord must not find me insensible to his kindness, or sorrowful when he snatches a visit to his recluse, after so long an absence. Be merry, Janet—the night wears on, and my lord must soon arrive. Call thy father hither, and call Varney also—I cherish resentment against neither; and though I may have some room to be displeased with both, it shall be their own fault if ever a complaint against them reaches the Earl through my means. Call them hither, Janet.'

Janet Foster obeyed her mistress; and in a few minutes after, Varney entered the withdrawing-room with the graceful ease and unclouded front of an accomplished courtier, skilled, under the veil of external politeness, to disguise his own feelings, and to penetrate into those of others. Anthony Foster plodded into the apartment after him, his natural gloomy vulgarity of aspect seeming to become yet more remarkable, from his clumsy attempt to conceal the anxious mixture of anxiety and dislike with which he looked on her, over whom he had hitherto exercised so severe a control, now so splendidly attired, and decked with so many pledges of the interest which she possessed in her husband's affection. The blundering reverence which he made, rather *at* than *to* the Countess, had confession in it—It was like the reverence which the criminal makes to the judge, when he at once confesses his guilt and implores mercy—which is at the same time an impudent and embarrassed attempt at defence or extenuation, a confession of a fault, and an entreaty for lenity.

Varney, who, in the right of his gentle blood, had pressed into the room before Anthony Foster, knew better what to say than he, and said it with more assurance and a better grace.

The Countess greeted him indeed with an appearance of cordiality, which seemed a complete amnesty for whatever she might have to complain of. She rose from her seat, and advanced two steps towards him, holding forth her hand as she said, 'Master

Richard Varney, you brought me this morning such welcome tidings, that I fear surprise and joy made me neglect my lord and husband's charge to receive you with distinction. We offer you our hand, sir, in reconciliation.'

'I am unworthy to touch it,' said Varney, dropping on one knee, 'save as a subject honours that of a prince.'

He touched with his lips those fair and slender fingers, so richly loaded with rings and jewels; then rising, with graceful gallantry, was about to hand her to the chair of state, when she said, 'No, good Master Richard Varney, I take not my place there until my lord himself conducts me. I am for the present but a disguised Countess, and will not take dignity on me until authorised by him whom I derive it from.'

'I trust, my lady,' said Foster, 'that in doing the commands of my lord your husband, in your restraint and so forth, I have not incurred your displeasure, seeing that I did but my duty towards your lord and mine; for Heaven, as holy writ saith, hath given the husband supremacy and dominion over the wife—I think it runs so, or something like it.'

'I receive at this moment so pleasant a surprise, Master Foster,' answered the Countess, 'that I cannot but excuse the rigid fidelity which secluded me from these apartments, until they had assumed an appearance so new and so splendid.'

'Ay, lady,' said Forster, 'it hath cost many a fair crown; and that more need not be wasted than is absolutely necessary, I leave you till my lord's arrival with good Master Richard Varney, who, as I think, hath somewhat to say to you from your most noble lord and husband. Janet, follow me, to see that all be in order.'

'No, Master Foster,' said the Countess, 'we will your daughter remains here in our apartment; out of earshot, however, in case Varney hath aught to say to me from my lord.'

Foster made his clumsy reverence, and departed, with an aspect that seemed to grudge the profuse expense which had been wasted upon changing his house from a bare and ruinous grange to an Asiatic palace. When he was gone, his daughter took her embroidery frame, and went to establish herself at the bottom of the apartment, while Richard Varney, with a profoundly humble courtesy, took the lowest stool he could find, and placing it by the side of the pile of cushions on which the Countess had now again seated herself, sat with his eyes for a time fixed on the ground, and in profound silence. 'I thought, Master Varney,' said the Countess, when she saw he was not likely to open the conversation, 'that you had something to communicate from my lord and husband: so at least I understood Master Foster, and therefore I removed my waiting-maid. If I am mistaken, I will recall her to my side; for her needle is not so absolutely perfect in tent and cross-stitch, but what my superintendence is advisable.'

'Lady,' said Varney, 'Foster was partly mistaken in my purpose. It was not *from*, but *of*, your noble husband, and my approved and most noble patron, that I am led, and indeed bound to speak.'

'The theme is most welcome, sir,' said the Countess, 'whether it be of or from my noble husband. But be brief, for I expect his hasty approach.'

'Briefly then, madam,' replied Varney, 'and boldly, for my argument requires both haste and courage. You have this day seen Tressilian.'

'I have, sir, and what of that?' answered the lady somewhat sharply.

'Nothing that concerns me, lady,' Varney replied with humility. 'But think you, honoured madam, that your lord will hear it with equal equanimity?'

'And wherefore should he not? To me alone was Tressilian's visit embarrassing and painful, for he brought news of my good father's illness.'

'Of your father's illness, madam!' answered Varney. 'It must have been sudden then—very sudden; for the messenger whom I despatched, at my lord's instance, found the good knight on the hunting-field, cheering his beagles with his wonted jovial field-cry. I trust Tressilian has but forged this news—He hath his reasons, madam, as you well know, for disquieting your present happiness.'

'You do him injustice, Master Varney,' replied the Countess with animation—'You do him much injustice. He is the freest, the most open, the most gentle heart that breathes—My honourable lord ever excepted, I know not one to whom falsehood is more odious than to Tressilian.'

'I crave your pardon, madam,' said Varney, 'I meant the gentleman no injustice—I knew not how nearly his cause affected you. A man may, in some circumstances, disguise the truth for fair and honest purpose; for were it to be for ever spoken, and upon all occasions, this were no world to live in.'

'You have a courtly conscience, Master Varney,' said the Countess, 'and your veracity will not, I think, interrupt your preferment in the world, such as it is. But touching Tressilian—I must do him justice, for I have done him wrong, as none knows better than thou. Tressilian's conscience is of other mould—The world thou speakest of has not that which could bribe him from the way of truth and honour; and for living in it with a soiled fame, the ermine would as soon seek to lodge in the den of the foul pole-cat. For this my father loved him—For this I would have loved him—if I could. And yet in this case he had what seemed to him, unknowing alike of my marriage, and to whom I was united, such powerful reasons to withdraw me from this place, that I well trust he exaggerated much my father's indisposition, and that thy better news may be the truer.'

'Believe me they are, madam,' answered Varney; 'I pretend not to be a champion of that same naked virtue called truth, to the very outrance. I can consent that her charms be hidden with a veil, were it but for decency's sake. But you must think lower of my head and heart, than is due to one whom my noble lord deigns to call his friend, if you suppose I could wilfully and unnecessarily palm upon your ladyship a falsehood, so soon to be detected in a matter which concerns your happiness.'

'Master Varney,' said the Countess, 'I know that my lord esteems you, and holds you a faithful and a good pilot in those seas in which he has spread so high and so venturous a sail. Do not suppose, therefore, I meant hardly by you, when I spoke the truth in Tressilian's vindication. I am, as you well know, country-bred, and like plain rustic truth better than courtly compliment, but I must change my fashions with my sphere, I presume.'

'True, madam,' said Varney, smiling, 'and though you speak now in jest, it will not be amiss that in earnest your present speech had some connection with your real purpose. A court-dame—take the most noble—the most virtuous—the most unimpeachable that stands around our Queen's throne—would, for example, have shunned to speak the truth, or what she thought such, in praise of a discarded suitor, before the dependant and confidant of her noble husband.'

'And wherefore,' said the Countess, colouring impatiently, 'should I not do justice to Tressilian's worth, before my husband's friend—before my husband himself—before the whole world?'

'And with the same openness,' said Varney, 'your ladyship will this night tell my noble lord your husband, that Tressilian has discovered your place of residence, so anxiously concealed from the world, and that he has had an interview with you?'

'Unquestionably,' said the Countess. 'It will be the first thing I tell him, together with every word that Tressilian said, and that I answered. I shall speak my own shame in this, for Tressilian's reproaches, less just than he esteemed them, were not altogether unmerited—I will speak, therefore, with pain, but I will speak, and speak all.'

'Your ladyship will do your pleasure,' answered Varney; 'but methinks it were as well, since nothing calls for so frank a disclosure, to spare yourself this pain, and my noble lord the disquiet, and Master Tressilian, since belike he must be thought of in the matter, the danger which is like to ensue.'

'I can see naught of all these terrible consequences,' said the lady, composedly, 'unless by imputing to my noble lord unworthy thoughts, which I am sure never harboured in his generous heart.'

'Far be it from me to do so,' said Varney—And then, after a moment's silence, he added, with a real or affected plainness of manner, very different from his usual smooth courtesy,—'Come, madam, I will show you that a courtier dare speak truth as well as another, when it concerns the weal of those whom he honours and regards, ay, and although it may infer his own danger.' He waited as if to receive commands, or at least permission to go on, but as the lady remained silent, he proceeded, but obviously with caution. 'Look around you,' he said, 'noble lady, and observe the barriers with which this place is surrounded, the studious mystery with which the brightest jewel that England possesses is secluded from the admiring gaze. See with what rigour your walks are circumscribed, and your movements restrained, at the beck of yonder churlish Foster. Consider all this, and judge for yourself what can be the cause.'

'My lord's pleasure,' answered the Countess; 'and I am bound to seek no other motive.'

'His pleasure it is indeed,' said Varney; 'and his pleasure arises out of a love worthy of the object which inspires it. But he who possesses a treasure, and who values it, is oft anxious, in proportion to the value he puts upon it, to secure it from the depredations of others.'

'What needs all this talk, Master Varney?' said the lady, in reply; 'you would have me believe that my noble lord is jealous—Suppose it true, I know a cure for jealousy.'

'Indeed, madam!' said Varney.

'It is,' replied the lady, 'to speak the truth to my lord at all times, to hold up my mind and my thoughts before him as pure as that polished mirror; so that when he looks into my heart, he shall only see his own features reflected there.'

'I am mute, madam,' answered Varney; 'and as I have no reason to grieve for Tressilian, who would have my heart's blood were he able, I shall reconcile myself easily to what may befall the gentleman, in consequence of your frank disclosure of his having presumed to intrude upon your solitude. You, who know my lord so much better than I, will judge if he be likely to bear the insult unavenged.'

'Nay, if I could think myself the cause of Tressilian's ruin,' said the Countess,—'I who have already occasioned him so much distress, I might be brought to be silent. And yet what will it avail, since he was seen by Foster and I think by some one else? No, no, Varney, urge it no more, I will tell the whole matter to my lord; and with such pleading for Tressilian's folly, as shall dispose my lord's generous heart rather to serve than to punish him.'

'Your judgment, madam,' said Varney, 'is far superior to mine, especially as you may, if you will, prove the ice before you step on it, by mentioning Tressilian's name to my lord, and observing how he endures it. For Foster and his attendant, they know not Tressilian by sight, and I can easily give them some reasonable excuse for the appearance of an unknown stranger.'

The lady paused for an instant, and then replied, 'If, Varney, it be indeed true that Foster knows not as yet that the man he saw was Tressilian, I own I were unwilling he should learn what no way concerns him. He bears himself already with austerity enough, and I wish him not to be judge or privy-councillor in my affairs.'

'Tush,' said Varney; 'what has the surly groom to do with your ladyship's concerns? No more, surely, than the ban-dog which watches his courtyard. If he is in ought distasteful to your ladyship, I have interest enough to have him exchanged for a seneschal that shall be more agreeable to you.'

'Master Varney,' said the Countess, 'let us drop this theme—when I complain of the attendants whom my lord has placed around me, it must be to my lord himself. Hark! I hear the trampling of horse—He comes! he comes!' she exclaimed, jumping up in ecstasy.'

'I cannot think it is he,' said Varney; 'or that you can hear the tread of his horse through the closely mantled casements.'

'Stop me not, Varney—my ears are keener than thine—it is he!'

'But, madam!—but, madam!' exclaimed Varney, anxiously, and still placing himself in her way—'I trust that what I have spoken in humble duty and service, will not be turned to my ruin? I hope that my faithful advice will not be bewrayed to my prejudice?—I implore that——'

'Content thee, man—content thee!' said the Countess, 'and quit my skirt—you are too bold to detain me—Content thyself, I think not of thee.'

At this moment the folding-doors flew open, and a man of majestic mien, muffled in the folds of a long dark riding-cloak, entered the apartment.

7

> ——This is he
> Who rides on the court gale; controls its tides;
> Knows all their secret shoals and fatal eddies;
> Whose frown abases, and whose smile exalts.
> He shines like any rainbow—and, perchance,
> His colours are as transient.—*Old Play.*

THERE was some little displeasure and confusion on the Countess's brow, owing to her struggle with Varney's pertinacity; but it was exchanged for an expression of the purest joy and affection, as she threw herself into the arms of the noble stranger who entered, and clasping him to her bosom, exclaimed, 'At length—at length thou art come!'

Varney discreetly withdrew as his lord entered, and Janet was about to do the same, when her mistress signed to her to remain. She took her place at the farther end of the apartment, and remained standing, as if ready for attendance.

Meanwhile, the Earl, for he was of no inferior rank, returned his lady's caress with the most affectionate ardour, but affected to resist when she strove to take his cloak from him.

'Nay,' she said, 'but I *will* unmantle you—I must see if you have kept your word to me, and come as the great Earl men call thee, and not as heretofore, like a private cavalier.'

'Thou art like the rest of the world, Amy,' said the Earl, suffering her to prevail in the playful contest; 'the jewels, and feathers, and silk, are more to them than the man whom they adorn—many a poor blade looks gay in a velvet scabbard.'

'But so cannot men say of thee, thou noble Earl,' said his lady, as the cloak dropped on the floor, and showed him dressed as princes when they ride abroad; 'thou art the good and well-tried steel, whose inly worth deserves, yet disdains, its outward ornaments. Do not think Amy can love thee better in this glorious garb, than she did when she gave her heart to him who wore the russet brown cloak in the woods of Devon.'

'And thou too,' said the Earl, as gracefully and majestically he led his beautiful Countess towards the chair of state which was prepared for them both,—'thou too, my love, hast donned a dress which becomes thy rank, though it cannot improve thy beauty. What think'st thou of our court taste?'

The lady cast a sidelong glance upon the great mirror as they passed it by, and then said, 'I know not how it is, but I think not of my own person while I look at the reflection of thine. Sit thou there,' she said, as they approached the chair of state, 'like a thing for men to worship and to wonder at.'

'Ay, love,' said the Earl, 'if thou wilt share my state with me.'

'Not so,' said the Countess; 'I will sit on this footstool at thy feet, that I may spell over thy splendour, and learn, for the first time, how princes are attired.'

And with a childish wonder, which her youth and rustic education rendered not only excusable but becoming, mixed as it was with a delicate show of the most tender conjugal affection, she examined and admired from head to foot the noble form and princely attire of him who formed the proudest ornament of the Court of England's Maiden Queen, renowned as it was for splendid courtiers, as well as for wise counsellors. Regarding affectionately his lovely bride, and gratified by her unrepressed admiration, the dark eye and noble features of the Earl expressed passions more gentle than the commanding and aspiring look, which usually sat upon his broad forehead, and in the piercing brilliancy of his dark eye, and he smiled at the simplicity which dictated the questions she put to him concerning the various ornaments with which he was decorated.

'The embroidered strap, as thou callest it, around my knee,' he said, 'is the English Garter, an ornament which kings are proud to wear. See, here is the star which belongs to it, and here the Diamond George, the jewel of the Order. You have heard how King Edward and the Countess of Salisbury——'

'Oh, I know all that tale,' said the Countess, slightly blushing, 'and how a lady's garter became the proudest badge of English chivalry.'

'Even so,' said the Earl; 'and this most honourable Order I had the good hap to receive at the same time with three most noble associates, the Duke of Norfolk, the Marquis of Northamptom, and the Earl of Rutland. I was the lowest of the four in rank—but what then?—he that climbs a ladder must begin at the first round.'

'But this other fair collar, so richly wrought, with some jewel like a sheep hung by the middle attached to it, what,' said the young Countess, 'does that emblem signify?'

'This collar,' said the Earl, 'with its double fusilles interchanged with these knobs, which are supposed to present flint-stones, sparkling with fire, and sustaining the jewel you inquire about, is the badge of the noble Order of the Golden Fleece, once appertaining to the House of Burgundy. It hath high privileges, my Amy, belonging to it, this most noble Order; for even the King of Spain himself, who hath now succeeded to the honours and demesnes of Burgundy, may not sit on judgment upon a knight of the Golden Fleece, unless by assistance, and consent of the Great Chapter of the Order.'

'And is this an Order belonging to the cruel King of Spain?' said the Countess. 'Alas! my noble lord, that you will defile your noble English breast by bearing such an emblem! Bethink you of the most unhappy Queen Mary's days, when this same Philip held sway with her in England, and of the piles which were built for our noblest, and our wisest, and our most truly sanctified prelates and divines—And will you, whom men call the standard-bearer of the true Protestant faith, be contented to wear the emblem and mark of such a Romish tyrant as he of Spain?'

'Oh, content you, my love,' answered the Earl; 'we who spread our sails to gales of court-favour, cannot always display the ensigns we love the best, or at all times refuse sailing under colours which we like not. Believe me, I am not the less good Protestant, that for policy I must accept the honour offered me by Spain, in admitting me to this his highest order of knighthood. Besides, it belongs properly to Flanders; and Egmont, Orange, and others, have pride in seeing it displayed on an English bosom.'

'Nay, my lord, you know your own path best,' replied the Countess. 'And this other collar, to what country does this fair jewel belong?'

'To a very poor one, my love,' replied the Earl; 'this is the Order of Saint Andrew, revived by the last James of Scotland. It was bestowed on me when it was thought the young widow of France and Scotland would gladly have wedded an English baron; but a free coronet of England is worth a crown matrimonial held at the humour of a woman, and owning only the poor rocks and bogs of the north.'

The Countess paused, as if what the Earl last said had excited some painful but interesting train of thought; and, as she still remained silent, the Earl proceeded.

'And now, loveliest, your wish is gratified, and you have seen your vassal in such of his trim array as accords with riding vestments; for robes of state and coronets are only for princely halls.'

'Well, then,' said the Countess, 'my gratified wish has, as usual, given rise to a new one.'

'And what is it thou canst ask that I can deny?' said the fond husband.

'I wished to see my Earl visit this obscure and secret bower,' said the Countess, 'in all his princely array; and now, methinks, I long to sit in one of his princely halls, and see him enter dressed in sober russet, as when he won poor Amy Robsart's heart.'

'That is a wish easily granted,' said the Earl; 'the sober russet shall be donned to-morrow if you will.'

'But shall I,' said the lady,' 'go with you to one of your castles, to see how the richness of your dwelling will correspond with your peasant habit?'

'Why, Amy,' said the Earl, looking around, 'are not these apartments decorated with sufficient splendour? I gave the most unbounded order, and, methinks, it has been indifferently well obeyed—but if thou canst tell me aught which remains to be done, I will instantly give direction.'

'Nay, my lord, now you mock me,' replied the Countess; 'the gaiety of this rich lodging exceeds my imagination as much as it does my desert. But shall not your wife, my love—at least one day soon—be surrounded with the honour, which arises neither from the toils of the mechanic who decks her apartment, nor from the silks and jewels with which your generosity adorns her, but which is attached to her place among the matronage, as the avowed wife of England's noblest Earl?'

'One day?' said her husband,—'Yes, Amy, my love, one day this shall surely happen; and, believe me, thou canst not wish for that day more fondly than I. With what rapture could I retire from labours of state, and cares and toils of ambition, to spend my life in dignity and honour of my own broad domains, with thee, my lovely Amy, for my friend and companion! But, Amy, this cannot yet be; and these dear but stolen interviews are all I can give to the loveliest and the best beloved of her sex.'

'But *why* can it not be?' urged the Countess, in the softest tones of persuasion,—'why can it not immediately take place—this more perfect, this uninterrupted union, for which you say you wish, and which the laws of God and man alike command? Ah! did you but desire it half so much as you say, mighty and favoured as you are, who, or what, shall bar your attaining your wish?'

The Earl's brow was overcast.

'Amy,' he said, 'you speak of what you understand not. We that toil in courts are like those who climb a mountain of loose sand—we dare make no halt until some projecting rock afford us a secure footing and resting-place—if we pause sooner, we slide down by our own weight, an object of universal derision. I stand high, but I stand not secure enough to follow my own inclination. To declare my marriage, were to be the artificer of my own ruin. But, believe me, I will reach a point, and that speedily, when I can do justice to thee and to myself. Meanwhile, poison not the bliss of the present moment, by desiring that which cannot at present be. Let me rather know whether all here is managed to thy liking. How does Foster bear himself to you?—in all things respectful, I trust, else the fellow shall dearly rue it.'

'He reminds me sometimes of the necessity of this privacy,' answered the lady with a sigh; 'but that is reminding me of your wishes, and therefore, I am rather bound to him than disposed to blame him for it.'

'I have told you the stern necessity which is upon us,' replied the Earl. 'Foster is, I note, somewhat sullen of mood, but Varney warrants to me his fidelity and devotion to my service. If thou hast aught, however, to complain of the mode in which he discharges his duty, he shall abye it.'

'Oh, I have naught to complain of,' answered the lady, 'so he discharges his task with fidelity to you; and his daughter Janet is the kindest and best companion of my solitude—her little air of precision sits so well upon her.'

'Is she indeed?' said the Earl; 'she who gives you pleasure must not pass unrewarded—Come hither, damsel.'

'Janet,' said the lady,' come hither to my lord.'

Janet, who, as we already noticed, had discreetly retired to some distance, that her presence might be no check upon the private conversation of her lord and lady, now came forward; and as she made her reverential courtesy, the Earl could not help smiling at the contrast which the extreme simplicity of her dress, and the prim demureness of her looks made, with a very pretty countenance and a pair of black eyes, that laughed in spite of their mistress's desire to look grave.

'I am bound to you, pretty damsel,' said the Earl, 'for the contentment which your service hath given to this lady.' As he said this, he took from his finger a ring of some price, and offered it to Janet Foster, adding. 'Wear this, for her sake and for mine.'

'I am well pleased, my lord,' answered Janet demurely, 'that my poor service hath gratified my lady, whom no one can draw nigh to without desiring to please; but we of the precious Mr Holdforth's congregation seek not, like the gay daughters of this world, to twine gold around our fingers, or wear stones upon our necks, like the vain women of Tyre and of Sidon.'

'Oh, what! you are a grave professor of the precise sisterhood, pretty Mrs Janet,' said the Earl, 'and I think your father is of the same congregation in sincerity. I like you both the better for it; for I have been prayed for, and wished well to, in your congregations. And you may the better afford the lack of ornament, Mrs Janet, because your fingers are slender, and your neck white. But here is what neither papist nor puritan, latitudinarian nor precisian, ever boggles or makes mouths at. E'en take it, my girl, and employ it as you list.'

So saying, he put into her hand five broad gold pieces of Philip and Mary.

'I would not accept this gold neither,' said Janet, 'but that I hope to find a use for it, which will bring a blessing on us all.'

'Even please thyself, pretty Janet,' said the Earl, 'and I shall be well satisfied—And I prithee let them hasten the evening collation.'

'I have bidden Master Varney and Master Foster to sup with us, my lord,' said the Countess, as Janet retired to obey the Earl's commands, 'has it your approbation?'

'What you do ever must have so, my sweet Amy,' replied her husband; 'and I am the better pleased thou hast done them this grace, because Richard Varney is my sworn man, and a close brother of my secret council; and for the present I must needs repose much trust in this Anthony Foster.'

'I had a boon to beg of thee, and a secret to tell thee, my dear lord,' said the Countess with a faltering accent.

'Let both be for to-morrow, my love,' replied the Earl. 'I see they open the folding-doors into the banqueting parlour, and, as I have ridden far and fast, a cup of wine will not be unacceptable.'

So saying, he led his lovely wife into the next apartment, where Varney and Foster received them with the deepest reverences, which the first paid with the fashion of the court, and the second after that of the congregation. The Earl returned their salutation with the negligent courtesy of one long used to such homage; while the Countess repaid it with a punctilious solicitude, which showed it was not quite so familiar to her.

The banquet, at which the company seated themselves, corresponded in magnificence with the splendour of the apartment in which it was served up, but no domestic gave his attendance. Janet alone stood ready to wait upon the company; and, indeed, the board was so well supplied with all that could be desired, that little or no assistance was necessary. The Earl and his lady occupied the upper end of the table, and Varney and Foster sat beneath the salt, as was the custom with inferiors. The latter, overawed perhaps by society to which he was altogether unused, did not utter a single syllable during the repast; while Varney, with great tact and discernment, sustained just so much of the conversation, as, without the appearance of intrusion on his part, prevented it from languishing, and maintained the good humour of the Earl at the highest pitch. This man was indeed highly qualified by nature to discharge the part in which he found himself placed, being discreet and cautious on the one hand, and on the other, quick, keen-witted, and imaginative; so that even the Countess, prejudiced as she was against him on many accounts, felt and enjoyed his powers of conversation, and was more disposed than she had ever hitherto found herself to join in the praises which the Earl lavished on his favourite. The hour of rest at length arrived, the Earl and Countess retired to their apartment, and all was silent in the castle for the rest of the night.

Early on the ensuing morning, Varney acted as the Earl's chamberlain as well as his master of horse, though the latter was his proper office in that magnificent household, where knights and gentlemen of good descent were well contented to hold such menial situations as nobles themselves held in that of the sovereign. The duties of each of these charges were familiar to Varney, who, sprung from an ancient but decayed family, was the Earl's page during his earlier and more obscure fortunes, and, faithful to him in adversity, had afterwards contrived to render himself no less useful to him in his rapid and splendid advance to fortune; thus establishing in him an interest resting both on present and past services, which rendered him an almost indispensable sharer of his confidence.

'Help me to do on a plainer riding-suit, Varney,' said the Earl, as he laid aside his morning-gown, flowered with silk, and lined with sables, 'and put these chains and fetters there (pointing to the collars of the various Orders which lay on the table) into their place of security—my neck last night was wellnigh broke with the weight of them. I am half of the mind that they shall gall me no more. They are bonds which knaves have invented to fetter fools. How think'st thou, Varney?'

'Faith, my good lord,' said his attendant, 'I think fetters of gold are like no other fetters—they are ever the weightier the welcomer.'

'For all that, Varney,' replied his master, 'I am half resolved they shall bind me to the court no longer. What can further service and higher favour give me, beyond the high rank and large estate which I have already secured? What brought my father to the block, but that he could not bound his wishes within right and reason? I have, you know, had mine own ventures and mine own escapes? I am wellnigh resolved to tempt the sea no further, but sit me down in quiet on the shore.'

'And gather cockle-shells, with Dan Cupid to aid you,' said Varney.

'How mean you by that, Varney?' said the Earl, somewhat hastily.

'Nay, my lord,' said Varney, 'be not angry with me. If your lordship is happy in a lady so rarely lovely, that in order to enjoy her company with somewhat more freedom, you are willing to part with all that you have hitherto lived for, some of your poor servants may be sufferers; but your bounty hath placed me so high, that I shall ever have enough to maintain a poor gentleman in the rank befitting the high office he has held in your lordship's family.'

'Yet you seem discontented when I propose throwing up a dangerous game, which may end in the ruin of both of us.'

'I, my lord?' said Varney; 'surely I have no cause to regret your lordship's retreat? It will not be Richard Varney who will incur the displeasure of majesty, and the ridicule of the court, when the stateliest fabric that ever was founded upon a prince's favour, melts away like a morning frost-work. I would only have you yourself to be assured, my lord, ere you take a step which cannot be retraced, that you consult your fame and happiness in the course you propose.'

'Speak on then, Varney,' said the Earl; 'I tell thee I have determined nothing, and will weigh all considerations on either side.'

'Well, then, my lord,' replied Varney, 'we will suppose the step taken, the frown frowned, the laugh laughed, and the moan moaned. You have retired, we will say, to some one of your most distant castles, so far from court that you hear neither the sorrow of your friends nor the glee of your enemies. We will suppose, too, that your successful rival will be satisfied (a thing greatly to be doubted) with abridging and cutting away the branches of the great tree, which so long kept the sun from him, and that he does not insist upon tearing you up by the roots. Well, the late prime favourite of England, who wielded her general's staff and controlled her parliaments, is now a rural baron, hunting, hawking, drinking fat ale with country esquires, and mustering his men at the command of the High Sheriff——'

'Varney, forbear!' said the Earl.

'Nay, my lord, you must give me leave to conclude my picture. Sussex governs England—the Queen's health fails—the succession is to be settled—a road is opened to ambition more splendid than ambition ever dreamed. You hear all this as you sit by the hob, under the shade of your hall-chimney—You then begin to think what hopes you have fallen from, and what insignificance you have embraced—and all that you might look babies in the eyes of your fair wife oftener than once a fortnight.'

'I say, Varney,' said the Earl, 'no more of this. I said not that the step, which my own ease and comfort would urge me to, was to be taken hastily, or without due consideration to the public safety. Bear witness to me, Varney, I subdue my wishes of retirement, not because I am moved by the call of private ambition, but that I may preserve the position in which I may best serve my country at the hour of need. Order our horses presently—I will wear, as formerly, one of the livery cloaks, and ride before the portmantle. Thou shalt be master for the day, Varney—neglect nothing that can blind suspicion. We will to horse ere men are stirring. I will but take leave of my lady, and be ready. I impose a restraint on my own poor heart, and wound one yet more dear to me; but the patriot must subdue the husband.'

Having said this in a melancholy but firm accent, he left the dressing apartment.

'I am glad thou art gone,' thought Varney, 'or, practised as I am in the follies of mankind, I had laughed in the very face of thee! Thou mayst tire as thou wilt of thy new bauble, thy pretty piece of painted Eve's flesh there, I will not be thy hindrance. But of thine old bauble, ambition, thou salt not tire, for as you climb the hill, my lord, you must drag Richard Varney up with you; and if he can urge you to the ascent he means to profit by, believe me he will spare neither whip nor spur.—And for you, my pretty lady, that would be Countess outright, you were best not thwart my counsels, lest you are called to an old reckoning on a new score. 'Thou shalt be master,' did he say—By my faith, he may find that he spoke truer than he is aware of—And thus he, who in the estimation of so many wise-judging men can match Burleigh and Walsingham in policy, and Sussex in war, becomes pupil to his own menial; and all for a hazel eye and a little cunning red and white, and so falls Ambition. And yet if the charms of mortal woman could excuse a man's politic pate for becoming bewildered, my lord had the excuse at his right hand on this blessed evening that has last passed over us. Well—let things roll as they may, he shall make me great, or will make myself happy; and for that softer piece of creation, if she speak not out her interview with Tressilian, as well I think she dare not, she also must traffic with me for concealment and mutual support in spite of all this scorn. I must to the stables. Well, my lord, I order your retinue now; the time may soon come that *my* master of the horse shall order mine own. What was Thomas Cromwell but a smith's son, and he died my lord—on a scaffold, doubtless, but that too was in character—And what was Ralph Saddler but the clerk of Cromwell, and he has gazed eighteen fair lordships—via! I know my steerage as well as they.'

So saying, he left the apartment.

In the meanwhile the Earl had re-entered the bed-chamber, bent on taking a hasty farewell of the lovely Countess, and scarce daring to trust himself in private with her, to hear requests again urged, which he found it difficult to parry, yet which his recent conversation with his master of horse had determined him not to grant.

He found her in a white cymar of silk lined with furs, her little feet unstockinged and hastily thrust into slippers; her unbraided hair escaping from under her midnight coif, with little array but her own loveliness, rather augmented than diminished by the grief which she felt at the approaching moment of separation.

'Now, God be with thee, my dearest and loveliest!' said the Earl, scarce tearing himself from her embrace, yet again returning to fold her again and again in his arms, and again bidding farewell, and again returning to kiss and bid adieu once more. 'The sun is on the verge of the blue horizon—I dare not stay. Ere this I should have been ten miles from hence.'

Such were the words with which at length he strove to cut short their parting interview.

'You will not grant my request then,' said the Countess. 'Ah, false knight! did ever lady, with bare foot in slipper, seek boon of a brave knight, yet return with denial?'

'Anything, Amy, anything thou canst ask I will grant,' answered the Earl—'always excepting,' he said, 'that which might ruin us both.'

'Nay,' said the Countess, 'I urge not my wish to be acknowledged in the character which would make me the envy of England—as the wife, that is, of my brave and noble lord, the first as the most fondly beloved of English nobles. Let me but share the secret with my dear father! Let me but end his misery on my unworthy account—they say he is ill, the good old kind-hearted man.'

'*They* say?' asked the Earl hastily, 'who says? Did not Varney convey to Sir Hugh all we dare at present tell him concerning your happiness and welfare? and has he not told you that the good old knight was following, with good heart and health, his favourite and wonted exercise? Who has dared put other thoughts into your head?'

'Oh, no one, my lord, no one,' said the Countess, something alarmed at the tone in which the question was put; 'but yet, my lord, I would fain be assured by my own eyesight that my father is well.'

'Be contented, Amy—thou canst not now have communication with thy father or his house. Were it not a deep course of policy to commit no secret unnecessarily to the custody of more than must needs be, it were sufficient reason for secrecy that yonder

Cornish man, yonder Trevanion, or Tressilian, or whatsoever his name is, haunts the old knight's house, and must necessarily know whatever is communicated there.'

'My lord,' answered the Countess, 'I do not think it so. My father has been long noted a worthy and honourable man; and for Tressilian, if we can pardon ourselves the ill we have wrought him, I will wager the coronet I am to share with you one day, that he is incapable of returning injury for injury.'

'I will not trust him, however, Amy,' said her husband; 'by my honour I will not trust him—I would rather the foul fiend intermingled in our secret than this Tressilian!'

'And why, my lord?' said the Countess, though she shuddered slightly at the tone of determination in which he spoke; 'let me but know why you think thus hardly of Tressilian?'

'Madam,' replied the Earl, 'my will ought to be a sufficient reason—If you desire more, consider how this Tressilian is leagued, and with whom. He stands high in the opinion of this Radcliffe, this Sussex, against whom I am barely able to maintain my ground in the opinion of our suspicious mistress; and if he had me at such advantage, Amy, as to become acquainted with the tale of our marriage before Elizabeth were fitly prepared, I were an outcast from her grace for ever—a bankrupt at once in favour and in fortune,—perhaps, for she hath in her a touch of her father Henry, a victim, a very victim, to her offended and jealous resentment.'

'But why, my lord,' again urged his lady, 'should you deem thus injuriously of a man of whom you know so little? What you do know of Tressilian is through me, and it is I who assure you that in no circumstances will he betray your secret. If I did him wrong in your behalf, my lord, I am now the more concerned you should do him justice. You are offended at my speaking of him; what would you say had I actually myself seen him?'

'If you had,' replied the Earl, 'you would do well to keep that interview as secret as that which is spoken in a confessional. I seek no one's ruin; but he who thrusts himself on my secret privacy, were better look well to his future walk. The bear brooks no one to cross his awful path.'

'Awful, indeed!' said the Countess, turning very pale.

'You are ill, my love,' said the Earl, supporting her in his arms; 'stretch yourself on your couch again, it is but an early day for you to leave it. Have you aught else, involving less than my fame, my fortune, and my life, to ask of me?'

'Nothing, my lord and love,' answered the Countess faintly; 'something there was that I would have told you, but your anger has driven it from my recollection.'

'Reserve it till our next meeting, my love,' said the Earl fondly, and again embracing her; 'and barring only those requests which I cannot and dare not grant, thy wish must be more than England and all its dependencies can fulfil, if it is not gratified to the letter.'

Thus saying, he took a final farewell. At the bottom of the staircase he received from Varney an ample livery cloak and slouched hat, in which he wrapped himself so as to disguise his person, and completely conceal his features. Horses were ready in the courtyard for himself and Varney; for one or two of his train, entrusted with the secret so far as to know or guess that the Earl intrigued with a beautiful lady at that mansion, though her name and quality were unknown to them, had already been dismissed overnight.

Anthony Foster himself held the rein of the Earl's palfrey, a stout and able nag for the road; while his old serving-man held the bridle of the more showy and gallant steed which Richard Varney was to occupy in the character of master.

As the Earl approached, however, Varney advanced to hold his master's bridle, and to prevent Foster from paying that duty to the Earl, which he probably considered as belonging to his own office. Foster scowled at an interference which seemed intended to prevent his paying his court to his patron, but gave place to Varney; and the Earl, mounting without further observation, and forgetting that his assumed character of a domestic threw him into the rear of his supposed master, rode pensively out of the quadrangle, not without waving his hand repeatedly in answer to the signals which were made by the Countess with her kerchief, from the windows of her appartment.

While his stately form vanished under the dark archway which led out of the quadrangle, Varney muttered, 'There goes fine policy—the servant before the master;' then as he disappeared, seized the moment to speak a word with Foster. 'Thou look'st dark on me, Anthony,' he said, 'as if I had deprived thee of a parting nod of my lord; but I have moved him to leave thee a better remembrance for thy faithful service. See here! a purse of as good gold as ever chinked under a miser's thumb and fore-finger. Ay, count them, lad,' said he, as Foster received the gold with a grim smile, 'and add to them the goodly remembrance he gave last night to Janet.'

'How's this! how's this!' said Anthony Foster hastily; 'gave he gold to Janet?'

'Ay, man, wherefore not?—does not her service to his fair lady require guerdon?'

'She shall have none on't,' said Foster; 'she shall return it. I know his dotage on one face is as brief as it is deep. His affections are as fickle as the moon.'

'Why, Foster, thou art mad—thou dost not hope for such good fortune, as that my lord should cast an eye on Janet? Who, in the fiend's name, would listen to the thrush when the nightingale is singing?'

'Thrush or nightingale, all is one to the fowler; and, Master Varney, you can sound the quail-pipe most daintily to wile wantons into his nets. I desire no such devil's preferment for Janet as you have brought many a poor maiden to—Dost thou laugh?—I will keep one limb of my family, at least, from Satan's clutches; that thou mayst rely on—She shall restore the gold.'

'Ay, or give it to thy keeping, Tony, which will serve as well,' answered Varney; 'but I have that to say which is more serious. Our lord is returning to court in an evil humour for us.'

'How meanest thou?' said Foster. 'Is he tired already of his pretty toy—his plaything yonder? He has purchased her at a monarch's ransom, and I warrant me he rues his bargain.'

'Not a whit, Tony; he dotes on her, and will forsake the court for her—then down go hopes, possessions, and safety—church-lands are resumed, Tony, and well if the holders be not called to account in Exchequer.'

'That were ruin,' said Foster, his brow darkening with apprehension; 'and all this for a woman! Had it been for his soul's sake, it were something; and I sometimes wish I myself could fling away the world that cleaves to me, and be as one of the poorest of our church.'

'Thou art like enough to be so, Tony,' answered Varney; 'but I think the devil will give thee little credit for thy compelled poverty, and so thou losest on all hands. But follow my counsel, and Cumnor Place shall be thy copyhold yet—Say nothing of this Tressilian's visit—not a word until I give thee notice.'

'And wherefore, I pray you?' said Foster suspiciously.

'Dull beast!' replied Varney; 'in my lord's present humour it were the ready way to confirm him in his resolution of retirement, should he know that his lady was haunted with such a spectre in his absence. He would be for playing the dragon himself over his golden fruit, and then, Tony, thy occupation is ended. A word to the wise. Farewell—I must follow him.'

He turned his horse, struck him with the spurs, and rode off under the archway in pursuit of his lord.

'Would thy occupation were ended, or thy neck broken, damned pander!' said Anthony Foster. 'But I must follow his beck, for his interest and mine are the same, and he can wind the proud Earl to his will. Janet shall give me these pieces though—they shall be laid out in some way for God's service, and I will keep them separate in my strong chest, till I can fall upon a fitting employment for them. No contagious vapour shall breathe on Janet—she shall remain pure as a blessed spirit, were it but to pray God for her father. I need her prayers, for I am at a hard pass. Strange reports are abroad concerning my way of life. The congregation look cold on me, and when Master Holdforth spoke of hypocrites being like a whited sepulchre, which within was full of dead men's bones, methought he looked full at me. The Romish was a comfortable faith; Lambourne spoke true in that. A man had but to follow his thrift by such ways as offered—tell his beads—hear a mass—confess, and be absolved. These puritans tread a harder and a rougher path; but I will try—I will read my Bible for an hour, ere I again open mine iron chest.'

Varney, meantime, spurred after his lord, whom he found waiting for him at the postern-gate of the path.

'You waste time, Varney,' said the Earl; 'and it presses. I must be at Woodstock before I can safely lay aside my disguise; and till then, I journey in some peril.'

'It is but two hours' brisk riding, my lord,' said Varney; 'for me, I only stopped to enforce your commands of care and secrecy on yonder Foster, and to inquire about the abode of the gentleman whom I would promote to your lordship's train, in the room of Trevors.'

'Is he fit for the meridian of the ante-chamber, think'st thou?' said the Earl.

'He promises well, my lord,' replied Varney; 'but if your lordship were pleased to ride on, I could go back to Cumnor, and bring him to your lordship at Woodstock, before you are out of bed.'

'Why, I am asleep there, thou know'st, at this moment,' said the Earl; 'and I pray you not to spare horse-flesh, that you may be with me at my levee.'

So saying, he gave his horse the spur, and proceeded on his journey, while Varney rode back to Cumnor by the public road, avoiding the park. The latter alighted at the door of the bonny Black Bear, and desired to speak with Master Michael Lambourne. That respectable character was not long of appearing before his new patron, but it was with downcast looks.

'Thou hast lost the scent,' said Varney, 'of thy comrade Tressilian. I know it by thy hang-dog visage. Is this thy alacrity, thou impudent knave?'

'Cogswounds!' said Lambourne, 'there was never a trail so finely hunted. I saw him to earth at mine uncle's here—stuck to him like beeswax—saw him at supper—watched him to his chamber, and presto—he is gone next morning, his very hostler knows not where.'

'This sounds like practice upon me, sir,' replied Varney; 'and if it prove so, by my soul you shall repent it.'

'Sir, the best hound will be sometimes at fault,' answered Lambourne; 'how should it serve me that this fellow should have thus evanished? You may ask mine host, Giles Gosling—ask the tapster and hostler—ask Cicely; and the whole household, how I kept eyes on Tressilian while he was on foot. On my soul, I could not be expected to watch him like a sick nurse, when I had seen him fairly a-bed in his chamber. That will be allowed me, surely.'

Varney did, in fact, make some inquiry among the household, which confirmed the truth of Lambourne's statement. Tressilian, it was unanimously agreed, had departed suddenly and unexpectedly, betwixt night and morning.

'But I will wrong no one,' said mine host; 'he left on the table in his lodging the full value of his reckoning, with some allowance to the servants of the house, which was the less necessary, that he saddled his own gelding, as it seems, without the hostler's assistance.'

Thus satisfied of the rectitude of Lambourne's conduct, Varney began to talk to him upon his future prospects and the mode in which he meant to bestow himself, intimating that he understood from Foster, he was not disinclined to enter into the household of a nobleman.

'Have you,' said he, 'ever been at court?'

'No,' replied Lambourne; 'but ever since I was ten years old, I have dreamt once a week that I was there, and made my fortune.'

'It may be your own fault if your dream comes not true,' said Varney. 'Are you needy?'

'Um!' replied Lambourne; 'I love pleasure.'

'That is a sufficient answer, and an honest one,' said Varney. 'Know you aught of the requisites expected from the retainer of a rising courtier?'

'I have imagined them to myself, sir,' answered Lambourne; 'as for example, a quick eye—a close mouth—a ready and bold hand—a sharp wit, and a blunt conscience.'

'And thine, I suppose,' said Varney, 'has had its edge blunted long since.'

'I cannot remember, sir, that its edge was ever overkeen,' replied Lambourne. 'When I was a youth, I had some few whimsies, but I rubbed them partly out of my recollection on the rough grindstone of the wars, and what remained, I washed out in the broad waves of the Atlantic.'

'Thou hast served, then, in the Indies?'

'In both East and West,' answered the candidate for court-service, 'by both sea and land; I have served both the Portugal and the Spaniard—both the Dutchman and the Frenchman, and have made war on our own account with a crew of jolly fellows, who held there was no 'peace beyond the Line.'

'Thou mayst do me, and my lord, and thyself, good service,' said Varney, after a pause. 'But observe, I know the world—and, answer me truly, canst thou be faithful?'

'Did you not know the world,' answered Lambourne, 'it were my duty to say ay, without further circumstance, and to swear it with life and honour, and so forth. But as it seems to me that your worship is one who desires rather honest truth than politic falsehood—I reply to you, that I can be faithful to the gallows' foot, ay, to the loop that dangles from it, if I am well used and well recompensed;—not otherwise.'

'To thy other virtues thou canst add, no doubt,' said Varney, in a jeering tone, 'the knack of seeming serious and religious, when the moment demands it?'

'It would cost me nothing,' said Lambourne, 'to say yes—but to speak on the square, I must needs say no. If you want a hypocrite, you may take Anthony Foster, who, from his childhood, had some sort of phantom haunting him, which he called religion, though it was that sort of godliness which always ended in being great gain. But I have no such knack of it.'

'Well,' replied Varney, 'if thou hast no hypocrisy, hast thou not a nag here in the stable?'

'Ay, sir,' said Lambourne, 'that shall take hedge and ditch with my Lord Duke's best hunters. When I made a little mistake on Shooter's Hill, and stopped an ancient grazier, whose pouches were better lined than his brain-pan, the bonny bay nag carried me sheer off, in spite of the whole hue and cry.'

'Saddle him then, instantly, and attend me,' said Varney. 'Leave thy clothes and baggage under charge of mine host, and I will conduct thee to a service, in which, if thou do not better thyself, the fault shall not be fortune's, but thine own.'

'Brave and hearty!' said Lambourne, 'and I am mounted in an instant. Knave, hostler, saddle my nag without the loss of one instant, as thou dost value the safety of thy noddle. Pretty Cicely, take half this purse, to comfort thee for my sudden departure.'

'Gogsnouns!' replied the father, 'Cicely wants no such token from thee—Go away, Mike, and gather grace if thou canst, though I think thou goest not to the land where it grows.'

'Let me look at this Cicely of thine, mine host,' said Varney; 'I have heard much talk of her beauty.'

'It is a sun-burnt beauty,' said mine host, 'well qualified to stand out rain and wind, but little calculated to please such critical gallants as yourself. She keeps her chamber, and cannot encounter the glance of such sunny-day courtiers, my noble guest.'

'Well, peace be with her, my good host,' answered Varney; 'our horses are impatient—we bid you good-day.'

'Does my nephew go with you, so please you?' said Gosling.

'Ay, such is his purpose,' answered Richard Varney.

'You are right—fully right,' replied mine host—'you are, I say, fully right, my kinsman. Thou hast got a gay horse, see thou light not unaware upon a halter—or if thou wilt needs be made immortal by means of a rope, which thy purpose of following this gentleman renders not unlikely, I charge thee to find a gallows as far from Cumnor as thou conveniently mayst; and so I commend you to your saddle.'

The master of the horse and his new retainer took horse accordingly, leaving the landlord to conclude his ill-omened farewell, to himself and at leisure; and set off together at a rapid pace, which prevented conversation until the ascent of a steep, sandy hill permitted them to resume it.

'You are contented then,' said Varney, to his companion, 'to take court-service?'

'Ay, worshipful sir, if you like my terms as well as I like yours.'

'And what are your terms?' demanded Varney.

'If I am to have a quick eye for my patron's interest, he must have a dull one towards my faults,' said Lambourne.

'Ay,' said Varney, 'so they lie not so grossly open that he must needs break his shins over them.'

'Agreed,' said Lambourne. 'Next, if I run down game, I must have the picking of the bones.'

'That is but reason,' replied Varney, 'so that your betters are served before you.'

'Good!' said Lambourne; 'and it only remains to be said, that if the law and I quarrel, my patron must bear me out, for that is a chief point.'

'Reason again,' said Varney, 'if the quarrel hath happened in your master's service.'

'For the wage and so forth, I say nothing,' proceeded Lambourne; 'it is the secret guerdon that I must live by.'

'Never fear,' said Varney; 'thou shalt have clothes and spending-money to ruffle it with the best of thy degree; for thou goest to a household where you have gold, as they say, by the eye.'

'That jumps all with my humour,' replied Michael Lambourne; 'and it only remains that you tell me my master's name.'

'My name is Master Richard Varney,' answered his companion.

'But I mean,' said Lambourne, 'the name of the noble lord to whose service you are to prefer me.'

'How, knave, art thou too good to call *me* master?' said Varney hastily; 'I would have thee bold to others, but not saucy to me.'

'I crave your worship's pardon,' said Lambourne; 'but you

seemed familiar with Anthony Foster; now I am familiar with Anthony myself.'

'Thou art a shrewd knave, I see,' replied Varney. 'Mark me—I do indeed propose to introduce thee into a nobleman's household; but it is upon my person thou wilt chiefly wait, and upon my countenance that thou wilt depend. I am his master of horse—Thou wilt soon know his name—it is one that shakes the council and wields the state.'

'By this light, a brave spell to conjure with,' said Lambourne, 'if a man would discover hidden treasures!'

'Used with discretion, it may prove so,' replied Varney; 'but mark—if thou conjure with it at thine own hand, it may raise a devil who will tear thee in fragments.'

'Enough said,' replied Lambourne; 'I will not exceed my limits.'

The travellers then resumed the rapid rate of travelling which their discourse had interrupted, and soon arrived at the Royal Park of Woodstock. This ancient possession of the crown of England was then very different from what it had been when it was the residence of the fair Rosamond, and the scene of Henry the Second's secret and illicit amours; and yet more unlike to the scene which it exhibits in the present day, when Blenheim House commemorates the victory of Marlborough, and no less the genius of Vanbrugh, though decried in his own time by persons of taste far inferior to his own. It was, in Elizabeth's time, an ancient mansion in bad repair, which had long ceased to be honoured with the royal residence, to the great impoverishment of the adjacent village. The inhabitants, however, had made several petitions to the Queen to have the favour of the sovereign's countenance occasionally bestowed upon them; and upon this very business, ostensibly at least, was the noble lord, whom we have already introduced to our readers, a visitor at Woodstock.

Varney and Lambourne galloped without ceremony into the courtyard of the ancient and dilapidated mansion, which presented on that morning a scene of bustle which it had not exhibited for two reigns. Officers of the Earl's household, livery-men and retainers, went and came with all the insolent fracas which attaches to their profession. The neigh of horses and the baying of hounds were heard; for my lord, in his occupation of inspecting and surveying the manor and demesne, was, of course, provided with the means of following his pleasures in the chase or park, said to have been the earliest that was enclosed in England, and which was well stocked with deer that had long roamed there unmolested. Several of the inhabitants of the village, in anxious hope of a favourable result from this unwonted visit, loitered about the courtyard, and awaited the great man's coming forth. Their attention was excited by the hasty arrival of Varney, and a murmur ran amongst them, 'The Earl's master of the horse!' while they hastened to bespeak favour by hastily unbonneting, and proffering to hold the bridle and stirrup of the favoured retainer and his attendant.

'Stand somewhat aloof, my masters!' said Varney, haughtily, 'and let the domestics do their office.'

The mortified peasants fell back at the signal; while Lambourne, who had his eye upon his superior's deportment, repelled the services of those who offered to assist him, with yet more discourtesy—'Stand back, Jack peasant, with a murrain to you, and let these knave footmen do their duty!'

While they gave their nags to the attendants of the household, and walked into the mansion with an air of superiority which long practice and consciousness of birth rendered natural to Varney, and which Lambourne endeavoured to imitate as well as he could, the poor inhabitants of Woodstock whispered to each other, 'Well-a-day—God save us from all such misproud princoxes! An the master be like the men, why the fiend may take all, and yet have no more than his due.'

'Silence, good neighbours!' said the Bailiff, 'keep tongue betwixt teeth—we shall know more by-and-by. But, ah! never will a lord come to Woodstock so welcome as bluff old King Harry! He would horsewhip a fellow one day with his own royal hand, and then fling him an handful of silver groats, with his own broad face on them, to 'noint the sore withal.'

'Ay, rest be with him!' echoed the auditors; 'it will be long ere this Lady Elizabeth horsewhip any of us.'

'There is no saying,' answered the Bailiff. 'Meanwhile, patience, good neighbours, and let us comfort ourselves by thinking that we deserve such notice at her grace's hands.'

Meanwhile, Varney, closely followed by his new dependant, made his way to the hall, where men of more note and consequence than those left in the courtyard awaited the appearance of the Earl, who as yet kept his chamber. All paid court to Varney, with more or less deference, as suited their own rank, or the urgency of the business which brought them to his lord's levee. To the general question of, 'When comes my lord forth, Master Varney?' he gave brief answers, as, 'See you not my boots? I am just returned from Oxford, and know nothing of it,' and the like, until the same query was put in a higher tone by a personage of more importance. 'I will inquire at the chamberlain, Sir Thomas Copely,' was the reply. The chamberlain, distinguished by his silver key, answered, that the Earl only awaited Master Varney's return to come down, but that he would first speak with him in his private chamber. Varney, therefore, bowed to the company, and took leave, to enter his lord's apartment.

There was a murmur of expectation which lasted a few minutes, and was at length hushed by the opening of the folding-doors at the upper end of the apartment, through which the Earl made his entrance, marshalled by his chamberlain and the steward of his family, and followed by Richard Varney. In his noble mien and princely features, men read nothing of that insolence which was practised by his dependants. His courtesies were indeed measured by the rank of those to whom they were addressed, but even the meanest person present had a share of his gracious notice. The inquiries which he made respecting the condition of the manor, of the Queen's rights there, and of the advantages and disadvantages which might attend her occasional residence at the royal seat of Woodstock, seemed to show that he had most earnestly investigated the matter of the petition of the inhabitants, and with a desire to forward the interest of the place.

'Now the Lord love his noble countenance,' said the Bailiff, who had thrust himself into the presence-chamber; 'he looks somewhat pale. I warrant him he hath spent the whole night in perusing our memorial. Master Toughyarn, who took six months to draw it up, said it would take a week to understand it; and see if the Earl hath not knocked the marrow out of it in twenty-four hours!'

The Earl then acquainted them that he should move their sovereign to honour Woodstock occasionally with her residence during her royal progresses, that the town and its vicinity might derive, from her countenance and favour, the same advantages as from those of her predecessors. Meanwhile, he rejoiced to be the expounder of her gracious pleasure, in assuring them that, for the increase of trade and encouragement of the worthy burgesses of

Woodstock, her majesty was reminded to erect the town into a Staple for wool.

This joyful intelligence was received with the acclamations not only of the better sort who were admitted to the audience-chamber, but of the commons who awaited without.

The freedom of the corporation was presented to the Earl upon knee by the magistrates of the place, together with a purse of gold pieces, which the Earl handed to Varney, who, on his part, gave a share to Lambourne, as the most acceptable earnest of his new service.

The Earl and his retinue took horse soon after, to return to court, accompanied by the shouts of the inhabitants of Woodstock, who made the old oaks ring with re-echoing, 'Long live Queen Elizabeth, and the noble Earl of Leicester!' The urbanity and courtesy of the Earl even threw a gleam of popularity over his attendants, as their haughty deportment had formerly obscured that of their master; and men shouted, 'Long life to the Earl, and to his gallant followers!' as Varney and Lambourne, each in his rank, rode proudly through the streets of Woodstock.

8

Host. I will hear you, Master Fenton; and I will, at least, keep your counsel.—*Merry Wives of Windsor.*

IT becomes necessary to return to the detail of those circumstances which accompanied, and indeed occasioned, the sudden disappearance of Tressilian from the sign of the Black Bear at Cumnor. It will be recollected that this gentleman, after his rencounter with Varney, had returned to Giles Gosling's caravansary, where he shut himself up in his own chamber, demanded pen, ink, and paper, and announced his purpose to remain private for the day. In the evening he appeared again in the public room, where Michael Lambourne, who had been on the watch for him, agreeably to his engagement to Varney, endeavoured to renew his acquaintance with him, and hoped he retained no unfriendly recollection of the part he had taken in the morning's scuffle.

But Tressilian repelled his advances firmly, though with civility —'Master Lambourne,' said he, 'I trust I have recompensed to your pleasure the time you have wasted on me. Under the show of wild bluntness which you exhibit, I know you have sense enough to understand me, when I say frankly, that the object of our temporary acquaintance having been accomplished, we must be strangers to each other in future.'

'*Voto!*' said Lambourne, twirling his whiskers with one hand, and grasping the hilt of his weapon with the other; 'if I thought that this usage was meant to insult me——'

'You would bear it with discretion, doubtless,' interrupted Tressilian, 'as you must do at anyrate. You know too well the distance that is betwixt us, to require me to explain myself further —Good-evening.'

So saying, he turned his back upon his former companion, and entered into discourse with the landlord. Michael Lambourne felt strongly disposed to bully; but his wrath died away in a few incoherent oaths and ejaculations, and he sank unresistingly under the ascendancy which superior spirits possess over persons of his habits and description. He remained moody and silent in a corner of the apartment, paying the most marked attention to every motion of his late companion, against whom he began now to nourish a quarrel on his own account, which he trusted to avenge by the execution of Varney's directions. The hour of supper arrived, and was followed by that of repose, when Tressilian, like others, retired to his sleeping apartment.

He had not been in bed long, when the train of sad reveries, which supplied the place of rest in his disturbed mind, was suddenly interrupted by the jar of a door on its hinges, and a light was seen to glimmer in the apartment. Tressilian, who was as brave as steel, sprang from his bed at this alarm, and had laid hand upon his sword, when he was prevented from drawing it by a voice which said, 'Be not too rash with your rapier, Master Tressilian—It is I, your host, Giles Gosling.'

At the same time, unshrouding the dark lantern, which had hitherto only emitted an indistinct glimmer, the goodly aspect and figure of the landlord of the Black Bear was visibly presented to his astonished guest.

'What mummery is this, mine host?' said Tressilian; 'have you supped as jollily as last night, and so mistaken your chamber? or is midnight a time for masquerading it in your guest's lodging?'

'Master Tressilian,' replied mine host, 'I know my place and my time as well as e'er a merry landlord in England. But here has been my hang-dog kinsman watching you as close as ever cat watched a mouse; and here have you, on the other hand, quarrelled and fought, either with him or with some other person, and I fear that danger will come of it.'

'Go to, thou art but a fool, man,' said Tressilian; 'thy kinsman is beneath my resentment; and besides, why shouldst thou think I had quarrelled with any one whomsoever?'

'Oh, sir,' replied the innkeeper, 'there was a red spot on thy very cheek-bone, which boded of a late brawl, as sure as the conjunction of Mars and Saturn threatens misfortune—and when you returned, the buckles of your girdle were brought forward, and your step was quick and hasty, and all things showed your hand and your hilt had been lately acquainted.'

'Well, good mine host, if I have been obliged to draw my sword,' said Tressilian, 'why should such a circumstance fetch thee out of thy warm bed at this time of night? Thou seest the mischief is all over.'

'Under favour, that is what I doubt. Anthony Foster is a

dangerous man, defended by strong court patronage, which hath borne him out in matters of very deep concernment. And then, my kinsman—why, I have told you what he is, and if these two old cronies have made up their old acquaintance, I would not, my worshipful guest, that it should be at thy cost. I promise you, Mike Lambourne has been making very particular inquiries at mine hostler, when and which way you ride. Now, I would have you think, whether you may not have done or said something for which you may be waylaid, and taken at disadvantage.'

'Thou art an honest man, mine host,' said Tressilian, after a moment's consideration, 'and I will deal frankly with thee. If these men's malice is directed against me—as I deny not but it may—it is because they are the agents of a more powerful villain than themselves.'

'You mean Master Richard Varney, do you not?' said the landlord; 'he was at Cumnor Place yesterday, and came not thither so private but what he was espied by one who told me.'

'I mean the same, mine host.'

'Then, for God's sake, worshipful Master Tressilian,' said honest Gosling, 'look well to yourself. This Varney is the protector and patron of Anthony Foster, who holds under him, and by his favour, some lease of yonder mansion and the park. Varney got a large grant of the lands of the Abbacy of Abingdon, and Cumnor Place amongst others, from his master, the Earl of Leicester. Men say he can do everything with him, though I hold the Earl too good a nobleman to employ him as some men talk of. And then the Earl can do anything (that is anything right or fitting) with the Queen, God bless her; so you see what an enemy you have made to yourself.'

'Well—it is done, and I cannot help it,' answered Tressilian.

'Uds precious, but it must be helped in some manner!' said the host. 'Richard Varney—why, what between his influence with my lord, and his pretending to so many old and vexatious claims in right of the Abbot here, men fear almost to mention his name, much more to set themselves against his practices. You may judge by our discourses the last night. Men said their pleasure of Tony Foster, but not a word of Richard Varney, though all men judge him to be at the bottom of yonder mystery about the pretty wench. But perhaps you know more of that matter than I do, for women, though they wear not swords, are occasion for many a blade's exchanging a sheath of neat's leather for one of flesh and blood.'

'I do indeed know more of that poor unfortunate lady than thou dost, my friendly host; and so bankrupt am I at this moment, of friends and advice, that I will willingly make a counsellor of thee, and tell thee the whole history, the rather that I have a favour to ask when my tale is ended.'

'Good Master Tressilian,' said the landlord, 'I am but a poor innkeeper, little able to adjust or counsel such a guest as yourself. But as surely as I have risen decently above the world, by giving good measure and reasonable charges, I am an honest man; and as such, if I may not be able to assist you, I am not, at least, capable to abuse your confidence. Say away, therefore, as confidently as if you spoke to your father; and thus far at least be certain, that my curiosity, for I will not deny that which belongs to my calling, is joined to a reasonable degree of discretion.'

'I doubt it not, mine host,' answered Tressilian; and while his auditor remained in anxious expectation, he meditated for an instant how he should commence his narrative. 'My tale,' he at length said, 'to be quite intelligible, must begin at some distance back. You have heard of the battle of Stoke, my good host, and perhaps of old Sir Roger Robsart, who, in that battle, valiantly took part with Henry the Seventh, the Queen's grandfather, and routed the Earl of Lincoln, Lord Geraldin and his wild Irish, and the Flemmings, whom the Duchess of Burgundy had sent over, in the quarrel of Lambert Simnel?'

'I remember both one and the other,' said Giles Gosling, 'it is sung of a dozen times a week in my ale-bench below. Sir Roger Robsart of Devon—Oh, ay,—'tis him of whom minstrels sing to this hour.—

'He was the flower of Stoke's red field,
    When Martin Swart on ground lay slain;
In raking rout he never reel'd,
    But like a rock did firm remain.

Ay, and then there was Martin Swart I have heard my grandfather talk of, and of the jolly Almains, whom he commanded, with their slashed doublets and quaint hose, all frounced with ribbons above the nether stocks. Here's a song goes of Martin Swart, too, an I had but memory for it:—

'Martin Swart and his men,
    Saddle them, saddle them,
Martin Swart and his men,
    Saddle them well.'

'True, good mine host—the day was long talked of; but if you sing so loud, you will awake more listeners than I care to commit my confidence unto.'

'I crave pardon, my worshipful guest,' said mine host, 'I was oblivious. When an old song comes across us merry old knights of the spigot, it runs away with discretion.'

'Well, mine host, my grandfather, like some other Cornish men, kept a warm affection to the House of York, and espoused the quarrel of this Simnel, assuming the title of Earl of Warwick, as the county afterwards, in great numbers, countenanced the cause of Perkin Warbeck, calling himself the Duke of York. My grandsire joined Simnel's standard, and was taken fighting desperately at Stoke, where most of the leaders of that unhappy army were slain in their harness. The good knight, to whom he rendered himself, Sir Roger Robsart, protected him from the immediate vengeance of the King, and dismissed him without ransom. But he was unable to guard him from other penalties of his rashness, being the heavy fines by which he was impoverished, according to Henry's mode of weakening his enemies. The good knight did what he might to mitigate the distresses of my ancestor; and their friendship became so strict, that my father was bred up as the sworn brother and intimate of the present Sir Hugh Robsart, the only son of Sir Roger, and the heir of his honest, and generous, and hospitable temper, though not equal to him in martial achievements.'

'I have heard of good Sir Hugh Robsart,' interrupted the host, 'many a time and oft. His huntsman and sworn servant, Will Badger, hath spoke of him an hundred times in this very house—a jovial knight he is, and hath loved hospitality and open house-keeping more than the present fashion, which lays as much gold-lace on the seams of a doublet as would feed a dozen of tall fellows with beef and ale for a twelvemonth, and let them have their evening at the ale-house once a week, to do good to the publican.'

'If you have seen Will Badger, mine host,' said Tressilian, 'you have heard enough of Sir Hugh Robsart; and, therefore, I will but say, that the hospitality you boast of hath proved somewhat detrimental to the estate of his family, which is perhaps of the less consequence as he has but one daughter to whom to bequeath it And here begins my share in the tale. Upon my father's death, now several years since, the good Sir Hugh would willingly have made me his constant companion. There was a time, however, at which I felt the kind knight's excessive love for field-sports detained me from studies, by which I might have profited more; but I ceased to regret the leisure which gratitude and hereditary friendship compelled me to bestow on these rural avocations. The exquisite beauty of Mistress Amy Robsart, as she grew up from childhood to woman, could not escape one whom circumstances obliged to be so constantly in her company—I loved her, in short, my good host, and her father saw it.'

'And crossed your true loves, no doubt?' said mine host; 'it is the way in all such cases, and I judge it must have been so in your instance from the heavy sigh you uttered even now.'

'The case was different, mine host. My suit was highly approved by the generous Sir Hugh Robsart—it was his daughter who was cold to my passion.'

'She was the more dangerous enemy of the two,' said the innkeeper. 'I fear your suit proved a cold one.'

'She yielded me her esteem,' said Tressilian, 'and seemed not unwilling that I should hope it might ripen into a warmer passion. There was a contract of future marriage executed betwixt us, upon her father's intercession; but to comply with her anxious request, the execution was deferred for a twelvemonth. During this period, Richard Varney appeared in the country, and, availing himself of some distant family connection with Sir Hugh Robsart, spent much of his time in his company, until, at length, he almost lived in the family.'

'That could bode no good to the place he honoured with his residence,' said Gosling.

'No, by the rood!' replied Tressilian. 'Misunderstanding and misery followed his presence, yet so strangely, that I am at this moment at a loss to trace the gradations of their encroachment upon a family, which had, till then, been so happy. For a time Amy Robsart received the attentions of this man Varney with the indifference attached to common courtesies; then followed a period in which she seemed to regard him with dislike, and even with disgust; and then an extraordinary species of connection appeared to grow up betwixt them. Varney dropped those airs of pretension and gallantry, which had marked his former approaches; and Amy, on the other hand, seemed to renounce the ill-disguised disgust with which she had regarded him. They seemed to have more of privacy and confidence together, than I fully liked; and I suspected that they met in private, where there was less restraint than in our presence. Many circumstances, which I noticed but little at the time—for I deemed her heart as open as her angelic countenance —have since arisen on my memory, to convince me of their private understanding. But I need not detail them—the fact speaks for itself. She vanished from her father's house—Varney disappeared at the same time—and this very day I have seen her in the character of his paramour, living in the house of his sordid dependant, Foster, and visited by him, muffled, and by a secret entrance.'

'And this, then, is the cause of your quarrel? Methinks, you should have been sure that the fair lady either desired or deserved your interference.'

'Mine host,' answered Tressilian, 'my father (such I must ever consider Sir Hugh Robsart) sits at home struggling with his grief, or if so far recovered, vainly attempting to drown, in the practice of his field-sports, the recollection that he had once a daughter—a recollection which ever and anon breaks from him under circumstances the most pathetic. I could not brook the idea that he should live in misery, and Amy in guilt; and I endeavoured to seek her out, with the hope of inducing her to return to her family. I have found her, and when I have either succeeded in my attempt, or have found it altogether unavailing, it is my purpose to embark for the Virginia voyage.'

'Be not so rash, good sir,' replied Giles Gosling; 'and cast not yourself away because a woman—to be brief—*is* a woman, and changes her lovers like her suit of ribbons, with no better reason than mere fantasy. And ere we probe this matter further, let me ask you what circumstances of suspicion directed you so truly to this lady's residence, or rather to her place of concealment?'

'The last is the better chosen word, mine host,' answered Tressilian; 'and touching your question, the knowledge that Varney held large grants of the demesnes formerly belonging to the Monks of Abingdon, directed me to this neighbourhood; and your nephew's visit to his old comrade Foster, gave me the means of conviction, on the subject.'

'And what is now your purpose, worthy sir?—excuse my freedom in asking the question so broadly.'

'I purpose, mine host,' said Tressilian, 'to renew my visit to the place of her residence to-morrow, and to seek a more detailed communication with her than I have had to-day. She must indeed be widely changed from what she once was, if my words make no impression upon her.'

'Under your favour, Master Tressilian,' said the landlord, 'you can follow no such course. The lady, if I understand you, has already rejected your interference in the matter.'

'It is but too true,' said Tressilian; 'I cannot deny it.'

'Then, marry, by what right or interest do you process a compulsory interference with her inclinations, disgraceful as it may be to herself and to her parents? Unless my judgment gulls me, those under whose protection she has thrown herself, would have small hesitation to reject your interference, even if it were that of a father or brother; but as a discarded lover, you expose yourself to be repelled with the strong hand, as well as with scorn. You can apply to no magistrate for aid or countenance; and you are hunting, therefore, a shadow in water, and will only (excuse my plainness) come by ducking and danger in attempting to catch it.'

'I will appeal to the Earl of Leicester,' said Tressilian, 'against the infamy of his favourite. He courts the severe and strict sect of puritans. He dare not, for sake of his own character, refuse my appeal, even although he were destitute of the principles of honour and nobleness with which fame invests him. Or I will appeal to the Queen herself.'

'Should Leicester,' said the landlord, 'be disposed to protect his dependant (as indeed he is said to be very confident with Varney), the appeal to the Queen may bring them both to reason. Her majesty is strict in such matters, and (if it be not treason to speak it) will rather, it is said, pardon a dozen courtiers for falling in love with herself, than one for giving preference to another woman. Coragio then, my brave guest! for if thou layest a petition from Sir Hugh at the foot of the throne, bucklered by the story of thine own wrongs, the favourite Earl dared as soon leap into the Thames, at the fullest and deepest, as offer to protect Varney in a cause of this nature. But to do this with any chance of success, you must go formally to work; and without staying here to tilt with the master of horse to a privy councillor, and expose yourself to the dagger of his cameradoes, you should hie you to Devonshire, get a petition drawn up for Sir Hugh Robsart, and make as many friends as you can to forward your interest at court.'

'You have spoken well, mine host,' said Tressilian, 'and I will profit by your advice, and leave you to-morrow early.'

'Nay, leave me to-night, sir, before to-morrow comes,' said the landlord. 'I never prayed for a guest's arrival more eagerly than I do to have you safely gone. My kinsman's destiny is most like to be hanged for something, but I would not that the cause were the murder of an honoured guest of mine. "Better ride safe in the dark," says the proverb, "than in daylight with a murderer at your elbow." Come, sir, I move you for your own safety. Your horse and all is ready, and here is your score.'

'It is somewhat under a noble,' said Tressilian, giving one to the host; 'give the balance to pretty Cicely, your daughter, and the servants of the house.'

'They shall taste of your bounty, sir,' said Gosling, 'and you should taste of my daughter's lips in grateful acknowledgment, but at this hour they cannot grace the porch to greet your departure.'

'Do not trust your daughter too far with your guests, my good landlord,' said Tressilian.

'Oh, sir, we will keep measure; but I wonder not that you are jealous of them all. May I crave to know with what aspect the fair lady at the Place yesterday received you?'

'I own,' said Tressilian, 'it was angry as well as confused, and affords me little hope that she is yet awakened from her unhappy delusion.'

'In that case, sir, I see not why you should play the champion of a wench that will none of you, and incur the resentment of a favourite's favourite, as dangerous a monster as ever a knight-adventurer encountered in the old story books.'

'You do me wrong in the supposition—gross wrong,' said Tressilian; 'I do not desire that Amy should ever turn thought upon me more. Let me but see her restored to her father, and all I have to do in Europe—perhaps in the world—is over and ended.'

'A wiser resolution were to drink a cup of sack, and forget her,' said the landlord. 'But five-and-twenty and fifty look on those matters with other eyes, especially when one case of peepers is set in the skull of a young gallant, and the other in those of an old publican. I pity you, Master Tressilian, but I see not how I can aid you in the matter.'

'Only thus far, mine host,' replied Tressilian—'Keep a watch on the motions of those at the Place, which thou canst easily learn without suspicion, as all men's news fly to the ale bench; and be pleased to communicate the tidings in writing to such person, and to no other, who shall bring you this ring as a special token—look at it—it is of value, and I will freely bestow it on you.'

'Nay, sir,' said the landlord, 'I desire no recompense—but it seems an unadvised course in me, being in a public line, to connect myself in a matter of this dark and perilous nature—I have no interest in it.'

'You, and every father in the land, who would have his daughter released from the snares of shame, and sin, and misery, have an interest deeper than aught concerning earth only could create.'

'Well, sir,' said the host, 'these are brave words; and I do pity from my soul the frank-hearted old gentleman, who has minished his estate in good house-keeping for the honour of his country, and now has his daughter, who should be the stay of his age, and so forth, whisked up by such a kite as this Varney. And though your part in the matter is somewhat of the wildest, yet I will e'en be a madcap for company, and help you in your honest attempt to get back the good man's child, so far as being your faithful intelligencer can serve. And as I shall be true to you, I pray you to be trusty to me, and keep my secret, for it were bad for the custom of the Black Bear, should it be said the bear-warder interfered in such matters. Varney has interest enough with the justices to dismount my noble emblem from the post on which he swings so gallantly, to call in my licence, and ruin me from garret to cellar.'

'Do not doubt my secrecy, mine host,' said Tressilian; 'I will retain, besides, the deepest sense of thy service, and of the risk thou dost run—remember the ring is my sure token. And now, farewell—for it was thy wise advice that I should tarry here as short a time as may be.'

'Follow me, then, Sir Guest,' said the landlord, 'and tread as gently as if eggs were under your foot, instead of deal boards. No one must know where or how you departed.'

By the aid of his dark lantern he conducted Tressilian, as soon as he made himself ready for his journey, through a long intricacy of passages, which opened to an outer court, and from thence to a remote stable, where he had already placed his guest's horse. He then aided him to fasten on the saddle the small portmantle which contained his necessaries, opened a postern-door, and with a hearty shake of the hand, and a reiteration of his promise to attend to what went on at Cumnor Place, he dismissed his guest to his solitary journey.

9

Far in the lane a lonely hut he found,
No tenant ventured on the unwholesome ground;
Here smokes his forge, he bares his sinewy arm,
And early strokes the sounding anvil warm;
Around his shop the steely sparkles flew,
As for the steed he shaped the bending shoe.
                                        Gay's 'Trivia.'

As it was deemed proper by the traveller himself, as well as by Giles Gosling, that Tressilian should avoid being seen in the neighbourhood of Cumnor by those whom accident might make early stirrers, the landlord had given him a route, consisting of various by-ways and lanes, which he was to follow in succession, and which, all the turns and short-cuts duly observed, was to conduct him to the public road to Marlborough.

But, like counsel of every other kind, this species of direction is much more easily given than followed; and what betwixt the intricacy of the way, the darkness of the night, Tressilian's ignorance of the country, and the sad and perplexing thoughts with which he had to contend, his journey proceeded so slowly, that morning found him only in the vale of Whitehorse, memorable for the defeat of the Danes in former days, with his horse deprived of a fore-foot shoe, an accident which threatened to put a stop to his journey, by laming the animal. The residence of a smith was his first object of inquiry, in which he received little satisfaction from the dullness or sullenness of one or two peasants, early bound for their labour, who gave brief and indifferent answers to his questions on the subject. Anxious at length, that the partner of his journey should suffer as little as possible from the unfortunate accident, Tressilian dismounted, and led his horse in the direction of a little hamlet, where he hoped either to find or hear tidings of such an artificer as he now wanted. Through a deep and muddy lane, he at length waded on to the place, which proved only an assemblage of five or six miserable huts, about the doors of which one or two people, whose appearance seemed as rude as that of their dwellings, were beginning the toils of the day. One cottage, however, seemed of rather superior aspect, and the old dame, who was sweeping her threshold, appeared something less rude than her neighbours. To her, Tressilian addressed the oft-repeated question, whether there was a smith in this neighbourhood, or any place where he could refresh his horse? The dame looked him in the face with a peculiar expression, as she replied, 'Smith! ay, truly, is there a smith—what wouldst ha' wi' un, mon?'

'To shoe my horse, good dame,' answered Tressilian; 'you may see that he has thrown a fore-foot shoe.'

'Master Holiday!' exclaimed the dame, without returning any direct answer—'Master Herasmus Holiday, come and speak to mon, and please you.'

'*Favete linguis*,' answered a voice from within; 'I cannot now come forth, Gammer Sludge, being in the very sweetest bit of my morning studies.'

'Nay, but, good now Master Holiday, come ye out, do ye— Here's a mon would to Wayland Smith, and I care not to show him way to devil—his horse hath cast shoe.'

'*Quid mihi cum caballo*,' replied the man of learning from within; 'I think there is but one wise man in the hundred, and they cannot shoe a horse without him!'

And forth came the honest pedagogue, for such his dress bespoke him. A long, lean, shambling, stooping figure was surmounted by a head thatched with lank black hair somewhat inclining to gray. His features had the cast of habitual authority, which I suppose Dionysius carried with him from the throne to the schoolmaster's pulpit, and bequeathed as a legacy to all of the same profession. A black buckram cassock was gathered at his middle with a belt, at which hung, instead of knife or weapon, a goodly leathern pen-and-ink case. His ferula was stuck on the other side, like Harlequin's wooden sword; and he carried in his hand the tattered volume which he had been busily perusing.

On seeing a person of Tressilian's appearance, which he was better able to estimate than the country-folks had been, the schoolmaster unbonneted, and accosted him with, '*Salve domine. Intelligisne linguam latinam?*'

Tressilian mustered his learning to reply, '*Linguæ latinæ haud penitus ignarus, venia tua, domine eruditissime, vernaculam libentius loquor.*'

The Latin reply had upon the schoolmaster the effect which the mason's sign is said to produce on the brethren of the trowel. He was at once interested in the learned traveller, listened with gravity to his story of a tired horse and lost shoe, and then replied with solemnity, 'It may appear a simple thing, most worshipful, to reply to you, that there dwells, within a brief mile of these *tuguria*, the best *faber ferrarius*, the most accomplished blacksmith that ever nailed iron upon horse. Now, were I to say so, I warrant me you would think yourself *compos voti*, or, as the vulgar have it, a made man.'

'I should at least,' said Tressilian, 'have a direct answer to a plain question, which seems difficult to be obtained in this country.'

'It is a mere sending of a sinful soul to the evil un,' said the old woman, 'the sending a living creature to Wayland Smith.'

'Peace, Gammer Sludge!' said the pedagogue; '*pauca verba*, Gammer Sludge; look to the furmity, Gammer Sludge; *curetur jentaculum*, Gammer Sludge, this gentleman is none of thy gossips.' Then turning to Tressilian, he resumed his lofty tone, 'And so, most worshipful, you would really think yourself *felix bis terque*, should I point out to you the dwelling of this same smith?'

'Sir,' replied Tressilian, 'I should in that case have all that I want at present—a horse fit to carry me forward out of hearing of your learning,' the last words he muttered to himself.

'*O cæca mens mortalium!*' said the learned man; 'well was it sung by Junius Juvenalis, "*numinibus vota exaudita malignis.*"'

'Learned Magister,' said Tressilian, 'your erudition so greatly exceeds my poor intellectual capacity, that you must excuse my seeking elsewhere for information which I can better understand.'

'There again now,' replied the pedagogue, 'how fondly you fly from him that would instruct you! Truly says Quinctilian'——

'I pray, sir, let Quinctilian be for the present, and answer, in a word and in English, if your learning can condescend so far, whether there is any place here where I can have opportunity to refresh my horse, until I can have him shod?'

'Thus much courtesy, sir,' said the schoolmaster, 'I can readily render you, that altogether there is in this poor hamlet (*nostra paupera regna*) no regular *hospitium*, as my namesake Erasmus calleth it, yet forasmuch as you are somewhat embued, or at least tinged as it were, with good letters, I will use my interest with the good woman of the house to accommodate you with a platter of furmity—an wholesome food, for which I have found no Latin phrase—your horse shall have a share of the cowhouse, with a bottle of sweet hay, in which the good woman Sludge so much abounds, that it may be said of her cow, *fœnum habet in cornu;* and if it please you to bestow on me the pleasure of your company, the banquet shall cost you *ne semissem quidem*, so much is Gammer Sludge bound to me for the pains I have bestowed on the top and bottom of her hopeful heir Dickie, whom I have painfully made to travel through the accidence.'

'Now, God yield ye for it, Master Herasmus,' said the good Gammer, 'and grant that little Dickie may be the better for his accident! And for the rest, if the gentleman list to stay, breakfast shall be on the board in the wringing of a dish-clout; and for horse-meat, and man's meat, I bear no such base mind as to ask a penny.'

Considering the state of his horse, Tressilian, upon the whole, saw no better course than to accept the invitation thus learnedly made and hospitably confirmed, and take chance that when the good pedagogue had exhausted every species of conversation, he might possibly condescend to tell him where he could find the smith they spoke of. He entered the hut accordingly, and sat down with the learned Magister Erasmus Holiday, partook of his furmity, and listened to his learned account of himself for a good half-hour, ere he could get him to talk upon any other topic. The reader will readily excuse our accompanying this man of learning into all the details with which he favoured Tressilian, of which the following sketch may suffice.

He was born at Hogsnorton, where, according to popular saying, the pigs play upon the organ, a proverb which he interpreted allegorically, as having reference to the herd of Epicurus, of which litter Horace confessed himself a porker. His name of Erasmus he derived partly from his father having been the son of a renowned washerwoman, who had held that great scholar in clean linen all the while he was at Oxford; a task of some difficulty, as he was only possessed of two shirts, 'the one,' as she expressed herself, 'to wash the other.' The vestiges of one of these *camiciæ*, as Master Holiday boasted, were still in his possession, having fortunately been detained by his grandmother to cover the balance of her bill. But he thought there was a still higher and overruling cause for his having had the name of Erasmus conferred on him, namely, the secret presentiment of his mother's mind, that, in the babe to be christened, was a hidden genius, which should one day lead him to rival the fame of the great scholar of Rotterdam. The schoolmaster's surname led him as far into dissertation as his Christian appellative. He was inclined to think that he bore the name of Holiday *quasi lucus a non lucendo*, because he gave such few holidays to his school; 'Hence,' said he, 'the schoolmaster is termed, classically, *Ludi Magister*, because he deprives boys of their play.' And yet, on the other hand, he thought it might bear a very different interpretation, and refer to his own exquisite art in arranging pageants, morris-dances, May-day festivities, and such-like holiday delights, for which he assured Tressilian he had positively the purest and the most inventive brain in England; insomuch, that his cunning in framing such pleasures had made him known to many honourable persons, both in country and in court, and especially to the noble Earl of Leicester. 'And although he may now seem to forget me,' he said, 'in the multitude of state affairs, yet I am well assured, that had he some pretty pastime to array for entertainment of the Queen's Grace, horse and man would be seeking the humble cottage of Erasmus Holiday. *Parvo contentus*, in the meanwhile, I hear my pupils parse, and construe, worshipful sir, and drive away my time with the aid of the Muses. And I have at all times, when in correspondence with foreign scholars, subscribed myself Erasmus ab Die Fausto, and have enjoyed the distinction due to the learned under that title; witness the erudite Diedrichus Buckers-chockius, who dedicated to me under that title his treatise on the letter *Tau*. In fine, sir, I have been a happy and distinguished man.'

'Long may it be so, sir,' said the traveller; 'but permit me to ask, in your own learned phrase, *Quid hoc ad Iphycli boves*, what has all this to do with the shoeing of my poor nag?'

'*Festina lente*,' said the man of learning, 'we will presently come to that point. You must know that some two or three years past, there came to these parts one who called himself Doctor Doboobie, although it may be he never wrote even *Magister artium*, save in right of his hungry belly. Or it may be that if he had any degrees, they were of the devil's giving, for he was what the vulgar call a white witch—a cunning man, and such like. Now, good sir, I perceive you are impatient; but if a man tell not his tale in his own way, how have you warrant that he can tell it yours?'

'Well, then, learned sir, take your way,' answered Tressilian; 'only let us travel at a sharper pace, for my time is somewhat of the shortest.'

'Well, sir,' resumed Erasmus Holiday, with the most provoking perseverance, 'I will not say that this same Demetrius, for so he wrote himself when in foreign parts, was an actual conjuror, but certain it is, that he professed to be a brother of the mystical Order of the Rosy Cross, a disciple of Geber (*ex nomine cujus venit verbum vernaculum, gibberish*). He cured wounds by salving the weapon instead of the sore—told fortunes by palmistry—discovered stolen goods by the sieve and shears—gathered the right maddow and the male fern seed, through use of which men walk invisible—pretended some advances towards the panacea, or universal elixir, and affected to convert good lead into sorry silver.'

'In other words,' said Tressilian, 'he was a quack salver and common cheat; but what has all this to do with my nag, and the shoe which he has lost?'

'With your worshipful patience,' replied the diffusive man of letters, 'you shall understand that presently—*patientia* then, right worshipful, which word, according to our Marcus Tullius, is "*difficilium rerum diurna perpessio.*" This same Demetrius Doboobie, after dealing with the country, as I have told you, began to acquire fame *inter magnates*, among the prime men of the land; and there is likelihood he might have aspired to great matters, had not, according to vulgar fame (for I aver not the thing as according with my certain knowledge), the devil claimed his right one dark night, and flown off with Demetrius, who was never seen or heard of afterwards. Now here comes the *medulla*, the very marrow of my tale. This Doctor Doboobie had a servant, a poor snake, whom he employed in trimming his furnace, regulating it by just measure —compounding his drugs—tracing his circles—cajoling his patients, *et sic de cæteris*. Well, right worshipful, the Doctor being removed thus strangely, and in a way which struck the whole country with terror, this poor Zany thinks to himself, in the words of Maro, "*Uno avulso non deficit alter;*" and, even as a tradesman's apprentice sets himself up in his master's shop when he is dead, or hath retired from business, so doth this Wayland assume the dangerous trade of his defunct master. But although, most worshipful sir, the world is ever prone to listen to the pretensions of such unworthy men, who are, indeed, mere *saltimbanqui* and *charlatani*, though usurping the style and skill of doctors of medicine, yet the pretensions of this poor Zany, this Wayland, were too gross to pass on them, nor was there a mere rustic, a villager, who was not ready to accost him in the sense of Persius, though in their own rugged words,—

'Diluis helleborum, certo compescere puncto
Nescius examen? vetat hoc natura medendi;'

which I have thus rendered in a poor paraphrase of mine own,—

Wilt thou mix hellebore, who doth not know
How many grains should to the mixture go?
The art of medicine this forbids, I trow.

Moreover, the evil reputation of the master, and his strange and doubtful end, or at least sudden disappearance, prevented any, excepting the most desperate of men, to seek any advice or opinion from the servant; wherefore, the poor vermin was likely at first to swarf for very hunger. But the devil that serves him, since the death of Demetrius or Doboobie, put him on a fresh device. This knave, whether from inspiration of the devil, or from early education, shoes horses better than e'er a man betwixt us and Iceland; and so he gives up his practice on the bipeds, the two-legged and unfledged species, called mankind, and betakes him entirely to shoeing of horses.'

'Indeed! and where does he lodge all this time?' said Tressilian. 'And does he shoe horses well?—show me his dwelling presently.'

The interruption pleased not the magister, who exclaimed, 'O cæca mens mortalium! though by the way I used that quotation before. But I would the classics could afford me any sentiment, of power to stop those who are so willing to rush upon their own destruction. Hear but, I pray you, the conditions of this man,' said he, in continuation, 'ere you are so willing to place yourself within his danger'——

'A' takes no money for a's work,' said the dame, who stood by, enraptured as it were with the fine words and learned apophthegms, which glided so fluently from her erudite inmate, Master Holiday. But this interruption pleased not the magister, more than that of the traveller.

'Peace,' said he, 'Gammer Sludge; know your place, if it be your will. Sufflamina, Gammer Sludge, and allow me to expound this matter to our worshipful guest. Sir,' said he, again addressing Tressilian, 'this old woman speaks true, though in her own rude style; for certainly this faberre frarius, or blacksmith, takes money of no one.'

'And that is a sure sign he deals with Satan,' said Dame Sludge; 'since no good Christian would ever refuse the wages of his labour.'

'The old woman hath touched it again,' said the pedagogue; '*rem acu tetigit*—she hath pricked it with her needle's point. This Wayland takes no money, indeed, nor doth he show himself to any one.'

'And can this madman, for such I hold him,' said the traveller, 'know aught like good skill of his trade?'

'Oh, sir, in that let us give the devil his due—Mulciber himself, with all his Cyclops, could hardly amend him. But assuredly there is little wisdom in taking counsel or receiving aid from one who is but too plainly in league with the author of evil.'

'I must take my chance of that, good Master Holiday,' said Tressilian, rising; 'and as my horse must now have eaten his provender, I must needs thank you for your good cheer, and pray you to show me this man's residence, that I may have the means of proceeding on my journey.'

'Ay, ay, do ye show him, Master Herasmus,' said the old dame, who was, perhaps, desirous to get her house freed of her guest; 'a' must needs go, when the devil drives.'

'*Do manus*,' said the magister, 'I submit—taking the world to witness, that I have possessed this honourable gentleman with the full injustice, which he has done and shall do to his own soul, if he becomes thus a trinketer with Satan. Neither will I go forth with our guest myself, but rather send my pupil. *Ricarde! Adsis, nebulo*.'

'Under your favour, not so,' answered the old woman; 'you may peril your own soul, if you list, but my son shall budge on no such errand; and I wonder at you, Dominie Doctor, to propose such a piece of service for little Dickie.'

'Nay, my good Gammer Sludge,' answered the preceptor, 'Ricardus shall go but to the top of the hill, and indicate with his digit to the stranger the dwelling of Wayland Smith. Believe not that any evil can come to him, he having read this morning, fasting, a chapter of the Septuagint, and, moreover, having had his lesson in the Greek Testament.'

'Ay,' said his mother, 'and I have sewn a sprig of witch's elm in the neck of un's doublet, ever since that foul thief has begun his practices on man and beast in these parts.'

'And as he goes oft (as I hugely suspect) towards this conjuror for his own pastime, he may for once go thither, or near it, to pleasure us, and to assist this stranger. *Ergo, heus Ricarde! adsis, quæso, mi didascule.'*

The pupil, thus affectionately invoked, at length came stumbling into the room; a queer, shambling, ill-made urchin, who, by his stunted growth, seemed about twelve or thirteen years old, though he was probably, in reality, a year or two older, with a carroty pate in huge disorder, a freckled sunburnt visage, with a snub nose, a long chin, and two peery gray eyes, which had a droll obliquity of vision, approaching to a squint, though perhaps not a decided one. It was impossible to look at the little man without some disposition to laugh, especially when Gammer Sludge, seizing upon and kissing him, in spite of his struggling and kicking in reply to her caresses, termed him her own precious pearl of beauty.

'*Ricarde,*' said the preceptor, 'you must forthwith (which is *profecto*) set forth so far as the top of the hill, and show this man of worship Wayland Smith's workshop.'

'A proper errand of a morning,' said the boy, in better language than Tressilian expected; 'and who knows but the devil may fly away with me before I come back?'

'Ay, marry may un,' said Dame Sludge, 'and you might have thought twice, Master Dominie, ere you sent my dainty darling on arrow such errand. It is not for such doings I feed your belly and clothe your back, I warrant you.'

'Pshaw—*nugæ*, good Gammer Sludge,' answered the preceptor; 'I ensure you that Satan, if there be Satan in the case, shall not touch a thread of his garment; for Dickie can say his *pater* with the best, and may defend the foul fiend—*Eumenides, Stygiumque nefas.*'

'Ay, and, as I said before, I have sewed a sprig of the mountain-ash into his collar,' said the good woman, 'which will avail more than your clerkship, I wus; but for all that, it is ill to seek the devil or his mates either.'

'My good boy,' said Tressilian, who saw, from a grotesque sneer on Dickie's face, that he was more like to act upon his own bottom, than by the instruction of his elders, 'I will give thee a silver groat, my pretty fellow, if you will but guide me to this man's forge.'

The boy gave him a knowing side-look, which seemed to promise acquiescence, while at the same time he exclaimed, 'I be your guide to Wayland Smith's! Why, man, did I not say that the devil might fly off with me, just as the kite there (looking to the window) is flying off with one of grandame's chicks?'

'The kite! the kite!' exclaimed the old woman in return, and forgetting all other matters in her alarm, hastened to the rescue of her chicken as fast as her old legs could carry her.

'Now for it,' said the urchin to Tressilian; 'snatch your beaver, get out your horse, and have at the silver groat you spoke of.'

'Nay, but tarry, tarry,' said the preceptor. '*Sufflamina, Ricarde.*'

'Tarry yourself,' said Dickie, 'and think what answer you are to make to grannie for sending me post to the devil.'

The teacher, aware of the responsibility he was incurring, bustled up in great haste to lay hold of the urchin, and to prevent his departure: but Dickie slipped through his fingers, bolted from the cottage, and sped him to the top of a neighbouring rising ground; while the preceptor, despairing, by well-taught experience, of recovering his pupil by speed of foot, had recourse to the most honied epithets the Latin vocabulary affords, to persuade his return. But to *mi anime, corculum meum*, and all such classical endearments, the truant turned a deaf ear, and kept frisking on the top of the rising ground like a goblin by moonlight, making signs to his new acquaintance, Tressilian, to follow him.

The traveller lost no time in getting out his horse, and departing to join his elvish guide, after half-forcing on the poor deserted teacher a recompense for the entertainment he had received, which partly allayed the terror he had for facing the return of the old lady of the mansion. Apparently this took place soon afterwards, for ere Tressilian and his guide had proceeded far on their journey, they heard the screams of a cracked female voice, intermingled with the classical objurgations of Master Erasmus Holiday. But Dickie Sludge, equally deaf to the voice of maternal tenderness and of magisterial authority, skipped on unconsciously before Tressilian, only observing, that 'if they cried themselves hoarse, they might go lick the honey-pot, for he had eaten up all the honeycomb himself on yesterday even.'

10

There entering in, they found the goodman selfe
Full busylie unto his work ybent,
Who was to weet a wretched wearish elf,
With hollow eyes and rawbone cheeks forspent,
As if he had been long in prison pent.—*The Faerie Queene.*

'Are we far from the dwelling of this smith, my pretty lad?' said Tressilian to his young guide.

'How is it you call me?' said the boy, looking askew at him with his sharp gray eyes.

'I call you my pretty lad—is there any offence in that, my boy?'

'No—but were you with my grandame and Dominie Holiday, you might sing chorus to the old song of—

'We three
Tom-fools be.'

'And why so, my little man?' said Tressilian.

'Because,' answered the ugly urchin, 'you are the only three ever called me pretty lad. Now my grandame does it because she is parcel blind by age, and whole blind by kindred—and my master, the poor Dominie, does it to curry favour, and have the fullest platter of furmity, and the warmest seat by the fire. But what you call me pretty lad for, you know best yourself.'

'Thou art a sharp wag at least, if not a pretty one. But what do thy playfellows call thee?'

'Hobgoblin,' answered the boy, readily; 'but for all that, I would rather have my own ugly viznomy than any of their jolter-heads, that have no more brains in them than a brick-bat.'

'Then you fear not this smith, whom you are going to see.'

'Me fear him!' answered the boy; 'if he were the devil folks think him, I would not fear him; but though there be something queer about him, he's no more a devil than you are, and that's what I would not tell to every one.'

'And why do you tell it to me then, my boy?' said Tressilian.

'Because you are another guess gentleman than those we see here every day,' replied Dickie; 'and though I am as ugly as sin,

I would not have you think me an ass, especially as I may have a boon to ask of you one day.'

'And what is that, my lad, whom I must not call pretty,' replied Tressilian.

'Oh, if I were to ask it just now,' said the boy, 'you would deny it me—but I will wait till we meet at court.'

'At court, Richard! are you bound for court?' said Tressilian.

'Ay, ay, that's just like the rest of them,' replied the boy; 'I warrant me you think, what should such an ill-favoured, scrambling urchin do at court? But let Richard Sludge alone; I have not been cock of the roost here for nothing. I will make sharp wit mend foul feature.'

'But what will your grandame say, and your tutor, Dominie Holiday?'

'E'en what they like,' replied Dickie; 'the one has her chickens to reckon, and the other has his boys to whip; I would have given them the candle to hold long since, and shown this trumpery hamlet a fair pair of heels, but that Dominie promises I should go with him to bear share in the next pageant he is to set forth, and they say there are to be great revels shortly.'

'And whereabout are they to be held, my little friend?' said Tressilian.

'Oh, at some castle far in the north,' answered his guide—'a world's breadth from Berkshire. But our old Dominie holds that they cannot go forward without him; and it may be he is right, for he has put in order many a fair pageant. He is not half the fool you would take him for, when he gets to work he understands; and so he can spout verses like a play-actor, when, God wot, if you set him to steal a goose's egg, he would be drubbed by the gander.'

'And you are to play a part in his next show?' said Tressilian, somewhat interested by the boy's boldness of conversation, and shrewd estimate of character.

'In faith,' said Richard Sludge, in answer, 'he hath so promised me; and if he break his word, it will be the worse for him; for let me take the bit between my teeth, and turn my head down hill, and I will shake him off with a fall that may harm his bones—And I should not like much to hurt him neither,' said he, 'for the tiresome old fool has painfully laboured to teach me all he could. But enough of that—here are we at Wayland Smith's forge-door.'

'You jest, my little friend,' said Tressilian; 'here is nothing but a bare moor, and that ring of stones, with a great one in the midst, like a Cornish barrow.'

'Ay, and that great flat stone in the midst, which lies across the top of these uprights,' said the boy, 'is Wayland Smith's counter, that you must tell down your money upon.'

'What do you mean by such folly?' said the traveller, beginning to be angry with the boy, and vexed with himself for having trusted such a hare-brained guide.

'Why,' said Dickie, with a grin, 'you must tie your horse to that upright stone that has the ring in't, and then you must whistle three times, and lay me down your silver groat on that other flat stone, walk out of the circle, sit down on the west side of that little thicket of bushes, and take heed you look neither to right nor to left for ten minutes, or so long as you shall hear the hammer clink, and whenever it ceases, say your prayers for the space you could tell a hundred,—or count over a hundred, which will do as well,—and then come into the circle, you will find your money gone and your horse shod.'

'My money gone to a certainty!' said Tressilian; 'but as for the rest—Hark ye, my lad, I am not your schoolmaster, but if you play off your waggery on me, I will take a part of his task off his hands, and punish you to purpose.'

'Ay, when you can catch me!' said the boy, and presently took to his heels across the heath, with a velocity which baffled every attempt of Tressilian to overtake him, loaded as he was with his heavy boots. Nor was it the least provoking part of the urchin's conduct, that he did not exert his utmost speed, like one who finds himself in danger, or who is frightened, but preserved just such a rate as to encourage Tressilian to continue the chase, and then darted away from him with the swiftness of the wind, when his pursuer supposed he had nearly run him down, doubling, at the same time, and winding so as always to keep near the place from which he started.

This lasted until Tressilian, from very weariness, stood still, and was about to abandon the pursuit with a hearty curse on the ill-favoured urchin, who had engaged him in an exercise so ridiculous. But the boy, who had, as formerly, planted himself on the top of a hillock close in front, began to clap his long thin hands, point with his skinny fingers, and twist his wild and ugly features into such extravagant expressions of laughter and derision, that Tressilian began half to doubt whether he had not in view an actual hobgoblin.

Provoked extremely, yet at the same time feeling an irresistible desire to laugh, so very odd were the boy's grimaces and gesticulations, the Cornish man returned to his horse, and mounted him with the purpose of pursuing Dickie at more advantage.

The boy no sooner saw him mount his horse, than he hallooed out to him, that rather than he should spoil his white-footed nag, he would come to him, on condition he would keep his fingers to himself.

'I will make no condition with thee, thou naughty varlet!' said Tressilian; 'I will have thee at my mercy in a moment.'

'Aha, Master Traveller,' said the boy, 'there is a marsh hard by would swallow all the horses of the Queen's Guard—I will into it, and see where you will go then—You shall hear the bittern bump, and the wild drake quack, ere you get hold of me without my consent, I promise you.'

Tressilian looked out, and from the appearance of the ground behind the hillock, believed it might be as the boy said, and accordingly determined to strike up a peace with so light-footed and ready-witted an enemy—'Come down,' he said, 'thou mischievous brat! Leave thy mopping and mowing, and come thither; I will do thee no harm, as I am a gentleman.'

The boy answered his invitation with the utmost confidence, and danced down from his stance with a galliard sort of step, keeping his eye at the same time fixed on Tressilian's, who, once more dismounted, stood with his horse's bridle in his hand, breathless, and half-exhausted with the fruitless exercise, though not one drop of moisture appeared on the freckled forehead of the urchin, which looked like a piece of dry and discoloured parchment, drawn tight across the brow of a fleshless skull.

'And tell me,' said Tressilian, 'why you use me thus, thou mischievous imp? or what your meaning is by telling me so absurd a legend as you wished but now to put on me? Or rather show me, in good earnest, this smith's forge, and I will give thee what will buy thee apples through the whole winter.'

'Were you to give me an orchard of apples,' said Dickie Sludge, 'I can guide thee no better than I have done. Lay down the silver token on the flat stone—whistle three times—then come sit down on the western side of the thicket of gorse; I will sit by you, and give you free leave to wring my head off, unless you hear the smith at work within two minutes after we are seated.'

'I may be tempted to take thee at thy word,' said Tressilian, 'if you make me do aught half so ridiculous for your own mischievous sport—however, I will prove your spell. Here, then, I tie my horse to this upright stone—I must lay my silver groat here, and whistle three times, sayest thou?'

'Ay, but thou must whistle louder than an unfledged owzle,' said the boy, as Tressilian, having laid down his money, and half-ashamed of the folly he practised, made a careless whistle—'You must whistle louder than that, for who knows where the smith is that you call for? He may be in the King of France's stables for what I know.'

'Why, you said but now he was no devil,' replied Tressilian.

'Man or devil,' said Dickie, 'I see that I must summon him for you;' and therewithal he whistled sharp and shrill, with an acuteness of sound that almost thrilled through Tressilian's brain—'That is what I call whistling,' said he, after he had repeated the signal thrice; 'and now to cover, to cover, or Whitefoot will not be shod this day.'

Tressilian, musing what the upshot of this mummery was to be, yet satisfied there was to be some serious result, by the confidence with which the boy had put himself in his power, suffered himself to be conducted to that side of the little thicket of gorse and brushwood which was farthest from the circle of stones, and there sat down: and as it occurred to him that, after all, this might be a trick for stealing his horse, he kept his hand on the boy's collar, determined to make him hostage for its safety.

'Now, hush and listen,' said Dickie, in a low whisper; 'you will soon hear the tack of a hammer that was never forged of earthly iron, for the stone it was made of was shot from the moon.' And in effect Tressilian did immediately hear the light stroke of a hammer, as when a farrier is at work. The singularity of such a sound, in so very lonely a place, made him involuntarily start; but looking at the boy, and discovering, by the arch malicious expression of his countenance, that the urchin saw and enjoyed his slight tremor, he became convinced that the whole was a concerted stratagem, and determined to know by whom, or for what purpose, the trick was played off.

Accordingly, he remained perfectly quiet all the time that the hammer continued to sound, being about the space usually employed in fixing a horse-shoe. But the instant the sound ceased, Tressilian, instead of interposing the space of time which his guide had requested, started up with his sword in his hand, ran round the thicket, and confronted a man in a farrier's leathern apron, but otherwise fantastically attired in a bear-skin dressed with the fur on, and a cap of the same, which almost hid the sooty and begrimed features of the wearer. 'Come back, come back!' cried the boy to Tressilian, 'or you will be torn to pieces—no man lives that looks on him.' In fact, the invisible smith (now fully visible) heaved up his hammer, and showed symptoms of doing battle.

But when the boy observed that neither his own entreaties, nor the menaces of the farrier appeared to change Tressilian's purpose, but that, on the contrary, he confronted the hammer with his drawn sword, he exclaimed to the smith in turn, 'Wayland, touch him not, or you will come by the worse!—the gentleman is a true gentleman, and a bold.'

'So thou hast betrayed me, Flibbertigibbet?' said the smith; 'it shall be the worst for thee.'

'Be who thou wilt,' said Tressilian, 'thou art in no danger from me, so thou tell me the meaning of this practice, and why thou drivest thy trade in this mysterious fashion.'

The smith, however, turning to Tressilian, exclaimed, in a threatening tone. 'Who questions the Keeper of the Crystal Castle of Light, the Lord of the Green Lion, the Rider of the Red Dragon? Hence!—avoid thee, ere I summon Talpack with his fiery lance, to quell, crush, and consume!' These words he uttered with violent gesticulation, mouthing, and flourishing his hammer.

'Peace, thou vile cozener, with thy gipsy cant!' replied Tressilian, scornfully, 'and follow me to the next magistrate, or I will cut thee over the pate.'

'Peace, I pray thee, good Wayland!' said the boy; 'credit me the swaggering vein will not pass here, you must cut boon whids.'*

'I think, worshipful sir,' said the smith, sinking his hammer and assuming a more gentle and submissive tone of voice, 'that when so poor a man does his day's job, he might be permitted to work it out after his own fashion. Your horse is shod, and your farrier

* 'Give good words.'—*Slang dialect.*

paid—What need you cumber yourself further, than to mount and pursue your journey?'

'Nay, friend, you are mistaken,' replied Tressilian; 'every man has a right to take the mask from the face of a cheat and juggler; and your mode of living arouses suspicion that you are both.'

'If you are so determined, sir,' said the smith, 'I cannot help myself save by force, which I were unwilling to use towards you, Master Tressilian; not that I fear your weapon, but because I know you to be a worthy, kind, and well-accomplished gentleman, who would rather help than harm a poor man, that is in a strait.'

'Well said, Wayland,' said the boy, who had anxiously awaited the issue of their conference. 'But let us to thy den, man, for it is ill for thy health to stand here talking in the open air.'

'Thou art right, Hobgoblin,' replied the smith; and going to the little thicket of gorse on the side nearest to the circle, and opposite to that at which his customer had so lately couched, he discovered a trap-door curiously covered with bushes, raised it, and, descending into the earth, vanished from their eyes. Notwithstanding Tressilian's curiosity, he had some hesitation at following the fellow into what might be a den of robbers, especially when he heard the smith's voice, issuing from the bowels of the earth, call out, 'Flibbertigibbet, do you come last, and be sure to fasten the trap!'

'Have you seen enough of Wayland Smith now?' whispered the urchin to Tressilian, with an arch sneer, as if marking his companion's uncertainty.

'Not yet,' said Tressilian firmly, and shaking off his momentary irresolution, he descended into the narrow staircase to which the entrance led, and was followed by Dickie Sludge, who made fast the trap-door behind him, and thus excluded every glimmer of daylight. The descent, however, was only a few steps, and led to a level passage of a few yards' length, at the end of which appeared the reflection of a lurid and red light. Arrived at this point, with his drawn sword in his hand, Tressilian found that a turn to the left admitted him and Hobgoblin, who followed closely, into a small square vault, containing a smith's forge glowing with charcoal, the vapour of which filled the apartment with an oppressive smell, which would have been altogether suffocating, but that by some concealed vent the smithy communicated with the upper air. The light afforded by the red fuel, and by a lamp suspended in an iron chain, served to show that, besides an anvil, bellows, tongs, hammers, a quantity of ready-made horse-shoes, and other articles proper to the profession of a farrier, there were also stoves, alembics, crucibles, retorts, and other instruments of alchemy. The grotesque figure of the smith, and the ugly but whimsical features of the boy, seen by the gloomy and imperfect light of the charcoal fire and the dying lamp, accorded very well with all this mystical apparatus, and in that age of superstition would have made some impression on the courage of most men. But nature had endowed Tressilian with firm nerves, and his education, originally good, had been too sedulously improved by subsequent study to give way to any imaginary terrors; and after giving a glance around him, he again demanded of the artist who he was, and by what accident he came to know and address him by his name.

'Your worship cannot but remember,' said the smith, 'that about three years since, upon Saint Lucy's Eve, there came a travelling juggler to a certain hall in Devonshire, and exhibited his skill before a worshipful knight and a fair company—I see from your worship's countenance, dark as this place is, that my memory has not done me wrong.'

'Thou hast said enough,' said Tressilian, turning away, as wishing to hide from the speaker the painful train of recollection which his discourse had unconsciously awakened.

'The juggler,' said the smith, 'played his part so bravely, that the clowns and clown-like squires in the company held his art to be little less than magical; but there was one maiden of fifteen, or thereby, with the fairest face I ever looked upon, whose rosy cheek grew pale, and her bright eyes dim, at the sight of the wonders exhibited.'

'Peace, I command thee, peace!' said Tressilian.

'I mean your worship no offence,' said the fellow; 'but I have cause to remember how, to relieve the young maiden's fears, you condescended to point out the mode in which these deceptions were practised, and to baffle the poor juggler by laying bare the mysteries of his art, as ably as if you had been a brother of his order. She was indeed so fair a maiden, that, to win a smile of her, a man might well——'

'Not a word more of her, I charge thee,' said Tressilian; 'I do well remember the night you speak of—one of the few happy evenings my life has known.'

'She is gone, then,' said the smith, interpreting after his own fashion the sigh with which Tressilian uttered these words—'She is gone, young, beautiful, and beloved as she was! I crave your worship's pardon—I should have hammered on another theme—I see I have unwarily driven the nail to the quick.'

This speech was made with a mixture of rude feeling, which inclined Tressilian favourably to the poor artisan, of whom before he was inclined to judge very harshly. But nothing can so soon attract the unfortunate, as real or seeming sympathy with their sorrows.

'I think,' proceeded Tressilian, after a minute's silence, 'thou wert in those days a jovial fellow, who could keep a company merry by song, and tale, and rebeck, as well as by thy juggling tricks—why do I find thee a laborious handicraftsman, plying thy trade in so melancholy a dwelling, and under such extraordinary circumstances?'

'My story is not long,' said the artist; 'but your honour had better sit while you listen to it.' So saying, he approached to the fire a three-footed stool, and took another himself, while Dickie Sludge, or Flibbertigibbet, as he called the boy, drew a cricket to the smith's feet, and looked up in his face with features which, as illuminated by the glow of the forge, seemed convulsed with intense curiosity. 'Thou too,' said the smith to him, 'shalt learn, as thou well deservest at my hand, the brief history of my life; and, in troth, it were as well tell it thee as leave thee to ferret it out, since Nature never packed a shrewder wit into a more ungainly casket. Well, sir, if my poor story may pleasure you, it is at your command—But will you not taste a stoup of liquor? I promise you that in even this poor cell I have some in store.'

'Speak not of it,' said Tressilian, 'but go on with thy story, for my leisure is brief.'

'You shall have no cause to rue the delay,' said the smith, 'for your horse shall be better fed in the meantime, than he hath been this morning, and made fitter for travel.'

With that the artist left the vault, and returned after a few minutes' interval. Here, also, we pause, that the narrative may commence in another chapter.

11

I say, my lord, can such a subtilty
(But all his craft ye must not wot of me,
And somewhat help I yet to his working),
That all the ground on which we ben riding,
Till that we come to Canterbury town,
He can all clean turnen so up so down,
And pave it all of silver and of gold.
        '*The Canon's Yeoman's Prologue*'—*Canterbury Tales.*

THE artist resumed his narrative in the following terms:— 'I was
bred a blacksmith, and knew my art as well as e'er a black-
thumb'd, leathern-apron'd, swart-faced knave of that noble
mystery. But I tired of ringing hammer-tunes on iron stithies, and
went out into the world, where I became acquainted with a
celebrated juggler, whose fingers had become rather too stiff for
legerdemain, and who wished to have the aid of an apprentice
in his noble mystery. I served him for six years, until I was master
of my trade—I refer myself to your worship, whose judgment
cannot be disputed, whether I did not learn to ply the craft
indifferently well?'

'Excellently,' said Tressilian; 'but be brief.'

'It was not long after I had performed at Sir Hugh Robsart's,
in your worship's presence,' said the artist, 'that I took myself to
the stage, and have swaggered with the bravest of them all, both
at the Black Bull, the Globe, the Fortune, and elsewhere; but I
know not how—apples were so plenty that year, that the lads in
the twopenny gallery never took more than one bite out of them,
and threw the rest of the pippin at whatsoever actor chanced to be
on the stage. So I tired of it—renounced my half share in the
company—gave my foil to my comrade—my buskins to the
wardrobe, and showed the theatre a clean pair of heels.'

'Well, friend, and what,' said Tressilian, 'was your next shift?'

'I became,' said the smith, 'half partner, half domestic, to a
man of much skill and little substance, who practised the trade
of a physician.'

'In other words,' said Tressilian, 'you were Jack Pudding to a
quack salver.'

'Something beyond that, let me hope, my good Master Tressilian,' replied the artist; 'and yet, to say truth, our practice was of an adventurous description, and the pharmacy which I had acquired in my first studies for the benefit of horses, was frequently applied to our human patients. But the seeds of all maladies are the same; and if turpentine, tar, pitch, and beef-suet, mingled with turmeric, gum-mastic, and one head of garlic, can cure the horse that hath been grieved with a nail, I see not but what it may benefit the man that hath been pricked with a sword. But my master's practice, as well as his skill, went far beyond mine, and dealt in more dangerous concerns. He was not only a bold and adventurous practitioner in physic, but also, if your pleasure so chanced to be, an adept, who read the stars and expounded the fortunes of mankind, genethliac-ally, as he called it, or otherwise. He was a learned distiller of simples, and a profound chemist—made several efforts to fix mercury,—and judged himself to have made a fair hit at the philosopher's stone. I have yet a programme of his on that subject, which, if your honour understandeth, I believe you have the better, not only of all who read, but also of him who wrote it.'

He gave Tressilian a scroll of parchment, bearing at top and bottom, and down the margin, the signs of the seven planets, curiously intermingled with talismanical characters and scraps of Greek and Hebrew. In the midst were some Latin verses from a cabalistical author, written out so fairly, that even the gloom of the place did not prevent Tressilian from reading them. The tenor of the original ran as follows:—

'Si fixum solvas, faciasque volare solutum,
    Et volucrem figas, facient te vivere tutum,
Si pariat ventum, valet auri pondere centum
Ventus ubi vult spirat—Capiat qui capere potest.'

'I protest to you,' said Tressilian, 'all I understand of this jargon is, that the last words seem to mean, "Catch who catch can."'

'That,' said the smith, 'is the very principle that my worthy friend and master, Doctor Doboobie, always acted upon; until, being besotted with his own imaginations, and conceited of his high chemical skill, he began to spend in cheating himself the money which he had acquired in cheating others, and either discovered or built for himself, I could never know which, this secret elaboratory, in which he used to seclude himself both from patients and disciples, who doubtless thought his long and mysterious absences from his ordinary residence in the town of Farringdon were occasioned by his progress in the mystic sciences, and his intercourse with the invisible world. Me also he tried to deceive; but though I contradicted him not, he saw that I knew too much of his secrets to be any longer a safe companion. Meanwhile, his name waxed famous, or rather infamous, and many of those who resorted to him did so under persuasion that he was a sorcerer. And yet his supposed advance in the occult sciences, drew to him the secret resort of men too powerful to be named, for purposes too dangerous to be mentioned. Men cursed and threatened him, and bestowed on me, the innocent assistant of his studies, the nickname of the Devil's foot-post, which procured me a volley of stones as soon as ever I ventured to show my face in the street of the village. At length, my master suddenly disappeared, pretending to me that he was about to visit his elaboratory in this place, and forbidding me to disturb him till two days were past. When this period had elapsed, I became anxious, and resorted to this vault, where I found the fires extinguished and the utensils in confusion, with a note from the learned Doboobius, as he was wont to style himself, acquainting me that we should never meet again, bequeathing me his chemical apparatus, and the parchment which I have just put into your hands, advising me strongly to prosecute the secret which it contained, which would infallibly lead me to the discovery of the grand magisterium.'

'And didst thou follow this sage advice?' said Tressilian.

'Worshipful sir, no,' replied the smith; 'for being by nature cautious and suspicious, from knowing with whom I had to do, I made so many perquisitions before I ventured even to light a fire, that I at length discovered a small barrel of gunpowder, carefully hid beneath the furnace, with the purpose, no doubt, that as soon as I should commence the grand work of the transmutation of metals, the explosion should transmute the vault and all in it into a heap of ruins, which might serve at once for my slaughter-house and my grave. This cured me of alchemy, and fain would I have returned to the honest hammer and anvil; but who would bring a horse to be shod by the Devil's post? Meanwhile, I had won the regard of my honest Flibbertigibbet here, he being then at Farringdon with his master, the sage Erasmus Holiday, by teaching him a few secrets, such as please youth at his age; and after much counsel together, we agreed, that since

I could get no practice in the ordinary way, I should try how I could work out business among those ignorant boors, by practising upon their silly fears; and thanks to Flibbertigibbet who hath spread my renown, I have not wanted custom. But it is won at too great risk, and I fear I shall be at length taken up for a wizard; so that I seek but an opportunity to leave this vault when I can have the protection of some worshipful person against the fury of the populace, in case they chance to recognise me.'

'And art thou,' said Tressilian, 'perfectly acquainted with the roads in this country?'

'I could ride them every inch by midnight,' answered Wayland Smith, which was the name this adept had assumed.

'Thou hast no horse to ride upon,' said Tressilian.

'Pardon me,' replied Wayland; 'I have as good a tit as ever yeoman bestrode; and I forgot to say it was the best part of the mediciner's legacy to me, excepting one or two of the choicest of his medical secrets, which I picked up without his knowledge and against his will.'

'Get thyself washed and shaven then,' said Tressilian; 'reform thy dress as well as thou canst, and fling away those grotesque trappings; and, so thou wilt be secret and faithful, thou shalt follow me for a short time, till thy pranks here are forgotten. Thou hast, I think, both address and courage, and I have matter to do that may require both.'

Wayland Smith eagerly embraced the proposal, and protested his devotion to his new master. In a very few minutes he had made so great an alteration in his original appearance, by change of dress, trimming his beard and hair and so forth, that Tressilian could not help remarking, that he thought he would stand in little need of a protector, since none of his old acquaintance were likely to recognise him.

'My debtors would not pay me money,' said Wayland, shaking his head; 'but my creditors of every kind would be less easily blinded. And, in truth, I hold myself not safe, unless under the protection of a gentleman of birth and character, as is your worship.'

So saying, he led the way out of the cavern. He then called loudly for Hobgoblin, who, after lingering for an instant, appeared with the horse furniture, when Wayland closed, and sedulously covered up, the trap-door, observing, it might again serve him at his need, besides that the tools were worth somewhat. A whistle from the owner brought to his side a nag that fed quietly on the common, and was accustomed to the signal. While he accoutred him for the journey, Tressilian drew his own girths faster, and in a few minutes both were ready to mount.

At this moment Sludge approached to bid them farewell.

'You are going to leave me then, my old playfellow,' said the boy; 'and there is an end of all our game at bo-peep with the cowardly lubbards whom I brought hither to have their broad-footed nags shod by the devil and his imps?'

'It is even so,' said Wayland Smith; 'the best friends must part, Flibbertigibbet; but thou, my boy, art the only thing in the Vale of Whitehorse which I shall regret to leave behind me.'

'Well, I bid thee not farewell,' said Dickie Sludge, 'for you will be at these revels, I judge, and so shall I; for if Dominie Holiday take me not thither, by the light of day, which we see not in yonder dark hole, I will take myself there.'

'In good time,' said Wayland; 'but I pray you to do naught rashly.'

'Nay, now you would make a child—a common child of me, and tell me of the risk of walking without leading strings. But before you are a mile from these stones, you shall know, by a sure token, that I have more of the hobgoblin about me than you credit; and I will so manage that, if you take advantage, you may profit by my prank.'

'What dost thou mean, boy?' said Tressilian; but Flibbertigibbet only answered with a grin and a caper, and bidding both of them farewell, and at the same time exhorting them to make the best of their way from the place, he set them the example by running homeward with the same uncommon velocity with which he had baffled Tressilian's former attempts to get hold of him.

'It is in vain to chase him,' said Wayland Smith; 'for unless your worship is expert in lark-hunting, we should never catch hold of him—and besides, what would it avail? Better make the best of our way hence, as he advises.'

They mounted their horses accordingly, and began to proceed at a round pace, as soon as Tressilian had explained to his guide the direction in which he desired to travel.

After they had trotted nearly a mile, Tressilian could not help observing to his companion, that his horse felt more lively under him than even when he mounted in the morning.

'Are you advised of that,' said Wayland Smith, smiling. 'That is owing to a little secret of mine. I mixed that with an handful of oats which shall save your worship's heels the trouble of spurring these six hours at least. Nay, I have not studied medicine and pharmacy for naught.'

'I trust,' said Tressilian, 'your drugs will do my horse no harm?'

'No more than the mare's milk which foaled him,' answered the artist; and was proceeding to dilate on the excellence of his recipe, when he was interrupted by an explosion as loud and tremendous as the mine which blows up the rampart of a beleaguered city. The horses started, and the riders were equally surprised. They turned to gaze in the direction from which the thunderclap was heard, and beheld, just over the spot they had left so recently, a huge pillar of dark smoke rising high into the clear blue atmosphere. 'My habitation is gone to wreck,' said Wayland, immediately conjecturing the cause of the explosion. 'I was a fool to mention the doctor's kind intention towards my mansion before that limb of mischief, Flibbertigibbet—I might have guessed he would long to put so rare a frolic into execution. But let us hasten on, for the sound will collect the country to the spot.

So saying he spurred his horse, and Tressilian also quickening his speed, they rode briskly forward.

'This, then, was the meaning of the little imp's token which he promised us,' said Tressilian; 'had we lingered near the spot, we had found it a love-token with a vengeance.'

'He would have given us warning,' said the smith; 'I saw him look back more than once to see if we were off—'tis a very devil for mischief, yet not an ill-natured devil either. It were long to tell your honour how I became first acquainted with him, and how many tricks he played me. Many a good turn he did me too, especially in bringing me customers; for his great delight was to see them sit shivering behind the bushes when they heard the click of my hammer. I think Dame Nature, when she lodged a double quantity of brains in that misshapen head of his, gave him the power of enjoying other people's distresses, as she gave them the pleasure of laughing at his ugliness.'

'It may be so,' said Tressilian; 'those who find themselves severed from society by peculiarities of form, if they do not hate the common bulk of mankind, are at least not altogether indisposed to enjoy their mishaps and calamities.'

'But Flibbertigibbet,' answered Wayland, 'hath that about him which may redeem his turn for mischievous frolic; for he is as faithful when attached, as he is tricky and malignant to strangers; and, as I said before, I have cause to say so.'

Tressilian pursued the conversation no further; and they continued their journey towards Devonshire without further adventure, until they alighted at an inn in the town of Marlborough, since celebrated for having given title to the greatest general (excepting one) whom Britain ever produced. Here the travellers received, in the same breath, an example of the truth of two old proverbs, namely, that 'Ill news fly fast,' and that 'Listeners seldom hear a good tale of themselves.'

The inn-yard was in a sort of combustion when they alighted; insomuch that they could scarce get man or boy to take care of their horses, so full were the whole household of some news which flew from tongue to tongue, the import of which they were for some time unable to discover. At length, indeed, they found it respected matters which touched them nearly.

'What is the matter, say you, master?' answered, at length, the head hostler, in reply to Tressilian's repeated questions—'Why, truly, I scarce know myself. But here was a rider but now, who says that the devil hath flown away with him they called Wayland Smith, that won'd about three miles from the Whitehorse of Berkshire, this very blessed morning, in a flash of fire and a pillar of smoke, and rooted up the place he dwelt in, near that old cockpit of upright stones, as cleanly as if it had all been delved up for a cropping.'

'Why, then,' said an old farmer, 'the more is the pity—for that Wayland Smith (whether he was the devil's crony or no I skill not) had a good notion of horse diseases, and it's to be thought the bots will spread in the country far and near, and Satan has not gi'en un time to leave his secret behind un.'

'You may say that, Gaffer Grimesby,' said the hostler in return; 'I have carried a horse to Wayland Smith myself, for he passed all farriers in this country.'

'Did you see him?' said Dame Alison Crane, mistress of the inn bearing that sign, and deigning to term *husband* the owner thereof, a mean-looking, hop-o'-my-thumb sort of person, whose halting gait, and long neck, and meddling hen-pecked insignificance, are supposed to have given origin to the celebrated old English tune of 'My Dame hath a lame tame Crane.'

On this occasion he chirped out a repetition of his wife's question, 'Did'st see the devil, Jack Hostler, I say?'

'And what if I did see un, Master Crane?' replied Jack Hostler,—for, like all the rest of the household, he paid as little respect to his master as his mistress herself did.

'Nay, naught, Jack Hostler,' replied the pacific Master Crane, 'only if you saw the devil, methinks I would like to know what un's like?'

'You will know that one day, Master Crane,' said his helpmate, an' ye mend not your manners, and mind your business, leaving off such idle palabras. But truly, Jack Hostler, I should be glad to know myself what like the fellow was.'

'Why, dame,' said the hostler, more respectfully, 'as for what he was like I cannot tell, nor no man else, for why I never saw un.'

'And how didst thou get thine errand done,' said Gaffer Grimesby, 'if thou seed'st him not?'

'Why, I had schoolmaster to write down ailment o' nag,' said Jack Hostler; 'and I went wi' the ugliest slip of a boy for my guide as ever man cut out o' lime-tree root to please a child withal.'

'And what was it?—and did it cure your nag, Jack Hostler?'—was uttered and echoed by all who stood around.

'Why, how can I tell you what it was?' said the hostler; 'simply it smelled and tasted—for I did make bold to put a pea's substance into my mouth—like hartshorn and savin mixed with vinegar—but then no hartshorn and savin ever wrought so speedy a cure—And I am dreading that if Wayland Smith be gone, the bots will have more power over horse and cattle.'

The pride of art, which is certainly not inferior in its influence to any other pride whatsoever, here so far operated on Wayland Smith, that, notwithstanding the obvious danger of his being recognised, he could not help winking to Tressilian, and smiling mysteriously, as if triumphing in the undoubted evidence of his veterinary skill. In the meanwhile, the discourse continued.

'E'en let it be so,' said a grave man in black, the companion of Gaffer Grimesby; 'e'en let us perish under the evil God sends us, rather than the devil be our doctor.'

'Very true,' said Dame Crane; 'and I marvel at Jack Hostler that he would peril his own soul to cure the bowels of a nag.'

'Very true, mistress,' said Jack Hostler, 'but the nag was my master's; and had it been yours, I think he would ha' held me cheap enow an I had feared the devil when the poor beast was in such a taking—For the rest, let the clergy look to it. Every man to his craft, says the proverb; the parson to the Prayer Book, and the groom to his curry-comb.'

'I vow,' said Dame Crane, 'I think Jack Hostler speaks like a good Christian and a faithful servant, who will spare neither body nor soul in his master's service. However, the devil has lifted him in time, for a Constable of the Hundred came hither this morning to get old Gaffer Pinniewinks, the trier of witches, to go with him to the Vale of Whitehorse to comprehend Wayland Smith, and put him to his probation. I helped Pinniewinks to sharpen his pincers and his poking-awl, and I saw the warrant from Justice Blindas.'

'Pooh—pooh—the devil would laugh both at Blindas and his warrant, constable, and witch-finder to boot,' said old Dame Crank, the papist laundress. 'Wayland Smith's flesh would mind Pinniewink's awl no more than a cambric ruff minds a hot piccadilloe-needle. But tell me, gentlefolks, if the devil ever had such a hand among ye, as to snatch away your smiths and your artists from under your nose, when the good Abbots of Abingdon had their own. By Our Lady, no!—they had their hallowed tapers, and their holy water, and their relics and what not, could send the foulest fiends a-packing. Go ask a heretic parson to do the like—But ours were a comfortable people.'

'Very true, Dame Crank,' said the hostler; 'so said Simpkins of Simonburn when the curate kissed his wife,—"They are a comfortable people," said he.'

'Silence, thou foul-mouthed vermin,' said Dame Crank; 'is it fit for a heretic horse-boy like thee to handle such a text as the Catholic clergy?'

'In troth no, dame,' replied the man of oats; 'and as you yourself are now no text for their handling, dame, whatever may have been the case in your day, I think we had e'en better leave un alone.'

At this last exchange of sarcasm, Dame Crank set up her throat, and began a horrible exclamation against Jack Hostler, under cover of which Tressilian and his attendant escaped into the house.

They had no sooner entered a private chamber, to which Goodman Crane himself had condescended to usher them, and despatched their worthy and obsequious host on an errand of procuring wine and refreshment, than Wayland Smith began to give vent to his self-importance.

'You see, sir,' said he, addressing Tressilian, 'that I nothing fabled in asserting that I possessed fully the mighty mystery of a farrier, or mareschal, as the French more honourably term us. These dog-hostlers, who, after all, are the better judges in such a case, know what credit they should attach to my medicaments. I call you to witness, worshipful Master Tressilian, that naught, save the voice of calumny and the hand of malicious violence hath driven me forth from a station in which I held a place alike useful and honoured.'

'I bear witness, my friend, but will reserve my listening,' answered Tressilian, 'for a safer time; unless, indeed, you deem it essential to your reputation, to be translated, like your late dwelling, by the assistance of a flash of fire. For you see your best friends reckon you no better than a mere sorcerer.'

'Now, Heaven forgive them,' said the artist, 'who confound learned skill with unlawful magic! I trust a man may be as skilful, or more so, than the best chirurgeon ever meddled with horse-flesh, and yet may be upon the matter little more than other ordinary men, or at the worst no conjurer.'

'God forbid else!' said Tressilian. 'But be silent just for the present, since here comes mine host with an assistant, who seems something of the least.'

Everybody about the inn, Dame Crane included, had been indeed so interested and agitated by the story they had heard of Wayland Smith, and by the new, varying, and more marvellous editions of the incident, which arrived from various quarters, that mine host, in his righteous determination to accommodate his guests, had been able to obtain the assistance of none of his household, saving that of a little boy, a junior tapster, of about twelve years old, who was called Sampson.

'I wish,' he said, apologising to his guests, as he set down a flagon of sack, and promising some food immediately,—'I wish the devil had flown away with my wife and my whole family instead of this Wayland Smith, who, I dare say, after all said and done, was much less worthy of the distinction that Satan has done him.'

'I hold opinion with you, good fellow,' replied Wayland Smith; 'and I will drink to you upon that argument.'

'Not that I would justify any man who deals with the devil,' said mine host, after having pledged Wayland in a rousing draught of sack, 'but that—Saw ye ever better sack, my masters?—but that, I say, a man had better deal with a dozen cheats and scoundrel fellows, such as this Wayland Smith, rather than with a devil incarnate, that takes possession of house and home, bed and board.'

The poor fellow's detail of grievances was here interrupted by the shrill voice of his helpmate, screaming from the kitchen, to which he instantly hobbled, craving pardon of his guests. He was no sooner gone, than Wayland Smith expressed, by every contemptuous epithet in the language, his utter scorn for a nincompoop, who stuck his head under his wife's apron-string; and intimated, that, saving for the sake of the horses, which required both rest and food, he would advise his worshipful Master Tressilian to push on a stage farther, rather than pay a reckoning to such a mean-spirited, crow-trodden, hen-pecked coxcomb, as Gaffer Crane.

The arrival of a large dish of good cowheel and bacon something smoothed the asperity of the artist, which wholly vanished before a choice capon, so delicately roasted, that the lard frothed on it, said Wayland, like May-dew on a lily; and both Gaffer Crane and his good dame became, in his eyes, very painstaking, accommodating, obliging persons.

According to the manners of the times, the master and his attendant sat at the same table, and the latter observed with regret, how little attention Tressilian paid to his meal. He recollected, indeed, the pain he had given by mentioning the maiden in whose company he had first seen him; but, fearful of touching upon a topic too tender to be tampered with, he chose to ascribe his abstinence to another cause.

'This fare is perhaps too coarse for your worship,' said Wayland, as the limbs of the capon disappeared before his own exertions; 'but had you dwelt as long as I have done in yonder dungeon, which Flibbertigibbet has translated to the upper element, a place where I dared hardly broil my food, lest the smoke should be seen without, you would think a fair capon a more welcome dainty.'

'If you are pleased, friend,' said Tressilian, 'it is well. Nevertheless, hasten thy meal if thou canst, for this place is unfriendly to thy safety, and my concerns crave travelling.'

Allowing, therefore, their horses no more rest than was absolutely necessary for them, they pursued their journey by a forced march as far as Bradford, where they reposed themselves for the night.

The next morning found them early travellers. And, not to fatigue the reader with unnecessary particulars, they traversed without adventure the counties of Wiltshire and Somerset, and about noon of the third day after Tressilian's leaving Cumnor, arrived at Sir Hugh Robsart's seat, called Lidcote Hall, on the frontiers of Devonshire.

12

Ah me! the flower and blossom of your house,
The wind hath blown away to other towers.
Joanna Baillie's 'Family Legend.'

THE ancient seat of Lidcote Hall was situated near the village of
the same name, and adjoined to the wild and extensive forest of
Exmoor, plentifully stocked with game, in which some ancient
rights belonging to the Robsart family entitled Sir Hugh to pursue
his favourite amusement of the chase. The old mansion was a low,
venerable building, occupying a considerable space of ground,
which was surrounded by a deep moat. The approach and drawbridge were defended by an octagonal tower, of ancient brick-
work, but so clothed with ivy and other creepers, that it was
difficult to discover of what materials it was constructed. The
angles of this tower were each decorated with a turret, whimsically
various in form and in size, and, therefore, very unlike the
monotonous stone pepper-boxes, which, in modern Gothic
architecture, are employed for the same purpose. One of these
turrets was square, and occupied as a clock-house. But the clock
was now standing still; a circumstance peculiarly striking to
Tressilian, because the good old Knight, among other harmless
peculiarities, had a fidgety anxiety about the exact measurement
of time, very common to those who have a great deal of that
commodity to dispose of, and find it lie heavy upon their hands,—
just as we see shopkeepers amuse themselves with taking an exact
account of their stock at the time there is least demand for it.

The entrance to the courtyard of the old mansion lay through
an archway, surmounted by the aforesaid tower, but the drawbridge was down, and one leaf of the iron-studded folding-doors
stood carelessly open. Tressilian hastily rode over the drawbridge,
entered the court, and began to call loudly on the domestics by
their names. For some time he was only answered by the echoes
and the howling of the hounds, whose kennel lay at no great
distance from the mansion, and was surrounded by the same moat.
At length Will Badger, the old and favourite attendant of the
Knight, who acted alike as squire of his body, and superintendent

of his sports, made his appearance. The stout, weather-beaten forester showed great signs of joy when he recognised Tressilian.

'Lord love you,' he said, 'Master Edmund, be it thou in flesh and fell? Then thou mayst do some good on Sir Hugh, for it passes the wit of man, that is of mine own, and the Curate's and Master Mumblazen's, to do aught wi' un.'

'Is Sir Hugh then worse since I went away, Will?' demanded Tressilian.

'For worse in body—no—he is much better,' replied the domestic; 'but he is clean mazed as it were—eats and drinks as he was wont—but sleeps not, or rather wakes not, for he is ever in a sort of twilight, that is neither sleeping nor waking. Dame Swineford thought it was like the dead palsy. But no, no, dame, said I, it is the heart, it is the heart.'

'Can you not stir his mind to any pastime?' said Tressilian.

'He is clean and quite off his sports,' said Will Badger; 'hath neither touched backgammon nor shovel-board—nor looked on the big book of harrowtry wi' Master Mumblazen. I let the clock run down, thinking the missing the bell might somewhat move him, for you know, Master Edmund, he was particular in counting time; but he never said a word on't, so I may e'en set the old chime a-towling again. I made bold to tread on Bungay's tail too, and you know what a round rating that would ha' cost me once a day—but he minded the poor tyke's whine no more than a madge howlet whooping down the chimney—so the case is beyond me.'

'Thou shalt tell me the rest within doors, Will. Meanwhile, let this person be taken to the buttery, and used with respect—He is a man of art.'

'White art or black art, I would,' said Will Badger, 'that he had any art which could help us. Here, Tom Butler, look to the man of art—and see that he steals none of thy spoons, lad,' he added, in a whisper to the butler, who showed himself at a low window, 'I have known as honest a faced fellow have art enough to do that.'

He then ushered Tressilian into a low parlour, and went, at his desire, to see in what state his master was, lest the sudden return of his darling pupil, and proposed son-in-law, should affect him too strongly. He returned immediately, and said that Sir Hugh was dozing in his elbow chair, but that Master Mumblazen would acquaint Master Tressilian the instant he awaked.

'But it is chance if he knows you, 'said the huntsman, 'for he has forgotten the name of every hound in the pack. I thought about a week since, he had gotten a favourable turn:—"Saddle me old Sorrel," said he, suddenly, after he had taken his usual night draught out of the great silver grace-cup, "and take the hounds to Mount Hazelhurst to-morrow." Glad men were we all, and out we had him in the morning, and he rode to cover as usual, with never a word spoken but that the wind was south, and the scent would lie. But ere we had uncoupled the hounds, he began to stare round him, like a man that wakes suddenly out of a dream—turns bridle and walks back to hall again, and leaves us to hunt at leisure by ourselves, if we listed.'

'You tell a heavy tale, Will,' replied Tressilian; 'but God must help us—there is no aid in man.'

'Then you bring us no news of young Mistress Amy? But what need I ask—your brow tells the story. Ever I hoped, that if any man could or would track her, it must be you. All's over and lost now. But if ever I have that Varney within reach of flight-shot, I will bestow a forked shaft on him; and that I will swear by salt and bread.'

As he spoke, the door opened, and Master Mumblazen appeared; a withered, thin, elderly gentleman, with a cheek like a winter apple, and his gray hair partly concealed by a small high hat, shaped like a cone, or rather like such a strawberry-basket as London fruiterers exhibit at their windows. He was too sententious a person to waste words on mere salutation; so, having welcomed Tressilian with a nod and shake of the hand, he beckoned him to follow to Sir Hugh's great chamber, which the good Knight usually inhabited. Will Badger followed, unasked, anxious to see whether his master would be relieved from his state of apathy by the arrival of Tressilian.

In a long, low parlour, amply furnished with implements of the chase, and with sylvan trophies, by a massive stone chimney, over which hung a sword and suit of armour, somewhat obscured by neglect, sat Sir Hugh Robsart of Lidcote, a man of large size, which had been only kept within moderate compass by the constant use of violent exercise. It seemed to Tressilian that the lethargy, under which his old friend appeared to labour, had, even during his few weeks' absence, added bulk to his person; at least it had obviously diminished the vivacity of his eye, which, as they entered, first followed Master Mumblazen slowly to a large oaken desk, on which a ponderous volume lay open, and then rested, as if in uncertainty, on the stranger who had entered along with him. The Curate, a gray-headed clergyman, who had been a confessor in the days of Queen Mary, sat with a book in his hand in another recess in the apartment. He, too, signed a mournful greeting to Tressilian, and laid his book aside, to watch the effect his appearance should produce on the afflicted old man.

As Tressilian, his own eyes filling fast with tears, approached more and more nearly to the father of his betrothed bride, Sir Hugh's intelligence seemed to revive. He sighed heavily, as one who awakens from a state of stupor, a slight convulsion passed over his features, he opened his arms without speaking a word, and as Tressilian threw himself into them, he folded him to his bosom.

'There is something left to live for yet,' were the first words he uttered; and while he spoke, he gave vent to his feelings in a paroxysm of weeping, the tears chasing each other down his sunburnt cheeks and long white beard.

'I ne'er thought to have thanked God to see my master weep,' said Will Badger; 'but now I do, though I am like to weep for company.'

'I will ask thee no questions,' said the old Knight; 'no questions— none, Edmund—thou hast not found her, or so found her, that she were better lost.'

Tressilian was unable to reply, otherwise than by putting his hands before his face.

'It is enough—it is enough. But do not thou weep for her, Edmund. I have cause to weep, for she was my daughter—thou hast cause to rejoice, that she did not become thy wife. Great God! Thou knowest best what is good for us—it was my nightly prayer that I should see Amy and Edmund wedded—had it been granted, it had now been gall added to bitterness.'

'Be comforted, my friend,' said the Curate, addressing Sir Hugh, 'it cannot be that the daughter of all our hopes and affections is the vile creature you would bespeak her.'

'Oh, no,' replied Sir Hugh, impatiently, 'I were wrong to name broadly the base thing she is become—there is some new court name for it, I warrant me. It is honour enough for the daughter of an old De'nshire clown to be the leman of a gay courtier; of

Varney too—of Varney, whose grandsire was relieved by my father, when his fortune was broken, at the battle of—the battle of—where Richard was slain—out on my memory!—and I warrant none of you will help me——'

'The battle of Bosworth,' said Master Mumblazen, 'stricken between Richard Crookback and Henry Tudor, grandsire of the Queen that now is, *primo Henrici Septimi;* and in the year one thousand four hundred and eighty-five, *post Christum natum.*'

'Ay, even so,' said the good Knight, 'every child knows it—But my poor head forgets all it should remember, and remembers only what it would most willingly forget. My brain has been at fault, Tressilian, almost ever since thou hast been away, and even yet it hunts counter.'

'Your worship,' said the good clergyman, 'had better retire to your apartment, and try to sleep for a little space,—the physician left a composing draught,—and our Great Physician has commanded us to use earthly means, that we may be strengthened to sustain the trials He sends us.'

'True, true, old friend,' said Sir Hugh, 'and we will bear our trials manfully—We have lost but a woman. See, Tressilian,'—he drew from his bosom a long ringlet of fair hair,—'see this lock!—I tell thee, Edmund, the very night she disappeared, when she bid me good-even, as she was wont, she hung about my neck, and fondled me more than usual; and I, like an old fool, held her by this lock, until she took her scissors, severed it, and left it in my hand,—as all I was ever to see more of her!'

Tressilian was unable to reply, well judging what a complication of feelings must have crossed the bosom of the unhappy fugitive at that cruel moment. The clergyman was about to speak, but Sir Hugh interrupted him.

'I know what you would say, Master Curate,—after all, it is but a lock of woman's tresses,—and by woman, shame, and sin, and death came into an innocent world—And learned Master Mumblazen, too, can say scholarly things of their inferiority.'

'*C'est l'homme,*' said Master Mumblazen, '*qui se bast et qui conseille.*'

'True,' said Sir Hugh, 'and we will bear us, therefore, like men who have both mettle and wisdom in us. Tressilian, thou art as welcome as if thou hadst brought better news. But we have spoken too long dry-lipped. Amy, fill a cup of wine to Edmund, and another to me.' Then instantly recollecting that he called upon her who could not hear, he shook his head, and said to the clergy-man, 'This grief is to my bewildered mind what the church of Lidcote is to our park; we may lose ourselves among the briers and thickets, for a little space, but from the end of each avenue we see the old gray steeple and the grave of my forefathers. I would I were to travel that road to-morrow.'

Tressilian and the Curate joined in urging the exhausted old man to lay himself to rest, and at length prevailed. Tressilian remained by his pillow till he saw that slumber at length sunk down on him, and then returned to consult with the Curate what steps should be adopted in these unhappy circumstances.

They could not exclude from these deliberations Master Michael Mumblazen; and they admitted him the more readily, that besides what hopes they entertained from his sagacity, they knew him to be so great a friend to taciturnity, that there was no doubt of his keeping counsel. He was an old bachelor of good family, but small fortune, and distinctly related to the House of Robsart; in virtue of which connection, Lidcote Hall had been honoured with his residence for the last twenty years. His company was agreeable to Sir Hugh, chiefly on account of his profound learning, which, though it only related to heraldry and genealogy, with such scraps of history as connected themselves with these subjects, was precisely of a kind to captivate the good old Knight; besides the convenience which he found in having a friend to appeal to, when his own memory, as frequently happened, proved infirm, and played him false concerning names and dates, which, and all similar deficiencies, Master Michael Mumblazen supplied with due brevity and discretion. And, indeed, in matters concerning the modern world, he often gave, in his enigmatical and heraldic phrase, advice which was well worth attending to, or, in Will Badger's language, started the game while others beat the bush.

'We have had an unhappy time of it with the good Knight, Master Edmund,' said the Curate. 'I have not suffered so much since I was torn away from my beloved flock, and compelled to abandon them to the Romish wolves.'

'That was *in tertio Mariæ*,' said Master Mumblazen.

'In the name of Heaven,' continued the Curate, 'tell us, has your time been better spent than ours? or have you any news of that unhappy maiden, who, being for so many years the principal joy of this broken-down house, is now proved our greatest unhappiness? Have you not at least discovered her place of residence?'

'I have,' replied Tressilian. 'Know you Cumnor Place, near Oxford?'

'Surely,' said the clergyman; 'it was a house of removal for the monks of Abingdon.'

'Whose arms,' said Master Michael, 'I have seen over a stone chimney in the hall,—a cross patonee betwixt four martlets.'

'There,' said Tressilian, 'this unhappy maiden resides in company with the villain Varney. But for a strange mishap, my sword had revenged all our injuries, as well as hers, on his worthless head.'

'Thank God, that kept thine hand from blood-guiltiness, rash young man,' answered the Curate. 'Vengeance is mine, saith the Lord, and I will repay. It were better study to free her from the villain's nets of infamy.'

'They are called, in heraldry, *laquei amoris*, or *lacs d'amour*,' said Mumblazen.

'It is in that I require your aid, my friends,' said Tressilian; 'I am resolved to accuse this villain, at the very foot of the throne, of falsehood, seduction, and breach of hospitable laws. The Queen shall hear me, though the Earl of Leicester, the villain's patron, stood at her right hand.'

'Her Grace,' said the Curate, 'hath set a comely example of continence to her subjects, and will doubtless do justice on this inhospitable robber. But wert thou not better apply to the Earl of Leicester, in the first place, for justice on his servant? If he grants it, thou dost save the risk of making thyself a powerful adversary, which will certainly chance, if, in the first instance, you accuse his master of the horse, and prime favourite before the Queen.

'My mind revolts from your counsel,' said Tressilian. 'I cannot brook to plead my noble patron's cause—the unhappy Amy's cause—before any one save my lawful Sovereign. Leicester, thou wilt say, is noble—be it so—he is but a subject like ourselves, and I will not carry my plaint to him, if I can do better. Still, I will think on what thou hast said,—but I must have your assistance to persuade the good Sir Hugh to make me his commissioner and fiduciary in this matter, for it is in his name I must speak, and not in my own. Since she is so far changed as to dote upon this empty profligate courtier, he shall at least do her the justice which is yet in his power.'

'Better she died *cœlebs* and *sine prole*,' said Mumblazen, with more animation than he usually expressed, 'than part, *per pale*, the noble coat of Robsart with that of such a miscreant.'

'If it be your object, as I cannot question,' said the clergyman, 'to save, as much as is yet possible, the credit of this unhappy young woman, I repeat, you should apply, in the first instance, to the Earl of Leicester. He is as absolute in his household as the Queen in her kingdom, and if he expresses to Varney that such is his pleasure, her honour will not stand so publicly committed.'

'You are right, you are right,' said Tressilian eagerly, 'and I thank you for pointing out what I overlooked in my haste. I little thought ever to have besought grace of Leicester; but I could kneel to the proud Dudley, if doing so could remove one shade of shame from this unhappy damsel. You will assist me then to procure the necessary powers from Sir Hugh Robsart?'

The Curate assured him of his assistance, and the herald nodded assent.

'You must hold yourselves also in readiness to testify, in case you are called upon, the open-hearted hospitality which our good patron exercised towards this deceitful traitor, and the solicitude with which he laboured to seduce his unhappy daughter.'

'At first,' said the clergyman, 'she did not, as it seemed to me, much affect his company, but latterly I saw them often together.'

'*Seiant* in the parlour,' said Michael Mumblazen, 'and *passant* in the garden.'

'I once came upon them by chance,' said the priest, 'in the South wood, in a spring evening—Varney was muffled in a russet cloak, so that I saw not his face,—they separated hastily, as they heard me rustle amongst the leaves, and I observed she turned her head and looked long after him.'

'With neck *reguardant*,' said the herald—'And on the day of her flight, and that was on Saint Austen's Eve, I saw Varney's groom, attired in his liveries, hold his master's horse and Mistress Amy's palfrey, bridled and saddled *proper*, behind the wall of the church-yard.'

'And now is she found mewed up in his secret place of retire-ment,' said Tressilian. 'The villain is taken in the manner, and I well wish he may deny his crime, that I may thrust conviction down his false throat. But I must prepare for my journey. Do you, gentlemen, dispose my patron to grant me such powers as are needful to act in his name.'

So saying, Tressilian left the room.

'He is too hot,' said the Curate; 'and I pray to God that He may grant him the patience to deal with Varney as is fitting.'

'Patience and Varney,' said Mumblazen, 'is worse heraldry than metal upon metal. He is more false than a siren, more rapacious than a griffin, more poisonous than a wyvern, and more cruel than a lion rampant.'

'Yet I doubt much,' said the Curate, 'whether we can with all right ask from Sir Hugh Robsart, being in his present condition, any deed deputing his paternal right in Mistress Amy to whomsoever——'

'Your reverence need not doubt that,' said Will Badger, who entered as he spoke, 'for I will lay my life he is another man when he wakes, than he has been these thirty days past.'

'Ay, Will,' said the Curate, 'hast thou then so much confidence in Doctor Diddleum's draught?'

'Not a whit,' said Will, 'because master ne'er tasted a drop on't, seeing it was emptied out by the housemaid. But here's a gentleman, who came attending on Master Tressilian, has given Sir Hugh a draught that is worth twenty of yon un. I have spoken cunningly with him, and a better farrier, or one who hath a more just notion of horse and dog ailment, I have never seen; and such a one would never be unjust to a Christian man.'

'A farrier! you saucy groom—and by whose authority, pray?' said the Curate, rising in surprise and indignation; 'or who will be warrant for this new physician?'

'For authority, an it like your reverence, he had mine; and for warrant, I trust I have not been five-and-twenty years in this house, without having right to warrant the giving of a draught to beast or body—I who can give a drench, and a ball, and bleed, or blister, if need, to my very self.'

The counsellors of the House of Robsart thought it meet to carry this information instantly to Tressilian, who as speedily summoned before him Wayland Smith, and demanded of him (in private, however) by what authority he had ventured to administer any medicine to Sir Hugh Robsart?

'Why,' replied the artist, 'your worship cannot but remember

that I told you I had made more progress into my master's—I
mean the learned Doctor Doboobie's—mystery than he was
willing to own; and indeed half of his quarrel and malice against
me was, that, besides that I got something too deep into his secrets,
several discerning persons, and particularly a buxom young widow
of Abingdon, preferred my prescriptions to his.'

'None of thy buffoonery, sir,' said Tressilian sternly. 'If thou
hast trifled with us—much more, if thou hast done aught that
may prejudice Sir Hugh Robsart's health, thou shalt find thy
grave at the bottom of a tin-mine.'

'I know too little of the great *arcanum* to convert the ore to
gold,' said Wayland firmly. 'But truce to your apprehensions,
Master Tressilian—I understood the good Knight's case, from
what Master William Badger told me; and I hope I am able
enough to administer a poor dose of mandragora, which, with
the sleep that must needs follow, is all that Sir Hugh Robsart
requires to settle his distraught brains.'

'I trust thou dealest fairly with me, Wayland?' said Tressilian.

'Most fairly and honestly, as the event shall show,' replied the
artist. 'What would it avail me to harm the poor old man for
whom you are interested? you, to whom I owe it, that Gaffer
Pinniewinks is not even now rending my flesh and sinews with
his accursed pincers, and probing every mole in my body with
his sharpened awl (a murrain on the hands which forged it!) in
order to find out the witch's mark! I trust to yoke myself as a
humble follower to your worship's train, and I only wish to have
my faith judged of by the result of the good Knight's slumbers.'

Wayland Smith was right in his prognostication. The sedative
draught which his skill had prepared, and Will Badger's confidence
had administered, was attended with the most beneficial effects.
The patient's sleep was long and healthful, and the poor old Knight
awoke, humbled indeed in thought, and weak in frame, yet a
much better judge of whatever was subjected to his intellect than
he had been for some time past. He resisted for a while the proposal
made by his friends, that Tressilian should undertake a journey
to court, to attempt the recovery of his daughter, and the redress
of her wrongs, in so far as they might yet be repaired. 'Let her
go,' he said; 'she is but a hawk that goes down the wind; I would
not bestow even a whistle to reclaim her.' But though he for some
time maintained this argument, he was at length convinced it was

his duty to take the part to which natural affection inclined him, and consent that such efforts as could yet be made should be used by Tressilian in behalf of his daughter. He subscribed, therefore, a warrant of attorney, such as the Curate's skill enabled him to draw up; for in those simple days the clergy were often the advisers of their flock in law, as well as in gospel.

All matters were prepared for Tressilian's second departure, within twenty-four hours after he had returned to Lidcote Hall; but one material circumstance had been forgotten, which was first called to the remembrance of Tressilian by Master Mumblazen. 'You are going to court, Master Tressilian,' said he; 'you will please remember that your blazonry must be *argent* and *or*—no other tinctures will pass current.' The remark was equally just and embarrassing. To prosecute a suit at court, ready money was as indispensable even in the golden days of Elizabeth as at any succeeding period; and it was a commodity little at the command of the inhabitants of Lidcote Hall. Tressilian was himself poor; and the revenues of good Sir Hugh Robsart were consumed, and even anticipated, in his hospitable mode of living; and it was finally necessary that the herald who started the doubt should himself solve it. Master Michael Mumblazen did so by producing a bag of money, containing nearly three hundred pounds in gold and silver of various coinage, the savings of twenty years; which he now, without speaking a syllable upon the subject, dedicated to the service of the patron whose shelter and protection had given him the means of making this little hoard. Tressilian accepted it without affecting a moment's hesitation, and a mutual grasp of the hand was all that passed betwixt them, to express the pleasure which the one felt in dedicating his all to such a purpose, and that which the other received from finding so material an obstacle to the success of his journey so suddenly removed, and in a manner so unexpected.

While Tressilian was making preparations for his departure early the ensuing morning, Wayland Smith desired to speak with him; and, expressing his hope that he had been pleased with the operation of his medicine in behalf of Sir Hugh Robsart, added his desire to accompany him to court. This was indeed what Tressilian himself had several times thought of; for the shrewdness, alertness of understanding, and variety of resource which this fellow had exhibited during the time they had travelled together, had made him sensible that his assistance might be of importance. But then Wayland was in danger from the grasp of law; and of this Tressilian reminded him, mentioning something, at the same time, of the pincers of Pinniewinks, and the warrant of Master Justice Blindas. Wayland Smith laughed both to scorn.

'See you, sir!' said he, 'I have changed my garb from that of a farrier to a serving-man; but, were it still as it was, look at my moustaches—they now hang down—I will but turn them up and dye them with a tincture that I know of, and the devil will scarce know me again.'

He accompanied these words with the appropriate action; and in less than a minute, by setting up his moustaches and his hair, he seemed a different person from him that had but now entered the room. Still, however, Tressilian hesitated to accept his services, and the artist became proportionately urgent.

'I owe you life and limb,' he said, 'and I would fain pay a part of the debt, especially as I know from Will Badger on what dangerous service your worship is bound. I do not indeed pretend to be what is called a man of mettle,—one of those ruffling tear-cats, who maintain their master's quarrel with sword and buckler. Nay, I am even one of those who hold the end of a feast better than the beginning of a fray. But I know that I can serve your worship better in such quest as yours, than any of these sword-and-dagger men, and that my head will be worth an hundred of their hands.'

Tressilian still hesitated. He knew not much of this strange fellow, and was doubtful how far he could repose in him the confidence necessary to render him an useful attendant upon the present emergency. Ere he had come to a determination, the trampling of a horse was heard in the courtyard, and Master Mumblazen and Will Badger both entered hastily into Tressilian's chamber, speaking almost at the same moment.

'Here is a serving-man on the bonniest gray tit I ever see'd in my life,' said Will Badger, who got the start;——'Having on his arm a silver cognisance, being a fire-drake, holding in his mouth a brick-bat, under a coronet of an Earl's degree,' said Master Mumblazen, 'and bearing a letter sealed of the same.'

Tressilian took the letter, which was addressed 'To the worshipful Master Edmund Tressilian, our loving kinsman—These—ride, ride, ride,—for thy life, for thy life, for thy life.' He then opened it, and found the following contents:—

'MASTER TRESSILIAN, OUR GOOD FRIEND AND COUSIN,

'We are at present so ill at ease, and otherwise so unhappily circumstanced, that we are desirous to have around us those of our friends on whose loving-kindness we can most especially repose confidence; amongst whom we hold our good Master Tressilian one of the foremost and nearest, both in good will and good ability. We therefore pray you, with your most convenient speed, to repair to our poor lodging, at Say's Court, near Deptford, where we will treat further with you of matters which we deem it not fit to commit unto writing. And so we bid you heartily farewell, being your loving kinsman to command,

RATCLIFFE, EARL OF SUSSEX.'

'Send up the messenger instantly, Will Badger,' said Tressilian; and, as the man entered the room, he exclaimed, 'Aha, Stevens, is it you? how does my good lord?'

'Ill, Master Tressilian,' was the messenger's reply; 'and having therefore the more need of good friends around him.'

'But what is my lord's malady?' said Tressilian anxiously; 'I heard nothing of his being ill.'

'I know not, sir,' replied the man. 'He is very ill at ease. The leeches are at a stand, and many of his household suspect foul practice; witchcraft, or worse.'

'What are the symptoms?' said Wayland Smith, stepping forward hastily.

'Anon?' said the messenger, not comprehending his meaning.

'What does he ail?' said Wayland; 'where lies his disease?'

The man looked at Tressilian, as if to know whether he should answer these inquiries from a stranger; and, receiving a sign in the affirmative, he hastily enumerated gradual loss of strength, nocturnal perspiration, and loss of appetite, faintness, etc.

'Joined,' said Wayland, 'to a gnawing pain in the stomach, and a low fever?'

'Even so,' said the messenger, somewhat surprised.

'I know how the disease is caused,' said the artist, 'and I know the cause. Your master has eaten of the manna of Saint Nicholas. I know the cure too—my master shall not say I studied in his laboratory for nothing.'

'How mean you?' said Tressilian, frowning; 'we speak of one

of the first nobles of England. Bethink you, this is no subject for buffoonery.'

'God forbid!' said Wayland Smith. 'I say that I know his disease, and can cure him. Remember what I did for Sir Hugh Robsart.'

'We will set forth instantly,' said Tressilian. 'God calls us.'

Accordingly, hastily mentioning this new motive for his instant departure, though without alluding to either the suspicions of Stevens or the assurances of Wayland Smith, he took the kindest leave of Sir Hugh and the family at Lidcote Hall, who accompanied him with prayers and blessings, and, attended by Wayland and the Earl of Sussex's domestic, travelled with the utmost speed towards London.

13

———Ay, I know you have arsenick,
Vitriol, sal-tartre, argaile, alkaly,
Cinoper: I know all. This fellow, Captain,
Will come in time to be a great distiller,
And give a say (I will not say directly,
But very near) at the philosopher's stone.
The Alchemist.

TRESSILIAN and his attendants pressed their route with all despatch. He had asked the smith, indeed, when their departure was resolved on, whether he would not rather choose to avoid Berkshire, in which he had played a part so conspicuous. But Wayland returned a confident answer. He had employed the short interval they passed at Lidcote Hall in transforming himself in a wonderful manner. His wild and overgrown thicket of beard was now restrained to two small moustachios on the upper lip, turned up in a military fashion. A tailor from the village of Lidcote (well paid) had exerted his skill, under his customer's directions, so as completely to alter Wayland's outward man, and take off from his appearance almost twenty years of age. Formerly, besmeared with soot and charcoal—overgrown with hair, and bent double with the nature of his labour—disfigured too, by his odd and fantastic dress, he seemed a man of fifty years old. But now, in a handsome suit of Tressilian's livery, with a sword by his side, and a buckler on his shoulder, he looked like a gay ruffling serving-man, whose age might be betwixt thirty and thirty-five, the very prime of human life. His loutish savage-looking demeanour seemed equally changed into a forward, sharp, and impudent alertness of look and action.

When challenged by Tressilian, who desired to know the cause of a metamorphosis so singular and so absolute, Wayland only answered by singing a stave from a comedy, which was then new, and was supposed, among the more favourable judges, to augur some genius on the part of the author. We are happy to preserve the couplet, which ran exactly thus,—

'Ban, ban, ca Caliban—
Get a new master—Be a new man.'

Although Tressilian did not recollect the verses, yet they reminded him that Wayland had once been a stage-player, a circumstance which, of itself, accounted indifferently well for the readiness with which he could assume so total a change of personal appearance. The artist himself was so confident of his disguise being completely changed, or of his having completely changed his disguise, which may be the more correct mode of speaking, that he regretted they were not to pass near his old place of retreat.

'I could venture,' he said, 'in my present dress, and with your worship's backing, to face Master Justice Blindas, even on a day of Quarter Sessions; and I would like to know what is become of Hobgoblin, who is like to play the devil in the world, if he can once slip the string, and leave his grannie and his Dominie.—Ay, and the scathed vault!' he said, 'I would willingly have seen what havoc the explosion of so much gunpowder has made among Doctor Demetrius Doboobie's retorts and phials. I warrant me, my fame haunts the Vale of the Whitehorse long after my body is rotten; and that many a lout ties up his horse, lays down his silver groat, and pipes like a sailor whistling in a calm, for Wayland Smith to come and shoe his tit for him. But the horse will catch the founders ere the smith answers the call.'

In this particular, indeed, Wayland proved a true prophet; and so easily do fables rise, that an obscure tradition of his extraordinary practice in farriery prevails in the Vale of Whitehorse even unto this day; and neither the tradition of Alfred's Victory, nor of the celebrated Pusey Horn, are better preserved in Berkshire than the wild legend of Wayland Smith. *

The haste of the travellers admitted their making no stay upon their journey, save what the refreshment of the horses required; and as many of the places through which they passed were under the influence of the Earl of Leicester, or persons immediately dependent on him, they thought it prudent to disguise their names, and the purpose of their journey. On such occasions the agency of Wayland Smith (by which name we shall continue to distinguish the artist, though his real name was Lancelot Wayland) was extremely serviceable. He seemed, indeed, to have a pleasure in displaying the alertness with which he could baffle investigation, and amuse himself by putting the curiosity of tapsters and inn-keepers on a false scent. During the course of their brief journey,

* Note B. Legend of Wayland Smith.

three different and inconsistent reports were circulated by him on their account; namely, first that Tressilian was the Lord Deputy of Ireland, come over in disguise to take the Queen's pleasure concerning the great rebel, Rory Oge MacCarthy MacMahon; secondly, that the said Tressilian was an agent of Monsieur, coming to urge his suit to the hand of Elizabeth; thirdly, that he was the Duke of Medina, come over, incognito, to adjust the quarrel betwixt Philip and that princess.

Tressilian was angry, and expostulated with the artist on the various inconveniences, and, in particular, the unnecessary degree of attention to which they were subjected by the figments he thus circulated; but he was pacified (for who could be proof against such an argument?) by Wayland's assuring him that a general importance was attached to his own (Tressilian's) striking presence, which rendered it necessary to give an extraordinary reason for the rapidity and secrecy of his journey.

At length they approached the metropolis, where, owing to the more general recourse of strangers, their appearance excited neither observation nor inquiry, and finally they entered London itself.

It was Tressilian's purpose to go down directly to Deptford, where Lord Sussex resided, in order to be near the court, then held at Greenwich, the favourite residence of Elizabeth, and honoured as her birthplace. Still a brief halt in London was necessary; and it was somewhat prolonged by the earnest entreaties of Wayland Smith, who desired permission to take a walk through the city.

'Take thy sword and buckler, and follow me, then,' said Tressilian; 'I am about to walk myself, and we will go in company.'

This he said, because he was not altogether so secure of the fidelity of his new retainer, as to lose sight of him at this interesting moment, when rival factions at the court of Elizabeth were running so high. Wayland Smith willingly acquiesced in the precaution, of which he probably conjectured the motive, but only stipulated, that his master should enter the shops, of such chemists or apothecaries as he should point out, in walking through Fleet Street, and permit him to make some necessary purchases. Tressilian agreed, and obeyed the signal of his attendant, walked successively into more than four or five shops, where he observed that Wayland purchased in each only one single drug, in various quantities. The medicines which he first asked for were readily furnished, each in succession, but those which he afterwards required were less easily supplied—and Tressilian observed, that Wayland more than once, to the surprise of the shopkeeper, returned the gum or herb that was offered to him, and compelled him to exchange it for the right sort, or else went on to seek it elsewhere. But one ingredient, in particular, seemed almost impossible to be found. Some chemists plainly admitted they had never seen it,—others denied that such a drug existed, excepting in the imagination of crazy alchemists,— and most of them attempted to satisfy their customer, by producing some substitute, which, when rejected by Wayland, as not being what he had asked for, they maintained possessed, in a superior degree, the self-same qualities. In general, they all displayed some curiosity concerning the purpose for which he wanted it. One old meagre chemist, to whom the artist put the usual question, in terms which Tressilian neither understood nor could recollect, answered frankly, there was none of that drug in London, unless Yoglan the Jew chanced to have some of it upon hand.

'I thought as much,' said Wayland. And as soon as they left the shop, he said to Tressilian, 'I crave your pardon, sir, but no artist can work without his tools. I must needs go to this Yoglan's; and I promise you, that if this detains you longer than your leisure seems to permit, you shall, nevertheless, be well repaid, by the use I will make of this rare drug. Permit me,' he added, 'to walk before you, for we are now to quit the broad street, and we will make double speed if I lead the way.'

Tressilian acquiesced, and, following the smith down a lane which turned to the left hand towards the river, he found that his guide walked on with great speed, and apparently perfect know-ledge of the town, through a labyrinth of by-streets, courts, and blind alleys, until at length Wayland paused in the midst of a very narrow lane, the termination of which showed a peep of the Thames, looking misty and muddy, which background was crossed saltirewise, as Master Mumblazen might have said, by the masts of two lighters that lay waiting for the tide. The shop under which he halted had not, as in modern days, a glazed window—but a paltry canvas screen surrounded such a stall as a cobbler now occupies, having the front open, much in the manner of a fish-monger's booth of the present day. A little old smock-faced man, the very reverse of a Jew in complexion, for he was very softhaired as well as beardless, appeared, and with many courtesies, asked Wayland what he pleased to want. He had no sooner named the drug, than the Jew started and looked surprised. 'And vat might your worship vant vith that drug which is not named, mein God, forty years I have been a chemist here?'

'These questions it is no part of my commission to answer,' said Wayland; 'I only wish to know if you have what I want, and having it, are willing to sell it?'

'Ay, mein God, for having it that I have, and for selling it I am chemist, and sell every drug.' So saying, he exhibited a powder, and then continued, 'But it will cost much monies—Vat I ave cost its weight in gold—ay, gold well refined—I vill say six times—It comes from Mount Sinai, where we had our blessed Law given forth, and the plant blossoms but once in one hundred year.'

'I do not know how often it is gathered on Mount Sinai,' said Wayland, after looking at the drug offered him with great disdain, 'but I will wager my sword and buckler against your gaberdine, that this trash you offer me instead of what I asked for, may be had for gathering any day of the week in the castle-ditch of Aleppo.'

'You are a rude man,' said the Jew; 'and, besides, I ave no better than that—or if I ave, I will not sell it without order of a physician —or without you tell me vat you make of it.'

The artist made brief answer in a language of which Tressilian could not understand a word, and which seemed to strike the Jew with the utmost astonishment. He stared upon Wayland like one who has suddenly recognised some mighty hero, or dreaded potentate, in the person of an unknown and unmarked stranger. 'Holy Elias!' he exclaimed, when he had recovered the first stunning effects of his surprise: and then passing from his former suspicions and surly manner to the very extremity of obsequiousness, he cringed low to the artist, and besought him to enter his poor house, to bless his miserable threshold by crossing it.

'Vill you not taste a cup with the poor Jew, Zacharias Yoglan? —Vill you Tokay ave?—vill you Lachrymæ taste?—vill you——'

'You offend in your proffers,' said Wayland; 'minister to me in what I require of you, and forbear further discourse.'

The rebuked Israelite took his bunch of keys, and opening with circumspection a cabinet which seemed more strongly secured than the other cases of drugs and medicines amongst which it stood, he drew out a little secret drawer, having a glass lid, and containing a small portion of a black powder. This he offered to Wayland, his manner conveying the deepest devotion towards him, though an avaricious and jealous expression, which seemed to grudge every grain of which his customer was about to possess himself, disputed ground in his countenance with the obsequious deference which he desired it should exhibit.

'Have you scales?' said Wayland.

The Jew pointed to those which lay ready for common use in the shop, but he did so with the puzzled expression of doubt and fear, which did not escape the artist.

'They must be other than these,' said Wayland sternly; 'know you not that holy things lose their virtue if weighed in an unjust balance?'

The Jew hung his head, took from a steel-plated casket a pair of scales beautifully mounted, and said, as he adjusted them for the artist's use,—'With these I do mine own experiment—one hair of the high-priest's beard would turn them.'

'It suffices,' said the artist; and weighed out two drachms for himself of the black powder, which he very carefully folded up, and put into his pouch with the other drugs. He then demanded the price of the Jew who answered, shaking his head and bowing,—

'No price—no, nothing at all from such as you.—But you will see the poor Jew again? you will look into his laboratory, where, God help him, he hath dried himself to the substance of the withered gourd of Jonah the holy prophet—You will ave pity on him, and show him one little step on the great road?'

'Hush!' said Wayland, laying his finger mysteriously on his mouth, 'it may be we shall meet again—thou hast already the *Schahmajm*, as thine own Rabbis call it—the general creation; watch therefore, and pray, for thou must attain the knowledge of Alchahest Elixir, Samech, ere I may commune further with thee.' Then returning with a slight nod the reverential congees of the Jew, he walked gravely up the lane, followed by his master, whose first observation on the scene he had just witnessed, was, that Wayland ought to have paid the man for his drug, whatever it was.

'I pay him!' said the artist; 'May the foul fiend pay me if I do! Had it not been that I thought it might displease your worship, I would have had an ounce or two of gold out of him, in exchange for the same just weight of brick-dust.'

'I advise you to practise no such knavery while waiting upon me,' said Tressilian.

'Did I not say,' answered the artist, 'that for that reason alone, I forbore him for the present? Knavery, call you it?—why, yonder wretched skeleton hath wealth sufficient to pave the whole lane he lives in with dollars, yet scarce miss them out of his own iron chest; yet he goes mad after the philosopher's stone—and besides, he would have cheated a poor serving-man, as he thought me at first, with trash that was not worth a penny—Match for match, quoth the devil to the collier; if his false medicine was worth my good crowns, my true brick-dust is as well worth his good gold.'

'It may be so for aught I know,' said Tressilian, 'in dealing amongst Jews and apothecaries; but understand, that to have such tricks of legerdemain practised by one attending on me, diminishes my honour, and that I will not permit them. I trust thou hast made up thy purchases?'

'I have, sir,' replied Wayland; 'and with these drugs will I, this very day, compound the true orvietan, that noble medicine which is so seldom found genuine and effective within these realms of Europe, for want of that most rare and precious drug which I got but now from Yoglan.'

'But why not have made all your purchases at one shop?' said his master; 'we have lost nearly an hour in running from one pounder of simples to another.'

'Content you, sir,' said Wayland. 'No man shall learn my secret; and it would not be mine long, were I to buy all my materials from one chemist.'

They now returned to their inn (the famous Bell-Savage), and while the Lord Sussex's servant prepared the horses for their journey, Wayland, obtaining from the cook the service of a mortar, shut himself up in a private chamber, where he mixed, pounded, and amalgamated the drugs which he had bought, each in its own proportion, with a readiness and address, that plainly showed him well practised in all the manual operations of pharmacy.

By the time Wayland's electuary was prepared, the horses were ready; and a short hour's riding brought them to the present habitation of Lord Sussex, an ancient house called Say's Court, near Deptford, which had long pertained to a family of that name, but had, for upwards of a century, been possessed by the ancient and honourable family of Evelyn. The present representative of that ancient house took a deep interest in the Earl of Sussex, and had willingly accommodated both him and his numerous retinue in his hospitable mansion. Say's Court was afterwards the residence of the celebrated Mr Evelyn, whose *Silva* is still the manual of British planters; and whose life, manners, and principles, as illustrated in his Memoirs, ought equally to be the manual of English gentlemen.

14

> This is rare news thou tell'st me, my good fellow;
> There are two bulls fierce battling on the green
> For one fair heifer—if the one goes down
> The dale will be more peaceful, and the herd,
> Which have small interest in their brulziement,
> May pasture there in peace.—*Old Play.*

SAY'S COURT was watched like a beleaguered fort; and so high rose the suspicions of the time, that Tressilian and his attendants were stopped and questioned repeatedly by sentinels, both on foot and horseback, as they approached the abode of the sick Earl. In truth, the high rank which Sussex held in Queen Elizabeth's favour, and his known and avowed rivalry of the Earl of Leicester, caused the utmost importance to be attached to his welfare; for, at that period we treat of, all men doubted whether he or the Earl of Leicester might ultimately have the higher rank in her regard.

Elizabeth, like many of her sex, was fond of governing by factions, so as to balance two opposing interests, and reserve in her own hand the power of making either predominate, as the interests of the state, or perhaps as her own female caprice (for to that foible even she was not superior), might finally determine. To finesse—to hold the cards—to oppose one interest to another—to bridle him who thought himself highest in her esteem, by the fears he must entertain of another equally trusted, if not equally beloved, were arts which she used throughout her reign, and which enabled her, though frequently giving way to the weakness of favouritism, to prevent most of its evil effects on her kingdom and government.

The two nobles, who at present stood as rivals in her favour, possessed very different pretensions to share it; yet it might be in general said, that the Earl of Sussex had been most serviceable to the Queen, while Leicester was most dear to the woman. Sussex was, according to the phrase of the times, a martialist; had done good service in Ireland and in Scotland, and especially in the great northern rebellion, in 1569, which was quelled, in a great measure, by his military talents. He was, therefore, naturally surrounded and looked up to by those who wished to make arms their road to distinction. The Earl of Sussex, moreover, was of more ancient and honourable descent than his rival, uniting in his person the representation of the Fitz-Walters, as well as of the Ratcliffes, while the scutcheon of Leicester was stained by the degradation of his grandfather, the oppressive minister of Henry the Seventh, and scarce improved by that of his father, the unhappy Dudley, Duke of Northumberland, executed on Tower Hill, August 22, 1553. But in person, features, and address, weapons so formidable in the court of a female sovereign, Leicester had advantages more than sufficient to counterbalance the military services, high blood, and frank bearing of the Earl of Sussex; and he bore in the eye of the court and kingdom the higher share in Elizabeth's favour, though (for such was her uniform policy) by no means so decidedly expressed as to warrant him against the final preponderance of his rival's pretensions. The illness of Sussex therefore happened so opportunely for Leicester, as to give rise to strange surmises among the public; while the followers of the one Earl were filled with the deepest apprehensions, and those of the other with the highest hopes of its probable issue. Meanwhile—for in that old time men never forgot the probability that the matter might be determined by length of sword,—the retainers of each noble flocked around their patron, appeared well armed in the vicinity of the court itself, and disturbed the ear of the sovereign by their frequent and alarming debates, held even within the precincts of her palace. This preliminary statement is necessary, to render what follows intelligible to the reader. *

On Tressilian's arrival at Say's Court, he found the place filled with the retainers of the Earl of Sussex, and of the gentlemen who came to attend their patron in his illness. Arms were in every hand, and a deep gloom on every countenance, as if they had apprehended an immediate and violent assault from the opposite faction. In the hall, however, to which Tressilian was ushered by one of the Earl's attendants, while another went to inform Sussex of his arrival, he found only two gentlemen in waiting. There was a remarkable contrast in their dress, appearance, and manners. The attire of the elder gentleman, a person as it seemed of quality and in the prime of life, was very plain and soldier-like, his stature low, his limbs stout, his bearing ungraceful, and his features of that kind which express sound common sense, without a grain of vivacity or imagination. The younger, who seemed about twenty, or upwards,

* *Note C.* Leicester and Sussex.

was clad in the gayest habit used by persons of quality at the period, wearing a crimson velvet cloak, richly ornamented with lace and embroidery, with a bonnet of the same, encircled with a gold chain turned three times round it, and secured by a medal. His hair was adjusted very nearly like that of some fine gentlemen of our own time; that is, it was combed upwards, and made to stand as it were on end, and in his ears he wore a pair of silver ear-rings, having each a pearl of considerable size. The countenance of this youth, besides being regularly handsome and accompanied by a fine person, was animated and striking in a degree, that seemed to speak at once the firmness of a decided and the fire of an enterprising character, the power of reflection, and the promptitude of determination.

Both these gentlemen reclined nearly in the same posture on benches near each other; but each seeming engaged in his own meditations, looked straight upon the wall which was opposite to them, without speaking to his companion. The looks of the elder were of that sort, which convinced the beholder, that, in looking on the wall, he saw no more than the side of an old hall hung around with cloaks, antlers, bucklers, old pieces of armour, partisans, and the similar articles which were usually the furniture of such a place. The look of the younger gallant had in it something imaginative; he was sunk in reverie, and it seemed as if the empty space of air betwixt him and the wall, were the stage of a theatre on which his fancy was mustering his own *dramatis personæ*, and treating him with sights far different from those which his awakened and earthly vision could have offered.

At the entrance of Tressilian, both started from their musing and bade him welcome; the younger, in particular, with great appearance of animation and cordiality.

'Thou art welcome, Tressilian,' said the youth; 'thy philosophy stole thee from us when this household had objects of ambition to offer—it is an honest philosophy, since it returns thee to us when there are only dangers to be shared.'

'Is my lord, then, so dangerously indisposed?' said Tressilian.

'We fear the very worst,' answered the elder gentleman, 'and by the worst practice.'

'Fie,' replied Tressilian, 'my Lord of Leicester is honourable.'

'What doth he with such attendants, then, as he hath about him?' said the younger gallant. 'The man who raises the devil may be honest, but he is answerable for the mischief which the fiend does, for all that.'

'And is this all that are of you, my mates,' said Tressilian, 'that are about my lord in his utmost straits?'

'No, no,' replied the elder gentleman, 'there are Tracy, Markham, and several more; but we keep watch here by two at once, and some are weary and are sleeping in the gallery above.'

'And some,' said the young man, 'are gone down to the Dock yonder at Deptford, to look out such a hulk as they may purchase by clubbing their broken fortunes; and so soon as all is over, we will lay our noble lord in a noble green grave, have a blow at those who have hurried him thither, if opportunity suits, and then sail for the Indies with heavy hearts and light purses.'

'It may be,' said Tressilian, 'that I will embrace the same purpose, so soon as I have settled some business at court.'

'Thou business at court!' they both exclaimed at once; 'and thou make the Indian voyage!'

'Why, Tressilian,' said the younger man, 'art thou not wedded, and beyond these flaws of fortune, that drive folks out to sea when their bark bears fairest for the haven?—What has become of the lovely Indamira that was to match my Amoret for truth and beauty?'

'Speak not of her,' said Tressilian, averting his face.

'Ay, stands it so with you?' said the youth, taking his hand very affectionately; 'then, fear not I will again touch the green wound— But it is strange as well as sad news. Are none of our fair and merry fellowship to escape shipwreck of fortune and happiness in this sudden tempest? I had hoped thou wert in harbour, at least, my dear Edmund—But truly says another dear friend of thy name,

> 'What man that sees the ever whirling wheel
> Of Chance, the which all mortal things doth sway,
> But that thereby doth find and plainly feel,
> How Mutability in them doth play
> Her cruel sports to many men's decay.'

The elder gentleman had risen from his bench, and was pacing the hall with some impatience, while the youth, with much earnestness and feeling, recited these lines. When he had done, the other wrapped himself in his cloak, and again stretched himself down, saying, 'I marvel, Tressilian, you will feed the lad in this silly humour. If there were aught to draw a judgment upon a virtuous and honourable household like my lord's, renounce me if I think not it were this piping, whining, childish trick of poetry that came among us with Master Walter Wittypate here and his comrades, twisting into all manner of uncouth and incomprehensible forms of speech, the honest plain English phrase which God gave us to express our meaning withal.'

'Blount believes,' said his comrade laughing, 'the devil woo'd Eve in rhyme, and that the mystic meaning of the Tree of Knowledge refers solely to the art of clashing rhymes and meting out hexameters.' *

At this moment the Earl's chamberlain entered, and informed Tressilian that his lord required to speak with him.

He found Lord Sussex dressed, but unbraced and lying on his couch, and was shocked at the alteration disease had made in his person. The Earl received him with the most friendly cordiality, and inquired into the state of his courtship. Tressilian evaded his inquiries for a moment, and turning his discourse on the Earl's own health, he discovered, to his surprise, that the symptoms of his disorder corresponded minutely with those which Wayland had predicated concerning it. He hesitated not, therefore, to communicate to Sussex the whole history of his attendant, and the pretensions he set up to cure the disorder under which he laboured. The Earl listened with incredulous attention until the name of Demetrius was mentioned, and then suddenly called to his secretary to bring him a certain casket which contained papers of importance. 'Take out from thence,' he said, 'the declaration of the rascal cook whom we had under examination, and look heedfully if the name of Demetrius be not there mentioned.'

The secretary turned to the passage at once, and read. 'And said declarant, being examined, saith, That he remembers having made the sauce to the said sturgeon-fish, after eating of which, the said noble Lord was taken ill; and he put the usual ingredients and condiments therein, namely——'

'Pass over his trash,' said the Earl, 'and see whether he had not been supplied with his materials by a herbalist called Demetrius.'

'It is even so,' answered the secretary. 'And he adds, he has not since seen the said Demetrius.'

'This accords with thy fellow's story, Tressilian,' said the Earl; 'call him hither.'

* *Note D.* Sir Walter Raleigh.

On being summoned to the Earl's presence, Wayland Smith told his former tale with firmness and consistency.

'It may be,' said the Earl, 'thou art sent by those who have begun this work, to end it for them; but bethink, if I miscarry under thy medicine, it may go hard with thee.'

'That were severe measure,' said Wayland, 'since the issue of medicine, and the end of life, are in God's disposal. But I will stand the risk. I have not lived so long under ground, to be afraid of a grave.'

'Nay, if thou be'st so confident,' said the Earl of Sussex, 'I will take the risk too, for the learned can do nothing for me. Tell me how this medicine is to be taken.'

'That will I do presently,' said Wayland; 'but allow me to condition that, since I incur all the risk of this treatment, no other physician shall be permitted to interfere with it.'

'That is but fair,' replied the Earl; 'and now prepare your drug.'

While Wayland obeyed the Earl's commands, his servants, by the artist's directions, undressed their master, and placed him in bed.

'I warn you,' he said, 'that the first operation of this medicine will be to produce a heavy sleep, during which time the chamber must be kept undisturbed, as the consequences may otherwise be fatal. I myself will watch by the Earl, with any of the gentlemen of his chamber.'

'Let all leave the room, save Stanley and this good fellow,' said the Earl.

'And saving me also,' said Tressilian. 'I too am deeply interested in the effects of this potion.'

'Be it so, good friend,' said the Earl; 'and now for our experiment; but first call my secretary and chamberlain.'

'Bear witness for me,' he continued, when these officers arrived, 'bear witness for me, gentlemen, that our honourable friend Tressilian is in no way responsible for the effects which this medicine may produce upon me, the taking it being my own free action and choice, in regard I believe it to be a remedy which God has furnished me by unexpected means, to recover me of my present malady. Commend me to my noble and princely Mistress; and say that I live and die her true servant, and wish to all about her throne the same singleness of heart and will to serve her, with more ability to do so, than hath been assigned to poor Thomas Ratcliffe.'

He then folded his hands, and seemed for a second or two absorbed in mental devotion, then took the potion in his hand, and, pausing, regarded Wayland with a look that seemed designed to penetrate his very soul, but which caused no anxiety or hesitation in the countenance or manner of the artist.

'Here is nothing to be feared,' said Sussex to Tressilian; and swallowed the medicine without further hesitation.

'I am now to pray your lordship,' said Wayland, 'to dispose yourself to rest as commodiously as you can; and of you, gentlemen, to remain as still and mute as if you waited at your mother's deathbed.'

The chamberlain and secretary then withdrew, giving orders that all doors be bolted, and all noise in the house strictly prohibited. Several gentlemen were voluntary watchers in the hall, but none remained in the chamber of the sick Earl, save his groom of the chamber, Stanley, the artist, and Tressilian. Wayland Smith's predictions were speedily accomplished, and a sleep fell upon the Earl, so deep and sound, that they who watched his bedside began to fear, that, in his weakened state, he might pass away without awakening from his lethargy. Wayland Smith himself appeared anxious, and felt the temples of the Earl slightly, from time to time, attending particularly to the state of respiration, which was full and deep but at the same time easy and uninterrupted.

15

> You logger-headed and unpolished grooms,
> What, no attendance, no regard, no duty?
> Where is the foolish knave I sent before?
> *Taming of the Shrew.*

THERE is no period at which men look worse in the eyes of each other, or feel more uncomfortable, than when the first dawn of daylight finds them watchers. Even a beauty of the first order, after the vigils of a ball are interrupted by the dawn, would do wisely to withdraw herself from the gaze of her fondest and most partial admirers. Such was the pale, inauspicious, and ungrateful light which began to beam upon those who kept watch all night, in the hall at Say's Court, and which mingled its cold, pale, blue diffusion with the red, yellow, and smoky beams of expiring lamps and torches. The young gallant, whom we noticed in our last chapter, had left the room for a few minutes, to learn the cause of a knocking at the outward gate, and on his return was so struck with the forlorn and ghastly aspects of his companions of the watch, that he exclaimed, 'Pity of my heart, my masters, how like owls you look! Methinks, when the sun rises, I shall see you flutter off with your eyes dazzled, to stick yourselves into the next ivy-trod or ruined steeple.'

'Hold thy peace, thou gibing fool,' said Blount, 'hold thy peace. Is this a time for jeering, when the manhood of England is perchance dying within a wall's breadth of thee?'

'There thou liest,' replied the gallant.

'How, lie!' exclaimed Blount, starting up, 'lie, and to me?'

'Why, so thou didst, thou peevish fool,' answered the youth; 'thou didst lie on that bench even now, didst thou not? But art thou not a hasty coxcomb, to pick up a wry word so wrathfully? Nevertheless, loving and honouring my lord as truly as thou, or any one, I do say, that should Heaven take him from us, all England's manhood dies not with him.'

'Ay,' replied Blount, 'a good portion will survive with thee, doubtless.'

'And a good portion with thyself, Blount, and with stout

Markham here, and Tracy, and all of us. But I am he will best employ the talent Heaven has given to us all.'

'As how, I prithee?' said Blount; 'tell us your mystery of multiplying.'

'Why, sirs,' answered the youth, 'ye are like goodly land, which bears no crop because it is not quickened by manure; but I have that rising spirit in me, which will make my poor faculties labour to keep pace with it. My ambition will keep my brain at work, I warrant thee.'

'I pray to God it does not drive thee mad,' said Blount; 'for my part if we lose our noble lord, I bid adieu to the court and to the camp both. I have five hundred foul acres in Norfolk, and thither will I, and change the court pantoufle for the country hobnail.'

'O base transmutation!' exclaimed his antagonist; 'thou hast already got the true rustic slouch—thy shoulders stoop, as if thine hands were at the stilts of the plough, and thou hast a kind of earthy smell about thee, instead of being perfumed with essence, as a gallant and courtier should. On my soul, thou hast stolen out to roll thyself on a hay mow. Thy only excuse will be to swear by thy hilts, that the farmer had a fair daughter.'

'I pray thee, Walter,' said another of the company, 'cease thy raillery, which suits neither time nor place, and tell us who was at the gate just now.'

'Doctor Masters, physician to her Grace in ordinary, sent by her special orders to inquire after the Earl's health,' answered Walter.

'Ha! what?' exclaimed Tracy, 'that was no slight mark of favour; if the Earl can but come through, he will match with Leicester yet. Is Masters with my lord at present?'

'Nay,' replied Walter, 'he is half-way back to Greenwich by this time, and in high dudgeon.'

'Thou didst not refuse him admittance?' exclaimed Tracy.

'Thou were not surely so mad?' ejaculated Blount.

'I refused him admittance as flatly, Blount, as you would refuse a penny to a blind beggar; as obstinately, Tracy, as thou didst ever deny access to a dun.'

'Why, in the fiend's name, did thou trust him to go to the gate?' said Blount to Tracy.

'It suited his years better than mine,' answered Tracy; 'but he has undone us all now thoroughly. My lord may live or die, he will never have a look of favour from her Majesty again.'

'Nor the means of making fortunes for his followers,' said the young gallant, smiling contemptuously; 'there lies the sore point, that will brook no handling. My good sirs, I sounded my lamentations over my lord somewhat less loudly than some of you; but when the point comes of doing him service, I will yield to none of you. Had this learned leech entered, think'st thou not there had been such a coil betwixt him and Tressilian's mediciner, that not the sleeper only, but the very dead might have awakened? I know what 'larum belongs to the discord of doctors.'

'And who is to take the blame of opposing the Queen's orders?' said Tracy; 'for undeniably, Doctor Masters came with her Grace's positive commands to cure the Earl.'

'I, who have done the wrong, will bear the blame,' said Walter.

'Thus, then, off fly the dreams of court favour thou hast nourished,' said Blount; 'and despite all thy boasted art and ambition, Devonshire will see thee shine a true younger brother, fit to sit low at the board, carve turn about with the chaplain, look that the hounds be fed, and see the squire's girths drawn when he goes a-hunting.'

'Not so,' said the young man, colouring, 'not while Ireland and the Netherlands have wars, and not while the sea hath pathless waves. The rich West hath lands undreamed of, and Britain contains bold hearts to venture on the quest of them. Adieu for a space, my masters. I go to walk in the court and look to the sentinels.'

'The lad hath quicksilver in his veins, that is certain,' said Blount, looking at Markham.

'He hath that both in brain and blood,' said Markham, 'which may either make or mar him. But, in closing the door against Masters, he hath done a daring and loving piece of service; for Tressilian's fellow hath ever averred, that to wake the Earl were death, and Masters would wake the Seven Sleepers themselves, if he thought they slept not by the regular ordinance of medicine.'

Morning was well advanced, when Tressilian, fatigued and over-watched, came down to the hall with the joyful intelligence that the Earl had awakened of himself, that he found his internal complaints much mitigated, and spoke with a cheerfulness, and looked round with a vivacity, which of themselves showed a material and favourable change had taken place. Tressilian at the same time commanded the attendance of one or two of his followers, to report what had passed during the night, and to relieve the watchers in the Earl's chamber.

When the message of the Queen was communicated to the Earl of Sussex, he at first smiled at the repulse which the physician had received from his zealous young follower, but instantly recollecting himself, he commanded Blount, his master of the horse, instantly to take boat, and go down the river to the palace of Greenwich, taking young Walter and Tracy with him, and make a suitable compliment, expressing his grateful thanks to his Sovereign, and mentioning the cause why he had not been enabled to profit by the assistance of the wise and learned Doctor Masters.

'A plague on it,' said Blount, as he descended the stairs, 'had he sent me with a cartel to Leicester, I think I should have done his errand indifferently well. But to go to our gracious Sovereign, before whom all words must be lacquered over either with gilding or with sugar, is such a confectionery matter as clean baffles my poor old English brain. Come with me, Tracy, and come you too, Master Walter Wittypate, that art the cause of our having all this ado. Let us see if thy neat brain, that frames so many flashy fireworks, can help out a plain fellow at need with some of thy shrewd devices.'

'Never fear, never fear,' exclaimed the youth, 'it is I will help you through—let me but fetch my cloak.'

'Why, thou hast it on thy shoulders,' said Blount—'the lad is mazed.'

'No, this is Tracy's old mantle,' answered Walter; 'I go not with thee to court unless as a gentleman should.'

'Why,' said Blount, 'thy braveries are like to dazzle the eyes of none but some poor groom or porter.'

'I know that,' said the youth; 'but I am resolved I will have my own cloak, ay, and brush my doublet to boot, ere I stir forth with you.'

'Well, well,' said Blount, 'here is a coil about a doublet and a cloak—get thyself ready, a God's name.'

They were soon launched on the princely bosom of the broad Thames, upon which the sun now shone forth in all its splendour.

'There are two things scarce matched in the universe,' said Walter to Blount, 'the sun in heaven, and the Thames on the earth.'

'The one will light us to Greenwich well enough,' said Blount, 'and the other would take us there a little faster if it were ebb tide.'

'And this is all thou think'st—all thou carest—all thou deem'st the use of the King of Elements, and the King of Rivers, to guide three such poor caitiffs as thyself, and me, and Tracy, upon an idle journey of courtly ceremony!'

'It is no errand of my seeking, faith,' replied Blount, 'and I could excuse both the sun and the Thames the trouble of carrying me where I have no great mind to go: and where I expect but dog's wages for my trouble—And by my honour,' he added, looking out from the head of the boat, 'it seems to me as if our message were a sort of labour in vain; for see, the Queen's barge lies at the stairs, as if her Majesty were about to take water.'

It was even so. The royal barge, manned with the Queen's watermen, richly attired in the regal liveries, and having the banner of England displayed, did indeed lie at the great stairs which ascended from the river, and along with it two or three other boats for transporting such part of her retinue as were not in immediate attendance on the royal person. The yeoman of the guard, the tallest and most handsome men whom England could produce, guarded with their halberds the passage from the palace-gate to the river side, and all seemed in readiness for the Queen's coming forth, although the day was yet so early.

'By my faith, this bodes us no good,' said Blount; 'it must be some perilous cause puts her Grace in motion thus untimeously. By my counsel, we were best put back again, and tell the Earl what we have seen.'

'Tell the Earl what we have seen?' said Walter, 'why, what have we seen but a boat, and men with scarlet jerkins, and halberds in their hands? Let us do his errand, and tell him what the Queen says in reply.'

So saying, he caused the boat to be pulled towards a landing-place at some distance from the principal one, which it would not, at that moment, have been thought respectful to approach, and jumped on shore, followed, though with reluctance, by his cautious and timid companions. As they approached the gate of the palace, one of the sergeant porters told them they could not at present enter, as her Majesty was in the act of coming forth. The gentleman used the name of the Earl of Sussex; but it proved no charm to subdue the officer, who alleged in reply, that it was as much as his post was worth, to disobey in the least title the commands which he had received.

'Nay, I told you as much before,' said Blount; 'do, I pray you, my dear Walter, let us take boat and return.'

'Not till I see the Queen come forth,' returned the youth, composedly.

'Thou art mad, stark mad, by the mass,' answered Blount.

'And thou,' said Walter, 'art turned coward of the sudden. I have seen thee face half a score of shag-headed Irish kernes to thy own share of them, and now thou wouldst blink and go back to shun the frown of a fair lady!'

At this moment the gates opened, and ushers began to issue forth in array, preceded and flanked by the band of Gentlemen Pensioners. After this, amid a crowd of lords and ladies, yet so disposed around her that she could see and be seen on all sides, came Elizabeth herself, then in the prime of womanhood, and in the full glow of what in a Sovereign was called beauty, and who would in the lowest rank of life have been truly judged a noble figure, joined to a striking and commanding physiognomy. She leant on the arm of Lord Hunsdon, whose relation to her by her mother's side often procured him such distinguished marks of Elizabeth's intimacy.

The young cavalier we have so often mentioned had probably never yet approached so near the person of his Sovereign, and he pressed forward as far as the line of warders permitted, in order to avail himself of the present opportunity. His companion, on the contrary cursing his imprudence, kept pulling him backwards, till Walter shook him off impatiently, and letting his rich cloak drop carelessly from one shoulder; a natural action, which served, however, to display to the best advantage his well-proportioned person. Unbonneting at the same time, he fixed his eager gaze on the Queen's approach, with a mixture of respectful curiosity and modest yet ardent admiration, which suited so well with his fine features, that the warders, struck with his rich attire and noble countenance, suffered him to approach the ground over which the Queen was to pass, somewhat closer than was permitted to ordinary spectators. Thus the adventurous youth stood full in Elizabeth's eye,—an eye never indifferent to the admiration which she deservedly excited among her subjects, or to the fair proportions of external form which chanced to distinguish any of her courtiers.

Accordingly, she fixed her keen glance on the youth, as she approached the place where he stood, with a look in which surprise at his boldness seemed to be unmingled with resentment, while a trifling accident happened which attracted her attention towards him yet more strongly. The night had been rainy, and just where the young gentleman stood, a small quantity of mud interrupted the Queen's passage. As she hesitated to pass on, the gallant, throwing his cloak from his shoulders, laid it on the miry spot, so as to ensure her stepping over it dry-shod. Elizabeth looked at the young man, who accompanied this act of devoted courtesy with a profound reverence, and a blush that overspread his whole countenance. The Queen was confused, and blushed in her turn, nodded her head, hastily passed on, and embarked in her barge without saying a word.

'Come along, Sir Coxcomb,' said Blount; 'your gay cloak will need the brush to-day, I wot. Nay, if you had meant to make a foot-cloth of your mantle, better have kept Tracy's old drap-de-bure, which despises all colours.'

'This cloak,' said the youth, taking it up and folding it, 'shall never be brushed while in my possession.'

'And that will not be long, if you learn not a little more economy—we shall have you in *cuerpo* soon, as the Spaniard says.'

Their discourse was here interrupted by one of the Band of Pensioners.

'I was sent,' said he, after looking at them attentively, 'to a gentleman who hath no cloak, or a muddy one. You, sir, I think,' addressing the younger cavalier, 'are the man; you will please to follow me.'

'He is in attendance on me,' said Blount, 'on me, the noble Earl of Sussex's master of horse.'

'I have nothing to say to that,' answered the messenger: 'my orders are directly from her Majesty, and concern this gentleman only.'

So saying, he walked away, followed by Walter, leaving the others behind, Blount's eyes almost starting from his head with the excess of his astonishment. At length he gave vent to it in an exclamation—'Who the good jere would have thought this!' And shaking his head with a mysterious air, he walked to his own boat, embarked and returned to Deptford.

The young cavalier was, in the meanwhile, guided to the

water-side by the Pensioner, who showed him considerable respect; a circumstance which, to persons in his situation, may be considered as an augury of no small consequence. He ushered him into one of the wherries which lay ready to attend the Queen's barge, which was already proceeding up the river, with the advantage of that flood-tide, of which, in the course of their descent, Blount had complained to his associates.

The two rowers used their oars with such expedition at the signal of the Gentleman Pensioner, that they very soon brought their little skiff under the stern of the Queen's boat, where she sat beneath an awning, attended by two or three ladies, and the nobles of her household. She looked more than once at the wherry in which the young adventurer was seated, spoke to those around her, and seemed to laugh. At length one of the attendants, by the Queen's order apparently, made a sign for the wherry to come alongside, and the young man was desired to step from his own skiff into the Queen's barge, which he performed with graceful agility at the fore part of the boat, and was brought aft to the Queen's presence, the wherry at the same time dropping into the rear. The youth underwent the gaze of Majesty, not the less gracefully that his self-possession was mingled with embarrassment. The muddied cloak still hung upon his arm, and formed the natural topic with which the Queen introduced the conversation.

'You have this day spoiled a gay mantle in our service, young man. We thank you for your service, though the manner of offering it was unusual, and something bold.'

'In a sovereign's need,' answered the youth, 'it is each liegeman's duty to be bold.'

'God's pity! that was well said, my lord,' said the Queen, turning to a grave person who sat by her, and answered with a grave inclination of the head, and something of a mumbled assent. 'Well, young man, your gallantry shall not go unrewarded. Go to the wardrobe-keeper, and he shall have orders to supply the suit which you have cast away in our service. Thou shalt have a suit, and that of the newest cut, I promise thee, on the word of a princess.'

'May it please your grace,' said Walter, hesitating, 'it is not for so humble a servant of your Majesty to measure out your bounties; but if it became me to choose——'

'Thou would'st have gold, I warrant me,' said the Queen,

interrupting him; 'fie, young man! I take shame to say, that, in our capital, such and so various are the means of thriftless folly, that to give gold to youth is giving fuel to fire, and furnishing them with the means of self-destruction. If I live and reign, these means of unchristian excess shall be abridged. Yet thou mayst be poor,' she added, 'or thy parents may be—It shall be gold, if thou wilt, but thou shalt answer to me for the use on't.'

Walter waited patiently until the Queen had done, and then modestly assured her, that gold was still less in his wish than the raiment her Majesty had before offered.

'How, boy!' said the Queen, 'neither gold nor garment? What is it thou wouldst have of me, then?'

'Only permission, Madam—if it is not asking too high an honour—permission to wear the cloak, which did you this trifling service.'

'Permission to wear thine own cloak, thou silly boy!' said the Queen.

'It is no longer mine,' said Walter; 'when your Majesty's foot touched it, it became a fit mantle for a prince, but far too rich a one for its former owner.'

The Queen again blushed; and endeavoured to cover, by laughing, a slight degree of not unpleasing surprise and confusion.

'Heard you ever the like, my lords? The youth's head is turned with reading romances—I must know something of him, that I may send him safe to his friends. What art thou?'

'A gentleman of the household of the Earl of Sussex, so please your grace, sent hither with his master of horse, upon a message to your Majesty.'

In a moment the gracious expression which Elizabeth's face had hitherto maintained, gave way to an expression of haughtiness and severity.

'My Lord of Sussex,' she said, 'has taught us how to regard his messages, by the value he places upon ours. We sent but this morning the physician in ordinary of our chamber, and that at no usual time, understanding his lordship's illness to be more dangerous than we had before apprehended. There is at no court in Europe a man more skilled in his holy and most useful science than Doctor Masters, and he came from us to our subject. Nevertheless, he found the gate of Say's Court defended by men with culverins, as if it had been on the Borders of Scotland, not in the vicinity of our court; and when he demanded admittance in our name, it was stubbornly refused. For this slight of kindness, which had but too much of condescension in it, we will receive, at present at least, no excuse; and some such we suppose to have been the purport of my Lord of Sussex's message.'

This was uttered in a tone, and with a gesture, which made Lord Sussex's friends who were within hearing tremble. He to whom the speech was addressed, however, trembled not; but with great deference and humility, as soon as the Queen's passion gave him an opportunity, he replied:—'So please your most gracious Majesty, I was charged with no apology from the Earl of Sussex.'

'With what were you then charged, sir?' said the Queen, with the impetuosity, which, amid nobler qualities, strongly marked her character; 'was it with a justification?—or, God's death! with a defiance?'

'Madam,' said the young man, 'my Lord of Sussex knew the offence approached towards treason, and could think of nothing save of securing the offender, and placing him in your Majesty's hands, and at your mercy. The noble Earl was fast asleep when your most gracious message reached him, a potion having been administered to that purpose by his physician; and his lordship knew not of the ungracious repulse your Majesty's royal and most comfortable message had received, until after he awoke this morning.'

'And which of his domestics then, in the name of Heaven, presumed to reject my message, without even admitting my own physician to the presence of him whom I sent him to attend?' said the Queen, much surprised.

'The offender, Madam, is before you,' replied Walter, bowing very low; 'the full and sole blame is mine; and my lord has most justly sent me to abye the consequences of a fault, of which he is innocent as a sleeping man's dreams can be of a waking man's actions.'

'What, was it thou?—thou thyself, that repelled my messenger and my physician from Say's Court?' said the Queen. 'What could occasion such boldness in one who seems devoted—that is, whose exterior bearing shows devotion—to his Sovereign?'

'Madam,' said the youth—who, notwithstanding an assumed appearance of severity, thought he saw something in the Queen's face that resembled not implacability—'we say in our country, that the physician is for the time the liege sovereign of his patient. Now, my noble master was then under dominion of a leech, by whose advice he hath greatly profited, who had issued his commands that his patient should not that night be disturbed, on the very peril of his life.'

'Thy master hath trusted some false varlet of an empiric,' said the Queen.

'I know not, Madam, but by the fact, that he is now—this very morning—awakened much refreshed and strengthened, from the only sleep he hath had for many hours.'

The nobles looked at each other, but more with the purpose to see what each thought of this news, than to exchange any remarks on what had happened. The Queen answered hastily, and without affecting to disguise her satisfaction, 'By my word, I am glad he is better. But thou wert over bold to deny the access of my Doctor Masters. Know'st thou not that the Holy Writ saith, "In the multitude of counsel there is safety?"'

'Ay, Madam,' said Walter, 'but I have heard learned men say, that the safety spoken of is for the physicians, not for the patient.'

'By my faith, child, thou hast pushed me home,' said the Queen, laughing; 'for my Hebrew learning does not come quite at a call.—How say you, my Lord of Lincoln? Hath the lad given a just interpretation of the text?'

'The word *safety*, most gracious Madam,' said the Bishop of Lincoln, 'for so hath been translated, it may be somewhat hastily, the Hebrew word, being——'

'My lord,' said the Queen, interrupting him, 'we said we had forgotten our Hebrew. But for thee, young man, what is thy name and birth?'

'Raleigh is my name, most gracious Queen, the youngest son of a large but honourable family of Devonshire.'

'Raleigh?' said Elizabeth, after a moment's recollection, 'have we not heard of your service in Ireland?'

'I have been so fortunate as to do some service there, Madam,' replied Raleigh, 'scarce, however, of consequence sufficient to reach your Grace's ears.'

'They hear farther than you think of,' said the Queen graciously, 'and have heard of a youth who defended a ford in Shannon against a whole band of wild Irish rebels, until the stream ran purple with their blood and his own.'

'Some blood I may have lost,' said the youth, looking down, 'but it was where my best is due; and that is in your Majesty's service.'

The Queen paused, and then said hastily, 'You are very young to have fought so well, and to speak so well. But you must not escape your penance for turning back Masters—the poor man hath caught cold on the river; for our order reached him when he was just returned from certain visits in London, and he held it matter of loyalty and conscience instantly to set forth again. So hark ye, Master Raleigh, see thou fail not to wear thy muddy cloak, in token of penitence, till our pleasure be further known. And here,' she added, giving him a jewel of gold, in the form of a chessman, 'I give thee this to wear at the collar.'

Raleigh, to whom nature had taught intuitively, as it were, those courtly arts which many scarce acquire from long experience, knelt, and, as he took from her hand the jewel, kissed the fingers which gave it. He knew, perhaps, better than almost any of the courtiers who surrounded her, how to mingle the devotion claimed by the Queen with the gallantry due to her personal beauty—and in this, his first attempt to unite them, he succeeded so well, as at once to gratify Elizabeth's personal vanity and her love of power. *

His master, the Earl of Sussex, had the full advantage of the satisfaction which Raleigh had afforded Elizabeth, on their first interview.

'My lords and ladies,' said the Queen, looking around to the retinue by whom she was attended, 'methinks since we are upon the river, it were well to renounce our present purpose of going to the city, and surprise this poor Earl of Sussex with a visit. He is ill, and suffering doubtless under the fear of our displeasure, from which he hath been honestly cleared by the frank avowal of this malapert boy. What think ye? were it not an act of charity to give him such consolation as the thanks of a Queen, much bound to him for his loyal service, may perchance best minister?'

It may be readily supposed, that none to whom this speech was addressed ventured to oppose its purport.

'Your Grace,' said the Bishop of Lincoln, 'is the breath of our nostrils.' The men of war averred, that the face of the Sovereign was a whetstone to the soldier's sword; while the men of state

* Note E. Court favour of Sir Walter Raleigh.

were not less of opinion, that the light of the Queen's countenance was a lamp to the paths of her councillors; and the ladies agreed, with one voice, that no noble in England so well deserved the regard of England's royal Mistress as the Earl of Sussex—the Earl of Leicester's right being reserved entire; so some of the more politic worded their assent—an exception to which Elizabeth paid no apparent attention. The barge had, therefore, orders to deposit its royal freight at Deptford, at the nearest and most convenient point of communication with Say's Court, in order that the Queen might satisfy her royal and maternal solicitude, by making personal inquiries after the health of the Earl of Sussex.

Raleigh, whose acute spirit foresaw and anticipated important consequences from the most trifling events, hastened to ask the Queen's permission to go in the skiff, and announce the royal visit to his master; ingeniously suggesting that the joyful surprise might prove prejudicial to his health, since the richest and most generous cordials may sometimes be fatal to those who have been long in a languishing state.

But whether the Queen deemed it too presumptuous in so young a courtier to interpose his opinion unasked, or whether she was moved by a recurrence of the feeling of jealousy, which had been instilled into her, by reports that the Earl kept armed men about his person, she desired Raleigh, sharply, to reserve his counsel till it was required of him, and repeated her former orders, to be landed at Deptford, adding, 'We will ourselves see what sort of household my Lord of Sussex keeps about him.'

'Now the Lord have pity on us!' said the young courtier to himself. 'Good hearts, the Earl hath many a one round him; but good heads are scarce with us—and he himself is too ill to give directions. And Blount will be at his morning meal of Yarmouth herrings and ale; and Tracy will have his beastly black puddings and Rhenish;—those thorough-paced Welshmen, Thomas ap Rice and Evan Evans, will be at work on their leek porridge and toasted cheese—and she detests, they say, all coarse meals, evil smells, and strong wines. Could they but think of burning some rosemary in the great hall! but *vogue la galère*, all must now be trusted to chance. Luck hath done indifferent well for me this morning, for I trust I have spoiled a cloak, and made a court fortune—May she do as much for my gallant patron!'

The royal barge soon stopped at Deptford, and, amid the loud shouts of the populace, which her presence never failed to excite, the Queen, with a canopy borne over her head, walked, accompanied by her retinue, towards Say's Court, where the distant acclamations of the people gave the first notice of her arrival. Sussex, who was in the act of advising with Tressilian how he should make up the supposed breach in the Queen's favour, was infinitely surprised at learning her immediate approach—not that the Queen's custom of visiting her more distinguished nobility, whether in health or sickness, could be unknown to him; but the suddenness of the communication left no time for those preparations with which he well knew Elizabeth loved to be greeted, and the rudeness and confusion of his military household, much increased by his late illness, rendered him altogether unprepared for her reception.

Cursing internally the chance which thus brought her gracious visitation on him unaware, he hastened down with Tressilian, to whose eventful and interesting story he had just given an attentive ear.

'My worthy friend,' he said, 'such support as I can give your accusation of Varney, you have a right to expect, alike from justice and gratitude. Chance will presently show whether I can do aught with our Sovereign, or whether, in very deed, my meddling in your affair may not rather prejudice than serve you.'

Thus spoke Sussex, while hastily casting around him a loose robe of sables, and adjusting his person in the best manner he could to meet the eye of his Sovereign. But no hurried attention bestowed on his apparel could remove the ghastly effects of long illness on a countenance which nature had marked with features rather strong than pleasing. Besides, he was low of stature, and though broad-shouldered, athletic, and fit for martial achievements, his presence in a peaceful hall was not such as ladies love to look upon; a personal disadvantage, which was supposed to give Sussex, though esteemed and honoured by his Sovereign, considerable disadvantage when compared with Leicester, who was alike remarkable for elegance of manners, and for beauty of person.

The Earl's utmost despatch only enabled him to meet the Queen as she entered the great hall, and he at once perceived there was a cloud on her brow. Her jealous eye had noticed the martial array of armed gentlemen and retainers with which the mansion-house was filled, and her first words expressed her disapprobation—'Is this a royal garrison, my Lord of Sussex, that it holds so many pikes and calivers? or have we by accident overshot Say's Court, and landed at our Tower of London?'

Lord Sussex hastened to offer some apology.

'It needs not,' she said. 'My lord, we intend speedily to take up a certain quarrel between your lordship and another great lord of our household, and at the same time to reprehend this uncivilised and dangerous practice of surrounding yourselves with armed, and even with ruffianly followers, as if, in the neighbourhood of our capital, nay, in the very verge of our royal residence, you were preparing to wage civil war with each other. We are glad to see you so well recovered, my lord, though without the assistance of the learned physician whom we sent to you—Urge no excuse— we know how that matter fell out, and we have corrected for it the wild slip, young Raleigh. By the way, my lord, we will speedily relieve your household of him, and take him into our own. Something there is about him which merits to be better nurtured than he is like to be amongst your very military followers.'

To this proposal Sussex, though scarce understanding how the Queen came to make it, could only bow and express his acquiescence. He then entreated her to remain till refreshment could be offered, but in this he could not prevail. And, after a few compliments of a much colder and more commonplace character than might have been expected from a step so decidedly favourable as a personal visit, the Queen took her leave of Say's Court, having brought confusion thither along with her, and leaving doubt and apprehension behind.

16

> Then call them to our presence. Face to face,
> And frowning brow to brow, ourselves will hear
> The accuser and accused freely speak;—
> High-stomach'd are they both and full of ire,
> In rage deaf as the sea, hasty as fire.—*Richard II.*

'I AM ordered to attend court to-morrow,' said Leicester, speaking to Varney, 'to meet, as they surmise, my Lord of Sussex. The Queen intends to take up matters betwixt us. This comes of her visit to Say's Court, of which you must needs speak so lightly.'

'I maintain it was nothing,' said Varney; 'nay, I know from a sure intelligencer, who was within ear-shot of much that was said, that Sussex has lost rather than gained by that visit. The Queen said, when she stepped into the boat, that Say's Court looked like a guard-house, and smelt like an hospital. "Like a cook's shop in Ram's Alley rather," said the Countess of Rutland, who is ever your lordship's good friend. And then my Lord of Lincoln must needs put in his holy oar, and say that my Lord of Sussex must be excused for his rude and old-world house-keeping, since he had as yet no wife.'

'And what said the Queen?' said Leicester hastily.

'She took him up roundly,' said Varney, 'and asked what my Lord Sussex had to do with a wife, or my Lord Bishop to speak on such a subject. If marriage is permitted, she said, I nowhere read that it is enjoined.'

'She likes not marriages, or speech of marriage, among churchmen,' said Leicester.

'Nor among courtiers neither,' said Varney; but, observing that Leicester changed countenance, he instantly added, that all the ladies who were present had joined in ridiculing Lord Sussex's house-keeping, and in contrasting it with the reception her Grace would have assuredly received at my Lord of Leicester's.

'You have gathered much tidings,' said Leicester, 'but you have forgotten or omitted the most important of all. She hath added another to those dangling satellites, whom it is her pleasure to keep revolving around her.'

'Your lordship meaneth that Raleigh, the Devonshire youth,' said Varney, 'the Knight of the Cloak, as they call him at the court?'

'He may be Knight of the Garter one day, for aught I know,' said Leicester, 'for he advances rapidly—She hath capped verses with him, and such fooleries. I would gladly abandon, of my own free will, the part I have in her fickle favour, but I will not be elbowed out of it by the clown Sussex, or this new upstart. I hear Tressilian is with Sussex also, and high in his favour—I would spare him for considerations, but he will thrust himself on his fate—Sussex, too, is almost as well as ever in his health.'

'My lord,' replied Varney, 'there will be rubs in the smoothest road, specially when it leads up hill. Sussex's illness was to us a god-send, from which I hoped much. He has recovered indeed, but he is not now more formidable than ere he fell ill, when he received more than one foil in wrestling with your lordship. Let not your heart fail you, my lord, and all shall be well.'

'My heart never failed me, sir,' replied Leicester.

'No, my lord,' said Varney; 'but it has betrayed you right often. He that would climb a tree, my lord, must grasp by the branches, not by the blossom.'

'Well, well, well!' said Leicester impatiently; 'I understand thy meaning—My heart shall neither fail me nor seduce me. Have my retinue in order—see that their array be so splendid as to put down, not only the rude companions of Ratcliffe, but the retainers of every other nobleman and courtier. Let them be well armed withal, but without any outward display of their weapons, wearing them as if more for fashion's sake than for use. Do thou thyself keep close to me, I may have business for you.'

The preparations of Sussex and his party were not less anxious than those of Leicester.

'Thy Supplication, impeaching Varney of seduction,' said the Earl to Tressilian, 'is by this time in the Queen's hand—I have sent it through a sure channel. Methinks your suit should succeed, being, as it is, founded in justice and honour, and Elizabeth being the very muster of both. But I wot not how—the gipsy' (so Sussex was wont to call his rival on account of his dark complexion) 'hath much to say with her in these holiday times of peace—Were war at the gates, I should be one of her white boys; but soldiers, like their bucklers and Bilboa blades, get out of fashion in peace time, and satin sleeves and walking rapiers bear the bell. Well, we must be gay since such is the fashion. Blount, hast thou seen our household put into their new braveries? But thou know'st as little of these toys as I do—thou wouldst be ready enough at disposing a stand of pikes.'

'My good lord,' answered Blount, 'Raleigh hath been here, and taken that charge upon him. Your train will glitter like a May morning. Marry, the cost is another question. One might keep an hospital of old soldiers at the charge of ten modern lackeys.'

'We must not count cost to-day, Nicholas,' said the Earl, in reply; 'I am beholden to Raleigh for his care—I trust though, he has remembered that I am an old soldier, and would have no more of these follies than needs must.'

'Nay, I understand naught about it,' said Blount; 'but here are your honourable lordship's brave kinsmen and friends coming in by scores to wait upon you to court, where, methinks, we shall bear as brave a front as Leicester, let him ruffle it as he will.'

'Give them the strictest charges,' said Sussex, 'that they suffer no provocation short of actual violence to provoke them into quarrel—they have hot bloods, and I would not give Leicester the advantage over me by any imprudence of theirs.'

The Earl of Sussex ran so hastily through these directions, that it was with difficulty Tressilian at length found opportunity to express his surprise that he should have proceeded so far in the affair of Sir Hugh Robsart as to lay his petition at once before the Queen—'It was the opinion of the young lady's friends,' he said, 'that Leicester's sense of justice should be first appealed to, as the offence had been committed by his officer; and so he had expressly told to Sussex.'

'This could have been done without applying to me,' said Sussex, somewhat haughtily. '*I*, at least, ought not to have been a counsellor when the object was a humiliating reference to Leicester; and I am surprised that you, Tressilian, a man of honour, and my friend, would assume such a mean course. If you said so, I certainly understood you not in a matter which sounded so unlike yourself.'

'My lord,' said Tressilian, 'the course I would prefer, for my own sake, is that you have adopted; but the friends of this most unhappy lady——'

'Oh, the friends—the friends,' said Sussex, interrupting him; 'they must let us manage this cause in the way which seems best. This is the time and the hour to accumulate every charge against

Leicester and his household, and yours the Queen will hold a heavy one. But at all events she hath the complaint before her.'

Tressilian could not help suspecting that, in his eagerness to strengthen himself against his rival, Sussex had purposely adopted the course most likely to throw odium on Leicester, without considering minutely whether it were the mode of proceeding most likely to be attended with success. But the step was irrevocable, and Sussex escaped from further discussing it by dismissing his company, with the command, 'Let all be in order at eleven o'clock; I must be at court and in the presence by high noon precisely.'

While the rival statesmen were thus anxiously preparing for their approaching meeting in the Queen's presence, even Elizabeth herself was not without apprehension of what might chance from the collision of two such fiery spirits, each backed by a strong and numerous body of followers, and dividing betwixt them, either openly or in secret, the hopes and wishes of most of her court. The band of Gentlemen Pensioners were all under arms, and a reinforcement of the Yeomen of the Guard was brought down the Thames from London. A royal proclamation was sent forth, strictly prohibiting nobles of whatever degree, to approach the Palace with retainers or followers, armed with shot, or with long weapons; and it was even whispered, that the High Sheriff of Kent had secret instructions to have a part of the array of the county ready on the shortest notice.

The eventful hour, thus anxiously prepared for on all sides, at length approached, and, each followed by his long and glittering train of friends and followers, the rival Earls entered the Palace-yard of Greenwich at noon precisely.

As if by previous arrangement, or perhaps by intimation that such was the Queen's pleasure, Sussex and his retinue came to the Palace from Deptford by water, while Leicester arrived by land; and thus they entered the courtyard from opposite sides. This trifling circumstance gave Leicester a certain ascendancy in the opinion of the vulgar, the appearance of his cavalcade of mounted followers showing more numerous and more imposing than those of Sussex's party, who were necessarily upon foot. No show or sign of greeting passed between the Earls, though each looked full at the other, both expecting perhaps an exchange of courtesies, which neither was willing to commence. Almost in the minute of their arrival the castle-bell tolled, the gates of the Palace were opened, and the Earls entered, each numerously attended by such gentlemen of their train whose rank gave them that privilege. The yeomen and inferior attendants remained in the courtyard, where the opposite parties eyed each other with looks of eager hatred and scorn, as if waiting with impatience for some cause of tumult, or some apology for mutual aggression. But they were restrained by the strict commands of their leaders, and overawed, perhaps, by the presence of an armed guard of unusual strength.

In the meanwhile, the more distinguished persons of each train followed their patrons into the lofty halls and antechambers of the royal Palace, flowing on in the same current, like two streams which are compelled into the same channel, yet shun to mix their waters. The parties arranged themselves, as it were instinctively, on the different sides of the lofty apartments, and seemed eager to escape from the transient union which the narrowness of the crowded entrance had for an instant compelled them to submit to. The folding doors at the upper end of the long gallery were immediately afterwards opened, and it was announced in a whisper that the Queen was in her presence-chamber, to which these gave access. Both Earls moved slowly and stately towards the entrance; Sussex followed by Tressilian, Blount, and Raleigh, and Leicester by Varney. The pride of Leicester was obliged to give way to court-forms, and with a grave and formal inclination of the head, he paused until his rival, a peer of older creation than his own, passed before him. Sussex returned the reverence with the same formal civility, and entered the presence-room. Tressilian and Blount offered to follow him, but were not permitted, the Usher of the Black Rod alleging in excuse, that he had precise orders to look to all admissions that day. To Raleigh, who stood back on the repulse of his companions, he said, 'You, sir, may enter,' and he entered accordingly.

'Follow me close, Varney,' said the Earl of Leicester, who had stood aloof for a moment to mark the reception of Sussex; and, advancing to the entrance, he was about to pass on, when Varney, who was close behind him, dressed out in the utmost bravery of the day, was stopped by the usher, as Tressilian and Blount had been before him. 'How is this, Master Bowyer?' said the Earl of Leicester; 'Know you who I am, and that this is my friend and follower?'

'Your lordship will pardon me,' replied Bowyer stoutly, 'my orders are precise, and limit me to a strict discharge of my duty.'

'Thou art a partial knave,' said Leicester, the blood mounting to his face, 'to do me this dishonour, when you but now admitted a follower of my Lord of Sussex.'

'My lord,' said Bowyer, 'Master Raleigh is newly admitted a sworn servant of her Grace, and to him my orders do not apply.'

'Thou art a knave—an ungrateful knave,' said Leicester; 'but he that hath done, can undo—thou shalt not prank thee in thy authority long!'

This threat he uttered aloud, with less than his usual policy and discretion, and having done so, he entered the presence-chamber, and made his reverence to the Queen, who, attired with even more than her usual splendour, and surrounded by those nobles and statesmen whose courage and wisdom have rendered her reign immortal, stood ready to receive the homage of her subjects. She graciously returned the obeisance of the favourite Earl, and looked alternately at him and at Sussex, as if about to speak, when Bowyer, a man whose spirit could not brook the insult he had so openly received from Leicester, in the discharge of his office, advanced with his black rod in his hand, and knelt down before her.

'Why, how now, Bowyer,' said Elizabeth, 'thy courtesy seems strangely timed!'

'My Liege Sovereign,' he said, while every courtier around trembled at his audacity, 'I come but to ask, whether, in the discharge of mine office, I am to obey your Highness's commands, or those of the Earl of Leicester, who has publicly menaced me with his displeasure, and treated me with disparaging terms, because I denied entry to one of his followers, in obedience to your Grace's precise orders?'

The spirit of Henry the Eighth was instantly aroused in the bosom of his daughter, and she turned on Leicester with a severity which appalled him, as well as all his followers.

'God's death, my lord,' such was her emphatic phrase, 'what means this? We have thought well of you, and brought you near to our person; but it was not that you might hide the sun from our other faithful subjects. Who gave you licence to contradict our orders, or control our officers? I will have in this court, ay, and in this realm, but one mistress, and no master. Look to it that Master Bowyer sustains no harm for his duty to me faithfully discharged; for, as I am Christian woman and crowned Queen, I will hold you dearly answerable. Go, Bowyer, you have done the part of an honest man and a true subject. We will brook no mayor of the Palace here.'

Bowyer kissed the hand which she extended towards him, and withdrew to his post, astonished at the success of his own audacity. A smile of triumph pervaded the faction of Sussex; that of Leicester seemed proportionally dismayed, and the favourite himself, assuming an aspect of the deepest humility, did not even attempt a word in his own exculpation.

He acted wisely; for it was the policy of Elizabeth to humble, not to disgrace him, and it was prudent to suffer her, without opposition or reply, to glory in the exertion of her authority. The dignity of the queen was gratified, and the woman began soon to feel for the mortification which she had imposed on her favourite. Her keen eye also observed the secret looks of congratulation exchanged amongst those who favoured Sussex, and it was no part of her policy to give either party a decisive triumph.

'What I say to my Lord of Leicester,' she said, after a moment's pause, 'I say also to you, my Lord of Sussex. You also must needs ruffle in the court of England, at the head of a faction of your own?'

'My followers, gracious Princess,' said Sussex, 'have indeed ruffled in your cause, in Ireland, in Scotland, and against yonder rebellious Earls in the north. I am ignorant that——'

'Do you bandy looks and words with me, my lord?' said the Queen, interrupting him; 'methinks you might learn of my Lord of Leicester the modesty to be silent, at least, under our censure. I say, my lord, that my grandfather and my father, in their wisdom, debarred the nobles of this civilised land from travelling with such disorderly retinues; and think you, that because I wear a coif, their sceptre has in my hand been changed into a distaff? I tell you, no king in Christendom will less brook his court to be cumbered, his people oppressed, and his kingdom's peace disturbed by the arrogance of over-grown power, than she who now speaks with you. My Lord of Leicester, and you, my Lord of Sussex, I command you both to be friends with each other; or, by the crown I wear, you shall find an enemy who will be too strong for both of you.'

'Madam,' said the Earl of Leicester, 'you, who are yourself the fountain of honour, know best what is due to mine. I place it at your disposal, and only say, that the terms on which I have stood with my Lord of Sussex have not been of my seeking; nor had he cause to think me his enemy, until he had done me gross wrong.'

'For me, Madam,' said the Earl of Sussex, 'I cannot appeal from your sovereign pleasure; but I were well content my Lord of Leicester should say in what I have, as he terms it, wronged him, since my tongue never spoke the word that I would not willingly justify either on foot or horseback.'

'And for me,' said Leicester, 'always under my gracious Sovereign's pleasure, my hand shall be as ready to make good my words, as that of any man who ever wrote himself Ratcliffe.'

'My lords,' said the Queen, 'these are no terms for this presence; and if you cannot keep your temper, we will find means to keep both that and you close enough. Let me see you join hands, my lords, and forget your idle animosities.'

The two rivals looked at each other with reluctant eyes, each unwilling to make the first advance to execute the Queen's will.

'Sussex,' said Elizabeth, 'I entreat—Leicester, I command you.'

Yet, so were the words accented, that the entreaty sounded like command, and the command like entreaty. They remained still and stubborn, until she raised her voice to a height which argued at once impatience and absolute command.

'Sir Henry Lee,' she said, to an officer in attendance, 'have a guard in present readiness, and man a barge instantly. My Lords of Sussex and Leicester, I bid you once more to join hands—and, God's death! he that refuses shall taste of our Tower fare ere he see our face again. I will lower your proud hearts ere we part, and that I promise, on the word of a Queen.'

'The prison,' said Leicester, 'might be borne, but to lose your Grace's presence, were to lose light and life at once. Here, Sussex, is my hand.'

'And here,' said Sussex, 'is mine, in truth and honesty; but——'

'Nay, under favour, you shall add no more,' said the Queen. 'Why, this is as it should be,' she added, looking on them more favourably, 'and when you, the shepherds of the people, unite to protect them, it shall be well with the flock we rule over. For, my lords, I tell you plainly, your follies and your brawls lead to strange disorders among your servants. My Lord of Leicester, you have a gentleman in your household, called Varney?'

'Yes, gracious Madam,' replied Leicester, 'I presented him to kiss your royal hand when you were last at Nonsuch.'

'His outside was well enough,' said the Queen, 'but scarce so fair, I should have thought, as to have caused a maiden of honourable birth and hopes to barter her fame for his good looks, and become his paramour. Yet so it is—this fellow of yours hath seduced the daughter of a good old Devonshire knight, Sir Hugh Robsart of Lidcote Hall, and she hath fled with him from her father's house like a castaway. My Lord of Leicester, are you ill, that you look so deadly pale?'

'No, gracious Madam,' said Leicester; and it required every effort he could make to bring forth these few words.

'You are surely ill, my lord?' said Elizabeth, going towards him with hasty speech and hurried step, which indicated the deepest concern. 'Call Masters—call our surgeon in ordinary. Where be these loitering fools? We lose the pride of our court through their negligence. Or is it possible, Leicester,' she continued, looking on him with a very gentle aspect, 'can fear of my displeasure have wrought so deeply on thee? Doubt not for a moment, noble Dudley, that we could blame *thee* for the folly of thy retainer—thee, whose thoughts we know to be far otherwise employed! He that would climb the eagle's nest, my lord, cares not who are catching linnets at the foot of the precipice.'

'Mark you that?' said Sussex, aside to Raleigh. 'The devil aids him surely; for all that would sink another ten fathom deep, seems but to make him float the more easily. Had a follower of mine acted thus——'

'Peace, my good lord,' said Raleigh, 'for God's sake, peace. Wait the change of the tide: it is even now on the turn.'

The acute observation of Raleigh, perhaps, did not deceive him; for Leicester's confusion was so great, and, indeed, for the moment, so irresistibly overwhelming, that Elizabeth, after looking at him with a wondering eye, and receiving no intelligible answer to the unusual expressions of grace and affection which had escaped from her, shot her quick glance around the circle of courtiers, and reading, perhaps, in their faces, something that accorded with her own awakened suspicions, she said suddenly, 'Or is there more in this than we see?—or than you, my lord, wish that we should see? Where is this Varney? Who saw him?'

'An it please your Grace,' said Bowyer, 'it is the same against whom I this instant closed the door of the presence-room.'

'An it please me?' repeated Elizabeth sharply, not at that moment in the humour of being pleased with anything, 'It does *not* please me that he should pass saucily into my presence, or that you should exclude from it one who came to justify himself from an accusation.'

'May it please you,' answered the perplexed usher, 'if I knew, in such case, how to bear myself, I would take heed——'

'You should have reported the fellow's desire to us, Master Usher, and taken our directions. You think yourself a great man, because but now we chid a nobleman on your account—yet, after all, we hold you but as the lead-weight that keeps the door fast. Call this Varney hither instantly—there is one Tressilian also mentioned in this petition—let them both come before us.'

She was obeyed, and Tressilian and Varney appeared accordingly. Varney's first glance was at Leicester, his second at the Queen. In the looks of the latter, there appeared an approaching storm, and in the downcast countenance of his patron, he could read no directions in what way he was to trim his vessel for the encounter —he then saw Tressilian, and at once perceived the peril of the situation in which he was placed. But Varney was as bold-faced and ready-witted as he was cunning and unscrupulous—a skilful pilot in extremity, and fully conscious of the advantages which he would obtain, could he extricate Leicester from his present peril, and of the ruin that yawned for himself, should he fail in doing so.

'Is it true, sirrah,' said the Queen, with one of those searching looks which few had the audacity to resist, 'that you have seduced to infamy a young lady of birth and breeding, the daughter of Sir Hugh Robsart of Lidcote Hall?'

Varney kneeled down, and replied, with a look of the most profound contrition, 'There had been some love-passages betwixt him and Mistress Amy Robsart.'

Leicester's flesh quivered with indignation as he heard his dependant make this avowal, and, for one moment, he manned himself to step forward, and, bidding farewell to the court and the royal favour, confess the whole mystery of his secret marriage. But he looked at Sussex, and the idea of the triumphant smile which would clothe his cheek upon hearing the avowal, sealed his lips. 'Not now, at least,' he thought, 'or in this presence, will I afford him so rich a triumph.' And pressing his lips close together, he stood firm and collected, attentive to each word which Varney uttered, and determined to hide to the last the secret on which his court favour seemed to depend. Meanwhile, the Queen proceeded in her examination of Varney.

'Love passages!' said she, echoing his last words; 'what passages, thou knave? and why not ask the wench's hand from her father, if thou hadst any honesty in thy love for her?'

'An it please your Grace,' said Varney, still on his knees, 'I dared not do so, for her father had promised her hand to a gentleman of birth and honour—I will do him justice, though I know he bears me ill will—one Master Edmund Tressilian, whom I now see in the presence.'

'So!' replied the Queen; 'and what was your right to make the simple fool break her worthy father's contract, through your love *passages*, as your conceit and assurance terms them?'

'Madam,' replied Varney, 'it is in vain to plead the cause of human frailty before a judge to whom it is unknown, or that of love, to one who never yields to the passion'—He paused an instant, and then added, in a very low and timid tone, 'which she inflicts upon all others.'

Elizabeth tried to frown, but smiled in her own despite, as she answered, 'Thou art a marvellously impudent knave—Art thou married to the girl?'

Leicester's feelings became so complicated and so painfully intense, that it seemed to him as if his life was to depend on the answer made by Varney, who, after a moment's real hesitation, answered, 'Yes.'

'Thou false villain!' said Leicester, bursting forth into rage, yet unable to add another word to the sentence, which he had begun with such emphatic passion.

'Nay, my lord,' said the Queen, 'we will, by your leave, stand between this fellow and your anger. We have not yet done with him. Knew your master, my Lord of Leicester, of this fair work of yours? Speak truth, I command thee, and I will be thy warrant from danger on every quarter.'

'Gracious Madam,' said Varney, 'to speak Heaven's truth, my lord was the cause of the whole matter.'

'Thou villain, wouldst thou betray me?' said Leicester.

'Speak on,' said the Queen hastily, her cheek colouring, and her eyes sparkling, as she addressed Varney; 'speak on—here no commands are heard but mine.'

'They are omnipotent, gracious Madam,' replied Varney; 'and to you there can be no secrets. Yet I would not,' he added, looking around him, 'speak of my master's concerns to other ears.'

'Fall back, my lords,' said the Queen to those who surrounded her, 'and do you speak on. What hath the Earl to do with this guilty intrigue of thine? See, fellow, that thou beliest him not.'

'Far be it from me to traduce my noble patron,' replied Varney; 'yet I am compelled to own that some deep, overwhelming, yet secret feeling, hath of late dwelt in my lord's mind, hath abstracted him from the cares of the household, which he was wont to govern with such religious strictness, and he hath left us opportunities to do follies, of which the shame, as in this case, partly falls upon our patron. Without this, I had not had means or leisure to commit the folly which has drawn on me his displeasure; the heaviest to endure by me, which I could by any means incur,— saving always the yet more dreaded resentment of your Grace.'

'And in this sense, and no other, hath he been accessory to thy fault?' said Elizabeth.

'Surely, Madam, in no other,' replied Varney; 'but since somewhat hath chanced to him, he can scarce be called his own man. Look at him, Madam, how pale and trembling he stands—how unlike his usual majesty of manner—yet what has he to fear from aught I can say to your Highness? Ah! Madam, since he received that fatal packet!'

'What packet, and from whence?' said the Queen eagerly.

'From whence, Madam, I cannot guess; but I am so near to his person, that I know he has ever since worn, suspended around his neck, and next to his heart, that lock of hair which sustains a small golden jewel shaped like a heart—he speaks to it when alone—he parts not from it when he sleeps—no heathen ever worshipped an idol with such devotion.'

'Thou art a prying knave to watch thy master so closely,' said Elizabeth, blushing, but not with anger; 'and a tattling knave to tell over again his fooleries. What colour might the braid of hair be that thou pratest of?'

Varney replied, 'A poet, Madam, might call it a thread from the golden web wrought by Minerva; but, to my thinking, it was paler than even the purest gold—more like the last parting sunbeam of the softest day of spring.'

'Why, you are a poet yourself, Master Varney,' said the Queen, smiling; 'but I have not genius quick enough to follow your rare metaphors—Look round these ladies—is there—(she hesitated, and endeavoured to assume an air of great indifference)—is there

here, in this presence, any lady, the colour of whose hair reminds thee of that braid? Methinks, without prying into my Lord of Leicester's amorous secrets, I would fain know what kind of locks are like the thread of Minerva's web, or the—what was it?—the last rays of the May-day sun.'

Varney looked round the presence-chamber, his eye travelling from one lady to another, until at length it rested upon the Queen herself, but with an aspect of the deepest veneration. 'I see no tresses,' he said, 'in this presence worthy of such similes, unless where I dare not look on them.'

'How, sir knave,' said the Queen, 'dare you intimate—'

'Nay, Madam,' replied Varney, shading his eyes with his hand, 'it was the beams of the May-day sun that dazzled my weak eyes.'

'Go to—go to,' said the Queen; 'thou art a foolish fellow'—and turning quickly from him she walked up to Leicester.

Intense curiosity, mingled with all the various hopes, fears, and passions which influence court-faction, had occupied the presence-chamber during the Queen's conference with Varney, as if with the strength of an eastern talisman. Men suspended every, even the slightest, external motion, and would have ceased to breathe, had Nature permitted such an intermission of her functions. The atmosphere was contagious, and Leicester, who saw all around wishing or fearing his advancement or his fall, forgot all that love had previously dictated, and saw nothing for the instant but the favour or disgrace which depended on the nod of Elizabeth and the fidelity of Varney. He summoned himself hastily, and prepared to play his part in the scene which was like to ensue, when, as he judged from the glances which the Queen threw towards him, Varney's communications, be they what they might, were operating in his favour. Elizabeth did not long leave him in doubt; for the more than favour with which she accosted him decided his triumph in the eyes of his rival, and of the assembled court of England—'Thou hast a prating servant of this same Varney, my lord,' she said; 'it is lucky you trust him with nothing that can hurt you in our opinion, for, believe me, he would keep no counsel.'

'From your Highness,' said Leicester, dropping gracefully on one knee, 'it were treason he should. I would that my heart itself lay before you, barer than the tongue of any servant could strip it.'

'What, my lord,' said Elizabeth, looking kindly upon him, 'is there no one little corner over which you would wish to spread a veil? Ah! I see you are confused at the question, and your Queen knows she should not look too deeply into her servants' motives for their faithful duty, lest she see what might, or at least ought, to displease her.'

Relieved by these last words, Leicester broke out into a torrent of expressions of deep and passionate attachment, which perhaps, at that moment, were not altogether fictitious. The mingled emotions which had at first overcome him, had now given way to the energetic vigour with which he had determined to support his place in the Queen's favour; and never did he seem to Elizabeth more eloquent, more handsome, more interesting, than while, kneeling at her feet, he conjured her to strip him of all his power, but to leave him the name of her servant—'Take from the poor Dudley,' he exclaimed, 'all that your bounty has made him, and bid him be the poor gentleman he was when your grace first shone on him; leave him no more than his cloak and his sword, but let him still boast he has—what in word or deed he never forfeited—the regard of his adored Queen and mistress!'

'No, Dudley!' said Elizabeth, raising him with one hand, while she extended the other that he might kiss it; 'Elizabeth hath not forgotten that, whilst you were a poor gentleman, despoiled of your hereditary rank, she was as poor a princess, and that in her cause you then ventured all that oppression had left you—your life and honour. Rise, my lord, and let my hand go! Rise, and be what you have ever been, the grace of our court, and the support of our throne. Your mistress may be forced to chide your misdemeanours, but never without owning your merits. And so help me God,' she added, turning to the audience, who, with various feelings, witnessed this interesting scene,—'So help me God, gentlemen, as I think never sovereign had a truer servant than I have in this noble Earl.'

A murmur of assent rose from the Leicesterian faction, which the friends of Sussex dared not oppose. They remained with their eyes fixed on the ground, dismayed as well as mortified by the public and absolute triumph of their opponents. Leicester's first use of the familiarity to which the Queen had so publicly restored him, was to ask her commands concerning Varney's offence. 'Although,' he said, 'the fellow deserves nothing from me but displeasure, yet, might I presume to intercede'——

'In truth, we had forgotten his matter,' said the Queen; 'and it was ill done of us, who owe justice to our meanest, as well as to our highest subject. We are pleased, my lord, that you were the first to recall the matter to our memory.—Where is Tressilian, the accuser?—let him come before us.'

Tressilian appeared, and made a low and beseeming reverence. His person, as we have elsewhere observed, had an air of grace and even of nobleness, which did not escape Queen Elizabeth's critical observation. She looked at him with attention as he stood before her unabashed, but with an air of the deepest dejection.

'I cannot but grieve for this gentleman,' she said to Leicester. 'I have inquired concerning him, and his presence confirms what I heard, that he is a scholar and a soldier, well accomplished both in arts and arms. We women, my lord, are fanciful in our choice— I had said now, to judge by the eye, there was no comparison to be held betwixt your follower and this gentleman. But Varney is a well-spoken fellow, and to say truth, that goes far with us of the weaker sex. Look you, Master Tressilian, a bolt lost is not a bow broken. Your true affection, as I will hold it to be, hath been, it seems, but ill requited; but you have scholarship, and you know there have been false Cressidas to be found, from the Trojan war downwards. Forget, good sir, this Lady Light-o'-Love—teach your affection to see with a wiser eye. This we say to you, more from the writings of learned men, than our own knowledge, being, as we are, far removed by station and will, from the enlargement of experience in such idle toys of humorous passion. For this dame's father, we can make his grief the less, by advancing his son-in-law to such station as may enable him to give an honourable support to his bride. Thou shalt not be forgotten thyself, Tressilian —follow our court, and thou shalt see that a true Troilus hath some claim on our grace. Think of what that arch-knave Shakespeare says—a plague on him, his toys come into my head when I should think of other matter—Stay, how goes it?

> 'Cressid was yours, tied with the bonds of heaven;
> These bonds of heaven are slipt, dissolved, and loosed,
> And with another knot five fingers tied,
> The fragments of her faith are bound to Diomed.'

You smile, my Lord of Southampton—perchance I make your player's verse halt through my bad memory—but let it suffice— let there be no more of this mad matter.'

And as Tressilian kept the posture of one who would willingly be heard, though, at the same time, expressive of the deepest reverence, the Queen added, with some impatience,—'What would the man have? The wench cannot wed both of you?—She has made her election—not a wise one perchance—but she is Varney's wedded wife.'

'My suit should sleep there, most gracious Sovereign,' said Tressilian, 'and with my suit my revenge. But I hold this Varney's word no good warrant for the truth.'

'Had that doubt been elsewhere urged,' answered Varney, 'my sword'——

'*Thy* sword!' interrupted Tressilian, scornfully; 'with her Grace's leave, my sword shall show'——

'Peace, you knaves both,' said the Queen; 'know you where you are? This comes of your feuds, my lords,' she added, looking towards Leicester and Sussex; 'your followers catch your own humour, and must bandy and brawl in my court, and in my very presence, like so many Matamoros. Look you, sirs, he that speaks of drawing swords in any other quarrel than mine or England's, by mine honour, I'll bracelet him with iron both on wrist and ankle!' She then paused a minute, and resumed in a milder tone, 'I must do justice betwixt the bold and mutinous knaves notwithstanding. My Lord of Leicester, will you warrant with your honour,—that is, to the best of your belief,—that your servant speaks truth in saying he hath married this Amy Robsart?'

This was a home-thrust, and had nearly staggered Leicester. But he had now gone too far to recede, and answered, after a moment's hesitation. 'To the best of my belief—indeed on my certain knowledge—she is a wedded wife.'

'Gracious Madam,' said Tressilian, 'may I yet request to know, when and under what circumstances this alleged marriage——'

'Out, sirrah,' answered the Queen; '*alleged* marriage!—Have you not the word of this illustrious Earl to warrant the truth of what his servant says? But thou art a loser—think'st thyself such at least—and thou shalt have indulgence—we will look into the matter ourself more at leisure. My Lord of Leicester, I trust you remember we mean to taste the good cheer of your Castle of Kenilworth, on this week ensuing—we will pray you to bid our good and valued friend the Earl of Sussex to hold company with us there.'

'If the noble Earl of Sussex,' said Leicester, bowing to his rival with the easiest and with the most graceful courtesy, 'will so far honour my poor house, I will hold it an additional proof of the amicable regard it is your Grace's desire we should entertain towards each other.'

Sussex was more embarrassed—'I should,' said he, 'Madam, but be a clog on your gayer hours since my late severe illness.'

'And have you been indeed so very ill?' said Elizabeth, looking on him with more attention than before; 'you are in faith strangely altered, and deeply am I grieved to see it. But be of good cheer— we will ourselves look after the health of so valued a servant, and to whom we owe so much. Masters shall order your diet; and that we ourselves may see that he is obeyed, you must attend us in this progress to Kenilworth.'

This was said so peremptorily, and at the same time with so much kindness, that Sussex, however unwilling to become the guest of his rival, had no resource but to bow low to the Queen in obedience to her commands, and to express to Leicester, with blunt courtesy, though mingled with embarrassment, his acceptance of his invitation. As the Earls exchanged compliments on the occasion, the Queen said to her High Treasurer, 'Methinks, my lord, the countenances of these our two noble peers resemble that of the two famed classic streams, the one so dark and sad, the other so fair and noble—My old Master Ascham would have chid me for forgetting the author—It is Cæsar, as I think. See what majestic calmness sits on the brow of the noble Leicester, while Sussex seems to greet him as if he did our will indeed, but not willingly.'

'The doubt of your Majesty's favour,' answered the Lord Treasurer, 'may perchance occasion the difference, which does not—as what does?—escape your Grace's eye.'

'Such doubt were injurious to us, my lord,' replied the Queen. 'We hold both to be near and dear to us, and will with impartiality employ both in honourable service for the weal of our kingdom. But we will break their further conference at present. My Lords of Sussex and Leicester, we have a word more with you. Tressilian and Varney are near your persons—you will see that they attend you at Kenilworth—And as we shall then have both Paris and Menelaus within our call, so we will have this same fair Helen also, whose fickleness has caused this broil. Varney, thy wife must be at

Kenilworth, and forthcoming at my order. My Lord of Leicester, we expect you will look to this.'

The Earl and his follower bowed low, and raised their heads, without daring to look at the Queen, or at each other; for both felt at the same instant as if the nets and toils which their own falsehood had woven, were in the act of closing around them. The Queen, however, observed not their confusion, but proceeded to say, 'My Lords of Sussex and Leicester, we require your presence at the privy-council to be presently held, where matters of importance are to be debated. We will then take the water for our divertisement, and you, my lords, will attend us. And that reminds us of a circumstance—Do you, Sir Squire of the Soiled Cassock' (distinguishing Raleigh by a smile), 'fail not to observe that you are to attend us on our progress. You shall be supplied with suitable means to reform your wardrobe.'

And so terminated the celebrated audience, in which, as throughout her life, Elizabeth united the occasional caprice of her sex, with that sense and sound policy, in which neither man nor woman ever excelled her.

17

> Well, then—our course is chosen—spread the sail—
> Heave oft the lead, and mark the soundings well—
> Look to the helm, good master—many a shoal
> Marks this stern coast, and rocks, where sits the Siren,
> Who, like ambition, lures men to their ruin.
>
> *The Shipwreck.*

DURING the brief interval that took place betwixt the dismissal of the audience and the sitting of the privy-council, Leicester had time to reflect that he had that morning sealed his own fate. 'It was impossible for him now,' he thought, 'after having, in the face of all that was honourable in England, pledged his truth (though in ambiguous phrase) for the statement of Varney, to contradict or disavow it, without exposing himself, not merely to the loss of court-favour, but to the highest displeasure of the Queen, his deceived mistress, and to the scorn and contempt at once of his rival and of all his compeers.' This certainly rushed at once on his mind, together with all the difficulties which he would necessarily be exposed to in preserving a secret, which seemed now equally essential to his safety, to his power, and to his honour. He was situated like one who walks upon ice, ready to give way around him, and whose only safety consists in moving onwards, by firm and unvacillating steps. The Queen's favour, to preserve which he had made such sacrifices, must now be secured by all means and at all hazards—it was the only plank which he could cling to in the tempest. He must settle himself, therefore, to the task of not only preserving, but augmenting the Queen's partiality—He must be the favourite of Elizabeth, or a man utterly shipwrecked in fortune and in honour. All other considerations must be laid aside for the moment, and he repelled the intrusive thoughts which forced on his mind the image of Amy, by saying to himself, there would be time to think hereafter how he was to escape from the labyrinth ultimately, since the pilot, who sees a Scylla under his bows, must not for the time think of the more distant dangers of Charybdis.

In this mood, the Earl of Leicester that day assumed his chair at the council-table of Elizabeth; and when the hours of business were over, in this same mood did he occupy an honoured place near her, during her pleasure excursion on the Thames. And never did he display to more advantage his powers as a politician of the first rank, or his parts as an accomplished courtier.

It chanced that in that day's council matters were agitated touching the affairs of the unfortunate Mary, the seventh year of whose captivity in England was now in doleful currency. There had been opinions in favour of this unhappy princess laid before Elizabeth's council, and supported with much strength of argument by Sussex and others, who dwelt more upon the law of nations and the breach of hospitality, than, however softened of qualified, was agreeable to the Queen's ear. Leicester adopted the contrary opinion with great animation and eloquence, and described the necessity of continuing the severe restraint of the Queen of Scots, as a measure essential to the safety of the kingdom, and particularly of Elizabeth's sacred person, the lightest hair of whose head, he maintained, ought, in their lordship's estimation, to be matter of more deep and anxious concern, than the life and fortunes of a rival, who, after setting up a vain and unjust pretence to the throne of England, was now, even while in the bosom of her country, the constant hope and theme of encouragement to all enemies to Elizabeth, whether at home or abroad. He ended by craving pardon of their lordships, if in the zeal of speech he had given any offence; but the Queen's safety was a theme which hurried him beyond his usual moderation of debate.

Elizabeth chid him, but not severely, for the weight which he attached unduly to her personal interests; yet she owned, that since it had been the pleasure of Heaven to combine those interests with the weal of her subjects, she did only her duty when she adopted such measures of self-preservation as circumstances forced upon her; and if the council in their wisdom should be of opinion, that it was needful to continue some restraint on the person of her unhappy sister of Scotland, she trusted they would not blame her if she requested of the Countess of Shrewsbury to use her with as much kindness as might be consistent with her safe keeping. And with this intimation of her pleasure, the council was dismissed.

Never was more anxious and ready way made for 'my Lord of Leicester,' than as he passed through the crowded ante-room to go towards the river-side, in order to attend her Majesty to her barge —Never was the voice of the ushers louder, to 'make room—make room for the noble Earl'—Never were these signals more promptly and reverentially obeyed—Never were more anxious eyes turned on him to obtain a glance of favour, or even of mere recognition, while the heart of many a humble follower throbbed betwixt the desire to offer his congratulations, and the fear of intruding himself on the notice of one so infinitely above him. The whole court considered the issue of this day's audience, expected with so much doubt and anxiety, as a decisive triumph on the part of Leicester, and felt assured that the orb of his rival satellite, if not altogether obscured by his lustre, must revolve hereafter in a dimmer and more distant sphere. So thought the court and courtiers, from high to low; and they acted accordingly.

On the other hand, never did Leicester return the general greeting with such ready and condescending courtesy, or endeavour more successfully to gather (in the words of one, who at that moment stood at no great distance from him) 'golden opinions from all sorts of men.'

For all the favourite Earl had a bow, a smile at least, and often a kind word. Most of these were addressed to courtiers, whose names have long gone down the tide of oblivion; but some, to such as sound strangely in our ears, when connected with the ordinary matters of human life, above which the gratitude of posterity has long elevated them. A few of Leicester's interlocutory sentences ran as follows:—

'Poynings, good morrow, and how does your wife and fair daughter? Why come they not to court?—Adams, your suit is naught—the Queen will grant no more monopolies but I may serve you in another matter.—My good Alderman Aylford, the suit of the City, affecting Queenhithe, shall be forwarded as far as my poor interest can serve.—Master Edmund Spenser, touching your Irish petition, I would willingly aid you, from my love to the muses; but thou hast nettled the Lord Treasurer.'

'My lord,' said the poet, 'were I permitted to explain——'

'Come to my lodging, Edmund,' answered the Earl—'not to-morrow, or next day, but soon.—Ha, Will Shakespeare—wild Will!—thou hast given my nephew, Philip Sidney, love-powder—he cannot sleep without thy Venus and Adonis under his pillow! We will have thee hanged for the veriest wizard in Europe. Hark thee, mad wag, I have not forgotten thy matter of the patent, and of the bears.'

The *player* bowed, and the Earl nodded and passed on—so that age would have told the tale—in ours, perhaps, we might say the immortal had done homage to the mortal. The next whom the favourite accosted, was one of his own zealous dependants.

'How now, Sir Francis Denning,' he whispered, in answer to his exulting salutation, 'that smile hath made they face shorter by one-third than when I first saw it this morning.—What, Master Bowyer, stand you back, and think you I bear malice? You did but your duty this morning; and, if I remember aught of the passage betwixt us, it shall be in thy favour.'

Then the Earl was approached, with several fantastic congees, by a person quaintly dressed in a doublet of black velvet, curiously slashed and pinked with crimson satin. A long cock's feather in the velvet bonnet, which he held in his hand, and an enormous ruff, stiffened to the extremity of the absurd taste of the times, joined with a sharp, lively, conceited expression of countenance, seemed to body forth a vain, harebrained coxcomb, and small wit; while the rod he held, and an assumption of formal authority, appeared to express some sense of official consequence, which qualified the natural pertness of his manner. A perpetual blush, which occupied rather the sharp nose than the thin cheek of this personage, seemed to speak more of 'good life,' as it was called, than of modesty; and the manner in which he approached the Earl confirmed that suspicion.

'Good-even to you, Master Robert Laneham,' said Leicester, and seemed desirous to pass forward, without further speech.

'I have a suit to your noble lordship,' said the figure, boldly following him.

'And what is it, good master keeper of the council-chamber door?'

'*Clerk* of the council-chamber door,' said Master Robert Laneham, with emphasis, by way of reply and of correction.

'Well, qualify thine office as thou wilt, man,' replied the Earl; 'what wouldst thou have with me?'

'Simply,' answered Laneham, 'that your lordship would be, as heretofore, my good lord, and procure me licence to attend the Summer Progress unto your lordship's most beautiful, and all-to-be unmatched Castle of Kenilworth.'

'To what purpose, good Master Laneham?' replied the Earl, 'bethink you my guests must needs be many.'

'Not so many,' replied the petitioner, 'but, that your nobleness will willingly spare your old servitor his crib and his mess. Bethink you, my lord, how necessary is this rod of mine, to fright away all those listeners, who else would play at bo-peep with the honourable council, and be searching for keyholes and crannies in the door of the chamber, so as to render my staff as needful as a fly-flap in a butcher's shop.'

'Methinks you have found out a fly-blown comparison for the honourable council, Master Laneham,' said the Earl; 'but seek not about to justify it. Come to Kenilworth, if you list; there will be store of fools there besides, and so you will be fitted.'

'Nay, and there be fools, my lord,' replied Laneham, with much glee, 'I warrant I will make sport among them; for no greyhound loves to cote a hare, as I to turn and course a fool. But I have another singular favour to beseech of your honour.'

'Speak it, and let me go,' said the Earl; 'I think the Queen comes forth instantly.'

'My very good lord, I would fain bring a bedfellow with me.'

'How, you irreverent rascal!' said Leicester.

'Nay, my lord, my meaning is within the canons,' answered his unblushing, or rather his ever-blushing petitioner. 'I have a wife as curious as her grandmother who ate the apple. Now, take her with me I may not, her Highness's orders being so strict against the officers bringing with them their wives in a progress, and so lumbering the court with womankind. But what I would crave of your lordship is, to find room for her in some mummery, or pretty pageant, in disguise, as it were; so that, not being known for my wife, there may be no offence.'

'The foul fiend seize ye both!' said Leicester, stung into uncontrollable passion by the recollections which this speech excited—'Why stop you me with such follies?'

The terrified clerk of the chamber-door, astonished at the burst of resentment he had so unconsciously produced, dropped his staff of office from his hand, and gazed on the incensed Earl with a foolish face of wonder and terror, which instantly recalled Leicester to himself.

'I meant but to try if thou hadst the audacity which befits thine office,' said he hastily. 'Come to Kenilworth, and bring the devil with thee, if thou wilt.'

'My wife, sir, hath played the devil ere now, in a Mystery, in Queen Mary's time—but we shall want a trifle for properties.'

'Here is a crown for thee,' said the Earl,—'make me rid of thee—the great bell rings.'

Master Robert Laneham stared a moment at the agitation which he had excited, and then said to himself, as he stooped to pick up his staff of office, 'The noble Earl runs wild humours to-day; but they who give crowns, expect us witty fellows to wink at their unsettled starts; and, by my faith, if they paid not for mercy, we would finger them tightly.' *

Leicester moved hastily on, neglecting the courtesies he had hitherto dispensed so liberally, and hurrying through the courtly crowd, until he paused in a small withdrawing-room, into which he plunged to draw a moment's breath unobserved, and in seclusion.

'What am I now,' he said to himself, 'that am thus jaded by the words of a mean, weather-beaten, goose-brained gull? Conscience, thou art a blood-hound, whose growl wakes as readily at the paltry stir of a rat or mouse, as at the step of a lion. Can I not quit myself by one bold stroke of a state so irksome, so unhonoured? What if I kneel to Elizabeth, and, owning the whole, throw myself on her mercy?'

As he pursued this train of thought, the door of the apartment opened, and Varney rushed in.

'Thank God, my lord, that I have found you,' was his exclamation.

'Thank the devil, whose agent thou art,' was the Earl's reply.

'Thank whom you will, my lord,' replied Varney; 'but hasten to the water-side. The Queen is on board, and asks for you.'

'Go, say I am taken suddenly ill,' replied Leicester, 'for, by Heaven, my brain can sustain this no longer.'

'I may well say so,' said Varney, with bitterness of expression; 'for your place, ay, and mine, who as your master of the horse was to have attended your lordship, is already filled up in the Queen's barge. The new minion, Walter Raleigh, and our old acquaintance, Tressilian, were called for, to fill our places just as I hastened away to seek you.'

'Thou art a devil, Varney,' said Leicester hastily; 'but thou hast the mastery for the present—I follow thee.'

Varney replied not, but led the way out of the Palace, and towards the river, while his master followed him, as if mechanically; until, looking back, he said in a tone which savoured of

* *Note F.* Robert Laneham.

familiarity at least, if not of authority, 'How is this, my lord?—your cloak hangs on one side,—your hose are unbraced—permit me——'

'Thou art a fool, Varney, as well as a knave,' said Leicester, shaking him off and rejecting his officious assistance; 'we are best thus, sir—when we require you to order our person, it is well, but now we want you not.'

So saying, the Earl resumed at once his air of command, and with it his self-possession—shook his dress into yet wilder disorder —passed before Varney with the air of a superior and master, and in his turn led the way to the river-side.

The Queen's barge was on the very point of putting off; the seat allotted to Leicester in the stern, and that to his master of the horse on the bow of the boat, being already filled up. But on Leicester's approach, there was a pause, as if the bargemen anticipated some alteration in their company. The angry spot was, however, in the Queen's cheek, as, in that cold tone with which superiors endeavour to veil their internal agitation, while speaking to those before whom it would be derogation to express it, she pronounced the chilling words—'We have waited, my Lord of Leicester.'

'Madam, and most gracious Princess,' said Leicester, 'you, who can pardon so many weaknesses which your own heart never knows, can best bestow your commiseration on the agitations of the bosom, which, for a moment, affect both head and limbs. I came to your presence, a doubting and an accused subject; your goodness penetrated the clouds of defamation, and restored me to my own honour, and, what is yet dearer, to your favour—is it wonderful, though for me it is most unhappy, that my master of the horse should have found me in a state which scarce permitted me to make the exertion necessary to follow him to this place, when one glance of your Highness, although, alas! an angry one, has had power to do that for me, on which Esculapius might have failed?'

'How is this?' said Elizabeth hastily, looking at Varney; 'hath your lord been ill?'

'Something of a fainting-fit,' answered the ready-witted Varney, 'as your Grace may observe from his present condition. My lord's haste would not permit me leisure even to bring his dress into order.'

'It matters not,' said Elizabeth, as she gazed on the noble face and form of Leicester, to which even the strange mixture of passions by which he had been so lately agitated, gave additional interest, 'make room for my noble lord—Your place, Master Varney, has been filled up; you must find a seat in another barge.'

Varney bowed, and withdrew.

'And you too, our young Squire of the Cloak,' added she, looking at Raleigh, 'must, for the time, go to the barge of our ladies of honour. As for Tressilian, he hath already suffered too much by the caprice of women, that I should aggrieve him by my change of plan, so far as he is concerned.'

Leicester seated himself in his place in the barge, and close to the sovereign; Raleigh rose to retire, and Tressilian would have been so ill-timed in his courtesy as to offer to relinquish his own place to his friend, had not the acute glance of Raleigh himself, who seemed now in his native element, made him sensible, that so ready a disclamation of the royal favour might be misinterpreted. He sat silent, therefore, whilst Raleigh, with a profound bow, and a look of the deepest humiliation, was about to quit his place.

A noble courtier, the gallant Lord Willoughby, read, as he thought, something in the Queen's face, which seemed to pity Raleigh's real or assumed semblance of mortification.

'It is not for us old courtiers,' he said, 'to hide the sunshine from the young ones. I will, with her Majesty's leave, relinquish for an hour that which her subjects hold dearest, the delight of her Highness's presence, and mortify myself by walking in starlight, while I forsake, for a brief season, the glory of Diana's own beams. I will take place in the boat which the ladies occupy, and permit this young cavalier his hour of promised felicity.'

The Queen replied, with an expression betwixt mirth and earnest, 'If you are so willing to leave us, my lord, we cannot help the mortification. But, under favour, we do not trust you—old and experienced as you may deem yourself—with the care of our young ladies of honour. Your venerable age, my lord', she continued, smiling, 'may be better assorted with that of my Lord Treasurer, who follows in the third boat, and by whose experience even my Lord Willoughby's may be improved.'

Lord Willoughby hid his disappointment under a smile— laughed, was confused, bowed, and left the Queen's barge to go on board my Lord Burleigh's. Leicester, who endeavoured to divert his thoughts from all internal reflection, by fixing them on what was passing around, watched this circumstance among others. But when the boat put off from the shore—when the music sounded from a barge which accompanied them—when the shouts of the populace were heard from the shore, and all reminded him of the situation in which he was placed, he abstracted his thoughts and feelings by a strong effort from everything but the necessity of maintaining himself in the favour of his patroness, and exerted his talents of pleasing captivation with such success, that the Queen, alternately delighted with his conversation, and alarmed for his health, at length imposed a temporary silence on him, with playful yet anxious care, lest his flow of spirits should exhaust him.

'My lords,' she said, 'having passed for a time our edict of silence upon our good Leicester, we will call you to counsel on a gamesome matter, more fitted to be now treated of, amidst mirth and music, than in the gravity of our ordinary deliberations. Which of you, my lords,' said she, smiling, 'know aught of a petition from Orson Pinnit, the keeper, as he qualifies himself, of our royal bears? Who stands godfather to his requests?'

'Marry, with your Grace's good permission, that do I,' said the Earl of Sussex. 'Orson Pinnit was a stout soldier before he was so mangled by the skenes of the Irish clan MacDonough, and I trust your grace will be, as you always have been, good mistress to your good and trusty servants.'

'Surely,' said the Queen, 'it is our purpose to be so, and in especial to our poor soldiers and sailors, who hazard their lives for little pay. We would give,' she said, with her eyes sparkling, 'yonder royal palace of ours to be an hospital for their use, rather than they should call their mistress ungrateful. But this is not the question,' she said, her voice, which had been awakened by her patriotic feelings, once more subsiding into the tone of gay and easy conversation; 'for this Orson Pinnit's request goes something further. He complains, that amidst the extreme delight with which men haunt the play houses, and in especial their eager desire for seeing the exhibitions of one Will Shakespeare (whom I think, my lords, we have all heard something of), the manly amusement of bear-baiting is falling into comparative neglect; since men will rather throng to see these roguish players kill each other in jest, than to see our royal dogs and bears worry each other in bloody earnest—What say you to this, my Lord of Sussex?'

'Why, truly, gracious Madam,' said Sussex, 'you must expect little from an old soldier like me in favour of battles in sport, when they are compared with battles in earnest; and yet, by my faith, I wish Will Shakespeare no harm. He is a stout man at quarter-staff and single falchion, though, as I am told, a halting fellow; and he stood, they say, a tough fight with the rangers of old Sir Thomas Lucy of Charlecot, when he broke his deerpark and kissed his keeper's daughter.'

'I cry you mercy, my Lord of Sussex,' said Queen Elizabeth, interrupting him; 'that matter was heard in council, and we will not have this fellow's offence exaggerated—there was no kissing in the matter, and the defendant hath put the denial on record. But what say you to his present practice, my lord, on the stage? for there lies the point, and not in any ways touching his former errors, in breaking parks, or the other follies you speak of.'

'Why, truly, Madam,' replied Sussex, 'as I said before, I wish the gamesome mad fellow no injury. Some of his whoreson poetry (I crave your Grace's pardon for such a phrase) has rung in mine ears as if the lines sounded to boot and saddle. But then it is all froth and folly—no substance or seriousness in it, as your grace has already well touched. What are half a dozen knaves, with rusty foils and tattered targets, making but a mere mockery of a stout fight, to compare to the royal game of bear-baiting, which has been graced by your Highness's countenance, and that of your royal predecessors, in this your princely kingdom, famous for matchless mastiffs, and bold bear-wards, over all Christendom? Greatly is it to be doubted that the race of both will decay, if men should throng to hear the lungs of an idle player belch forth nonsensical bombast, instead of bestowing their pence in encouraging the bravest image of war that can be shown in peace, and that is the sports of the Bear-garden. There you may see the bear lying at guard with his red pinky eyes, watching the onset of the mastiff, like a wily captain, who maintains his defence that an assailant may be tempted to venture within his danger. And then comes Sir Mastiff, like a worthy champion, in full career at the throat of his adversary—and then shall Sir Bruin teach him the reward for those who, in their over-courage, neglect the policies of war, and, catching him in his arms, strain him to his breast like a lusty wrestler, until rib after rib crack like the shot of a pistolet. And then another mastiff, as bold, but with better aim and sounder judgment, catches Sir Bruin by the nether lip, and hangs fast, while he tosses about his blood and slaver, and tries in vain to shake Sir Talbot from his hold. And then——'

'Nay, by my honour, my lord,' said the Queen, laughing, 'you have described the whole so admirably, that, had we never seen a bear-baiting (as we have beheld many, and hope, with Heaven's allowance to see many more), your words were sufficient to put the whole Bear-garden before our eyes. But come, who speaks next in this case? My Lord of Leicester, what say you?'

'Am I then to consider myself as unmuzzled, please your Grace?' replied Leicester.

'Surely, my lord—that is, if you feel hearty enough to take part in our game,' answered Elizabeth; 'and yet, when I think of your cognisance of the Bear and Ragged Staff, methinks we had better hear some less partial orator.'

'Nay, on my word, gracious Princess,' said the Earl, 'though my brother Ambrose of Warwick and I do carry the ancient cognisance your Highness deigns to remember, I nevertheless desire nothing but fair play on all sides; or, as they say, "fight dog, fight bear." And in behalf of the players, I must needs say that they are witty knaves, whose rants and jests keep the minds of the commons from busying themselves with state affairs, and listening to traitorous speeches, idle rumours, and disloyal insinuations. When men are agape to see how Marlowe, Shakespeare, and other play artificers, work out their fanciful plots as they call them, the mind of the spectators is withdrawn from the conduct of their rulers.'

'We would not have the mind of our subjects withdrawn from the consideration of our own conduct, my lord,' answered Elizabeth; 'because the more closely it is examined, the true motives by which we are guided will apear the more manifest.'

'I have heard, however, Madam,' said the Dean of St Asaph's, an eminent Puritan, 'that these players are wont, in their plays, not only to introduce profane and lewd expressions, tending to foster sin and harlotry, but even to bellow out such reflections on government, its origin and its object, as tend to render the subject discontented, and shake the solid foundations of civil society. And it seems to be, under your Grace's favour, far less than safe to permit these naughty foul-mouthed knaves to ridicule the godly for their decent gravity, and in blaspheming Heaven, and slandering its earthly rulers, to set at defiance the laws both of God and man.'

'If we could think this were true, my lord,' said Elizabeth, 'we should give sharp correction for such offences. But it is ill arguing against the use of anything from its abuse. And touching this Shakespeare, we think there is that in his plays that is worth twenty Bear-gardens; and that this new undertaking of his Chronicles, as he calls them, may entertain, with honest mirth, mingled with useful instruction, not only our subjects, but even the generation which may succeed to us.'

'Your Majesty's reign will need no such feeble aid to make it remembered to the latest posterity,' said Leicester. 'And yet, in his way, Shakespeare hath so touched some incidents of your Majesty's happy government, as may countervail what has been spoken by his reverence the Dean of St Asaph's. There are some lines for example—I would my nephew, Philip Sidney, were here, they are scarce ever out of his mouth—they are spoken in a mad tale of fairies, love-charms, and I wot not what besides; but beautiful they are, however short they may and must fall of the subject to which they bear a bold relation—and Philip murmurs them, I think, even in his dreams.'

'You tantalise us, my lord,' said the Queen—'Master Philip Sidney is, we know, a minion of the Muses, and we are pleased it should be so. Valour never shines to more advantage than when united with the true taste and love of letters. But surely there are some others among our young courtiers who can recollect what your lordship has forgotten amid weightier affairs.—Master Tressilian, you are described to me as a worshipper of Minerva—remember you aught of these lines?'

Tressilian's heart was too heavy, his prospects in life too fatally blighted, to profit by the opportunity which the Queen thus offered to him of attracting her attention, but he determined to transfer the advantage to his more ambitious young friend; and, excusing himself on the score of want of recollection, he added, that he believed the beautiful verses of which my Lord of Leicester had spoken, were in the remembrance of Master Walter Raleigh.

At the command of the Queen, that cavalier repeated, with accent and manner which even added to their exquisite delicacy of tact and beauty of description, the celebrated vision of Oberon:—

> 'That very time I saw (but thou couldst not),
> Flying between the cold moon and the earth,
> Cupid, all arm'd: a certain aim he took

At a fair vestal, throned by the west;
And loos'd his love-shaft smartly from his bow,
As it should pierce a hundred thousand hearts:
But I might see young Cupid's fiery shaft
Quench'd in the chaste beams of the wat'ry moon;
And the imperial vot'ress passed on,
In maiden meditation, fancy free.'

The voice of Raleigh as he repeated the last lines, became a little tremulous, as if diffident how the Sovereign to whom the homage was addressed might receive it, exquisite as it was. If this diffidence was affected, it was good policy; but if real, there was little occasion for it. The verses were not probably new to the Queen, for when was ever such elegant flattery long in reaching the royal ear to which it was addressed? But they were not the less welcome when repeated by such a speaker as Raleigh. Alike delighted with the matter, the manner, and the graceful form and animated countenance of the gallant young reciter, Elizabeth kept time to every cadence, with look and with finger. When the speaker had ceased, she murmured over the last lines as if scarce conscious that she was overheard, and as she uttered the words,

'In maiden meditation, fancy free,'

she dropped into the Thames the supplication of Orson Pinnit, keeper of the royal bears, to find more favourable acceptance at Sheerness, or wherever the tide might waft it.

Leicester was spurred to emulation by the success of the young courtier's exhibition, as the veteran racer is roused when a high-mettled colt passes him on the way. He turned the discourse on shows, banquets, pageants, and on the character of those by whom these gay scenes were then frequented. He mixed acute observation with light satire, in that just proportion which was free alike from malignant slander and insipid praise. He mimicked with ready accent the manners of the affected or the clownish, and made his own graceful tone and manner seem doubly such when he resumed it. Foreign countries—their customs—their manners—the rules of their courts—the fashions, and even the dress of their ladies, were equally his theme; and seldom did he conclude without conveying some compliment, always couched in delicacy, and expressed with propriety, to the Virgin Queen, her court and her government. Thus passed the conversation during this pleasure voyage, seconded by the rest of the attendants upon the royal person, in gay discourse, varied by remarks upon ancient classics and modern authors, and enriched by maxims of deep policy and sound morality, by the statesmen and sages who sat around, and mixed wisdom with the lighter talk of a female court.

When they returned to the palace, Elizabeth accepted, or rather selected, the arm of Leicester to support her, from the stairs where they landed, to the great gate. It even seemed to him (though that might arise from the flattery of his own imagination), that during this short passage, she leaned on him somewhat more than the slipperiness of the way necessarily demanded. Certainly her actions and words combined to express a degree of favour, which, even in his proudest days, he had not till then attained. His rival, indeed, was repeatedly graced by the Queen's notice; but it was in a manner that seemed to flow less from spontaneous inclination, than as extorted by a sense of his merit. And, in the opinion of many experienced courtiers, all the favour she showed him was overbalanced by her whispering in the ear of the Lady Derby, that 'now she saw sickness was a better alchemist than she before wotted of, seeing it had changed my Lord of Sussex's copper nose into a golden one.'

The jest transpired, and the Earl of Leicester enjoyed his triumph, as one to whom court favour had been both the primary and the ultimate motive of life, while he forgot, in the intoxication of the moment, the perplexities and dangers of his own situation. Indeed, strange as it may appear, he thought less at that moment of the perils arising from his secret union, than of the marks of grace which Elizabeth from time to time showed to young Raleigh. They were indeed transient, but they were conferred on one accomplished in mind and body, with grace, gallantry, literature, and valour. An accident occurred in the course of the evening which riveted Leicester's attention to this object.

The nobles and courtiers who had attended the Queen on her pleasure expedition, were invited, with royal hospitality, to a splendid banquet in the hall of the palace. The table was not, indeed, graced by the presence of the Sovereign; for, agreeable to her idea of what was at once modest and dignified, the Maiden Queen, on such occasions, was wont to take in private, or with one or two favourite ladies, her light and temperate meal. After a moderate interval, the court again met in the splendid gardens of the palace; and it was while thus engaged, that the Queen suddenly asked a lady, who was near to her both in place and favour, what had become of the young Squire Lack-Cloak.

The Lady Paget answered. 'She had seen Master Raleigh but two or three minutes since, standing at the window of a small pavilion or pleasure house, which looked out on the Thames, and writing on the glass with a diamond ring.'

'That ring,' said the Queen, 'was a small token I gave him, to make amends for his spoiled mantle. Come, Paget, let us see what use he has made of it, for I can see through him already. He is a marvellously sharp-witted spirit.'

They went to the spot, within sight of which, but at some distance, the young cavalier still lingered, as the fowler watches the net which he has set. The Queen approached the window, on which Raleigh had used her gift, to inscribe the following lines:—

'Fain would I climb, but that I fear to fall.'

The Queen smiled, read it twice over, once with deliberation to Lady Paget, and once again to herself. 'It is a pretty beginning,' she said, after the consideration of a moment or two; 'but methinks the Muse hath deserted the young wit, at the very outset of his task. It were good-natured—were it not, Lady Paget,—to complete it for him? Try your rhyming faculties.'

Lady Paget, prosaic from her cradle upwards, as ever any lady of the bedchamber before or after her, disclaimed all possibility of assisting the young poet.

'Nay, then, we must sacrifice to the Muses ourselves,' said Elizabeth.

'The incense of no one can be more acceptable,' said Lady Paget; 'and your Highness will impose such obligation on the ladies of Parnassus——'

'Hush, Paget,' said the Queen, 'you speak sacrilege against the immortal Nine—yet virgins themselves, they should be exorable to a Virgin Queen—and, therefore—let me see how runs his verse—

'Fain would I climb, but that I fear to fall.

Might not the answer (for fault of a better) run thus,—

'If thy mind fail thee, do not climb at all.'

The dame of honour uttered an exclamation of joy and surprise at so happy a termination; and certainly a worse had been applauded, even when coming from a less distinguished author.

The Queen, thus encouraged, took off a diamond ring, and saying, 'We will give this gallant some cause of marvel, when he finds his couplet perfected without his own interference,' she wrote her own line beneath that of Raleigh.

The Queen left the pavilion—but retiring slowly, and often looking back, she could see the young cavalier steal, with the flight of a lapwing, towards the place where he had seen her make a pause;—'She stayed but to observe,' as she said, 'that her train had taken;' and then, laughing at the circumstance with the Lady Paget, she took the way slowly towards the palace. Elizabeth, as they returned, cautioned her companion not to mention to any one the aid which she had given to the young poet—and Lady Paget promised scrupulous secrecy. It is to be supposed that she made a mental reservation in favour of Leicester, to whom her ladyship transmitted without delay an anecdote, so little calculated to give him pleasure.

Raleigh, in the meanwhile, stole back to the window, and read, with a feeling of intoxication, the encouragement thus given him by the Queen in person to follow out his ambitious career, and returned to Sussex and his retinue, then on the point of embarking to go up the river, his heart beating high with gratified pride, and with hope of future distinction.

The reverence due to the person of the Earl prevented any notice being taken of the reception he had met with at court, until they had landed, and the household were assembled in the great hall at Say's Court; while that lord, exhausted by his late illness, and the fatigues of the day, had retired to his chamber, demanding the attendance of Wayland, his successful physician. Wayland, however, was nowhere to be found; and, while some of the party were, with military impatience, seeking him and cursing his absence, the rest flocked round Raleigh, to congratulate him on his prospects of court favour.

He had the good taste and judgment to conceal the decisive circumstance of the couplet, to which Elizabeth had deigned to find a rhyme; but other circumstances had transpired, which plainly intimated that he had made some progress in the Queen's favour. All hastened to wish him joy on the mended appearance of his fortune: some from real regard; some, perhaps, from hopes that his preferment might hasten their own; and most from a mixture of these motives, and a sense that the countenance shown to any one of Sussex's household, was, in fact, a triumph to the whole. Raleigh returned the kindest thanks to them all, disowning, with becoming modesty, that one day's fair reception made a favourite, any more than one swallow a summer. But he observed that Blount did not join in the general congratulation, and, somewhat hurt at his apparent unkindness, he plainly asked him the reason.

Blount replied with equal sincerity—'My good Walter, I wish thee as well as do any of those chattering gulls, who are whistling and whooping congratulations in thine ear, because it seems fair weather with thee. But I fear for thee, Walter (and he wiped his honest eye), I fear for thee with all my heart. These court tricks, and gambols, and flashes of fine women's favour, are the tricks and trinkets that bring fair fortunes to farthings, and fine faces and witty coxcombs to the acquaintance of dull blocks and sharp axes.'

So saying, Blount arose and left the hall, while Raleigh looked after him with an expression that blanked for a moment his bold and animated countenance.

Stanley just then entered the hall, and said to Tressilian, 'My lord is calling for your fellow Wayland, and your fellow Wayland is just come hither in a sculler, and is calling for you, nor will he go to my lord till he sees you. The fellow looks as he were mazed, methinks—I would you would see him immediately.'

Tressilian instantly left the hall, and causing Wayland Smith to be shown into a withdrawing apartment, and lights placed, he conducted the artist thither, and was surprised when he observed the emotion of his countenance.

'What is the matter with you, Smith?' said Tressilian; 'have you seen the devil?'

'Worse, sir, worse,' replied Wayland, 'I have seen a basilisk. Thank God, I saw him first, for being so seen, and seeing not me, he will do the less harm.'

'In God's name, speak sense,' said Tressilian, 'and say what you mean.'

'I have seen my old master,' said the artist. 'Last night, a friend, whom I had acquired, took me to see the palace clock, judging me to be curious in such works of art. At the window of a turret next to the clock-house I saw my old master.'

'Thou must have needs been mistaken,' said Tressilian.

'I was not mistaken,' said Wayland. 'He that once hath his features by heart would know him amongst a million. He was anticly habited; but he cannot disguise himself from me, God be praised, as I can from him. I will not, however, tempt Providence by remaining within his ken. Tarleton the player himself could not so disguise himself, but that, sooner or later, Doboobie would find him out. I must away to-morrow; for, as we stand together, it were death to me to remain within reach of him.'

'But the Earl of Sussex?' said Tressilian.

'He is in little danger from what he has hitherto taken, providing he swallow the matter of a bean's size of the orvietan, every morning fasting—but let him beware of a relapse.'

'And how is that to be guarded against?' said Tressilian.

'Only by such caution as you would use against the devil,' answered Wayland. 'Let my lord's clerk of the kitchen kill his lord's meat himself, and dress it himself, using no spice but what he procures from the surest hands—Let the sewer serve it up himself, and let the master of my lord's household see that both clerk and sewer taste the dishes which the one dresses and the other serves. Let my lord use no perfumes which come not from well-accredited persons; no unguents—no pomades. Let him, on no account, drink with strangers, or eat fruit with them, either in the way of nooning or otherwise. Especially, let him observe such caution, if he goes to Kenilworth—the excuse of his illness, and his being under diet, will, and must, cover the strangeness of such practice.'

'And thou,' said Tressilian, 'what dost thou think to make of thyself?'

'France, Spain, either India, East or West, shall be my refuge,' said Wayland, 'ere I venture my life by residing within ken of Doboobie, Demetrius, or whatever else he calls himself for the time.'

'Well,' said Tressilian, 'this happens not inopportunely—I had business for you in Berkshire, but in the opposite extremity to the place where thou art known: and ere thou hadst found out this new reason for living private, I had settled to send thee thither upon a secret embassage.'

The artist expressed himself willing to receive his commands, and Tressilian, knowing he was well acquainted with the outline of his business at court, frankly explained to him the whole, mentioned the agreement which subsisted betwixt Giles Gosling and him, and told what had that day been averred in the presence-chamber by Varney, and supported by Leicester.

'Thou seest,' he added, 'that, in the circumstances in which I am placed, it behoves me to keep a narrow watch on the motions of these unprincipled men, Varney and his complices, Foster and Lambourne, as well as on those of my Lord Leicester himself, who, I suspect, is partly a deceiver, and not altogether the deceived in that matter. Here is my ring, as a pledge to Giles Gosling—here is besides gold, which shall be trebled if thou serve me faithfully. Away down to Cumnor, and see what happens there.'

'I go with double good will,' said the artist; 'first, because I serve your honour, who has been so kind to me, and then, that I may escape my old master, who, if not an absolute incarnation of the devil, has, at least, as much of the demon about him, in will, word, and action, as ever polluted humanity. And yet let him take care of me. I fly him now, as heretofore; but if, like the Scottish wild cattle, I am vexed by frequent pursuit, I may turn on him in hate and desperation. Will your honour command my nag to be saddled? I will but give the medicine to my lord, divided in its proper proportions, with a few instructions. His safety will then depend on the care of his friends and domestics—for the past he is guarded, but let him beware of the future.'

Wayland Smith accordingly made his farewell visit to the Earl of Sussex, dictated instructions as to his regimen, and precautions concerning his diet, and left Say's Court without waiting for morning.

18

> The moment comes—
> It is already come—when thou must write
> The absolute total of thy life's vast sum.
> The constellations stand victorious o'er thee,
> The planets shoot good fortune in fair junctions,
> And tell thee, 'Now's the time.'
> *Schiller's 'Wallenstein,' by Coleridge.*

WHEN Leicester returned to his lodgings, after a day so important and so harassing, in which, after riding out more than one gale, and touching on more than one shoal, his bark had finally gained the harbour with banner displayed, he seemed to experience as much fatigue as a mariner after a perilous storm. He spoke not a word while his chamberlain exchanged his rich court-mantle for a furred night-robe, and when this officer signified that Master Varney desired to speak with his lordship, he replied only by a sullen nod. Varney, however, entered, accepting this signal as a permission, and the chamberlain withdrew.

The Earl remained silent and almost motionless in his chair, his head reclined on his hand, and his elbow resting on the table which stood beside him, without seeming to be conscious of the entrance, or of the presence, of his confidant. Varney waited for some minutes until he should speak, desirous to know what was the finally predominant mood of a mind through which so many powerful emotions had that day taken their course. But he waited in vain, for Leicester continued still silent, and the confidant saw himself under the necessity of being the first to speak. 'May I congratulate your lordship,' he said, 'on the deserved superiority you have this day attained over your most formidable rival?'

Leicester raised his head, and answered sadly, but without anger, 'Thou, Varney, whose ready invention has involved me in a web of most mean and perilous falsehood, knowest best what small reason there is for gratulation on the subject.'

'Do you blame me, my lord,' said Varney, 'for not betraying, on the first push, the secret on which your fortunes depended, and which you have so oft and so earnestly recommended to my safe keeping? Your lordship was present in person, and might have contradicted me and ruined yourself by an avowal of the truth; but surely it was no part of a faithful servant to have done so without your commands.'

'I cannot deny it, Varney,' said the Earl, rising and walking across the room; 'my own ambition has been traitor to my love.'

'Say rather, my lord, that your love has been traitor to your greatness, and barred you from such a prospect of honour and power as the world cannot offer to any other. To make my honoured lady a Countess, you have missed the chance of being yourself——'

He paused and seemed unwilling to complete the sentence.

'Of being myself *what?*' demanded Leicester: 'speak out thy meaning, Varney.'

'Of being yourself a KING, my lord,' replied Varney; 'and King of England to boot! It is no treason to our Queen to say so. It would have chanced by her obtaining that which all true subjects wish her—a lusty, noble, and gallant husband.'

'Thou ravest, Varney,' answered Leicester. 'Besides, our times have seen enough to make men loathe the Crown Matrimonial which men take from their wives' lap. There was Darnley in Scotland.'

'He!' said Varney; 'a gull, a fool, a thrice-sodden ass, who suffered himself to be fired off into the air like a rocket on a rejoicing day. Had Mary had the hap to have wedded the noble Earl *once* destined to share her throne, she had experienced a husband of different metal; and her husband had found in her a wife as complying and loving as the mate of the meanest squire, who follows the hounds a-horseback, and holds her husband's bridle as he mounts.'

'It might have been as thou say'st, Varney,' said Leicester, a brief smile of self-satisfaction passing over his anxious countenance. 'Henry Darnley knew little of women—with Mary, a man who knew her sex might have had some chance of holding his own. But not with Elizabeth, Varney—for I think God, when he gave her the heart of a woman, gave her the head of a man to control its follies. No, I know her. She will accept love-tokens, ay, and requite them with the like—put sugared sonnets in her bosom—ay, and answer them too—push gallantry to the very verge where it becomes exchange of affection—but she writes *nil ultra* to all which is to follow, and would not barter one iota of her own supreme power for all the alphabet of both Cupid and Hymen.'

'The better for you, my lord,' said Varney, 'that is, in the case supposed, if such be her disposition; since you think you cannot aspire to become her husband. Her favourite you are, and may remain, if the lady at Cumnor Place remains in her present obscurity.'

'Poor Amy!' said Leicester, with a deep sigh; 'she desires so earnestly to be acknowledged in presence of God and man!'

'Ay, but, my lord,' said Varney, 'is her desire reasonable?—that is the question. Her religious scruples are solved—she is an honoured and beloved wife—enjoying the society of her husband at such times as his weightier duties permit him to afford her his company —What would she more? I am right sure that a lady so gentle and so loving would consent to live her life through in a certain obscurity—which is, after all, not dimmer than when she was at Lidcote Hall—rather than diminish the least jot of her lord's honour and greatness by a premature attempt to share them.'

'There is something in what thou say'st,' said Leicester; 'and her appearance here were fatal—yet she must be seen at Kenilworth; Elizabeth will not forget that she has so appointed.'

'Let me sleep on that hard point,' said Varney; 'I cannot else perfect the device I have on the stithy, which I trust will satisfy the Queen and please my honoured lady, yet leave this fatal secret where it is now buried. Has your lordship further commands for the night?'

'I would be alone,' said Leicester. 'Leave me, and place my steel casket on the table. Be within summons.'

Varney retired—and the Earl, opening the window of his apartment, looked out long and anxiously upon the brilliant host of stars which glimmered in the splendour of a summer firmament. The words burst from him as at unawares—'I had never more need that the heavenly bodies should befriend me, for my earthly path is darkened and confused.'

It is well known that the age reposed a deep confidence in the vain predictions of judicial astrology, and Leicester, though exempt from the general control of superstition, was not in this respect superior to his time; but, on the contrary, was remarkable for the encouragement which he gave to the professors of this pretended science. Indeed, the wish to pry into futurity, so general among the human race, is peculiarly to be found amongst those who trade in state mysteries and the dangerous intrigues and cabals of courts.

With heedful precaution to see that it had not been opened, or its locks tampered with, Leicester applied a key to the steel casket, and drew from it, first, a parcel of gold pieces, which he put into a silk purse; then a parchment inscribed with planetary signs, and the lines and calculations used in framing horoscopes, on which he gazed intently for a few moments; and, lastly, took forth a large key, which, lifting aside the tapestry, he applied to a little concealed door in the corner of the apartment, and, opening it, disclosed a stair constructed in the thickness of the wall.

'Alasco,' said the Earl, with a voice raised, yet no higher raised than to be heard by the inhabitant of the small turret to which the stair conducted—'Alasco, I say, descend.'

'I come, my lord,' answered a voice from above. The foot of an aged man was heard, slowly descending the narrow stair, and Alasco entered the Earl's apartment. The astrologer was a little man, and seemed much advanced in age, for his beard was long and white, and reached over his black doublet down to his silken girdle. His hair was of the same venerable hue. But his eyebrows were as dark as the keen and piercing black eyes which they shaded, and this peculiarity gave a wild and singular cast to the physiognomy of the old man. His cheek was still fresh and ruddy, and the eyes we have mentioned resembled those of a rat, in acuteness, and even fierceness of expression. His manner was not without a sort of dignity; and the interpreter of the stars, though respectful, seemed altogether at his ease, and even assumed a tone of instruction and command, in conversing with the prime favourite of Elizabeth.

'Your prognostications have failed, Alasco,' said the Earl, when they had exchanged salutations. 'He is recovering.'

'My son,' replied the astrologer, 'let me remind you I warranted not his death—nor is there any prognostication that can be derived from the heavenly bodies, their aspects and their conjunctions, which is not liable to be controlled by the will of Heaven. *Astra regunt homines, sed regit astra Deus.*'

'Of what avail, then, is your mystery?' replied the Earl.

'Of much, my son,' replied the old man, 'since it can show the natural and probable course of events, although that course moves in subordination to an Higher Power. Thus, in reviewing the horoscope which your lordship subjected to my skill, you will observe that Saturn, being in the sixth House in opposition to

236

Mars, retrograde in the House of Life, cannot but denote long and dangerous sickness, the issue whereof is in the will of Heaven, though death may probably be inferred—Yet, if I knew the name of the party, I would erect another scheme.'

'His name is a secret,' said the Earl; 'yet I must own, thy prognostication hath not been unfaithful. He has been sick and dangerously so, not however to death. But hast thou again cast my horoscope as Varney directed thee, and art thou prepared to say what the stars tell of my present fortune?'

'My art stands at your command,' said the old man; 'and here, my son, is the map of thy fortunes, brilliant in aspect as ever beamed from those blessed signs whereby our life is influenced, yet not unchequered with fears, difficulties, and dangers.'

'My lot were more than mortal were it otherwise,' said the Earl. 'Proceed, father; and believe you speak with one ready to undergo his destiny in action and in passion, as may beseem a noble of England.'

'Thy courage to do and to suffer must be wound up yet a strain higher,' said the old man. 'The stars intimate yet a prouder title, yet a higher rank. It is for thee to guess their meaning, not for me to name it.'

'Name it, I conjure you—name it, I command you,' said the Earl, his eyes brightening as he spoke.

'I may not, and I will not,' replied the old man. 'The ire of princes is as the wrath of the lion. But mark, and judge for thyself. Here Venus, ascendant in the House of Life, and conjoined with Sol, showers down that flood of silver light, blent with gold, which promises power, wealth, dignity, all that the proud heart of man desires, and in such abundance, that never the future Augustus of that old and mighty Rome heard from his *Haruspices* such a tale of glory, as from this rich text my lore might read to my favourite son.'

'Thou dost but jest with me, father,' said the Earl, astonished at the strain of enthusiasm in which the astrologer delivered his prediction.

'Is it for him to jest who hath his eye on heaven, who hath his foot in the grave?' returned the old man solemnly.

The Earl made two or three strides through the apartment, with his hand outstretched, as one who follows the beckoning signal of some phantom, waving him on to deeds of high import. As he turned, however, he caught the eye of the astrologer fixed on him, while an observing glance of the most shrewd penetration shot from under the penthouse of his shaggy dark eyebrows. Leicester's haughty and suspicious soul at once caught fire; he darted towards the old man from the farther end of the lofty apartment, only standing still when his extended hand was within a foot of the astrologer's body.

'Wretch!' he said, 'if you dare to palter with me, I will have your skin stripped from your living flesh! Confess thou hast been hired to deceive and to betray me—that thou art a cheat, and I thy silly prey and booty!'

The old man exhibited some symptoms of emotion, but not more than the furious deportment of his patron might have extorted from innocence itself.

'What means this violence, my lord?' he answered, 'or in what can I have deserved it at your hand?'

'Give me proof,' said the Earl vehemently, 'that you have not tampered with mine enemies.'

'My lord,' replied the old man, with dignity, 'you can have no better proof than that which you yourself elected. In that turret I have spent the last twenty-four hours, under the key which has been in your own custody. The hours of darkness I have spent in gazing on the heavenly bodies with these dim eyes, and during those of light I have toiled this aged brain to complete the calculations arising from their combinations. Earthly food I have not tasted—earthly voice I have not heard—you are yourself aware I had no means of doing so—and yet I tell you—I who have been thus shut up in solitude and study—that within these twenty-four hours your star has become predominant in the horizon, and either the bright book of heaven speaks false, or there must have been a proportionate revolution in your fortunes upon earth. If nothing has happened within that space to secure your power, or advance your favour, then am I indeed a cheat, and the divine art, which was first devised in the plains of Chaldea, is a foul imposture'.

'It is true,' said Leicester, after a moment's reflection, 'thou wert closely immured—and it is also true that the change has taken place in my situation which thou say'st the horoscope indicates.'

'Wherefore this distrust then, my son,' said the astrologer, assuming a tone of admonition; 'the celestial intelligences brook not diffidence, even in their favourites.'

'Peace, father,' answered Leicester, 'I have erred in doubting thee. Not to mortal man, nor to celestial intelligence—under that which is supreme—will Dudley's lips say more in condescension or apology. Speak rather to the present purpose. Amid these bright promises thou hast said there was a threatening aspect—Can thy skill tell whence, or by whose means, such danger seems to impend?'

'Thus far only,' answered the astrologer, 'does my art enable me to answer your query. The infortune is threatened by the malignant and adverse aspect, through means of a youth,—and, as I think, a rival; but whether in love or in prince's favour, I know not; nor can I give further indication respecting him, save that he comes from the western quarter.'

'The western—ha!' replied Leicester, 'it is enough—the tempest does indeed brew in that quarter!—Cornwall and Devon—Raleigh and Tressilian—one of them is indicated—I must beware of both.— Father, if I have done thy skill injustice, I will make thee a lordly recompense.'

He took a purse of gold from the strong casket which stood before him—'Have thou double the recompense which Varney promised. Be faithful—be secret—obey the directions thou shalt receive from my master of the horse, and grudge not a little seclusion or restraint in my cause—it shall be richly considered. Here, Varney—conduct this venerable man to thine own lodging— tend him heedfully in all things, but see that he holds communication with no one.'

Varney bowed, and the astrologer kissed the Earl's hand in token of adieu, and followed the master of the horse to another apartment, in which were placed wine and refreshments for his use.

The astrologer sat down to his repast, while Varney shut two doors with great precaution, examined the tapestry, lest any listener lurked behind it; and then, sitting down opposite to the sage, began to question him.

'Saw you my signal from the court beneath?'

'I did,' said Alasco, for by such name he was at present called, 'and shaped the horoscope accordingly.'

'And it passed upon the patron without challenge?' continued Varney.

'Not without challenge,' replied the old man, 'but it did pass; and I added, as before agreed, danger from a discovered secret, and a western youth.'

'My lord's fear will stand sponsor to the one, and his conscience to the other, of these prognostications,' replied Varney. 'Sure never man chose to run such a race as his, yet continued to retain those silly scruples! I am fain to cheat him to his own profit. But, touching your matters, sage interpreter of the stars, I can tell you more of your own fortune than plan or figure can show. You must be gone from hence forthwith.'

'I will not,' said Alasco peevishly. 'I have been too much hurried up and down of late—immured for day and night in a desolate turret-chamber—I must enjoy my liberty, and pursue my studies, which are of more import than the fate of fifty statesmen, and favourites, that rise and burst like bubbles in the atmosphere of a court.'

'At your pleasure,' said Varney, with a sneer that habit had rendered familiar to his features, and which forms the principal characteristic that painters have assigned to those of Satan—'At your pleasure,' he said, 'you may enjoy your liberty, and your studies, until the daggers of Sussex's followers are clashing within your doublet, and against your ribs.' The old man turned pale, and Varney proceeded. 'Wot you not he hath offered a reward for the arch-quack and poison-vendor, Demetrius, who sold certain precious species to his lordship's cook? What! turn you pale, old friend? Does Hali already see an infortune in the House of Life? Why, hark thee, we will have thee down to an old house of mine in the country, where thou shalt live with a hob-nailed slave, whom thy alchemy may convert into ducats, for to such conversion alone is thy art serviceable.'

'It is false, thou foul-mouthed railer,' said Alasco, shaking with impotent anger; 'it is well known that I have approached more nearly to projection than any hermetic artist who now lives. There are not six chemists in the world who possess so near an approximation to the grand arcanum——'

'Come, come,' said Varney, interrupting him, 'what means this, in the name of Heaven? Do we not know one another? I believe thee to be so perfect,—so very perfect, in the mystery of cheating, that, having imposed upon all mankind, thou hast at length, in some measure, imposed upon thyself; and without ceasing to dupe others, hast become a species of dupe to thine own imagination. Blush not for it, man—thou art learned, and shalt have classical comfort:—

'Ne quisquam Ajacem possit superare nisi Ajax.'
No one but thyself could have gulled thee—and thou hast gulled
the whole brotherhood of the Rosy Cross besides—none so deep
in the mystery as thou. But hark thee in thine ear;—had the
seasoning which spiced Sussex's broth wrought more surely, I
would have thought better of the chemical science thou dost boast
so highly.'

'Thou art an hardened villain, Varney,' replied Alasco; 'many
will do those things, who dare not speak of them,'

'And many speak of them, who dare not do them,' answered
Varney; 'but be not wroth—I will not quarrel with thee—if I did,
I were fain to live on eggs for a month, that I might feed without
fear. Tell me at once, how came thine art to fail thee at this great
emergency?'

'The Earl of Sussex's horoscope intimates,' replied the astrologer,
'that the sign of the ascendant being in combustion——'

'Away with your gibberish,' replied Varney; 'think'st thou it is
the patron thou speak'st with?'

'I crave your pardon,' replied the old man, 'and swear to you,
I know but one medicine that could have saved the Earl's life; and
as no man living in England knows that antidote save myself,—
moreover, as the ingredients, one of them in particular, are scarce
possible to be come by, I must needs suppose his escape was owing
to such a constitution of lungs and vital parts, as was never before
bound up in a body of clay.'

'There was some talk of a quack who waited on him,' said
Varney, after a moment's reflection. 'Are you sure there is no one
in England who has this secret of thine?'

'One man there was,' said the doctor, 'once my servant, who
might have stolen this of me, with one or two other secrets of art.
But content you, Master Varney; it is no part of my policy to
suffer such interlopers to interfere in my trade. He pries into no
mysteries more, I warrant you; for, as I well believe, he hath been
wafted to heaven on the wing of a fiery dragon—Peace be with
him. But in this retreat of mine, shall I have the use of mine
elaboratory?'

'Of a whole workshop, man,' said Varney; 'for a reverend
father Abbot, who was fain to give place to bluff King Hal, and
some of his courtiers, a score of years since, had a chemist's
complete apparatus, which he was obliged to leave behind him

to his successors. Thou shalt there occupy, and melt, and puff, and blaze, and multiply, until the Green Dragon become a golden goose, or whatever the newer phrase of the brotherhood may testify.'

'Thou art right, Master Varney,' said the alchemist, setting his teeth close, and grinding them together—'thou art right, even in thy very contempt of right and reason. For what thou say'st in mockery, may in sober verity chance to happen ere we meet again. If the most venerable sages of ancient days have spoken the truth—if the most learned of our own have rightly received it,—if I have been accepted wherever I travelled, in Germany, in Poland, in Italy, and in the farther Tartary, as one to whom Nature has unveiled her darkest secrets—If I have acquired the most secret signs and passwords of the Jewish Cabala, so that the grayest beard in the synagogue would brush the steps to make them clean for me—if all this is so, and if there remain but one step—one little step—betwixt my long, deep, and dark and subterranean progress, and that blaze of light which shall show Nature watching her richest and her most glorious productions in the very cradle—one step betwixt dependence and the power of sovereignty—one step betwixt poverty and such a sum of wealth as earth, without that noble secret, cannot minister from all her minds in the old or the new-found world—if this be all so, is it not reasonable that to this I dedicate my future life, secure, for a brief period of studious patience, to rise above the mean dependence upon favourites, and *their* favourites, by which I am now enthralled!'

'Now, bravo! bravo! my good father,' said Varney, with the usual sardonic expression of ridicule on his countenance; 'yet all this approximation to the philosopher's stone wringeth not one single crown out of my Lord Leicester's pouch, and far less out of Richard Varney's—*We* must have earthly and substantial services, man, and care not whom else thou canst delude with thy philosophical charlatanry.'

'My son Varney,' said the alchemist, 'the unbelief, gathered around thee like a frost-fog, hath dimmed thine acute perception to that which is a stumbling-block to the wise, and which yet, to him who seeketh knowledge with humility, extends a lesson so clear, that he who runs may read. Hath not Art, think'st thou, the means of completing Nature's imperfect concoctions in her attempts to form the precious metals, even as by art we can perfect those other operations, of incubation, distillation, fermentation, and similar processes of an ordinary description, by which we extract life itself out of a senseless egg, summon purity and vitality out of muddy dregs, or call into vivacity the inert substance of a sluggish liquid?'

'I have heard all this before,' said Varney; 'and my heart is proof against such cant ever since I sent twenty good gold pieces (marry, it was in the nonage of my wit) to advance the grand magisterium, all which, God help the while, vanished *in fumo*. Since that moment, when I paid for my freedom, I defy chemistry, astrology, palmistry, and every other occult art, were it as secret as hell itself, to unloose the stricture of my purse-strings. Marry, I neither defy the manna of Saint Nicholas, nor can I dispense with it. Thy first task must be to prepare some when thou get'st down to my little sequestered retreat yonder, and then make as much gold as thou wilt.'

'I will make no more of that dose,' said the alchemist, resolutely.

'Then,' said the master of the horse, 'thou shalt be hanged for what thou hast made already, and so were the great secret for ever lost to mankind. Do not humanity this injustice, good father, but e'en bend to thy destiny, and make us an ounce or two of this same stuff, which cannot prejudice above one or two individuals, in order to gain life-time to discover the universal medicine, which shall clear away all mortal diseases at once. But cheer up, thou grave, learned, and most melancholy jackanapes! Hast thou not told me, that a moderate portion of thy drug hath mild effects, no ways ultimately dangerous to the human frame, but which produce depression of spirits, nausea, headache, an unwillingness to change of place—even such a state of temper as would keep a bird from flying out of a cage, were the door left open?'

'I have said so, and it is true,' said the alchemist; 'this effect will it produce, and the bird, who partakes of it in such proportion, shall sit for a season drooping on her perch, without thinking either of the free blue sky, or of the fair greenwood, though the one be lighted by the rays of the rising sun, and the other ringing with the newly awakened song of all the feathered inhabitants of the forest.'

'And this without danger to life?' said Varney, somewhat anxiously.

'Ay, so that proportion and measure be not exceeded; and so that one who knows the nature of the manna be ever near to watch the symptoms, and succour in case of need.'

'Thou shalt regulate the whole,' said Varney; 'thy reward shall be princely, if thou keep'st time and touch, and exceedest not the due proportion to the prejudice of her health—otherwise thy punishment shall be as signal.'

'The prejudice of *her* health!' repeated Alasco; 'it is, then, a woman I am to use my skill upon?'

'No, thou fool,' replied Varney, 'said I not it was a bird—a reclaimed linnet, whose pipe might soothe a hawk when in mid stoop? I see thine eye sparkle, and I know thy beard is not altogether so white as art has made it—*that*, at least, thou hast been able to transmute to silver. But mark me, this is no mate for thee. This caged bird is dear to one who brooks no rivalry, and far less such rivalry as thine, and her health must over all things be cared for. But she is in the case of being commanded down to yonder Kenilworth revels; and it is most expedient—most needful—most necessary, that she fly not thither. Of these necessities and their causes, it is not needful that she should know aught, and it is to be thought that her own wish may lead her to combat all ordinary reasons which can be urged for her remaining a house-keeper.'

'That is but natural,' said the alchemist with a strange smile, which yet bore a greater reference to the human character, than the uninterested and abstracted gaze which his physiognomy had hitherto expressed, where all seemed to refer to some world distant from that which was existing around him.

'It is so,' answered Varney; 'you understand women well, though it may have been long since you were conversant amongst them. Well, then, she is not to be contradicted—yet she is not to be humoured. Understand me—a slight illness, sufficient to take away the desire of removing from thence, and to make such of your wise fraternity as may be called in to aid, recommend a quiet residence at home will, in one word, be esteemed good service, and remunerated as such.'

'I am not to be asked to affect the House of Life?' said the chemist.

'On the contrary, we will have thee hanged if thou dost,' replied Varney.

'And I must,' added Alasco, 'have opportunity to use my turn, and all facilities for concealment or escape, should there be detection?'

'All, all, and everything, thou infidel in all but the impossibilities of alchemy. Why, man, for what dost thou take me?'

The old man rose, and taking a light, walked towards the end of the apartment, where was a door that led to the small sleeping room destined for his reception during that night. At the door he turned round, and slowly repeated Varney's question ere he answered it. 'For what do I take thee, Richard Varney? Why, for a worse devil than I have been myself. But I am in your toils and must serve you till my term be out.'

'Well, well,' answered Varney hastily, 'be stirring with gray light. It may be we shall not need thy medicine—Do naught till I myself come down—Michael Lambourne shall guide you to the place of your destination.' *

When Varney heard the adept's door shut and carefully bolted within, he stepped towards it, and with similar precaution carefully locked it on the outside, and took the key from the lock, muttering to himself, 'Worse than *thee*, thou poisoning quacksalver and witch-monger, who, if thou art not a bounden slave to the devil, it is only because he disdains such an apprentice; I am a mortal man, and seek by mortal means the gratification of my passions, and advancement of my prospects—Thou art a vassal of hell itself. So ho, Lambourne!' he called at another door; and Michael made his appearance with a flushed cheek and an unsteady step.

'Thou art drunk, thou villain!' said Varney to him.

'Doubtless, noble sir,' replied the unabashed Michael, 'we have been drinking all even to the glories of the day, and to my noble Lord of Leicester, and his valiant master of the horse. Drunk! odds blades and poniards, he that would refuse to swallow a dozen healths on such an evening, is a base besognio, and a puckfoist, and shall swallow six inches of my dagger!'

'Hark ye, scoundrel,' said Varney, 'be sober on the instant—I command thee. I know thou canst throw off they drunken folly, like a fool's coat, at pleasure; and if not, it were the worse for thee.'

Lambourne drooped his head, left the apartment, and returned in two or three minutes with his face composed, his hair adjusted, his dress in order, and exhibiting as great a difference from his former self as if the whole man had been changed.

'Art thou sober now, and dost thou comprehend me?' said Varney sternly.

Lambourne bowed in acquiescence.

'Thou must presently down to Cumnor Place with the reverend

* *Note* G. Dr Julio.

man of art, who sleeps yonder in the little vaulted chamber. Here is the key, that thou mayst call him by times. Take another trusty fellow with you. Use him well on the journey, but let him not escape you—pistol him if he attempt it, and I will be your warrant. I will give thee letters to Foster. The doctor is to occupy the lower apartments of the eastern quadrangle, with freedom to use the old elaboratory and its implements. He is to have no access to the lady but such as I shall point out—only she may be amused to see his philosophical jugglery. Thou wilt await at Cumnor Place my further orders; and, as thou livest, beware of the ale-bench and the aquavitæ flask. Each breath drawn in Cumnor Place must be kept severed from common air.'

'Enough, my lord—I mean my worshipful master—soon, I trust, to be my worshipful knightly master. You have given me my lesson and my licence; I will execute the one, and not abuse the other. I will be in the saddle by daybreak.'

'Do so, and deserve favour. Stay—ere thou goest fill me a cup of wine—not out of that flask, sirrah,'—as Lambourne was pouring out from that which Alasco had left half finished, 'fetch me a fresh one.'

Lambourne obeyed, and Varney, after rinsing his mouth with the liquor, drank a full cup, and said, as he took up a lamp to retreat to his sleeping apartment, 'It is strange—I am as little the slave of fancy as any one, yet I never speak for a few minutes with this fellow Alasco, but my mouth and lungs feel as if soiled with the fumes of calcined arsenic—pah!'

So saying, he left the apartment. Lambourne lingered, to drink a cup of the freshly opened flask. 'It is from Saint-John's-Berg,' he said, as he paused on the draught to enjoy its flavour, 'and has the true relish of the violet. But I must forbear it now, that I may one day drink it at my own pleasure.' And he quaffed a goblet of water to quench the fumes of the Rhenish wine, retired slowly towards the door, made a pause, and then, finding the temptation irresistible, walked hastily back, and took another long pull at the wine-flask, without the formality of a cup.

'Were it not for this accursed custom,' he said, 'I might climb as high as Varney himself. But who can climb when the room turns round with him like a parish-top? I would the distance were greater, or the road rougher, betwixt my hand and mouth! But I will drink nothing to-morrow, save water—nothing save fair water.'

19

Pistol. And tidings do I bring, and lucky joys,
    And happy news of price.
Falstaff. I prithee, now, deliver them like to men of
    this world.
Pistol. A foutra for the world, and worldlings base!
    I speak of Africa, and golden joys.
                  Henry IV, Part. 2.

THE public room of the Black Bear at Cumnor, to which the scene
of our story now returns, boasted, on the evening we now treat
of, no ordinary assemblage of guests. There had been a fair in the
neighbourhood, and the cutting mercer of Abingdon, with some
of the other personages whom the reader has already been made
acquainted with, as friends and customers of Giles Gosling, had
already formed their wonted circle around the evening fire, and
were talking over the news of the day.

A lively, bustling, arch fellow, whose pack and oaken ell wand,
studded duly with brass points, denoted him to be of Autolycus's
profession, occupied a good deal of the attention, and furnished
much of the amusement of the evening. The pedlars of those days,
it must be remembered, were men of far greater importance than
the degenerate and degraded hawkers of our modern times. It was
by means of these peripatetic venders that the country trade, in the
finer manufactures used in female dress particularly, was almost
entirely carried on; and if a merchant of this description arrived
at the dignity of travelling with a pack-horse, he was a person of
no small consequence, and company for the most substantial
yeoman or Franklin whom he might meet in his wanderings.

The pedlar of whom we speak bore, accordingly, an active and
unrebuked share in the merriment to which the rafters of the bonny
Black Bear of Cumnor resounded. He had his smile with pretty
Mistress Cicely, his broad laugh with mine host, and his jest upon
dashing Master Goldthred, who, though indeed without any such
benevolent intention on his own part, was the general butt of the
evening. The pedlar and he were closely engaged in a dispute upon
the preference due to the Spanish nether-stock over the black
Gascoigne hose, and mine host had just winked to the guests around

him, as who should say, 'You will have mirth presently, my masters,' when the trampling of horses was heard in the courtyard, and the hostler was loudly summoned, with a few of the newest oaths then in vogue, to add force to the invocation. Out tumbled Will Hostler, John Tapster, and all the militia of the inn, who had slunk from their posts in order to collect some scattered crumbs of the mirth which was flying about among the customers. Out into the yard sallied mine host himself also, to do fitting salutation to his new guests; and presently returned, ushering into the apartment his own worthy nephew, Michael Lambourne, pretty tolerably drunk, and having under his escort the astrologer. Alasco, though still a little old man, had, by altering his gown to a riding-dress, trimming his beard and eyebrows, and so forth, struck at least a score of years from his apparent age, and might now seem an active man of sixty, or little upwards. He appeared at present exceedingly anxious, and had insisted much with Lambourne that they should not enter the inn, but go straight forward to the place of their destination. But Lambourne would not be controlled. 'By Cancer and Capricorn,' he vociferated, 'and the whole heavenly host—besides all the stars that these blessed eyes of mine have seen sparkle in the southern heavens, to which these northern blinkers are but farthing candles, I will be unkindly for no one's humour—I will stay and salute my worthy uncle here.—Chesu! that good blood should ever be forgotten betwixt friends!—A gallon of your best, uncle, and let it go round to the health of the noble Earl of Leicester! What! Shall we not collogue together, and warm the cockles of our ancient kindness? Shall we not collogue, I say?'

'With all my heart, kinsman,' said mine host, who obviously wished to be rid of him; 'but are you to stand shot to all this good liquor?'

This is a question has quelled many a jovial toper, but it moved not the purpose of Lambourne's soul. 'Question my means, uncle?' he said, producing a handful of mixed gold and silver pieces; 'question Mexico and Peru —question the Queen's exchequer—God save her Majesty!—She is my good Lord's good mistress.'

'Well, kinsman,' said mine host, 'it is my business to sell wine to those who can buy it—So, Jack Tapster, do me thine office. But I would I knew how to come by money as lightly as thou dost, Mike.'

'Why, uncle,' said Lambourne, 'I will tell thee a secret —Dost see this little old fellow here? as old and withered a chip as ever the devil put into his porridge—and yet, uncle, between you and me, he hath Potosi in that brain of his—'Sblood! he can coin ducats faster than I can vent oaths.'

'I will have none of his coinage in my purse though, Michael,' said mine host; 'I know what belongs to falsifying the Queen's coin.'

'Thou art an ass, uncle, for as old as thou art—Pull me not by the skirts, doctor, thou art an ass thyself to boot—so, being both asses, I tell ye I spoke but metaphorically

'Are you mad?' said the old man; 'Is the devil in you?—can you not let us begone without drawing all men's eyes on us?'

'Say'st thou?' said Lambourne; 'Thou art deceived now—no man shall see you an I give the word. By heavens, masters, an any one dare to look on this old gentleman, I will slash the eyes out of his head with my poniard—So sit down, old friend, and be merry—these are mine ingles—mine ancient inmates, and will betray no man.'

'Had you not better withdraw to a private apartment, nephew?' said Giles Gosling; 'you speak strange matter,' he added, 'and there be intelligencers everywhere.'

'I care not for them,' said the magnanimous Michael—'intelligencers? pshaw! I serve the noble Earl of Leicester—Here comes the wine—Fill round, Master Skinker, a carouse to the health of the flower of England, the noble Earl of Leicester! I say, the noble Earl of Leicester! He that does me not reason is a swine of Sussex, and I'll make him kneel to the pledge, if I should cut his hams and smoke them for bacon.'

None disputed a pledge given under such formidable penalties; and Michael Lambourne, whose drunken humour was not of course diminished by this new potation, went on in the same wild way, renewing his acquaintance with such of the guests as he had formerly known, and experiencing a reception in which there was now something of deference, mingled with a good deal of fear; for the least servitor of the favourite Earl, especially such a man as Lambourne, was, for very sufficient reasons, an object both of the one and of the other.

In the meanwhile, the old man, seeing his guide in this uncontrollable humour, ceased to remonstrate with him, and sitting down in the most obscure corner of the room, called for a small measure of sack, over which he seemed, as it were, to slumber, withdrawing himself as much as possible from general observation, and doing nothing which could recall his existence to the recollection of his fellow-traveller, who by this time had got into close intimacy with his ancient comrade, Goldthred of Abingdon.

'Never believe me, bully Mike,' said the mercer, 'if I am not as glad to see thee as ever I was to see a customer's money! Why, thou canst give a friend a sly place at a mask or a revel now, Mike; ay, or, I warrant thee, thou canst say in my lord's ear, when my honourable lord is down in these parts, and wants a Spanish ruff or the like—thou canst say in his ear, There is mine old friend, young Lawrence Goldthred of Abingdon, has as good wares, lawn, tiffany, cambric, and so forth—ay, and is as pretty a piece of man's flesh, too, as is in Berkshire, and will ruffle it for your lordship with any man of his inches; and thou mayst say'——

'I can say a hundred d—d lies besides, mercer,' answered Lambourne; 'what, one must not stand upon a good word for a friend!'

'Here is to thee, Mike, with all my heart,' said the mercer; 'and thou canst tell one the reality of the new fashions too—Here was a rogue pedlar but now, was crying up the old-fashioned Spanish nether-stock over the Gascoigne hose, although thou seest how well the French hose set off the leg and knee, being adorned with parti-coloured garters and garniture in conformity.'

'Excellent, excellent,' replied Lambourne; 'why, thy limber bit of a thigh, thrust through that bunch of slashed buckram and tiffany, shows like a housewife's distaff, when the flax is half spun off.'

'Said I not so?' said the mercer, whose shallow brain was now overflowed in his turn; 'where then, where be this rascal pedlar?—there was a pedlar here but now, methinks—Mine host, where the foul fiend is this pedlar?'

'Where wise men should be, Master Goldthred,' replied Giles Gosling; 'even shut up in his private chamber, telling over the sales of to-day, and preparing for the custom of to-morrow.'

'Hang him, a mechanical chuff,' said the mercer; 'but for shame, it were a good deed to ease him of his wares, —a set of peddling knaves, who stroll through the land, and hurt the established trader. There are good fellows in Berkshire yet, mine host—your pedlar may be met withal on Maiden Castle.'

'Ay,' replied mine host, laughing, 'and he who meets him may meet his match—the pedlar is a tall man.'

'Is he?' said Goldthred.

'Is he?' replied the host; 'ay, by cock and pye is he—the very pedlar he who raddled Robin Hood so tightly, as the song says,—

"Now Robin Hood drew his sword so good,
  The pedlar drew his brand,
And he hath raddled him, Robin Hood,
  Till he neither could see nor stand."'

'Hang him, foul scroyle, let him pass,' said the mercer; 'if he be such a one, there were small worship to be won upon him. And now tell me, Mike—my honest Mike, how wears the Hollands you won of me?'

'Why, well, as you may see, Master Goldthred,' answered Mike; 'I will bestow a pot on thee for the handsel. Fill the flagon, Master Tapster.'

'Thou wilt win no more Hollands, I think, on such wager, friend Mike,' said the mercer; 'for the sulky swain, Tony Foster, rails at thee all to naught, and swears you shall ne'er darken his doors again, for that your oaths are enough to blow the roof off a Christian man's dwelling.'

'Doth he say so, the mincing, hypocritical miser?' vociferated Lambourne;—'Why, then, he shall come down and receive my commands here, this blessed night, under my uncle's roof! And I will ring him such a black sanctus, that he shall think the devil hath him by the skirts for a month to come, for barely hearing me.'

'Nay, now the pottle-pot is uppermost, with a witness,' said the mercer. 'Tony Foster obey thy whistle!—Alas! good Mike, go sleep —go sleep.'

'I tell thee what, thou thin-faced gull,' said Michael Lambourne, in high chafe, 'I will wager thee fifty angels against the first five shelves of thy shop, numbering upward from the false light, with all that is on them, that I make Tony Foster come down to this public-house before we have finished three rounds.'

'I will lay no bet to that amount,' said the mercer, something sobered by an offer which intimated rather too private a knowledge, on Lambourne's part, of the secret recesses of his shop,—'I will lay no such wager,' he said; 'but I will take five angels against thy five, if thou wilt, that Tony Foster will not leave his own roof, or come to ale-house after prayer-time, for thee, or any man.'

'Content,' said Lambourne. 'Here, uncle, hold stakes, and let one of your young bleed-barrels there—one of your infant tapsters, trip presently up to The Place, and give this letter to Master Foster, and say that I, his ingle, Michael Lambourne, pray to speak with him at mine uncle's castle here, upon business of grave import. Away with thee, child, for it is now sundown, and the wretch goeth to bed with the birds, to save mutton-suet—faugh!'

Shortly after this messenger was despatched—an interval which was spent in drinking and buffoonery,—he returned with the answer, that Master Foster was coming presently.

'Won, won!' said Lambourne, darting on the stake.

'Not till he comes, if you please,' said the mercer, interfering.

'Why, 'sblood, he is at the threshold,' replied Michael—'What said he, boy?'

'If it please your worship,' answered the messenger, 'he looked out of window, with a musquetoon in his hand, and when I delivered your errand, which I did with fear and trembling, he said, with a vinegar aspect, that your worship might be gone to the infernal regions.'

'Or to hell, I suppose,' said Lambourne—'it is there he disposes of all that are not of the congregation.'

'Even so,' said the boy; 'I used the other phrase, as being the more poetical.'

'An ingenious youth,' said Michael; 'shalt have a drop to whet thy poetical whistle—And what said Foster next?'

'He called me back,' answered the boy, 'and bid me say you might come to him, if you had aught to say to him.'

'And what next?' said Lambourne.

'He read the letter, and seemed in a fluster, and asked if your worship was in drink—and I said you were speaking a little Spanish, as one who had been in the Canaries.'

'Out, you diminutive pint-pot, whelped of an overgrown reckoning!' replied Lambourne—'Out!—But what said he then?'

'Why,' said the boy, 'he muttered, that if he came not, your worship would bolt out what were better kept in; and so he took his old flat cap, and threadbare blue cloak, and, as I said before, he will be here incontinent.'

'There is truth in what he said,' replied Lambourne, as if speaking to himself—'My brain has played me its old dog's trick—but corragio—let him approach!—I have not rolled about in the world, for many a day, to fear Tony Foster, be I drunk or sober. Bring me a flagon of cold water to christen my sack withal.'

While Lambourne, whom the approach of Foster seemed to have recalled to a sense of his own condition, was busied in preparing to receive him, Giles Gosling stole up to the apartment of the pedlar, whom he found traversing the room in much agitation.

'You withdrew yourself suddenly from the company,' said the landlord to the guest.

'It was time, when the devil became one among you,' replied the pedlar.

'It is not courteous in you to term my nephew by such a name,' said Gosling, 'nor is it kindly in me to reply to it; and yet, in some sort, Mike may be considered as a limb of Satan.'

'Pooh—I talk not of the swaggering ruffian,' replied the pedlar, 'it is of the other, who, for aught I know—But when go they? or wherefore come they?'

'Marry, these are questions I cannot answer,' replied the host. 'But, look you, sir, you have brought me a token from worthy Master Tressilian—a pretty stone it is.' He took out the ring, and looked at it, adding, as he put it into his purse again, that it was too rich a guerdon for anything he could do for the worthy donor. He was, he said, in the public line, and it ill became him to be too inquisitive into other folks' concerns; he had already said, that he could hear nothing, but that the lady lived still at Cumnor Place, in the closest seclusion, and, to such as by chance had a view of her, seemed pensive and discontended with her solitude. 'But here,' he said, 'if you are desirous to gratify your master, is the rarest chance that hath occurred for this many a day. Tony Foster is coming down hither, and it is but letting Mike Lambourne smell another wine-flask, and the Queen's command would not move him from the ale-bench. So they are fast for an hour or so—Now, if you will don your pack, which will be your best excuse, you may, per-chance, win the ear of the old servant, being assured of the master's absence, to let you try to get some custom of the lady, and then you may learn more of her condition than I or any other can tell you.'

'True—very true,' answered Wayland, for he it was; 'an excellent device, but methinks something dangerous—for, say Foster should return?'

'Very possible indeed,' replied the host.

'Or say,' continued Wayland, 'the lady should render me cold thanks for my exertions?'

'As is not unlikely,' replied Giles Gosling. 'I marvel Master Tressilian will take such heed of her that cares not for him.'

'In either case I were foully sped,' said Wayland; 'and therefore I do not, on the whole, much relish your device.'

'Nay, but take me with you, good master serving-man,' replied mine host, 'this is your master's business and not mine; you best know the risk to be encountered, or how far you are willing to brave it. But that which you will not yourself hazard, you cannot expect others to risk.'

'Hold, hold,' said Wayland; 'tell me but one thing—Goes yonder old man up to Cumnor?'

'Surely, I think so,' said the landlord; 'their servant said he was to take their baggage thither, but the ale-tap has been as potent for him as the sack-spiggot has been for Michael.'

'It is enough,' said Wayland, assuming an air of resolution—'I will thwart that old villain's projects—my affright at his baleful aspect begins to abate, and my hatred to arise. Help me on with my pack, good mine host—And look to thyself, old Albumazar—there is a malignant influence in thy horoscope, and it gleams from the constellation Ursa Major.'

So saying, he assumed his burden, and, guided by the landlord through the postern-gate of the Black Bear, took the most private way from thence to Cumnor Place.

20

Clown. You have of these pedlars, that have more in 'em than you'd think, sister.—*Winter's Tale*, Act. IV. Scene 3.

IN his anxiety to obey the Earl's repeated charges of secrecy, as well as from his own unsocial and miserly habits, Anthony Foster was more desirous, by his mode of housekeeping, to escape observation, than to resist intrusive curiosity. Thus, instead of a numerous household to secure his charge, and defend his house, he studied, as much as possible, to elude notice, by diminishing his attendants; so that, unless when there were attendants of the Earl, or of Varney, in the mansion, one old male domestic, and two aged cronies, who assisted in keeping the Countess's apartments in order, were the only servants of the family. It was one of these old women who opened the door when Wayland knocked, and answered his petition to be admitted to exhibit his wares to the ladies of the family, with a volley of vituperation, couched in what is there called the *jowring* dialect. The pedlar found the means of checking this vociferation by slipping a silver groat into her hand, and intimating the present of some stuff for a coif, if the lady would buy of his wares.

'God ield thee, for mine is aw in littocks—Slocket with thy pack into gharn, mon—Her walks in gharn.' Into the garden she ushered the pedlar accordingly, and pointing to an old ruinous garden-house, said, 'Yonder be's her, mon,—yonder be's her—Zhe will buy changes an zhe loikes stuffs.'

'She has left me to come off as I may,' thought Wayland, as he heard the hag shut the garden-door behind him. 'But they shall not be at me, and they dare not murder me, for so little trespass, and by this fair twilight. Hang it, I will on—a brave general never thought of his retreat till he was defeated. I see two females in the old garden-house yonder—but how to address them? Stay—Will Shakespeare, be my friend in need. I will give them a taste of Autolycus.' He then sung, with a good voice, and becoming audacity, the popular play-house ditty,

> "Lawn as white as driven snow
> Cyprus black as e'er was crow,
> Gloves as sweet as damask roses,
> Masks for faces and for noses."

'What hath fortune sent us here for an unwonted sight, Janet?' said the lady.

'One of these merchants of vanity, called pedlars,' answered Janet demurely, 'who utters his light wares in lighter measures—I marvel old Dorcas let him pass.'

'It is a lucky chance, girl,' said the Countess; 'we lead a heavy life here, and this may while off a weary hour.'

'Ay, my gracious lady,' said Janet; 'but my father?'

'He is not *my* father, Janet, nor I hope my master,' answered the lady—'I say, call the man hither—I want some things.'

'Nay,' replied Janet, 'your ladyship has just to say so in the next packet, and if England can furnish them, they will be sent. There will come mischief on't—Pray, dearest lady, let me bid the man begone!'

'I will have thee bid him come hither,' said the Countess,—'or stay, thou terrified fool, I will bid him myself, and spare thee a chiding.'

'Ah! well-a-day, dearest lady, if that were the worst,' said Janet sadly, while the lady called to the pedlar, 'Good fellow, step forward—undo thy pack—if thou hast good wares, chance has sent thee hither for my convenience, and thy profit.'

'What may your ladyship please to lack?' said Wayland, unstrapping his pack, and displaying its contents with as much dexterity as if he had been bred to the trade. Indeed, he had occasionally pursued it in the course of his roving life, and now commended his wares with all the volubility of a trader, and showed some skill in the main art of placing prices upon them.

'What do I please to lack?' said the lady; 'why, considering I have not for six long months bought one yard of lawn or cambric, or one trinket, the most inconsiderable, for my own use, and at my own choice, the better question is, what hast thou got to sell? Lay aside for me that cambric partlet and pair of sleeves—and those roundells of gold fringe, drawn out with cyprus—and that short cloak of cherry-coloured fine cloth, garnished with gold buttons and loops—is it not of an absolute fancy, Janet?'

'Nay, my lady,' replied Janet, 'if you consult my poor judgment, it is, methinks, over gaudy for a graceful habit.'

'Now, out upon thy judgment, if it be no brighter, wench,' said the Countess; 'thou shalt wear it thyself for penance sake; and I promise thee the gold buttons, being somewhat massive, will comfort thy father, and reconcile him to the cherry-coloured body. See that he snap them not away, Janet, and send them to bear company with the imprisoned angels which he keeps captive in his strong box.'

'May I pray your ladyship to spare my poor father!' said Janet.

'Nay, but why should any one spare him that is so sparing of his own nature?' replied the lady. 'Well, but to our gear—That head garniture for myself, and that silver bodkin, mounted with pearl;—and take off two gowns of that russet cloth for Dorcas and Alison, Janet, to keep the old wretches warm against winter comes—And stay, has thou no perfumes and sweet bags, or any handsome casting bottles of the newest mode?'

'Were I a pedlar in earnest, I were a made merchant,' thought Wayland, as he busied himself to answer the demands which she thronged one on another, with the eagerness of a young lady, who has been long secluded from such a pleasing occupation. 'But how to bring her to a moment's serious reflection.' Then as he exhibited his choicest collection of essences and perfumes, he at once arrested her attention by observing, that these articles had almost risen to double value, since the magnificent preparations made by the Earl of Leicester to entertain the Queen and court at his princely castle of Kenilworth.

'Ha!' said the Countess hastily; 'that rumour then is true, Janet.'

'Surely, madam,' answered Wayland; 'and I marvel it hath not reached your noble ladyship's ears. The Queen of England feasts with the noble Earl for a week during the Summer's Progress; and there are many who will tell you, England will have a king, and England's Elizabeth—God save her—a husband, ere the Progress be over.'

'They lie like villains!' said the Countess, bursting forth impatiently.

'For God's sake, madam, consider,' said Janet, trembling with apprehension; 'who would cumber themselves about pedlar's tidings?'

'Yes, Janet!' exclaimed the Countess; 'right, thou hast corrected me justly. Such reports, blighting the reputation of England's brightest and noblest peer, can only find currency amongst the mean, the abject, and the infamous.'

'May I perish, lady,' said Wayland Smith, observing that her violence directed itself towards him, 'if I have done anything to merit this strange passion! I have said but what many men say.'

By this time the Countess had recovered her composure, and endeavoured, alarmed by the anxious hints of Janet, to suppress all appearance of displeasure. 'I were loath,' she said, 'good fellow, that our Queen should change the virgin style, so dear to us her people—think not of it.' And then, as if desirous to change the subject, she added, 'And what is this paste, so carefully put up in the silver box?' as she examined the contents of a casket in which drugs and perfumes were contained in separate drawers.

'It is a remedy, madam, for a disorder, of which I trust your ladyship will never have reason to complain. The amount of a small turkey-bean, swallowed daily for a week, fortifies the heart against those black vapours which arise from solitude, melancholy, unrequited affection, disappointed hope——'

'Are you a fool, friend?' said the Countess sharply; 'or do you think, because I have good-naturedly purchased your trumpery goods at your roguish prices, that you may put any gullery you will on me?—who ever heard that affections of the heart were cured by medicines given to the body?'

'Under your honourable favour,' said Wayland, 'I am an honest man, and I have sold my goods at an honest price—As to this most precious medicine, when I told its qualities, I asked you not to purchase it, so why should I lie to you? I say not it will cure a rooted affection of the mind, which only God and time can do; but I say, that this restorative relieves the black vapours which are engendered in the body of that melancholy which broodeth on the mind. I have relieved many with it, both in court and city; and of late, one Master Edmund Tressilian, a worshipful gentleman in Cornwall, who, on some slight, received, it was told me, where he had set his affections, was brought into that state of melancholy which made his friends alarmed for his life.'

He paused, and the lady remained silent for some time, and then asked, with a voice she strove in vain to render firm and indifferent in its tone, 'Is the gentleman you have mentioned perfectly recovered?'

'Passably, madam,' answered Wayland; 'he hath at least no bodily complaint.'

'I will take some of the medicine, Janet,' said the Countess. 'I too have sometimes that dark melancholy which overclouds the brain.'

'You shall not do so, madam,' said Janet; 'who shall answer that this fellow vends what is wholesome?'

'I will myself warrant my good faith,' said Wayland; and, taking a part of the medicine, he swallowed it before them. The Countess now bought what remained, a step to which Janet, by further objections, only determined her the more obstinately. She even took the first dose upon the instant, and professed to feel her heart lightened and her spirits augmented—a consequence which, in all probability, existed only in her own imagination. The lady then piled the purchases she had made together, flung her purse to Janet, and desired her to compute the amount and to pay the pedlar; while she herself, as if tired of the amusement she at first found in conversing with him, wished him good-evening, and walked carelessly into the house, thus depriving Wayland of every opportunity to speak with her in private. He hastened, however, to attempt an explanation with Janet.

'Maiden,' he said, 'thou hast the face of one who should love her mistress. She hath much need of faithful service.'

'And well deserves it at my hands,' replied Janet; 'but what of that?'

'Maiden, I am not altogether what I seem,' said the pedlar, lowering his voice.

'The less like to be an honest man,' said Janet.

'The more so,' answered Wayland, 'since I am no pedlar.'

'Get thee gone then instantly, or I will call for assistance,' said Janet; 'my father must ere this time be returned.'

'Do not be so rash,' said Wayland; 'you will do what you may repent of. I am one of your mistress's friends; and she had need of more, not that thou shouldst ruin those she hath.'

'How shall I know that?' said Janet.

'Look me in the face,' said Wayland Smith, 'and see if thou dost not read honesty in my looks.'

And in truth, though by no means handsome, there was in his physiognomy the sharp, keen expression of inventive genius and prompt intellect, which, joined to quick and brilliant eyes, a well-formed mouth, and an intelligent smile, often gives grace and interest to features which are both homely and irregular. Janet looked at him with the sly simplicity of her sect, and replied, 'Notwithstanding thy boasted honesty, friend, and although I am not accustomed to read and pass judgment on such volumes as thou hast submitted to my perusal, I think I see in thy countenance something of the pedlar—something of the picaroon.'

'On a small scale, perhaps,' said Wayland Smith, laughing. 'But this evening, or to-morrow, will an old man come hither with thy father, who has the stealthy step of the cat, the shrewd and vindictive eye of the rat, the fawning wile of the spaniel, the determined grasp of the mastiff—of him beware, for your own sake and that of your mistress. See you, fair Janet, he brings the venom of the aspic under the assumed innocence of the dove. What precise mischief he meditates towards you I cannot guess, but death and disease have ever dogged his footsteps. Say naught of this to thy mistress—my art suggests to me that in her state, the fear of evil may be as dangerous as its operation—But see that she take my specific, for'—(he lowered his voice and spoke low but impressively in her ear) 'it is an antidote against poison—Hark, they enter the garden!'

In effect, a sound of noisy mirth and loud talking approached the garden door, alarmed by which Wayland Smith sprung into the midst of a thicket of overgrown shrubs, while Janet withdrew to the garden-house, that she might not incur observation, and that she might at the same time conceal, at least for the present, the purchases made from the supposed pedlar, which lay scattered on the floor of the summer-house.

Janet, however, had no occasion for anxiety. Her father, his old attendant, Lord Leicester's domestic, and the astrologer entered the garden in tumult and in extreme perplexity, endeavouring to quiet Lambourne, whose brain had now become completely fired with liquor, and who was one of those unfortunate persons, who, being once stirred with the vinous stimulus, do not fall asleep like other drunkards, but remain partially influenced by it for many hours, until at length, by successive draughts, they are elevated into a state of uncontrollable frenzy. Like many men in this state also, Lambourne neither lost the power of motion, speech, or expression; but, on the contrary, spoke with unwonted emphasis and readiness, and told all that at another time he would have been most desirous to have kept secret.

'What!' ejaculated Michael, at the full extent of his voice, 'am I to have no welcome—no carouse, when I have brought fortune to your old ruinous dog-house in the shape of a devil's ally, that can change slate-shivers into Spanish dollars? Here, you Tony Fire-the-Fagot, papist, puritan, hypocrite, miser, profligate, devil, compounded of all men's sins, bow down and reverence him who has brought into thy house the very mammon thou worshippest.'

'For God's sake,' said Foster, 'speak low—come into the house—thou shalt have wine, or whatever thou wilt.'

'No, old puckfoist, I will have it here,' thundered the inebriated ruffian—'here, *al fresco*, as the Italian hath it. No, no, I will not drink with that poisoning devil within doors, to be choked with the fumes of arsenic and quicksilver; I learned from villain Varney to beware of that.'

'Fetch him wine, in the name of all the fiends,' said the alchemist.

'Aha! and thou wouldst spice it for me, old Truepenny, wouldst thou not? Ay, I should have copperas, and hellebore, and vitriol, and aquafortis, and twenty devilish materials, bubbling in my brain-pan like a charm to raise the devil in a witch's cauldron. Hand me the flask thyself, old Tony Fire-the-Fagot—and let it be cool—I will have no wine mulled at the pile of the old burned bishops—Or stay, let Leicester be king if he will—good—and Varney, villain Varney, grand vizier—why, excellent,—and what shall I be, then? —why, emperor—Emperor Lambourne! I will see this choice piece of beauty that they have walled up here for their private pleasures— I will have her this very night to serve my wine-cup, and put on my nightcap. What should a fellow do with two wives, were he twenty times an Earl?—answer me that, Tony boy, you old reprobate, hypocritical dog, whom God struck out of the book of life, but tormented with the constant wish to be restored to it. You old bishop-burning, blasphemous fanatic, answer me that.'

'I will stick my knife to the haft in him,' said Foster, in a low tone, which trembled with passion.

'For the love of Heaven, no violence,' said the astrologer. 'It cannot but be looked closely into. Here, honest Lambourne, wilt thou pledge me to the health of the noble Earl of Leicester, and Master Richard Varney?'

'I will, mine old Albumazar—I will, my trusty vendor of ratsbane —I would kiss thee, mine honest infractor of the Lex Julia (as they said at Leyden), didst thou not flavour so damnably of sulphur, and such fiendish apothecary's stuff. Here goes it, up seyes—to Varney and Leicester!—two more noble mounting spirits—and more dark-seeking, deep-diving, high-flying, malicious, ambitious miscreants —well, I say no more, but I will whet my dagger on his heart-spone, that refuses to pledge me! And so, my masters——'

Thus speaking, Lambourne exhausted the cup which the astrologer had handed him, and which contained not wine, but distilled spirits.

He swore half an oath, dropped the empty cup from his grasp, laid his hand on his sword without being able to draw it, reeled, and fell without sense or motion into the arms of the domestic, who dragged him off to his chamber and put him to bed.

In the general confusion, Janet regained her lady's chamber unobserved, trembling like an aspen leaf, but determined to keep secret from the Countess the dreadful surmises which she could not help entertaining from the drunken ravings of Lambourne. Her fears, however, though they assumed no certain shape, kept pace with the advice of the pedlar; and she confirmed her mistress, in her purpose of taking the medicine which he had recommended, from which it is probable she would otherwise have dissuaded her. Neither had these intimations escaped the ears of Wayland, who knew much better how to interpret them. He felt much compassion at beholding so lovely a creature as the Countess, and whom he had first seen in the bosom of domestic happiness, exposed to the machinations of such a gang of villains. His indignation, too, had been highly excited, by hearing the voice of his old master, against whom he felt, in equal degree, the passions of hatred and fear. He nourished also a pride in his own art and resources; and dangerous as the task was, he that night formed a determination to attain the bottom of the mystery, and to aid the distressed lady, if it were yet possible. From some words which Lambourne had dropped among his ravings, Wayland now, for the first time, felt inclined to doubt that Varney had acted entirely on his own account, in wooing and winning the affections of this beautiful creature. Fame asserted of this zealous retainer that he had accommodated his lord in former love-intrigues; and it occurred to Wayland Smith, that Leicester himself might be the party chiefly interested. Her marriage with the Earl he could not suspect; but even the discovery of such a passing intrigue with a lady of Mistress Amy Robsart's rank, was a secret of the deepest importance to the stability of the favourite's power over Elizabeth. 'If Leicester should hesitate to stifle such a rumour by very strange means,' said he to himself, 'he has those about him who would do him that favour without waiting for his consent. If I would meddle in this business, it must be in such guise as my old master uses when he compounds his manna of Satan, and that is with a close mask on my face. So I will quit Giles Gosling to-morrow, and change my course and place of residence as often as a hunted fox. I should like to see this little puritan, too, once more.

She looks both pretty and intelligent, to have come of such a caitiff as Anthony Fire-the-Fagot.'

Giles Gosling received the adieus of Wayland rather joyfully than otherwise. The honest publican saw so much peril in crossing the course of the Earl of Leicester's favourite, that his virtue was scarce able to support him in the task, and he was well pleased when it was likely to be removed from his shoulders; still, however, professing his good will, and readiness, in case of need, to do Mr Tressilian or his emissary any service, in so far as consisted with his character of a publican.

21

Vaulting ambition, that o'erleaps itself,
And falls on the other side.—*Macbeth*.

THE splendour of the approaching revels at Kenilworth was now the conversation through all England; and everything was collected at home, or from abroad, which could add to the gaiety or glory of the prepared reception of Elizabeth, at the house of her most distinguished favourite. Meantime Leicester appeared daily to advance in the Queen's favour. He was perpetually by her side in council, willingly listened to in the moments of courtly recreation —favoured with approaches even to familiar intimacy—looked up to by all who had aught to hope at court—courted by foreign ministers with the most flattering testimonies of respect from their sovereigns—the *Alter Ego*, as it seemed, of the stately Elizabeth, who was now very generally supposed to be studying the time and opportunity for associating him, by marriage, into her sovereign power.

Amid such a tide of prosperity, this minion of fortune, and of the Queen's favour, was probably the most unhappy man in the realm which seemed at his devotion. He had the Fairy King's superiority over his friends and dependants, and saw much which they could not. The character of his mistress was intimately known to him; it was his minute and studied acquaintance with her humours, as well as her noble faculties, which, joined to his powerful mental qualities, and his eminent external accomplishments, had raised him so high in her favour; and it was that very knowledge of her disposition which led him to apprehend at every turn some sudden and overwhelming disgrace. Leicester was like a pilot possessed of a chart, which points out to him all the peculiarities of his navigation, but which exhibits so many shoals, breakers, and reefs of rocks, that his anxious eye reaps little more from observing them, than to be convinced that his final escape can be little else than miraculous.

In fact, Queen Elizabeth had a character strangely compounded of the strongest masculine sense, with those foibles which are chiefly supposed proper to the female sex.

Her subjects had the full benefits of her virtues, which far predominated over her weaknesses; but her courtiers, and those about her person, had often to sustain sudden and embarrassing turns of caprice, and the sallies of a temper which was both jealous and despotic. She was the nursing mother of her people, but she was also the true daughter of Henry the Eighth; and though early sufferings and an excellent education had repressed and modified, they had not altogether destroyed, the hereditary temper of that 'hard-ruled King.' 'Her mind,' says her witty godson, Sir John Harrington, who had experienced both the smiles and the frowns which he describes, 'was oft-time like the gentle air, that cometh from the western point in a summer's morn—'twas sweet and refreshing to all around her. Her speech did win all affections. And again, she could put forth such alterations, when obedience was lacking, as left no doubting *whose* daughter she was. When she smiled, it was a pure sunshine, that every one did choose to bask in, if they could; but anon came a storm, from a sudden gathering of clouds, and the thunder fell, in a wondrous manner, on all alike.' *

This variability of disposition, as Leicester well knew, was chiefly formidable to those who had a share in the Queen's affections, and who depended rather on her personal regard, than on the indispensable services which they could render to her councils and her crown. The favour of Burleigh, or of Walsingham, of a description far less striking than that by which he was himself upheld, was founded, as Leicester was well aware, on Elizabeth's solid judgment, not on her partiality; and was, therefore, free from all those principles of change and decay, necessarily incident to that which chiefly arose from personal accomplishments and female predilection. These great and sage statesmen were judged of by the Queen only with reference to the measure they suggested, and the reasons by which they supported their opinions in council; whereas the success of Leicester's course depended on all those light and changeable gales of caprice and humour, which thwart or favour the progress of a lover in the favour of his mistress, and she, too, a mistress who was ever and anon becoming fearful lest she should forget the dignity, or compromise the authority of the Queen, while she indulged the affections of the woman. Of the difficulties which surrounded his power, 'too great to keep or to resign,' Leicester was fully sensible; and, as he looked anxiously round for the means of maintaining himself in his precarious situation, and sometimes contemplated

* 'Nugæ Antiquæ,' Vol. I., pp. 356–362.

those of descending from it in safety, he saw but little hope of either. At such moments, his thoughts turned to dwell upon his secret marriage, and its consequences; and it was in bitterness against himself, if not against his unfortunate Countess, that he ascribed to that hasty measure, adopted in the ardour of what he now called inconsiderate passion, at once the impossibility of placing his power on a solid basis, and an imminent prospect of its precipitate downfall.

'Men say,' thus ran his thoughts, in these anxious and repentant moments, 'that I might marry Elizabeth, and become king of England. All things suggest this. The match is carolled in ballads, while the rabble throw their caps up. It has been touched upon in the schools—whispered in the presence-chamber—recommended from the pulpit—prayed for in the Calvinistic churches abroad—touched on by statists in the very council at home. These bold insinuations have been rebutted by no rebuke, no resentment, no chiding, scarce even by the usual female protestation that she would live and die a Virgin princess. Her words have been more courteous than ever, though she knows such rumours are abroad—her actions more gracious—her looks more kind—naught seems wanting to make me King of England, and place me beyond the storms of court favour, excepting the putting forth of mine own hand to take that crown imperial, which is the glory of the universe! And when I might stretch that hand out most boldly, it is fettered down by a secret and inextricable bond! And here I have letters from Amy,' he would say, catching them up with a movement of peevishness, 'persecuting me to acknowledge her openly—to do justice to her and to myself—and I wot not what. Methinks I have done less than justice to myself already. And she speaks as if Elizabeth were to receive the knowledge of this matter with the glee of a mother hearing of the happy marriage of a hopeful son!—She, the daughter of Henry, who spared neither man in his anger, nor woman in his desire,—she to find herself tricked, drawn on with toys of passion to the verge of acknowledging her love to a subject, and he discovered to be a married man!—Elizabeth to learn that she had been dallied with in such fashion, as a gay courtier might trifle with a country wench—We should then see to our ruin *furens quid fœmina*!'

He would then pause, and call for Varney, whose advice was now more frequently resorted to than ever, because the Earl remembered the remonstrances which he had made against his secret contract. And their consultation usually terminated in anxious deliberation, how, or in what manner, the Countess was to be produced at Kenilworth. These communings had for some time ever ended always in a resolution to delay the Progress from day to day. But at length a peremptory decision became necessary.

'Elizabeth will not be satisfied without her presence,' said the Earl; 'whether any suspicion hath entered her mind, as my own apprehensions suggest, or whether the petition of Tressilian is kept in her memory by Sussex, or some other secret enemy, I know not; but amongst all the favourable expressions which she uses to me, she often recurs to the story of Amy Robsart. I think that Amy is the slave in the chariot, who is placed there by my evil fortune, to dash and to confound my triumph, even when at the highest. Show me thy device, Varney, for solving the inextricable difficulty. I have thrown every such impediment in the way of these accursed revels, as I could propound even with a shade of decency, but to-day's interview has put all to a hazard. She said to me kindly, but peremptorily. "We will give you no further time for preparations, my lord, lest you should altogether ruin yourself. On Saturday, the 9th of July, we will be with you at Kenilworth—We pray you to forget none of our appointed guests and suitors, and in especial this light-o'-love, Amy Robsart. We would wish to see the woman who could postpone yonder poetical gentleman, Master Tressilian, to your man, Richard Varney." Now, Varney, ply thine invention, whose forge hath availed us so often; for sure as my name is Dudley, the danger menaced by my horoscope is now darkening around me.'

'Can my lady be by no means persuaded to bear for a brief space the obscure character which circumstances impose on her?' said Varney, after some hesitation.

'How, sirrah! my Countess term herself *thy* wife!—that may neither stand with my honour nor with hers.'

'Alas! my lord,' answered Varney, 'and yet such is the quality in which Elizabeth now holds her; and to contradict this opinion is to discover all.'

'Think of something else, Varney,' said the Earl, in great agitation; 'this invention is naught—If I could give way to it, she would not; for I tell thee, Varney, if thou know'st it not, that not Elizabeth on the throne has more pride than the daughter of this obscure gentleman of Devon. She is flexible in many things, but where she holds her honour brought in question, she hath a spirit and temper as apprehensive as lightning, and as swift in execution.'

'We have experienced that, my lord, else had we not been thus circumstanced,' said Varney. 'But what else to suggest I know not —Methinks she whose good fortune in becoming your lordship's bride gives rise to the danger, should do somewhat towards parrying it.'

'It is impossible,' said the Earl, waving his hand; 'I know neither authority nor entreaties would make her endure thy name for an hour.'

'It is somewhat hard though,' said Varney, in a dry tone; and, without pausing on that topic, he added, 'Suppose some one were found to represent her? Such feats have been performed in the courts of as sharp-eyed monarchs as Queen Elizabeth.'

'Utter madness, Varney,' answered the Earl; 'the counterfeit would be confronted with Tressilian, and discovery become inevitable.'

'Tressilian might be removed from court,' said the unhesitating Varney.

'And by what means?'

'There are many,' said Varney, 'by which a statesman in your situation, my lord, may remove from the scene one who pries into your affairs, and places himself in perilous opposition to you.'

'Speak not to me of such policy, Varney,' said the Earl hastily; 'which, besides, would avail nothing in the present case. Many others may be at court, to whom Amy may be known; and besides, on the absence of Tressilian, her father or some of her friends would be instantly summoned hither. Urge thine invention once more.'

'My lord, I know not what to say,' answered Varney; 'but were I myself in such perplexity, I would ride post down to Cumnor Place, and compel my wife to give her consent to such measures as her safety and mine required.'

'Varney,' said Leicester, 'I cannot urge her to aught so repugnant to her noble nature, as a share in this stratagem—it would be a base requital for the love she bears me.'

'Well, my lord,' said Varney, 'your lordship is a wise and an honourable man, and skilled in those high points of romantic scruple, which are current in Arcadia, perhaps, as your nephew Philip Sidney, writes. I am your humble servitor—a man of this world, and only happy that my knowledge of it, and its ways, is such as your lordship has not scorned to avail yourself of. Now I would fain know, whether the obligation lies on my lady or on you, in this fortunate union; and which has most reason to show complaisance to the other, and to consider that other's wishes, conveniences, and safety?'

'I tell thee, Varney,' said the Earl, 'that all it was in my power to bestow upon her, was not merely deserved, but a thousand times overpaid, by her own virtue and beauty; for never did greatness descend upon a creature so formed by nature to grace and adorn it.'

'It is well, my lord, you are so satisfied,' answered Varney, with his usual sardonic smile, which even respect to his patron could not at all times subdue—'you will have time enough to enjoy undisturbed the society of one so gracious and beautiful,—that is, as soon as such confinement in the Tower be over, as may correspond to the crime of deceiving the affections of Elizabeth Tudor—A cheaper penalty, I presume, you do not expect.'

'Malicious fiend!' answered Leicester, 'do you mock me in my misfortune? Manage it as thou wilt.'

'If you are serious, my lord,' said Varney, 'you must set forth instantly, and post for Cumnor Place.'

'Do thou go thyself, Varney; the devil has given thee that sort of eloquence, which is most powerful in the worst cause. I should stand self-convicted of villainy, were I to urge such a deceit. Begone, I tell thee—Must I entreat thee to mine own dishonour?'

'No, my lord,' said Varney—'but if you are serious in entrusting me with the task of urging this most necessary measure, you must give me a letter to my lady, as my credentials, and trust to me for backing the advice it contains with all the force in my power. And such is my opinion of my lady's love for your lordship, and of her willingness to do that which is at once to contribute to your pleasure and your safety, that I am sure she will condescend to bear, for a few brief days, the name of so humble a man as myself, especially since it is not inferior in antiquity to that of her own paternal house.'

Leicester seized on writing materials, and twice or thrice commenced a letter to the Countess, which he afterwards tore into fragments. At length he finished a few distracted lines, in which he conjured her, for reasons nearly concerning his life and honour, to consent to bear the name of Varney for a few days, during the revels at Kenilworth. He added, that Varney would communicate all the reasons which rendered this deception indispensable; and having signed and sealed these credentials, he flung them over the table to Varney, with a motion that he should depart, which his adviser was not slow to comprehend and to obey.

Leicester remained like one stupefied, till he heard the trampling of the horses, as Varney, who took no time even to change his dress, threw himself into the saddle, and, followed by a single servant, set off for Berkshire. At the sound, the Earl started from his seat, and ran to the window, with the momentary purpose of recalling the unworthy commission with which he had entrusted one, of whom he used to say, he knew no virtuous property save affection to his patron. But Varney was already beyond call—and the bright starry firmament, which the age considered as the Book of Fate, lying spread before Leicester when he opened the casement, diverted him from his better and more manly purpose.

'There they roll, on their silent but potential course,' said the Earl, looking around him, 'without a voice which speaks to our ear, but with influences which affect, at every change, the indwellers of this vile earthly planet. This, if astrologers fable not, is the very crisis of my fate! The hour approaches, of which I was taught to beware—the hour, too, which I was encouraged to hope for. A King was the word—but how?—the crown matrimonial—all hopes of that are gone—let them go. The rich Netherlands have demanded me for their leader, and, would Elizabeth consent, would yield me to *their* crown. And have I not such a claim, even in this kingdom? That of York, descending from George of Clarence to the House of Huntingdon, which, this lady failing, may have a fair chance—Huntingdon is of my house. But I will plunge no deeper in these high mysteries. Let me hold my course in silence for a while, and in obscurity, like a subterranean river—the time shall come that I will burst forth in my strength, and bear all opposition before me.'

While Leicester was thus stupefying the remonstrances of his own conscience, by appealing to political necessity for his apology, or losing himself amidst the wild dreams of ambition, his agent left town and tower behind him, on his hasty journey to Berkshire. *He* also nourished high hope. He had brought Lord Leicester to the point which he had desired, of committing to him the most intimate recesses of his breast, and of using him as the channel of his most confidential intercourse with his lady. Henceforward it would, he foresaw, be difficult for his patron either to dispense with his services, or refuse his requests, however unreasonable. And if this disdainful dame, as he termed the Countess, should comply with the request of her husband, Varney, her pretended husband, must needs become so situated with respect to her, that there was no knowing where his audacity might be bounded; perhaps not till circumstances enabled him to obtain a triumph, which he thought of with a mixture of fiendish feelings, in which revenge for her previous scorn was foremost and predominant. Again he contemplated the possibility of her being totally intractable, and refusing obstinately to play the part assigned to her in the drama at Kenilworth.

'Alasco must then do his part,' he said—'Sickness must serve her Majesty as an excuse for not receiving the homage of Mrs. Varney —ay, and a sore and a wasting sickness it may prove, should Elizabeth continue to cast so favourable an eye on my Lord of Leicester. I will not forgo the chance of being favourite of a monarch for want of determined measures, should these be necessary. Forward, good horse, forward—ambition, and haughty hope of power, pleasure, and revenge, strike their stings as deep through my bosom as I plunge the rowels in thy flanks. On, good horse, on—the devil urges us both forward.'

22

If that my beauty is but small,
　　Among court ladies all despised,
Why didst thou rend it from that hall,
　　Where, scornful Earl, 'twas dearly prized?

No more thou comest with lover's speed,
　　Thy once beloved bride to see;
But be she alive, or be she dead,
　　I fear, stern Earl, 's the same to thee.

　　　　　'Cumnor Hall,' by William Julius Mickle.

THE ladies of fashion of the present, or of any other period, must have allowed that the young and lovely Countess of Leicester had, besides her youth and beauty, two qualities which entitled her to a place amongst women of rank and distinction. She displayed, as we have seen in her interview with the pedlar, a liberal promptitude to make unnecessary purchases, solely for the pleasure of acquiring useless and showy trifles which ceased to please as soon as they were possessed; and she was, besides, apt to spend a considerable space of time every day in adorning her person, although the varied splendour of her attire could only attract the half satirical praise of the precise Janet, or an approving glance from the bright eyes which witnessed their own beams of triumph reflected from the mirror.

The Countess Amy had, indeed, to plead for indulgence in those frivolous tastes, that the education of the times had done little or nothing for a mind naturally gay and averse to study. If she had not loved to collect finery and to wear it, she might have woven tapestry or sewed embroidery, till her labours spread in gay profusion all over the walls and seats at Lidcote Hall; or she might have varied Minerva's labours with the task of preparing a mighty pudding against the time that Sir Hugh Robsart returned from the greenwood. But Amy had no natural genius either for the loom, the needle, or the receipt-book. Her mother had died in infancy; her father contradicted her in nothing; and Tressilian, the only one that approached her who was able or desirous to attend to the cultivation of her mind, had much hurt his interest with her, by assuming too eagerly the task of a preceptor; so that he was regarded by the lively, indulged, and idle girl with some fear and much respect; but with little or nothing of that softer emotion which it had been his hope and his ambition to inspire. And thus her heart lay readily open, and her fancy became easily captivated by the noble exterior and graceful deportment and complacent flattery of Leicester, even before he was known to her as the dazzling minion of wealth and power.

The frequent visits of Leicester at Cumnor, during the earlier part of their union, had reconciled the Countess to the solitude and privacy to which she was condemned; but when these visits became rarer and more rare, and when the void was filled up with letters of excuse, not always very warmly expressed, and generally extremely brief, discontent and suspicion began to haunt those splendid apartments which love had fitted up for beauty. Her answers to Leicester conveyed these feelings too bluntly, and pressed more naturally than prudently that she might be relieved from this obscure and secluded residence, by the Earl's acknowledgement of their marriage: and in arranging her arguments with all the skill she was mistress of, she trusted chiefly to the warmth of the entreaties with which she urged them. Sometimes she even ventured to mingle reproaches, of which Leicester conceived he had good reason to complain.

'I have made her Countess,' he said to Varney; 'surely she might wait till it consisted with my pleasure that she should put on a coronet.'

The Countess Amy viewed the subject in directly an opposite light.

'What signifies,' she said, 'that I have rank and honour in reality, if I am to live an obscure prisoner, without either society or observance, and suffering in my character, as one of dubious or disgraced reputation? I care not for all those strings of pearl, which you fret me by warping into my tresses, Janet. I tell you, that at Lidcote Hall, if I put but a fresh rosebud among my hair my good father would call me to him, that he might see it more closely; and the kind old curate would smile, and Master Mumblazen would say something about roses gules; and now I sit here, decked out like an image with gold and gems, and no one to see my finery but you, Janet. There was the poor Tressilian too—but it avails not speaking of him.'

'It doth not, indeed, madam,' said her prudent attendant; 'and verily you make me sometimes wish you would not speak of him so often, or so rashly.'

'It signifies nothing to warn me, Janet,' said the impatient and incorrigible Countess; 'I was born free, though I am now mewed up like some fine foreign slave, rather than the wife of an English noble. I bore it all with pleasure while I was sure he loved me; but now, my tongue and heart shall be free, let them fetter my limbs as they will. I tell thee, Janet, I love my husband—I will love him till my latest breath—I cannot cease to love him, even if I would, or if he—which, God knows, may chance—should cease to love me. But I will say, and loudly, I would have been happier than I now am, to have remained in Lidcote Hall; even although I must have married poor Tressilian, with his melancholy look, and his head full of learning, which I cared not for. He said if I would read his favourite volumes, there would come a time that I should be glad of having done so—I think it is come now.'

'I bought you some books, madam,' said Janet, 'from a lame fellow who sold them in the Market-place—and who stared something boldly at me, I promise you.'

'Let me see them, Janet,' said the Countess; 'but let them not be of your own precise cast. How is this, most righteous damsel? "A Pair of Snuffers for the Golden Candlestick"—"A Handful of Myrrh and Hyssop to put a Sick Soul to Purgation"—"A Draught of Water from the Valley of Baca"—"Foxes and Firebrands"—What gear call you this, maiden?'

'Nay, madam,' said Janet, 'it was but fitting and seemly to put grace in your ladyship's way; but an you will none of it, there are play-books, and poet-books, I trow.'

The Countess proceeded carelessly in her examination, turning over such rare volumes as would now make the fortune of twenty retail booksellers. Here was a "Boke of Cookery, imprinted by Richard Lant," and "Sketon's Books"—"The Passtime of the People"—"The Castle of Knowledge," etc. But neither to this lore did the Countess's heart incline, and joyfully did she start up from the listless task of turning over the leaves of the pamphlets, and hastily did she scatter them through the floor, when the hasty clatter of horses' feet, heard in the courtyard, called her to the window, exclaiming. 'It is Leicester!—it is my noble Earl!—it is my Dudley! Every stroke of his horse's hoof sounds like a note of lordly music!'

There was a brief bustle in the mansion, and Foster, with his downward look and sullen manner, entered the apartment to say, 'That Master Richard Varney was arrived from my lord, having ridden all night, and craved to speak with her ladyship instantly.'

'Varney?' said the disappointed Countess, 'and to speak with me? —pshaw! But he comes with news from Leicester—so admit him instantly.'

Varney entered her dressing apartment, where she sat arrayed in her native loveliness, adorned with all that Janet's art, and a rich and tasteful undress, could bestow. But the most beautiful part of her attire was her profuse and luxuriant light-brown locks, which floated in such rich abundance around a neck that resembled a swan's, and over a bosom heaving with anxious expectation, which communicated a hurried tinge of red to her whole countenance.

Varney entered the room in the dress in which he had waited on his master that morning to court, the splendour of which made a strange contrast with the disorder arising from hasty riding during a dark night and foul ways. His brow bore an anxious and hurried expression, as one who has that to say of which he doubts the reception, and who hath yet posted on from the necessity of communicating his tidings.

The Countess's anxious eye at once caught the alarm, as she exclaimed. 'You bring news from my lord, Master Varney— Gracious Heaven, is he ill?'

'No, madam, thank Heaven!' said Varney. 'Compose yourself, and permit me to take breath ere I communicate my tidings.'

'No breath, sir,' replied the lady impatiently; 'I know your theatrical arts. Since your breath hath sufficed to bring you hither, it may suffice to tell your tale, at least briefly, and in the gross.'

'Madam,' answered Varney, 'we are not alone, and my lord's message was for your ear only.'

'Leave us, Janet, and Master Foster,' said the lady; 'but remain in the next apartment, and within call.'

Foster and his daughter retired, agreeably to the Lady Leicester's commands, into the next apartment, which was the withdrawing-room. The door which led from the sleeping chamber was then carefully shut and bolted, and the father and daughter remained both in a posture of anxious attention, the first with a stern, suspicious, lowering cast of countenance, and Janet with folded hands, and looks which seemed divided betwixt her desire to know the fortunes of her mistress, and her prayers to Heaven for her safety.

Anthony Foster seemed himself to have some idea of what was passing through his daughter's mind, for he crossed the apartment and took her anxiously by the hand, saying, 'That is right—pray, Janet, pray—we have all need of prayers, and some of us more than others. Pray, Janet—I would pray myself, but I must listen to what goes on within—evil has been brewing, love—evil has been brewing. God forgive our sins, but Varney's sudden and strange arrival bodes us no good.'

Janet had never before heard her father excite or even permit her attention to anything which passed in their mysterious family, and now that he did so, his voice sounded in her ear—she knew not why—like that of a screech-owl denouncing some deed of terror and of woe. She turned her eyes fearfully towards the door, almost as if she expected some sounds of horror to be heard, or some sight of fear to display itself.

All, however, was as still as death, and the voices of those who spoke in the inner-chamber, were, if they spoke at all, carefully subdued to a tone which could not be heard in the next. At once, however, they were heard to speak fast, thick, and hastily; and presently after the voice of the Countess was heard exclaiming, at the highest pitch to which indignation could raise it, 'Undo the door, sir, I command you! Undo the door! I will have no other reply!' she continued, drowning with her vehement accents the low and muttered sounds which Varney was heard to utter betwixt whiles. 'What, ho! without there!' she persisted, accompanying her words with shrieks, 'Janet, alarm the house! Foster, break open the door—I am detained here by a traitor! Use axe and lever, Master Foster—I will be your warrant!'

'It shall not need, madam,' Varney was at length distinctly heard to say. 'If you please to expose my lord's important concerns and your own to the general ear, I will not be your hindrance.'

The door was unlocked and thrown open, and Janet and her father rushed in, anxious to learn the cause of these reiterated exclamations.

When they entered the apartment, Varney stood by the door grinding his teeth, with an expression in which rage, and shame, and fear had each their share. The Countess stood in the midst of her apartment like a juvenile Pythoness, under the influence of the prophetic fury. The veins in her beautiful forehead started into swollen blue lines through the hurried impulse of her articulation

—her cheek and neck glowed like scarlet—her eyes were like those of an imprisoned eagle, flashing red lightning on the foes whom it cannot reach with its talons. Were it possible for one of the Graces to have been animated by a Fury, the countenance could not have united such beauty with so much hatred, scorn, defiance, and resentment. The gesture and attitude corresponded with the voice and looks, and altogether presented a spectacle which was at once beautiful and fearful; so much of the sublime had the energy of passion united with Countess Amy's natural loveliness. Janet, as soon as the door was open, ran to her mistress; and more slowly, yet with more haste than he was wont, Anthony Foster went to Richard Varney.

'In the Truth's name, what ails your ladyship?' said the former.

'What, in the name of Satan, have you done to her?' said Foster to his friend.

'Who, I?—nothing,' answered Varney, but with sunken head and sullen voice; 'nothing but communicated to her her lord's commands, which, if the lady list not to obey, she knows better how to answer it than I may pretend to do.'

'Now, by Heaven, Janet!' said the Countess, 'the false traitor lies in his throat! He must needs lie, for he speaks to the dishonour of my noble lord—he must needs lie doubly, for he speaks to gain ends of his own, equally execrable and unattainable.'

'You have misapprehended me, lady,' said Varney, with a sulky species of submission and apology; 'let this matter rest till your passion be abated, and I will explain all.'

'Thou shalt never have an opportunity to do so,' said the Countess. 'Look at him, Janet. He is fairly dressed, hath the outside of a gentleman, and hither he came to persuade me it was my lord's pleasure—nay, more, my wedded lord's commands, that I should go with him to Kenilworth; and before the Queen and nobles, and in presence of my own wedded lord, that I should acknowledge him—*him* there—that very cloak-brushing, shoe-cleaning fellow—*him* there, my lord's lackey, for my liege lord and husband; furnishing against myself, great God! whenever I was to vindicate my right and my rank, such weapons as would hew my just claim from the root, and destroy my character to be regarded as an honourable matron of the English nobility!'

'You hear her, Foster, and you, young maiden, hear this lady,' answered Varney, taking advantage of the pause which the Countess had made in her charge, more for lack of breath than for lack of matter—'You hear that her heart only objects to me the course which our good lord, for the purpose to keep certain matters secret, suggests in the very letter which she holds in her hands.'

Foster here attempted to interfere with a face of authority, which he thought became the charge entrusted to him, 'Nay, lady, I must needs say you are over hasty in this—Such deceit is not utterly to be condemned when practised for a righteous end; and thus even the patriarch Abraham feigned Sarah to be his sister when they went down to Egypt.'

'Ay, sir,' answered the Countess; 'but God rebuked that deceit even in the father of His chosen people, by the mouth of the heathen Pharaoh. Out upon you, that will read Scripture only to copy those things which are held out to us as warnings, not as examples!'

'But Sarah disputed not the will of her husband, an it be your pleasure,' said Foster, in reply; 'but did as Abraham commanded, calling herself his sister, that it might be well with her husband for her sake, and that his soul might live because of her beauty.'

'Now, so Heaven pardon me my useless anger,' answered the Countess, 'thou art as daring a hypocrite as yonder fellow is an impudent deceiver. Never will I believe that the noble Dudley gave countenance to so dastardly, so dishonourable a plan. Thus I tread on his infamy, if indeed it be, and thus destroy its remembrance for ever!'

So saying, she tore in pieces Leicester's letter, and stamped, in the extremity of impatience, as if she would have annihilated the minute fragments into which she had rent it.

'Bear witness,' said Varney, collecting himself, 'she has torn my lord's letter, in order to burden me with the scheme of his devising; and although it promises naught but danger and trouble to me, she would lay it to my charge, as if I had any purpose of mine own in it.'

'Thou liest, thou treacherous slave!' said the Countess, in spite of Janet's attempts to keep her silent, in the sad foresight that her vehemence might only furnish arms against herself. 'Thou liest,' she continued. 'Let me go, Janet—Were it the last word I have to speak, he lies—he had his own foul ends to seek; and broader he would have displayed them, had my passion permitted me to preserve the silence which at first encouraged him to unfold his vile projects.'

'Madam,' said Varney, overwhelmed in spite of his effrontery, 'I entreat you to believe yourself mistaken.'

'As soon will I believe light darkness,' said the ensnared Countess. 'Have I drunk of oblivion? Do I not remember former passages, which, known to Leicester, had given thee the preferment of a gallows, instead of the honour of his intimacy. I would I were a man but for five minutes! It were space enough to make a craven like thee confess his villainy. But go—begone—Tell thy master, that when I take the foul course to which such scandalous deceits as thou hast recommended on his behalf must necessarily lead me, I will give him a rival something worthy of the name. He shall not be supplanted by an ignominious lackey, whose best fortune is to catch a gift of his master's last suit of clothes ere it is threadbare, and who is only fit to seduce a suburb-wench by the bravery of new roses in his master's old pantofles. Go, begone, sir—I scorn thee so much, that I am ashamed to have been angry with thee.'

Varney left the room with a mute expression of rage, and was followed by Foster, whose apprehension, naturally slow, was overpowered by the eager and abundant discharge of indignation, which, for the first time, he had heard burst from the lips of a being, who had seemed till that moment too languid, and too gentle, to nurse an angry thought, or utter an intemperate expression. Foster, therefore, pursued Varney from place to place, persecuting him with interrogatories, to which the other replied not until they were in the opposite side of the quadrangle, and in the old library, with which the reader has already been made acquainted. Here he turned round on his persevering follower, and thus addressed him, in a tone tolerably equal; that brief walk having been sufficient to give one so habituated to command his temper, time to rally and recover his presence of mind.

'Tony,' he said, with his usual sneering laugh, 'it avails not to deny it. The Woman and the Devil, who, as thine oracle Holdforth will confirm to thee, cheated man at the beginning, have this day proved more powerful than my discretion. Yon termagant looked so tempting, and had the art to preserve her countenance so naturally, while I communicated my lord's message, that, by my faith, I thought I might say some little thing for myself. She thinks she hath my head under her girdle now, but she is deceived. Where is Doctor Alasco?'

'In his laboratory,' answered Foster; 'it is the hour he is not spoken withal—we must wait till noon is past, or spoil his important—What said I, important?—I would say interrupt his divine studies.'

'Ay, he studies the devil's divinity,' said Varney—'but when I want him, one hour must suffice as well as another. Lead the way to his pandemonium.'

So spoke Varney, and with hasty and perturbed steps followed Foster, who conducted him through private passages, many of which were wellnigh ruinous, to the opposite side of the quadrangle, where, in a subterranean apartment, now occupied by the chemist Alasco, one of the Abbots of Abingdon, who had a turn for the occult sciences, had, much to the scandal of his convent, established a laboratory, in which like other fools of the period, he spent much precious time, and money besides, in the pursuit of the grand arcanum.

Anthony Foster paused before the door, which was scrupulously secured within, and again showed a marked hesitation to disturb the sage in his operations. But Varney, less scrupulous, roused him, by knocking and voice, until at length, slowly and reluctantly, the inmate of the apartment undid the door. The chemist appeared with his eyes bleared with the heat and vapours of the stove or alembic over which he brooded, and the interior of his cell displayed the confused assemblage of heterogeneous substances, and extraordinary implements belonging to his profession. The old man was muttering. with spiteful impatience, 'Am I for ever to be recalled to the affairs of earth from those of heaven?'

'To the affairs of hell,' answered Varney, 'for that is thy proper element. Foster, we need thee at our conference.'

Foster slowly entered the room. Varney, following, barred the door, and they betook themselves to secret council.

In the meanwhile, the Countess traversed the apartment, with shame and anger contending on her lovely cheek.

'The villain,' she said, 'the cold-blooded calculating slave! But I unmasked him, Janet—I made the snake uncoil all his folds before me, and crawl abroad in his naked deformity—I suspended my resentment, at the danger of suffocating under the effort, until he had let me see the very bottom of a heart more foul than hell's darkest corner. And thou, Leicester, is it possible thou couldst bid me for a moment deny my wedded right in thee, or thyself yield it to another? But it is impossible—the villain has lied in all. Janet, I will not remain here longer—I fear him—I fear thy father—I grieve to say it, Janet—but I fear thy father, and, worst of all, this odious Varney. I will escape from Cumnor.'

'Alas! madam, whither would you fly, or by what means will you escape from these walls?'

'I know not, Janet,' said the unfortunate young lady, looking upwards, and clasping her hands together, 'I know not where I shall fly, or by what means; but I am certain the God I have served will not abandon me in this dreadful crisis, for I am in the hands of wicked men.'

'Do not think so, dear lady,' said Janet; 'my father is stern and strict in his temper, and severely true to his trust—but yet?——'

At this moment, Anthony Foster entered the apartment, bearing in his hand a glass cup, and a small flask. His manner was singular; for, while approaching the Countess with the respect due to her rank, he had till this time suffered to become visible, or had been unable to suppress, the obdurate sulkiness of his natural disposition, which, as is usual with those of his unhappy temper, was chiefly exerted towards those over whom circumstances gave him control. But at present he showed nothing of that sullen consciousness of authority which he was wont to conceal under a clumsy affectation of civility and deference, as a ruffian hides his pistols and bludgeon under his ill-fashioned gaberdine. And yet it seemed as if his smile was more in fear than in courtesy, and as if, while he pressed the Countess to taste of the choice cordial, which should refresh her spirits after her late alarm, he was conscious of meditating some further injury. His hand trembled also, his voice faltered, and his whole outward behaviour exhibited so much that was suspicious, that his daughter Janet, after she had stood looking at him in astonishment for some seconds, seemed at once to collect herself to execute some hardy resolution, raised her head, assumed an attitude and gait of determination and authority, and walking slowly betwixt her father and her mistress, took the salver from the hand of the former, and said in a low, but marked and decided tone, 'Father, *I* will fill for my noble mistress, when such is her pleasure.'

'Thou, my child?' said Foster, eagerly and apprehensively; 'no, my child—it is not *thou* shalt render the lady this service.'

'And why, I pray you,' said Janet, 'if it be fitting that the noble lady should partake of the cup at all?'

'Why—why,' said the seneschal, hesitating, and then bursting into passion, as the readiest mode of supplying the lack of all other reason—'Why, because it is my pleasure, minion, that you should not—Get you gone to the evening lecture.'

'Now, as I hope to hear lecture again,' replied Janet, 'I will not go thither this night, unless I am better assured of my mistress's safety. Give me that flask, father;'—and she took it from his reluctant hand, while he resigned it as if conscience-struck—'And now,' she said, 'father, that which shall benefit my mistress, cannot do *me* prejudice. Father, I drink to you.'

Foster, without speaking a word, rushed on his daughter and wrested the flask from her hand; then, as if embarrassed by what he had done, and totally unable to resolve what he should do next, he stood with it in his hand, one foot advanced and the other drawn back, glaring on his daughter with a countenance in which rage, fear, and convicted villainy formed a hideous combination.

'This is strange, my father,' said Janet, keeping her eye fixed on his, in the manner in which those who have the charge of lunatics are said to overawe their unhappy patients; 'will you neither let me serve my lady nor drink to her myself?'

The courage of the Countess sustained her through this dreadful scene, of which the import was not the less obvious that it was not even hinted at. She preserved even the rash carelessness of her temper, and though her cheek had grown pale at the first alarm, her eye was calm and almost scornful. 'Will *you* taste this rare cordial, Master Forster? Perhaps you will not yourself refuse to pledge us, though you permit not Janet to do so—Drink, sir, I pray you.'

'I will not,' answered Foster.

'And for whom, then, is this precious beverage reserved, sir?' said the Countess.

'For the devil who brewed it,' answered Foster; and, turning on his heel, he left the chamber.

Janet looked at her mistress with a countenance expressive, in the highest degree, of shame, dismay, and sorrow.

'Do not weep for me, Janet,' said the Countess kindly.

'No, madam,' replied her attendant, in a voice broken by sobs, 'it is not for you I weep, it is for myself—it is for that unhappy man. Those who are dishonoured before man—those who are condemned by God, have cause to mourn—not those who are innocent! Farewell, madam!' she said, hastily assuming the mantle in which she was wont to go abroad.

'Do you leave me, Janet?' said her mistress—'desert me in such an evil strait?'

'Desert you, madam!' exclaimed Janet; and, running back to her mistress, she imprinted a thousand kisses on her hand—'desert you! —may the Hope of my trust desert me when I do so! No, madam; well you said the God you serve will open you a path for deliverance. There is a way of escape; I have prayed night and day for light, that I might see how to act betwixt my duty to yonder unhappy man, and that which I owe to you. Sternly and fearfully that light has now dawned, and I must not shut the door which God opens.—Ask me no more. I will return in brief space.'

So speaking, she wrapped herself in her mantle, and saying to the old woman whom she passed in the outer room, that she was going to evening prayer, she left the house. Meanwhile her father had reached once more the laboratory, where he found the accomplices of his intended guilt.

'Has the sweet bird sipped?' said Varney, with half a smile; while the astrologer put the same question with his eyes, but spoke not a word.

'She has not, nor she shall not from my hands,' replied Foster; 'would you have me do murder in my daughter's presence?'

'Wert thou not told, thou sullen and yet faint-hearted slave,' answered Varney with bitterness, 'that no *murder*, as thou call'st it, with that staring look and stammering tone, is designed in the matter? Wert thou not told, that a brief illness, such as woman puts on in very wantonness, that she may wear her night-gear at noon, and lie on a settle when she should mind her domestic business, is all here aimed at? Here is a learned man will swear it to thee by the key of the Castle of Wisdom.'

'I swear it,' said Alasco, 'that the elixir thou hast there in the flask will not prejudice life! I swear it, by that immortal and indestructible quintessence of gold, which pervades every substance in nature, though its secret existence can be traced by him only to whom Tresmigistus renders the key of the Cabala.'

'An oath of force,' said Varney. 'Foster, thou wert worse than a pagan to disbelieve it. Believe me, moreover, who swear by nothing but by my own word, that if you be not conformable, there is no hope, no, not a glimpse of hope, that this thy leasehold may be transmuted into a copyhold. Thus, Alasco will leave your pewter artillery untransmigrated, and I, honest Anthony, will still have thee for my tenant.'

'I know not, gentlemen,' said Foster, 'where your designs tend to; but in one thing I am bound up—that, fall back fall edge, I will have one in this place that may pray for me, and that one shall be my daughter. I have lived ill, and the world has been too weighty with me; but she is as innocent as ever she was when on her mother's lap, and she, at least, shall have her portion in that happy city whose walls are of pure gold, and the foundations garnished with all manner of precious stones.'

'Ah, Tony,' said Varney, 'that were a paradise to thy heart's content. Debate the matter with him, Doctor Alasco; I will be with you anon.'

So speaking, Varney arose, and, taking the flask from the table, he left the room.

'I tell thee, my son,' said Alasco to Foster, as soon as Varney had left them, 'that whatever this bold and profligate railer may say of the mighty science, in which, by Heaven's blessing, I have advanced so far, that I would not call the wisest of living artists my better or my teacher—I say, howsoever yonder reprobate may scoff at things too holy to be apprehended by men merely of carnal and evil thoughts, yet believe, that the city beheld by St John, in that bright vision of the Christian Apocalypse, that new Jerusalem, of which all Christian men hope to partake, sets forth typically the discovery of the GRAND SECRET, whereby the most precious and perfect of nature's works are elicited out of her basest and most crude productions; just as the light and gaudy butterfly, the most beautiful child of the summer's breeze, breaks forth from the dungeon of a sordid chrysalis.'

'Master Holdforth said naught of this exposition,' said Foster, doubtfully; 'and moreover, Doctor Alasco, the Holy Writ says, that the gold and precious stones of the Holy City are in no sort for those who work abomination, or who frame lies.'

'Well, my son,' said the Doctor, 'and what is your inference from thence?'

'That those,' said Forster, 'who distil poisons, and administer them in secrecy, can have no portion in those unspeakable riches.'

'You are to distinguish, my son,' replied the alchemist, 'betwixt that which is necessarily evil in its progress and in its end also, and that which, being evil, is, nevertheless, capable of working forth good. If, by the death of one person, the happy period shall be brought nearer to us, in which all that is good shall be attained, by wishing its presence—all that is evil escaped, by desiring its absence —in which sickness, and pain, and sorrow shall be the obedient servants of human wisdom, and made to fly at the slightest signal of a sage,—in which that which is now richest and rarest shall be within the compass of every one who shall be obedient to the voice of wisdom,—when the art of healing shall be lost and absorbed in the one universal medicine,—when sages shall become monarchs of the earth, and death itself retreat before their crown,—if this blessed consummation of all things can be hastened by the slight circumstance, that a frail earthly body, which must needs partake corruption, shall be consigned to the grave a short space earlier than in the course of nature, what is such a sacrifice to the advancement of the holy Millennium?'

'Millennium is the reign of the Saints,' said Foster, somewhat doubtfully.

'Say it is the reign of the Sages, my son,' answered Alasco; 'or rather the reign of Wisdom itself.'

'I touched on the question with Master Holdforth last exercising night,' said Forster; 'but he says your doctrine is heterodox, and a damnable and false exposition.'

'He is in the bonds of ignorance, my son,' answered Alasco, 'and as yet burning bricks in Egypt; or, at best, wandering in the dry desert at Sinai. Thou didst ill to speak to such a man of such matters. I will, however, give the proof, and that shortly, which I will defy that peevish divine to confute, though he should strive with me as the magicians strove with Moses before King Pharaoh. I will do projection in thy presence, my son,——in thy very presence,—and thine eyes shall witness the truth.'

'Stick to that, learned sage,' said Varney, who at this moment entered the apartment; 'if he refuse the testimony of thy tongue, yet how shall he deny that of his own eyes?'

'Varney!' said the adept—'Varney already returned! Hast thou—' he stopped short.

'Have I done mine errand, thou wouldst say,' replied Varney—'I have! And thou,' he added, showing more symptoms of interest than he had hitherto exhibited, 'art thou sure thou hast poured forth neither more nor less than the just measure?'

'Ay,' replied the alchemist, 'as sure as men can be in these nice proportions; for there is diversity of constitutions.'

'Nay, then,' said Varney, 'I fear nothing. I know thou wilt not go a step farther to the devil than thou art justly considered for. Thou were paid to create illness, and would esteem it thriftless prodigality to do murder at the same price. Come, let us each to our chamber—We shall see the event to-morrow.'

'What didst thou do to make her swallow it?' said Foster, shuddering.

'Nothing,' answered Varney, 'but looked on her with the aspect which governs madmen, women, and children. They told me, in Saint Luke's Hospital, that I have the right look for overpowering a refractory patient. The keepers made me their compliments on't; so I know how to win my bread, when my court favour fails me.'

'And art thou not afraid,' said Foster, 'lest the dose be dispro-portioned?'

'If so,' replied Varney, 'she will but sleep the sounder, and the fear of that shall not break my rest. Good-night, my masters.'

Anthony Foster groaned heavily, and lifted up his hands and eyes. The alchemist intimated his purpose to continue some experiment of high import during the greater part of the night, and the others separated to their places of repose.

23

Now God be good to me in this wild pilgrimage!
All hope in human aid I cast behind me.
Oh, who would be a woman?—who that fool,
A weeping, pining, faithful, loving woman?
She hath hard measures still where she hopes kindest,
And all her bounties only make ingrates.

Love's Pilgrimage.

THE summer evening was closed, and Janet, just when her longer stay might have occasioned suspicion and inquiry in that jealous household, returned to Cumnor Place, and hastened to the apartment in which she had left her lady. She found her with her head resting on her arms, and these crossed upon a table which stood before her. As Janet came in, she neither looked up nor stirred.

Her faithful attendant ran to her mistress with the speed of lightning, and rousing her at the same time with her hand, conjured the Countess in the most earnest manner to look up, and say what thus affected her. The unhappy lady raised her head accordingly, and looking on her attendant with a ghastly eye, and cheek as pale as clay, 'Janet,' she said, 'I have drunk it.'

'God be praised!' said Janet hastily—'I mean God be praised that it is no worse—the potion will not harm you.—Rise, shake this lethargy from your limbs, and this despair from your mind.'

'Janet,' repeated the Countess again, 'disturb me not—leave me at peace—let life pass quietly—I am poisoned.'

'You are not, my dearest lady,' answered the maiden eagerly. 'What you have swallowed cannot injure you, for the antidote has been taken before it, and I hastened hither to tell you that the means of escape are open to you.'

'Escape!' exclaimed the lady, as she raised herself hastily in her chair, while light returned to her eye and life to her cheek; 'but ah! Janet, it comes too late.'

'Not so, dearest lady. Rise, take mine arm, walk through the apartment—Let not fancy do the work of poison! So; feel you not now that you are possessed of the full use of your limbs?'

'The torpor seems to diminish', said the Countess, as, supported by Janet, she walked to and fro in the apartment; 'but is it then so, and have I not swallowed a deadly draught? Varney was here since thou wert gone, and commanded me, with eyes in which I read my fate, to swallow yon horrible drug. Oh, Janet! it must be fatal; never was harmless draught served by such a cup-bearer!'

'He did not deem it harmless, I fear,' replied the maiden; 'but God confounds the devices of the wicked. Believe me, as I swear by the dear Gospel in which we trust, your life is safe from his practice. Did you not debate with him?'

'The house was silent,' answered the lady—'thou gone—no other but he in the chamber—and he capable of every crime. I did but stipulate he would remove his hateful presence, and I drank whatever he offered. But you spoke of escape, Janet; can I be so happy?'

'Are you strong enough to bear the tidings, and make the effort?' said the maiden.

'Strong?' answered the Countess. 'Ask the hind, when the fangs of the deerhound are stretched to gripe her, if she is strong enough to spring over a chasm. I am equal to every effort that may relieve me from this place.'

'Hear me, then,' said Janet. 'One whom I deem an assured friend of yours has shown himself to me in various disguises, and sought speech of me, which—for my mind was not clear on the matter until this evening—I have ever declined. He was the pedlar who brought you goods—the itinerant hawker who sold me books; whenever I stirred abroad I was sure to see him. The event of this night determined me to speak with him. He awaits even now at the postern-gate of the park with means for your flight. But have you strength of body? Have you courage of mind?—Can you undertake the enterprise?'

'She that flies from death,' said the lady, 'finds strength of body— she that would escape from shame, lacks no strength of mind. The thoughts of leaving behind me the villain who menaces both my life and honour, would give me strength to rise from my deathbed.'

'In God's name, then, lady,' said Janet, 'I must bid you adieu, and to God's charge I must commit you.'

'Will you not fly with me, then, Janet?' said the Countess anxiously—'Am I to lose thee? Is this thy faithful service?'

'Lady, I would fly with you as willingly as bird ever fled from cage, but my doing so would occasion instant discovery and pursuit. I must remain, and use means to disguise the truth for some time— May heaven pardon the falsehood, because of the necessity!'

'And am I then to travel alone with this stranger?' said the lady—
'Bethink thee, Janet, may not this prove some deeper and darker
scheme to separate me perhaps from you, who are my only friend?'

'No, madam, do not suppose it,' answered Janet readily; 'the
youth is an honest youth in his purpose to your and a friend to
Master Tressilian, under whose direction he is come hither.'

'If he be a friend of Tressilian,' said the Countess, 'I will commit
myself to his charge, as to that of an angel sent from heaven; for
than Tressilian, never breathed mortal man more free of whatever
was base, false, or selfish. He forgot himself whenever he could be
of use to others—Alas! and how was he requited!'

With eager haste they collected the few necessaries which it was
thought proper the Countess should take with her, and which
Janet, with speed and dexterity, formed into a small bundle, not
forgetting to add such ornaments of intrinsic value as came most
readily in her way, and particularly a casket of jewels, which she
wisely judged might prove of service in some future emergency.
The Countess of Leicester next changed her dress for one which
Janet wore upon any brief journey, for they judged it necessary to
avoid every external distinction which might attract attention. Ere
these preparations were fully made, the moon had arisen in the
summer heaven, and all in the mansion had betaken themselves to
rest, or at least to the silence and retirement of their chambers.

There was no difficulty anticipated in escaping, whether from the
house or garden, provided only they could elude observation.
Anthony Foster had accustomed himself to consider his daughter
as a conscious sinner might regard a visible guardian angel, which,
notwithstanding his guilt, continued to hover around him; and
therefore his trust in her knew no bounds. Janet commanded her
own motions during the daytime, and had a master-key which
opened the postern-door of the park, so that she could go to the
village at pleasure, either upon the household affairs, which were
entirely confided to her management, or to attend her devotions at
the meeting-house of her sect. It is true, the daughter of Foster was
thus liberally entrusted, under the solemn condition that she should
not avail herself of these privileges, to do anything inconsistent with
the safe-keeping of the Countess; for so her residence at Cumnor
place had been termed, since she began of late to exhibit impatience
of the restrictions to which she was subjected. Nor is there reason to
suppose, that anything short of the dreadful suspicions which the

scene of that evening had excited, could have induced Janet to violate her word or deceive her father's confidence. But from what she had witnessed, she now conceived herself not only justified, but imperatively called upon to make her lady's safety the principal object of her care, setting all other considerations aside.

The fugitive Countess, with her guide, traversed with hasty steps the broken and interrupted path, which had once been an avenue, now totally darkened by the boughs of spreading trees which met above their head, and now receiving a doubtful and deceiving light from the beams of the moon, which penetrated where the axe had made openings in the wood. Their path was repeatedly interrupted by felled trees, or the large boughs which had been left on the ground till time served to make them into fagots and billets. The inconveniences and difficulty attending these interruptions, the breathless haste of the first part of their route, the exhausting sensations of hope and fear, so much affected the Countess's strength, that Janet was forced to propose that they should pause for a few minutes to recover breath and spirits. Both therefore stood still beneath the shadow of a huge old gnarled oak-tree, and both naturally looked back to the mansion which they had left behind them, whose long, dark front was seen in the gloomy distance, with its huge stalks of chimneys, turrets, and clock-house, rising above the line of the roof, and definedly visible against the pure azure blue of the summer sky. One light only twinkled from the extended and shadowy mass, and it was placed so low that it rather seemed to glimmer from the ground in front of the mansion, than from one of the windows. The Countess's terror was awakened. 'They follow us!' she said, pointing out to Janet the light which thus alarmed her.

Less agitated than her mistress. Janet perceived that the gleam was stationary, and informed the Countess, in a whisper, that the light proceeded from the solitary cell in which the alchemist pursued his occult experiments. 'He is of those,' she added, 'who sit up and watch by night that they may commit iniquity. Evil was the chance which sent hither a man, whose mixed speech of earthly wealth and unearthly or superhuman knowledge hath in it what does so especially captivate my poor father. Well spoke the good Master Holdforth—and, methought, not without meaning, that those of our household should find therein a practical use. "There be those," he said, "and their number is legion, who will rather, like the wicked Ahab, listen to the dreams of the false prophet Zedekiah, than to the words of him by whom the Lord has spoken." And he further insisted—"Ah, my brethren, there be many Zedekiahs among you—men that promise you the light of their carnal knowledge, so you will surrender to them that of your heavenly understanding. What are they better than the tyrant Naas, who demanded the right eye of those who were subjected to him?" and further he insisted——'

It is uncertain how long the fair Puritan's memory might have supported her in the recapitulation of Master Holdforth's discourse; but the Countess now interrupted her, and assured her she was so much recovered that she could now reach the postern without the necessity of a second delay.

They set out accordingly, and performed the second part of their journey with more deliberation, and of course more easily, than the first hasty commencement. This gave them leisure for reflection; and Janet now, for the first time, ventured to ask her lady which way she proposed to direct her flight. Receiving no immediate answer—for perhaps, in the confusion of her mind, this very obvious subject of deliberation had not occurred to the Countess—Janet ventured to add. 'Probably to your father's house, where you are sure of safety and protection?'

'No, Janet,' said the lady mournfully, 'I left Lidcote Hall while my heart was light and my name was honourable; and I will not return thither till my lord's permission and public acknowledgment of our marriage restore me to my native home, with all the rank and honour which he has bestowed on me.'

'And whither will you then, madam?' said Janet.

'To Kenilworth, girl,' said the Countess, boldly and freely. 'I will see these revels—these princely revels—the preparation for which makes the land ring from side to side. Methinks, when the Queen of England feasts within my husband's halls, the Countess of Leicester should be no unbeseeming guest.'

'I pray God you may be a welcome one!' said Janet hastily.

'You abuse my situation, Janet,' said the Countess angrily, 'and you forget your own.'

'I do neither, dearest madam,' said the sorrowful maiden; 'but have you forgotten that the noble Earl has given such strict charges to keep your marriage secret, that he may preserve his court favour? and can you think that your sudden appearance at his castle, at such a juncture, and in such a presence, will be acceptable to him?'

'Thou thinkest I would disgrace him,' said the Countess; 'nay, let go my arm, I can walk without aid and work without counsel.'

'Be not angry with me, lady,' said Janet meekly, 'and let me still support you; the road is rough, and you are little accustomed to walk in darkness.'

'If you deem me not so mean as may disgrace my husband,' said the Countess, in the same resentful tone, 'you suppose my Lord of Leicester capable of abetting, perhaps of giving aim and authority to the base proceedings of your father and Varney, whose errand I will do to the good Earl!'

'For God's sake, madam, spare my father in your report,' said Janet; 'let my services, however poor, be some atonement for his errors.'

'I were most unjust, dearest Janet, were it otherwise,' said the Countess, resuming at once the fondness and confidence of her manner towards her faithful attendant. 'No, Janet, not a word of mine shall do your father prejudice. But thou seest, my love, I have no desire but to throw myself on my husband's protection. I have left the abode he assigned for me, because of the villainy of the persons by whom I was surrounded—but I will disobey his commands in no other particular. I will appeal to him alone—I will be protected by him alone; to no other, than at his pleasure, have I or will I communicate the secret union which combines our hearts and our destinies. I will see him, and receive from his own lips the directions for my future conduct. Do not argue against my resolution, Janet; you will only confirm me in it—And to own the truth, I am resolved to know my fate at once, and from my husband's own mouth; and to seek him at Kenilworth is the surest way to attain my purpose.'

While Janet hastily revolved in her mind the difficulties and uncertainties attendant on the unfortunate lady's situation, she was inclined to alter her first opinion, and to think, upon the whole, that since the Countess had withdrawn herself from the retreat in which she had been placed by her husband, it was her first duty to repair to his presence, and possess him with the reasons of such conduct. She knew what importance the Earl attached to the concealment of their marriage, and could not but own, that by taking any step to make it public without his permission, the Countess would incur, in a high degree, the indignation of her husband. If she retired to her father's house without an explicit avowal of her rank, her situation was likely greatly to prejudice her character; and if she made such an avowal, it might occasion an irreconcilable breach with her husband. At Kenilworth, again, she might plead her cause with her husband himself, whom Janet, though distrusting him more than the Countess did, believed incapable of being accessory to the base and desperate means which his dependants, from whose power the lady was now escaping, might resort to, in order to stifle her complaints of the treatment she had received at their hands. But at the worst, and were the Earl himself to deny her justice and protection, still at Kenilworth, if she chose to make her wrongs public, the Countess might have Tressilian for her advocate, and the Queen for her judge, for so much Janet had learned in her short conference with Wayland. She was, therefore, on the whole, reconciled to her lady's proposal of going towards Kenilworth, and so expressed herself; recommending, however, to the Countess the utmost caution in making her arrival known to her husband.

'Hast thou thyself been cautious, Janet?' said the Countess; 'this guide, in whom I must put my confidence, hast thou not entrusted to him the secret of my condition?'

'From me he has learned nothing,' said Janet; 'nor do I think that he knows more than what the public in general believe of your situation.'

'And what is that?' said the lady.

'That you left your father's house—but I shall offend you again if I go on,' said Janet, interrupting herself.

'Nay, go on,' said the Countess; 'I must learn to endure the evil report which my folly has brought upon me. They think, I suppose, that I have left my father's house to follow lawless pleasure. It is an error which will soon be removed,—indeed it shall, for I will live with spotless fame, or I shall cease to live. I am accounted, then, the paramour of my Leicester?'

'Most men say of Varney,' said Janet; 'yet some call him only the convenient cloak of his master's pleasures; for reports of the profuse expense in garnishing yonder apartments have secretly gone abroad, and such doings far surpass the means of Varney. But this latter opinion is little prevalent; for men dare hardly even hint suspicion when so high a name is concerned, lest the Star Chamber should punish them for scandal of the nobility.'

'They do well to speak low,' said the Countess, 'who would mention the illustrious Dudley as the accomplice of such a wretch as Varney. We have reached the postern. Ah! Janet, I must bid thee farewell! Weep not, my good girl,' said she, endeavouring to cover her own reluctance to part with her faithful attendant under an attempt at playfulness; 'and against we meet again, reform me, Janet, that precise ruff of thine for an open rabatine of lace and cut work, that will let men see thou hast a fair neck; and that kirtle of Philippine chency, with that bugle lace which befits only a chambermaid, into three-piled velvet and cloth of gold—thou wilt find plenty of stuffs in my chamber, and I freely bestow them on you. Thou must be brave, Janet; for though thou art now but the attendant of a distressed and errant lady, who is both nameless and fameless, yet, when we meet again, thou must be dressed as becomes the gentlewoman nearest in love and in service to the first Countess in England.'

'Now, may God grant it, dear lady!' said Janet,—'not that I may go with gayer apparel, but that we may both wear our kirtles over lighter hearts.'

By this time the lock of the postern-door had, after some hard wrenching, yielded to the master-key; and the Countess, not without internal shuddering, saw herself beyond the walls which her husband's strict commands had assigned to her as the boundary of her walks. Waiting with much anxiety for their appearance, Wayland Smith stood at some distance, shrouding himself behind a hedge which bordered the high-road.

'Is all safe?' said Janet to him anxiously, as he approached them with caution.

'All,' he replied; 'but I have been unable to procure a horse for the lady. Giles Gosling, the cowardly hilding, refused me one on any terms whatever; lest, forsooth, he should suffer—but no matter. She must ride on my palfrey, and I must walk by her side until I come by another horse. There will be no pursuit if you, pretty Mistress Janet, forget not thy lesson.'

'No more than the wise widow of Tekoa forgot the words which Joab put into her mouth,' answered Janet. 'To-morrow, I say that my lady is unable to rise.'

'Ay; and that she hath aching and heaviness of the head—a throbbing at the heart, and lists not to be disturbed. Fear not; they will take the hint, and trouble thee with few questions—they understand the disease.'

'But,' said the lady, 'my absence must be soon discovered, and they will murder her in revenge. I will rather return than expose her to such danger.'

'Be at ease on my account, madam,' said Janet; 'I would you were as sure of receiving the favour you desire from those to whom you must make appeal, as I am that my father, however angry, will suffer no harm to befall me.'

The Countess was now placed by Wayland upon his horse, around the saddle of which he had placed his cloak, so folded as to make her a commodious seat.

'Adieu, and may the blessing of God wend with you!' said Janet, again kissing her mistress's hand, who returned her benediction with a mute caress. They then tore themselves asunder, and Janet, addressing Wayland, exclaimed, 'May Heaven deal with you at your need, as you are true or false to this most injured and most helpless lady!'

'Amen! dearest Janet,' replied Wayland; 'and believe me, I will so acquit myself of my trust, as may tempt even your pretty eyes, saint-like as they are, to look less scornfully on me when we next meet.'

The latter part of this adieu was whispered into Janet's ear; and, although she made no reply to it directly, yet her manner, influenced no doubt by her desire to leave every motive in force which could operate towards her mistress's safety, did not discourage the hope which Wayland's words expressed. She re-entered the postern-door, and locked it behind her, while Wayland, taking the horse's bridle in his hand, and walking close by its head, they began in silence their dubious and moonlight journey.

Although Wayland Smith used the utmost despatch which he could make, yet his mode of travelling was so slow, that when morning began to dawn through the eastern mist, he found himself not farther than about ten miles distant from Cumnor. 'Now, a plague upon all smooth spoken hosts!' said Wayland, unable longer to suppress his mortification and uneasiness. 'Had the false loon, Giles Gosling, but told me plainly two days since, that I was to reckon naught upon him, I had shifted better for myself. But your hosts have such a custom of promising whatever is called for, that it is not till the steed is to be shod you find they are out of iron. Had I but known, I could have made twenty shifts; nay, for that matter, and in so good a cause, I would have thought little to have prigged a prancer from the next common—it had but been sending back the brute to the headborough. The farcy and the founders confound every horse in the stables of the Black Bear!'

The lady endeavoured to comfort her guide, observing that the dawn would enable him to make more speed.

'True, madam,' he replied: 'but then it will enable other folk to take note of us, and that may prove an ill beginning of our journey. I had not cared a spark from anvil about the matter, had we been farther advanced on our way. But this Berkshire has been notoriously haunted ever since I knew the country, with that sort of malicious elves who sit up late and rise early for no other purpose than to pry into other folk's affairs. I have been endangered by them ere now. But do not fear,' he added, 'good madam; for wit, meeting with opportunity, will not miss to find a salve for every sore.'

The alarms of her guide made more impression on the Countess's mind than the comfort which he judged fit to administer along with it. She looked anxiously around her, and as the shadows withdrew from the landscape, and the heightening glow of the eastern sky promised the speedy rise of the sun, expected at every turn that the increasing light would expose them to the view of the vengeful pursuers, or present some dangerous and insurmountable obstacle to the prosecution of their journey. Wayland Smith perceived her uneasiness, and, displeased with himself for having given her cause of alarm, strode on with affected alacrity, now talking to the horse as one expert in the language of the stable, now whistling to himself low and uninterrupted snatches of tunes, and now assuring the lady there was no danger, while at the same time he looked sharply around to see that there was nothing in sight which might give the lie to his words while they were issuing from his mouth. Thus did they journey on, until an unexpected incident gave them the means of continuing their pilgrimage with more speed and convenience.

24

Richard. A horse!—a horse!—my kingdom for a horse!
Catesby. ——My lord, I'll help you to a horse.
Richard III.

OUR travellers were in the act of passing a small thicket of trees close by the roadside, when the first living being presented himself whom they had seen since their departure from Cumnor Place. This was a stupid lout, seemingly a farmer's boy, in a gray jerkin, with his head bare, his hose about his heels, and huge startups upon his feet. He held by the bridle what of all things they most wanted, a palfrey, namely, with a side-saddle, and all other garniture for a woman's mounting; and he hailed Wayland Smith with 'Zur, be ye zure the party?'

'Ay, that I be, my lad,' answered Wayland, without an instant's hesitation; and it must be owned that consciences trained in a stricter school of morality might have given way to an occasion so tempting. While he spoke, he caught the rein out of the boy's hand, and almost at the same time helped down the Countess from his own horse, and aided her to mount on that which chance had thus presented for her acceptance. Indeed, so naturally did the whole take place, that the Countess, as it afterwards appeared, never suspected but that the horse had been placed there to meet them by the precaution of the guide, or some of his friends.

The lad, however, who was thus hastily dispossessed of his charge, began to stare hard, and scratch his head as if seized with some qualms of conscience for delivering up the animal on such brief explanation.—'I be right zure thou be'st the party,' said he, muttering to himself, 'but thou shouldst ha' zaid *Beans*, thou knaw'st.'

'Ay, ay,' said Wayland, speaking at a venture; 'and thou *Bacon*, thou know'st.'

'Noa, noa,' said the lad; 'bide ye—bide ye—it was *Peas* a should ha' said.'

'Well, well,' answered Wayland, 'peas be it, a' God's name, though bacon were the better password.'

And being by this time mounted on his own horse, he caught the rein of the palfrey from the uncertain hold of the hesitating young boor, flung him a small piece of money, and made amends for lost time by riding briskly off without further parley. The lad was still visible from the hill up which they were riding, and Wayland, as he looked back, beheld him standing with his fingers in his hair as immovable as a guide-post, and his head turned in the direction in which they were escaping from him. At length, just as they topped the hill, he saw the clown stoop to lift up the silver groat which his benevolence had imparted. 'Now this is what I call a Godsend,' said Wayland; 'this is a bonny well-ridden bit of a going thing, and it will carry us so far till we get you as well mounted, and then we will send it back time enough to satisfy the Hue and Cry.'

But he was deceived in his expectations; and fate, which seemed at first to promise so fairly, soon threatened to turn the incident, which he thus gloried in, into the cause of their utter ruin.

They had not ridden a short mile from the place where they left the lad, before they heard a man's voice shouting on the wind behind them, 'Robbery! robbery! Stop thief!' and similar exclamations, which Wayland's conscience readily assured him must arise out of the transaction to which he had been just accessory.

'I had better have gone barefoot all my life,' he said; 'it is the Hue and Cry, and I am a lost man. Ah! Wayland, Wayland, many a time thy father said horse-flesh would be the death of thee. Were I once safe among the horse-coursers in Smithfield, or Turnball Street, they should have leave to hang me as high as St. Paul's, if I e'er meddled more with nobles, knights, or gentlewomen.'

Amidst these dismal reflections, he turned his head repeatedly to see by whom he was chased, and was much comforted when he could only discover a single rider, who was, however, well mounted, and came after them at a speed which left them no chance of escaping, even had the lady's strength permitted her to ride as fast as her palfrey might have been able to gallop.

'There may be fair play betwixt us sure,' thought Wayland, 'where there is but one man on each side, and yonder fellow sits on his horse more like a monkey than a cavalier. Pshaw! if it come to the worst, it will be easy unhorsing him. Nay, 'snails! I think his horse will take the matter in his own hand, for he has the bridle betwixt his teeth. Oons, what care I for him?' said he, as the pursuer drew yet nearer; 'it is but the little animal of a mercer from Abingdon, when all is over.'

Even so it was, as the experienced eye of Wayland had descried at a distance. For the valiant mercer's horse, which was a beast of mettle, feeling himself put to his speed, and discerning a couple of horses riding fast, at some hundred yards distance before him, betook himself to the road with such alacrity as totally deranged the seat of his rider, who not only came up with, but passed, at full gallop, those whom he had been pursuing, pulling the reins with all his might, and ejaculating, 'Stop! stop!' an interjection which seemed rather to regard his own palfrey, than what seamen call 'the chase.' With the same involuntary speed, he shot ahead (to use another nautical phrase) about a furlong, ere he was able to stop and turn his horse, and then rode back towards our travellers, adjusting, as well as he could, his disordered dress, resettling himself in the saddle, and endeavouring to substitute a bold and martial frown for the confusion and dismay which sat upon his visage during his involuntary career.

Wayland had just time to caution the lady not to be alarmed, adding, 'This fellow is a gull, and I will use him as such.'

When the mercer had recovered breath and audacity enough to confront them, he ordered Wayland, in a menacing tone, to deliver up his palfrey.

'How?' said the smith, in King Cambyses' vein, 'are we commanded to stand and deliver on the king's highway? Then out, Excalibur, and tell this knigh of prowess that dire blows must decide between us.'

'Haro and help, and hue and cry, every true man!' said the mercer, 'I am withstood in seeking to recover mine own.'

'Thou swearest thy gods in vain, foul paynim,' said Wayland, 'for I will through with my purpose, were death at the end on't. Nevertheless, know, thou false man of frail cambric and ferrateen, that I am he, even the pedlar, whom thou didst boast to meet on Maiden Castle moor, and despoil of his pack; wherefore betake thee to thy weapons presently.'

'I spoke but in jest, man,' said Goldthred; 'I am an honest shopkeeper and citizen, who scorns to leap forth on any man from behind a hedge.'

'Then, by my faith, most puissant mercer,' answered Wayland, 'I am sorry for my vow, which was, that wherever I met thee, I would despoil thee of thy palfrey, and bestow it upon my leman, unless thou couldst defend it by blows of force. But the vow is passed and registered— and all I can do for thee is to leave the horse at Donnington, in the nearest hostelry.'

'But I tell thee, friend,' said the mercer, 'it is the very horse on which I was this day to carry Jane Thackham, of Shottesbrok, as far as the parish church yonder, to become Dame Goldthred. She hath jumped out of the shot-window of old Gaffer Thackham's grange; and lo ye, yonder she stands, at the place where she should have met the palfrey, with her camlet riding-cloak and ivory-handled whip, like a picture of Lot's wife. I pray you, in good terms, let me have back the palfrey.'

'Grieved am I,' said Wayland, 'as much for the fair damsel, as for thee, most noble imp of muslin. But vows must have their course— thou wilt find the palfrey at the Angel yonder at Donnington. It is all I may do for thee, with a safe conscience.'

'To the devil with thy conscience!' said the dismayed mercer— 'Wouldst thou have a bride walk to church on foot?'

'Thou mayst take her on thy crupper, Sir Goldthred,' answered Wayland; 'it will take down thy steed's mettle.'

'And how if you—if you forget to leave my horse, as you propose?' said Goldthred, not without hesitation, for his soul was afraid within him.

'My pack shall be pledged for it—yonder it lies with Giles Gosling, in his chamber with the damasked leathern hangings, stuffed full with velvet, single, double, treble-piled—rash-taffeta, and parapa— shag, damask, and mockado, plush, and grogram——'

'Hold! hold!' exclaimed the mercer; 'nay, if there be, in truth and sincerity, but the half of these wares—but if ever I trust bumpkin with bonny Bayard again!'

'As you list for that, good Master Goldthred, and so good-morrow to you—and well parted,' he added, riding on cheerfully with the lady, while the discountenanced mercer rode back much slower than he came, pondering what excuse he should make to the disappointed bride, who stood waiting for her gallant groom in the midst of the king's highway.

'Methought,' said the lady, as they rode on, 'yonder fool stared at me, as if he had some remembrance of me; yet I kept my muffler as high as I might.'

'If I thought so,' said Wayland, 'I would ride back, and cut him over the pate—there would be no fear of harming his brains, for he never had so much as would make pap to a sucking gosling. We must now push on, however, and at Donnington we will leave the oaf's horse, that he may have no further temptation to pursue us, and endeavour to assume such a change of shape as may baffle his pursuit, if he should persevere in it.'

The travellers reached Donnington without further alarm, where it became matter of necessity that the Countess should enjoy two or three hours' repose, during which Wayland disposed himself with equal address and alacrity, to carry through those measures on which the safety of their future journey seemed to depend.

Exchanging his pedlar's gaberdine for a smock-frock, he carried the palfrey of Goldthred to the Angel Inn, which was at the other end of the village from that where our travellers had taken up their quarters. In the progress of the morning, as he travelled about his other business, he saw the steed brought forth and delivered, to the cutting mercer himself, who, at the head of a valorous posse of the Hue and Cry, came to rescue by force of arms what was delivered to him without any other ransom than the price of a huge quantity of ale, drunk out by his assistants, thirsty, it would seem, with their walk, and concerning the price of which Master Goldthred had a fierce dispute with the headborough, whom he had summoned to aid him in raising the country.

Having made this act of prudent, as well as just restitution, Wayland procured such change of apparel for the lady, as well as himself, as gave them both the appearance of country people of the better class; it being further resolved, that, in order to attract the less observation, she should pass upon the road for the sister of her guide. A good but not a gay horse, fit to keep pace with his own, and gentle enough for a lady's use, completed the preparations for their journey; for making which, and for other expenses, he had been furnished with sufficient funds by Tressilian. And thus, about noon, after the Countess had been refreshed by the sound repose of several hours, they resumed their journey, with the purpose of making the best of their way to Kenilworth, by Coventry and Warwick. They were not, however, destined to travel far without meeting some cause of apprehension.

It is necessary to premise, that the landlord of the inn had informed them that a jovial party, intended, as he understood, to present some of the masques or mummeries, which made a part of the entertainment with which the Queen was usually welcomed on the royal Progresses, had left the village of Donnington an hour or two before them, in order to proceed to Kenilworth. Now it had occurred to Wayland, that, by attaching themselves in some sort to this group, as soon as they should overtake them on the road, they would be less likely to attract notice, than if they continued to travel entirely by themselves. He communicated his idea to the Countess, who, only anxious to arrive at Kenilworth without interruption, left him free to choose the manner in which this was to be accomplished. They pressed forward their horses, therefore, with the purpose of overtaking the party of intended revellers, and making the journey in their company; and had just seen the little party, consisting partly of riders, partly of people on foot, crossing the summit of a gentle hill, at about half a mile's distance, and disappearing on the other side, when Wayland, who maintained the most circumspect observation of all that met his eye in every direction, was aware that a rider was coming up behind them on a horse of uncommon action, accompanied by a serving-man, whose utmost efforts were unable to keep up with his master's trotting hackney, and who, therefore, was fain to follow him at a hand gallop. Wayland looked anxiously back at these horsemen, became considerably disturbed in his manner, looked back again, and became pale, as he said to the lady—'That is Richard Varney's trotting gelding—I would know him among a thousand nags—this is a worse business than meeting the mercer.'

'Draw your sword,' answered the lady, 'and pierce my bosom with it, rather than I should fall into his hands!'

'I would rather by a thousand times,' answered Wayland, 'pass it through his body, or even mine own. But to say truth, fighting is not my best point, though I can look on cold iron like another, when needs must be. And indeed, as for my sword, (put on, I pray you) it is a poor provant rapier, and I warrant you he has a special Toledo. He has a serving-man too, and I think it is the drunken ruffian Lambourne, upon the horse on which men say—(I pray you heartily to put on)—he did the great robbery of the west-country grazier. It is not that I fear either Varney or Lambourne in a good cause—(your palfrey will go yet faster if you urge him)—But yet—(nay, I pray you let him not break off into the gallop, lest they should see we fear them, and give chase—keep him only at the full trot)—But yet, though I fear them not, I would we were well rid of them, and that rather by policy than by violence. Could we once reach the party before us, we may herd among them, and pass unobserved, unless Varney be really come in express pursuit of us, and then, happy man be his dole.'

While he thus spoke, he alternately urged and restrained his horse, desirous to maintain the fleetest pace that was consistent with the idea of an ordinary journey on the road, but to avoid such rapidity of movement as might give rise to suspicion that they were flying.

At such a pace, they ascended the gentle hill we have mentioned, and, looking from the top, had the pleasure to see that the party which had left Donnington before them, were in the little valley or bottom on the other side, where the road was traversed by a rivulet, beside which was a cottage or two. In this place they seemed to have made a pause, which gave Wayland the hope of joining them, and becoming a part of their company, ere Varney should overtake them. He was the more anxious, as his companion, though she made no complaints, and expressed no fear, began to look so deadly pale, that he was afraid she might drop from her horse. Notwithstanding this symptom of decaying strength, she pushed on her palfrey so briskly, that they joined the party in the bottom of the valley ere Varney appeared on the top of the gentle eminence which they descended.

They found the company to which they meant to associate themselves in great disorder. The women, with dishevelled locks and looks of great importance, ran in and out of one of the cottages, and the men stood around holding the horses, and looking silly enough, as is usual in cases where their assistance is not wanted.

Wayland and his charge paused, as if out of curiosity, and then gradually, without making any inquiries, or being asked any questions, they mingled with the group, as if they had always made part of it.

They had not stood there above five minutes, anxiously keeping as much to the side of the road as possible, so as to place the other travellers betwixt them and Varney, when Lord Leicester's master of the horse, followed by Lambourne, came riding fiercely down the hill, their horses' flanks and the rowels of their spurs showing bloody tokens of the rate at which they travelled. The appearance of the stationary group around the cottages, wearing their buckram suits in order to protect their masquing dresses, having their light cart for transporting their scenery, and carrying various fantastic properties in their hands for the more easy conveyance, let the riders at once into the character and purpose of the company.

'You are revellers,' said Varney, 'designing for Kenilworth?'

'*Recte quidem, Domine spectatissime*,' answered one of the party.

'And why the devil stand you here,' said Varney, 'when your utmost despatch will but bring you to Kenilworth in time? The Queen dines at Warwick to-morrow, and you loiter here, ye knaves.'

'In very truth, sir,' said a little diminutive urchin, wearing a vizard with a couple of sprouting horns of an elegant scarlet hue, having moreover a black serge jerkin drawn close to his body by lacing, garnished with red stockings, and shoes so shaped as to resemble cloven feet —'in very truth, sir, and you are in the right on't. It is my father, the Devil, who, being taken in labour, has delayed our present purpose, by increasing our company with an imp too many.'

'The devil he has!' answered Varney, whose laugh, however, never exceeded a sarcastic smile.

'It is even as the juvenal hath said,' added the masquer who spoke first; 'our major devil, for this is but our minor one, is even now at *Lucina fer opem*, within that very *tugurium*.'

'By Saint George, or rather by the Dragon, who may be a kins-man of the fiend in the straw, a most comical chance!' said Varney. 'How say'st thou, Lambourne, wilt thou stand godfather for the nonce?—if the devil were to choose a gossip, I know no one more fit for the office.'

'Saving always when my betters are in presence,' said Lambourne with the civil impudence of a servant who knows his services to be so indispensable that his jest will be permitted to pass muster.

'And what is the name of this devil, or devil's dam, who has timed her turns so strangely?' said Varney. 'We can ill afford to space any of our actors.'

'*Gaudet nomine Sibyllae*,' said the first speaker, 'she is called Sibyl Laneham, wife of Master Richard Laneham—'

'Clerk to the Council-chamber door,' said Varney; 'why, she is inexcusable, having had experience how to have ordered her matters better. But who were those, a man and a woman I think, who rode so hastily up the hill before me even now?—do they belong to your company?'

Wayland was about to hazard a reply to this alarming inquiry, when the little diablotin again thrust in his oar.

'So please you,' he said, coming close up to Varney, and speaking so as not to be overheard by his companions, 'the man was our devil major, who has tricks enough to supply the lack of a hundred such as Dame Laneham; and the woman—if you please—is the sage person whose assistance is more particularly necessary to our distressed comrade.'

'Oh, what, you have got the wise woman then?' said Varney. 'Why, truly, she rode like one bound to a place where she was needed. And you have a spare limb of Satan, besides, to supply the place of Mistress Laneham?'

'Ay, sir,' said the boy, 'they are not so scarce in this world as your honour's virtuous eminence would suppose —This master-fiend shall spit a few flashes of fire, and eruct a volume or two of smoke on the spot, if it will do you pleasure—you would think he had Ætna in his abdomen.'

'I lack time just now, most hopeful imp of darkness, to witness this performance,' said Varney; 'but here is something for you all to drink the lucky hour—and so, as the play says, "God be with your labour!"'

Thus speaking, he struck his horse with the spurs, and rode on his way.

Lambourne tarried a moment or two behind his master, and rummaged his pouch for a piece of silver, which he bestowed on the communicative imp, as he said, for his encouragement on his path to the infernal regions, some sparks of whose fire, he said, he could discover flashing from him already. Then having received the boy's thanks for his generosity, he also spurred his horse, and rode after his master as fast as the fire flashes from flint.

'And now,' said the wily imp, sidling close up to Wayland's horse, and cutting a gambol in the air, which seemed to vindicate his title to relationship with the prince of that element, 'I have told them who you are, do you in return tell me who I am?'

'Either Flibbertigibbet,' answered Wayland Smith, 'or else an imp of the devil in good earnest.'

'Thou hast hit it,' answered Dickie Sludge; 'I am thine own Flibbertigibbet, man; and I have broken forth of bounds, along with my learned preceptor, as I told thee I would do, whether he would or not. But what lady hast thou got with thee? I saw thou wert at fault the first question was asked, and so I drew up for thy assistance. But I must know all who she is, dear Wayland.'

'Thou shalt know fifty finer things, my dear ingle,' said Wayland; 'but a truce to thine inquiries just now; and since you are bound for Kenilworth, thither will I too, even for the love of thy sweet face and waggish company.'

'Thou shouldst have said my waggish face and sweet company,' said Dickie; 'but how wilt thou travel with us—I mean in what character?'

'E'en in that thou hast assigned me, to be sure—as a juggler; thou know'st I am used to the craft,' answered Wayland.

'Ay, but the lady?' answered Flibbertigibbet; 'credit me, I think she *is* one, and thou art in a sea of troubles about her at this moment, as I can perceive by thy fidgeting.'

'Oh, she man!—she is a poor sister of mine,' said Wayland—'she can sing and play o' the lute, would win the fish out o' the stream.'

'Let me hear her instantly,' said the boy; 'I love the lute rarely; I love it of all things, though I never heard it.'

'Then how canst thou love it, Flibbertigibbet?' said Wayland.

'As knights love ladies in old tales,' answered Dickie—'on hearsay.'

'Then love it on hearsay a little longer, till my sister is recovered from the fatigue of her journey,' said Wayland;—muttering afterwards betwixt his teeth, 'The devil take the imp's curiosity! I must keep fair weather with him, or we shall fare the worse.'

He then proceeded to state to Master Holiday his own talents as a juggler, with those of his sister as a musician. Some proof of his dexterity was demanded, which he gave in such a style of excellence, that, delighted at obtaining such an accession to their party, they readily acquiesced in the apology which he offered, when a display of his sister's talents was required. The newcomers were invited to partake of the refreshments with which the party were provided; and it was with some difficulty that Wayland Smith obtained an opportunity of being apart with his supposed sister during the meal, of which interval he availed himself to entreat her to forget for the present both her rank and her sorrows, and condescend, as the most probable chance of remaining concealed, to mix in the society of those with whom she was to travel.

The Countess allowed the necessity of the case, and when they resumed their journey, endeavoured to comply with her guide's advice, by addressing herself to a female near her, and expressing her concern for the woman whom they were thus obliged to leave behind them.

'Oh, she is well attended, madam,' replied the dame whom she addressed, who, from her jolly and laughter-loving demeanour, might have been the very emblem of the Wife of Bath; 'and my gossip Laneham thinks as little of these matters as any one. By the ninth day, an the revels last so long, we shall have her with us at Kenilworth, even if she should travel with her bantling on her back.'

There was something in this speech which took away all desire on the Countess of Leicester's part to continue the conversation; but having broken the charm by speaking to her fellow-traveller first, the good dame, who was to play Rare Gillian of Croydon in one of the interludes, took care that silence did not again settle on the journey, but entertained her mute companion with a thousand anecdotes of revels, from the days of King Harry downwards, with the reception given them by the great folks, and all the names of those who played the principal characters; but ever concluding with 'they would be nothing to the princely pleasures of Kenilworth.'

'And when shall we reach Kenilworth?' said the Countess, with an agitation which she in vain attempted to conceal.

'We that have horses may, with late riding, get to Warwick to-night, and Kenilworth may be distant some four or five miles,—but then we must wait till the foot-people come up; although it is like my good Lord of Leicester will have horses or light carriages to meet them, and bring them up without being travel toiled, which last is no good preparation, as you may suppose, for dancing before your betters—And yet, Lord help me, I have seen the day I would have tramped five leagues of lea-land, and turned on my toe the whole evening after, as a juggler spins a pewter platter on the point of a needle. But age has clawed me somewhat in his clutch, as the song says; though, if I like the tune and like my partner, I'll dance the heys yet with any merry lass in Warwickshire, that writes that unhappy figure four with a round O after it.'

If the Countess was overwhelmed with the garrulity of this good dame, Wayland Smith, on his part, had enough to do to sustain and parry the constant attacks made upon him by the indefatigable curiosity of his old acquaintance Richard Sludge. Nature had given that arch youngster a prying cast of disposition, which matched admirably with his sharp wit; the former inducing him to plant himself as a spy on other people's affairs, and the latter quality leading him perpetually to interfere after he had made himself master of that which concerned him not. He spent the livelong day in attempting to peer under the Countess's muffler, and apparently what he could there discern greatly sharpened his curiosity.

'That sister of thine, Wayland,' he said, 'has a fair neck to have been born in a smithy, and a pretty taper hand to have been used for twirling a spindle—faith, I'll believe in your relationship when the crow's egg is hatched into a cygnet.'

'Go to,' said Wayland, 'thou art a prating boy, and should be breeched for thine assurance.'

'Well,' said the imp, drawing off, 'all I say is,—remember you have kept a secret from me! and if I give thee not a Rowland for thine Oliver, my name is not Dickon Sludge.'

This threat, and the distance at which Hobgoblin kept from him for the rest of the way, alarmed Wayland very much, and he suggested to his pretended sister that, on pretext of weariness, she should express a desire to stop two or three miles short of the fair town of Warwick, promising to rejoin the troop on the morning. A small village inn afforded them a resting-place; and it was with secret pleasure that Wayland saw the whole party, including Dickon, pass on, after a courteous farewell, and leave them behind.

'To-morrow, madam,' he said to his charge, 'we will, with your leave, again start early, and reach Kenilworth before the rout which are to assemble there.'

The Countess gave assent to the proposal of her faithful guide; but, somewhat to his surprise, said nothing further on the subject, which left Wayland under the disagreeable uncertainty whether or no she had formed any plan for her own future proceedings, as he knew her situation demanded circumspection, although he was but imperfectly acquainted with all its peculiarities. Concluding, however, that she must have friends within the castle, whose advice and assistance she could safely trust, he supposed his task would be best accomplished by conducting her thither in safety, agreeably to her repeated commands.

25

Hark, the bells summon, and the bugle calls,
But she the fairest answers not—the tide
Of nobles and of ladies throngs the halls,
But she the loveliest must in secret hide.
What eyes were thine, proud Prince, which in the gleam
Of yon gay meteors lost that better sense,
That o'er the glow-worm doth the star esteem,
And merit's modest blush o'er courtly insolence?
                                        The Glass Slipper.

THE unfortunate Countess of Leicester had, from her infancy upwards, been treated by those around her with indulgence as unbounded as injudicious. The natural sweetness of her disposition had saved her from becoming insolent and ill-humoured; but the caprice which preferred the handsome and insinuating Leicester before Tressilian, of whose high honour and unalterable affection she herself entertained so firm an opinion—that fatal error, which ruined the happiness of her life, had its origin in the mistaken kindness that had spared her childhood the painful, but most necessary lesson, of submission and self-command. From the same indulgence, it followed that she had only been accustomed to form and to express her wishes, leaving to others the task of fulfilling them; and thus, at the most momentous period of her life, she was alike destitute of presence of mind, and of ability to form for herself any reasonable or prudent plan of conduct.

These difficulties pressed on the unfortunate lady with overwhelming force, on the morning which seemed to be the crisis of her fate. Overlooking every intermediate consideration, she had only desired to be at Kenilworth, and to approach her husband's presence; and now, when she was in the vicinity of both, a thousand considerations arose at once upon her mind, startling her with accumulated doubts and dangers, some real, some imaginary, and all exalted and exaggerated by a situation alike helpless, and destitute of aid and counsel.

A sleepless night rendered her so weak in the morning, that she was altogether unable to attend Wayland's early summons. The trusty guide became extremely distressed on the lady's account, and somewhat alarmed on his own, and was on the point of going alone to Kenilworth, in the hope of discovering Tressilian, and intimating to him the lady's approach, when about nine in the morning he was summoned to attend her. He found her dressed, and ready for resuming her journey, but with a paleness of countenance which alarmed him for her health. She intimated her desire that the horses might be got instantly ready, and resisted with impatience her guide's request, that she would take some refreshment before setting forward. 'I have had,' she said, 'a cup of water —the wretch who is dragged to execution needs no stronger cordial, and that may serve me which suffices for him—do as I command you.' Wayland Smith still hesitated. 'What would you have?' said she—'Have I not spoken plainly?'

'Yes, madam,' answered Wayland; 'but may I ask what is your further purpose? I only wish to know, that I may guide myself by your wishes. The whole country is afloat, and streaming towards the Castle of Kenilworth. It will be difficult travelling thither, even if we had the necessary passports for safe-conduct and free-admittance—Unknown and unfriended, we may come by mishap. Your ladyship will forgive my speaking my poor mind—Were we not better try to find out the masquers, and again join ourselves with them?' The Countess shook her head, and her guide proceeded, 'Then I see but one other remedy.'

'Speak out, then,' said the lady, not displeased, perhaps, that he should thus offer the advice which she was ashamed to ask; 'I believe thee faithful—what wouldst thou counsel?'

'That I should warn Master Tressilian,' said Wayland, 'that you are in this place. I am right certain he would get to horse with a few of Lord Sussex's followers, and ensure your personal safety.'

'And it is to *me* you advise,' aid the Countess, 'to put myself under the protection of Sussex, the unworthy rival of the noble Leicester?' Then, seeing the surprise with which Wayland stared upon her, and afraid of having too strongly intimated her interest in Leicester, she added, 'and for Tressilian, it must not be—mention not to him, I charge you, my unhappy name; it would but double *my* misfortunes, and involve *him* in dangers beyond the power of rescue.' She paused; but when she observed that Wayland continued to look on her with that anxious and uncertain gaze, which indicated a doubt whether her brain was settled, she assumed an air of composure, and added, 'Do thou but guide me to Kenilworth

Castle, good fellow, and thy task is ended, since I will then judge what further is to be done. Thou hast yet been true to me—here is something that will make thee rich amends.'

She offered the artist a ring, containing a valuable stone. Wayland looked at it, hesitated a moment, and then returned it. 'Not,' he said, 'that I am above your kindness, madam, being but a poor fellow, who have been forced, God help me! to live by worse shifts than the bounty of such a person as you. But as my old master the farrier used to say to his customers, "No cure, no pay." We are not yet in Kenilworth Castle, and it is time enough to discharge your guide, as they say, when you take your boots off. I trust in God your ladyship is as well assured of fitting reception when you arrive, as you may hold yourself certain of my best endeavours to conduct you thither safely. I go to get the horses; meantime let me pray you once more, as your poor physician as well as guide, to take some sustenance.'

'I will—I will,' said the lady, hastily. 'Begone, begone instantly! —It is in vain I assume audacity,' said she, when he left the room; 'even this poor groom sees through my affectation of courage, and fathoms the very ground of my fears.'

She then attempted to follow her guide's advice by taking some food, but was compelled to desist, as the effort to swallow even a single morsel gave her so much uneasiness as amounted well-nigh to suffocation. A moment afterwards the horses appeared at the latticed window—the lady mounted, and found that relief from the free air and change of place, which is frequently experienced in similar circumstances.

It chanced well for the Countess's purpose that Wayland Smith, whose previous wandering and unsettled life had made him acquainted with almost all England, was intimate with all the by-roads, as well as direct communications, through the beautiful county of Warwick. For such and so great was the throng which flocked in all directions towards Kenilworth, to see the entry of Elizabeth into that splendid mansion of her prime favourite, that the principal roads were actually blocked up and interrupted, and it was only by circuitous by-paths that the travellers could proceed on their journey.

The Queen's purveyors had been abroad, sweeping the farms and villages of those articles usually exacted during a royal progress, and for which the owners were afterwards to obtain a tardy payment from the Board of Green Cloth. The Earl of Leicester's household officers had been scouring the country for the same purpose; and many of his friends and allies, both near and remote, took this opportunity of ingratiating themselves, by sending large quantities of provisions and delicacies of all kinds, with game in huge quantities, and whole tuns of the best liquors, foreign and domestic. Thus the high-roads were filled with droves of bullocks, sheep, calves, and hogs, and choked with loaded wains, whose axle-trees cracked under their burdens of wine-casks and hogsheads of ale, and huge hampers of grocery goods, and slaughtered game, and salted provision, and sacks of flour. Perpetual stoppages took place as these wains became entangled; and their rude drivers, swearing and brawling till their wild passions were fully raised, began to debate precedence with their wagon-whips and quarter-staves, which occasional riots were usually quieted by a purveyor, deputy-marshall's man, or some other person in authority, breaking the heads of both parties.

Here were, besides, players and mummers, jugglers and showmen, of every description, traversing in joyous bands the paths which led to the Palace of Princely Pleasure; for so the travelling minstrels had termed Kenilworth in the songs which already had come forth in anticipation of the revels, which were there expected. In the midst of this motley show, mendicants were exhibiting their real or pretended miseries, forming a strange though common contrast betwixt the vanities and the sorrows of human existence. All these floated along with the immense tide of population, whom mere curiosity had drawn together; and where the mechanic, in his leathern apron, elbowed the dink and dainty dame, his city mistress; where clowns, with hobnailed shoes, were treading on the kibes of substantial burghers and gentlemen of worship; and where Joan of the dairy, with robust pace, and red sturdy arms, rowed her way onward, amongst those prim and pretty moppets whose sires were knights and squires.

The throng and confusion was, however, of a gay and cheerful character. All came forth to see and to enjoy, and all laughed at the trifling inconveniences which at another time might have chafed their temper. Excepting the occasional brawls which we have mentioned among that irritable race the carmen, the mingled sounds which arose from the multitude were those of light-hearted mirth and tiptoe jollity. The musicians preluded on their instruments—the minstrels hummed their songs—the licensed jester whooped betwixt mirth and madness, as he brandished his bauble —the morrice-dancers jangled their bells—the rustics halloo'd and whistled—men laughed loud, and maidens giggled shrill; while many a broad jest flew like a shuttle-cock from one party to be caught in the air and returned from the opposite side of the road by another, at which it was aimed.

No infliction can be so distressing to a mind absorbed in melancholy, as being plunged into a scene of mirth and revelry, forming an accompaniment so dissonant from its own feelings. Yet, in the case of the Countess of Leicester, the noise and tumult of this giddy scene distracted her thoughts, and rendered her this sad service, that it became impossible for her to brood on her own misery, or to form terrible anticipations of her approaching fate. She travelled on, like one in a dream, following implicitly the guidance of Wayland, who, with great address, now threaded his way through the general throng of passengers, now stood still until a favourable opportunity occurred of again moving forward, and frequently turning altogether out of the direct road, followed some circuitous by-path, which brought them into the high road again, after having given them the opportunity of traversing a considerable way with greater ease and rapidity.

It was thus he avoided Warwick, within whose castle (that fairest monument of ancient and chivalrous splendour which yet remains uninjured by time) Elizabeth had passed the previous night, and where she was to tarry until past noon, at that time the general hour of dinner throughout England, after which repast she was to proceed to Kenilworth. In the meanwhile, each passing group had something to say in the Sovereign's praise, though not absolutely without the usual mixture of satire which qualifies more or less our estimate of our neighbours, especially if they chance to be also our betters.

'Heard you,' said one, 'how graciously she spoke to Master Bailiff and the Recorder, and to good Master Griffin the preacher, as they kneeled down at her coach-window?

'Ay, and how she said to little Aglionby, "Master Recorder, men would have persuaded me that you were afraid of me, but truly I think, so well did you reckon up to me the virtues of a sovereign, that I have more reason to be afraid of you,"—And then with what grace she took the fair-wrought purse with the twenty gold sovereigns, seeming as though she would not willingly handle it, and yet taking it withal.'

'Ay, ay,' said another, 'her fingers closed on it pretty willingly methought, when all was done; and methought, too, she weighed them for a second in her hand, as she would say, I hope they be avoirdupois.'

'She needed not, neighbour,' said a third; 'it is only when the corporation pay the accounts of a poor handicraft like me, that they put him off with clipt coin. Well, there is a God above all—Little Master Recorder, since that is the word, will be greater now than ever.'

'Come, good neighbour,' said the first speaker, 'be not envious— She is a good Queen, and a generous—She gave the purse to the Earl of Leicester.'

'I envious?—beshrew thy heart for the word!' replied the handicraft—'But she will give all to the Earl of Leicester anon, methinks.'

'You are turning ill, lady,' said Wayland Smith to the Countess of Leicester, and proposed that she should draw off from the road, and halt till she recovered. But, subduing her feelings at this, and different speeches to the same purpose, which caught her ear as they passed on, she insisted that her guide should proceed to Kenilworth with all the haste which the numerous impediments of their journey permitted. Meanwhile, Wayland's anxiety at her repeated fits of indisposition, and her obvious distraction of mind, was hourly increasing, and he became extremely desirous that, according to her reiterated requests, she should be safely introduced into the castle, where, he doubted not, she was secure of a kind reception, though she seemed unwilling to reveal on whom she reposed her hopes.

'An I were once rid of this peril,' thought he, 'and if any man shall find me playing squire of the body to a damosel-errant, he shall have leave to beat my brains out with my own sledgehammer!'

At length the princely castle appeared, upon improving which, and the domains around, the Earl of Leicester had, it is said, expended sixty thousand pounds sterling, a sum equal to half a million of our present money.

The outer wall of this splendid and gigantic structure enclosed seven acres, a part of which was occupied by extensive stables, and by a pleasure garden, with its trim arbours and parterres, and the rest formed the large base-court, or outer yard, of the noble castle.

The lordly structure itself, which rose near the centre of this spacious enclosure, was composed of a huge pile of magnificent castellated buildings, apparently of different ages, surrounding an inner court, and bearing in the names attached to each portion of the magnificent mass, and in the armorial bearings which were there blazoned, the emblems of mighty chiefs who had long passed away, and whose history, could Ambition have lent ear to it, might have read a lesson to the haughty favourite who had now acquired and was augmenting the fair domain. A large and massive keep, which formed the citadel of the castle, was of uncertain though great antiquity. It bore the name of Cæsar, perhaps from its resemblance to that in the Tower of London so called. Some antiquaries ascribed its foundation to the time of Kenelph, from whom the castle had its name, a Saxon King of Mercia, and others to an early era after the Norman Conquest. On the exterior walls frowned the scutcheon of the Clintons, by whom they were founded in the reign of Henry the First, and of the yet more redoubted Simon de Montfort, by whom, during the Barons' Wars, Kenilworth was long held out against Henry the Third. Here Mortimer, Earl of March, famous alike for his rise and his fall, had once gaily revelled in Kenilworth, while his dethroned sovereign, Edward the Second, languished in its dungeons. Old John of Gaunt, 'time-honoured Lancaster,' had widely extended the castle, erecting that noble and massive pile which yet bears the name of Lancaster's Buildings; and Leicester himself had outdone the former possessors, princely and powerful as they were, by erecting another immense structure, which now lies crushed under its own ruins, the monument of its owner's ambition. The external wall of this royal castle was, on the south and west sides, adorned and defended by a lake partly artificial, across which Leicester had constructed a stately bridge, that Elizabeth might enter the castle by a path hitherto untrodden, instead of the usual entrance to the northward, over which he had erected a gate house or barbican, which still exists, and is equal in extent, and superior in architecture, to the baronial castle of many a nothern chief.

Beyond the lake lay an extensive Chase, full of red deer, fallow deer, roes, and every species of game, and abounding with lofty trees, from amongst which the extended front and massive towers of the castle were seen to rise in majesty and beauty. We cannot but add, that of this lordly palace, where princes feasted and heroes fought, now in the bloody earnest of storm and siege, and now in the games of chivalry, where beauty dealt the prize which valour won, all is now desolate. The bed of the lake is but a rushy swamp; and the massive ruins of the castle only serve to show what their splendour once was, and to impress on the musing visitor the transitory value of human possessions, and the happiness of those who enjoy a humble lot in virtuous contentment.

It was with far different feelings that the unfortunate Countess of Leicester viewed those gray and massive towers, when she first beheld them rise above the embowering and richly shaded woods, over which they seemed to preside. She, the undoubted wife of the great Earl, of Elizabeth's minion, and England's mighty favourite, was approaching the presence of her husband, and that husband's sovereign, under the protection, rather than the guidance, of a poor juggler; and though unquestioned Mistress of that proud castle, whose lightest word ought to have had force sufficient to make its gates leap from their massive hinges to receive her, yet she could not conceal from herself the difficulty and peril which she must experience in gaining admission into her own halls.

The risk and difficulty, indeed, seemed to increase every moment, and at length threatened altogether to put a stop to her further progress, at the great gate leading to a broad and fair road, which, traversing the breadth of the Chase for the space of two miles, and commanding several most beautiful views of the castle and lake, terminated at the newly constructed bridge, to which it was an appendage, and which was destined to form the Queen's approach to the castle on that memorable occasion.

Here the Countess and Wayland found the gate at the end of this avenue, which opened on the Warwick road, guarded by a body of the Queen's mounted Yeomen of the Guard, armed in corslets richly carved and gilded, and wearing morions instead of bonnets, having their carabines resting with the butt-end on their thighs. These Guards, distinguished for strength and stature, who did duty wherever the Queen went in person, were here stationed under the direction of a pursuivant, graced with the Bear and Ragged Staff on his arm, as belonging to the Earl of Leicester, and peremptorily refused all admittance, excepting to such as were guests invited to the festival, or persons who were to perform some part in the mirthful exhibitions which were proposed.

The press was of consequence great around the entrance, and

persons of all kinds presented every sort of plea for admittance; to which the guards turned an inexorable ear, pleading, in return to fair words and even to fair offers, the strictness of their orders, founded on the Queen's well-known dislike to the rude pressing of a multitude. With those whom such reasons did not serve, they dealt more rudely, repelling them without ceremony by the pressure of powerful, barbed horses, and good round blows from the stocks of their carabines. These last manœuvres produced undulations amongst the crowd, which rendered Wayland much afraid that he might perforce be separated from his charge in the throng. Neither did he know what excuse to make in order to obtain admittance, and he was debating the matter in his head with great uncertainty, when the Earl's pursuivant, having cast an eye upon him, exclaimed, to his no small surprise, 'Yeomen, make room for the fellow in the orange-tawny cloak—Come forward, Sir Coxcomb, and make haste. What, in the fiend's name has kept you waiting? Come forward with your bale of woman's gear.'

While the pursuivant gave Wayland this pressing yet un-courteous invitation, which, for a minute or two, he could not imagine was applied to him, the Yeomen speedily made a free passage for him, while, only cautioning his companion to keep the muffler close around her face, he entered the gate leading her palfrey, but with such a drooping crest, and such a look of conscious fear and anxiety, that the crowd, not greatly pleased at any rate with the preference bestowed upon them, accompanied their admission with hooting, and a loud laugh of derision.

Admitted thus within the Chase, though with no very flattering notice or distinction, Wayland and his charge rode forward, musing what difficulties it would be next their lot to encounter, through the broad avenue, which was sentinelled on either side by a long line of retainers armed with swords, and partisans richly dressed in the Earl of Leicester's liveries, and bearing his cognisance of the Bear and Ragged Staff, each placed within three paces of each other, so as to line the whole road from the entrance into the park to the bridge. And, indeed, when the lady obtained the first commanding view of the castle, with its stately towers rising from within a long sweeping line of outward walls, ornamented with battlements, and turrets, and platforms, at every point of defence, with many a banner streaming from its walls, and such a bustle of gay crests and waving plumes disposed on the terraces and battlements, and all the gay and gorgeous scene, her heart, unaccustomed to such splendour, sank as if it died within her, and for a moment she asked herself, what she had offered up to Leicester to deserve to become the partner of this princely splendour. But her pride and generous spirit resisted the whisper which bade her despair.

'I have given him', she said, 'all that woman has to give. Name and fame, heart and hand, have I given the lord of all this magnificence at the altar, and England's Queen could give him no more. He is my husband—I am his wife—Whom God hath joined, man cannot sunder. I will be bold in claiming my right; even the bolder, that I come thus unexpected, and thus forlorn. I know my noble Dudley well! He will be something impatient at my disobeying him; but Amy will weep, and Dudley will forgive her.'

These meditations were interrupted by a cry of surprise from her guide Wayland, who suddenly felt himself grasped firmly round the body by a pair of long thin black arms, belonging to some one who had dropped himself out of an oak-tree upon the croupe of his horse, amidst the shouts of laughter which burst from the sentinels.

'This must be the devil, or Flibbertigibbet again!' said Wayland, after a vain struggle to disengage himself, and unhorse the urchin who clung to him. 'Do Kenilworth oaks bear such acorns?'

'In sooth do they, Master Wayland,' said his unexpected adjunct, 'and many others, too hard for you to crack, for as old as you are, without my teaching you. How would you have passed the pursuivant at the upper gate yonder, had not I warned him our principal juggler was to follow us? and here have I waited for you, having clambered up into the tree from the spot of the wain, and I suppose they are all mad for want of me by this time.'

'Nay, then, thou art a limb of the devil in good earnest,' said Wayland. 'I give thee way, good imp, and will walk by thy counsel; only, as thou art powerful, be merciful.'

As he spoke, they approached a strong tower, at the south extremity of the long bridge we have mentioned, which served to protect the outer gateway of the castle of Kenilworth.

Under such disastrous circumstances, and in such singular company, did the unfortunate Countess of Leicester approach, for the first time, the magnificent abode of her almost princely husband.

26

Snug. Have you the lion's part written? pray, if it be, give it me, for I am slow of study.

Quince. You may do it extempore, for it is nothing but roaring.
Midsummer-Night's Dream.

WHEN the Countess of Leicester arrived at the outer gate of the Castle of Kenilworth, she found the tower, beneath which its ample portal arch opened, guarded in a singular manner. Upon the battlements were placed gigantic warders, with clubs, battle-axes, and other implements of ancient warfare, designed to represent the soldiers of King Arthur; those primitive Britons, by whom, according to romantic tradition, the castle had been first tenanted, though history carried back its antiquity only to the times of the Heptarchy. Some of these tremendous figures were real men, dressed up with vizards and buskins; others were mere pageants composed of pasteboard and buckram, which, viewed from beneath, and mingled with those that were real, formed a sufficiently striking representation of what was intended. But the gigantic porter who waited at the gate beneath, and actually discharged the duties of warder, owed none of his terrors to fictitious means. He was a man whose huge stature, thews, sinews, and bulk in proportion, would have enabled him to enact Colbrand, Ascapart, or any other giant of romance, without raising himself nearer to heaven even by the altitude of a chopin. The legs and knees of this son of Anak were bare, as were his arms from a span below the shoulder; but his feet were defended with sandals, fastened with cross straps of scarlet leather, studded with brazen knobs. A close jerkin of scarlet velvet, looped with gold, with short breeches of the same, covered his body and a part of his limbs; and he wore on his shoulders, instead of a cloak, the skin of a black bear. The head of this formidable person was uncovered, excepting by his shaggy black hair, which descended on either side around features of that huge, lumpish, and heavy cast, which are often annexed to men of very uncommon size, and which, notwithstanding some distinguished exceptions, have created a general prejudice against giants, as being a dull and sullen kind of persons. This tremendous warder was appropriately armed with a heavy club, spiked with steel. In fine, he represented excellently one of those giants of popular romance, who figure in every fairy tale, or legend of knight-errantry.

The demeanour of this modern Titan, when Wayland Smith bent his attention to him, had in it something arguing much mental embarrassment and vexation; for sometimes, he sat down for an instant on a massive stone bench, which seemed placed for his accommodation beside the gateway, and then ever and anon he started up, scratching his huge head, and striding to and fro on his post, like one under a fit of impatience and anxiety. It was while the porter was pacing before the gate in this agitated manner, that Wayland, modestly, yet as a matter of course (not however without some mental misgiving), was about to pass him, and enter the portal arch. The porter, however, stopped his progress, bidding him, in a thundering voice, 'Stand back!' and enforcing his injunction by heaving up his steel-shod mace, and dashing it on the ground before Wayland's horse's nose with such vehemence, that the pavement flashed fire, and the archway rang to the clamour. Wayland, availing himself of Dickie's hint, began to state that he belonged to a band of performers to which his presence was indispensable, that he had been accidentally detained behind, and much to the same purpose. But the warder was inexorable, and kept muttering and murmuring something betwixt his teeth, which Wayland could make little of; and addressing betwixt whiles a refusal of admittance, couched in language which was but too intelligible. A specimen of his speech might run thus:—'What, how now, my masters? (to himself)—Here's a stir—here's a coil.—(Then to Wayland)—You are a loitering knave, and shall have no entrance—(Again to himself)—Here's a throng—here's a thrusting. —I shall never get through with it—Here's a—hunph—ha—(To Wayland)—Back from the gate, or I'll break the pate of thee—(Once more to himself)—Here's a—no—I shall never get through it.'

'Stand still,' whispered Flibbertigibbet into Wayland's ear, 'I know where the shoe pinches, and will tame him in an instant.'

He dropped down from the horse, and skipping up to the porter, plucked him by the tail of the bear-skin, so as to induce him to decline his huge head, and whispered something in his ear. Not at the command of the lord of some eastern talisman did ever

Afrite change his horrid frown into a look of smooth submission, more suddenly than the gigantic porter of Kenilworth relaxed the terrors of his look, at the instant Flibbertigibbet's whisper reached his ears. He flung his club upon the ground, and caught up Dickie Sludge, raising him to such a distance from the earth, as might have proved perilous had he chanced to let him slip.

'It is even so,' he said, with a thundering sound of exultation—'it is even so, my little dandieprat—But who the devil could teach it thee?'

'Do not thou care about that,' said Flibbertigibbet;'but'——he looked at Wayland and the lady, and then sunk what he had to say in a whisper, which needed not to be a loud one, as the giant held him for his convenience close to his ear. The porter than gave Dickie a warm caress, and set him on the ground with the same care which a careful housewife uses in replacing a cracked china cup upon her mantelpiece, calling out at the same time to Wayland and the lady, 'In with you—in with you—and take heed how you come too late another day when I chance to be porter.'

'Ay, ay, in with you,' added Flibbertigibbet; 'I must stay a short space with mine honest Philistine, my Goliath of Gath here; but I will be with you anon, and at the bottom of all your secrets, were they as deep and dark as the castle dungeon.'

'I do believe thou wouldst,' said Wayland; 'but I trust the secret will be soon out of my keeping, and then I shall care the less whether thou or any one knows it.'

They now crossed the entrance tower, which obtained the name of the Gallery Tower, from the following circumstance:—The whole bridge, extending from the entrance to another tower on the opposite side of the lake, called Mortimer's Tower, was so disposed as to make a spacious tilt-yard, about one hundred and thirty yards in length, and ten in breadth, strewed with the finest sand, and defended on either side by strong and high palisades. The broad and fair gallery, destined for the ladies who were to witness the feats of chivalry presented on this area, was erected on the nothern side of the outer tower, to which it gave name. Our travellers passed slowly along the bridge or tilt-yard, and arrived at Mortimer's Tower, at its farthest extremity, through which the approach led into the outer, or base court of the castle. Mortimer's Tower bore on its front the scutcheon of the Earl of March, whose daring ambition overthrew the throne of Edward the Second, and aspired to share his power with the 'She-wolf of France,' to whom the unhappy monarch was wedded. The gate, which opened under this ominous memorial, was guarded by many warders in rich liveries; but they offered no opposition to the entrance of the Countess and her guide, who, having passed by licence of the principal porter at the Gallery Tower, were not, it may be supposed, liable to interruption from his deputies. They entered accordingly, in silence, the great outward court of the castle, having then full before them that vast and lordly pile, with all its stately towers, each gate open, as if in sign of unlimited hospitality, and the apartments filled with noble guests of every degree, besides dependants, retainers, domestics of every description, and all the appendages and promoters of mirth and revelry.

Amid this stately and busy scene. Wayland halted his horse, and looked upon the lady, as if waiting her commands what was next to be done, since they had safely reached the place of destination. As she remained silent, Wayland, after waiting a minute or two, ventured to ask her in direct terms, what were her next commands. She raised her hand to her forehead, as if in the act of collecting her thoughts and resolution, while she answered him in a low and suppressed voice, like the murmurs of one who speaks in a dream— 'Commands? I may indeed claim right to command, but who is there will obey me?'

Then suddenly raising her head like one who has formed a decisive resolution, she addressed a gaily-dressed domestic, who was crossing the court with importance and bustle in his countenance. 'Stop, sir,' she said, 'I desire to speak with the Earl of Leicester.'

'With whom, an it please you?' said the man, surprised at the demand; and then looking upon the mean equipage of her who used towards him such a tone of authority, he added with insolence, 'Why, what Bess of Bedlam is this, would ask to see my lord on such a day as the present?'

'Friend,' said the Countess, 'be not insolent—my business with the Earl is most urgent.'

'You must get some one else to do it, were it thrice as urgent,' said the fellow. 'I should summon my lord from the Queen's royal presence to do *your* business, should I? I were like to be thanked with a horse-whip. I marvel our old porter took not measure of such ware with his club, instead of giving them passage; but his brain is addled with getting his speech by heart.'

Two or three persons stopped, attracted by the fleering way in which the serving-man expressed himself; and Wayland, alarmed both for himself and the lady, hastily addressed himself to one who appeared the most civil, and thrusting a piece of money into his hand, held a moment's counsel with him, on the subject of finding a place of temporary retreat for the lady. The person to whom he spoke, being one of some authority, rebuked the others for their incivility, and commanding one fellow to take care of the strangers' horses, he desired them to follow him. The Countess retained presence of mind sufficient to see that it was absolutely necessary she should comply with his request; and, leaving the rude lackeys and grooms to crack their brutal jests about light heads, light heels, and so forth, Wayland and she followed in silence the deputy-usher, who undertook to be their conductor.

They entered the inner court of the castle by the great gateway, which extended betwixt the principal keep or donjon, called Cæsar's Tower, and a stately building which passed by the name of King Henry's Lodging, and were thus placed in the centre of the noble pile, which presented on its different fronts magnificent specimens of every species of castellated architecture, from the Conquest to the reign of Elizabeth, with the appropriate style and ornaments of each.

Across this inner court also they were conducted by their guide to a small but strong tower, occupying the north-east angle of the building, adjacent to the great hall, and filling up a space betwixt the immense range of kitchens and the end of the great hall itself. The lower part of this tower was occupied by some of the household officers of Leicester, owing to its conveneint vicinity to the places where their duty lay; but in the upper story, which was reached by a narrow winding stair, was a small chamber, which, in the great demand for lodgings, had been on the present occasion fitted up for the reception of guests, though generally said to have been used as a place of confinement for some unhappy person who had been there murdered. Tradition called this prisoner Mervyn, and transferred his name to the tower. That it had been used as a prison was not improbable; for the floor of each story was arched, the walls of tremendous thickness, while the space of the chamber did not exceed fifteen feet in diameter. The window, however, was pleasant, though narrow, and commanded a delightful view of what was called the *Pleasance*; a space of ground enclosed and decorated with arches, trophies, statues, fountains, and other architectural monuments, which formed one access from the castle itself to the garden. There was a bed in the apartment, and other preparations for the reception of a guest, to which the Countess paid but slight attention, her notice being instantly arrested by the sight of writing materials placed on the table (not very commonly to be found in the bedrooms of those days), which instantly suggested the idea of writing to Leicester, and remaining private until she had received his answer.

The deputy-usher having introduced them into this commodious apartment, courteously asked Wayland, whose generosity he had experienced, whether he could do anything further for his service. Upon receiving a gentle hint that some refreshment would not be unacceptable, he presently conveyed the smith to the buttery-hatch, where dressed provisions of all sorts were distributed, with hospitable profusion, to all who asked for them. Wayland was readily supplied with some light provisions, such as he thought would best suit the faded appetite of the lady, and did not omit the opportunity of himself making a hasty but hearty meal on more substantial fare. He then returned to the apartment in the turret, where he found the Countess, who had finished her letter to Leicester; and, in lieu of a seal and silken thread, had secured it with a braid of her own beautiful tresses, fastened by what is called a true-love knot.

'Good friend,' said she to Wayland, 'whom God hath sent to aid me at my utmost need, I do beseech thee, as the last trouble you shall take for an unfortunate lady, to deliver this letter to the noble Earl of Leicester. Be it received as it may,' she said, with features agitated betwixt hope and fear, 'thou, good fellow, shalt have no more cumber with me. But I hope the best; and if ever lady made a poor man rich, thou hast surely deserved it at my hand, should my happy days ever come round again. Give it, I pray you, into Lord Leicester's own hand, and mark how he looks on receiving it.'

Wayland, on his part, readily undertook the commission, but anxiously prayed the lady, in his turn, to partake of some refreshment; in which he at length prevailed, more through importunity, and her desire to see him begone on his errand, than from any inclination the Countess felt to comply with his request. He then left her, advising her to lock her door on the inside, and not to stir from her little apartment—and went to seek an opportunity of discharging her errand, as well as of carrying into effect a purpose of his own, which circumstances had induced him to form.

In fact, from the conduct of the lady during the journey—her long fits of profound silence—the irresolution and uncertainty which seemed to pervade all her movements, and the obvious incapacity of thinking and acting for herself, under which she seemed to labour, Wayland had formed the not improbable opinion, that the difficulties of her situation had in some degree affected her understanding.

When she had escaped from the seclusion of Cumnor Place, and the dangers to which she was there exposed, it would have seemed her most rational course to retire to her father's, or elsewhere, at a distance from the power of those by whom these dangers had been created. When, instead of doing so, she demanded to be conveyed to Kenilworth, Wayland had been only able to account for her conduct, by supposing that she meant to put herself under the tutelage of Tressilian, and to appeal to the protection of the Queen. But now, instead of following this natural course, she entrusted him with a letter to Leicester, the patron of Varney, and within whose jurisdiction at least, if not under his express authority, all the evils she had already suffered were inflicted upon her. This seemed an unsafe, and even desperate measure, and Wayland felt anxiety for his own safety, as well as that of the lady, should he execute her commission, before he had secured the advice and countenance of a protector. He therefore resolved, before delivering the letter to Leicester, that he would seek out Tressilian, and communicate to him the arrival of the lady at Kenilworth, and thus at once rid himself of all further responsibility, and devolve the task of guiding and protecting this unfortunate lady upon the patron who had at first employed him on her service.

'He will be a better judge than I am,' said Wayland, 'whether she is to be gratified in this humour of appeal to my Lord of Leicester, which seems like an act of insanity; and, therefore, I will turn the matter over on his hands, deliver him the letter, receive what they list to give me by way of guerdon, and then show the Castle of Kenilworth a pair of light heels; for, after the work I have been engaged in, it will be, I fear, neither a safe not wholesome place of residence; and I would rather shoe colts on the coldest common in England, than share in their gayest revels.'

27

In my time I have seen a boy do wonders.
Robin, the red tinker, had a boy
Would ha' run through a cat-hole.—*The Coxcomb.*

AMID the universal bustle which filled the castle and its environs, it was no easy matter to find out any individual; and Wayland was still less likely to light upon Tressilian, whom he sought so anxiously, because, sensible of the danger of attracting attention, in the circumstances in which he was placed, he dared not make general inquiries among the retainers or domestics of Leicester. He learned, however, by indirect questions, that, in all probability, Tressilian must have been one of a large party of gentlemen in attendance on the Earl of Sussex, who had accompanied their patron that morning to Kenilworth, when Leicester had received them with marks of the most formal respect and distinction. He further learned, that both Earls, with their followers, and many other nobles, knights and gentlemen, had taken horse, and gone towards Warwick several hours since, for the purpose of escorting the Queen to Kenilworth.

Her Majesty's arrival, like other great events, was delayed from hour to hour; and it was now announced by a breathless post, that her Majesty being detained by her gracious desire, to receive the homage of her lieges who had thronged to wait upon her at Warwick, it would be the hour of twilight ere she entered the castle. The intelligence released for a time those who were upon duty, in the immediate expectation of the Queen's appearance, and ready to play their part in the solemnities with which it was to be accompanied; and Wayland, seeing several horsemen enter the castle, was not without hopes that Tressilian might be of the number. That he might not lose an opportunity of meeting his patron in case this should be the case, Wayland placed himself in the base-court of the castle, near Mortimer's Tower, and watched every one who went or came by the bridge, the extremity of which was protected by that building. Thus stationed, nobody could enter or leave the castle without his observation, and most anxiously did he study the garb and countenance of every horseman, as, passing from under the opposite Gallery Tower, they paced slowly, or curveted, along the tilt-yard, and approached the entrance of the base-court.

But while Wayland gazed thus eagerly to discover him whom he saw not, he was pulled by the sleeve by one by whom he himself would not willingly have been seen.

This was Dickie Sludge, or Flibbertigibbet, who, like the imp whose name he bore, and whom he had been accoutred in order to resemble, seemed to be ever at the ear of those who thought least of him. Whatever were Wayland's internal feelings, he judged it necessary to express pleasure at their unexpected meeting.

'Ha! it is thou, my minikin—my miller's thumb—my prince of cacodemons—my little mouse?'

'Ay,' said Dickie, 'the mouse which gnawed asunder the toils, just when the lion who was caught in them began to look wonderfully like an ass.'

'Why, thou little hop-the-gutter, thou art as sharp as vinegar this afternoon. But tell me, how didst thou come off with yonder jolter-headed giant whom I left thee with? I was afraid he would have stripped thy clothes, and so swallowed thee as men peel and eat a roasted chestnut.'

'Had he done so', replied the boy, 'he would have had more brains in his guts than ever he had in his noddle. But the giant is a courteous monster, and more grateful than many other folks whom I have helped at a pinch, Master Wayland Smith.'

'Beshrew me, Flibbertigibbet,' replied Wayland, 'but thou art sharper than a Sheffield whittle! I would I knew by what charm you muzzled yonder old bear?'

'Ay, that is in your own manner,' answered Dickie; 'you think fine speeches will pass muster instead of goodwill. However, as to this honest porter, you must know, that when we presented ourselves at the gate yonder, his brain was overburdened with a speech that had been penned for him, and which proved rather an overmatch for his gigantic faculties. Now this same pithy oration had been indited, like sundry others, by my learned magister, Erasmus Holiday, so I had heard it often enough to remember every line. As soon as I heard him blundering, and floundering like a fish upon dry land, through the first verse, and perceived him at stand, I knew where the shoe pinched, and helped him to the next word, when he caught me up in an ecstasy, even as you saw but now. I promised, as the price of your admission, to hide me under his bearish gaberdine, and prompt him in the hour of need. I have just now been getting some food in the castle, and am about to return to him.'

'That's right—that's right, my dear Dickie,' replied Wayland; 'haste thee, for Heaven's sake, else the poor giant will be utterly disconsolate for want of his dwarfish auxiliary—Away with thee, Dickie.'

'Ay, ay!' asnwered the boy—'Away with Dickie, when we have got what good of him we can.—You will not let me know the story of this lady, then, who is as much a sister of thine as I am?'

'Why, what good would it do thee, thou silly elf?' said Wayland.

'Oh, stand ye on these terms?' said the boy; 'well, I care not greatly about the matter,—only, I never smell out a secret, but I try to be either at the right or the wrong end of it, and so good-evening to ye.'

'Nay, but Dickie,' said Wayland, who knew the boy's reckless and intriguing disposition too well not to fear his enmity—'stay, my dear Dickie—part not with old friends so shortly! Thou shalt know all I know of the lady one day.'

'Ay!' said Dickie; 'and that day may prove a nigh one. Fare thee well, Wayland—I will to my large-limbed friend, who, if he have not so sharp a wit as some folks, is at least more grateful for the service which other folks render him. And so again, good-evening to ye.'

So saying, he cast a somersault through the gateway, and, lighting on the bridge, ran with the extraordinary agility which was one of his distinguishing attributes, towards the Gallery Tower, and was out of sight in an instant.

'I would to God I were safe out of this castle again!' prayed Wayland internally; 'for now that this mischievous imp has put his finger in the pie, it cannot but prove a mess fit for the devil's eating. I would to Heaven Master Tressilian would appear!'

Tressilian, whom he was thus anxiously expecting in one direction, had returned to Kenilworth by another access. It was indeed true, as Wayland had conjectured, that, in the earlier part of the day, he had accompanied the Earls on their cavalcade towards Warwick, not without hope that he might in that town hear some tidings of his emissary. Being disappointed in this expectation, and observing Varney amongst Leicester's attendants, seeming as if he had some purpose of advancing to and addressing him, he conceived, in the present circumstances, it was wisest to avoid the interview. He, therefore, left the presence-chamber when the High Sheriff of the county was in the very midst of his dutiful address to her Majesty; and, mounting, his horse rode back to Kenilworth by a remote and circuitous road, and entered the castle by a small sallyport in the western wall, at which he was readily admitted as one of the followers of the Earl of Sussex, towards whom Leicester had commanded the utmost courtesy to be exercised. It was thus that he met not Wayland, who was impatiently watching his arrival, and whom he himself would have been, at least, equally desirous to see.

Having delivered his horse to the charge of his attendant, he walked for a space in the Pleasance, and in the garden rather to indulge in comparative solitude his own reflections, than to admire those singular beauties of nature and art which the magnificence of Leicester had there assembled. The greater part of the persons of condition had left the castle for the present, to form part of the Earl's cavalcade; others, who remained behind, were on the battlements, outer walls, and towers, eager to view the splendid spectacle of the royal entry. The garden, therefore, while every other part of the castle resounded with the human voice, was silent, but for the whispering of the leaves, the emulous warbling of the tenants of a large aviary, with their happier companions who remained denizens of the free air, and the plashing of the fountains, which, forced into the air from sculptures of fantastic and grotesque forms, fell down with ceaseless sound into the great basins of Italian marble.

The melancholy thoughts of Tressilian cast a gloomy shade on all the objects with which he was surrounded. He compared the magnificent scenes which he here traversed, with the deep woodland and wild moorland which surrounded Lidcote Hall, and the image of Amy Robsart glided like a phantom through every landscape which his imagination summoned up. Nothing is perhaps more dangerous to the future happiness of men of deep thought and retired habits, than the entertaining an early, long, and unfortunate attachment. It frequently sinks so deep into the mind, that it becomes their dream by night and their vision by day—mixes itself with every source of interest and enjoyment; and when blighted and withered by final disappointment, it seems as if the strings of the heart were dried up along with it. This aching of the heart, this languishing after a shadow which has lost all the gaiety of its colouring, this dwelling on the remembrance of a dream from which we have been long roughly awakened, is the weakness of a gentle and generous heart, and it was that of Tressilian.

He himself at length became sensible of the necessity of forcing other objects upon his mind; and for this purpose he left the Pleasance, in order to mingle with the noisy crowd upon the walls, and viewed the preparation for the pageants. But as he left the garden, and heard the busy hum mixed with music and laughter, which floated around him, he felt an uncontrollable reluctance to mix with society, whose feelings were in a tone so different from his own, and resolved, instead of doing so, to retire to the chamber assigned him, and employ himself in study until the tolling of the great castle-bell should announce the arrival of Elizabeth.

Tressilian crossed accordingly by the passage betwixt the immense range of kitchens and the great hall, and ascended to the third story of Mervyn's Tower, and applying himself to the door of the small apartment which had been allotted to him, was surprised to find it was locked. He then recollected that the deputy-chamberlain had given him a master-key, advising him, in the present confused state of the castle, to keep his door as much shut as possible. He applied this key to the lock, the bolt revolved, he entered, and in the same instant saw a female form seated in the apartment, and recognised that form to be Amy Robsart. His first idea was, that a heated imagination had raised the image on which it doted into visible existence; his second, that he beheld an apparition—the third and abiding conviction, that it was Amy herself, paler, indeed, and thinner than in the days of heedless happiness, when she possessed the form and hue of a wood nymph, with the beauty of a sylph; but still Amy, unequalled in loveliness by aught which had ever visited his eyes.

The astonishment of the Countess was scarce less than that of Tressilian, although it was of shorter duration, because she had heard from Wayland that he was in the castle. She had started up on his first entrance, and now stood facing him, the paleness of her cheeks having given way to a deep blush.

'Tressilian,' she said, at length, 'why come you here?'

'Nay, why come *you* here, Amy,' returned Tressilian, 'unless it be at length to claim that aid, which, as far as one man's heart and arm can extend, shall instantly be rendered to you?'

She was silent for a moment, and then answered in a sorrowful, rather than an angry tone,—'I require no aid, Tressilian, and would rather be injured than benefited by any which your kindness can offer me. Believe me, I am near one whom law and love oblige to protect me.'

'The villain, then, hath done you the poor justice which remained in his power,' said Tressilian; 'and I behold before me the wife of Varney!'

'The wife of Varney!' she replied, with all the emphasis of scorn. 'With what base name, sir, does your boldness stigmatise the—the—the'—She hesitated, dropped her tone of scorn, looked down, and was confused and silent, for she recollected what fatal consequences might attend her completing the sentence with 'the Countess of Leicester,' which were the words that had naturally suggested themselves. It would have been a betrayal of the secret, on which her husband had assured her that his fortunes depended, to Tressilian, to Sussex, to the Queen, and to the whole assembled court. 'Never,' she thought, 'will I break my promised silence. I will submit to every suspicion rather than that.'

The tears rose to her eyes, as she stood silent before Tressilian; while, looking on her with mingled grief and pity, he said, 'Alas! Amy, your eyes contradict your tongue. That speaks of a protector, willing and able to watch over you; but these tell me you are ruined and deserted by the wretch to whom you have attached yourself.'

She looked on him, with eyes in which anger sparkled through her tears, but only repeated the word 'wretch!' with a scornful emphasis.

'Yes, *wretch!*' said Tressilian; 'for were he aught better, why are you here, and alone in my apartment? why was not fitting provision made for your honourable reception?'

'In your apartment?' repeated Amy; 'in *your* apartment? It shall instantly be relieved of my presence.' She hastened towards the door; but the sad recollection of her deserted state at once pressed on her mind, and pausing on the threshold, she added, in a tone unutterably pathetic, 'Alas! I had forgot—I know not where to go.——'

'I see—I see it all,' said Tressilian, springing to her side, and leading her back to the seat, on which she sunk down—'You *do* need aid—you *do* need protection, though you will not own it; and you shall not need it long. Leaning on my arm, as the representative of your excellent and broken-hearted father, on the very threshold of the castle-gate, you shall meet Elizabeth; and the first deed she shall do in the halls of Kenilworth, shall be an act of justice to her sex and her subjects. Strong in my good cause, and in the Queen's justice, the power of her minion shall not shake my resolution. I will instantly seek Sussex.'

'Not for all that is under heaven!' said the Countess, much alarmed, and feeling the absolute necessity of obtaining time, at least, for consideration. 'Tressilian, you were wont to be generous—Grant me one request, and believe, if it be your wish to save me from misery, and from madness, you will do more by making me the promise I ask of you, than Elizabeth can do for me with all her power.'

'Ask me anything for which you can allege reason,' said Tressilian 'but demand not of me——'

'Oh, limit not your boon, dear Edmund!' exclaimed the Countess—'you once loved that I should call you so—Limit not your boon to reason! for my case is all madness, and frenzy must guide the counsels which alone can aid me.'

'If you speak thus wildly,' said Tressilian, astonishment again overpowering both his grief and his resolution, 'I must believe you indeed incapable of thinking or acting for yourself.'

'Oh, no!' she exclaimed, sinking on one knee before him, 'I am not mad—I am but a creature unutterably miserable, and, from circumstances the most singular, dragged on to a precipice by the arm of him who thinks he is keeping me from it—even by yours, Tressilian—by yours, whom I have honoured, respected—all but loved—and yet loved too—loved too, Tressilian—though not as you wished to be.'

There was an energy—a self-possession—an abandonment in her voice and manner—a total resignation of herself to his generosity, which, together with the kindness of her expressions to himself, moved him deeply. He raised her, and, in broken accents, entreated her to be comforted.

'I cannot,' she said, 'I will not be comforted, till you grant me my request! I will speak as plainly as I dare—I am now awaiting the commands of one who has a right to issue them—The interference of a third person—of you in especial, Tressilian, will be ruin—utter ruin to me. Wait but four-and-twenty hours, and it may be that the poor Amy may have the means to show that she values, and can reward, your disinterested friendship—that she is happy herself, and has the means to make you so—It is surely worthy your patience, for so short a space?'

Tressilian paused, and weighing in his mind the various probabilities which might render a violent interference on his part more prejudicial than advantageous, both to the happiness and reputation of Amy; considering also that she was within the walls of Kenilworth, and could suffer no injury in a castle honoured with the Queen's residence, and filled with her guards and attendants,—he conceived, upon the whole, that he might render her more evil than good service, by intruding upon her his appeal to Elizabeth in her behalf. He expressed his resolution cautiously, however, doubting naturally whether Amy's hopes of extricating herself from her difficulties rested on anthing stronger than a blinded attachment to Varney, whom he supposed to be her seducer.

'Amy,' he said, while he fixed his sad and expressive eyes on hers, which, in her ecstasy of doubt, terror, and perplexity, she cast up towards him, 'I have ever remarked that when others called thee girlish and wilful, there lay under that external semblance of youthful and self-willed folly, deep feeling and strong sense. In this I will confide, trusting your own fate in your own hands for the space of twenty-four hours, without my interference by word or act.'

'Do you promise me this, Tressilian?' said the Countess. 'Is it possible you can yet repose so much confidence in me? Do you promise, as you are a gentleman and man of honour, to intrude in my matters, neither by speech nor action, whatever you may see or hear that seems to you to demand your interference? Will you so far trust me?'

'I will, upon my honour,' said Tressilian; 'but when that space is expired——'

'When that space is expired,' she said, interrupting him, 'you are free to act as your judgment shall determine.'

'Is there naught besides which I can do for you, Amy?' said Tressilian.

'Nothing,' said she, 'save to leave me—that is, if—I blush to acknowledge my helplessness by asking it—if you can spare me the use of this apartment for the next twenty-four hours.'

'This is most wonderful!' said Tressilian; 'what hope or interest can you have in a castle, where you cannot command even an apartment?'

'Argue not, but leave me,' she said; and added, as he slowly and unwillingly retired, 'Generous Edmund; the time may come, when Amy may show she deserved thy noble attachment.'

28

What, man, ne'er lack a draught, when the full can
Stands at thine elbow, and craves emptying!
Nay, fear not me, for I have no delight
To watch men's vices, since I have myself
Of virtue naught to boast of.—I'm a striker,
Would have the world strike with me, pell-mell, all.
                                                    Pandæmonium.

TRESSILIAN, in strange agitation of mind, had hardly stepped down the first two or three steps of the winding staircase, when, greatly to his surprise and displeasure, he met Michael Lambourne, wearing an impudent familiarity of visage, for which Tressilian felt much disposed to throw him downstairs; until he remembered the prejudice which Amy, the only object of his solicitude, was likely to receive from his engaging in any act of violence at that time, and in that place.

He therefore contented himself with looking sternly upon Lambourne, as upon one whom he deemed unworthy of notice, and attempted to pass him in his way downstairs, without any symptom of recognition. But Lambourne, who, amidst the profusion of that day's hospitality, had not failed to take a deep, though not an overpowering cup of sack, was not in the humour of humbling himself before any man's looks. He stopped Tressilian upon the staircase without the least bashfulness or embarrassment, and addressed him as if he had been on kind and intimate terms:—
'What, no grudge between us, I hope, upon old scores, Master Tressilian?—nay, I am one who remember former kindness rather than later feud—I'll convince you that I meant honestly and kindly, ay, and comfortably by you.'

'I desire none of your intimacy,' said Tressilian—'keep company with your mates.'

'Now, see how hasty he is!' said Lambourne; 'and how these gentles, that are made questionless out of the porcelain clay of the earth, look down upon poor Michael Lambourne! You would take Master Tressilian now for the most maid-like, modest, simpering squire of dames, that ever made love when candles were long i' the stuff —snuff—call you it? Why, you would play the saint on us,

Master Tressilian, and forget that even now thou hast a commodity in thy very bedchamber, to the shame of my Lord's castle, ha! ha! ha! Have I touched you, Master Tressilian?'

'I know not what you mean,' said Tressilian, inferring, however, too surely, that this licentious ruffian must have been sensible of Amy's presence in his apartment; 'but if,' he continued, 'thou art varlet of the chambers, and lackest a fee, there is one to leave mine unmolested.'

Lambourne looked at the piece of gold, and put it in his pocket, saying—'Now, I know not but you might have done more with me by a kind word, than by this chiming rogue. But after all he pays well that pays with gold—and Mike Lambourne was never a make-bate, or a spoil sport, or the like. E'en live and let others live, that is my motto—only, I would not let some folks cock their beaver at men either, as if they were made of silver ore, and I of Dutch pewter. So if I keep your secret, Master Tressilian, you may look sweet on me at least; and were I to want a little backing or countenance, being caught, as you see the best of us may be, in a sort of peccadillo—why, you owe it me—and so e'en make your chamber serve you and that same bird in bower beside—it's all one to Mike Lambourne.'

'Make way, sir,' said Tressilian, unable to bridle his indignation, 'you have had your fee.'

'Um!' said Lambourne, giving place, however, while he sulkily muttered between his teeth, repeating Tressilian's words—'Make way—and you have had your fee —but it matters not, I will spoil no sport, as I said before; I am no dog in the manger—mind that.'

He spoke louder and louder, as Tressilian, by whom he felt himself overawed, got farther and farther out of hearing.

'I am no dog in the manger—but I will not carry coals neither—mind that, my Master Tressilian; and I will have a peep at this wench, whom you have quartered so commodiously in your old haunted room—afraid of ghosts belike, and not too willing to sleep alone. If *I* had done this now in a strange lord's castle, the word had been,—The porter's lodge for the knave! and,—Have him flogged—trundle him downstairs like a turnip! Ay, but your virtuous gentlemen take strange privileges over us, who are downright servants of our senses. Well—I have my Master Tressilian's head under my belt by this lucky discovery, that is one thing certain; and I will try to get a sight of this Lindabrides of his, that is another.'

29

Now fare thee well, my master—if true service
Be guerdon'd with hard looks, e'en cut the tow-line,
And let our barks across the pathless flood
Hold different courses.—*Shipwreck.*

TRESSILIAN walked into the outer yard of the castle, scarce knowing what to think of his late strange and most unexpected interview with Amy Robsart, and dubious if he had done well, being entrusted with the delegated authority of her father, to pass his word so solemnly to leave her to her own guidance for so many hours. Yet how could he have denied her request,—dependent as she had too probably rendered herself upon Varney? Such was his natural reasoning. The happiness of her future life might depend upon his not driving her to extremities, and since no authority of Tressilian's could extricate her from the power of Varney, supposing he was to acknowledge Amy to be his wife, what title had he to destroy the hope of domestic peace, which might yet remain to her by setting enmity betwixt them? Tressilian resolved, therefore, scrupulously to observe his word pledged to Amy, both because it had been given, and because, as he still thought, while he considered and reconsidered that extraordinary interview, it could not with justice or propriety have been refused.

In one respect, he had gained much towards securing effectual protection for this unhappy and still beloved object of his early affection. Amy was no longer mewed up in a distant and solitary retreat, under the charge of persons of doubtful reputation. She was in the castle of Kenilworth, within the verge of the Royal Court for the time, free from all risk of violence, and liable to be produced before Elizabeth on the first summons. These were circumstances which could not but assist greatly the efforts which he might have occasion to use on her behalf.

While he was thus balancing the advantages and perils which attended her unexpected presence in Kenilworth, Tressilian was hastily and anxiously accosted by Wayland, who, after ejaculating, 'Thank God, your worship is found at last!' proceeded with breathless caution to pour into his ear the intelligence, that the lady had escaped from Cumnor Place.

'And is at present in this castle,' said Tressilian; 'I know it, and I have seen her—Was it by her own choice she found refuge in my apartment?'

'No,' answered Wayland; 'but I could think of no other way of safely bestowing her, and was but too happy to find a deputy-usher who knew where you were quartered—in jolly society truly, the hall on the one hand and the kitchen on the other!'

'Peace, this is no time for jesting,' answered Tressilian, sternly.

'I wot that but too well,' said the artist, 'for I have felt these three days as if I had an halter round my neck. This lady knows not her own mind—she will have none of your aid—commands you not to be named to her—and is about to put herself into the hands of my Lord Leicester. I had never got her safe under your chamber, had she known the owner of it.'

'Is it possible?' said Tressilian. 'But she may have hopes the Earl will exert his influence in her favour over his villainous dependant.'

'I know nothing of that,' said Wayland—'but I believe, if she is to reconcile herself with either Leicester or Varney, the side of the Castle of Kenilworth, which will be safest for us, will be the outside from which we can fastest fly away. It is not my purpose to abide an instant after delivery of the letter to Leicester, which waits but your commands to find its way to him. See, here it is—but no —a plague on it—I must have left it in my dog-hole, in the hay-loft yonder, where I am to sleep.'

'Death and fury!' said Tressilian, transported beyond his usual patience; 'thou hast not lost that on which may depend a stake more important than a thousand such lives as thine?'

'Lost it!' answered Wayland readily; 'that were a jest indeed! No, sir, I have it carefully put up with my night-sack, and some matters I have occasion to use—I will fetch it in an instant.'

'Do so,' said Tressilian; 'be faithful, and thou shalt be well rewarded. But if I have reason to suspect thee, a dead dog were in better case than thou.'

Wayland bowed, and took his leave with seeming confidence and alacrity; but, in fact, filled with the utmost dread and confusion. The letter was lost, that was certain, notwithstanding the apology which he had made to appease the impatient displeasure of Tressilian. It was lost—it might fall into wrong hands—it would then, certainly, occasion a discovery of the whole intrigue in which he had been engaged; nor, indeed, did Wayland see much prospect of its remaining concealed in any event. He felt much hurt, besides, at Tressilian's burst of impatience.

'Nay, if I am to be paid in this coin, for services where my neck is concerned, it is time I should look to myself. Here have I offended, for aught I know, to the death, the Lord of this stately castle, whose word were as powerful to take away my life, as the breath which speaks it to blow out a farthing candle. And all this for a mad lady, and a melancholy gallant; who, on the loss of a four-nooked bit of paper, has his hand on his poignado, and swears death and fury! Then there is the Doctor and Varney—I will save myself from the whole mess of them—Life is dearer than gold—I will fly this instant, though I leave my reward behind me.'

These reflections naturally enough occurred to a mind like Wayland's, who found himself engaged far deeper than he had expected in a train of mysterious and unintelligible intrigues in which the actors seemed hardly to know their own course. And yet, to do him justice, his personal fears were, in some degree, counterbalanced by his compassion for the deserted state of the lady.

'I care not a groat for Master Tressilian,' he said; 'I have done more than bargain by him, and I have brought his errant-damozel within his reach, so that he may look after her himself; but I fear the poor thing is in much danger amongst these stormy spirits. I will to her chamber, and tell her the fate which has befallen her letter, that she may write another if she list. She cannot lack a messenger, I trow, where there are so many lackeys that can carry a letter to their lord. And I will tell her also that I leave the castle, trusting her to God, her own guidance, and Master Tressilian's care and looking after. Perhaps she may remember the ring she offered me—it was well earned, I trow; but she is a lovely creature, and—marry hang the ring! I will not bear a base spirit for the matter. If I fare ill in this world for my good nature, I will have better chance in the next. So now for the lady, and then for the road.'

With the stealthy step and jealous eye of the cat that steals on her prey, Wayland resumed the way to the Countess's chamber, sliding along by the side of the courts and passages, alike observant of all around him, and studious himself to escape observation. In this manner he crossed the outward and inward castle-yard, and the great arched passage, which, running betwixt the range of kitchen offices and the hall, led to the bottom of the little winding stair that gave access to the chambers of Mervyn's Tower.

The artist congratulated himself on having escaped the various perils of his journey, and was in the act of ascending by two steps at once, when he observed that the shadow of a man, thrown from a door which stood ajar, darkened the opposite wall of the staircase. Wayland drew back cautiously, went down to the inner courtyard, spent about a quarter of an hour, which seemed at least quadruple its usual duration, in walking from place to place, and then returned to the tower, in hopes to find that the lurker had disappeared. He ascended as high as the suspicious spot—there was no shadow on the wall—he ascended a few yards farther—the door was still ajar, and he was doubtful whether to advance or retreat, when it was suddenly thrown wide open, and Michael Lambourne bolted out upon the astonished Wayland. 'Who the devil art thou? and what seek'st thou in this part of the castle? March into that chamber and be hanged to thee!'

'I am no dog, to go at every man's whistle,' said the artist, affecting a confidence which was belied by a timid shake in his voice.

'Say'st thou me so? Come hither, Lawrence Staples.'

A huge, ill-made, and ill-looked fellow, upwards of six feet high, appeared at the door, and Lambourne proceeded: 'If thou be'st so fond of this tower, my friend, thou shalt see its foundations, good twelve feet below the bed of the lake, and tenanted by certain jolly toads, snakes, and so forth, which thou wilt find mighty good company. Therefore, once more I ask you in fair play, who thou art, and what thou seek'st here?'

'If the dungeon grate once clashes behind me,' thought Wayland, 'I am a gone man.' He therefore answered submissively, 'He was the poor juggler whom his honour had met yesterday in Weatherly-bottom.'

'And what juggling trick art thou playing in this tower? Thy gang,' said Lambourne, 'lie over against Clinton's buildings.'

'I came here to see my sister,' said the juggler, 'who is in Master Tressilian's chamber, just above.'

'Aha!' said Lambourne, smiling, 'here be truths—upon my honour, for a stranger, this same Master Tressilian makes himself at home among us, and furnishes out his cell handsomely, with all sort of commodities. This will be a precious tale of the sainted Master Tressilian, and will be welcome to some folks, as a purse of broad pieces to me—Hark ye, fellow,' he continued, addressing Wayland, 'thou shalt not give Puss a hint to steal away—we must catch her in her form. So, back with that pitiful sheep-biting visage of thine, or I will fling thee from the window of the tower, and try if your juggling skill can save your bones.'

'Your worship will not be so hard-hearted, I trust,' said Wayland; 'poor folks must live. I trust your honour will allow me to speak with my sister?'

'Sister on Adam's side, I warrant,' said Lambourne; 'or, if otherwise, the more knave thou. But sister or no sister, thou diest on point of fox, if thou, if thou comest a-prying to this tower once more. And now I think of it—uds daggers and death!—I will see thee out of the castle, for this is a more main concern than thy jugglery.'

'But please your worship,' said Wayland, 'I am to enact Arion in the pageant upon the lake this very evening.

'I will act it myself, by Saint Christopher!' said Lambourne— 'Orion, call'st thou him? I will act Orion, his belt and his seven stars to boot. Come along, for a rascal knave as thou art—follow me! Or stay—Lawrence, do thou bring him along.'

Lawrence seized by the collar of the cloak the unresisting juggler, while Lambourne, with hasty steps, led the way to that same sallyport, or secret postern, by which Tressilian had returned to the castle, and which opened in the western wall, at no great distance from Mervyn's Tower.

While traversing with a rapid foot the space betwixt the tower and the sallyport, Wayland in vain racked his brain for some device which might avail the poor lady, for whom, notwithstanding his own imminent danger, he felt deep interest. But when he was thrust out of the castle, and informed by Lambourne, with a tremendous oath, that instant death would be the consequence of his again approaching it, he cast up his hands and eyes to heaven, as if to call God to witness he had stood to the uttermost in defence of the oppressed; then turned his back on the proud towers of Kenilworth, and went his way to seek a humbler and safer place of refuge.

Lawrence and Lambourne gazed a little while after Wayland, and then turned to go back to their tower, when the former thus addressed his companion: 'Never credit me, Master Lambourne, if I can guess why thou hast driven this poor caitiff from the castle, just when he was to bear a part in the show that was beginning, and all this about a wench.'

'Ah, Lawrence,' replied Lambourne, 'thou art thinking of Black Joan Jugges of Slingdon, and hast sympathy with human frailty. But corragio, most noble Duke of the Dungeon and Lord of Limbo, for thou art as dark in this matter as thine own dominions of Little-ease. My most reverend Signior of the Low Countries of Kenilworth, know that our most notable master, Richard Varney, would give as much to have a hole in this same Tressilian's coat, as would make us some fifty midnight carousals, with the full leave of bidding the steward go snick up, if he came to startle us too soon from our goblets.'

'Nay, an that be the case, thou hast right,' said Lawrence Staples, the upper-warder, or, in common phrase, the first jailer of Kenilworth Castle, and of the liberty and honour belonging thereto; 'but how will you manage when you are absent at the Queen's entrance, Master Lambourne; for methinks thou must attend thy master there?'

'Why, thou, mine honest prince of prisons, must keep ward in my absence—Let Tressilian enter if he will, but see thou let no one come out. If the damsel herself would make a break, as 'tis not unlike she may, scare her back with rough words—she is but a paltry player's wench after all.'

'Nay, for that matter,' said Lawrence, 'I might shut the iron wicket upon her, that stands without the double door, and so force perforce she will be bound to her answer without more trouble.'

'Then Tressilian will not get access to her,' said Lambourne, reflecting a moment. 'But 'tis no matter —she will be detected in his chamber, and that is all one. But confess, thou old bat's-eyed dungeon-keeper, that you fear to keep awake by yourself in that Mervyn's Tower of thine?'

'Why, as to fear, Master Lambourne,' said the fellow, 'I mind it not the turning of a key, but strange things have been heard and seen in that tower. You have heard, for as short time as you have been in Kenilworth, that it is haunted by the spirit of Arthur ap Mervyn, a wild chief taken by fierce Lord Mortimer, when he was one of the Lord Marchers of Wales, and murdered, as they say, in that same tower which bears his name?'

'Oh, I have heard the tale five hundred times,' said Lambourne, 'and how the ghost is always most vociferous when they boil leeks and stirabout, or fry toasted cheese in the culinary regions. Santo Diavolo, man, hold thy tongue, I know all about it.'

'Ay, but thou dost not though,' said the turnkey, 'for as wise as thou wouldst make thyself. Ah, it is an awful thing to murder a prisoner in his ward! You, that may have given a man a stab in a dark street, know nothing of it. To give a mutinous fellow a knock on the head with the keys, and bid him be quiet, that's what I call keeping order in the ward; but to draw weapon and slay him, as was done to this Welsh lord, *that* raises you a ghost that will render your prison-house untenantable by any decent captive for some hundred years. And I have that regard for my prisoners, poor things, that I have put good squires and men of worship, that have taken a ride on the highway, or slandered my Lord of Leicester, or the like, fifty feet under ground, rather than I would put them into that upper chamber yonder, that they call Mervyn's Bower. Indeed, by good Saint Peter of the Fetters, I marvel my noble lord, or Master Varney, would think of lodging guests there; and if this Master Tressilian could get any one to keep him company, and in especial a pretty wench, why, truly, I think he was in the right on't.'

'I tell thee,' said Lambourne, leading the way into the turnkey's apartment, 'thou art an ass—Go bolt the wicket on the stair, and trouble not thy noddle about ghosts. Give me the wine-stoup, man; I am somewhat heated with chafing with yonder rascal.'

While Lambourne drew a long draught from a pitcher of claret, which he made use of without any cup, the warder went on, vindicating his own belief in the supernatural.

'Thou hast been few hours in this castle, and hast been for the whole space so drunk, Lambourne, that thou art deaf, dumb, and blind. But we should hear less of your bragging, were you to pass a night with us at full moon, for then the ghost is busiest; and more especially when a rattling wind sets in from the north-west, with some sprinkling of rain, and now and then a growl of thunder. Body o' me, what crackings and clashings, what groanings and what howlings will there be at such times in Mervyn's Bower, right as it were over our heads, till the matter of two quarts of distilled waters has not been enough to keep my lads and me in some heart!'

'Pshaw, man!' replied Lambourne, on whom his last draught,

joined to repeated visitations of the pitcher upon former occasions, began to make some innovation, 'thou speak'st thou know'st not what about spirits. No one knows justly what to say about them; and, in short, least said may in that matter be soonest mended. Some men believe in one thing, some in another—it is all matter of fancy. I have known them of all sorts, my dear Lawrence Lock-the-Door, and sensible men too. There's a great lord—we'll pass his name, Lawrence—he believes in the stars and the moon, the planets and their courses, and so forth, and that they tinkle exclusively for his benefit; when in sober, or rather in drunken truth, Lawrence, they are only shining to keep honest fellows like me out of the kennel. Well, sir, let his humour pass, he is great enough to indulge it. Then look ye, there is another—a very learned man, I promise you, and can vent Greek and Hebrew as I can Thieves'-Latin—he has an humour of sympathies and antipathies—of changing lead into gold and the like—why, via, let that pass too, and let him pay those in transmigrated coin, who are fools enough to let it be current with them. Then here comest thou thyself, another great man, though neither learned nor noble, yet full six feet high, and thou, like a purblind mole, must needs believe in ghosts and goblins, and such like.—Now, there is, besides, a great man—that is, a great little man, or a little great man, my dear Lawrence—and his name begins with V, and what believes he? Why, nothing, honest Lawrence—nothing in earth, heaven, or hell; and for my part, if I believe there is a devil, it is only because I think there must be some one to catch our aforesaid friend by the back "when soul and body sever," as the ballad says—for your antecedent will have a consequent—*raro antecedentem*, as Doctor Bircham was wont to say—But this is Greek to you now, honest Lawrence, and in sooth learning is dry work—Hand me the pitcher once more.'

'In faith, if you drink more, Michael,' said the warder, 'you will be in sorry case either to play Arion or to wait on your master on such a solemn night; and I expect each moment to hear the great bell toll for the muster at Mortimer's Tower, to receive the Queen.'

While Staples remonstrated, Lambourne drank; and then setting down the pitcher, which was nearly emptied, with a deep sigh, he said, in an undertone, which soon rose to a high one as his speech proceeded, 'Never mind, Lawrence—if I be drunk, I know that shall make Varney uphold me sober. But, as I said, never mind, I can carry my drink discreetly. Moreover, I am to go on the water as Orion, and shall take cold unless I take something comfortable beforehand. Not play Orion! Let us see the best roarer that ever strained his lungs for twelve pence out-mouth me. What if they see me a little disguised? Wherefore should any man be sober to-night? answer me that—It is matter of loyalty to be merry—and I tell thee, there are those in the castle, who if they are not merry when drunk, have little chance to be merry when sober—I name no names, Lawrence. But your pottle of sack is a fine shoeing-horn to pull on a loyal humour, and a merry one. Huzza for Queen Elizabeth!—for the noble Leicester!—for the worshipful Master Varney!—and for Michael Lambourne, that can turn them all round his finger!'

So saying, he walked downstairs, and across the inner court.

The warder looked after him, shook his head, and, while he drew close and locked a wicket, which, crossing the staircase, rendered it impossible for any one to ascend higher than the story immediately beneath Mervyn's Bower, as Tressilian's chamber was named, he thus soliloquised with himself—'It's a good thing to be a favourite —I wellnigh lost mine office, because one frosty morning Master Varney thought I smelled of aquavitæ; and this fellow can appear before him drunk as a wine-skin, and yet meet no rebuke. But then he is a pestilent clever fellow withal, and no one can understand above one-half of what he says.'

30

Now bid the steeple rock—she comes, she comes!
Speak for us, bells—speak for us, shrill-tongued tuckets
Stand to thy linstock, gunner; let thy cannon
Play such a peal, as if a paynim foe
Came stretch'd in turban'd ranks to storm the ramparts.
We will have pageants too—but that craves wit,
And I'm a rough-hewn soldier.
The Virgin Queen—A Tragi-Comedy.

TRESSILIAN, when Wayland had left him, as mentioned in the last chapter, remained uncertain what he ought next to do, when Raleigh and Blount came up to him arm in arm, yet, according to their wont, very eagerly disputing together. Tressilian had no great desire for their society in the present state of his feelings, but there was no possibility of avoiding them; and indeed he felt that, bound by his promise not to approach Amy, or take any step in her behalf, it would be his best course at once to mix with general society, and to exhibit on his brow as little as he could of the anguish and uncertainty which sat heavy at his heart. He therefore made a virtue of necessity, and hailed his comrades with, 'All mirth to you, gentlemen. Whence come ye?'

'From Warwick, to be sure,' said Blount; 'we must needs home to change our habits, like poor players, who are fain to multiply their persons to outward appearance by change of suits; and you had better do the like, Tressilian.'

'Blount is right,' said Raleigh; 'the Queen loves such marks of deference, and notices, as wanting in respect, those who, not arriving in her immediate attendance, may appear in their soiled and ruffled riding-dress. But look at Blount himself, Tressilian, for the love of laughter, and see how his villainous tailor hath apparelled him—in blue, green, and crimson, with carnation ribbons, and yellow roses in his shoes!'

'Why, what wouldst thou have?' said Blount, 'I told the crosslegged thief to do his best, and spare no cost; and methinks these things are gay enough—gayer than thine own—I'll be judged by Tressilian,

'I agree—I agree,' said Walter Raleigh. 'Judge betwixt us, Tressilian, for the love of Heaven!'

Tressilian, thus appealed to, looked at them both, and was immediately sensible at a single glance, that honest Blount had taken upon the tailor's warrant the pied garments which he had chosen to make, and was as much embarrassed by the quantity of points and ribbons which garnished his dress, as a clown is in his holiday clothes, while the dress of Raleigh was a well-fancied and rich suit, which the wearer bore as a garb too well adapted to his elegant person to attract particular attention. Tressilian said, therefore, 'That Blount's dress was finest, but Raleigh's the best fancied.'

Blount was satisfied with his decision. 'I knew mine was finest,' he said; 'if that knave Doublestitch had brought me home such a simple doublet as that of Raleigh's I would have beat his brains out with his own pressing-iron. Nay, if we must be fools, ever let us be fools of the first head, say I.'

'But why gettest thou not on thy braveries, Tressilian?' said Raleigh.

'I am excluded from my apartment by a silly mistake,' said Tressilian, 'and separated for the time from my baggage. I was about to seek thee, to beseech a share of thy lodging.'

'And welcome,' said Raleigh; 'it is a noble one. My Lord of Leicester has done us that kindness, and lodged us in princely fashion. If his courtesy be extorted reluctantly, it is at least extended far. I would advise you to tell your strait to the Earl's chamberlain— you will have instant redress.'

'Nay, it is not worth while, since you can spare me room,' replied Tressilian—'I would not be troublesome.—Has any one come hither with you?'

'Oh, ay,' said Blount; 'Varney and a whole tribe of Leicesterians, besides about a score of us honest Sussex folks.—We are all, it seems, to receive the Queen at what they call the Gallery Tower, and witness some fooleries there; and then we're to remain in attendance upon the Queen in the Great Hall, God bless the mark, while those who are now waiting upon her Grace get rid of their slough, and doff their riding-suits. Heaven help me, if her Grace should speak to me, I shall never know what to answer!'

'And what has detained them so long at Warwick?' said Tressilian, unwilling that their conversation should return to his own affairs.

'Such a succession of fooleries,' said Blount, 'as were never seen at Bartholomew-fair. We have had speeches and players, and dogs and bears, and men making monkeys and women moppets of themselves—I marvel the Queen could endure it. But ever and anon came in something of "the lovely light of her gracious countenance," or some such trash. Ah! vanity makes a fool of the wisest. But, come, let us on to this same Gallery Tower,—though I see not what thou, Tressilian, canst do with thy riding-dress and boots.'

'I will take my station behind thee, Blount,' said Tressilian, who saw that his friend's unusual finery had taken a strong hold of his imagination; 'thy goodly size and gay dress will cover my defects.'

'And so thou shalt, Edmund,' said Blount. 'In faith I am glad thou think'st my garb well-fancied, for all Master Wittypate here; for when one does a foolish thing, it is right to do it handsomely.'

So saying, Blount cocked his beaver, threw out his leg, and marched manfully forward, as if at the head of his brigade of pikemen, ever and anon looking with complaisance on his crimson stockings, and the huge yellow roses which blossomed on his shoes. Tressilian followed, wrapped in his own sad thoughts, and scarce minding Raleigh, whose quick fancy, amused by the awkward vanity of his respectable friend, vented itself in jests, which he whispered into Tressilian's ear.

In this manner they crossed the long bridge, or tilt-yard, and took their station, with other gentlemen of quality, before the outer gate of the Gallery or Entrance Tower. The whole amounted to about forty, persons all selected as of the first rank under that of knighthood, and were disposed in double rows on either side of the gate, like a guard of honour, within the close hedge of pikes and partisans, which was formed by Leicester's retainers, wearing his liveries. The gentlemen carried no arms, save their swords and daggers. These gallants were as gaily dressed as imagination could devise; and as the garb of the time permitted a great display of expensive magnificence, naught was to be seen but velvet and cloth of gold, and silver, ribbons, feathers, gems, and golden chains. In spite of his more serious subjects of distress, Tressilian could not help feeling, that he, with his riding-suit, however handsome it might be, made rather an unworthy figure among these 'fierce vanities,' and the rather because he saw that his dishabille was the subject of wonder among his own friends, and of scorn among the partisans of Leicester.

We could not suppress this fact, though it may seem something at variance with the gravity of Tressilian's character; but the truth is, that a regard for personal appearance is a species of self-love, from which the wisest are not exempt, and to which the mind clings so instinctively, that not only the soldier advancing to almost inevitable death, but even the doomed criminal who goes to certain execution, shows an anxiety to array his person to the best advantage. But this is a digression.

It was the twilight of a summer night (9th July, 1575), the sun having for some time set, and all were in anxious expectation of the Queen's immediate approach. The multitude had remained assembled for many hours, and their numbers were still rather on the increase. A profuse distribution of refreshments, together with roasted oxen, and barrels of ale set a-broach in different places of the road, had kept the populace in perfect love and loyalty towards the Queen and her favourite, which might have somewhat abated had fasting been added to watching. They passed away the time, therefore, with the usual popular amusements of whooping, hallooing, shrieking, and playing rude tricks upon each other, forming the chorus of discordant sounds usual on such occasions. These prevailed all through the crowded roads and fields, and especially beyond the gate of the Chase, where the greater number of the common sort were stationed; when, all of a sudden, a single rocket was seen shoot into the atmosphere, and, at the instant, far heard over flood and field, the great bell of the castle tolled.

Immediately there was a pause of dead silence, succeeded by a deep hum of expectation, the united voice of many thousands, none of whom spoke above their breath; or, to use a singular expression, the whisper of an immense multitude.

'They come now, for certain,' said Raleigh. 'Tressilian, that sound is grand. We hear it from this distance, as mariners, after a long voyage, hear, upon their night watch, the tide rush upon some distant and unknown shore.'

'Mass!' answered Blount; 'I hear it rather as I used to hear mine own kine lowing from the close of Wittenswestlowe.'

'He will assuredly graze presently,' said Raleigh to Tressilian; 'his thought is all of fat oxen and fertile meadows—he grows little better than one of his own beeves, and only becomes grand when he is provoked to pushing and goring.'

'We shall have him at that presently,' said Tressilian, 'if you spare not your wit.'

'Tush, I care not,' answered Raleigh; 'but thou too, Tressilian, hast turned a kind of owl, that flies only by night; hast exchanged thy songs for screechings, and good company for an ivy-tod.'

'But what manner of animal art thou thyself, Raleigh,' said Tressilian, 'that thou holdest us all so lightly?'

'Who, I?' replied Raleigh. 'An eagle am I, that never will think of dull earth, while there is a heaven to soar in, and a sun to gaze upon.'

'Well bragged, by Saint Barnaby!' said Blount; 'but, good Master Eagle, beware the cage, and beware the fowler. Many birds have flown as high, that I have seen stuffed with straw, and hung up to scare kites. But hark, what a dead silence hath fallen on them at once!'

'The procession pauses,' said Raleigh, 'at the gate of the Chase, where a sibyl, one of the *Fatidicae*, meets the Queen, to tell her fortune. I saw the verses; there is little savour in them, and her Grace has been already crammed full with such poetical compliments. She whispered to me during the Recorder's speech yonder, at Ford-mill, as she entered the liberties of Warwick, how she was *"pertæsa barbaræ loquelæ."*'

'The Queen whispered to *him!*' said Blount, in a kind of soliloquy; 'Good God, to what will this world come!'

His further meditations were interrupted by a shout of applause from the multitude, so tremendously vociferous, that the country echoed for miles round. The guards, thickly stationed upon the road by which the Queen was to advance, caught up the acclamation, which ran like wildfire to the castle, and announced to all within that Queen Elizabeth had entered the Royal Chase of Kenilworth. The whole music of the castle sounded at once, and a round of artillery, with a salvo of small arms, was discharged from the battlements; but the noise of drums and trumpets, and even of the cannon themselves, was but faintly heard, amidst the roaring and reiterated welcome of the multitude.

As the noise began to abate, a broad glare of light was seen to appear from the gate of the Park, and, broadening and brightening as it came nearer, advanced along the open and fair avenue that led towards the Gallery Tower; and which, as we have already noticed, was lined on either hand by the retainers of the Earl of Leicester. The word was passed along the line, 'The Queen! The Queen! Silence, and stand fast!' Onward came the cavalcade, illuminated by two hundred thick waxen torches, in the hands of as many horsemen, which cast a light like that of broad day all around the procession, but especially on the principal group, of which the Queen herself, arrayed in the most splendid manner, and blazing with jewels, formed the central figure. She was mounted on a milk-white horse, which she reined with peculiar grace and dignity; and in the whole of her stately and noble carriage, you saw the daughter of an hundred kings.

The ladies of the court, who rode beside her Majesty, had taken especial care that their own external appearance should not be more glorious than their rank and the occasion altogether demanded, so that no inferior luminary might appear to approach the orbit of royalty. But their personal charms, and the magnificence by which, under every prudential restraint, they were necessarily distinguished, exhibited them as the very flower of a realm so far famed for splendour and beauty. The magnificence of the courtiers, free from such restraints as prudence imposed on the ladies, was yet more unbounded.

Leicester, who glittered like a golden image with jewels and cloth of gold, rode on her Majesty's right hand, as well in quality of her host, as of her Master of the Horse. The black steed which he mounted had not a single white hair on his body, and was one of the most renowned chargers in Europe, having been purchased by the Earl at large expense for this royal occasion. As the noble steed chafed at the slow pace of the procession, and, arching his stately neck, champed on the silver bits which restrained him, the foam flew from his mouth, and speckled his well-formed limbs as if with spots of snow. The rider well became the high place which he held, and the proud animal which he bestrode; for no man in England, or perhaps in Europe, was more perfect than Dudley in horsemanship, and all other exercises belonging to his quality. He was bare-headed, as were all the courtiers in the train; and the red torch-light shone upon his long curled tresses of dark hair, and on his noble features, to the beauty of which even the severest criticism could only object the lordly fault, as it may be termed, of a forehead somewhat too high. On that proud evening, those features wore all the graceful solicitude of a subject, to show himself sensible of the high honour which the Queen was conferring on him, and all the pride and satisfaction which became so glorious a moment. Yet, though neither eye nor feature betrayed aught but feelings which suited the occasion, some of the Earl's personal attendants remarked, that he was unusually pale, and they expressed to each other their fear that he was taking more fatigue than consisted with his health.

Varney followed close behind his master, as the principal squire in waiting, and had charge of his lordship's black velvet bonnet, garnished with a clasp of diamonds, and surmounted by a white plume. He kept his eye constantly on his master; and, for reasons with which the reader is not unacquainted, was, among Leicester's numerous dependants, he who was most anxious that his lord's strength and resolution should carry him successfully through a day so agitating. For although Varney was one of the few—the very few moral monsters, who contrive to lull to sleep the remorse of their own bosoms, and are drugged into moral insensibility by atheism, as men in extreme agony are lulled by opium, yet he knew that in the breast of his patron there was already awakened the fire that is never quenched, and that his lord felt, amid all the pomp and magnificence we have described, the gnawing of the worm that dieth not. Still, however, assured as Lord Leicester stood, by Varney's own intelligence, that his Countess laboured under an indisposition which formed an unanswerable apology to the Queen for her not appearing at Kenilworth, there was little danger, his wily retainer thought, that a man so ambitious would betray himself by giving way to any external weakness.

The train, male and female, who attended immediately upon the Queen's person, were of course of the bravest and the fairest,—the highest born nobles, and the wisest counsellors, of that distinguished reign, to repeat whose names were but to weary the reader. Behind came a long crowd of knights and gentlemen, whose rank and birth, however distinguished, were thrown into shade, as their persons into the rear of a procession, whose front was of such august majesty.

Thus marshalled, the cavalcade approached the Gallery Tower, which formed, as we have often observed, the extreme barrier of the castle.

It was now the part of the huge porter to step forward; but the lubbard was so overwhelmed with confusion of spirit,—the contents of one immense black jack of double ale, which he had just drunk to quicken his memory, having at the same time treacherously confused the brain it was intended to clear,—that he only groaned piteously, and remained sitting on his stone seat; and the Queen would have passed on without greeting, had not the gigantic warder's secret ally, Flibbertigibbet, who lay perdue behind him, thrust a pin into the rear of the short femoral garment which we elsewhere described.

The porter uttered a sort of a yell, which came not amiss into his part, started up with his club, and dealt a sound douse or two on each side of him; and then, like a coach-horse pricked by the spur, started off at once into the full career of his address, and by dint of active prompting on the part of Dickie Sludge, delivered, in sounds of gigantic intonation, a speech which may be thus abridged;—the reader being to suppose that the first lines were addressed to the throng who approached the gateway; the conclusion at the approach of the Queen, upon the sight of whom, as struck by some heavenly vision, the gigantic warder dropped his club, resigned his keys, and gave open way to the Goddess of the night, and all her magnificent train.

> 'What stir, what turmoil, have we for the nones?
> Stand back, my masters, or beware your bones!
> Sirs, I'm a warder, and no man of straw,
> My voice keeps order, and my club gives law.
> Yet soft—nay stay—what vision have we here?
> What dainty darling's this—what peerless peer?
> What loveliest face, that loving ranks enfold,
> Like brightest diamond chased in purest gold?
> Dazzled and blind, mine office I forsake,
> My club, my key, my knee, my homage take,
> Bright paragon, pass on in joy and bliss;—
> Beshrew the gate that opes not wide at such a sight as this!'

Elizabeth received most graciously the homage of the herculean porter, and, bending her head to him in requital, passed through his guarded tower, from the top of which was poured a clamorous blast of warlike music, which was replied to by other bands of minstrelsy placed at different points on the castle walls, and by others again stationed in the Chase; while the tones of the one, as they yet vibrated on the echoes, were caught up and answered by new harmony from different quarters.

Amidst these bursts of music, which, as if the work of enchantment, seemed now close at hand, now softened by distant space, now wailing so low and sweet as if that distance were gradually prolonged until only the last lingering strains alone could reach the ear, Queen Elizabeth crossed the Gallery Tower, and came upon the long bridge, which extended from thence to Mortimer's Tower, and which was already as light as day, so many torches had been fastened to the palisades on either side. Most of the nobles here alighted, and sent their horses to the neighbouring village of Kenilworth, following the Queen on foot, as did the gentlemen who had stood in array to receive her at the Gallery Tower.

On this occasion, as at different times during the evening, Raleigh addressed himself to Tressilian, and was not a little surprised at his vague and unsatisfactory answers; which, joined to his leaving his apartment without any assigned reason, appearing in an undress when it was likely to be offensive to the Queen, and some other symptoms of irregularity which he thought he discovered, led him to doubt whether his friend did not labour under some temporary derangement.

Meanwhile, the Queen had no sooner stepped on the bridge than a new spectacle was provided; for as soon as the music gave signal that she was so far advanced, a raft, so disposed as to resemble a small floating island, illuminated by a great variety of torches, and surrounded by floating pageants formed to represent sea-horses, on which sat Tritons, Nereids, and other fabulous deities of the seas and rivers, made its appearance upon the lake, and issuing from behind a small heronry where it had been concealed, floated gently towards the farther end of the bridge.

On the islet appeared a beautiful woman, clad in a watchet-coloured silken mantle, bound with a broad girdle, inscribed with characters like the phylacteries of the Hebrews. Her feet and arms were bare, but her wrists and ankles were adorned with gold bracelets of uncommon size. Amidst her long silky black hair, she wore a crown or chaplet of artificial mistletoe, and bore in her hand a rod of ebony tipped with silver. Two nymphs attended on her, dressed in the same antique and mystical guise.

The pageant was so well managed, that this Lady of the Floating Island, having performed her voyage with much picturesque effect, landed at Mortimer's Tower with her two attendants, just as Elizabeth presented herself before that out-work. The stranger then, in a well-penned speech, announced herself as that famous Lady of the Lake, renowned in the stories of King Arthur, who had nursed the youth of the redoubted Sir Lancelot, and whose beauty had proved too powerful both for the wisdom and the spells of the mighty Merlin. Since that early period she had remained possessed of her crystal dominions, she said, despite the various men of fame and might by whom Kenilworth had been successively tenanted. The Saxons, the Danes, the Normans, the Saintlowes, the Clintons, the Mountforts, the Mortimers, the Plantagenets, great though they were in arms and magnificence, had never, she said, caused her to raise her head from the waters which hid her crystal palace. But a greater than all these great names had now appeared, and she came in homage and duty to welcome the peerless Elizabeth to all sport, which the castle and its environs, which lake or land, could afford.

The Queen received this address also with great courtesy, and made answer in raillery, 'We thought this lake had belonged to our own dominions, fair dame; but since so famed a lady claims it for hers, we will be glad at some other time to have further communing with you touching our joint interests.'

With this gracious answer, the Lady of the Lake vanished, and Arion, who was amongst the maritime deities, appeared upon his dolphin. But Lambourne, who had taken upon him the part in the absence of Wayland, being chilled with remaining immersed in an element to which he was not friendly, having never got his speech by heart, and not having, like the porter, the advantage of a prompter, paid if off with impudence, tearing off his vizard, and swearing, 'Cogs bones! he was none of Arion or Orion either, but honest Mike Lambourne, that had been drinking her Majesty's health from morning till midnight, and was come to bid her heartily welcome to Kenilworth Castle.'

This unpremeditated buffoonery answered the purpose probably better than the set speech would have done. The Queen laughed heartily, and swore (in her turn) that he had made the best speech she had heard that day. Lambourne, who instantly saw his jest had saved his bones, jumped on shore, gave his dolphin a kick, and declared he would never meddle with fish again, except at dinner.

At the same time that the Queen was about to enter the castle, that memorable discharge of fireworks by water and land took place, which Master Laneham, formerly introduced to the reader, has strained all his eloquence to describe.

'Such,' says the Clerk of the Council-chamber door, 'was the blaze of burning darts, the gleams of stars coruscant, the streams and hail of fiery sparks, lightnings of wildfire, and flightshot of thunderbolts, with continuance, terror, and vehemency, that the heavens thundered, the waters surged, and the earth shook; and for my part, hardy as I am, it made me very vengeably afraid.' *

* See Laneham's Account of the Queen's Entertainment at Killingworth Castle, in 1575, a very diverting tract, written by as great a coxcomb as ever blotted paper. The original is extremely rare, but it has been twice reprinted; once in Mr Nichols's very curious and interesting collection of the Progresses and Public Processions of Queen Elizabeth, Vol. i; and more lately in No I of a work termed 'Kenilworth Illustrated,' beautifully printed at Chiswick, for Meridew of Coventry and Radcliffe of Birmingham.

31

Nay, this is matter for the month of March,
When hares are maddest. Either speak in reason,
Giving cold argument the wall of passion,
Or I break up the court.—*Beaumont and Fletcher.*

IT is by no means our purpose to describe minutely all the princely
festivities of Kenilworth, after the fashion of Master Robert Laneham, whom we quoted in the conclusion of the last chapter. It is
sufficient to say, that under discharge of the splendid fire-works,
which we have borrowed Laneham's eloquence to describe, the
Queen entered the base-court of Kenilworth, through Mortimer's
Tower, and moving on through pageants of heathen gods and
heroes of antiquity, who offered gifts and compliments on the
bended knee, at length found her way to the great hall of the castle,
gorgeously hung for her reception with the richest silken tapestry,
blazing with torches, misty with perfumes, and sounding to strains
of soft and delicious music. From the highly-carved oaken roof
hung a superb chandelier of gilt bronze, formed like a spread eagle,
whose outstretched wings supported three male and three female
figures, grasping a pair of branches in each hand. The hall was thus
illuminated by twenty-four torches of wax. At the upper end of
the splendid apartment was a state canopy, overshadowing a royal
throne, and beside it was a door, which opened to a long suite
of apartments, decorated with the utmost magnificence for the
Queen and her ladies, whenever it should be her pleasure to be
private.

The Earl of Leicester having handed the Queen up to the throne,
and seated her there, knelt down before her, and kissing the hand
which she held out, with an air in which romantic and respectful
gallantry was happily mingled with loyal devotion, he thanked
her, in terms of the deepest gratitude, for the highest honour which
a sovereign could render to a subject. So handsome did he look
when kneeling before her, that Elizabeth was tempted to prolong
the scene a little longer than there was, strictly speaking, necessity
for; and ere she raised him, she passed her hand over his head, so
near, as almost to touch his long curled and perfumed hair, and

with a movement of fondness, that seemed to intimate she would, if she dared, have made the motion a slight caress.*

She at length raised him, and, standing beside the throne, he explained to her the various preparations which had been made for her amusement and accommodation, all of which received her prompt and gracious approbation. The Earl then prayed her Majesty for permission, that he himself, and the nobles who had been in attendance upon her during the journey, might retire for a few minutes, and put themselves into a guise more fitting for dutiful attendance, during which space, those gentlemen of worship (pointing to Varney, Blount, Tressilian, and others), who had already put themselves into fresh attire, would have the honour of keeping her presence-chamber.

'Be it so, my lord,' answered the Queen; 'you could manage a theatre well, who can thus command a double set of actors. For ourselves, we will receive your courtesies this evening but clownishly, since it is not our purpose to change our riding attire, being in effect something fatigued with a journey, which the concourse of our good people hath rendered slow, though the love they have shown our person hath, at the same time, made it delightful.'

Leicester, having received this permission, retired accordingly, and was followed by those nobles who had attended the Queen to Kenilworth in person. The gentlemen who had preceded them, and were of course dressed for the solemnity, remained in attendance. But being most of them of rather inferior rank, they remained at an awful distance from the throne which Elizabeth occupied. The Queen's sharp eye soon distinguished Raleigh amongst them, with one or two others who were personally known to her, and she instantly made them a sign to approach, and accosted them very graciously. Raleigh, in particular, the adventure of whose cloak, as well as the incident of the verses, remained on her mind, was very graciously received; and to him she most frequently applied for information concerning the names and rank of those who were in presence. These he communicated concisely, and not without some traits of humorous satire, by which Elizabeth seemed much amused. 'And who is yonder clownish fellow?' she said, looking at Tressilian, whose soiled dress on this occasion greatly obscured his good mien.

'A poet, if it please your Grace,' replied Raleigh.

* *Note H.* Sir James Melville.

'I might have guessed that from his careless garb,' said Elizabeth. 'I have known some poets so thoughtless as to throw their cloaks into gutters.'

'It must have been when the sun dazzled both their eyes and their judgment,' answered Raleigh.

Elizabeth smiled and proceeded, 'I asked that slovenly fellow's name, and you only told me his profession.'

'Tressilian is his name,' said Raleigh, with internal reluctance, for he foresaw nothing favourable to his friend from the manner in which she took notice of him.

'Tressilian!' answered Elizabeth. 'Oh, the Menelaus of our romance. Why, he has dressed himself in a guise that will go far to exculpate his fair and false Helen. And where is Farnham, or whatever his name is—my Lord of Leicester's man, I mean—the Paris of this Devonshire tale?'

With still greater reluctance Raleigh named and pointed out to her Varney, for whom the tailor had done all that art could perform in making his exterior agreeable; and who, if he had not grace, had a sort of tact and habitual knowledge of breeding, which came in place of it.

The Queen turned her eye from the one to the other—'I doubt,' she said, 'this same poetical Master Tressilian, who is too learned, I warrant me, to remember what presence he was to appear in, may be one of those of whom Geoffrey Chaucer says wittily, the wisest clerks are not the wisest men. I remember that Varney is a smooth-tongued varlet. I doubt this fair runaway had reasons for breaking her faith.'

To this Raleigh durst make no answer, aware how little he should benefit Tressilian by contradicting the Queen's sentiments, and not at all certain, on the whole, whether the best thing that could befall him, would not be that she should put an end at once by her authority to this affair, upon which it seemed to him Tressilian's thoughts were fixed with unavailing and distressing pertinacity. As these reflections passed through his active brain, the lower door of the hall opened, and Leicester, accompanied by several of his kinsmen, and of the nobles who had embraced his faction, re-entered the castle hall.

The favourite Earl was now apparelled all in white; his shoes being of white velvet; his understocks (or stockings) of knit silk; his upper stocks of white velvet lined with cloth of silver, which was shown at the slashed part of the middle thigh; his doublet of cloth of silver, the close jerkin of white velvet, embroidered with silver and seed-pearl; his girdle and the scabbard of his sword of white velvet with golden buckles; his poniard and sword hilted and mounted with gold; and over all, a rich loose robe of white satin, with a border of golden embroidery a foot in breadth. The collar of the Garter, and the azure Garter itself around his knee, completed the appointments of the Earl of Leicester; which were so well matched by his fair stature, graceful gesture, fine proportion of body, and handsome countenance, that at that moment he was admitted by all who saw him, as the goodliest person whom they had ever looked upon. Sussex and the other nobles were also richly attired; but in point of splendour and gracefulness, Leicester far exceeded them all.

Elizabeth received him with great complacency. 'We have one piece of royal justice,' she said, 'to attend to. It is a piece of justice, too, which interests us as a woman, as well as in the character of mother and guardian of the English people.'

An involuntary shudder came over Leicester, as he bowed low, expressive of his readiness to receive her royal commands; and a similar cold fit came over Varney, whose eyes (seldom during that evening removed from his patron) instantly perceived, from the change in his looks, slight as that was, of what the Queen was speaking. But Leicester had wrought his resolution up to the point which, in his crooked policy, he judged necessary; and when Elizabeth added—'It is of the matter of Varney and Tressilian we speak—is the lady here, my lord?' His answer was ready. 'Gracious madam, she is not.'

Elizabeth bent her brows and compressed her lips. 'Our orders were strict and positive, my lord,' was her answer——

'And should have been obeyed, good my liege,' answered Leicester, 'had they been expressed in the form of the lightest wish. But—Varney, step forward—this gentleman will inform your Grace of the cause why the lady' (he could not force his rebellious tongue to utter the words—*his wife*) 'cannot attend on your royal presence.'

Varney advanced, and pleaded with readiness, what indeed he firmly believed, the absolute incapacity of the party (for neither did he dare, in Leicester's presence, term her his wife) to wait on her Grace

'Here,' said he, 'are attestations from a most learned physician, whose skill and honour are well known to my good lord of Leicester; and from an honest and devout Protestant, a man of credit and substance, one Anthony Foster, the gentleman in whose house she is at present bestowed, that she now labours under an illness which altogether unfits her for such a journey as betwixt this castle and the neighbourhood of Oxford.'

'This alters the matter,' said the Queen, taking the certificates in her hand, and glancing at their contents—'Let Tressilian come forward. Master Tressilian, we have much sympathy for your situation, the rather that you seem to have set your heart deeply on this same Amy Robsart, or Varney. Our power, thanks to God and the willing obedience of a loving people, is worth something, but there are some things which it cannot compass. We cannot, for example, command the affections of a giddy young girl, or make her love sense and learning better than a courtier's fine doublet; and we cannot control sickness, with which it seems this lady is afflicted, who may not, by reason of such infirmity, attend our court here, as we had required her to do. Here are the testimonials of the physician who hath her under his charge, and the gentleman in whose house she resides, so setting forth.'

'Under your Majesty's favour,' said Tressilian hastily, and, in his alarm for the consequence of the imposition practised on the Queen, forgetting, in part at least, his own promise to Amy, 'these certificates speak not the truth.'

'How, sir!' said the Queen,—'Impeach my Lord of Leicester's veracity! But you shall have a fair hearing. In our presence the meanest of our subjects shall be heard against the proudest, and the least known against the most favoured; therefore you shall be heard fairly, but beware you speak not without a warrant. Look at these certificates in your own hand, and say manfully if you impugn the truth of them, and upon what evidence.'

As the Queen spoke, his promise and all its consequences rushed on the mind of the unfortunate Tressilian, and while it controlled his natural inclination to pronounce that a falsehood which he knew from the evidence of his senses to be untrue, gave an indecision and irresolution to his appearance and utterance, which made strongly against him in the mind of Elizabeth, as well as of all who beheld him. He turned the papers over and over, as if he had been an idiot, incapable of comprehending their contents. The Queen's impatience began to become visible. 'You are a scholar, sir,' she said, 'and of some note, as I have heard; yet you seem wondrous slow in reading text hand—How say you, are these certificates true or no?'

'Madam,' said Tressilian, with obvious embarrassment and hesitation, anxious to avoid admitting evidence which he might afterwards have reason to confute, yet equally desirous to keep his word to Amy, and to give her, as he had promised, space to plead her own cause in her own way—'Madam—Madam, your Grace calls on me to admit evidence which ought to be proved valid by those who found their defence upon them.'

'Why, Tressilian, thou art critical as well as poetical,' said the Queen, bending on him a brow of displeasure; 'methinks, these writings, being produced in the presence of the noble Earl to whom this castle pertains, and his honour being appealed to as the guarantee of their authenticity, might be evidence enough for thee. But since thou lists to be so formal—Varney, or rather my Lord of Leicester, for the affair becomes yours' (these words, though spoken at random, thrilled through the Earl's marrow and bones), 'what evidence have you as touching these certificates?'

Varney hastened to reply, preventing Leicester—'So please your Majesty, my young Lord of Oxford, who is here in presence, knows Master Anthony Foster's hand and his character.'

The Earl of Oxford, a young unthrift, whom Foster had more than once accommodated with loans on usurious interest, acknowledged, on this appeal, that he knew him as a wealthy and independent franklin, supposed to be worth much money, and verified the certificate produced to be his handwriting.

'And who speaks to the Doctor's certificate?' said the Queen. 'Alasco, methinks, is his name.'

Masters, her Majesty's physician (not the less willingly that he remembered his repulse from Say's Court, and thought that his present testimony might gratify Leicester, and mortify the Earl of Sussex and his faction), acknowledged he had more than once consulted with Doctor Alasco, and spoke of him as a man of extraordinary learning and hidden acquirements, though not altogether in the regular course of practice. The Earl of Huntingdon, Lord Leicester's brother-in-law, and the old Countess of Rutland, next sang his praises, and both remembered the thin beautiful Italian hand in which he was wont to write his receipts, and which corresponded to the certificate produced as his.

'And now, I trust, Master Tressilian, this matter is ended,' said the Queen. 'We will do something ere the night is older to reconcile old Sir Hugh Robsart to the match. You have done your duty something more than boldly; but we were no woman had we not compassion for the wounds which true love deals; so we forgive your audacity, and your uncleansed boots withal, which have wellnigh overpowered my Lord of Leicester's perfumes.'

So spoke Elizabeth, whose nicety of scent was one of the characteristics of her organisation, as appeared long afterwards when she expelled Essex from her presence, on a charge against his boots, similar to that which she now expressed against those of Tressilian.

But Tressilian had by this time collected himself, astonished as he had at first been by the audacity of the falsehood so feasibly supported, and placed in array against the evidence of his own eyes. He rushed forward, kneeled down, and caught the Queen by the skirt of her robe. 'As you are Christian woman,' he said, 'Madam, as you are crowned Queen, to do equal justice among your subjects —as you hope yourself to have fair hearing (which God grant you) at that last bar at which we must all plead, grant me one small request! Decide not this matter so hastily. Give me but twenty-four hours' interval, and I will, at the end of that brief space, produce evidence which will show to demonstration, that these certificates, which state this unhappy lady to be now ill at ease in Oxfordshire, are false as hell!'

'Let go my train, sir!' said Elizabeth, who was startled at his vehemence, though she had too much of lion in her to fear; 'the fellow must be distraught—that witty knave, my godson Harrington, must have him into his rhymes of Orlando Furioso! And yet, by this light, there is something strange in the vehemence of his demand. Speak, Tressilian; what wilt thou do if, at the end of these four-and-twenty hours, thou canst not confute a fact so solemnly proved as this lady's illness?'

'I will lay down my head on the block,' answered Tressilian.

'Pshaw!' replied the Queen. 'God's light! thou speak'st like a fool. What head falls in England but by just sentence of English law? I ask thee, man, if thou hast sense to understand me—wilt thou, if thou shalt fail in this improbable attempt of thine, render me a good and sufficient reason why thou dost undertake it?'

Tressilian paused, and again hesitated; because he felt convinced, that if, within the interval demanded, Amy should become reconciled to her husband, he would in that case do her the worst of offices, by again ripping up the whole circumstances before Elizabeth, and showing how that wise and jealous princess had been imposed upon by false testimonials. The consciousness of this dilemma renewed his extreme embarrassment of look, voice, and manner; he hesitated, looked down, and on the Queen repeating her question with a stern voice and flashing eye, he admitted with faltering words, 'That it might be—he could not positively—that is, in certain events—explain the reasons and grounds on which he acted.'

'Now, by the soul of King Henry,' said the Queen, 'this is either moonstruck madness, or very knavery! Seest thou, Raleigh, thy friend is far too Pindaric for this presence. Have him away, and make us quit of him, or it shall be the worse for him; for his flights are too unbridled for aught but Parnassus, or Saint Luke's hospital. But come back instantly thyself, when he is placed under fitting restraint. We wish we had seen the beauty which could make such havoc in a wise man's brain.'

Tressilian was again endeavouring to address the Queen, when Raleigh, in obedience to the orders he had received, interfered, and, with Blount's assistance, half led, half forced him out of the presence chamber, where he himself indeed began to perceive his presence did his cause more harm than good.

When they had attained the antechamber, Raleigh entreated Blount to see Tressilian safely conducted into the apartments allotted to the Earl of Sussex's followers, and, if necessary, recommended that a guard should be mounted on him.

'This extravagant passion,' he said, 'and, as it would seem, the news of the lady's illness, has utterly wrecked his excellent judgment. But it will pass away if he be kept quiet. Only let him break forth again at no rate; for he is already far in her Highness's displeasure, and should she be again provoked, she will find for him a worse place of confinement and sterner keepers.'

'I judged as much as that he was mad,' said Nicholas Blount, looking down upon his own crimson stockings and yellow roses, 'whenever I saw him with these damned boots, which stunk so in her nostrils. I will but see him stowed, and be back with you presently. But, Walter, did the Queen ask who I was?—methought she glanced an eye at me.'

'Twenty—twenty eye-glances she sent, and I told her all how

thou wert a brave soldier, and a——But, for God's sake, get off Tressilian.'

'I will—I will,' said Blount; 'but methinks this court-haunting is no such bad pastime, after all. We shall rise by it, Walter, my brave lad. Thou said'st I was a good soldier, and a—What besides, dearest Walter?'

'An all unutterable—codshead.—For God's sake, begone.'

Tressilian, without further resistance or expostulation, followed, or rather suffered himself to be conducted by Blount to Raleigh's lodging, where he was formally installed into a small truckle-bed, placed in a wardrobe, and designed for a domestic. He saw but too plainly, that no remonstrances would avail to procure the help or sympathy of his friends, until the lapse of the time for which he had pledged himself to remain inactive should enable him either to explain the whole circumstances to them, or remove from him every pretext or desire of further interference with the fortunes of Amy, by her having found means to place herself in a state of reconciliation with her husband.

With great difficulty, and only by the most patient and mild remonstrances with Blount, he escaped the disgrace and mortification of having two of Sussex's stoutest yeomen quartered in his apartment. At last, however, when Nicholas had seen him fairly deposited in his trucklebed, and had bestowed one or two hearty kicks, and as hearty curses, on the boots, which, in his lately acquired spirit of foppery, he considered as a strong symptom, if not the cause, of his friend's malady, he contented himself with the modified measure of locking the door on the unfortunate Tressilian; whose gallant and disinterested efforts to save a female who had treated him with ingratitude, thus terminated, for the present, in the displeasure of his Sovereign, and the conviction of his friends, that he was little better than a madman.

32

The wisest Sovereigns err like private men,
And royal hand has sometimes laid the sword
Of chivalry upon a worthless shoulder,
Which better had been branded by the hangman.
What then?—Kings do their best—and they and we
Must answer for the intent, and not the event.—*Old Play.*

'It is a melancholy matter,' said the Queen, when Tressilian was withdrawn, 'to see a wise and learned man's wit thus pitifully unsettled. Yet this public display of his imperfection of brain plainly shows us that his supposed injury and accusation were fruitless; and, therefore, my Lord of Leicester, we remember your suit formerly made to us in behalf of your faithful servant Varney, whose good gifts and fidelity, as they are useful to you, ought to have due reward from us, knowing well that your lordship, and all you have, are so earnestly devoted to our service. And we render Varney the honour more especially, that we are a guest, and we fear a chargeable and troublesome one, under your lordship's roof; and also for the satisfaction of the good old Knight of Devon, Sir Hugh Robsart, whose daughter he hath married; and we trust the especial mark of grace which we are about to confer, will reconcile him to his son-in-law. Your sword, my Lord of Leicester.'

The Earl unbuckled his sword, and, taking it by the point, presented on bended knee the hilt to Elizabeth.

She took it slowly, drew it from the scabbard, and while the ladies who stood around turned away their eyes with real or affected shuddering, she noted with a curious eye the high polish and rich damasked ornaments upon the glittering blade.

'Had I been a man,' she said, 'methinks, none of my ancestors would have loved a good sword better. As it is with me, I like to look on one, and could, like the Fairy of whom I have read in some Italian rhymes—were my godson Harrington here, he could tell me the passage *—even trim my hair, and arrange my head-gear, in such a steel mirror as this is. Richard Varney, come forth and kneel down. In the name of God and Saint George, we dub thee knight! Be Faithful, Brave, and Fortunate.—Arise, Sir Richard Varney.'

* *Note I.* Italian Rhymes.

Varney arose and retired, making a deep obeisance to the Sovereign who had done him so much honour.

'The buckling of the spur, and what other rites remain,' said the Queen, 'may be finished to-morrow in the chapel; for we intend Sir Richard Varney a companion in his honours. And as we must not be partial in conferring such distinction, we mean on this matter to confer with our cousin of Sussex.'

That noble Earl, who since his arrival at Kenilworth, and indeed since the commencement of this Progress, had found himself in a subordinate situation to Leicester, was now wearing a heavy cloud on his brow—a circumstance which had not escaped the Queen, who hoped to appease his discontent, and to follow out her system of balancing policy by a mark of peculiar favour, the more gratifying as it was tendered at a moment when his rival's triumph appeared to be complete.

At the summons of Queen Elizabeth, Sussex hastily approached her person; and being asked on which of his followers, being a gentleman and of merit, he would wish the honour of knighthood to be conferred, he answered with more sincerity than policy, that he would have ventured to speak for Tressilian, to whom he conceived he owed his own life, and who was a distinguished soldier, and scholar, besides a man of unstained lineage, 'only' he said, 'he feared the events of that night'——And then he stopped.

'I am glad your lordship is thus considerate,' said Eliazbeth; 'the events of this night would make us, in the eyes of our subjects, as mad as this poor brain-sick gentleman himself—for we ascribe his conduct to no malice—should we choose this moment to do him grace.'

'In that case,' said the Earl of Sussex, somewhat discountenanced, 'your Majesty will allow me to name my master of the horse, Master Nicholas Blount, a gentleman of fair estate and ancient name, who has served your Majesty both in Scotland and Ireland, and brought away bloody marks on his person, all honourably taken and requited.'

The Queen could not help shrugging her shoulders slightly even at this second suggestion; and the Duchess of Rutland, who read in the Queen's manner that she had expected Sussex would have named Raleigh, and thus would have enabled her to gratify her own wish while she honoured his recommendation, only waited the Queen's assent to what he had proposed, and then said, that she hoped, since these two high nobles had been each permitted to suggest a candidate for the honours of chivalry, she, in behalf of the ladies in presence, might have a similar indulgence.

'I were no woman to refuse you such a boon,' said the Queen, smiling.

'Then', pursued the Duchess, 'in the name of these fair ladies present, I request your Majesty to confer the rank of knighthood on Walter Raleigh, whose birth, deeds of arms, and promptitude to serve our sex with sword or pen deserve such distinction from us all.'

'Gramercy, fair ladies,' said Elizabeth, smiling, 'your boon is granted; and the gentle Squire Lack-Cloak shall become the good Knight Lack-Cloak, at your desire. Let the two aspirants for the honour of chivalry step forward.'

Blount was not as yet returned from seeing Tressilian, as he conceived, safely disposed of; but Raleigh came forth and, kneeling down, received at the hand of the Virgin Queen that title of honour, which was never conferred on a more distinguished or more illustrious object.

Shortly afterwards, Nicholas Blount entered, and, hastily apprised by Sussex, who met him at the door of the hall, of the Queen's gracious purpose towards him, he was desired to advance towards the throne. It is a sight sometimes seen, and it is both ludicrous and pitiable, when an honest man of plain common sense is surprised, by the coquetry of a pretty woman, or any other cause, into those frivolous fopperies which only sit well upon the youthful, the gay, and those to whom long practice has rendered them a second nature. Poor Blount was in this situation. His head was already giddy from a consciousness of unusual finery, and the supposed necessity of suiting his manners to the gaiety of his dress; and now this sudden view of promotion altogether completed the conquest of the newly inhaled spirit of foppery over his natural disposition, and converted a plain, honest, awkward man into a coxcomb of a new and most ridiculous kind.

The knight-expectant advanced up the hall, the whole length of which he had unfortunately to traverse, turning out his toes, with so much zeal, that he presented his leg at every step with its broadside foremost, so that it greatly resembled an old-fashioned knife with a curved point, when seen sideways. The rest of his gait was in proportion to this unhappy amble; and the implied mixture of bashful fear, and self-satisfaction, was so unutterably ridiculous, that Leicester's friends did not suppress a titter, in which many of Sussex's partisans were unable to resist joining, though ready to eat their nails with mortification. Sussex himself lost all patience, and could not forbear whispering into the ear of his friend, 'Curse thee! can'st thou not walk like a man and a soldier?' an interjection which only made honest Blount start and stop, until a glance at his yellow roses and crimson stockings restored his self-confidence, when on he went at the same pace as before.

The Queen conferred on poor Blount the honour of knighthood with a marked sense of reluctance. That wise Princess was fully aware of the propriety of using great circumspection and economy in bestowing those titles of honour, which the Stewarts, who succeeded to her throne, distributed with such imprudent liberality as greatly diminished their value. Blount had no sooner arisen and retired, than she turned to the Duchess of Rutland, 'Our woman wit,' she said, 'dear Rutland, is sharper than that of those proud things in doublet and hose. See'st thou, out of these three knights, thine is the only true metal to stamp chivalry's imprint upon?'

'Sir Richard Varney, surely—the friend of my Lord of Leicester—surely *he* has merit,' replied the Duchess.

'Varney has a sly countenance, and a smooth tongue,' replied the Queen. 'I fear me he will prove a knave—but the promise was of ancient standing. My Lord of Sussex must have lost his own wits, I think, to recommend to us first a madman like Tressilian, and then a clownish fool like this other fellow. I protest, Rutland, that while he sat on his knees before me, mopping and mowing as if he had scalding porridge in his mouth, I had much to forbear cutting him over the pate, instead of striking his shoulder.'

'Your Majesty gave him a smart *accolade*,' said the Duchess; 'we who stood behind heard the blade clatter on his collar-bone, and the poor man fidgeted too as if he felt it.'

'I could not help it, wench,' said the Queen, laughing; 'but we will have this same Sir Nicholas sent to Ireland or Scotland, or somewhere, to rid our court of so antic a chevalier; he may be a good soldier in the field, though a preposterous ass in a banqueting-hall.'

The discourse became then more general, and soon after there was a summons to the banquet.

In order to obey this signal, the company were under the necessity of crossing the inner court of the castle, that they might reach the new buildings, containing the large banqueting-room, in which preparations for supper were made upon a scale of profuse magnificence, corresponding to the occasion.

The livery cupboards were loaded with plate of the richest description, and the most varied—some articles tasteful, some perhaps grotesque, in the invention and decoration, but all gorgeously magnificent, both from the richness of the work and value of the materials. Thus the chief table was adorned by a salt, ship-fashion, made of mother-of-pearl, garnished with silver and divers warlike ensigns and other ornaments, anchors, sails, and sixteen pieces of ordnance. It bore a figure of Fortune, placed on a globe, with a flag in her hand. Another salt was fashioned of silver, in form of a swan in full sail. That chivalry might not be omitted amid this splendour, a silver Saint George was presented, mounted and equipped in the usual fashion in which he bestrides the dragon. The figures were moulded to be in some sort useful. The horse's tail was managed to hold a case of knives, while the breast of the dragon presented a similar accommodation for oyster knives.

In the course of the passage from the hall of reception to the banqueting-room, and especially in the courtyard, the new-made knights were assailed by the heralds, pursuivants, minstrels, etc., with the usual cry of *Largesse, largesse, chevaliers très hardis!* an ancient invocation, intended to awaken the bounty of the acolytes of chivalry towards those whose business it was to register their armorial bearings, and celebrate the deeds by which they were illustrated. The call was of course liberally and courteously answered by those to whom it was addressed. Varney gave his largesse with an affectation of complaisance and humility. Raleigh bestowed his with the graceful ease peculiar to one who has attained his own place, and is familiar with its dignity. Honest Blount gave what his tailor had left him of his half-year's rent, dropping some pieces in his hurry, then stooping down to look for them, and then distributing them amongst the various claimants, with the anxious face and mien of the parish beadle dividing a dole among paupers.

These donations were accepted with the usual clamour and *vivats* of applause common on such occasions; but as the parties gratified were chiefly dependants of Lord Leicester, it was Varney whose name was repeated with the loudest acclamations. Lambourne, especially, distinguished himself by his vociferations of 'Long life to Sir Richard Varney!—Health and honour to Sir Richard!—Never was a more worthy knight dubbed!'—then, suddenly sinking his voice, he added,—'since the valiant Sir Pandarus of Troy,'—a winding up of his clamorous applause, which set all men a-laughing who were within hearing of it.

It is unnecessary to say anything further of the festivities of the evening, which were so brilliant in themselves and received with such obvious and willing satisfaction by the Queen, that Leicester retired to his own apartment, with all the giddy raptures of successful ambition. Varney, who had changed his splendid attire, and now waited on his patron in a very modest and plain undress, attended to do the honours of the Earl's *coucher*.

'How! Sir Richard,' said Leicester, smiling, 'your new rank scarce suits the humility of this attendance.'

'I would disown that rank, my lord,' said Varney, 'could I think it was to remove me to a distance from your lordship's person.'

'Thou art a grateful fellow,' said Leicester; 'but I must not allow you to do what would abate you in the opinion of others.'

While thus speaking, he still accepted, without hesitation, the offices about his person, which the new-made knight seemed to render as eagerly as if he had really felt, in discharging the task, that pleasure which his words expressed.

'I am not afraid of men's misconstruction,' he said, in answer to Leicester's remark, 'since there is not—(permit me to undo the collar)—a man within the castle, who does not expect very soon to see persons of a rank far superior to that which, by your goodness, I now hold, rendering the duties of the bed-chamber to you, and accounting it an honour.'

'It might, indeed, so have been,' said the Earl, with an involuntary sigh; and then presently added, 'My gown, Varney—I will look out on the night. Is not the moon near to the full?'

'I think so, my lord, according to the calendar,' answered Varney.

There was an abutting window, which opened on a small projecting balcony of stone, battlemented as is usual in Gothic castles. The Earl undid the lattice, and stepped out into the open air. The station he had chosen commanded an extensive view of the lake, and woodlands beyond, where the clear moonlight rested on the clear blue waters, and the distant masses of oak and elm trees. The moon rode high in the heavens, attended by thousands and thousands of inferior luminaries. All seemed already to be hushed in the nether world, excepting occasionally the voice of the watch (for the Yeomen of the Guard performed that duty wherever the Queen was present in person), and the distant baying of the hounds, disturbed by the preparations amongst the grooms and prickers for a magnificent hunt, which was to be the amusement of the next day.

Leicester looked out on the blue arch of heaven, with gestures and a countenance expressive of anxious exultation, while Varney, who remained within the darkened apartment, could (himself unnoticed), with a secret satisfaction, see his patron stretch his hand with earnest gesticulation towards the heavenly bodies.

'Ye distant orbs of living fire,' so ran the muttered invocation of the ambitious Earl, 'ye are silent while you wheel your mystic rounds, but Wisdom has given to you a voice. Tell me, then, to what end is my high course destined. Shall the greatness to which I have aspired be bright, pre-eminent, and stable as your own; or am I but doomed to draw a brief and glittering train along the nightly darkness, and then to sink down to earth, like the base refuse of those artificial fires with which men emulate your rays?'

He looked on the heavens in profound silence for a minute or two longer, and then again stepped into the apartment, where Varney seemed to have been engaged in putting the Earl's jewels into a casket.

'What said Alasco of my horoscope?' demanded Leicester. 'You already told me, but it has escaped me, for I think but lightly of that art.'

'Many learned and great men have thought otherwise,' said Varney; 'and, not to flatter your lordship, my own opinion leans that way.'

'Ay, Saul among the prophets?' said Leicester—'I thought thou wert sceptical in all such matters as thou couldst neither see, hear, smell, taste, or touch, and that thy belief was limited by thy senses.'

'Perhaps, my lord,' said Varney, 'I may be misled on the present occasion by my wish to find the predictions of astrology true. Alasco says, that your favourite planet is culminating, and that the adverse influence—he would not use a plainer term—though not overcome, was evidently combust, I think he said, or retrograde.'

'It is even so,' said Leicester, looking at an abstract of astrological calculations which he had in his hand; 'the stronger influence will prevail, and, as I think, the evil hour pass away.—Lend me your hand, Sir Richard, to doff my gown—and remain an instant, if it is

not too burdensome to your knighthood, while I compose myself
to sleep. I believe the bustle of this day has fevered my blood, for it
streams through my veins like a current of molten lead—remain an
instant, I pray you—I would fain feel my eyes heavy ere I closed
them.'

Varney officiously assisted his lord to bed, and placed a massive
silver night-lamp, with a short sword, on a marble table which stood
close by the head of the couch. Either in order to avoid the light
of the lamp, or to hide his countenance from Varney, Leicester
drew the curtain, heavy with entwined silk and gold, so as completely to shade his face. Varney took a seat near the bed, but with
his back towards his master, as if to intimate that he was not
watching him, and quietly waited till Leicester himself led the way
to the topic by which his mind was engrossed.

'And so, Varney,' said the Earl, after waiting in vain till his
dependant should commence the conversation, 'men talk of the
Queen's favour towards me?'

'Ay, my good lord,' said Varney, 'of what can they else, since it
is so strongly manifested?'

'She is indeed my good and gracious mistress,' said Leicester,
after another pause; 'but it is written, "Put not thy trust in princes."'

'A good sentence and a true,' said Varney, 'unless you can unite
their interest with yours so absolutely, that they must needs sit on
your wrist like hooded hawks.'

'I know what thou meanest,' said Leicester impatiently, 'though
thou art to-night so prudentially careful of what thou say'st to me.
—Thou wouldst intimate, I might marry the Queen if I would?'

'It is your speech, my lord, not mine,' answered Varney; 'but
whose soever be the speech, it is the thought of ninety-nine out of
an hundred men throughout broad England.'

'Ay, but,' said Leicester, turning himself in his bed, 'the hun-
dreth man knows better. Thou, for example, knowest the obstacle
that cannot be overleaped.'

'It must, my lord, if the stars speak true,' said Varney composedly.

'What! talk'st thou of them,' said Leicester, 'that believest not
in them or in aught else?'

'You mistake, my lord, under your gracious pardon,' said Varney;
'I believe in many things that predict the future. I believe, if
showers fall in April, that we shall have flowers in May; that if the
sun shines, grain will ripen; and I believe in much natural philos-

ophy to the same effect, which, if the stars swear to me, I will say the stars speak the truth. And in like manner, I will not disbelieve that which I see wished for and expected on earth, solely because the astrologers have read it in the heavens.'

'Thou art right,' said Leicester, again tossing himself on his couch—'Earth does wish for it. I have had advices from the reformed churches of Germany—from the Low Countries—from Switzerland, urging this as a point on which Europe's safety depends. France will not oppose it. The ruling party in Scotland look to it as their best security—Spain fears it, but cannot prevent it—and yet thou knowest it is impossible.'

'I know not that, my lord,' said Varney, 'the Countess is indisposed.'

'Villain!' said Leicester, starting up on his couch, and seizing the sword which lay on the table beside him, 'go thy thoughts that way?—thou wouldst not do murder!'

'For whom, or what, do you hold me, my lord?' said Varney, assuming the superiority of an innocent man subjected to unjust suspicion. 'I said nothing to deserve such a horrid imputation as your violence infers. I said but that the Countess was ill. And Countess though she be—lovely and beloved as she is—surely your lordship must hold her to be mortal? She may die, and your lordship's hand become once more your own.'

'Away! away!' said Leicester; 'let me have no more of this.'

'Good-night, my lord,' said Varney, seeming to understand this as a command to depart; but Leicester's voice interrupted his purpose.

'Thou 'scapest me not thus, Sir Fool,' said he; 'I think thy knighthood has addled thy brains—Confess, thou hast talked of impossibilities, as of things which may come to pass.'

'My lord, long live your fair Countess,' said Varney; 'but neither your love nor my good wishes can make her immortal. But God grant she live long to be happy herself, and to render you so. I see not but you may be King of England notwithstanding.'

'Nay, now, Varney, thou art stark-mad,' said Leicester.

'I would I were myself within the same nearness to a good estate of freehold,' said Varney. 'Have we not known in other countries, how a left-handed marriage might subsist betwixt persons of differing degree?—ay, and be no hindrance to prevent the husband from conjoining himself afterwards with a more suitable partner.'

'I have heard of such things in Germany,' said Leicester.

'Ay, and the most learned doctors in foreign universities justify the practice from the Old Testament,' said Varney. 'And after all, where is the harm? The beautiful partner, whom you have chosen for true love, has your secret hours of relaxation and affection. Her fame is safe—her conscience may slumber securely—You have wealth to provide royally for your issue, should Heaven bless you with offspring. Meanwhile you may give to Elizabeth ten times the leisure, and ten thousand times the affection, that ever Don Philip of Spain spared to her sister Mary; yet you know how she doted on him, though so cold and neglectful. It requires but a close mouth and an open brow, and you keep your Eleanor and your fair Rosamond far enough separate. Leave me to build you a bower to which no jealous Queen shall find a clue.'

Leicester was silent for a moment, then sighed, and said, 'It is impossible. Good night, Sir Richard Varney—yet stay—Can you guess what meant Tressilian by showing himself in such careless guise before the Queen to-day?—to strike her tender heart, I should guess, with all the sympathies due to a lover, abandoned by his mistress, and abandoning himself.'

Varney, smothering a sneering laugh, answered, 'He believed Master Tressilian had no such matter in his head.'

'How,' said Leicester; 'what mean'st thou? There is ever knavery in that laugh of thine, Varney.'

'I only meant, my lord,' said Varney, 'that Tressilian has taken the sure way to avoid heart-breaking. He hath had a companion— a female companion—a mistress—a sort of player's wife or sister, as I believe,—with him in Mervyn's Bower, where I quartered him for certain reasons of my own.'

'A mistress!—mean'st thou a paramour?'

'Ay, my lord; who else waits for hours in a gentleman's chamber?'

'By my faith, time and space fitting, this were a good tale to tell,' said Leicester. 'I ever distrusted those bookish, hypocritical, seeming-virtuous scholars. Well—Master Tressilian makes somewhat familiar with my house—If I look it over, he is indebted to it for certain recollections. I would not harm him more than I can help. Keep eye on him, however, Varney.'

'I lodged him for that reason,' said Varney, 'in Mervyn's Bower, where he is under the eye of my very vigilant, if he were not also my very drunken servant, Michael Lambourne, whom I have told your Grace of.'

'Grace!' said Leicester: 'what mean'st thou by that epithet?'

'It came unawares, my lord; and yet it sounds so very natural, that I cannot recall it.'

'It is thine own preferment that hath turned thy brain,' said Leicester, laughing; 'new honours are as heady as new wine.'

'May your lordship soon have cause to say so from experience,' said Varney; and, wishing his patron good night, he withdrew.*

* *Note J.* Furniture of Kenilworth.

33

Here stands the victim—there the proud betrayer,
E'en as the hind pull'd down by strangling dogs
Lies at the hunter's feet—who courteous proffers
To some high dame, the Dian of the chase,
To whom he looks for guerdon, his sharp blade,
To gash the sobbing throat.—*The Woodman.*

WE are now to return to Mervyn's Bower, the apartment, or rather
the prison, of the unfortunate Countess of Leicester, who for some
time kept within bounds her uncertainty and her impatience. She
was aware that, in the tumult of the day, there might be some delay
ere her letter could be safely conveyed to the hands of Leicester, and
that some time more might elapse ere he could extricate himself
from the necessary attendance on Elizabeth, to come and visit her
in her secret bower. 'I will not expect him,' she said, 'till night—he
cannot be absent from his royal guest, even to see me. He will, I
know, come earlier if it be possible, but I will not expect him
before night.' And yet all the while she did expect him and, while
she tried to argue herself into a contrary belief, each hasty noise, of
the hundred which she heard, sounded like the hurried step of
Leicester on the staircase, hasting to fold her in his arms.

The fatigue of body which Amy had lately undergone, with the
agitation of mind natural to so cruel a state of uncertainty, began
by degrees strongly to affect her nerves, and she almost feared her
total inability to maintain the necessary self-command through the
scenes which might lie before her. But, although spoiled by an
over-indulgent system of education, Amy had naturally a mind
of great power, united with a frame which her share in her father's
woodland exercises had rendered uncommonly healthy. She
summoned to her aid such mental and bodily resources; and not
unconscious how much the issue of her fate might depend on her
own self-possession, she prayed internally for strength of body and
for mental fortitude, and resolved, at the same time, to yield to no
nervous impulse which might weaken either.

Yet when the great bell of the castle, which was placed in
Cæsar's Tower, at no great distance from that called Mervyn's,
began to send its pealing clamour abroad, in signal of the arrival

of the royal procession, the din was so painfully acute to ears rendered nervously sensitive by anxiety, that she could hardly forbear shrieking with anguish, in answer to every stunning clash of the relentless peal.

Shortly afterwards, when the small apartment was at once enlightened by the shower of artificial fires with which the air was suddenly filled, and which crossed each other like fiery spirits, each bent on his own separate mission, or like salamanders executing a frolic dance in the region of the Sylphs, the Countess felt at first as if each rocket shot close by her eyes, and discharged its sparks and flashes so nigh that she could feel a sense of the heat. But she struggled against these fantastic terrors, and compelled herself to arise, stand by the window, look out, and gaze upon a sight, which at another time would have appeared to her at once captivating and fearful. The magnificent towers of the castle were enveloped in garlands of artificial fire, or shrouded with tiaras of pale smoke. The surface of the lake glowed like molten iron, while many fireworks (then thought extremely wonderful, though now common), whose flame continued to exist in the opposing element, dived and rose, hissed and roared, and spouted fire, like so many dragons of enchantment sporting upon a burning lake.

Even Amy was for a moment interested by what was to her so new a scene. 'I had thought it magical art,' she said, 'but poor Tressilian taught me to judge of such things as they are. Great God! and may not these idle splendours resemble my own hoped-for happiness,—a single spark, which is instantly swallowed up by surrounding darkness,—a precarious glow, which rises but for a brief space into the air, that its fall may be the lower? Oh, Leicester! after all—all that thou hast said—hast sworn—that Amy was thy love, thy life, can it be that thou art the magician at whose nod these enchantments arise, and that she sees them, as an outcast, if not a captive?'

The sustained, prolonged, and repeated bursts of music, from so many different quarters, and at so many varying points of distance, which sounded as if not the Castle of Kenilworth only, but the whole country around, had been at once the scene of solemnising some high national festival, carried the same oppressive thought still closer to her heart, while some notes would melt in distant and falling tones, as if in compassion for her sorrows, and some burst close and near upon her, as if mocking her misery, with all the insolence of unlimited mirth. 'These sounds,' she said, 'are mine—mine, because they are HIS; but I cannot say,—Be still, these loud strains suit me not; and the voice of the meanest peasant that mingles in the dance, would have more power to modulate the music, than the command of her who is mistress of all.'

By degrees the sounds of revelry died away, and the Countess withdrew from the window at which she had sat listening to it. It was night, but the moon afforded considerable light in the room, so that Amy was able to make the arrangement which she judged necessary. There was hope that Leicester might come to her apartment as soon as the revel in the castle had subsided; but there was also risk she might be disturbed by some unauthorised intruder. She had lost confidence in the key, since Tressilian had entered so easily, though the door was locked on the inside; yet all the additional security she could think of, was to place the table across the door, that she might be warned by the noise should any one attempt to enter. Having taken these necessary precautions, the unfortunate lady withdrew to her couch, stretched herself down on it, mused in anxious expectation, and counted more than one hour after midnight, till exhausted nature proved too strong for love, for grief, for fear, nay even for uncertainty, and she slept.

Yes, she slept. The Indian sleeps at the stake, in the intervals between his tortures; and mental torments, in like manner, exhaust by long continuance the sensibility of the sufferer, so that an interval of lethargic repose must necessarily ensue, ere the pangs which they inflict can again be renewed.

The Countess slept, then, for several hours, and dreamed that she was in the ancient house at Cumnor Place, listening for the low whistle with which Leicester often used to announce his presence in the courtyard, when arriving suddenly on one of his stolen visits. But on this occasion, instead of a whistle, she heard the peculiar blast of a bugle-horn, such as her father used to wind on the fall of the stag, and which huntsmen then called a *mort*. She ran, as she thought, to a window that looked into the courtyard, which she saw filled with men in mourning garments. The old Curate seemed about to read the funeral service. Mumblazen, tricked out in an antique dress, like an ancient herald, held aloft a scutcheon, with its usual decorations of skulls, cross-bones, and hour-glasses, surrounding a coat-of-arms, of which she could only distinguish that it was surmounted with an Earl's coronet. The old man looked at her with a ghastly smile, and said, 'Amy, are they not rightly quartered?' Just as he spoke, the horns again poured on her ears the melancholy yet wild strain of the *mort*, or death-note, and she awoke.

The Countess awoke to hear a real bugle-note, or rather the combined breath of many bugles, sounding not the *mort*, but the jolly *reveille*, to remind the inmates of the Castle of Kenilworth, that the pleasures of the day were to commence with a magnificent stag-hunting in the neighbouring chase. Amy started up from her couch, listened to the sound, saw the first beams of the summer morning already twinkle through the lattice of her window, and recollected, with feelings of giddy agony, where she was, and how circumstanced.

'He thinks not of *me*,' she said—'he will not come nigh me! A Queen is his guest, and what cares he in what corner of his huge castle a wretch like me pines in doubt, which is fast fading into despair?' At once, a sound at the door, as of some one attempting to open it softly, filled her with an ineffable mixture of joy and fear; and, hastening to remove the obstacle she had placed against the door, and to unlock it, she had the precaution to ask 'Is it thou, my love?'

'Yes, my Countess,' murmured a whisper in reply.

She threw open the door, and exclaiming, 'Leicester!' flung her arms around the neck of the man who stood without, muffled in his cloak.

'No—not quite Leicester,' answered Michael Lambourne, for he it was, returning the caress with vehemence,—'not quite Leicester, my lovely and most loving duchess, but as good a man.'

With an exertion of force of which she would at another time have thought herself incapable, the Countess freed herself from the profane and profaning grasp of the drunken debauchee, and retreated into the midst of her apartment, where despair gave her courage to make a stand.

As Lambourne, on entering, dropped the lap of his cloak from his face, she knew Varney's profligate servant; the very last person, excepting his detested master, by whom she would have wished to be discovered. But she was still closely muffled in her travelling dress, and as Lambourne had scarce ever been admitted to her presence at Cumnor Place, her person, she hoped, might not be so well known to him as his was to her, owing to Janet's pointing him frequently out as he crossed the court, and telling stories of his wickedness. She might have had still greater confidence in her disguise, had her experience enabled her to discover that he was much intoxicated; but this could scarce have consoled her for the risk which she might incur from such a character, in such a time, place, and circumstances.

Lambourne flung the door behind him as he entered, and folding his arms, as if in mockery of the attitude of distraction into which Amy had thrown herself, he proceeded thus: 'Hark ye, most fair Callipolis—or most lovely Countess of clouts, and divine Duchess of dark corners—if thou takest all that trouble of skewering thyself together, like a trussed fowl, that there may be more pleasure in the carving, even save thyself the labour. I like thy first frank manner the best—like thy present as little'—(he made a step towards her and staggered)—'as little as—such a damned uneven floor as this, where a gentleman may break his neck, if he does not walk as upright as a posture-master on the tight-rope.'

'Stand back!' said the Countess; 'do not approach nearer to me, on thy peril.'

'My peril!—and stand off—Why, how now, Madam? Must you have a better mate than honest Mike Lambourne? I have been in America, girl, where the gold grows, and have brought off such a load on't——'

'Good friend,' said the Countess, in great terror at the ruffian's determined and audacious manner, 'I prithee begone, and leave me.'

'And so I will, pretty one, when we are tired of each other's company—not a jot sooner.' He seized her by the arm, while, incapable of further defence, she uttered shriek upon shriek. 'Nay, scream away if you like it,' said he, still holding her fast; 'I have heard the sea at the loudest, and I mind a squalling woman no more than a miauling kitten—Damn me!—I have heard fifty or a hundred screaming at once, when there was a town stormed.'

The cries of the Countess, however, brought unexpected aid, in the person of Lawrence Staples, who had heard her exclamations from his apartment below, and entered in good time to save her from being discovered, if not from more atrocious violence. Lawrence was drunk also, from the debauch of the preceding night; but fortunately his intoxication had taken a different turn from that of Lambourne.

'What the devil's noise is this in the ward?' he said—'What! man and woman together in the same cell? that is against rule. I will have decency under my rule, by Saint Peter of the Fetters.'

'Get thee downstairs, thou drunken beast,' said Lambourne; 'seest thou not the lady and I would be private?'

'Good sir, worthy sir!' said the Countess, addressing the jailer, 'do but save me from him, for the sake of mercy!'

'She speaks fairly,' said the jailer, 'and I will take her part. I love my prisoners; and I have had as good prisoners under my key, as they have had in Newgate or the Compter. And so, being one of my lambkins, as I say, no one shall disturb her in her pen-fold. So, let go the woman, or I'll knock your brains out with my keys.'

'I will make a blood-pudding of thy midriff first,' answered Lambourne, laying his left hand on his dagger, but still detaining the Countess by the arm with his right—'So have at thee, thou old ostrich, whose only living is upon a bunch of iron keys.'

Lawrence raised the arm of Michael, and prevented him from drawing his dagger, and as Lambourne struggled and strove to shake him off, the Countess made a sudden exertion on her side, and slipping her hand out of the glove on which the ruffian still kept hold, she gained her liberty, and escaping from the apartment ran downstairs; while, at the same moment, she heard the two combatants fall on the floor with a noise which increased her terror. The outer wicket offered no impediment to her flight, having been opened for Lambourne's admittance; so that she succeeded in escaping down the stair, and fled into the Pleasance, which seemed to her hasty glance the direction in which she was most likely to avoid pursuit.

Meanwhile, Lawrence and Lambourne rolled on the floor of the apartment, closely grappled together. Neither had, happily, opportunity to draw their daggers; but Lawrence found space enough to dash his heavy keys across Michael's face, and Michael, in return, grasped the turnkey so felly by the throat, that the blood gushed from nose and mouth; so that they were both gory and filthy spectacles, when one of the other officers of the household, attracted by the noise of the fray, entered the room, and with some difficulty effected the separation of the combatants.

'A murrain on you both,' said the charitable mediator, 'and especially on you, Master Lambourne! What the fiend lie you here for, fighting on the floor like two butchers' curs in the kennel of the shambles?'

Lambourne arose, and, somewhat sobered by the interposition of a third party, looked with something less than his usual brazen impudence of visage. 'We fought for a wench an thou must know,' was his reply.

'A wench! Where is she?' said the officer.

'Why, vanished, I think,' said Lambourne, looking around him; 'unless Lawrence hath swallowed her. That filthy paunch of his swallows as many distressed damsels and oppressed orphans, as e'er a giant in King Arthur's history; they are his prime food; he worries them body, soul, and substance.'

'Ay, ay! It's no matter,' said Lawrence, gathering up his huge ungainly form from the floor, 'but I have had your betters, Master Michael Lambourne, under the little turn of my forefinger and thumb; and I shall have thee, before all's done, under my hatches. The impudence of thy brow will not always save thy shin-bones from iron, and thy foul thirsty gullet from a hempen cord.' The words were no sooner out of his mouth, when Lambourne again made at him.

'Nay, go not to it again,' said the sewer, 'or I will call for him shall tame you both, and that is Master Varney—Sir Richard, I mean—he is stirring, I promise you—I saw him cross the court just now.'

'Didst thou, by G—!' said Lambourne, seizing on the basin and ewer which stood in the apartment; 'Nay, then, element do thy work—I thought I had enough of thee last night, when I floated about for Orion, like a cork on a fermenting cask of ale.'

So saying, he fell to work to cleanse from his face and hands the signs of the fray, and get his apparel into some order.

'What hast thou done to him?' said the sewer, speaking aside to the jailer; 'his face is fearfully swelled.'

'It is but the imprint of the key of my cabinet—too good a mark for his gallows face. No man shall abuse or insult my prisoners; they are my jewels, and I lock them in safe casket accordingly. And so, mistress, leave off your wailing—Hey! why, surely there was a woman here!'

'I think you are all mad this morning,' said the sewer; 'I saw no woman here, nor no man neither in a proper sense, but only two beasts rolling on the floor.'

'Nay, then I am undone,' said the jailer; 'the prison's broken, that is all. Kenilworth prison is broken,' he continued, in a tone of maudlin lamentation, 'which was the strongest jail betwixt this and the Welsh marches—ay, and a house that has had knights, and earls, and kings sleeping in it, as secure as if they had been in the Tower of London. It is broken, the prisoners fled, and the jailer in much danger of being hanged!'

So saying, he retreated down to his own den to conclude his lamentations, or to sleep himself sober. Lambourne and the sewer followed him close, and it was well for them, since the jailer, out of mere habit, was about to lock the wicket after him; and had they not been within the reach of interfering, they would have had the pleasure of being shut up in the turret-chamber, from which the Countess had been just delivered.

That unhappy lady, as soon as she found herself at liberty, fled, as we have already mentioned, into the Pleasance. She had seen this richly ornamented space of ground from the window of Mervyn's Tower; and it occurred to her, at the moment of her escape, that, among its numerous arbours, bowers, fountains, statues, and grottos, she might find some recess, in which she could lie concealed until she had an opportunity of addressing herself to a protector, to whom she might communicate as much as she dared of her forlorn situation, and through whose means she might supplicate an interview with her husband.

'If I could see my guide,' she thought, 'I would learn if he had delivered my letter. Even did I but see Tressilian, it were better to risk Dudley's anger, by confiding my whole situation to one who is the very soul of honour, than to run the hazard of further insult among the insolent menials of this ill-ruled place. I will not again venture into an enclosed apartment. I will wait, I will watch—amidst so many human beings there must be some kind heart which can judge and compassionate what mine endures.'

In truth, more than one party entered and traversed the Pleasance. But they were in joyous groups of four or five persons together, laughing and jesting in their own fullness of mirth and lightness of heart.

The retreat which she had chosen gave her the easy alternative of avoiding observation. It was but stepping back to the farthest recess of a grotto, ornamented with rustic work and moss-seats, and terminated by a fountain, and she might easily remain concealed, or at her pleasure discover herself to any solitary wanderer, whose curiosity might lead him to that romantic retirement.

Anticipating such an opportunity, she looked into the clear basin, which the silent fountain held up to her like a mirror, and felt shocked at her own appearance, and doubtful at the same time, muffled and disfigured as her disguise made her seem to herself, whether any female (and it was from the compassion of her own sex that she chiefly expected sympathy) would engage in conference with so suspicious an object. Reasoning thus like a woman, to whom external appearance is scarcely in any circumstances a matter of unimportance, and like a beauty, who had some confidence in the power of her own charms she laid aside her own travelling cloak and capotaine hat, and placed them beside her, so that she could assume them in an instant, ere one could penetrate from the entrance of the grotto to its extremity, in case the intrusion of Varney or of Lambourne should render such disguise necessary. The dress which she wore under these vestments was somewhat of a theatrical cast, so as to suit the assumed personage of one of the females who was to act in the pageant. Wayland had found the means of arranging it thus upon the second day of their journey, having experienced the service arising from the assumption of such a character on the preceding day. The fountain, acting both as a mirror and ewer, afforded Amy the means of a brief toilet, of which she availed herself as hastily as possible; then took in her hand her small casket of jewels, in case she might find them useful inter-cessors, and retiring to the darkest and most sequestered nook, sat down on a seat of moss, and awaited till fate should give her some chance of rescue, or of propitiating an intercessor.

34

> Have you not seen the partridge quake,
> Viewing the hawk approaching nigh?
> She cuddles close beneath the brake,
> Afraid to sit, afraid to fly.—*Prior.*

IT chanced upon that memorable morning, that one of the earliest of the huntress train, who appeared from her chamber in full array for the chase, was the Princess for whom all these pleasures were instituted, England's Maiden Queen. I know not if it were by chance, or out of the befitting courtesy due to a mistress by whom he was so much honoured, that she had scarcely made one step beyond the threshold of her chamber, ere Leicester was by her side, and proposed to her, until the preparations for the chase had been completed, to view the Pleasance, and the gardens which it connected with the castle-yard.

To this new scene of pleasure they walked; the Earl's arm affording his Sovereign the occasional support which she required, where flights of steps, then a favourite ornament in a garden, conducted them from terrace to terrace, and from parterre to parterre. The ladies in attendance, gifted with prudence, or endowed perhaps with the amiable desire of acting as they would be done by, did not conceive their duty to the Queen's person required them, though they lost not sight of her, to approach so near as to share, or perhaps disturb, the conversation betwixt the Queen and the Earl, who was not only her host, but also her most trusted, esteemed, and favoured servant. They contented themselves with admiring the grace of this illustrious couple, whose robes of state were now exchanged for hunting suits, almost equally magnificent.

Elizabeth's sylvan dress, which was of a pale blue silk, with silver lace and *aiguillettes*, approached in form to that of the ancient Amazons; and was, therefore, well suited at once to her height, and to the dignity of her mien, which her conscious rank and long habits of authority had rendered in some degree too masculine to be seen to the best advantage in ordinary female weeds. Leicester's hunting suit of Lincoln-green, richly embroidered with gold, and

crossed by the gay baldric, which sustained a bungle-horn, and a
wood-knife instead of a sword, became its master, as did his other
vestments of court or of war. For such were the perfections of his
form and mien, that Leicester was always supposed to be seen to
the greatest advantage in the character and dress which for the time
he represented or wore.

The conversation of Elizabeth and the favourite Earl has not
reached us in detail. But those who watched at some distance (and
the eyes of courtiers and court ladies are right sharp) were of
opinion, that on no occasion did the dignity of Elizabeth, in gesture
and motion, seem so decidedly to soften away into a mien expressive
of indecision and tenderness. Her step was not only slow, but even
unequal, a thing most unwonted in her carriage; her looks seemed
bent on the ground, and there was a timid disposition to withdraw
from her companion, which external gesture in females often
indicates exactly the opposite tendency in the secret mind. The
Duchess of Rutland, who ventured nearest, was even heard to aver,
that she discerned a tear in Elizabeth's eye, and a blush on her
cheek; and still further, 'She bent her looks on the ground to avoid
mine,' said the Duchess; 'she who, in her ordinary mood, could
look down a lion.' To what conclusion these symptoms led is
sufficiently evident; nor were they probably entirely groundless.
The progress of a private conversation, betwixt two persons of
different sexes, is often decisive of their fate, and gives it a turn very
different perhaps from what they themselves anticipated. Gallantry
becomes mingled with conversation, and affection and passion
come gradually to mix with gallantry. Nobles, as well as shepherd
swains, will, in such a trying moment, say more than they intended;
and Queens, like village maidens, will listen longer than they
should.

Horses in the meanwhile neighed, and champed the bits with
impatience in the base-court; hounds yelled in couples, and yeomen,
rangers, and prickers, lamented the exhaling of the dew, which
would prevent the scent from lying. But Leicester had another
chase in view, or, to speak more justly towards him, had become
engaged in it without premeditation, as the high-spirited hunter
which follows the cry of the hounds that have crossed his path by
accident. The Queen—an accomplished and handsome woman—
the pride of England, the hope of France and Holland, and the
dread of Spain, had probably listened with more than usual favour

to that mixture of romantic gallantry with which she always loved to be addressed; and the Earl had, in vanity, in ambition, or in both, thrown in more and more of that delicious ingredient, until his importunity became the language of love itself.

'No, Dudley,' said Elizabeth, yet it was with broken accents—'No, I must be the mother of my people. Other ties, that make the lowly maiden happy, are denied to her Sovereign—No, Leicester, urge it no more—Were I as others, free to seek my own happiness—then, indeed—but it cannot—cannot be. Delay the chase—delay it for half an hour—and leave me, my lord.'

'How, leave you, Madam!' said Leicester,—'Has my madness offended you?'

'No, Leicester, not so!' answered the Queen hastily; 'but it *is* madness, and must not be repeated. Go—but go not far from hence—and meantime let no one intrude on my privacy.'

While she spoke thus, Dudley bowed deeply, and retired with a slow and melancholy air. The Queen stood gazing after him, and murmured to herself—'Were it possible—were it *but* possible!—no—no—Elizabeth must be the wife and mother of England alone.'

As she spoke thus, and in order to avoid some one whose step she heard approaching, the Queen turned into the grotto in which her hapless, and yet but too successful, rival lay concealed.

The mind of England's Elizabeth, if somewhat shaken by the agitating interview to which she had just put a period, was of that firm and decided character which soon recovers its natural tone. It was like one of those ancient druidical monuments called rocking-stones. The finger of Cupid, boy as he is painted, could put her feelings in motion, but the power of Hercules could not have destroyed their equilibrium. As she advanced with a slow pace towards the inmost extremity of the grotto, her countenance, ere she had proceeded half the length, had recovered its dignity of look, and her mien its air of command.

It was then the Queen became aware that a female figure was placed beside, or rather partly behind, an alabaster column, at the foot of which arose the pellucid fountain, which occupied the inmost recess of the twilight grotto. The classical mind of Elizabeth suggested the story of Numa and Egeria, and she doubted not that some Italian sculptor had here represented the Naiad, whose inspirations gave laws to Rome. As she advanced, she became doubtful whether she beheld a statue, or a form of flesh and blood.

The unfortunate Amy, indeed, remained motionless, betwixt the desire which she had to make her condition known to one of her own sex, and her awe for the stately form which approached her, and which, though her eyes had never before beheld, her fears instantly suspected to be the personage she really was. Amy had risen from her seat with the purpose of addressing the lady, who entered the grotto alone, and, as she at first thought, so opportunely. But when she recollected the alarm which Leicester had expressed at the Queen knowing aught of their union, and became more and more satisfied that the person whom she now beheld was Elizabeth herself, she stood with one foot advanced and one withdrawn, her arms, head, and hands perfectly motionless, and her cheek as pallid as the alabaster pedestal against which she leaned. Her dress was of pale sea-green silk, little distinguished in that imperfect light, and somewhat resembled the drapery of a Grecian nymph, such an antique disguise having been thought the most secure, where so many masquers and revellers were assembled; so that the Queen's doubt of her being a living form was well justified by all contingent circumstances, as well as by the bloodless cheek and the fixed eye.

Elizabeth remained in doubt, even after she had approached within a few paces, whether she did not gaze on a statue so cunningly fashioned, that by that doubtful light it could not be distinguished from reality. She stopped, therefore, and fixed upon this interesting object her princely look, with so much keenness that the astonishment which had kept Amy immovable gave way to awe, and she gradually cast down her eyes, and drooped her head under the commanding gaze of the Sovereign. Still, however, she remained in all respects, saving this slow and profound inclination of the head, motionless and silent.

From her dress, and the casket which she instinctively held in her hand, Elizabeth naturally conjectured that the beautiful but mute figure which she beheld, was a performer in one of the various theatrical pageants which had been placed in different situations to surprise her with their homage, and that the poor player, overcome with awe at her presence, had either forgot the part assigned her, or lacked courage to go through it. It was natural and courteous to give her some encouragement; and Elizabeth accordingly said, in a tone of condescending kindness,—'How now, fair nymph of this lovely grotto—art thou spell-bound and struck with dumbness by the charms of the wicked enchanter whom men termed Fear?

We are his sworn enemy, maiden, and can reverse his charm. Speak, we command thee.'

Instead of answering her by speech, the unfortunate Countess dropped on her knee before the Queen, let her casket fall from her hand, and clasping her palms together, looked up in the Queen's face with such a mixed agony of fear and supplication, that Elizabeth was considerably affected.

'What may this mean?' she said; 'this is a stronger passion than befits the occasion. Stand up, damsel—what wouldst thou have with us?'

'Your protection, Madam,' faltered forth the unhappy petitioner,

'Each daughter of England has it while she is worthy of it,' replied the Queen; 'but your distress seems to have a deeper root than a forgotten task. Why, and in what, do you crave our protection?'

Amy hastily endeavoured to recall what she were best to say, which might secure herself from the imminent dangers that surrounded her, without endangering her husband; and plunging from one thought to another, amidst the chaos which filled her mind, she could at length, in answer to the Queen's repeated inquiries, in what she sought protection, only falter out, 'Alas! I know not.'

'This is folly, maiden,' said Elizabeth impatiently; for there was something in the extreme confusion of the suppliant, which irritated her curiosity as well as interested her feelings. 'The sick man must tell his malady to the physician, nor are *we* accustomed to ask questions so oft, without receiving an answer.'

'I request—I implore,' stammered forth the unfortunate Countess,—'I beseech your gracious protection—against—against one Varney.' She choked wellnigh as she uttered the fatal word, which was instantly caught up by the Queen.

'What, Varney—Sir Richard Varney—the servant of Lord Leicester! What, damsel, are you to him, or he to you?'

'I—I—was his prisoner—and he practised on my life—and I broke forth to—to——'

'To throw thyself on my protection, doubtless,' said Elizabeth. 'Thou shalt have it—that is, if thou art worthy; for we will sift this matter to the uttermost. Thou art,' she said, bending on the Countess an eye which seemed designed to pierce her very inmost soul,—'thou art Amy, daughter of Sir Hugh Robsart of Lidcote Hall?'

'Forgive me—forgive me—most gracious Princess!' said Amy, dropping once more on her knee, from which she had arisen.

'For what should I forgive thee, silly wench?' said Elizabeth; 'for being the daughter of thine own father? Thou art brain-sick, surely. Well, I see I must wring the story from thee by inches— Thou didst deceive thine old and honoured father—thy look confesses it—cheated Master Tressilian—thy blush avouches it— and married this same Varney.'

Amy sprang on her feet, and interrupted the Queen eagerly, with, 'No, Madam, no—as there is a God above us, I am not the sordid wretch you would make me! I am not the wife of that contemptible slave—of that most deliberate villain! I am not the wife of Varney! I would rather be the bride of Destruction!'

The Queen, overwhelmed in her turn by Amy's vehemence, stood silent for an instant, and then replied, 'Why, God ha' mercy, woman!—I see thou canst talk fast enough when the theme likes thee. Nay, tell me, woman,' she continued, for to the impulse of curiosity was now added that of an undefined jealousy that some deception had been practised on her,—'tell me, woman—for by God's day, I WILL know—whose wife, or whose paramour, art thou? Speak out, and be speedy—Thou wert better dally with a lioness than with Elizabeth.'

Urged to this extremity, dragged as it were by irresistible force to the verge of the precipice, which she saw but could not avoid,— permitted not a moment's respite by the eager words and menacing gestures of the offended Queen, Amy at length uttered in despair, 'The Earl of Leicester knows it all.'

'The Earl of Leicester!' said Elizabeth, in utter astonishment— 'The Earl of Leicester!' she repeated, with kindling anger,— 'Woman, thou art set on to this—thou dost belie him—he takes no keep of such things as thou art. Thou art suborned to slander the noblest lord, and the truest-hearted gentleman, in England! But were he the right hand of our trust, or something yet dearer to us, thou shalt have thy hearing, and that in his presence. Come with me—come with me instantly!'

As Amy shrunk back with terror, which the incensed Queen interpreted as that of conscious guilt, Elizabeth rapidly advanced, seized on her arm, and hastened with swift and long steps out of the grotto, and along the principal alley of the Pleasance, dragging with her the terrified Countess, whom she still held by the arm, and whose utmost exertions could but just keep pace with those of the indignant Queen.

Leicester was at this moment the centre of a splendid group of lords and ladies, assembled together under an arcade, or portico, which closed the alley. The company had drawn together in that place to attend the commands of her Majesty when the hunting party should go forward, and their astonishment may be imagined, when, instead of seeing Elizabeth advance towards them with her usual measured dignity of motion, they beheld her walking so rapidly, that she was in the midst of them ere they were aware; and then observed, with fear and surprise, that her features were flushed betwixt anger and agitation, that her hair was loosened by her haste of motion, and that her eyes sparkled as they were wont when the spirit of Henry the Eighth mounted highest in his daughter. Nor were they less astonished at the appearance of the pale, attenuated, half-dead, yet still lovely female, whom the Queen upheld by main strength with one hand, while with the other she waved aside the ladies and nobles who pressed towards her, under the idea that she had taken suddenly ill. 'Where is my Lord of Leicester?' she said, in a tone that thrilled with astonishment all the courtiers who stood around—'Stand forth, my Lord of Leicester!'

If, in the midst of the most serene day of summer, when all is light and laughing around, a thunderbolt were to fall from the clear blue vault of heaven, and rend the earth at the very feet of some careless traveller, he could not gaze upon the smouldering chasm, which so unexpectedly yawned before him, with half the astonishment and fear which Leicester felt at the sight that so suddenly presented itself. He had that instant been receiving, with a political affectation of disavowing and misunderstanding their meaning, the half uttered, half intimated congratulations of their courtiers upon the favour of the Queen, carried apparently to its highest pitch during the interview of that morning; from which most of them seemed to augur, that he might soon arise from their equal in rank to become their master. And now, while the subdued yet proud smile with which he disclaimed those inferences was yet curling his cheek, the Queen shot into the circle, her passions excited to the uttermost; and, supporting with one hand, and apparently without an effort, the pale and sinking form of his almost expiring wife, and pointing with the finger of the other to her half-dead features, demanded in a voice that sounded to the ears of the astounded statesman like the last dread trumpet-call, that is to summon body and spirit to the judgment-seat, 'Knowest thou this woman?'

As, at the blast of that last trumpet, the guilty shall call upon the mountains to cover them, Leicester's inward thoughts invoked the stately arch which he had built in his pride, to burst its strong conjunction, and overwhelm them in its ruins. But the cemented stones, architrave and battlement, stood fast; and it was the proud master himself, who, as if some actual pressure had bent him to the earth, kneeled down before Elizabeth, and prostrated his brow to the marble flag-stones on which she stood.

'Leicester,' said Elizabeth, in a voice which trembled with passion, 'could I think thou hast practised on me—on me, thy Sovereign—on me thy confiding, thy too partial mistress, the base and ungrateful deception which thy present confusion surmises—by all that is holy, false lord, that head of thine were in as great peril as ever was thy father's!'

Leicester had not conscious innocence, but he had pride to support him. He raised slowly his brow and features, which were black and swollen with contending emotions, and only replied, 'My head cannot fall but by the sentence of my peers—to them I will plead, and not to a princess who thus requites my faithful service.'

'What! my lords,' said Elizabeth, looking around, 'we are defied, I think—defied in the castle we have ourselves bestowed on this proud man! My Lord Shrewsbury, you are Marshal of England, attach him of high treason.'

'Whom does your Grace mean?' said Shrewsbury, much surprised, for he had that instant joined the astonished circle.

'Whom should I mean, but that traitor, Dudley, Earl of Leicester! Cousin of Hunsdon, order out your band of Gentlemen Pensioners, and take him into instant custody. I say, villain, make haste!'

Hunsdon, a rough old noble, who, from his relationship to the Boleyns, was accustomed to use more freedom with the Queen than almost any other dared to do, replied bluntly, 'And it is like your Grace might order me to the Tower to-morrow, for making too much haste. I do beseech you to be patient.'

'Patient—God's life!' exclaimed the Queen—'name not the word to me—thou know'st not of what he is guilty!'

Amy, who had by this time in some degree recovered herself,

and who saw her husband, as she conceived, in the utmost danger from the rage of an offended Sovereign, instantly (and, alas! how many women have done the same) forgot her own wrongs, and her own danger, in her apprehensions for him, and throwing herself before the Queen, embraced her knees, while she exclaimed, 'He is guiltless, Madam—he is guiltless—no one can lay aught to the charge of the noble Leicester.'

'Why, minion,' answered the Queen, 'didst not thou, thyself, say that the Earl of Leicester was privy to thy whole history?'

'Did I say so?' repeated the unhappy Amy, laying aside every consideration of consistency and of self interest; 'Oh, if I did I foully belied him. May God so judge me, as I believe he was never privy to a thought that would harm me!'

'Woman!' said Elizabeth, 'I will know who has moved thee to this; or my wrath—and the wrath of kings is a flaming fire—shal! wither and consume thee like a weed in the furnace.'

As the Queen uttered this threat, Leicester's better angel called his pride to his aid, and reproached him with the utter extremity of meanness which would overwhelm him for ever, if he stooped to take shelter under the generous interposition of his wife, and abandoned her, in return for her kindness, to the resentment of the Queen. He had already raised his head, with the dignity of a man of honour, to avow his marriage, and proclaim himself the protector of his Countess, when Varney, born, as it appeared, to be his master's evil genius, rushed into the presence, with every mark of disorder on his face and apparal.

'What means this saucy intrusion?' said Elizabeth.

Varney, with the air of a man altogether overwhelmed with grief and confusion, prostrated himself before her feet, exclaiming, 'Pardon, my Liege, pardon!—or at least let your justice avenge itself on me, where it is due; but spare my noble, my generous, my innocent patron and master!'

Amy, who was yet kneeling, started up as she saw the man whom she deemed most odious place himself so near her, and was about to fly towards Leicester, when, checked at once by the uncertainty and even timidity which his looks had reassumed as soon as the appearance of his confidant seemed to open a new scene, she hung back, and, uttering a faint scream, besought of her Majesty to cause her to be imprisoned in the lowest dungeon of the castle—to deal with her as the worst of criminals—'but spare,' she exclaimed, 'my sight and hearing, what will destroy the little judgment I have left—the sight of that unutterable and most shameless villain!'

'And why, sweetheart?' said the Queen, moved by a new impulse; 'what hath he, this false knight, since such thou accountest him, done to thee?'

'Oh, worse than sorrow, madam, and worse than injury—he has sown dissension where most there should be peace. I shall go mad if I look longer on him.'

'Beshrew me, but I think thou art distraught already,' answered the Queen. 'My Lord Hunsdon, look to this poor distressed young woman, and let her be safely bestowed, and in honest keeping, till we require her to be forthcoming.'

Two or three of the ladies in attendance, either moved by compassion for a creature so interesting, or by some other motive, offered their service to look after her; but the Queen briefly answered, 'Ladies, under favour, no. You have all (give God thanks) sharp ears and nimble tongues—our kinsman Hunsdon has ears of the dullest, and a tongue somewhat rough, but yet of the slowest. Hunsdon, look to it that none have speech of her.'

'By Our Lady!' said Hunsdon, taking in his strong sinewy arms the fading and almost swooning form of Amy, 'she is a lovely child; and though a rough nurse, your Grace hath given her a kind one. She is safe with me as one of my own ladybirds of daughters.'

So saying, he carried her off, unresistingly and almost unconsciously; his war-worn locks and long gray beard mingling with her light-brown tresses, as her head reclined on his strong square shoulder. The Queen followed him with her eye—she had already, with that self-command which forms so necessary a part of a Sovereign's accomplishments, suppressed every appearance of agitation, and seemed as if she desired to banish all traces of her burst of passion from the recollection of those who had witnessed it. 'My Lord of Hunsdon says well,' she observed, 'he is indeed but a rough nurse for so tender a babe.'

'My Lord of Hunsdon,' said the Dean of St. Asaph, 'I speak it not in defamation of his more noble qualities, hath a broad licence in speech, and garnishes his discourse somewhat too freely with the cruel and superstitious oaths, which savour both of profaneness and of old Papistrie.'

'It is the fault of his blood, Mr Dean,' said the Queen, turning sharply round upon the reverend dignitary as she spoke; 'and you may blame mine for the same distemperature. The Boleyns were ever a hot and plain-spoken race, more hasty to speak their mind than careful to choose their expressions. And by my word—I hope there is no sin in that affirmation—I question if it were much cooled by mixing with that of Tudor.'

As she made this last observation she smiled graciously, and stole her eyes almost insensibly round to seek those of the Earl of Leicester, to whom she now began to think she had spoken with hasty harshness upon the unfounded suspicion of a moment.

The Queen's eye found the Earl in no mood to accept the implied offer of conciliation. His own looks had followed, with late and rueful repentance, the faded form which Hunsdon had just borne from the presence; they now reposed gloomily on the ground, but more—so at least it seemed to Elizabeth—with the expression of one who had received an unjust affront, than of him who is conscious of guilt. She turned her face angrily from him, and said to Varney, 'Speak, Sir Richard, and explain these riddles—thou hast sense and the use of speech, at least, which elsewhere we look for in vain.'

As she said this, she darted another resentful glance towards Leicester, while the wily Varney hastened to tell his own story.

'Your Majesty's piercing eye,' he said, 'has already detected the cruel malady of my beloved lady; which, unhappy that I am, I would not suffer to be expressed in the certificate of her physician, seeking to conceal what has now broken out with so much the more scandal.'

'She is then distraught?' said the Queen—'indeed we doubted not of it—her whole demeanour bears it out. I found her moping in a corner of yonder grotto; and every word which she spoke—which indeed I dragged from her as by the rack—she instantly recalled and forswore. But how came she hither? Why had you her not in safe keeping?'

'My gracious Liege,' said Varney, 'the worthy gentleman under whose charge I left her, Master Anthony Foster, has come hither but now, as fast as man and horse can travel, to show me of her escape, which she managed with the art peculiar to many who are afflicted with this malady. He is at hand for examination.'

'Let it be for another time,' said the Queen. 'But, Sir Richard, we envy you not your domestic felicity; your lady railed on you bitterly, and seemed ready to swoon at beholding you.'

'It is the nature of persons in her disorder, so please your Grace,' answered Varney, 'to be ever most inveterate in their spleen against those, whom, in their better moments, they hold nearest and dearest.'

'We have heard so, indeed,' said Elizabeth, 'and give faith to the saying.'

'May your Grace then be pleased,' said Varney, 'to command my unfortunate wife to be delivered into the custody of her friends?'

Leicester partly started; but, making a strong effort, he subdued his emotion, while Elizabeth answered sharply, 'You are something too hasty, Master Varney; we will have first a report of the lady's health and state of mind from Masters, our own physician, and then determine what shall be thought just. You shall have licence, however, to see her, that if there be any matrimonial quarrel betwixt you—such things we have heard do occur, even betwixt a loving couple—you may make it up, without further scandal to our court, or trouble to ourselves.'

Varney bowed low, and made no other answer.

Elizabeth again looked towards Leicester, and said, with a degree of condescension which could only arise out of the most heartfelt interest, 'Discord, as the Italian poet says, will find her way into peaceful convents, as well as into the privacy of families, and we fear our own guards and ushers will hardly exclude her from courts. My Lord of Leicester, you are offended with us, and we have right to be offended with you. We will take the lion's part upon us, and be the first to forgive.'

Leicester smoothed his brow, as by an effort, but the trouble was too deep-seated that its placidity should at once return. He said, however, that which fitted the occasion, 'that he could not have the happiness of forgiving, because she who commanded him to do so, could commit no injury towards him.'

Elizabeth seemed content with this reply, and intimated her pleasure that the sports of the morning should proceed. The bugles sounded—the hounds bayed—the horses pranced—but the courtiers and ladies sought the amusement to which they were summoned with hearts very different from those which had leaped to the morning's *reveille*. There was doubt, and fear, and expectation on every brow, and surmise and intrigue in every whisper.

Blount took an opportunity to whisper into Raleigh's ear, 'This storm came like a levanter in the Mediterranean.'

'*Varium et mutabile*'—answered Raleigh, in a similar tone.

'Nay, I know naught of your Latin,' said Blount; 'but I thank God, Tressilian took not the sea during that hurricane. He could scarce have missed shipwreck, knowing as he does so little how to trim his sails to a court gale.'

'Thou wouldst have instructed him?' said Raleigh.

'Why, I have profited by my time as well as thou, Sir Walter,' replied honest Blount. 'I am knight as well as thou, and of the earlier creation.'

'Now, God further thy wit,' said Raleigh; 'but for Tressilian, I would I knew what were the matter with him. He told me this morning he would not leave his chamber for the space of twelve hours, or thereby, being bound by a promise. This lady's madness, when he shall learn it, will not, I fear, cure his infirmity. The moon is at the fullest, and men's brains are working like yeast. But hark! they sound to mount. Let us to horse, Blount; we young knights must deserve our spurs.'

35

——Sincerity,
Thou first of virtues! let no mortal leave
The onward path, although the earth should gape,
And from the gulf of hell destruction cry,
To take dissimulation's winding way.—*Douglas*.

IT was not till after a long and successful morning's sport, and a prolonged repast which followed the return of the Queen to the castle, that Leicester at length found himself alone with Varney, from whom he now learned the whole particulars of the Countess's escape, as they had been brought to Kenilworth by Foster, who, in his terror for the consequences, had himself posted thither with the tidings. As Varney, in his narrative, took especial care to be silent concerning those practices on the Countess's health which had driven her to so desperate a resolution, Leicester, who could only suppose that she had adopted it out of jealous impatience, to attain the avowed state and appearance belonging to her rank, was not a little offended at the levity with which his wife had broken his strict commands, and exposed him to the resentment of Elizabeth.

'I have given,' he said, 'to this daughter of an obscure Devonshire gentleman, the proudest name in England. I have made her sharer of my bed and of my fortunes. I ask but of her a little patience, ere she launches forth upon the full current of her grandeur, and the infatuated woman will rather hazard her own shipwreck and mine, will rather involve me in a thousand whirlpools, shoals, and quicksands, and compel me to a thousand devices which shame me in mine own eyes, than tarry for a little space longer in the obscurity to which she was born.—So lovely, so delicate, so fond, so faithful —yet to lack in so grave a matter the patience which one might hope from the veriest fool—it puts me beyond my patience.'

'We may post it over yet well enough,' said Varney, 'if my lady will be but ruled, and take on her the character which the time commands.'

'It is but too true, Sir Richard,' said Leicester, 'there is indeed no other remedy. I have heard her termed thy wife in my presence, without contradiction. She must bear the title until she is far from Kenilworth.'

'And long afterwards, I trust,' said Varney; then instantly added, 'For I cannot but hope it will be long after ere she bear the title of Lady Leicester—I fear me it may scarce be with safety during the life of this Queen. But your lordship is best judge, you alone knowing what passages have taken place betwixt Elizabeth and you.'

'You are right, Varney,' said Leicester; 'I have this morning been both fool and villain; and when Elizabeth hears of my unhappy marriage, she cannot but think herself treated with that premeditated slight which women never forgive. We have once this day stood upon terms little short of defiance; and to those, I fear, we must again return.'

'Is her resentment, then, so implacable?' said Varney.

'Far from it,' replied the Earl; 'for being what she is in spirit and in station, she has even this day been but too condescending, in giving me opportunities to repair what she thinks my faulty heat of temper.'

'Ay,' answered Varney, 'the Italians say right—in lovers' quarrels, the party that loves most is always most willing to acknowledge the greater fault. So then, my lord, if this union with the lady could be concealed, you stand with Elizabeth as you did?'

Leicester sighed, and was silent for a moment, ere he replied.

'Varney, I think thou art true to me, and I will tell thee all. I do *not* stand where I did. I have spoken to Elizabeth—under what mad impulse I know not—on a theme which cannot be abandoned without touching every female feeling to the quick, and which yet I dare not and cannot prosecute. She can never, never forgive me, for having caused and witnessed those yieldings of human passion.'

'We must do something, my lord,' said Varney, 'and that speedily.'

'There is naught to be done,' answered Leicester, despondingly; 'I am like one that has long toiled up a dangerous precipice, and when he is within one perilous stride of the top, finds his progress arrested when retreat has become impossible. I see above me the pinnacle which I cannot reach—beneath me the abyss into which I must fall, as soon as my relaxing and dizzy brain join to hurl me from my present precarious stance.'

'Think better of your situation, my lord,' said Varney—'let us try the experiment in which you have but now acquiesced. Keep we your marriage from Elizabeth's knowledge, and all may yet be well. I will instantly go to the lady myself—She hates me, because I have been earnest with your lordship, as she truly suspects, in opposition to what she terms her rights. I care not for her prejudices —She *shall* listen to me; and I will show her such reasons for yielding to the pressure of the times that I doubt not to bring back her consent to whatever measures these exigencies may require.'

'No, Varney,' said Leicester; 'I have thought upon what is to be done, and I will myself speak with Amy.'

It was now Varney's turn to feel, upon his own account, the terrors which he affected to participate solely on account of his patron. 'Your lordship will not yourself speak with the lady?'

'It is my fixed purpose,' said Leicester; 'fetch me one of the livery-cloaks; I will pass the sentinel as thy servant. Thou art to have free access to her.'

'But, my lord——'

'I will have no *buts*,' replied Leicester; 'it shall be even thus, and not otherwise. Hunsdon sleeps, I think, in Saintlowe's Tower. We can go thither from these apartments by the private passage, without risk of meeting any one. Or what if I do meet Hunsdon? he is more my friend than enemy, and thick-witted enough to adopt any belief that is thrust on him. Fetch me the cloak instantly.'

Varney had no alternative save obedience. In a few minutes Leicester was muffled in the mantle, pulled his bonnet over his brows, and followed Varney along the secret passage of the castle which communicated with Hunsdon's apartments, in which there was scarce a chance of meeting any inquisitive person, and hardly light enough for any such to have satisfied their curiosity. They emerged at a door where Lord Hunsdon had, with military precaution, placed a sentinel, one of his own northern retainers as it fortuned, who readily admitted Sir Richard Varney, and his attendant, saying only, in his northern dialect, 'I would, man, thou couldst make the mad lady be still yonder; for her moans do sae dirl through my head, that I would rather keep watch on a snow-drift, in the wastes of Catlowdie.'

They hastily entered, and shut the door behind them.

'Now, good devil, if there be one,' said Varney within himself, 'for once help a votary at a dead pinch, for my boat is amongst the breakers.'

The Countess Amy, with her hair and her garments dishevelled, was seated upon a sort of couch, in an attitude of the deepest affliction, out of which she was startled by the opening of the door. She turned hastily round, and fixing her eye on Varney, exclaimed, 'Wretch! art thou come to frame some new plan of villainy?'

Leicester cut short her reproaches by stepping forward, and dropping his cloak, while he said, in a voice rather of authority than of affection, 'It is with me, madam, you have to commune, not with Sir Richard Varney.'

The change effected on the Countess's look and manner was like magic. 'Dudley!' she exclaimed, 'Dudley! and art thou come at last?' And with the speed of lightning she flew to her husband, clung around his neck, and, unheeding the presence of Varney, overwhelmed him with caresses, while she bathed his face in a flood of tears; muttering, at the same time, but in broken and disjointed monosyllables, the fondest expressions which love teaches his votaries.

Leicester, as it seemed to him, had reason to be angry with his lady for transgressing his commands, and thus placing him in the perilous situation in which he had that morning stood. But what displeasure could keep its ground before these testimonies of affection from a being so lovely, that even the negligence of dress, and the withering effects of fear, grief, and fatigue, which would have impaired the beauty of others, rendered hers but the more interesting! He received and repaid her caresses with fondness, mingled with melancholy, the last of which she seemed scarcely to observe, until the first transport of her own joy was over; when, looking anxiously in his face, she asked if he was ill.

'Not in my body, Amy,' was his answer.

'Then I will be well too. Oh Dudley! I have been ill!—very ill, since we last met!—for I call not this morning's horrible vision a meeting. I have been in sickness, in grief, and in danger—But thou art come, and all is joy, and health, and safety.'

'Alas! Amy,' said Leicester, 'thou hast undone me!'

'I, my lord?' said Amy; her cheek at once losing its transient flush of joy—'how could I injure that which I love better than myself?'

'I would not upbraid you, Amy,' replied the Earl; 'but are you not here contrary to my express commands—and does not your presence here endanger both yourself and me?'

'Does it, does it indeed!' she exclaimed eagerly; 'then why am I here a moment longer? Oh, if you knew by what fears I was urged to quit Cumnor Place!—but I will say nothing of myself—only

that if it might be otherwise, I would not willingly return *thither*;—
yet if it concern your safety——'

'We will think, Amy, of some other retreat,' said Leicester; 'and
you shall go to one of my northern castles, under the personage—it
will be but needful, I trust, for a very few days—of Varney's wife.'

'How, my Lord of Leicester!' said the lady, disengaging herself
from his embraces; 'is it to your wife you give the dishonourable
counsel to acknowledge herself the bride of another—and of all
men, the bride of that Varney?'

'Madam, I speak it in earnest—Varney is my true and faithful
servant, trusted in my deepest secrets. I had better lose my right
hand than his service at this moment. You have no cause to scorn
him as you do.'

'I could assign one, my lord,' replied the Countess; 'and I see he
shakes even under that assured look of his. But he that is necessary
as your right hand to your safety, is free from any accusation of
mine. May he be true to you; and that he may be true, trust him
not too much or too far. But it is enough to say, that I will not go
with him unless by violence, nor would I acknowledge him as my
husband, were all——'

'It is a temporary deception, madam,' said Leicester, irritated by
her opposition, 'necessary for both our safeties, endangered by you
through female caprice, or the premature desire to seize on a rank
to which I gave you title, only under condition that our marriage,
for a time, should continue secret. If my proposal disgust you, it is
yourself has brought it on both of us. There is no other remedy—
you must do what your own impatient folly hath rendered
necessary—I command you.'

'I cannot put your commands, my lord,' said Amy, 'in balance
with those of honour and conscience. I will NOT, in this instance,
obey you. You may achieve your own dishonour, to which these
crooked policies naturally tend, but I will do naught that can
blemish mine. How could you again, my lord, acknowledge me as
a pure and chaste matron, worthy to share your fortunes, when,
holding that high character, I had strolled the country the acknowledged wife of such a profligate fellow as your servant Varney!'

'My lord,' said Varney, interposing, 'my lady is too much
prejudiced against me, unhappily, to listen to what I can offer; yet
it may please her better than what she proposes. She has good
interest with Master Edmund Tressilian, and could doubtless prevail

on him to consent to be her companion to Lidcote Hall, and there she might remain in safety, until time permitted the development of this mystery.'

Leicester was silent, but stood looking eagerly on Amy, with eyes which seemed suddenly to glow as much with suspicion as displeasure.

The Countess only said, 'Would to God I were in my father's house! When I left it, I little thought I was leaving peace of mind and honour behind me.'

Varney proceeded with a tone of deliberation, 'Doubtless this will make it necessary to take strangers into my lord's counsels; but surely the Countess will be warrant for the honour of Master Tressilian, and such of her father's family——'

'Peace, Varney,' said Leicester; 'by Heaven, I will strike my dagger into thee, if again thou namest Tressilian as a partner of my counsels!'

'And wherefore not?' said the Countess; 'unless they be counsels fitter for such as Varney, than for a man of stainless honour and integrity. My lord, my lord, bend no angry brows on me—it is the truth, and it is I who speak it. I once did Tressilian wrong for your sake—I will not do him the further injustice of being silent when his honour is brought in question. I can forbear,' she said, looking at Varney, 'to pull the mask off hypocrisy, but I will not permit virtue to be slandered in my hearing.'

There was a dead pause. Leicester stood displeased, yet undetermined, and too conscious of the weakness of his cause; while Varney, with a deep and hypocritical affectation of sorrow, mingled with humility, bent his eyes on the ground.

It was then that the Countess Amy displayed, in the midst of distress and difficulty, the natural energy of character, which would have rendered her, had fate allowed, a distinguished ornament of the rank which she held. She walked up to Leicester with a composed step, a dignified air, and looks in which strong affection essayed in vain to shake the firmness of conscious truth and rectitude of principle. 'You have spoke your mind, my lord,' she said, 'in these difficulties, with which, unhappily, I have found myself unable to comply. This gentleman—this person, I would say—has hinted at another scheme, to which I object not but as it displeases you. Will your lordship be pleased to hear what a young and timid woman, but your most affectionate wife, can suggest in the present extremity?'

Leicester was silent, but bent his head towards the Countess, as an intimation that she was at liberty to proceed.

'There hath been but one cause for all these evils, my lord,' she proceeded, 'and it resolves itself into the mysterious duplicity with which you have been induced to surround yourself. Extricate yourself at once, my lord, from the tyranny of these disgraceful trammels. Be like a true English gentleman, knight, and earl, who holds that truth is the foundation of honour, and that honour is dear to him as the breath of his nostrils. Take your ill-fated wife by the hand, lead her to the footstool of Elizabeth's throne—Say, that in a moment of infatuation, moved by supposed beauty, of which none perhaps can now trace even the remains, I gave my hand to this Amy Robsart. You will then have done justice to me, my lord, and to your own honour; and should law or power require you to part from me, I will oppose no objection—since I may then with honour hide a grieved and broken heart in those shades from which your love withdrew me. Then—have but a little patience, and Amy's life will not long darken your brighter prospects.'

There was so much of dignity, so much of tenderness, in the Countess's remonstrance, that it moved all that was noble and generous in the soul of her husband. The scales seemed to fall from his eyes, and the duplicity and tergiversation of which he had been guilty stung him at once with remorse and shame.

'I am not worthy of you, Amy,' he said, 'that could weigh aught which ambition has to give against such a heart as thine. I have a bitter penance to perform, in disentangling, before sneering foes and astounded friends, all the meshes of my own deceitful policy. And the Queen—but let her take my head, as she has threatened.'

'Your head, my lord!' said the Countess; 'because you used the freedom and liberty of an English subject in choosing a wife? For shame; it is this distrust of the Queen's justice, this apprehension of danger, which cannot but be imaginary, that, like scarecrows, have induced you to forsake the straightforward path, which, as it is the best, is also the safest.'

'Ah, Amy, thou little knowest!' said Dudley; but instantly checking himself, he added, 'Yet she shall not find in me a safe or easy victim of arbitrary vengeance. I have friends—I have allies—I will not, like Norfolk, be dragged to the block, as a victim to sacrifice. Fear not, Amy; thou shalt see Dudley bear himself worthy of his name. I must instantly communicate with some of those friends on whom I can best rely; for, as things stand, I may be made prisoner in my own castle.'

'Oh, my good lord,' said Amy, 'make no faction in a peaceful state! There is no friend can help us so well as our own candid truth and honour. Bring but these to our assistance, and you are safe amidst a whole army of the envious and malignant. Leave these behind you, and all other defence will be fruitless—Truth, my noble lord, is well painted unarmed.'

'But Wisdom, Amy,' answered Leicester, 'is arrayed in panoply of proof. Argue not with me on the means I shall use to render my confession—since it must be called so—as safe as may be; it will be fraught with enough of danger, do what we will. Varney, we must hence. Farewell, Amy, whom I am to vindicate as mine own, at an expense and risk of which thou alone couldst be worthy. You shall soon hear further from me.'

He embraced her fervently, muffled himself as before, and accompanied Varney from the apartment. The latter, as he left the room, bowed low, and, as he raised his body, regarded Amy with a peculiar expression, as if he desired to know how far his own pardon was included in the reconciliation which had taken place betwixt her and her lord. The Countess looked upon him with a fixed eye, but seemed no more conscious of his presence, than if there had been nothing but vacant air on the spot where he stood.

'She has brought me to the crisis,' he muttered—'She or I are lost. There was something—I wot not if it was fear or pity—that prompted me to avoid this fatal crisis. It is now decided—She or I must *perish*.'

While he thus spoke, he observed, with surprise, that a boy, repulsed by the sentinel, made up to Leicester, and spoke with him. Varney was one of those politicians, whom not the slightest appearances escape without inquiry. He asked the sentinel what the lad wanted with him, and received for answer, that the boy had wished him to transmit a parcel to the mad lady, but that he cared not to take charge of it, such communication being beyond his commission. His curiosity satisfied in that particular, he approached his patron, and heard him say—'Well, boy, the packet shall be delivered.'

'Thanks, good Master Serving-man,' said the boy, and was out of sight in an instant.

Leicester and Varney returned with hasty steps to the Earl's private apartment, by the same passage which had conducted them to Saintlowe's Tower.

36

————I have said
This is an adultress—I have said with whom—
More, she's a traitor, and Camillo is
A federary with her, and one that knows
What she should shame to know herself.—*Winter's Tale.*

THEY were no sooner in the Earl's cabinet, than, taking his tablets from his pocket, he began to write, speaking partly to Varney and partly to himself:—'There are many of them close bounden to me, and especially those in good estate and high office; many who, if they look back towards my benefits, or forward towards the perils which may befall themselves, will not, I think, be disposed to see me stagger unsupported. Let me see—Knollis is sure, and through his means Guernsey and Jersey—Horsey commands in the Isle of Wight—My brother-in-law, Huntingdon, and Pembroke, have authority in Wales—Through Bedford I lead the Puritans, with their interest, so powerful in all the boroughs—My brother of Warwick is equal wellnigh to myself, in wealth, followers, and dependencies—Sir Owen Hopton is at my devotion; he commands the Tower of London, and the national treasure deposited there—My father and grandfather needed never to have stooped their heads to the block, had they thus forecast their enterprises. Why look you so sad, Varney? I tell thee, a tree so deep-rooted is not easily to be torn up by the tempest.'

'Alas! my lord,' said Varney, with well-acted passion, and then resumed the same look of despondency which Leicester had before noted.

'Alas!' repeated Leicester, 'and wherefore alas, Sir Richard? Doth your new spirit of chivalry supply no more vigorous ejaculation, when a noble struggle is impending? Or, if *alas* means thou wilt flinch from the conflict, thou mayst leave the castle, or go join mine enemies, whichsoever thou think'st best.'

'Not so, my lord,' answered his confidant; 'Varney will be found fighting or dying by your side. Forgive me, if, in love to you, I see more fully than your noble heart permits you to do, the inextricable difficulties with which you are surrounded. You are strong, my lord, and powerful; yet, let me say it without offence, you are so only by the reflected light of the Queen's favour. While you are Elizabeth's favourite, you are all, save in name, like an actual sovereign. But let her call back the honours she has bestowed, and the Prophet's gourd did not wither more suddenly. Declare against the Queen, and I do not say that in the wide nation, or in this province alone, you would find yourself instantly deserted and out-numbered; but I will say, that even in this very castle, and in the midst of your vassals, kinsmen, and dependants, you would be a captive, nay, a sentenced captive, should she please to say the word. Think upon Norfolk, my lord,—upon the powerful Northumberland,—the splendid Westmoreland;—think on all who have made head against this sage Princess. They are dead, captive, or fugitive. This is not like other thrones, which can be overturned by a combination of powerful nobles; the broad foundations which support it are in the extended love and affections of the people. You might share it with Elizabeth if you would; but neither yours, nor any other power, foreign or domestic, will avail to overthrow, or even to shake it.'

He paused, and Leicester threw his tablets from him with an air of reckless despite. 'It may be as thou say'st,' he said; 'and, in sooth, I care not whether truth or cowardice dictate thy forebodings. But it shall not be said I fell without a struggle. Give orders that those of my retainers who served under me in Ireland be gradually drawn into the main keep, and let our gentlemen and friends stand on their guard, and go armed, as if they expected an onset from the followers of Sussex. Possess the town's-people with some apprehension; let them take arms, and be ready, at a signal given, to master the Pensioners and Yeomen of the Guard.'

'Let me remind you, my lord,' said Varney, with the same appearance of deep and melancholy interest, 'that you have given me order to prepare for disarming the Queen's guard. It is an act of high treason, but you shall nevertheless be obeyed.'

'I care not,' said Leicester desperately;—'I care not. Shame is behind me, ruin before me; I must on.'

Here there was another pause, which Varney at length broke with the following words: 'It is come to the point I have long dreaded. I must either witness, like an ungrateful beast, the downfall of the best and kindest of masters, or I must speak what I would have buried in the deepest oblivion, or told by any other mouth than mine.'

'What is that thou say'st, or would say?' replied the Earl; 'we have no time to waste on words, when the time calls us to action.'

'My speech is soon made, my lord—would to God it were as soon answered. Your marriage is the sole cause of the threatened breach with your Sovereign, my lord, is it not?'

'Thou knowest it is!' replied Leicester.' What needs so fruitless a question?'

'Pardon me, my lord,' said Varney; 'the use lies here. Men will wager their lands and lives in defence of a rich diamond, my lord; but were it not first prudent to look if there is no flaw in it?'

'What means this?' said Leicester, with his eyes sternly fixed on his dependant; 'of whom dost thou dare to speak?'

'It is——of the Countess Amy, my lord, of whom I am unhappily bound to speak; and of whom I *will* speak, were your lordship to kill me for my zeal.'

'Thou mayst happen to deserve it at my hand,' said the Earl; 'but speak on, I will hear thee.'

'Nay, then, my lord, I will be bold. I speak for my own life, as well as for your lordship's. I like not this lady's tampering and trickstering with this same Edmund Tressilian. You know him, my lord. You know he had formerly an interest in her, which it cost your lordship some pains to supersede. You know the eagerness with which he has pressed on the suit against me in behalf of this lady, the open object of which is to drive your lordship to an avowal of what I must ever call your most unhappy marriage, the point to which my lady also is willing, at any risk, to urge you.'

Leicester smiled constrainedly. 'Thou meanest well, good Sir Richard, and would, I think, sacrifice thine own honour, as well as that of any other person, to save me from what thou think'st a step so terrible. But, remember,'—he spoke these words with the most stern decision,—'you speak of the Countess of Leicester.'

'I do, my lord,' said Varney; 'but it is for the welfare of the Earl of Leicester. My tale is but begun. I do most strongly believe that this Tressilian has, from the beginning of his moving in her cause, been in connivance with her ladyship the Countess.'

'Thou speak'st wild madness, Varney, with the sober face of a preacher. Where, or how, could they communicate together?'

'My lord,' said Varney, 'unfortunately I can show that but too well. It was just before the supplication was presented to the Queen, in Tressilian's name, that I met him, to my utter astonishment, at the postern gate, which leads from the demesne at Cumnor Place.'

'Thou met'st him, villain! and why didst thou not strike him dead?' exclaimed Leicester.

'I drew on him, my lord, and he on me; and had not my foot slipped, he would not, perhaps, have been again a stumbling-block in your lordship's path.'

Leicester seemed struck dumb with surprise. At length he answered, 'What other evidence hast thou of this, Varney, save thine own assertion?—for, as I will punish deeply, I will examine coldly and warily. Sacred Heaven! but no—I will examine coldly and warily—coldly and warily.' He repeated these words more than once to himself, as if in the very sound there was a sedative quality; and again compressing his lips, as if he feared some violent expression might escape from them, he asked again, 'What further proof?'

'Enough, my lord,' said Varney, 'and to spare. I would it rested with me alone, for with me it might have been silenced for ever. But my servant, Michael Lambourne, witnessed the whole, and was, indeed, the means of the first introducing Tressilian into Cumnor Place; and therefore I took him into my service and retained him in it, though something of a debauched fellow, that I might have his tongue always under my own command.' He then acquainted Lord Leicester how easy it was to prove the circumstance of their interview true, by evidence of Anthony Foster, with the corroborative testimonies of the various persons at Cumnor, who had heard the wager laid, and had seen Lambourne and Tressilian set off together. In the whole narrative, Varney hazarded nothing fabulous, excepting that, not indeed by direct assertion, but by inference, he led his patron to suppose that the interview betwixt Amy and Tressilian at Cumnor Place, had been longer than the few minutes to which it was in reality limited.

'And wherefore was I not told of all this?' said Leicester sternly. 'Why did all of ye—and in particular thou, Varney—keep back from me such material information?'

'Because, my lord,' replied Varney, 'the Countess pretended to Foster and to me, that Tressilian had intruded himself upon her; and I concluded their interview had been in all honour, and that she would at her own time tell it to your lordship. Your lordship knows with what unwilling ears we listen to evil surmises against those whom we love; and I thank Heaven, I am no make-bate or informer, to be the first to sow them.'

'You are but too ready to receive them, however, Sir Richard,' replied his patron. 'How know'st thou that this interview was not in all honour, as thou hast said? Methinks the wife of the Earl of Leicester might speak for a short time with such a person as Tressilian, without injury to me, or suspicion to herself.'

'Questionless, my lord,' answered Varney; 'had I thought otherwise, I had been no keeper of the secret. But here lies the rub—Tressilian leaves not the place without establishing a correspondence with a poor man, the landlord of an inn in Cumnor, for the purpose of carrying off the lady. He sent down an emissary of his, whom I trust soon to have in right sure keeping under Mervyn's Tower. Killigrew and Lambsbey are scouring the country in quest of him. The host is rewarded with a ring for keeping counsel—your lordship may have noted it on Tressilian's hand—here it is. This fellow, this agent, makes his way to the Place as a pedlar, holds conference with the lady, and they make their escape together by night—rob a poor fellow of a horse by the way, such was their guilty haste; and at length reach this castle, where the Countess of Leicester finds refuge—I dare not say in what place.'

'Speak, I command thee,' said Leicester; 'speak, while I retain sense enough to hear thee.'

'Since it must be so,' answered Varney, 'the lady resorted immediately to the apartment of Tressilian, where she remained many hours, partly in company with him, and partly alone. I told you Tressilian had a paramour in this chamber—I little dreamed that paramour was——'

'Amy, thou wouldst say,' answered Leicester; 'but it is false, false as the smoke of hell! Ambitious she may be—fickle and impatient—'tis a woman's fault; but false to me!—never, never. The proof—the proof of this!' he exclaimed hastily.

'Carrol, the deputy-marshal, ushered her thither by her own desire, on yesterday afternoon,—Lambourne and the warder both found her there at an early hour this morning.'

'Was Tressilian there with her?' said Leicester, in the same hurried tone.

'No, my lord. You may remember,' answered Varney, 'that he was that night placed with Sir Nicholas Blount, under a species of arrest.'

'Did Carrol, or the other fellows, know who she was?' demanded Leicester.

'No, my lord,' replied Varney; 'Carrol and the warder had never seen the Countess, and Lambourne knew her not in her disguise; but, in seeking to prevent her leaving the cell, he obtained possession of one of her gloves, which, I think, your lordship may know.'

He gave the glove, which had the Bear and Ragged Staff, the Earl's impress, embroidered upon it in seed-pearls.

'I do, I do recognise it,' said Leicester. 'They were my own gift. The fellow of it was on the arm which she threw this very day around my neck!' He spoke this with violent agitation.

'Your lordship,' said Varney, 'might yet further inquire of the lady herself, respecting the truth of these passages.'

'It needs not—it needs not,' said the tortured Earl; 'it is written in characters of burning light, as if they were branded on my very eyeballs! I see her infamy—I can see naught else; and,—gracious Heaven!—for this vile woman was I about to commit to danger the lives of so many noble friends—shake the foundation of a lawful throne—carry the sword and torch through the bosom of a peaceful land—wrong the kind mistress who made me what I am—and would, but for that hell-framed marriage, have made me all that man can be! All this I was ready to do for a woman who trinkets and traffics with my worst foes! And thou, villain, why didst thou not speak sooner?'

'My lord,' said Varney, 'a tear from my lady would have blotted out all I could have said. Besides, I had not these proofs until this very morning, when Anthony Foster's sudden arrival, with the examinations and declarations, which he had extorted from the innkeeper Gosling, and others, explained the manner of her flight from Cumnor Place, and my own researches discovered the steps which she had taken here.'

'Now, may God be praised for the light He has given! so full, so satisfactory, that there breathes not a man in England who shall call my proceeding rash, or my revenge unjust. And yet, Varney, so young, so fair, so fawning, and so false! Hence, then, her hatred to thee, my trusty, my well-beloved servant, because you withstood her plots, and endangered her paramour's life?'

'I never gave her any other cause of dislike, my lord,' replied Varney; 'but she knew that my counsels went directly to diminish her influence with your lordship; and that I was, and have been, ever ready to peril my life against your enemies.'

'It is too, too apparent,' replied Leicester; 'yet, with what an air of magnanimity she exhorted me to commit my head to the Queen's mercy, rather than wear the veil of falsehood a moment longer! Methinks, the angel of truth himself can have no such tones of high-souled impulse. Can it be so, Varney? Can falsehood use thus boldly the language of truth? Can infamy thus assume the guise of purity? Varney, thou hast been my servant from a child— I have raised thee high—can raise thee higher. Think, think for me! Thy brain was ever shrewd and piercing—May she not be innocent? Prove her so, and all I have yet done for thee shall be as nothing— nothing—in comparison of thy recompense!'

The agony with which his master spoke had some effect even on the hardened Varney, who, in the midst of his own wicked and ambitious designs, really loved his patron as well as such a wretch was capable of loving anything; but he comforted himself, and subdued his self-reproaches with the reflection, that if he inflicted upon the Earl some immediate and transitory pain, it was in order to pave his way to the throne, which, were this marriage dissolved by death or otherwise, he deemed Elizabeth would willingly share with his benefactor. He, therefore, persevered in his diabolical policy; and, after a moment's consideration, answered the anxious queries of the Earl with a melancholy look, as if he had in vain sought some exculpation for the Countess; then suddenly raising his head, he said, with an expression of hope, which instantly commu-nicated itself to the countenance of his patron,—'Yet, wherefore, if guilty, should she have perilled herself by coming hither? Why not rather have fled to her father's or elsewhere?—though that, indeed, might have interfered with her desire to be acknowledged as Countess of Leicester.'

'True, true, true!' exclaimed Leicester, his transient gleam of hope giving way to the utmost bitterness of feeling and expression; 'thou art not fit to fathom a woman's depth of wit, Varney. I see it all. She would not quit the estate and title of the wittol who had wedded her. Ay, and if in my madness I had started into rebellion, or if the angry Queen had taken my head, as she this morning threatened, the wealthy dower, which law would have assigned to the Countess Dowager of Leicester, had been no bad windfall to the beggarly Tressilian. Well might she goad me on to danger, which could not end otherwise than profitably to her. Speak not for her, Varney! I will have her blood!'

'My lord,' replied Varney, 'the wildness of your distress breaks forth in the wildness of your language.'

'I say, speak not for her,' replied Leicester; 'she has dishonoured me—she would have murdered me—all ties are burst between us. She shall die the death of a traitress and adulteress, well merited both by the laws of God and man! And—what is this casket,' he said, 'which was even now thrust into my hand by a boy, with the desire I would convey it to Tressilian, as he could not give it to the Countess? By Heaven! the words surprised me as he spoke them, though other matters chased them from my brain; but now they return with double force. It is her casket of jewels! Force it open, Varney; force the hinges open with thy poniard.'

'She refused the aid of my dagger once,' thought Varney, as he unsheathed the weapon, 'to cut the string which bound a letter; but now it shall work a mightier ministry in her fortunes.'

With this reflection, by using the three-cornered stiletto-blade as a wedge, her forced open the slender silver hinges of the casket. The Earl no sooner saw them give way, than he snatched the casket from Sir Richard's hand, wrenched off the cover, and tearing out the splendid contents, flung them on the floor in a transport of rage, while he eagerly searched for some letter or billet, which should make the fancied guilt of his innocent Countess yet more apparent. Then stamping furiously on the gems, he exclaimed, 'Thus I annihilate the miserable toys for which thou hast sold thyself, body and soul, consigned thyself to an early and timeless death, and me to misery and remorse for ever! Tell me not of forgiveness, Varney—She is doomed!'

So saying, he left the room, and rushed into an adjacent closet, the door of which he locked and bolted.

Varney looked after him, while something of a more human feeling seemed to contend with his habitual sneer. 'I am sorry for his weakness,' he said, 'but love has made him a child. He throws down and treads on these costly toys—with the same vehemence would he dash to pieces this frailest toy of all, of which he used to rave so fondly. But that taste also will be forgotten when its object is no more. Well, he has no eye to value things as they deserve, and that nature has given to Varney. When Leicester shall be a sovereign, he will think as little of the gales of passion, through which he gained that royal port, as ever did sailor in harbour of the perils of a voyage. But these tell-tale articles must not remain here —they are rather too rich vails for the drudges who dress the chamber.'

While Varney was employed in gathering together and putting them into a secret drawer of a cabinet that chanced to be open, he saw the door of Leicester's closet open, the tapestry pushed aside, and the Earl's face thrust out, but with eyes so dead, and lips and cheeks so bloodless and pale, that he started at the sudden change. No sooner did his eyes encounter the Earl's than the latter withdrew his head, and shut the door of the closet. This manoeuvre Leicester repeated twice, without speaking a word, so that Varney began to doubt whether his brain was not actually affected by his mental agony. The third time, however, he beckoned, and Varney obeyed the signal. When he entered, he soon found his patron's perturbation was not caused by insanity, but by the fellness of purpose which he entertained, contending with various contrary passions. They passed a full hour in close consultation; after which the Earl of Leicester, with an incredible exertion, dressed himself, and went to attend his royal guest.

37

You have displaced the mirth, broke the good meeting
With most admired disorder.—*Macbeth*.

It was afterwards remembered, that during the banquets and revels
which occupied the remainder of this eventful day, the bearing of
Leicester and of Varney were totally different from their usual
demeanour. Sir Richard Varney had been held rather a man of
counsel and of action, than a votary of pleasure. Business, whether
civil or military, seemed always to be his proper sphere; and while
in festivals and revels, although he well understood how to trick
them up and present them, his own part was that of a mere
spectator; or of he exercised his wit, it was in a rough, caustic,
and severe manner, rather as if he scoffed at the exhibition and the
guests, than shared the common pleasure.

But upon the present day his character seemed changed. He
mixed among the younger courtiers and ladies, and appeared for
the moment to be actuated by a spirit of light-hearted gaiety, which
rendered him a match for the liveliest. Those who had looked
upon him as a man given up to graver and more ambitious pursuits,
a bitter sneerer and passer of sarcasms at the expense if those who,
taking life as they find it, were disposed to snatch at each pastime it
presents, now perceived with astonishment that his wit could
carry as smooth an edge as their own, his laugh be as lively, and
his brow as unclouded. By what art of damnable hypocrisy he
could draw this veil of gaiety over the black thoughts of one of the
worst of human bosoms, must remain unintelligible to all but his
compeers, if any such ever existed; but he was a man of extraordinary powers, and those powers were unhappily dedicated in
all their energy to the very worst of purposes.

It was entirely different with Leicester. However habituated his
mind usually was to play the part of a good courtier, and appear
gay, assiduous, and free from all care but that of enhancing the
pleasure of the moment, while his bosom internally throbbed with
the pangs of unsatisfied ambition, jealousy, or resentment, his heart
had now a yet more dreadful guest, whose workings could not be
overshadowed or suppressed; and you might read in his vacant eye

and troubled brow, that his thoughts were far absent from the scenes in which he was compelling himself to play a part. He looked, moved, and spoke as if by a succession of continued efforts; and it seemed as if his will had, in some degree, lost the promptitude of command over the acute mind and goodly form of which it was the regent. His actions and gestures, instead of appearing the consequence of simple volition, seemed, like those of an automaton, to wait the revolution of some internal machinery ere they could be performed; and his words fell from him piecemeal, interrupted, as if he had first to think what he was to say, then how it was to be said, and as if, after all, it was only by an effort of continued attention that he completed a sentence without forgetting both the one and the other.

The singular effects which these distractions of mind produced upon the behaviour and conversation of the most accomplished courtier of England, as they were visible to the lowest and dullest menial who approached his person, could not escape the notice of the most intelligent princess of the age. Nor is there the least doubt, that the alternate negligence and irregularity of his manner would have called down Elizabeth's severe displeasure on the Earl of Leicester, had it not occurred to her to account for it, by supposing that the apprehension of that displeasure which she had expressed towards him with such vivacity that very morning, was dwelling upon the spirits of her favourite, and, spite of his efforts to the contrary, distracted the usual graceful tenor of his mien, and the charms of his conversation. When this idea, so flattering to female vanity, had once obtained possession of her mind, it proved a full and satisfactory apology for the numerous errors and mistakes of the Earl of Leicester; and the watchful circle around observed with astonishment, that, instead of resenting his repeated negligence, and want of even ordinary attention (although these were points on which she was usually extremely punctilious), the Queen sought, on the contrary, to afford him time and means to recollect himself, and deigned to assist him in doing so, with an indulgence which seemed altogether inconsistent with her usual character. It was clear, however, that this could not last much longer, and that Elizabeth must finally put another and more severe construction on Leicester's uncourteous conduct, when the Earl was summoned by Varney to speak with him in a different apartment.

After having had the message twice delivered to him, he rose, and was about to withdraw, as it were, by instinct—then stopped, and turning round, entreated permission of the Queen to absent himself for a brief space upon matters of pressing importance.

'Go, my lord,' said the Queen; 'we are aware our presence must occasion sudden and unexpected occurrences, which require to be provided for on the instant. Yet, my lord, as you would have us believe ourself your welcome and honoured guest, we entreat you to think less of our good cheer, and favour us with more of your good countenance than we have this day enjoyed; for whether prince or peasant be the guest, the welcome of the host will always be the better part of the entertainment. Go, my lord, and we trust to see you return with an unwrinkled brow, and those free thoughts which you are wont to have at the disposal of your friends.'

Leicester only bowed low in answer to this rebuke, and retired. At the door of the apartment he was met by Varney, who eagerly drew him apart and whispered in his ear, 'All is well!'

'Has Masters seen her?' said the Earl.

'He has, my lord; and as she would neither answer his queries, nor allege any reason for her refusal, he will give full testimony that she labours under a mental disorder, and may be best committed to the charge of her friends. The opportunity is therefore free to remove her as we propose.'

'But Tressilian?' said Leicester.

'He will not know of her departure for some time,' replied Varney; 'it shall take place this very evening, and to-morrow he shall be cared for.'

'No, by my soul,' answered Leicester; 'I will take vengeance on him with mine own hand!'

'You, my lord, and on so inconsiderable a man as Tressilian!— No, my lord, he hath long wished to visit foreign parts. Trust him to me—I will take care he returns not hither to tell tales.'

'Not so, by Heaven, Varney!' exclaimed Leicester.—'Inconsiderable do you call an enemy, that hath had power to wound me so deeply, that my whole after life must be one scene of remorse and misery? No; rather than forgo the right of doing myself justice with my own hand on that accursed villain, I will unfold the whole truth at Elizabeth's footstool, and let her vengeance descend at once on them and on myself.'

Varney saw with great alarm that his lord was wrought up to such a pitch of agitation, that if he gave no way to him, he was perfectly capable of adopting the desperate resolution which he had announced, and which was instant ruin to all the schemes of ambition which Varney had formed for his patron and for himself. But the Earl's rage seemed at once uncontrollable and deeply concentrated; and while he spoke, his eyes shot fire, his voice trembled with excess of passion, and the light foam stood on his lip.

His confidant made a bold and successful effort to obtain the mastery of him even in this hour of emotion. 'My lord,' he said, leading him to a mirror, 'behold your reflection in that glass, and think if these agitated features belong to one who, in a condition so extreme, is capable of forming a resolution for himself.'

'What, then, wouldst thou make me?' said Leicester, struck at the change in his own physiognomy, though offended at the freedom with which Varney made the appeal. 'Am I to be thy ward, thy vassal,—the property and subject of my servant?'

'No, my lord,' said Varney, firmly, 'but be master of yourself, and of your own passion. My lord, I, your born servant, am ashamed to see how poorly you bear yourself in the storm of fury. Go to Elizabeth's feet, confess your marriage—impeach your wife and her paramour of adultery—and avow yourself, amongst all your peers, the wittol who married a country girl, and was cozened by her and her book-learned gallant. Go, my lord—but first take farewell of Richard Varney, with all the benefits you ever conferred on him. He served the noble, the lofty, the high-minded Leicester, and was more proud of depending on him, than he would be of commanding thousands. But the abject lord who stoops to every adverse circumstance, whose judicious resolves are scattered like chaff before every wind of passion, him Richard Varney serves not. He is as much above him in constancy of mind, as beneath him in rank and fortune.'

Varney spoke thus without hypocrisy, for, though the firmness of mind which he boasted was hardness and impenetrability, yet he really felt the ascendency which he vaunted; while the interest which he actually felt in the fortunes of Leicester, gave unusual emotion to his voice and manner.

Leicester was overpowered by his assumed superiority; it seemed to the unfortunate Earl as if his last friend was about to abandon him. He stretched his hand towards Varney, as he uttered the words, 'Do not leave me—What wouldst thou have me do?'

'Be thyself, my noble master,' said Varney, touching the Earl's hand with his lips, after having respectfully grasped it in his own; 'be yourself, superior to those storms of passion which wreck inferior minds. Are you the first who has been cozened in love? The first whom a vain and licentious woman has cheated into an affection, which she has afterwards scorned and misused? And will you suffer yourself to be driven frantic, because you have not been wiser than the wisest men whom the world has seen? Let her be as if she had not been—let her pass from your memory, as unworthy of ever having held a place there. Let your strong resolve of this morning, which I have both courage, zeal, and means enough to execute, be like the fiat of a superior being, a passionless act of justice. She hath deserved death—let her die!'

While he was speaking, the Earl held his hand fast, compressed his lips hard, and frowned, as if he laboured to catch from Varney a portion of the cold, ruthless, and dispassionate firmness which he recommended. When he was silent, the Earl still continued to grasp his hand, until, with an effort at calm decision, he was able to articulate, 'Be it so—she dies! But one tear might be permitted.'

'Not one, my lord,' interrupted Varney, who saw by the quivering eye and convulsed cheek of his patron, that he was about to give way to a burst of emotion,—'Not a tear—the time permits it not—Tressilian must be thought of——'

'That indeed is a name,' said the Earl, 'to convert tears into blood. Varney, I have thought on this, and I have determined—neither entreaty nor argument shall move me—Tressilian shall be my own victim.'

'It is madness, my lord; but you are too mighty for me to bar your way to your revenge. Yet resolve at least to choose fitting time and opportunity, and to forbear him until those shall be found.'

'Thou shalt order me in what thou wilt,' said Leicester, 'only thwart me not in this.'

'Then, my lord,' said Varney, 'I first request of you to lay aside the wild, suspected, and half-frenzied demeanour, which hath this day drawn the eyes of all the court upon you; and which, but for the Queen's partial indulgence, which she hath extended towards you in a degree far beyond her nature, she had never given you the opportunity to atone for.'

'Have I indeed been so negligent?' said Leicester, as one who awakes from a dream; 'I thought I had coloured it well; but fear nothing, my mind is now eased—I am calm. My horoscope shall be fulfilled; and that it may be fulfilled, I will tax to the highest every faculty of my mind. Fear me not, I say—I will to the Queen instantly—not thine own looks and language shall be more impenetrable than mine. Hast thou aught else to say?'

'I must crave your signet-ring,' said Varney gravely, 'in token to those of your servants whom I must employ, that I possess your full authority in commanding their aid.'

Leicester drew off the signet-ring which he commonly used, and gave it to Varney with a haggard and stern expression of countenance, adding only, in a low, half-whispered tone, but with terrific emphasis, the words, 'What thou doest, do quickly.'

Some anxiety and wonder took place, meanwhile, in the presence-hall, at the prolonged absence of the noble lord of the castle, and great was the delight of his friends, when they saw him enter as a man, from whose bosom, to all human seeming, a weight of care had been just removed. Amply did Leicester that day redeem the pledge he had given to Varney, who soon saw himself no longer under the necessity of maintaining a character so different from his own, as that which he had assumed in the earlier part of the day, and gradually relapsed into the same grave, shrewd, caustic, observer of conversation and incident, which constituted his usual part in society.

With Elizabeth, Leicester played his game as one to whom her natural strength of talent, and her weakness in one or two particular points, were well known. He was too wary to exchange on a sudden the sullen personage which he had played before he retired with Varney; but on approaching her, it seemed softened into a melancholy, which had a touch of tenderness in it, and which, in the course of conversing with Elizabeth, and as she dropped in compassion one mark of favour after another to console him, passed into a flow of affectionate gallantry, the most assiduous, the most delicate, the most insinuating, yet at the same time the most respectful, with which a Queen was ever addressed by a subject. Elizabeth listened, as in a sort of enchantment; her jealousy of power was lulled asleep; her resolution to forsake all social or domestic ties, and dedicate herself exclusively to the care of her people, began to be shaken, and once more the star of Dudley culminated in the court horizon.

But Leicester did not enjoy this triumph over nature, and over conscience, without its being embittered to him, not only by the internal rebellion of his feelings against the violence which he exercised over them, but by many accidental circumstances, which in the course of the banquet, and during the subsequent amusements of the evening, jarred upon that nerve, the least vibration of which was agony.

The courtiers were, for example, in the great hall, after having left the banqueting-room, awaiting the appearance of a splendid masque, which was the expected entertainment of this evening, when the Queen interrupted a wild career of wit, which the Earl of Leicester was running against Lord Willoughby, Raleigh, and some other courtiers, by saying—'We will impeach you of high treason, my lord, if you proceed in this attempt to slay us with laughter. And here comes a thing may make us all grave at his pleasure, our learned physician Masters, with news belike of our poor suppliant, Lady Varney—nay, my lord, we will not have you leave us, for this being a dispute betwixt married persons, we do not hold our own experience deep enough to decide thereon, without good counsel. How now, Masters, what think'st thou of the runaway bride?'

The smile with which Leicester had been speaking when the Queen interrupted him, remained arrested on his lips, as if it had been carved there by the chisel of Michael Angelo, or of Chantrey; and he listened to the speech of the physician with the same immovable cast of countenance.

'The Lady Varney, gracious Sovereign,' said Masters, 'is sullen, and would hold little conference with me touching the state of her health, talking wildly of being soon to plead her own cause before your own presence, and of answering no meaner person's inquiries.'

'Now, the heavens forfend!' said the Queen; 'we have already suffered from the misconstructions and broils which seem to follow this poor brain-sick lady wherever she comes. Think you not so, my lords?' she added, appealing to Leicester, with something in her look that indicated regret, even tenderly expressed, for their disagreement of that morning. Leicester compelled himself to bow low. The utmost force he could exert was inadequate to the further effort of expressing in words his acquiescence in the Queen's sentiment.

'You are vindictive,' she said, 'my lord; but we will find time and place to punish you. But once more to this same trouble-mirth, this Lady Varney—What of her health, Masters?'

'She is sullen, Madam, as I already said,' replied Masters, 'and refuses to answer interrogatories, or be amenable to the authority of the mediciner. I conceive her to be possessed with a delirium, which I incline to term rather *hypochondria* than *phrenesis;* and I think she were best cared for by her husband in his own house, and removed from all this bustle of pageants, which disturbs her weak brain with the most fantastic phantoms. She drops hints as if she were some great person in disguise—some Countess or Princess perchance. God help them, such are the hallucinations of these infirm persons.'

'Nay, then,' said the Queen, 'away with her with all speed. Let Varney care for her with fitting humanity; but let them rid the castle of her forthwith. She will think herself lady of all, I warrant you. It is pity so fair a form, however, should have an infirm understanding.—What think you, my lord?'

'It is pity indeed,' said the Earl, repeating the words like a task which was set him.

'But perhaps,' said Elizabeth, 'you do not join with us in our opinion of her beauty; and indeed we have known men prefer a statelier and more Juno-like form, to that drooping fragile one, that hung its head like a broken lily. Ay, men are tyrants, my lord, who esteem the animation of the strife above the triumph of an unresisting conquest, and, like sturdy champions, love best those women who can wage contest with them. I could think with you, Rutland, that give my Lord of Leicester such a piece of painted wax for a bride, he would have wished her dead ere the end of the honeymoon.'

As she said this, she looked on Leicester so expressively, that, while his heart revolted against the egregious falsehood, he did himself so much violence as to reply in a whisper, that Leicester's love was more lowly than her Majesty deemed, since it was settled where he could never command, but must ever obey.

The Queen blushed, and bid him be silent; yet looked as if she expected that he would not obey her commands. But at that moment the flourish of trumpets and kettledrums from a high balcony which overlooked the hall, announced the entrance of the masquers, and relieved Leicester from the horrible state of constraint and dissimulation in which the result of his own duplicity had placed him.

The masque which entered consisted of four separate bands,

which followed each other at brief intervals, each consisting of six principal persons and as many torch-bearers, and each representing one of the various nations by which England had at different times been occupied.

The aboriginal Britons, who first entered, were ushered in by two ancient Druids, whose hoary hair was crowned with a chaplet of oak, and who bore in their hands branches of mistletoe. The masquers who followed these venerable figures were succeeded by two bards, arrayed in white, and bearing harps, which they occasionally touched, singing at the same time certain stanzas of an ancient hymn to Belus, or the Sun. The aboriginal Britons had been selected from amongst the tallest and most robust young gentlemen in attendance on the court. Their masks were accommodated with long shaggy beards and hair; their vestments were of the hides of wolves and bears; while their legs, arms, and the upper parts of their bodies, being sheathed in flesh-coloured silk, on which were traced in grotesque lines representations of the heavenly bodies, and of animals and other terrestrial objects, gave them the lively appearance of our painted ancestors, whose freedom was first trenched upon by the Romans.

The sons of Rome, who came to civilise as well as to conquer, were next produced before the princely assembly; and the manager of the revels had correctly imitated the high crest and military habits of that celebrated people, accommodating them with the light yet strong buckler, and the short two-edged sword, the use of which had made them victors of the world. The Roman eagles were borne before them by two standard-bearers, who recited a hymn to Mars, and the classical warriors followed with the grave and haughty step of men who aspired at universal conquest.

The third quadrille represented the Saxons, clad in the bearskins which they had brought with them from the German forests, and bearing in their hands the redoubtable battle-axes which made such havoc among the natives of Britain. They were preceded by two Scalds, who chanted the praises of Odin.

Last came the knightly Normans, in their mail shirts and hoods of steel, with all the panoply of chivalry, and marshalled by two minstrels, who sung of war and ladies' love.

These four bands entered the spacious hall with the utmost order, a short pause being made, that the spectators might satisfy their curiosity as to each quadrille before the appearance of the next.

They then marched completely round the hall, in order the more fully to display themselves, regulating their steps to organs, shalms, hautboys, and virginals, the music of the Lord Leicester's household. At length the four quadrilles of masquers, ranging their torch-bearers behind them, drew up in their several ranks, on the two opposite sides of the hall, so that the Romans confronting the Britons, and the Saxons the Normans, seemed to look on each other with eyes of wonder, which presently appeared to kindle into anger, expressed by menacing gestures. At the burst of a strain of martial music from the gallery, the masquers drew their swords on all sides, and advanced against each other in the measured steps of a sort of Pyrrhic or military dance, clashing their swords against their adversaries' shields, and clattering them against their blades as they passed each other in the progress of the dance. It was a very pleasant spectacle to see how the various bands, preserving regularity amid motions which seemed to be totally irregular, mixed together, and then disengaging themselves, resumed each their own original rank as the music varied.

In this symbolical dance were presented the conflicts which had taken place among the various nations which had anciently inhabited Britain.

At length, after many mazy evolutions, which afforded great pleasure to the spectators, the sound of a loud-voiced trumpet was heard, as if it blew for instant battle, or for victory won. The masquers instantly ceased their mimic strife, and collecting themselves under their original leaders, or presenters, for such was the appropriate phrase, seemed to share the anxious expectation which the spectators experienced concerning what was next to appear.

The doors of the hall were thrown wide, and no less a person entered than the fiend-born Merlin, dressed in a strange and mystical attire, suited to his ambiguous birth and magical power. About him and behind him fluttered or gambolled many extraordinary forms, intended to represent the spirits who waited to do his powerful bidding; and so much did this part of the pageant interest the menials and others of the lower class then in the castle, that many of them forgot even the reverence due to the Queen's presence, so far as to thrust themselves into the lower part of the hall.

The Earl of Leicester, seeing his officers had some difficulty to repel these intruders, without more disturbance than was fitting where the Queen was in presence, arose and went himself to the bottom of the hall; Elizabeth at the same time, with her usual feeling for the common people, requesting that they might be permitted to remain undisturbed to witness the pageant. Leicester went under this pretext; but his real motive was to gain a moment to himself, and to relieve his mind, were it but for one instant, from the dreadful task of hiding, under the guise of gaiety and gallantry, the lacerating pangs of shame, anger, remorse, and thirst for vengeance. He imposed silence by his look and sign upon the vulgar crowd, at the lower end of the apartment; but, instead of instantly returning to wait on her Majesty, he wrapped his cloak around him, and mixing with the crowd, stood in some degree an undistinguished spectator of the progress of the masque.

Merlin having entered and advanced into the midst of the hall, summoned the presenters of the contending bands around him by a wave of his magical rod, and announced to them, in a poetical speech, that the isle of Britain was now commanded by a Royal Maiden, to whom it was the will of fate that they should all do homage, and request of her to pronounce on the various pretensions which each set forth to be esteemed the pre-eminent stock, from which the present natives, the happy subjects of that angelical Princess, derived their lineage.

In obedience to this mandate, the bands, each moving to solemn music, passed in succession before Elizabeth; doing her as they passed, each after the fashion of the people whom they represented, the lowest and most devotional homage, which she returned with the same gracious courtesy that had marked her whole conduct since she came to Kenilworth.

The presenters of the several masques, or quadrilles, then alleged, each in behalf of his own troop, the reasons which they had for claiming pre-eminence over the rest; and when they had been all heard in turn, she returned them this gracious answer: 'That she was sorry she was not better qualified to decide upon the doubtful question which had been propounded to her by the direction of the famous Merlin; but that it seemed to her that no single one of these celebrated nations could claim pre-eminence over the others, as having most contributed to form the Englishman of her own time, who unquestionably derived from each of them some worthy attribute of his character. 'Thus,' she said, 'the Englishman had from the ancient Briton his bold and tameless spirit of freedom, from the

Roman his disciplined courage in war, with his love of letters and civilisation in time of peace,—from the Saxon his wise and equitable laws,—and from the chivalrous Norman his love of honour and courtesy, with his generous desire for glory.'

Merlin answered with readiness, that it did indeed require that so many choice qualities should meet in the English, as might render them in some measure the muster of the perfections of other nations, since that alone could render them in some degree deserving of the blessings they enjoyed under the reign of England's Elizabeth.

The music then sounded, and the quadrilles, together with Merlin and his assistants, had begun to remove from the crowded hall, when Leicester, who was, as we have mentioned, stationed for the moment near the bottom of the hall, and consequently engaged in some degree in the crowd, felt himself pulled by the cloak, while a voice whispered in his ear, 'My lord, I do desire some instant conference with you.'

38

How is't with me, when every noise appals me?—*Macbeth*.

'I DESIRE some conference with you.' The words were simple in themselves, but Lord Leicester was in that alarmed and feverish state of mind, when the most ordinary occurrences seem fraught with alarming import; and he turned hastily round to survey the person by whom they had been spoken. There was nothing remarkable in the speaker's appearance, which consisted of a black silk doublet and short mantle with a black vizard on his face; for it appeared he had been among the crowd of masks who had thronged into the hall in the retinue of Merlin, though he did not wear any of the extravagant disguises by which most of them were distinguished.

'Who are you, and what do you want with me?' said Leicester not without betraying, by his accents, the hurried state of his spirits.

'No evil, my lord,' answered the mask, 'but much good and honour, if you will rightly understand my purpose. But I must speak with you more privately.'

'I can speak with no nameless stranger,' answered Leicester, dreading he knew not precisely what from the request of the unknown; 'and those who are known to me must seek another and a fitter time to ask an interview.'

He would have hurried away, but the mask still detained him.

'Those who talk to your lordship of what your own honour demands, have a right over your time, whatever occupations you may lay aside in order to indulge them.'

'How! my honour? Who dare impeach it?' said Leicester.

'Your own conduct alone can furnish grounds for accusing it, my lord, and it is that topic on which I would speak with you.'

'You are insolent,' said Leicester, 'and abuse the hospitable licence of the time, which prevents me from having you punished. I demand your name!'

'Edmund Tressilian of Cornwall,' answered the mask. 'My tongue has been bound by a promise for four-and-twenty hours,—the space is passed,—I now speak, and do your lordship the justice to address myself first to you.'

The thrill of astonishment which had penetrated to Leicester's very heart at hearing that name pronounced by the voice of the man he most detested, and by whom he conceived himself so deeply injured, at first rendered him immovable, but instantly gave way to such a thirst for revenge as the pilgrim in the desert feels for the water-brooks. He had but sense and self-government enough left to prevent his stabbing to the heart the audacious villain, who, after the ruin he had brought upon him, dared, with such unmoved assurance, thus to practise upon him further. Determined to suppress for the moment every symptom of agitation, in order to perceive the full scope of Tressilian's purpose, as well as to secure his own vengeance, he answered in a tone so altered by restrained passion as scarce to be intelligible,—'And what does Master Edmund Tressilian require at my hand?'

'Justice, my lord,' answered Tressilian, calmly but firmly.

'Justice,' said Leicester, 'all men are entitled to—You, Master Tressilian, are peculiarly so, and be assured you shall have it.'

'I expect nothing less from your nobleness,' answered Tressilian; 'but time presses, and I must speak with you to-night—May I wait on you in your chamber?'

'No,' answered Leicester sternly, 'not under a roof, and that roof mine own—We will meet under the free cope of heaven.'

'You are discomposed or displeased, my lord,' replied Tressilian; 'yet there is no occasion for distemperature. The place is equal to me, so you allow me one half-hour of your time uninterrupted.'

'A shorter time will, I trust, suffice,' answered Leicester—'Meet me in the Pleasance, when the Queen has retired to her chamber.'

'Enough,' said Tressilian, and withdrew; while a sort of rapture seemed for the moment to occupy the mind of Leicester.

'Heaven,' he said, 'is at last favourable to me, and has put within my reach the wretch who has branded me with this deep ignominy —who has inflicted on me this cruel agony. I will blame fate no more, since I am afforded the means of tracing the wiles by which he means still further to practise on me, and then of at once convicting and punishing his villainy. To my task—to my task! I will not sink under it now, since midnight, at furthest, will bring me vengeance.'

While these reflections thronged through Leicester's mind, he again made his way amid the obsequious crowd which divided to give him passage, and resumed his place, envied and admired, beside the person of his Sovereign. But, could the bosom of him thus admired and envied, have been laid open before the inhabitants of that crowded hall, with all its dark thoughts of guilty ambition, blighted affection, deep vengeance, and conscious sense of meditated cruelty, crossing each other like spectres in the circle of some foul enchantress,—which of them, from the most ambitious noble in the courtly circle, down to the most wretched menial who lived by shifting of trenchers, would have desired to change characters with the favourite of Elizabeth and the Lord of Kenilworth!

New tortures awaited him as soon as he had rejoined Elizabeth.

'You come in time, my lord,' she said, 'to decide a dispute between us ladies. Here has Sir Richard Varney asked our permission to depart from the castle with his infirm lady, having, as he tells us, your lordship's consent to his absence, so he can obtain ours. Certes, we have no will to withhold him from the affectionate charge of this poor young person—but you are to know, that Sir Richard Varney hath this day shown himself so much captivated with these ladies of ours, that here is our Duchess of Rutland says, he will carry his poor insane wife no farther than the lake, plunge her in, to tenant the crystal palaces that the enchanted nymph told us of and return a jolly widower, to dry his tears, and to make up the loss among our train. How say you, my lord? We have seen Varney under two or three different guises—you know what are his proper attributes—think you he is capable of playing his lady such a knave's trick?'

Leicester was confounded, but the danger was urgent, and a reply absolutely necessary. 'The ladies,' he said, 'think too lightly of one of their own sex, in supposing she could deserve such a fate, or too ill of ours, to think it could be inflicted upon an innocent female.'

'Hear him, my ladies,' said Elizabeth; 'like all his sex, he would excuse their cruelty by imputing fickleness to us.'

'Say not *us*, Madam,' replied the Earl; 'we say that meaner women, like the lesser lights of heaven, have revolutions and phases, but who shall impute mutability to the sun, or to Elizabeth?'

The discourse presently afterwards assumed a less perilous tendency, and Leicester continued to support his part in it with spirit, at whatever expense of mental agony. So pleasing did it seem to Elizabeth, that the castle bell had sounded midnight ere she retired from the company, a circumstance unusual in her quiet and regular habits of disposing of time. Her departure was of course the signal for breaking up the company, who dispersed to their several places of repose, to dream over the pastimes of the day, or to anticipate those of the morrow.

The unfortunate lord of the castle, and founder of the proud festival, retired to far different thoughts. His direction to the valet who attended him, was to send Varney instantly to his apartment. The messenger returned after some delay, and informed him that an hour had elapsed since Sir Richard Varney had left the castle by the postern gate, with three other persons, one of whom was transported in a horse-litter.

'How came he to leave the castle after the watch was set?' said Leicester; 'I thought he went not till daybreak.'

'He gave satisfactory reasons, as I understand,' said the domestic, 'to the guard, and as I hear, showed your lordship's signet——'

'True—true,' said the Earl; 'yet he has been hasty—Do any of his attendants remain behind?'

'Michael Lambourne, my lord,' said the valet, 'was not to be found when Sir Richard Varney departed, and his master was much incensed at his absence. I saw him but now saddling his horse to gallop after his master.'

'Bid him come hither instantly,' said Leicester; 'I have a message to his master.'

The servant left the apartment, and Leicester traversed it for some time in deep meditation—'Varney is over zealous,' he said, 'over pressing—He loves me, I think—but he hath his own ends to serve, and he is inexorable in pursuit of them. If I rise he rises, and he hath shown himself already but too eager to rid me of this obstacle which seems to stand betwixt me and sovereignty. Yet I will not stoop to bear this disgrace. She shall be punished, but it shall be more advisedly. I already feel, even in anticipation, that over-haste would light the flames of hell in my bosom. No—one victim is enough at once, and that victim already waits me.'

He seized upon writing materials, and hastily traced these words:—

'Sir Richard Varney, we have resolved to defer the matter entrusted to your care, and strictly command you to proceed no further in relation to our Countess, until our further order. We also command your instant return to Kenilworth, as soon as you have safely bestowed that with which you are entrusted. But if the safe-placing of your present charge shall detain you longer than we think for, we command you, in that case, to send back our signet-ring by a trusty and speedy messenger, we having present need of the same. And requiring your strict obedience in these things, and commending you to God's keeping, we rest your assured good friend and master,

'R. LEICESTER.

'Given at our Castle of Kenilworth, the tenth of July, in the year of Salvation one thousand five hundred and seventy-five.'

As Leicester had finished and sealed this mandate, Michael Lambourne, booted up to mid-thigh, having his riding cloak girthed around him with a broad belt, and a felt cap on his head, like that of a courier, entered his apartment, ushered in by the valet.

'What is thy capacity of service?' said the Earl.

'Equerry to your lordship's master of the horse,' answered Lambourne, with his customary assurance.

'Tie up thy saucy tongue, sir,' said Leicester; 'the jests that may suit Sir Richard Varney's presence, suit not mine. How soon will thou overtake thy master?'

'In one hour's riding, my lord, if man and horse hold good,' said Lambourne, with an instant alteration of demeanour, from an approach to familiarity to the deepest respect. The Earl measured him with his eye from top to toe.

'I have heard of thee,' he said; 'men say thou art a prompt fellow in thy service, but too much given to brawling and to wassail to be trusted with things of moment.'

'My lord,' said Lambourne, 'I have been soldier, sailor, traveller, and adventurer; and these are all trades in which men enjoy to-day, because they have no surety of to-morrow. But though I may misuse mine own leisure, I have never neglected the duty I owe my master.'

'See that it be so in this instance,' said Leicester, 'and it shall do thee good. Deliver this letter speedily and carefully into Sir Richard Varney's hands.'

'Does my commission reach no further?' said Lambourne.

'No,' answered Leicester; 'but it deeply concerns me that it be carefully as well as hastily executed.'

'I will spare neither care nor horse-flesh,' answered Lambourne, and immediately took his leave.

'So, this is the end of my private audience, from which I hoped so much,' he muttered to himsèlf, as he went through the long

430

gallery and down the back staircase. 'Cogs bones! I thought the Earl had wanted a cast of mine office in some secret intrigue, and it all ends in carrying a letter! Well, his pleasure shall be done, however, and as his lordship well says, it may do me good another time. The child must creep ere he walk, and so must your infant courtier. I will have a look into this letter, however, which he hath sealed so sloven-like.'—Having accomplished this, he clapped his hands together in ecstasy, exclaiming 'The Countess—the Countess!—I have the secret that shall make or mar me. But come forth, Bayard,' he added, leading his horse into the courtyard, 'for your flanks and my spur must be presently acquainted.'

Lambourne mounted accordingly, and left the castle by the postern-gate, where his free passage was permitted, in consequence of a message to that effect left by Sir Richard Varney.

As soon as Lambourne and the valet had left the apartment, Leicester proceeded to change his dress for a very plain one, threw his mantle around him, and taking a lamp in his hand, went by the private passage of communication to a small secret postern-door which opened into the courtyard, near to the entrance of the Pleasance. His reflections were of a more calm and determined character than they had been at any late period, and he endeavoured to claim, even in his own eyes, the character of a man more sinned against than sinning.

'I have suffered the deepest injury,' such was the tenor of his meditations, 'yet I have restricted the instant revenge which was in my power, and have limited it to that which is manly and noble. But shall the union which this false woman has this day disgraced, remain an abiding fetter on me, to check me in the noble career to which my destinies invite me? No—there are other means of disengaging such ties, without unloosing the cords of life. In the sight of God, I am no longer bound by the union she has broken. Kingdoms shall divide us—oceans roll betwixt us, and their waves, whose abysses have swallowed whole navies, shall be the so'e depositories of the deadly mystery.'

By such a train of argument did Leicester labour to reconcile his conscience to the prosecution of plans of vengeance, so hastily adopted, and of schemes of ambition, which had become so woven in with every purpose and action of his life, that he was incapable of the effort of relinquishing them; until his vengeance appeared to him to wear a face of justice, and even of generous moderation.

In this mood, the vindictive and ambitious Earl entered the superb precincts of the Pleasance, then illuminated by the full moon. The broad yellow light was reflected on all sides from the white freestone, of which the pavement, balustrades, and architectural ornaments of the place were constructed; and not a single fleecy cloud was visible in the azure sky, so that the scene was nearly as light as if the sun had but just left the horizon. The numerous statues of white marble glimmered in the pale light, like so many sheeted ghosts just arisen from their sepulchres, and the fountains threw their jets into the air, as if they sought that their waters should be brightened by the moonbeams, ere they fell down again upon their basins in showers of sparkling silver. The day had been sultry, and the gentle night-breeze, which sighed along the terrace of the Pleasance, raised not deeper breath than the fan in the hand of youthful beauty. The bird of summer night had built many a nest in the bowers of the adjacent garden, and the tenants now indemnified themselves for silence during the day, by a full chorus of their own unrivalled warblings, now joyous, now pathetic, now united, now responsive to each other, as if to express their delight in the placid and delicious scene to which they poured their melody.

Musing on matters far different from the fall of waters, the gleam of moonlight, or the song of the nightingale, the stately Leicester walked slowly from the one end of the terrace to the other, his cloak wrapped around him, and his sword under his arm, without seeing anything resembling the human form.

'I have been fooled by my own generosity,' he said, 'if I have suffered the villain to escape me—ay, and perhaps to go to the rescue of the adulteress, who is so poorly guarded.'

These were his thoughts, which were instantly dispelled when, turning to look back towards the entrance, he saw a human form advancing slowly from the portico, and darkening the various objects with its shadow, as passing them successively, in its approach towards him.

'Shall I strike ere I again hear his detested voice?' was Leicester's thought, as he grasped the hilt of his sword. 'But no! I will see which way his vile practice tends. I will watch, disgusting as it is, the coils and mazes of the loathsome snake, ere I put forth my strength and crush him.' His hand quitted the sword-hilt, and he advanced slowly towards Tressilian, collecting, for their meeting, all the self-possession he could command, until they came front to front with each other.

Tressilian made a profound reverence, to which the Earl replied with a haughty inclination of the head, and the words, 'You sought secret conference with me, sir—I am here, and attentive.'

'My lord,' said Tressilian, 'I am so earnest in that which I have to say, and so desirous to find a patient, nay, a favourable, hearing, that I will stoop to exculpate myself from whatever might prejudice your lordship against me. You think me your enemy?'

'Have I not some apparent cause?' answered Leicester, perceiving that Tressilian paused for a reply.

'You do me wrong, my lord. I am a friend, but neither a dependant not partisan of the Earl of Sussex, whom courtiers call your rival; and it is some considerable time since I ceased to consider either courts, or court-intrigues, as suited to my temper or genius.'

'No doubt, sir,' answered Leicester; 'there are other occupations more worthy a scholar, and for such the world holds Master Tressilian—Love has his intrigues as well as ambition.'

'I perceive, my lord,' replied Tressilian, 'you give much weight to my early attachment for the unfortunate young person of whom I am about to speak, and perhaps think I am prosecuting her cause out of rivalry, more than a sense of justice.'

'No matter for my thoughts, sir,' said the Earl; 'proceed. You have as yet spoken of yourself only; an important and worthy subject doubtless, but which, perhaps, does not altogether so deeply concern me, that I should postpone my repose to hear it. Spare me further prelude, sir, and speak to the purpose, if indeed you have aught to say that concerns me. When you have done, I, in my turn, have something to communicate.'

'I will speak, then, without further prelude, my lord,' answered Tressilian; 'having to say that which, as it concerns your lordship's honour, I am confident you will not think your time wasted in listening to. I have to request an account from your lordship of the unhappy Amy Robsart, whose history is too well known to you. I regret deeply that I did not at once take this course, and make yourself judge between me and the villain by whom she is injured. My lord, she extricated herself from an unlawful and most perilous state of confinement, trusting to the effects of her own remonstrance upon her unworthy husband, and extorted from me a promise, that I would not interfere in her behalf until she had used her own efforts to have her rights acknowledged by him.'

'Ha!' said Leicester, 'remember you to whom you speak?'

'I speak of her unworthy husband, my lord,' repeated Tressilian, 'and my respect can find no softer language. The unhappy young woman is withdrawn from my knowledge, and sequestered in some secret place of this castle—if she be not transferred to some place of seclusion better fitted for bad designs. This must be reformed, my lord,—I speak it as authorised by her father,—and this ill-fated marriage must be avouched and proved in the Queen's presence, and the lady placed without restraint, and at her own free disposal. And, permit me to say, it concerns no one's honour that these most just demands of mine should be complied with, so much as it does that of your lordship.'

The Earl stood as if he had been petrified, at the extreme coolness with which the man, whom he considered as having injured him so deeply, pleaded the cause of his criminal paramour, as if she had been an innocent woman, and he a disinterested advocate; nor was his wonder lessened by the warmth with which Tressilian seemed to demand for her the rank and situation which she had disgraced, and the advantages of which she was doubtless to share with the lover who advocated her cause with such effrontery. Tressilian had been silent for more than a minute ere the Earl recovered from the excess of his astonishment; and, considering the prepossessions with which his mind was occupied, there is little wonder that his passion gained the mastery of every other consideration. 'I have heard you, Master Tressilian,' said he, 'without interruption, and I bless God that my ears were never before made to tingle by the words of so frontless a villain. The task of chastising you is fitter for the hangman's scourge than the sword of a nobleman, but yet—— Villain, draw and defend thyself!'

As he spoke the last words, he dropped his mantle on the ground, struck Tressilian smartly with his sheathed sword, and instantly drawing his rapier, put himself into a posture of assault. The vehement fury of his language at first filled Tressilian, in his turn, with surprise equal to what Leicester had felt when he addressed him. But astonishment gave rise to resentment, when the unmerited insults of his language were followed by a blow, which immediately put to flight every thought save that of instant combat. Tressilian's sword was instantly drawn, and though perhaps somewhat inferior to Leicester in the use of the weapon, he understood it well enough to maintain the contest with great spirit, the rather that of the two he was for the time the more cool, since he could not help imputing Leicester's conduct either to actual frenzy, or to the influence of some strong delusion .

The rencontre had continued for several minutes, without either party receiving a wound, when of a sudden voices were heard beneath the portico, which formed the entrance of the terrace, mingled with the steps of men advancing hastily. 'We are interrupted,' said Leicester to his antagonist; 'follow me.'

At the same time a voice from the portico said , 'The jackanapes is right—they are tilting here.'

Leicester, meanwhile, drew off Tressilian into a sort of recess behind one of the fountains, which served to conceal them, while six of the Yeomen of the Queen's Guard passed along the middle walk of the Pleasance, and they could hear one say to the rest, 'We will never find them to-night amongst all these squirting funnels, squirrel cages, and rabbit-holes; but if we light not on them before we reach the farther end, we will return, and mount a guard at the entrance, and so secure them till morning.'

'A proper matter,' said another, 'the drawing of swords so near the Queen's presence, ay, and in her very Palace as 'twere!—Hang it, they must be some poor drunken game-cocks fallen to sparring —'twere pity almost we should find them—the penalty is chopping off a hand, is it not?—'twere hard to lose hand for handling a bit of steel, that comes so natural to one's grip.'

'Thou art a brawler thyself, George,' said another; 'but take heed, for the law stands as thou sayest.'

'Ay,' said the first, 'an the act be not mildly construed; for thou know'st 'tis not the Queen's Palace, but my Lord of Leicester's.'

'Why, for that matter, the penalty may be as severe,' said another; 'for an our gracious Mistress be Queen, as she is, God save her, my Lord of Leicester is as good as King.'

'Hush! thou knave!' said a third; 'how know'st thou who may be within hearing?'

They passed on, making a kind of careless search, but seemingly more intent on their own conversation than bent on discovering the persons who had created the nocturnal disturbance.

They had no sooner passed forward along the terrace, than Leicester, making a sign to Tressilian to follow him, glided away

in an opposite direction, and escaped through the portico un-
discovered. He conducted Tressilian to Mervyn's Tower, in which
he was now again lodged; and then, ere parting with him, said
these words. 'If thou hast courage to continue and bring to an end
what is thus broken off, be near me when the court goes forth to-
morrow—we shall find a time, and I will give you a signal when it
is fitting.'

'My lord,' said Tressilian, 'at another time I might have inquired
the meaning of this strange and furious inveteracy against me. But
you have laid that on my shoulder, which only blood can wash
away; and were you as high as your proudest wishes ever carried
you, I would have from you satisfaction for my wounded honour.'

On these terms they parted, but the adventures of the night were
not yet ended with Leicester. He was compelled to pass by Saintlowe's Tower, in order to gain the private passage which led to his
own chamber, and in the entrance thereof he met Lord Hunsdon
half-clothed, and with a naked sword under his arm.

'Are you awakened, too, with this 'larm, my Lord of Leicester?'
said the old soldier. ''Tis well—By gog's nails the nights are as noisy
as the day in this castle of yours. Some two hours since, I was waked
by the screams of that poor brain-sick Lady Varney, whom her
husband was forcing away. I promise you, it required both your
warrant and the Queen's to keep me from entering into the game,
and cutting that Varney of yours over the head; and now there is
a brawl down in the Pleasance, or what call you the stone terrace
walk, where all yonder gimcracks stand?'

The first part of the old man's speech went through the Earl's
heart like a knife; to the last he answered that he himself had heard
the clash of swords, and had come down to take order with those
who had been so insolent so near the Queen's presence.

'Nay then,' said Hunsdon, 'I will be glad of your lordship's
company.'

Leicester was thus compelled to turn back with the rough old
lord to the Pleasance, where Hunsdon heard from the Yeomen of
the Guard, who were under his immediate command, the un-
successful search they had made for the authors of the disturbance;
and bestowed for their pains some round dozen of curses on them,
as lazy knaves and blind whoresons. Leicester also thought it
necessary to seem angry that no discovery had been effected; but
at length suggested to Lord Hunsdon, that after all it could only be

some foolish young men, who had been drinking healths pottle-deep, and who would be sufficiently scared by the search which had taken place after them. Hunsdon, who was himself attached to his cup, allowed that a pint-flagon might cover many of the follies which it had caused. 'But,' added he, 'unless your lordship will be less liberal in your housekeeping, and restrain the overflow of ale, and wine, and wassail, I foresee it will end in my having some of these good fellows into the guard-house, and treating them to a dose of the strappado—And with this warning, good-night to you.'

Joyful at being rid of his company, Leicester took leave of him at the entrance of his lodging, where they had first met, and entering the private passage, took up the lamp which he had left there, and by its expiring light found the way to his own apartment.

39

Room! room! for my horse will wince
If he come within so many yards of a prince; . . .
For to tell you true, and in rhyme,
He was foal'd in Queen Elizabeth's time;
When the great Earl of Lester
In his castle did feast her.—'*Masque of Owls*'—*Ben Jonson.*

THE amusement with which Elizabeth and her court were next day to be regaled, was an exhibition by the true-hearted men of Coventry, who were to represent the strife between the English and the Danes, agreeably to a custom long preserved in their ancient borough, and warranted for truth by old histories and chronicles. In this pageant, one party of the town's folks presented the Saxons and the other the Danes, and set forth, both in rude rhymes and with hard blows, the contentions of these two fierce nations, and the Amazonian courage of the English women, who, according to the story, were the principal agents in the general massacre of the Danes, which took place at Hocktide, in the year of God 1012. This sport, which had been long a favourite pastime with the men of Coventry, had, it seems, been put down by the influence of some zealous clergymen, of the more precise cast, who chanced to have considerable influence with the magistrates. But the generality of the inhabitants had petitioned the Queen that they might have their play again, and be honoured with permission to represent it before her Highness. And when the matter was canvassed in the little council, which usually attended the Queen for despatch of business, the proposal, although opposed by some of the stricter sort, found favour in the eyes of Elizabeth, who said that such toys occupied, without offence, the minds of many, who, lacking them, might find worse subjects of pastime; and that their pastors, however commendable for learning and godliness, were somewhat too sour in preaching against the pastimes of their flocks, and so the pageant was permitted to proceed.

Accordingly, after a morning repast, which Master Laneham calls an ambrosial breakfast, the principal persons of the court, in attendance upon her Majesty, pressed to the Gallery Tower, to witness the approach of the two contending parties of English and Danes; and after a signal had been given, the gate which opened in the circuit of the Chase was thrown wide, to admit them. On they came, foot and horse; for some of the more ambitious burghers and yeomen had put themselves into fantastic dresses, imitating knights, in order to resemble the chivalry of the two different nations. However, to prevent fatal accidents, they were not permitted to appear on real horses, but had only licence to accoutre themselves with those hobby-horses, as they are called, which anciently formed the chief delight of a morrice-dance, and which still are exhibited on the stage, in the grand battle fought at the conclusion of Mr Baye's tragedy. The infantry followed in similar disguises. The whole exhibition was to be considered as a sort of anti-masque, or burlesque of the more stately pageants, in which the nobility and gentry bore part in the show, and, to the best of their knowledge, imitated with accuracy the personages whom they represented. The Hocktide play was of a different character, the actors being persons of inferior degree, and their habits the better fitted for the occasion, the more incongruous and ridiculous that they were in themselves. Accordingly their array, which the progress of our tale allows us no time to describe, was ludicrous enough, and their weapons, though sufficiently formidable to deal sound blows, were long alder-poles instead of lances, and sound cudgels for swords; and for fence, both cavalry and infantry were well equipped with stout headpieces, and targets of thick leather.

Captain Coxe, that celebrated humorist of Coventry, whose library of ballads, almanacs, and penny histories, fairly wrapped up in parchment, and tied round for security with a piece of whipcord, remains still the envy of antiquaries, being himself the ingenious person under whose direction the pageant had been set forth, rode valiantly on his hobby-horse before the bands of English, high-trussed, saith Laneham, and brandishing his long sword, as became an experienced man of war, who had fought under the Queen's father, bluff King Henry, at the siege of Boulogne. This chieftain was, as right and reason craved, the first to enter the lists, and, passing the Gallery at the head of his myrmidons, kissed the hilt of his sword to the Queen, and executed at the same time a gambade, the like whereof had never been practised by two-legged hobby-horse. Then passing on with all his followers of cavaliers and infantry, he drew them up with martial skill at the opposite extremity of the bridge, or tilt-yard, until his antagonists should be fairly prepared for the onset.

This was no long interval; for the Danish cavalry and infantry, no way inferior to the English in number, valour, and equipment, instantly arrived, with the northern bagpipe blowing before them in token of their country, and headed by a cunning master of defence, only inferior to the renowned Captain Coxe, if to him, in the discipline of war. The Danes, as invaders, took their station under the Gallery Tower, and opposite to that of Mortimer; and, when their arrangements were completely made, a signal was given for the encounter.

This first charge upon each other was rather moderate, for either party had some dread of being forced into the lake. But as reinforcements came up on either side, the encounter grew from a skirmish into a blazing battle. They rushed upon one another, as Master Laneham testifies, like rams inflamed by jealousy, with such furious encounter, that both parties were often overthrown, and the clubs and targets made a most horrible clatter. In many instances, that happened which had been dreaded by the more experienced warriors, who began the day of strife. The rails which defended the ledges of the bridge, had been, perhaps of purpose, left but slightly fastened and gave way under the pressure of those who thronged to the combat; so that the hot courage of many of the combatants received a sufficient cooling. These incidents might have occasioned more serious damage than became such an affray, for many of the champions who met with this mischance could not swim, and those who could were encumbered with their suits of leathern and of paper armour; but the case had been provided for, and there were several boats in readiness to pick up the unfortunate warriors, and convey them to the dry land, where, dripping and dejected, they comforted themselves with the hot ale and strong waters which were liberally allowed to them, without showing any desire to re-enter so desperate a conflict.

Captain Coxe alone, that paragon of Black-letter Antiquaries, after twice experiencing, horse and man, the perilous leap from the bridge into the lake, equal to any extremity to which the favourite heroes of chivalry, whose exploits he studied in an abridged form, whether Amadis, Belianis, Bevis, or his own Guy of Warwick, had ever been subjected to—Captain Coxe, we repeat, did alone, after two such mischances, rush again into the heat of conflict, his bases and the footcloth of his hobby-horse dropping water, and twice reanimated by voice and example the drooping spirits of the English, so that at length their victory over the Danish invaders became, as was just and reasonable, complete and decisive. Worthy he was to be rendered immortal by the pen of Ben Jonson, who, fifty years afterwards, deemed that a masque, exhibited at Kenilworth, could be ushered in by none with so much propriety, as by the ghost of Captain Coxe, mounted upon his redoubted hobby-horse.

These rough, rural gambols may not altogether agree with the reader's preconceived idea of an entertainment presented before Elizabeth, in whose reign letters revived with such brilliancy, and whose court, governed by a female whose sense of propriety was equal to her strength of mind, was no less distinguished for delicacy and refinement, than her counsels for wisdom and fortitude. But whether from the political wish to seem interested in popular sports, or whether from a spark of old Henry's rough masculine spirit, which Elizabeth sometimes displayed, it is certain the Queen laughed heartily at the imitation, or rather burlesque of chivalry, which was presented in the Coventry play. She called near her person the Earl of Sussex and Lord Hunsdon, partly perhaps to make amends to the former for the long and private audiences with which she had indulged the Earl of Leicester, by engaging him in conversation upon a pastime which better suited his taste than those pageants that were furnished forth from the stores of antiquity. The disposition which the Queen showed to laugh and jest with her military leaders, gave the Earl of Leicester the opportunity he had been watching for withdrawing from the royal presence, which to the court around, so well had he chosen his time, had the graceful appearance of leaving his rival free access to the Queen's person, instead of availing himself of his right as her landlord, to stand perpetually betwixt others and the light of her countenance.

Leicester's thoughts, however, had a far different object from mere courtesy; for no sooner did he see the Queen fairly engaged in conversation with Sussex and Hunsdon, behind whose back stood Sir Nicholas Blount, grinning from ear to ear at each word which was spoken, than, making a sign to Tressilian, who, according to appointment, watched his motions at a little distance, he extricated himself from the press, and walking towards the Chase, made his way through the crowds of ordinary spectators, who, with open mouth, stood gazing on the battle of the English and the

Danes. When he had accomplished this, which was a work of some difficulty, he shot another glance behind him to see that Tressilian had been equally successful and as soon as he saw him also free from the crowd, he led the way to a small thicket, behind which stood a lackey, with two horses ready saddled. He flung himself on the one, and made signs to Tressilian to mount the other, who obeyed without speaking a single word.

Leicester then spurred his horse, and galloped without stopping until he reached a sequestered spot, environed by lofty oaks, about a mile's distance from the castle, and in an opposite direction from the scene to which curiosity was drawing every spectator. He there dismounted, bound his horse to a tree, and only pronouncing the words, 'Here there is no risk of interruption,' laid his cloak across his saddle, and drew his sword.

Tressilian imitated his example punctually, yet could not forbear saying, as he drew his weapon, 'My lord, as I have been known to many as one who does not fear death, when placed in balance with honour, methinks I may, without derogation, ask, wherefore, in the name of all that is honourable, your lordship has dared to offer me such a mark of disgrace, as places us on these terms with respect to each other?'

'If you like not such marks of my scorn,' replied the Earl, 'betake yourself instantly to your weapon, lest I repeat the usage you complain of.'

'It shall not need, my lord,' said Tressilian. 'God judge betwixt us! and your blood, if you fall, be on your own head.'

He had scarce completed the sentence when they instantly closed in combat.

But Leicester, who was a perfect master of defence among all other exterior accomplishments of the time, had seen, on the preceding night, enough of Tressilian's strength and skill, to make him fight with more caution than therefore, and prefer a secure revenge to a hasty one. For some minutes they fought with equal skill and fortune, till, in a desperate lunge which Leicester successfully put aside, Tressilian exposed himself at disadvantage; and, in a subsequent attempt to close, the Earl forced his sword from his hand, and stretched him on the ground. With a grim smile he held the point of his rapier within two inches of the throat of his fallen adversary, and placing his foot at the same time upon his breast, bid him confess his villainous wrongs towards him, and prepare for death.

'I have no villainy nor wrong towards thee to confess,' answered Tressilian, 'and am better prepared for death than thou. Use thine advantage as thou wilt, and may God forgive you. I have given you no cause for this.'

'No cause!' exclaimed the Earl, 'no cause!—but why parley with such a slave?—Die a liar, as thou hast lived!'

He had withdrawn his arm for the purpose of striking the fatal blow, when it was suddenly seized from behind.

The Earl turned in wrath to shake off the unexpected obstacle, but was surprised to find that a strange-looking boy had hold of his sword-arm, and clung to it with such tenacity of grasp, that he could not shake him off without a considerable struggle; in the course of which, Tressilian had opportunity to rise and possess himself once more of his weapon. Leicester again turned towards him with looks of unabated ferocity, and the combat would have recommenced with still more desperation on both parts, had not the boy clung to Lord Leicester's knees, and in a shrill tone implored him to listen one moment ere he prosecuted this quarrel.

'Stand up, and let me go,' said Leicester, 'or by Heaven, I will pierce thee with my rapier! What hast thou to do to bar my way to revenge?'

'Much—much!' exclaimed the undaunted boy; 'since my folly has been the cause of these bloody quarrels between you, and perchance of worse evils. Oh, if you would ever again enjoy the peace of an innocent mind, if you hope again to sleep in peace and unhaunted by remorse, take so much leisure as to peruse this letter, and then do as you list.'

While he spoke in this eager and earnest manner, to which his singular features and voice gave a goblin-like effect, he held up to Leicester a packet, secured with a long tress of woman's hair, of a beautiful light-brown colour. Enraged as he was, nay, almost blinded with fury to see his destined revenge so strangely frustrated, the Earl of Leicester could not resist this extraordinary supplicant. He snatched the letter from his hand—changed colour as he looked on the superscription—undid, with faltering hand, the knot which secured it—glanced over the contents, and staggering back, would have fallen, had he not rested against the trunk of a tree, where he stood for an instant, his eyes bent on the letter, and his sword-point turned to the ground, without seeming to be conscious of the presence of an antagonist, towards whom he had shown little mercy, and who might in turn have taken him at advantage. But for such revenge Tressilian was too noble-minded—he also stood still in surprise, waiting the issue of this strange fit of passion, but holding his weapon ready to defend himself in case of need, against some new and sudden attack on the part of Leicester, whom he began to suspect to be under the influence of actual frenzy. The boy, indeed, he easily recognised as his old acquaintance Dickon, whose face, once seen, was scarcely to be forgotten; but how he came hither at so critical a moment, why his interference was so energetic, and, above all, how it came to produce so powerful an effect upon Leicester, were questions which he could not solve.

But the letter was of itself powerful enough to work effects yet more wonderful. It was that which the unfortunate Amy had written to her husband, in which she alleged the reasons and manner of her flight from Cumnor Place, informed him of her having taken refuge at Kenilworth to enjoy his protection, and mentioned the circumstances which had compelled her to take refuge in Tressilian's apartment, earnestly requesting he would, without delay, assign her a more suitable asylum. The letter concluded with the most earnest expressions of devoted attachment, and submission to his will in all things, and particularly respecting her situation and place of residence, conjuring him only that she might not be placed under the guardianship or restraint of Varney.

The letter dropped from Leicester's hand when he had perused it. 'Take my sword,' he said, 'Tressilian, and pierce my heart, as I would but now have pierced yours!'

'My lord,' said Tressilian, 'you have done me great wrong; but something within my breast ever whispered that it was by egregious error.'

'Error, indeed!' said Leicester, and handed him the letter; 'I have been made to believe a man of honour a villain, and the best and purest of creatures a false profligate: Wretched boy, why comes this letter now, and where has the bearer lingered?'

'I dare not tell you, my lord,' said the boy, withdrawing, as if to keep beyond his reach; 'but here comes one who was the messenger.'

Wayland at the same moment came up; and, interrogated by Leicester, hastily detailed all the circumstances of his escape with Amy,—the fatal practices which had driven her to flight,—and her anxious desire to throw herself under the instant protection of her husband, pointing out the evidence of the domestics of Kenilworth,

444

'who could not,' he observed, 'but remember her eager inquiries after the Earl of Leicester on her first arrival.'

'The villains!' ecxlaimed Leicester; 'but oh, that worst of villains, Varney!—and she is even now in his power!'

'But not, I trust in God,' said Tressilian, 'with any commands of fatal import?'

'No, no, no!' exclaimed the Earl hastily. 'I said something in madness—but it was recalled, fully recalled, by a hasty messenger; and she is now—she must now be safe.'

'Yes,' said Tressilian, 'she *must* be safe, and I *must* be assured of her safety. My own quarrel with you is ended, my lord; but there is another to begin with the seducer of Amy Robsart, who has screened his guilt under the cloak of the infamous Varney.'

'The *seducer* of Amy!' replied Leicester, with a voice like thunder; 'say her husband!—her misguided, blinded, most unworthy husband! She is as surely Countess of Leicester, as I am belted Earl. Nor can you, sir, point out that manner of justice which I will not render her at my own free will. I need scarce say, I fear not your compulsion.'

The generous nature of Tressilian was instantly turned from consideration of anything personal to himself, and entered at once upon Amy's welfare. He had by no means undoubting confidence in the fluctuating resolutions of Leicester, whose mind seemed to him agitated beyond the government of calm reason; neither did he, notwithstanding the assurances he had received, think Amy safe in the hands of his dependants. 'My lord,' he said calmly, 'I mean you no offence, and am far from seeking a quarrel. But my duty to Sir Hugh Robsart compels me to carry this matter instantly to the Queen, that the Countess's rank may be acknowledged in her person.'

'You shall not need, sir,' replied the Earl haughtily; 'do not dare to interfere. No voice but Dudley's shall proclaim Dudley's infamy. —To Elizabeth herself will I tell it, and then for Cumnor Place with the speed of life and death!'

So saying, he unbound his horse from the tree, threw himself into the saddle, and rode at full gallop towards the castle.

'Take me before you, Master Tressilian,' said the boy, seeing Tressilian mount in the same haste—'my tale is not all told out, and I need your protection.'

Tressilian complied, and followed the Earl, though at a less furious rate. By the way the boy confessed, with much contrition, that in resentment at Wayland's evading all his inquiries concerning the lady, after Dickon conceived he had in various ways merited his confidence, he had purloined from him, in revenge, the letter with which Amy had entrusted him for the Earl of Leicester. His purpose was to have restored it to him that evening, as he reckoned himself sure of meeting with him, in consequence of Wayland's having to perform the part of Arion in the pageant. He was indeed something alarmed when he saw to whom the letter was addressed; but he argued that, as Leicester did not return to Kenilworth until that evening, it would be again in the possession of the proper messenger as soon as, in the nature of things, it could possibly be delivered. But Wayland came not to the pageant, having been in the interim expelled by Lambourne from the castle; and the boy, not being able to find him, or to get speech of Tressilian, and finding himself in possession of a letter addressed to no less a person than the Earl of Leicester, became much afraid of the consequences of his frolic. The caution, and indeed the alarm, which Wayland had expressed respecting Varney and Lambourne, led him to judge that the letter must be designed for the Earl's own hand, and that he might prejudice the lady, by giving it to any of the domestics. He made an attempt or two to obtain an audience of Leicester, but the singularity of his features, and the meanness of his appearance, occasioned his being always repulsed by the insolent menials whom he applied to for that purpose. Once, indeed, he had nearly succeeded, when, in prowling about, he found in the grotto the casket, which he knew to belong to the unlucky Countess, having seen it on her journey; for nothing escaped his prying eye. Having strove in vain to restore it either to Tressilian or the Countess, he put it into the hands, as we have seen, of Leicester himself, but unfortunately did not recognise him in his disguise.

At length the boy thought he was on the point of succeeding, when the Earl came down to the lower part of the hall; but just as he was about to accost him, he was prevented by Tressilian. As sharp in ear as in wit, the boy heard the appointment settled betwixt them, to take place in the Pleasance, and resolved to add a third to the party, in hopes that, either in coming or in returning, he might find an opportunity of delivering the letter to Leicester; for strange stories began to flit among the domestics, which alarmed him for the lady's safety. Accident, however, detained Dickon a little behind the Earl, and, as he reached the arcade, he saw them engaged in combat; in consequence of which he hastened to alarm the guard, having little doubt, that what bloodshed took place betwixt them, might arise out of his own frolic. Continuing to lurk in the portico, he heard the second appointment, which Leicester, at parting, assigned to Tressilian, and was keeping them in view during the encounter of the Coventry-men, when, to his surprise, he recognised Wayland in the crowd, much disguised, indeed, but not sufficiently so to escape the prying glance of his old comrade. They drew aside out of the crowd to explain their situation to each other. The boy confessed to Wayland what we have above told, and the artist, in return, informed him, that his deep anxiety for the fate of the unfortunate lady had brought him back to the neighbourhood of the castle, upon his learning that morning, at a village about ten miles distant, that Varney and Lambourne, whose violence he dreaded, had both left Kenilworth over-night.

While they spoke, they saw Leicester and Tressilian separate themselves from the crowd, dogged them until they mounted their horses, when the boy, whose speed of foot has been before mentioned, though he could not possibly keep up with them, yet arrived, as we have seen, soon enough to save Tressilian's life. The boy had just finished his tale when they arrived at the Gallery Tower.

40

High o'er the eastern steep the sun is beaming,
And darkness flies with her deceitful shadows;—
So truth prevails o'er falsehood.— *Old Play.*

As Tressilian rode along the bridge, lately the scene of so much riotous sport, he could not but observe that men's countenances had singularly changed during the space of his brief absence. The mock fight was over, but the men, still habited in their masquing suits, stood together in groups, like the inhabitants of a city who have been just startled by some strange and alarming news.

When he reached the base-court, appearances were the same—domestics, retainers, and under officer's, stood together and whispered, bending their eyes towards the windows of the great hall, with looks which seemed at once alarmed and mysterious.

Sir Nicholas Blount was the first person of his own particular acquaintance Tressilian saw, who left him no time to make inquiries, but greeted him with, 'God help thy heart, Tressilian, thou art fitter for a clown than a courtier—thou canst not attend, as becomes one who follows her Majesty. Here you are called for, wished for, waited for—no man but you will serve the turn; and hither you come with a misbegotten brat on thy horse's neck, as if thou wert dry nurse to some sucking devil, and were just returned from airing.'

'Why, what is the matter?' said Tressilian, letting go the boy, who sprung to ground like a feather, and himself dismounted at the same time.

'Why, no one knows the matter,' replied Blount; 'I cannot smell it out myself, though I have a nose like other courtiers. Only, my Lord of Leicester has galloped along the bridge, as if he would have rode over all in his passage, demanded an audience of the Queen, and is closeted even now with her, and Burleigh and Walsingham—and you are called for—but whether the matter be treason or worse, no one knows.'

'He speaks true, by Heaven,' said Raleigh, who that instant appeared; 'you must immediately to the Queen's presence.'

'Be not rash, Raleigh,' said Blount, 'remember his boots—For

Heaven's sake, go to my chamber, dear Tressilian, and don my new bloom-coloured silken hose—I have worn them but twice.'

'Pshaw!' answered Tressilian; 'do thou take care of this boy, Blount; be kind to him, and look he escapes you not—much depends on him.'

So saying, he followed Raleigh hastily, leaving honest Blount with the bridle of his horse in one hand, and the boy in the other. Blount gave a long look after him.

'Nobody,' he said, 'calls me to these mysteries,—and he leaves me here to play horse-keeper and child-keeper at once. I could excuse the one, for I love a good horse naturally; but to be plagued with a bratchet whelp!—Whence come ye, my fair-favoured little gossip?'

'From the Fens,' answered the boy.

'And what didst thou learn there, forward imp?'

'To catch gulls, with their webbed feet and yellow stockings,' said the boy.

'Umph!' said Blount, looking down on his own immense roses. 'Nay, then the devil take him that asks thee more questions!'

Meanwhile Tressilian traversed the full length of the great hall, in which the astonished courtiers formed various groups, and were whispering mysteriously together, while all kept their eyes fixed on the door which led from the upper end of the hall into the Queen's withdrawing apartment. Raleigh pointed to the door—Tressilian knocked, and was instantly admitted. Many a neck was stretched to gain a view into the interior of the apartment; but the tapestry which covered the door on the inside was dropped too suddenly to admit the slightest gratification of curiosity.

Upon entrance, Tressilian found himself, not without a strong palpitation of heart, in the presence of Elizabeth, who was walking to and fro in a violent agitation, which she seemed to scorn to conceal, while two or three of her most sage and confidential counsellors exchanged anxious looks with each other, but delayed speaking till her wrath had abated. Before the empty chair of state in which she had been seated, and which was half pushed aside by the violence with which she had started from it, knelt Leicester, his arms crossed, and his brows bent on the ground, still and motionless as the effigies upon a sepulchre. Beside him stood the Lord Shrewsbury, then Earl Marshal of England, holding his baton of office—the Earl's sword was unbuckled, and lay before him on the floor.

'Ho, sir!' said the Queen, coming close up to Tressilian, and stamping on the floor with the action and manner of Henry himself; '*you* knew of this fair work—*you* are an accomplice in this deception which has been practised on us—*you* have been a main cause of our doing injustice?' Tressilian dropped on his knee before the Queen, his good sense showing him the risk of attempting any defence at that moment of irritation. 'Art dumb, sirrah!' she continued; 'thou know'st of this affair—dost thou not?'

'Not, gracious Madam, that this poor lady was Countess of Leicester.'

'Nor shall any one know her for such,' said Elizabeth. 'Death of my life! Countess of Leicester!—I say Dame Amy Dudley—and well if she have not cause to write herself widow of the traitor Robert Dudley.'

'Madam,' said Leicester, 'do with me what it may be your will to do—but work no injury on this gentlemen—he hath in no way deserved it.'

'And will he be the better for thy intercession,' said the Queen, leaving Tressilian, who slowly arose, and rushing to Leicester, who continued kneeling,—'the better for *thy* intercession, thou doubly false—thou doubly forsworn? —of thy intercession, whose villainy hath made me ridiculous to my subjects, and odious to myself?—I could tear out mine own eyes for their blindness!'

Burleigh here ventured to interpose.

'Madam,' he said, 'remember that you are a Queen—Queen of England—mother of your people. Give not way to this wild storm of passion.'

Elizabeth turned round to him, while a tear actually twinkled in her proud and angry eye. 'Burleigh,' she said, 'thou art a statesman —thou dost not, thou canst not, comprehend half the scorn—half the misery, that man has poured on me.'

With the utmost caution—with the deepest reverence, Burleigh took her hand at the moment he saw her heart was at the fullest, and led her aside to an oriel window, apart from the others.

'Madam,' he said, 'I am a statesman but I am also a man—a man already grown old in your councils, who have not and cannot have a wish on earth but your glory and happiness—I pray you to be composed.'

'Ah, Burleigh,' said Elizabeth, 'thou little knowest'—here her tears fell over her cheeks in despite of her.

'I do—I do know, my honoured Sovereign. Oh, beware that you lead not others to guess that which they know not!'

'Ha!' said Elizabeth, pausing as if a new train of thought had suddenly shot across her brain. 'Burleigh, thou art right—thou art right—anything but disgrace—anything but a confession of weakness—anything rather than seem the cheated—slighted— 'Sdeath! to think on it is distraction!'

'Be but yourself, my Queen,' said Burleigh; 'and soar far above a weakness which no Englishman will ever believe his Elizabeth could have entertained, unless the violence of her disappointment carries a sad conviction to his bosom.'

'What weakness, my lord?' said Elizabeth haughtily; 'would you too insinuate that the favour in which I held yonder proud traitor, derived its source from aught'—But here she could no longer sustain the proud tone which she had assumed, and again softened as she said, 'But why would I strive to deceive even thee, my good and wise servant!'

Burleigh stooped to kiss her hand with affection, and—rare in the annals of courts—a tear of true sympathy dropped from the eye of the minister on the hand of his Sovereign.

It is probable that the consciousness of possessing this sympathy aided Elizabeth in supporting her mortification and suppressing her extreme resentment; but she was still more moved by fear that her passion should betray to the public the affront and the disappointment which, alike as a woman and a Queen, she was so anxious to conceal. She turned from Burleigh, and sternly paced the hall till her features had recovered their usual dignity, and her mien its wonted stateliness of regular motion.

'Our Sovereign is her noble self once more,' whispered Burleigh to Walsingham; 'mark what she does, and take heed you thwart her not.'

She then approached Leicester, and said, with calmness, 'My Lord Shrewsbury, we discharge you of your prisoner.—My Lord of Leicester, rise and take up your sword—a quarter of an hour's restraint, under the custody of our Marshal, my lord, is, we think, no high penance for months of falsehood practised upon us. We will now hear the progress of this affair.' She then seated herself in her chair, and said, 'You, Tressilian, step forward, and say what you know.'

Tressilian told his story generously, suppressing as much as he could what affected Leicester, and saying nothing of their having twice actually fought together. It is very probable that, in doing so, he did the Earl good service; for had the Queen at that instant found anything on account of which she could vent her wrath upon him, without laying open sentiments of which she was ashamed, it might have fared hard with him. She paused when Tressilian had finished his tale.

'We will take that Wayland,' she said, 'into our own service, and place the boy in our Secretary-office for instruction, that he may in future use discretion towards letters. For you, Tressilian, you did wrong in not communicating the whole truth to us, and your promise not to do so was both imprudent and undutiful. Yet, having given your word to this unhappy lady, it was the part of a man and a gentleman to keep it; and, on the whole, we esteem you for the character you have sustained in this matter. My Lord of Leicester, it is now your turn to tell us the truth, an exercise to which you seem of late to have been too much a stranger.'

Accordingly, she extorted by successive questions, the whole history of his first acquaintance with Amy Robsart—their marriage —his jealousy—the causes on which it was founded, and many particulars besides. Leicester's confession, for such it might be called, was wrenched from him piecemeal, yet was upon the whole accurate, excepting that he totally omitted to mention that he had, by implication, or otherwise, assented to Varney's designs upon the life of his Countess. Yet the consciousness of this was what at that moment lay nearest to his heart; and although he trusted in great measure to the very positive counter-orders which he had sent by Lambourne, it was his purpose to set out for Cumnor Place in person, as soon as he should be dismissed from the presence of the Queen, who, he concluded, would presently leave Kenilworth.

But the Earl reckoned without his host. It is true, his presence and his communications were gall and wormwood to his once partial mistress. But, barred from every other and more direct mode of revenge, the Queen perceived that she gave her false suitor torture by these inquiries, and dwelt on them for that reason; no more regarding the pain which she herself experienced, than the savage cares for the searing of his own hands by grasping the hot pincers with which he tears the flesh of his captive enemy.

At length, however, the haughty lord, like a deer that turns to bay, gave intimation that his patience was failing, 'Madam,' he said, 'I have been much to blame—more than even your just resentment has expressed. Yet, Madam, let me say, that my guilt, if it be unpardonable, was not unprovoked; and that if beauty and condescending dignity could seduce the frail heart of a human being, I might plead both, as the causes of my concealing this secret from your Majesty.'

The Queen was so much struck by this reply, which Leicester took care should be heard by no one but herself, that she was for the moment silenced, and the Earl had the temerity to pursue his advantage. 'Your Grace, who has pardoned so much, will excuse my throwing myself on your royal mercy for those expressions, which were yester-morning accounted but a slight offence.'

The Queen fixed her eyes on him while she replied, 'Now, by Heaven, my lord, thy effrontery passes the bounds of belief, as well as patience! But it shall avail thee nothing. What, ho! my lords, come all and hear the news. My Lord of Leicester's stolen marriage has cost me a husband and England a King. His lordship is patriarchal in his tastes—one wife at a time was insufficient, and he designed us the honour of his left hand. Now, is not this too insolent,—that I could not grace him with a few marks of court favour, but he must presume to think my hand and crown at his disposal? You, however, think better of me; and I can pity this ambitious man, as I could a child, whose bubble of soap has burst between his hands. We go to the presence-chamber—My Lord of Leicester, we command your close attendance on us.'

All was eager expectation in the hall, and what was the universal astonishment, when the Queen said to those next her, 'The revels of Kenilworth are not yet exhausted, my lords and ladies—we are to solemnise the noble owner's marriage.'

There was a universal expression of surprise.

'It is true, on our royal word,' said the Queen; 'he hath kept this a secret even from us, that he might surprise us with it at this very place and time. I see you are dying of curiosity to know the happy bride. It is Amy Robsart, the same who, to make up the May-game yesterday, figured in the pageant as the wife of his servant Varney.'

'For God's sake, Madam,' said the Earl, approaching her with a mixture of humility, vexation, and shame in his countenance, and speaking so low as to be heard by no one else, 'take my head, as you threatened in your anger, and spare me these taunts! Urge not a falling man—tread not on a crushed worm.'

'A worm, my lord?' said the Queen, in the same tone; 'nay, a snake is the nobler reptile, and the more exact similitude—the frozen snake you wot of, which was warmed in a certain bosom——'

'For your own sake—for mine, Madam,' said the Earl—'while there is yet some reason left in me——'

'Speak aloud, my lord,' said Elizabeth, 'and at farther distance, so please you—your breath thaws our ruff. What have you to ask of us?'

'Permission,' said the unfortunate Earl humbly, 'to travel to Cumnor Place.'

'To fetch home your bride belike? Why, ay,—that is but right—for, as we have heard, she is.indifferently cared for there. But, my lord, you go not in person—we have counted upon passing certain days in this castle of Kenilworth, and it were a slight courtesy to leave us without a landlord during our residence here. Under your favour, we cannot think to incur such disgrace in the eyes of our subjects. Tressilian shall go to Cumnor Place instead of you, and with him some gentleman who hath been sworn of our chamber, lest my Lord of Leicester should be again jealous of his old rival.—Whom wouldst thou have to be in commission with thee, Tressilian?'

Tressilian, with humble deference, suggested the name of Raleigh.

'Why, ay,' said the Queen; 'so God ha' me, thou hast made a good choice. He is a young knight besides, and to deliver a lady from prison is an appropriate first adventure.—Cumnor Place is little better than a prison, you are to know, my lords and ladies. Besides, there are certain faitours there whom we would willingly have in fast keeping. You will furnish them, Master Secretary, with the warrant necessary to secure the bodies of Richard Varney and the foreign Alasco, dead or alive. Take a sufficient force with you, gentlemen—bring the lady here in all honour—lose no time, and God be with you.'

They bowed, and left the presence.

Who shall describe how the rest of that day was spent at Kenilworth? The Queen, who seemed to have remained there for the sole purpose of mortifying and taunting the Earl of Leicester, showed herself as skilful in that female art of vengeance, as she was in the science of wisely governing her people. The train of state soon caught the signal, and, as he walked among his own splendid preparations, the Lord of Kenilworth, in his own castle, already experienced the lot of a disgraced courtier, in the slight regard and cold manners of alienated friends, and the ill-concealed triumph of avowed and open enemies. Sussex, from his natural military frankness of disposition, Burleigh and Walsingham, from their

penetrating and prospective sagacity, and some of the ladies, from
the compassion of their sex, were the only persons in the crowded
court who retained towards him the countenance they had borne
in the morning.

So much had Leicester been accustomed to consider court favour
as the principal object of his life, that all other sensations were, for
the time, lost in the agony which his haughty spirit felt at the
succession of petty insults and studied neglects to which he had been
subjected; but when he retired to his own chamber for the night,
that long fair tress of hair which had once secured Amy's letter fell
under his observation, and, with the influence of a counter-charm,
awakened his heart to nobler and more natural feelings. He kissed
it a thousand times; and while he recollected that he had it always
in his power to shun the mortifications which he had that day
undergone, by retiring into a dignified and even prince-like
seclusion, with the beautiful and beloved partner of his future life,
he felt that he could rise above the revenge which Elizabeth had
condescended to take.

Accordingly, on the following day, the whole conduct of the
Earl displayed so much dignified equanimity; he seemed so
solicitous about the accommodations and amusements of his
guests, yet so indifferent to their personal demeanour towards him,
so respectfully distant to the Queen, yet so patient of her harassing
displeasure, that Elizabeth changed her manner to him, and though
cold and distant, ceased to offer him any direct affront. She intimated also with some sharpness to others around her, who thought
they were consulting her pleasure in showing a neglectful conduct
to the Earl, that while they remained at Kenilworth, they ought to
show the civility due from guests to the lord of the castle. In short,
matters were so far changed in twenty-four hours, that some of the
more experienced and sagacious courtiers foresaw a strong possibility of Leicester's restoration to favour, and regulated their demeanour towards him, as those who might one day claim merit for not
having deserted him in adversity. It is time, however, to leave these
intrigues, and to follow Tressilian and Raleigh on their journey.

The troop consisted of six persons; for, besides Wayland, they
had in company a royal pursuivant and two stout serving-men.
All were well armed, and travelled as fast as it was possible with
justice to their horses, which had a long journey before them. They
endeavoured to procure some tidings as they rode along of Varney

and his party, but could hear none, as they had travelled in the dark. At a small village about twelve miles from Kenilworth, where they gave some refreshment to their horses, a poor clergyman, the curate of the place, came out of a small cottage, and entreated any of the company who might know aught of surgery, to look in for an instant on a dying man.

The empiric Wayland undertook to do his best, and as the curate conducted him to the spot, he learned that the man had been found on the high-road, about a mile from the village, by labourers, as they were going to their work on the preceding morning, and the curate had given him shelter in his house. He had received a gun-shot wound which seemed to be obviously mortal, but whether in a brawl or from robbers they could not learn, as he was in a fever, and spoke nothing connectedly. Wayland entered the dark and lowly apartment, and no sooner had the curate drawn aside the curtain, than he knew in the distorted features of the patient the countenance of Michael Lambourne. Under pretence of seeking something which he wanted. Wayland hastily apprised his fellow-travellers of this extraordinary circumstance; and both Tressilian and Raleigh, full of boding apprehensions, hastened to the curate's house to see the dying man.

The wretch was by this time in the agonies of death, from which a much better surgeon than Wayland could not have rescued him, for the bullet had passed clear through the body. He was sensible, however, at least in part, for he knew Tressilian, and made signs that he wished him to stoop over his bed. Tressilian did so, and after some inarticulate murmurs, in which the names of Varney and Lady Leicester were alone distinguishable, Lambourne bade him 'make haste, or he would come too late.' It was in vain Tressilian urged the patient for further information; he seemed to become in some degree delirious, and when he again made a signal to attract Tressilian's attention, it was only for the purpose of desiring him to inform his uncle, Giles Gosling of the Black Bear, that 'he had died without his shoes after all.' A convulsion verified his words a few minutes after, and the travellers derived nothing from having met with him, saving the obscure fears concerning the fate of the Countess, which his dying words were calculated to convey, and which induced them to urge their journey with the utmost speed, pressing horses in the Queen's name, when those which they rode became unfit for service.

41

The death-bell thrice was heard to ring,
An aerial voice was heard to call;
And thrice the raven flapp'd its wing,
Around the towers of Cumnor Hall.—*Mickle*.

WE are now to return to that part of our story where we intimated that Varney, possessed of the authority of the Earl of Leicester, and of the Queen's permission to the same effect, hastened to secure himself against discovery of his perfidy, by removing the Countess from Kenilworth Castle. He had proposed to set forth early in the morning, but reflecting that the Earl might relent in the interim, and seek another interview with the Countess, he resolved to prevent, by immediate departure, all chance of what would probably have ended in his detection and ruin. For this purpose he called for Lambourne, and was exceedingly incensed to find that his trusty attendant was abroad on some ramble in the neighbouring village, or elsewhere. As his return was expected, Sir Richard commanded that he should prepare himself for attending him on an immediate journey, and follow him in case he returned after his departure.

In the meanwhile, Varney used the ministry of a servant called Robin Tider, one to whom the mysteries of Cumnor Place were already in some degree known, as he had been there more than once in attendance on the Earl. To this man, whose character resembled that of Lambourne, though he was neither quite so prompt nor altogether so profligate, Varney gave command to have three horses saddled, and to prepare a horse-litter, and have them in readiness at the postern-gate. The natural enough excuse of his lady's insanity, which was now universally believed, accounted for the secrecy with which she was to be removed from the castle, and he reckoned on the same apology in case the unfortunate Amy's resistance or screams should render such necessary. The agency of Anthony Foster was indispensable, and that Varney now went to secure.

This person, naturally of a sour, unsocial disposition, and somewhat tired, besides, with his journey from Cumnor to Warwickshire, in order to bring the news of the Countess's escape, had long extricated himself from the crowd of wassailers, and betaken himself to his chamber, where he lay asleep, when Varney, completely equipped for travelling, and with a dark lantern in his hand, entered his apartment. He paused an instant to listen to what his associate was murmuring in his sleep, and could plainly distinguish the words, 'Ave Maria—ora pro nobis—No—it runs not so—deliver us from evil—Ay, so it goes.'

'Praying in his sleep,' said Varney; 'and confounding his old and new devotions. He must have more need of prayer ere I have done with him. What ho! holy man—most blessed penitent! Awake—awake! The devil has not discharged you from service yet.'

As Varney at the same time shook the sleeper by the arm, it changed the current of his ideas, and he roared out, 'Thieves!—thieves! I will die in defence of my gold—my hard-won gold, that hast cost me so dear. Where is Janet? Is Janet safe?'

'Safe enough, thou bellowing fool,' said Varney; 'art thou not ashamed of thy clamour?'

Foster by this time was broad awake, and, sitting up in his bed, asked Varney the meaning of so untimely a visit. 'It augurs nothing good,' he added.

'A false prophecy, most sainted Anthony,' returned Varney; 'it augurs that the hour is come for converting thy leasehold into copyhold—What say'st thou to that?'

'Hadst thou told me in broad day,' said Foster, 'I had rejoiced—but at this dead hour, and by this dim light, and looking on thy pale face, which is a ghastly contradiction to thy light words, I cannot but rather think of the work that is to be done, than the guerdon to be gained by it.'

'Why, thou fool, it is but to escort thy charge back to Cumnor Place.'

'Is that indeed all?' said Foster; 'thou looked deadly pale, and thou art not moved by trifles—is that indeed all?'

'Ay, that—and may be a trifle more,' said Varney.

'Ah, that trifle more!' said Foster; 'still thou look'st paler and paler.'

'Heed not my countenance,' said Varney, 'you see it by this wretched light. Up and be doing, man—Think of Cumnor Place—thine own proper copyhold—Why, thou mayst found a weekly lectureship, besides endowing Janet like a baron's daughter. Seventy pounds and odds.'

'Seventy-nine pounds, five shillings and fivepence halfpenny, besides the value of the wood,' said Foster; 'and I am to have it all as copyhold?'

'All, man—squirrels and all—no gipsy shall cut the value of a broom—no boy so much as take a bird's nest, without paying thee a quittance. Ay, that is right—don thy matters as fast as possible—horses and everything are ready, all save that accursed villain Lambourne, who is out on some infernal gambol.'

'Ay, Sir Richard,' said Foster, 'you would take no advice. I ever told you that a drunken profligate would fail you at need. Now I could have helped you to a sober young man.

'What, some slow-spoken, long-breathed brother of the congregation? Why we shall have use for such also, man—Heaven be praised, we shall lack labourers of every kind. Ay, that is right—forget not your pistols—Come now, and let us away.'

'Whither?' said Anthony.

'To my lady's chamber—and, mind—she *must* along with us. Thou art not a fellow to be startled by a shriek?'

'Not if Scripture-reason can be rendered for it; and it is written, "wives, obey your husbands." But will my lord's commands bear us out if we use violence?'

'Tush, man! here is his signet,' answered Varney; and, having thus silenced the objections of his associate, they went together to Lord Hunsdon's apartment, and, acquainting the sentinel with their purpose, as a matter sanctioned by the Queen and the Earl of Leicester, they entered the apartment of the unfortunate Countess.

The horror of Amy may be conceived, when, starting from a broken slumber, she saw at her bedside Varney, the man on earth she most feared and hated. It was even a consolation to see that he was not alone, though she had so much reason to dread his sullen companion.

'Madam,' said Varney, 'there is no time for ceremony. My Lord of Leicester, having fully considered the exigencies of the time, sends you his orders immediately to accompany us on our return to Cumnor Place. See, here is his signet, in token of his instant and pressing commands.'

'It is false!' said the Countess; 'thou hast stolen the warrant,—thou, who art capable of every villainy, from the blackest to the basest!'

'It is TRUE, madam,' replied Varney; 'so true, that if you do not instantly arise, and prepare to attend us, we must compel you to obey our orders.'

'Compel!—thou darest not put it to that issue, base as thou art!' exclaimed the unhappy Countess.

'That remains to be proved, madam,' said Varney, who had determined on intimidation as the only means of subduing her high spirit; 'if you put me to it, you will find me a rough groom of the chambers.'

It was at this threat that Amy screamed so fearfully, that had it not been for the received opinion of her insanity, she would quickly have had Lord Hunsdon and others to her aid. Perceiving, however, that her cries were vain, she appealed to Foster in the most affecting terms, conjuring him, as his daughter Janet's honour and purity were dear to him, not to permit her to be treated with un-womanly violence.

'Why, madam, wives must obey their husbands,—there's Scripture-warrant for it,' said Foster; 'and if you will dress yourself, and come with us patiently, there's no one shall lay finger on you while I can draw a pistol-trigger.'

Seeing no help arrive, and comforted even by the dogged language of Foster, the Countess promised to arise and dress herself, if they would agree to retire from the room. Varney at the same time assured her of all safety and honour while in their hands, and promised, that he himself would not approach her, since his presence was so displeasing. Her husband, he added, would be at Cumnor Place within twenty-four hours after they had reached it.

Somewhat comforted by this assurance, upon which, however, she saw little reason to rely, the unhappy Amy made her toilet by the assistance of the lantern, which they left with her when they quitted the apartment.

Weeping, trembling, and praying, the unfortunate lady dressed herself,—with sensations how different from the days in which she was wont to decorate herself in all the pride of conscious beauty! She endeavoured to delay the completing her dress as long as she could, until, terrified by the impatience of Varney, she was obliged to declare herself ready to attend them.

When they were about to move, the Countess clung to Foster with such an appearance of terror at Varney's approach, that the latter protested to her, with a deep oath, that he had no intention whatsoever of even coming near her. 'If you do but consent to execute your husband's will in quietness, you shall,' he said, 'see but little of me. I will leave you undisturbed to the care of the usher whom your good taste prefers.'

'My husband's will!' she exclaimed. 'But it is the will of God, and let that be sufficient to me. I will go with Master Foster as unresistingly as ever did a literal sacrifice. He is a father at least; and will have decency, if not humanity. For thee, Varney, were it my latest word, thou art an equal stranger to both.

Varney replied only, she was at liberty to choose, and walked some paces before them to show the way; while, half leaning on Foster, and half carried by him, the Countess was transported from Saintlowe's Tower to the postern-gate, where Tider waited with the litter and horses.

The Countess was placed in the former without resistance. She saw with some satisfaction, that while Foster and Tider rode close by the litter, which the latter conducted, the dreaded Varney lingered behind, and was soon lost in darkness. A little while she strove, as the road winded round the verge of the lake, to keep sight of those stately towers which called her husband lord, and which still, in some places, sparkled with lights, where wassailers were yet revelling. But when the direction of the road rendered this no longer possible, she drew back her head, and sinking down in the litter, recommended herself to the care of Providence.

Besides the desire of inducing the Countess to proceed quietly on her journey, Varney had it also in view to have an interview with Lambourne, by whom he every moment expected to be joined without the presence of any witnesses. He knew the character of this man, prompt, bloody, resolute, and greedy, and judged him the most fit agent he could employ in his further designs. But ten miles of their journey had been measured ere he heard the hasty clatter of horse's hoofs behind him, and was overtaken by Michael Lambourne.

Fretted as he was with his absence, Varney received his profligate servant with a rebuke of unusual bitterness. 'Drunken villain,' he said, 'thy idleness and debauched folly will stretch a halter ere it be long; and, for me, I care not how soon.'

This style of objurgation, Lambourne, who was elated to an unusual degree, not only by an extraordinary cup of wine, but by the sort of confidential interview he had just had with the Earl, and the secret of which he had made himself master, did not receive with his wonted humility. 'He would take no insolence of language,' he said, 'from the best knight that ever wore spurs. Lord Leicester had detained him on some business of import, and that was enough for Varney, who was but a servant like himself.'

Varney was not a little surprised at his unusual tone of insolence; but, ascribing it to liquor, suffered it to pass as if unnoticed, and then began to tamper with Lambourne, touching his willingness to aid in removing out of the Earl of Leicester's way an obstacle to a rise, which would put it in his power to reward his trusty followers to their utmost wish. And upon Michael Lambourne's seeming ignorant what was meant, he plainly indicated 'the litter-load, yonder,' as the impediment which he desired should be removed.

'Look you, Sir Richard, and so forth,' said Michael, 'some are wiser than some, that is one thing, and some are worse than some, that's another. I know my lord's mind on this matter better than thou, for he hath trusted me fully in the matter. Here are his mandates, and his last words were, Michael Lambourne,—for his lordship speaks to me as a gentleman of the sword, and useth not the words drunken villain, or such like phrases, of those who know not how to bear new dignities. Varney, says he, must pay the utmost respect to my Countess—I trust to you for looking to it, Lambourne, says his lordship, and you must bring back my signet from him peremptorily.'

'Ay,' replied Varney, 'said he so, indeed? You know all, then?'

'All—all—and you were as wise to make a friend of me while the weather is fair betwixt us.'

'And was there no one present,' said Varney, 'when my lord so spoke?'

'Not a breathing creature,' replied Lambourne. 'Think you my lord would trust any one with such matters, save an approved man of action like myself?'

'Most true,' said Varney; and, making a pause, he looked forward on the moonlight road. They ware traversing a wide and open heath. The litter being at least a mile before them, was both out of sight and hearing. He looked behind, and there was an expanse, lighted by the moonbeams, without one human being in sight. He resumed his speech to Lambourne: 'And will you turn upon your master, who has introduced you to this career of court favour—whose apprentice you have been, Michael—who has taught you the depths and shallows of court intrigue?'

'Michael not me,' said Lambourne, 'I have a name will brook a

462

master before it as well as another; and as to the rest, if I have been an apprentice, my indenture is out, and I am resolute to set up for myself.'

'Take thy quittance first, thou fool!' said Varney; and with a pistol, which he had for some time held in his hand, shot Lambourne through the body.

The wretch fell from his horse, without a single groan, and Varney, dismounting, rifled his pockets, turning out the lining, that it might appear he had fallen by robbers. He secured the Earl's packet, which was his chief object, but he also took Lambourne's purse, containing some gold pieces, the relics of what his debauchery had left him, and, from a singular combination of feelings, carried it in his hand only the length of a small river, which crossed the road, into which he threw it as far as he could fling. Such are the strange remnants of conscience which remain after she seems totally subdued, that this cruel and remorseless man would have felt himself degraded had he pocketed the few pieces belonging to the wretch whom he had thus ruthlessly slain.

The murderer reloaded his pistol, after cleansing the lock and barrel from the appearances of late explosion, and rode calmly after the litter, satisfying himself that he had so adroitly removed a troublesome witness to many of his intrigues, and the bearer of mandates which he had no intention to obey, and which, therefore, he was desirous it should be thought had never reached his hand.

The remainder of the journey was made with a degree of speed, which showed the little care they had for the health of the unhappy Countess. They paused only at places where all was under their command, and where the tale they were prepared to tell of the insane Lady Varney would have obtained ready credit, had she made any attempt to appeal to the compassion of the few persons admitted to see her. But Amy saw no chance of obtaining a hearing from any to whom she had an opportunity of addressing herself, and, besides, was too terrified for the presence of Varney, to violate the implied condition under which she was to travel free from his company. The authority of Varney, often so used, during the Earl's private journeys to Cumnor, readily procured relays of horses where wanted, so that they approached Cumnor Place upon the night after they left Kenilworth.

At this period of the journey, Varney came up to the rear of the litter, as he had done before repeatedly during their progress, and asked, 'What does she?'

'She sleeps,' said Foster; 'I would we were home—her strength is exhausted.'

'Rest will restore her,' answered Varney. 'She shall soon sleep sound and long—we must consider how to lodge her in safety.'

'In her own apartments, to be sure,' said Foster. 'I have sent Janet to her aunts', with a proper rebuke, and the old women are truth itself—for they hate this lady cordially.'

'We shall not trust them, however, friend Anthony,' said Varney; 'we must secure her in that stronghold where you keep your gold.'

'My gold!' said Anthony, much alarmed; 'why, what gold have I? God help me, I have no gold—I would I had.'

'Now, marry hang thee, thou stupid brute—who thinks of, or cares for, thy gold? If I did, could I not find an hundred better ways to come at it? In one word, thy bedchamber, which thou hast fenced so curiously, must be her place of seclusion; and thou, thou hind, shalt press her pillows of down. I dare to say the Earl will never ask after the rich furniture of these four rooms.'

This last consideration rendered Foster tractable; he only asked permission to ride before, to make matters ready, and, spurring his horse, he posted before the litter, while Varney falling about three-score paces behind, it remained only attended by Tider.

When they had arrived at Cumnor Place, the Countess asked eagerly for Janet, and showed much alarm when informed that she was no longer to have the attendance of that amiable girl.

'My daughter is dear to me, madam,' said Foster gruffly; 'and I desire not that she could get the court-tricks of lying and 'scaping—somewhat too much of that has she learned already, and it please your ladyship.'

The Countess, much fatigued and greatly terrified by the circumstances of her journey, made no answer to this insolence, but mildly expressed a wish to retire to her chamber.

'Ay, ay,' muttered Foster, "tis but reasonable; but, under favour, you go not to your gew-gaw toy-house yonder—you will sleep to-night in better security.'

'I would it were in my grave,' said the Countess; 'but that mortal feelings shiver at the idea of soul and body parting.'

'You, I guess, have no chance to shiver at that,' replied Foster. 'My lord comes hither to-morrow, and doubtless you will make your own ways good with him.'

'But does he come hither?—does he indeed, good Foster?'

'Oh ay, good Foster!' replied the other. 'But what Foster shall I be to-morrow, when you speak of me to my lord—though all I have done was to obey his own orders?'

'You shall be my protector—a rough one indeed—but still a protector,' answered the Countess. 'Oh that Janet were but here!'

'She is better where she is,' answered Foster—'one of you is enough to perplex a plain head—but will you taste any refreshment?'

'Oh no, no—my chamber—my chamber. I trust,' she said, 'I may secure it on the inside.'

'With all my heart,' answered Foster, 'so I may secure it on the outside;' and taking a light, he led the way to a part of the building where Amy had never been, and conducted her up a stair of great height, preceded by one of the old women with a lamp. At the head of the stair, which seemed of almost immeasurable height, they crossed a short wooden gallery, formed of black oak, and very narrow, at the farther end of which was a strong oaken door, which opened and admitted them into the miser's apartment, homely in its accommodations in the very last degree, and, except in name, little different from a prison-vault.

Foster stopped at the door, and gave the lamp to the Countess, without either offering or permitting the attendance of the old woman who had carried it. The lady stood not on ceremony, but taking it hastily, barred the door, and secured it with the ample means provided on the inside for that purpose.

Varney, meanwhile, had lurked behind on the stairs, but hearing the door barred, he now came up on tiptoe, and Foster, winking to him, pointed with self-complacence to a piece of concealed machinery in the wall, which, playing with much ease and little noise, dropped a part of the wooden gallery, after the manner of a drawbridge, so as to cut off all communication between the door of the bedroom, which he usually inhabited, and the landing-place of the high winding-stair which ascended to it. The rope by which this machinery was wrought was generally carried within the bedchamber, it being Foster's object to provide against invasion from without; but now that it was intended to secure the prisoner within, the cord had been brought over to the landing-place, and was there made fast, when Foster, with much complacency, had dropped the unsuspected trap-door.

Varney looked with great attention at the machinery, and peeped more than once down the deep abyss which was opened by the fall of the trap-door. It was dark as pitch, and seemed profoundly deep, going, as Foster informed his confederate in a whisper, nigh to the lowest vault of the castle. Varney cast once more a fixed and long look down into this sable gulf, and then followed Foster to the part of the manor-house most usually inhabited.

When they arrived in the parlour which we have mentioned, Varney requested Foster to get them supper, and some of the choicest wine. 'I will seek Alasco,' he added; 'we have work for him to do, and we must put him into good heart.'

Foster groaned at this intimation, but made no remonstrance. The old woman assured Varney that Alasco had scarce eaten or drunken since her master's departure, living perpetually shut up in the laboratory, and talking as if the world's continuance depended on what he was doing there.

'I will teach him that the world hath other claims on him,' said Varney, seizing a light, and going in quest of the alchemist. He returned, after a considerable absence, very pale, but yet with his habitual sneer on his cheek and nostril—'Our friend,' he said, 'has exhaled.'

'How!—what mean you?' said Foster. 'Run away—fled with my forty pounds, that should have been multiplied a thousand-fold? I will have Hue and Cry.'

'I will tell thee a surer way,' said Varney.

'How! which way?' exclaimed Foster; 'I will have back my forty pounds—I deemed them as surely a thousand times multiplied —I will have back my in-put, at the least.'

'Go hang thyself then, and sue Alasco in the Devil's Court of Chancery, for thither he has carried the cause.'

'How!—what dost thou mean—is he dead?'

'Ay, truly is he,' said Varney; 'and properly swollen already in the face and body—He had been mixing some of the devil's medicines, and the glass mask which he used constantly had fallen from his face, so that the subtle poison entered the brain, and did its work.'

'Sancta Maria!' said Foster;—'I mean, God in His mercy preserve us from covetousness and deadly sin!—Had he not had projection, think you? Saw you no ingots in the crucibles?'

'Nay, I looked not but at the dead carrion,' answered Varney; 'an ugly spectacle—he was swollen like a corpse three days exposed on the wheel—Pah! give me a cup of wine.'

'I will go,' said Foster, 'I will examine myself——' He took the lamp and hastened to the door, but there hesitated, and paused. 'Will you not go with me?' said he to Varney.

'To what purpose?' said Varney; 'I have seen and smelled enough to spoil my appetite. I broke the window, however, and let in the air—it reeked of sulphur, and such like suffocating steams, as if the very devil had been there.'

'And might it not be the act of the Demon himself?' said Foster, still hesitating; 'I have heard he is powerful at such times, and with such people.'

'Still, if it *were* that Satan of thine,' answered Varney, 'who thus jades thy imagination, thou art in perfect safety, unless he is a most unconscionable devil indeed. He hath had two good sops of late.'

'How, *two* sops—what mean you?' said Foster—'what mean you?'

'You will know in time,' said Varney;—'and then this other banquet—but thou will esteem Her too choice a morsel for the fiend's tooth—she must have her psalms, and harps, and seraphs.'

Anthony Foster heard, and came slowly back to the table: 'God! Sir Richard, and must that then be done?'

'Ay, in very truth, Anthony, or there comes no copyhold thy way,' replied his inflexible associate.

'I always foresaw it would land there,' said Foster, 'but how, Sir Richard, how?—for not to win the world would I put hands on her.'

'I cannot blame thee,' said Varney; 'I should be reluctant to do that myself—we miss Alasco and his manna sorely; ay, and the dog Lambourne.'

'Why, where tarries Lambourne?' said Anthony.

'Ask no questions,' said Varney, 'thou wilt see him one day, if thy creed be true. But to our graver matter. I will teach thee a springe, Tony, to catch a pewit,—yonder trap-door—yonder gimcrack of thine, will remain secure in appearance, will it not, though the supports are withdrawn beneath?'

'Ay, marry, will it,' said Foster; 'so long as it is not trodden on.'

'But were the lady to attempt an escape over it,' replied Varney; 'her weight would carry it down?'

'A mouse's weight would do it,' said Foster.

'Why, then, she dies in attempting her escape, and how could you or I help it, honest Tony? Let us to bed, we will adjust our project to-morrow.'

On the next day, when evening approached, Varney summoned Foster to the execution of their plan. Tider and Foster's old man-servant were sent on a feigned errand down to the village, and Anthony himself, as if anxious to see that the Countess suffered no want of accommodation, visited her place of confinement. He was so much staggered at the mildness and patience with which she seemed to endure her confinement, that he could not help earnestly recommending to her not to cross the threshold of her room on any account whatsoever, until Lord Leicester should come, 'which,' he added, 'I trust in God, will be very soon.' Amy patiently promised that she would resign herself to her fate, and Foster returned to his hardened companion with his conscience half-eased of the perilous load that weighed on it. 'I have warned her,' he said; 'surely in vain is the snare set in the sight of any bird.'

He left, therefore, the Countess's door unsecured on the outside, and, under the eye of Varney, withdrew the supports which sustained the falling trap, which, therefore, kept its level position merely by a slight adhesion. They withdrew to wait the issue on the ground-floor adjoining, but they waited long in vain. At length Varney, after walking long to and fro, with his face muffled in his cloak, threw it suddenly back, and said, 'Surely never was a woman fool enough to neglect so fair an opportunity of escape!'

'Perhaps she is resolved,' said Foster, 'to await her husband's return.'

'True!—most true,' said Varney, rushing out, 'I had not thought of that before.'

In less than two minutes, Foster, who remained behind, heard the tread of a horse in the courtyard, and then a whistle similar to that which was the Earl's usual signal;—the instant after the door of the Countess's chamber opened, and in the same moment the trap-door gave way. There was a rushing sound—a heavy fall—a faint groan—and all was over.

At the same instant, Varney called in at the window, in an accent and tone which was an indescribable mixture betwixt horror and raillery, 'Is the bird caught?—is the deed done?'

'O God, forgive us!' replied Anthony Foster.

'Why, thou fool,' said Varney, 'thy toil is ended, and thy reward secure. Look down into the vault—what seest thou?'

'I see only a heap of white clothes, like a snow-drift,' said Foster,— 'O God, she moves her arm!'

'Hurl something down on her. Thy gold chest, Tony—it is an heavy one.'

'Varney, thou art an incarnate fiend!' replied Foster;—'There needs nothing more—she is gone!'

'So pass our troubles,' said Varney, entering the room; 'I dreamed not I could have mimicked the Earl's call so well.'

'Oh, if there be judgment in Heaven, thou hast deserved it,' said Foster, 'and wilt meet it! Thou hast destroyed her by means of her best affections—It is a seething of the kid in the mother's milk.'

'Thou art a fanatical ass,' replied Varney; 'let us now think how the alarm should be given,—the body is to remain where it is.'

But their wickedness was to be permitted no longer;—for even while they were at this consultation, Tressilian and Raleigh broke in upon them, having obtained admittance by means of Tider and Foster's servant, whom they had secured at the village.

Anthony Foster fled on their entrance; and, knowing each corner and pass of the intricate old house, escaped all search. But Varney was taken on the spot; and, instead of expressing compunction for what he had done, seemed to take a fiendish pleasure in pointing out to them the remains of the murdered Countess, while at the same time he defied them to show that he had any share in her death. The despairing grief of Tressilian, on viewing the mangled and yet warm remains of what had lately been so lovely and so beloved, was such, that Raleigh was compelled to have him removed from the place by force, while he himself assumed the direction of what was to be done.

Varney, upon a second examination, made very little mystery either of the crime or of its motives; alleging, as a reason for his frankness, that though much of what he confessed could only have attached to him by suspicion, yet such suspicion would have been sufficient to deprive him of Leicester's confidence, and to destroy all his towering plans of ambition. 'I was not born,' he said, 'to drag on the remainder of life a degraded outcast,—nor will I so die, that my fate shall make a holiday to the vulgar herd.'

From these words it was apprehended he had some design upon himself, and he was carefully deprived of all means by which such could be carried into execution. But, like some of the heroes of antiquity, he carried about his person a small quantity of strong poison, prepared probably by the celebrated Demetrius Alasco. Having swallowed this portion over-night, he was found next morning dead in his cell; nor did he appear to have suffered much agony, his countenance presenting, even in death, the habitual expression of sneering sarcasm which was predominant while he lived. 'The wicked man,' saith Scripture, 'hath no bonds in his death.'

The fate of his colleague in wickedness was long unknown. Cumnor Place was deserted immediately after the murder; for, in the vicinity of what was called the Lady Dudley's Chamber, the domestics pretended to hear groans and screams, and other supernatural noises. After a certain length of time, Janet, hearing no tidings of her father, became the uncontrolled mistress of his property, and conferred it with her hand upon Wayland, now a man of settled character, and holding a place in Elizabeth's household. But it was after they had been both dead for some years, that their eldest son and heir, in making some researches about Cumnor Hall, discovered a secret passage, closed by an iron door, which, opening from behind the bed in the Lady Dudley's Chamber, descended to a sort of cell, in which they found an iron chest containing a quantity of gold, and a human skeleton stretched above it. The fate of Anthony Foster was now manifest. He had fled to this place of concealment, forgetting the key of the spring-lock; and being barred from escape by the means he had used for preservation of that gold for which he had sold his salvation, he had there perished miserably. Unquestionably the groans and screams heard by the domestics were not entirely imaginary, but were those of this wretch, who, in his agony, was crying for relief and succour.

The news of the Countess's dreadful fate put a sudden period to the pleasures of Kenilworth. Leicester retired from court, and for a considerable time abandoned himself to his remorse. But as Varney in his last declaration had been studious to spare the character of his patron, the Earl was the object rather of compassion then resentment. The Queen at length recalled him to court; he was once more distinguished as a statesman and favourite, and the rest of his career is well known to history. But there was something retributive in his death, if, according to an account very generally received, it took place from his swallowing a draught of poison which was designed for another person *.

Sir Hugh Robsart died very soon after his daughter, having settled his estate on Tressilian. But neither the prospect of rural

* *Note K.* Death of the Earl of Leicester.

independence, nor the promises of favour which Elizabeth held out to induce him to follow the court, could remove his profound melancholy. Wherever he went, he seemed to see before him the disfigured corpse of the early and only object of his affection. At length, having made provision for the maintenance of the old friends and old servants who formed Sir Hugh's family at Lidcote Hall, he himself embarked with his friend Raleigh for the Virginia expedition, and, young in years, but old in griefs, died before his day in that foreign land.

Of inferior persons it is only necessary to say, that Blount's wit grew brighter as his yellow roses faded; that, doing his part as a brave commander in the wars, he was much more in his element than during the short period of his following the court; and that Fibbertigibbet's acute genius raised him to favour and distinction, in the employment both of Burleigh and Walsingham.

NOTES

Note A, p. 53.—*Foster, Lambourne, and the Black Bear*

If faith is to be put in epitaphs, Anthony Foster was something the very reverse of the character represented in the novel. Ashmole gives this description of his tomb. I copy from the 'Antiquities of Berkshire,' vol. i. p. 143.

'In the north wall of the chancel at Cumnor Church is a monument of gray marble, whereon, in brass plates, are engraved a man in armour, and his wife in the habit of her times, both kneeling before a fald-stoole, together with the figures of three sons kneeling behind their mother. Under the figure of the man is this inscription:—

> Antonius Forster, generis generosa propago,
>   Cumneræ Dominus, Bercheriensis erat.
> Armiger, Armigero prognatus patre Ricardo,
>   Qui quondam Iphlethæ Salopiensis erat.
> Quatuor ex isto fluxerunt stemmate nati,
>   Ex isto Antonius stemmate quartus erat.
> Mente sagax, animo precellens, corpore promptus,
>   Eloquii dulcis, ore disertus erat.
> In factis probitas; fuit in sermone venustas,
>   In vultu gravitas, religione fides,
> In patriam pietas, in egenos grata voluntas,
>   Accedunt reliquis annumeranda bonis.
> Si quod cuncta rapit, rapuit non omnia Lethum,
>   Si quod Mors rapuit, vivida fama dedit.

'These verses following are writ at length, two by two, in praise of him:—

> Argute resonas Cithare pretendere chordas
>   Novit, et Aonia concrepuisse Lyra.
> Gaudebat terre teneras defigere plantas;
>   Et mira pulchras construere arte domos
> Composita varias lingua formare loquelas
>   Doctus, et edocta scribere multa manu.

The arms over it thus:—

Quart. { I. 3 *Hunter's Horns* stringed.
       { II. 3 *Pinions* with their points upwards.

'The crest is a *Stag* couchant, vulnerated through the neck by a broad arrow; on his side is a *Martlett* for a difference.'

From this monumental inscription it appears that Anthony Foster, instead of being a vulgar, low-bred, puritanical churl, was in fact a gentleman of birth and consideration, distinguished for his skill in the arts of music and horticulture, as also in languages. In so far, therefore, the Anthony Foster of the romance has nothing but the name in common with the real individual. But notwithstanding the charity, benevolence, and religious faith imputed by the monument of gray marble to its tenant, tradition, as well as secret history name him as the active agent in the death of the Countess; and it is added, that from being a jovial and convivial gallant, as we may infer from some expressions in the epitaph, he sunk, after the fatal deed, into a man of gloomy and retired habits, whose looks and manners indicated that he suffered under the pressure of some atrocious secret.

The name of Lambourne is still known in the vicinity, and it is said some of the clan partake the habits, as well as name, of the Michael Lambourne of the romance. A man of this name lately murdered his wife, outdoing Michael in this respect, who only was concerned in the murder of the wife of another man.

I have only to add, that the jolly Black Bear has been restored to his predominance over bowl and bottle, in the village of Cumnor.

473

Note B, p. 167.—Legend of Wayland Smith

The great defeat, given by Alfred to the Danish invaders, is said, by Mr Gough, to have taken place near Ashdown, in Berkshire. 'The burial place of Baereg, the Danish chief, who was slain in this fight, is distinguished by a parcel of stones, less than a mile from the hill, set on edge, enclosing a piece of ground somewhat raised. On the east side of the southern extremity stands three squarish flat stones, of about four or five feet over either way, supporting a fourth, and now called by the vulgar Wayland Smith, from an idle tradition about an invisible smith replacing lost horse-shoes there.'—Gough's 'Edition of Camden's Britannia,' vol. i. p. 221.

The popular belief still retains memory of this wild legend, which, connected as it is with the site of a Danish sepulchre, may have arisen from some legend concerning the northern Duergar, who resided in the rocks, and were cunning workers in steel and iron. It was believed that Wayland Smith's fee was sixpence, and that, unlike other workmen, he was offended if more was offered. Of late his offices have been again called to memory; but fiction has in this, as in other cases, taken the liberty to pillage the stores of oral tradition. This monument must be very ancient, for it has been kindly pointed out to me that it is referred to in an ancient Saxon charter, as a landmark. The monument has been of late cleared out, and made considerably more conspicuous.

Note C, p. 175.—Leicester and Sussex

Naunton gives us numerous and curious particulars of the jealous struggle which took place between Ratcliffe, Earl of Sussex, and the rising favourite Leicester. The former, when on his deathbed, predicted to his followers that, after his death, the gipsy (so he called Leicester, from his dark complexion) would prove too many for them.

Note D, p. 178.—Sir Walter Raleigh

Among the attendants and adherents of Sussex, we have ventured to introduce the celebrated Raleigh, in the dawn of his court favour.

In Aubrey's 'Correspondence' there are some curious particulars of Sir Walter Raleigh. 'He was a tall, handsome, bold man; but his naeve was that he was damnably proud. Old Sir Robert Harley of Brampton Brian Castle, who knew him, would say, it was a great question who was the proudest, Sir Walter, or Sir Thomas Overbury; but the difference that was, was judged in Sir Thomas's side. In the great parlour at Downton, at Mr Raleigh's, is a good piece, an original of Sir Walter, in a white satin doublet, all embroidered with rich pearls, and a mighty rich chain of great pearls about his neck. The old servants have told me that the pearls were near as big as the painted ones. He had a most remarkable aspect, an exceeding high forehead, long faced, and sour-eyelidded.' A rebus is added to this purpose:—

> The enemy to the stomach and the word of disgrace,
> Is the name of the gentleman with the bold face.

Sir Walter Raleigh's beard turned up naturally, which gave him an advantage over the gallants of the time, whose moustaches received a touch of the barber's art to give them the air then most admired.—See Aubrey's 'Correspondence,' vol. ii. part ii. p. 500.

Note E, p. 192.—Court Favour of Sir Walter Raleigh

The gallant incident of the cloak is the traditional account of this celebrated statesman's rise at court. None of Elizabeth's courtiers knew better than he how to make his court to her personal vanity, or could more justly estimate the quantity of flattery which she could condescend to swallow. Being confined in the Tower for some offence, and understanding the Queen was about to pass to Greenwich in her barge, he insisted on approaching the window, that he might see, at whatever distance, the Queen of his Affections, the most beautiful object which the earth bore on its surface. The lieutenant of the Tower (his own particular friend) threw himself between his prisoner and the window; while Sir Walter, apparently influenced by a fit of unrestrainable passion, swore he would not be debarred from seeing his light, his life, his goddess! A scuffle ensued, *got up* for effect's sake, in which the lieutenant and his captive grappled and struggled with fury—tore each other's hair—and at length drew daggers, and were only separated by force. The

Queen being informed of this scene exhibited by her frantic adorer, it wrought, as was to be expected, much in favour of the captive Paladin. There is little doubt that his quarrel with the lieutenant was entirely contrived for the purpose which it produced.

Note F, p. 219.—Robert Laneham

Little is known of Robert Laneham, save in his curious letter to a friend in London, giving an account of Queen Elizabeth's entertainments at Kenilworth, written in a style of the most intolerable affectation, both in point of composition and orthography. He describes himself as a *bon vivant*, who was wont to be jolly and dry in the morning, and by his goodwill would be chiefly in the company of the ladies. He was, by the interest of Lord Leicester, clerk of the council-chamber door, and also keeper of the same. 'When Council sits,' says he, 'I am at hand. If any makes a babbling, *Peace*, say I. If I see a listener or a pryer in at the chinks or lockhole, I am presently on the bones of him. If a friend comes, I make him sit down by me on a form or chest. The rest may walk, a God's name!' There has been seldom a better portrait of the pragmatic conceit and self-importance of a small man in office.

Note G, p. 245.—Dr. Julio

The Earl of Leicester's Italian physician, Julio, was affirmed by his contemporaries to be a skilful compounder of poisons, which he applied with such frequency, that the Jesuit Parsons extols ironically the marvellous good luck of this great favourite, in the opportune deaths of those who stood in the way of his wishes. There is a curious passage on the subject:—

'Long after this, he fell in love with the Lady Sheffield, whom I signified before, and then also had he the same fortune to have her husband dye quickly, with an extreame rheume in his head (as it was given out), but as others say, of an artificiall catarre that stopped his breath.

'The like good chance had he in the death of my Lord of Essex (as I have said before), and that at a time most fortunate for his purpose; for when he was coming home from Ireland, with intent to revenge himselfe upon my Lord of Leicester for begetting his wife with childe in his absence (the childe was a daughter, and brought up by the Lady Shandoes, W. Knooles, his wife) my Lord of Leicester hearing thereof, wanted not a friend or two to accompany the deputy, as among other a couple of the Earles own servants, Crompton (if I misse not his name), yeoman of his bottles, and Lloid his secretary, entertained afterward by my Lord of Leicester, and so he dyed in the way, of an extraeme flax, caused by an Italian receipe, as all his friends are well assured, the maker whereof was a chyrurgeon (as it is beleeved) that then was newly come to my Lord from Italy—a cunning man and sure in operation, with whom, if the good Lady had been sooner acquainted, and used his help, she should not have needed to sitten so pensive at home, and fearful of her husband's former returne out of the same country .... Neither must you marvaile though all these died in divers manners of outward diseases, for this is the excellency of the Italian art, for which this chyrurgeon and Dr Julio were entertained so carefully, who can make a man dye in what manner or show of sickness you will—by whose instructions, no doubt; but his lordship is now cunning, especially adding also to these the counsel of his Doctor Bayly, a man also not a little studied (as he seemeth) in his art; for I heard him once myselfe, in a publique act in Oxford, and that in presence of my Lord of Leicester (if I be not deceived) maintain that poyson might be so tempered and given as it should not appear presently, and yet should kill the party afterward, at what time should be appointed; which argument belike pleased well his lordship, and therefore was chosen to be discussed in his audience, if I be not deceived of his being that day present. So, though one dye of a flux, and another of a catarre, yet this importeth little to the matter, but showeth rather the great cunning and skill of the artificer.'—Parsons' 'Leicester's Commonwealth,' p. 23.

It is unneccessary to state the numerous reasons why the Earl is stated in the tale to be rather the dupe of villains than the unprincipled author of their atrocities. In the latter capacity, which a part at least of his contemporaries imputed to him, he would have made a character too disgustingly wicked to to be useful for the purposes of fiction.

I have only to add, that the union of the poisoner, the quacksalver, the alchemist, and the astrologer, in the same person, was familiar to the pretenders to the mystic sciences.

Note H, p. 356.—Sir James Melville

To justify what may be considered as a high-coloured picture, the author quotes the original of the courtly and shrewd Sir James Melville, being then Queen Mary's envoy at the Court of London.

'I was required,' says Sir James, 'to stay till I had seen him made Earle of Leicester, and Baron of Denbigh, with great solemnity; herself (Elizabeth) helping to put on his ceremonial, he sitting on his knees before her, keeping a great gravity and discreet behaviour; but she could not refrain from putting her hand to his neck to kittle (*i.e.*, tickle) him, smilingly, the French Ambassador and I standing beside her.'—Melville's 'Memoirs, Bannatyne Edition,' p. 120.

Note I, p. 364.—Italian Rhymes

The incident alluded to occurs in the poem of Orlando Innamorato of Boiardo, libro ii. canto 4, stanza 25.

'Non era per ventura,' etc.

It may be rendered thus:—

As then, perchance, unguarded was the tower,
    So enter'd free Anglante's dauntless knight.
No monster and no giant guard the bower
    In whose recess reclined the fairy light,
Robed in a loose cymar of lily white,
    And on her lap a sword of breadth and might,
In whose broad blade, as in a mirror bright,
    Like maid that trims her for a festal night,
The fairy deck'd her hair, and placed her coronet aright.

Elizabeth's attachment to the Italian school of poetry was singularly manifested on a well-known occasion. Her godson, Sir John Harrington, having offended her delicacy by translating some of the licentious passages of the Orlando Furioso, she imposed on him, as a penance, the task of rendering the *whole* poem into English.

Note J, p. 374.—Furniture of Kenilworth

In revising this work, I have had the means of making some accurate additions to my attempt to describe the princely pleasures of Kenilworth, by the kindness of my friend William Harper, Esq., who had the goodness to communicate to me an inventory of the furniture of Kenilworth in the days of the magnificent Earl of Leicester. I have adorned the text with some of the splendid articles mentioned in the inventory, but antiquaries, especially, will be desirous to see a more full specimen than the story leaves room for.

EXTRACTS FROM KENILWORTH INVENTORY, A.D. 1584.

A salte, ship-fashion, of the mother of perle, garnished with silver and divers workes, warlike ensignes, and ornaments, with xvj peeces of ordinance, whereof ij on wheles, two anckers on the foreparte, and on the stearne the image of Dame Fortune standing on a globe with a flag in her hand. Pois xxxij oz.

A gilte salte like a swann, mother of perle. Pois xxx oz. iij quarters.

A George on horseback, of wood, painted and gilt, with a case for knives in the tayle of the horse, and a case for oyster knives in the brest of the Dragon.

A green barge-cloth, embroider'd with white lions and beares.

A perfuming pann, of silver. Pois xix oz.

In the halle. Tabells, long and short, vj. Formes, long and short, xiiij.

Hangings

(These are minutely specified, and consisted of the following subjects, in tapestry. and gilt, and red leather).

Flowers, beasts, and pillars arched. Forest worke. Historie. Storie of Susanna, the Prodigall Childe, Saule, Tobie, Hercules, Lady Fame, Hawking and Hunting, Jezabell, Judith and Holofernes, David, Abraham, Sampson, Hippolitus, Alexander the Great, Naaman the Assyrian, Jacob, etc.

NOTES

Bedsteds, with their Furniture

(These are magnificent and numerous. 1 shall copy, *verbatim* the description of what appears to have been one of the best.)

A bedsted of wallnut-tree, toppe fashion, the pillers redd and varnished, the ceelor, tester, and single vallance of crimson sattin, paned with a broad border of bone lace of golde and silver. The tester richlie embrothered with my Lo. armes in a garland of hoppes, roses, and pomegranetts, and lyned with buckerom. Fyve curteins of crimson sattin to the same bedsted, striped downe with a bone lace of gold and silver, garnished with buttons and loops of crimson silk and golde, containing xiij bredths of sattin, and one yarde iij quarters deepe. The ceelor, vallance, and curteins lyned with crymson taffata sarsenet.

A crymson sattin counterpointe, quilted and embr. with a golde twiste, and lyned with redd sarsenet, being in length iij yards good, and in breadth iij scant.

A chaise of crymson sattin, suteable.

A fayre quilte of crymson sattin, vj breadths, iij yardes 3 quarters naile deepe, all lozenged over with silver twiste, in the midst a cinquefoile within a garland of ragged staves, fringed rounde aboute with a small fringe of crymson silbe, lyned throughe with white fustian.

Fyve plumes of coolered feathers, garnished with bone lace and spangells of goulde and silver, standing in cups[1] knitt all over with goulde, silver and crymson silk.

A carpett for a cupboarde of crymson sattin, embrothered with a border of goulde twiste, about iij parts of it fringed with silk and goulde, lyned with bridges[2] sattin, in length ij yards, and ij bredths of sattin.

(There were eleven down beds and ninety feather beds, besides thirty-seven mattresses.)

Chayres, Stooles, and Cushens

(These were equally splendid with the beds, etc. I shall here copy that which stands at the head of the list).

A chaier of crimson velvet, the seate and backe partlie embrothered, with R.L. in cloth of goulde, the beare and ragged staffe in clothe of silver, garnished with lace and fringe of goulde, silver, and crimson silck. The frame covered with velvet, bounde about the edge with goulde lace, and studded with gilte nailes.

A square stoole and a foote stoole, of crimson velvet, fringed and garnished suteable.

A long cushen of crimson velvet, embr. with the ragged staffe in a wreathe of goulde, with my Lo. posie 'Droyte et Loyall' written in the same, and the letters R. L. in clothe of goulde, being garnished with lace, fringe, buttons, and tassels, of gold, silver, and crimson silck, lyned with crimson taff., being in length 1 yard quarter.

A square cushen, of the like velvet, embr. suteable to the long cushen.

Carpets

(There were 10 velvet carpets for tables and windows, 49 Turkey carpets for floors, and 32 cloth carpets. One of each I will now specify.)

A carpett of crimson velvet, richly embr. with my Lo. posie, beares and ragged staves, etc., of clothe of goulde and silver, garnished upon the seames and aboute with golde lace, fringed accordinglie, lyned with crimson taffata sarsenett, being 3 breadths of velvet, one yard 3 quarters long.

A great Turquoy carpett, the grounde blew, with a list of yelloe at each end, being in length x yards, in bredthe iij yards and quarter.

A long carpett of blew clothe, lyned with bridges sattin, fringed with blew silck and goulde, in length vj yards lack a quarter, the whole bredth of the clothe.

Pictures

(Chiefly described as having curtains.)

The Queene's Majestie (2 great tables), 3 of my Lord. St Jerome. Lo. of Arundell. Lord Mathevers. Lord of Pembroke. Counte Egmondt. The Queene of Scotts.

1. Probably on the centre and four corners of the bedstead. Four bears and ragged staves occupied a similar position on another of these sumptuous pieces of furniture.

2. *i.e.* Bruges.

477

King Philip. The Baker's Daughters. The Duke of Feria. Alexander Magnus. Two Yonge Ladies. Pompæa Sabina. Fred. D. of Saxony. Emp. Charles. K. Philip's Wife. Prince of Orange and his Wife. Marq. of Berges and his Wife. Counte de Horne. Count Holstrate. Monsr. Brederode. Duke Alva. Cardinal Grandville. Duches of Parma. Henrie E. of Pembroke and his young Countess. Countis of Essex. Occacion and Repentance. Lord Mowntacute. S. Jas. Crofts. Sir Wr. Mildmay. Sr. Wm. Pickering. Edwin Abp. of York.

A tabell of an historie of men, women, and children, molden in wax.

A little foulding table of ebanie, garnished with white bone, wherein are written verses with lres. of goulde.

A table of my Lord's armes.

Fyve of the plannetts, painted in frames.

Twentie-three cardes, [1] or maps of countries.

Instruments

(I shall give two specimens.)

An instrument of organs, regalls, and virginalls, covered with crimson velvet, and garnished with goulde lace.

A fair pair of double virginalls.

Cabonetts

A cabonett of crimson sattin, richlie embr. with a device of hunting the stagg, in goulde, silver, and silck, with iiij glasses in the topp thereof, xvj cupps of flowers made of goulde, silver, and silck, in a case of leather, lyned with greene sattin of bridges.

(Another of purple velvet. A desk of red leather).

A Chess Boarde of ebanie, with checkars of christall and other stones, layed with silver, garnished with beares and ragged staves, and cinque-foiles of silver. The xxxij men likewyse of christall and other stones sett, the one sort in silver white, the other gilte, in a case gilded and lyned with green cotton.

(Another of bone and ebanie. A pair of tabells of bone.)

A Great Brason Candlestick to hang in the roofe of the howse, verie fayer and curiously wrought, with xxiij branches, xij greate and xij of lesser size, 6 rowlers and ij wings for the spread eagle, xxiiij socketts for candells, xij greater and xij of a lesser sorte, xxiiij sawcers, or candlecupps, of like proporcion to put under the socketts, iij images of men and iij of weomen, of brass, verie finely and artificiallie done.

These specimens of Leicester's magnificence may serve to assure the reader that it scarce lay in the power of a modern author to exaggerate the lavish style of expense displayed in the princely pleasures of Kenilworth.

Note K, p. 471.—Death of the Earl of Leicester

In a curious manuscript copy of the information given by Ben Jonson to Drummond of Hawthornden, as transcribed by Sir Robert Sibbald, Leicester's death is ascribed to poison administered as a cordial by his Countess, to whom he had given it, representing it to be a restorative in any faintness, in the hope that she herself might be cut off by using it. We have already quoted Jonson's account of this merited stroke of retribution in a note to the introduction, p. 18. It may be here added, that the following satirical epitaph on Leicester occurs in Drummond's Collection, but is evidently not of his composition:—

EPITAPH ON THE ERLE OF LEISTER

Here lies a valiant warriour,
Who never drew a sword;
Here lies a noble courtier,
Who never kept his word;
Here lies the Erle of Leister,
Who governed the Estates,
Whom the earth could never living love,
And the just heaven now hates.

1. *i.e.* Charts.

BIBLIOGRAPHY

Poems, Sketches and Translations

1796   *The Chase, William and Helen* (From the German of Bürger)
1799   *Goetz von Berlichingen* (Goethe)
1800   *The Eve of St. John*
1805   *The Lay of the Last Minstrel*
1807   *Ballads and Lyrical Pieces*
1808   *Marmion*
1810   *The Lady of the Lake*
1811   *The Vision of Don Roderick*
1813   *Rokeby—The Bridal of Triermain*
1815   *The Lord of the Isles—The Field of Waterloo*
1817   *Harold the Dauntless*
1830   *The Doom of Devergoil*

Novels and Tales

1814   *Waverley*
1815   *Guy Mannering*
1816   *The Antiquary—Tales of My Landlord*
1817   *The Search After Happiness*
1818   *Tales of My Landlord* (2nd series) (*The Heart of Midlothian*)
        —Rob Roy—Tales of My Landlord (3rd series) (*The Bride
        of Lammermoor* and *The Legend of Montrose*)
1820   *Ivanhoe—The Monastery—The Abbot*
1821   *Kenilworth*
1822   *The Pirate—The Fortunes of Nigel—Peveril of the Peak*
1823   *Quentin Durward*
1824   *St. Ronan's Well—Redgauntlet*
1825   *The Tales of the Crusaders* (*The Betrothed* and *The Talisman*)
1827   *Woodstock—The Chronicles of Canongate*
1828   *My Aunt Margaret's Mirror—The Chronicles of Canongate*
        (2nd series)
1832   *Tales of My Landlord* (4th series) (*Count Robert of Paris*, and
        Castle Dangerous)

BIBLIOGRAPHY

Collected Editions of Scott's works

First Collected Edition (Edinburgh) 1819–33 (41 vols.)
1821–33 (53 vols.)
1823–33 (41 vols.)

Edinburgh Edition of Collected Poems. 1820 (12 vols.)
Collected Poems edited by J. G. Lockhart. 1833–34 (12 vols.)

The following contain information on his life and works:

Memoirs of the Life of Sir Walter Scott Bt. (2 vols.) by J. G. Lockhart. 1837–39
Journal of Sir Walter Scott by A. C. Swinburne (in 'Studies in Prose and Poetry'). 1896.
Sir Walter Scott by G. Saintsbury. 1897.
The Story of Scott's Ruin by Sir Leslie Stephen (in 'Studies of a biographer' vol. 2). 1898.
Life of Sir Walter Scott by Stephen Gwynn. 1930.
Life of Sir Walter Scott by John Buchan. 1932.
The Laird of Abbotsford by Una Pope-Hennessy. 1932.
Sir Walter Scott, Bt. by Sir H. J. C. Grierson. 1938.
Sir Walter Scott by Una Pope-Hennessy (The English Novelists Series). 1948.
A Bibliography of Sir Walter Scott by James Clarkson Corson.
Walter Scott by H. Pearson. 1954.
The Heyday of Sir Walter Scott by D. Davie. 1961.
Sir Walter Scott by J. Buchan. 1961.
The Hero of The Waverley Novels by A. Welsh. 1963.
Sir Walter Scott by I. Jack (Writers and Their Works Series). 1962.